ANDRE GONZALEZ

Wealth of Time Series: Books 1-3

First published by M4L Publishing 2019

This novel is entirely a work of fiction. The names, characters and incidents portrayed in it are the work of the author's imagination. Any resemblance to actual persons, living or dead, events or localities is entirely coincidental.

Andre Gonzalez asserts the moral right to be identified as the author of this work.

Second edition

ISBN: 978-1-951762-03-2

Editing by Stephanie Cohen
Cover art by ebooklaunch.com
Cover art by Natasha Gonzalez (paperback)

This book was professionally typeset on Reedsy.
Find out more at reedsy.com

To my mom, Julie, for always believing in this wild dream.

To my dad, Larry. You may not remember, but you were my very first reader in 2002.

For my Auntie Chris. You helped me through a dark and confusing time of my life. Thank you for helping me see the road ahead more clearly.

"Time slips away like grains of sand never to return again."

-Robin Sharma

Contents

II Warm Souls

GET EXCLUSIVE BONUS CONTENT

Connecting with readers is the best part of this job. Releasing a book into the world is a truly frightening moment every time it happens! Hearing your feedback, whether good or bad, goes a long in shaping future projects and helping me grow as a writer. I also like to take readers behind the scenes on occasion and share what is happening in my wild world of writing. If you're interested, please consider joining my mailing list. If you do so, I'll send you the following as a thank you:

1. A free copy of *Revolution,* a prequel story that goes back in time before Chris Speidel ever knew about the mysterious world of time travel.
2. A free copy of *Road Runners*, a prequel story that looks at the rise of the Road Runners.

You can get your content **for free,** by signing up HERE.
https://dl.bookfunnel.com/zb03c72679

I

Wealth of Time

Wealth of Time Series, Book #1

1

Wealth of Time Cover

BOOK ONE OF THE WEALTH OF TIME SERIES

WEALTH OF TIME

ANDRE GONZALEZ

2

Chapter 1

One squeeze of the trigger and it's all over.

The pistol was cold on his tongue, like a metallic popsicle. It weighed upon his jaw, keeping it pried open as saliva pooled between his tongue and the small hole where the slug would come blasting out to end his life.

Pull it, you coward. Darkness is waiting just on the other side. No more pain, no more regret. Just darkness.

His hands didn't shake this time, nerves long gone after going through this same routine for the tenth time in just as many years. He already knew that this would play out with him removing the pistol, cursing the world, and passing out on the couch. The pills in his stomach swirled around the tide pool of whiskey, along for another ride.

Every September reminded Martin Briar of how much he hated his life. His once-normal life waited 22 years in the past. It was Labor Day of 2018 when Martin sat in his apartment with his pistol between his teeth. He had cried the first two years of attempting this, and knew that it was only a matter of time before the good graces of death would finally help him pull the trigger.

Minutes ago, he had smoked a cheap cigar while washing down a handful of colorful pills with a glass of whiskey. From the balcony of his rundown apartment, he had a view of the sunset with its blue mountains and orange glowing sky, but he took it for granted. Whiskey and tobacco came from the Earth, and that was the extent he cared for Mother Nature.

It was Monday the 3rd, and the upcoming Sunday would officially mark 22 years since his daughter's disappearance. The Imagine Dragons sang through his cell phone speakers from the balcony's chipped and rough handrail. He stood with his elbows on it, the only other neighboring object being an ashtray he never used.

Lela, his ex-wife from many moons ago, had gifted him the ashtray. The bottom of the tray was a yellow circle with black lettering that read: *World's Greatest Dad!*

He *had* been the world's greatest dad, too, at least according to Izzy. Izzy, formally named Isabel, had grown up to be quite the daddy's girl, always running to him when he arrived home from work and jumping into his embrace. She was only 12 years old when she had gone missing in 1996.

Kids have a way of distracting you from the fact that you are getting older with each passing day, and Izzy provided the same fountain of youth effect for Martin.

He was 32 when she disappeared. His entire twenties had gone by in a blur, thanks to Isabel. While his friends went out drinking and partying every weekend, Martin stayed home and watched shows like *Rugrats* and *Arthur*. He wouldn't have traded it for a single night out, loving every moment with his little family in their first home, a small ranch-style house just north of Denver in Larkwood.

Martin grew up in Larkwood, his parents having moved there well before he was born. His mother still lived in his childhood home, just two blocks away. While most people would flee the quiet town after such a tragedy like losing a child, Martin couldn't picture life anywhere else in the world. Larkwood was home and always would be. Going away wouldn't bring Isabel back. If she were ever to return, it would likely be to the last place she could remember.

Now at the age of 54, Martin didn't know if he'd even recognize his daughter. She would be 34 years old, a beautiful woman approaching the tail end of her prime. *Of course you'll know her face. You stare at it every day.*

From the small picture he kept in his wallet, to the 8x10 on his nightstand, he would damn well know his own daughter if she showed up all of these years later.

Martin stood in front of a mirror in his living room, staring at his pathetic self. His body had swollen over the years. What was once an athletic, six-foot frame of muscle was now a round collection of fast food and booze. His brown hair was plastered across his forehead with sweat. He started to wheeze, feeling his heart rate increase by the second as he stared at himself. His pale skin was now a light shade of red.

"Isabel," he mumbled around the muzzle. Tears welled up in his eyes, but he fought their attempt to run down his face.

He ripped the pistol out of his mouth and threw it aside, falling into the soft couch waiting to catch him from behind.

Well, here we are again. You chickened out. Is the temptation really that hard to resist?

As he had done the previous nine times, Martin couldn't pull the trigger, knowing that his mother would have to clean up the mess and bury her son. His brother had moved across the country years ago, around the same time that Izzy went missing, and had remained mostly estranged to the family. His father had passed when they were younger, leaving Marilyn Briar all alone, should Martin end his shitty life.

Just wait until she passes away – then we can ride off into the darkness together.

His mom was in great shape and nowhere near death, so it would take a few more years to reach that point. Once she was gone, though, there would be no more roadblocks, no hesitations from entering the darkness and leaving his lifelong sorrow behind.

Tuesday awaited with a full day of work at the post office, as if he needed an additional reason to shoot himself. He took the job for the guarantee of having Sundays and holidays off. Days off were all he looked forward to anymore. The customers were needy and whiny.

So many goddamn entitled little shits! he thought at the end of each shift. The days felt longer than eight hours as the clock on the wall teased him all day. His coworkers lacked any sort of personality and seemed to hate life as much as he did. At least they had that much in common.

Martin had fallen into the trap of monotonously going through the daily grind. Leave for work at seven in the morning, slog through five hours of mind-numbingly boring tasks until lunchtime, eat a bland sandwich made half-assed while drunk the night before, slog through until four o'clock, go home to drink booze and eat microwaveable dinners, make the bland sandwich for the next day, and then go to sleep. *Work. Drink. Sleep. Repeat.*

Sometimes he fantasized about being adventurous, but he had no clue what he would do. The numbness that remained in his chest since 1996 wasn't going anywhere and made everyday life difficult to enjoy. He'd tried going to sporting events, the shooting range, even a book club. They all had the same result in leaving him unsatisfied and longing for the next day, one day closer to death where he could forget all of his problems and either start over or enjoy the darkness. *Whatever the hell happens after this life can't be worse.*

The pistol was somewhere in the corner of the room as he started to doze off. He knew he wouldn't have the urge to use it again until next year. The intensity of sticking an instrument of death in his mouth was enough to last him a full three hundred and sixty-five days.

Work. Drink. Sleep. Repeat. Tomorrow is another day in the glorious life of Martin Briar.

3

Chapter 2

Martin had a nail jammed into the back of his head when his alarm buzzed obnoxiously at six the next morning. *God, I hate that fucking sound.* He downed his usual breakfast of two aspirin pills and a glass of water to remedy the situation.

He slid into his uniform of a dark blue shirt and gray slacks. *Larkwood Postal Services* and his name were stitched across the shirt on opposite sides. "Hi, I'm Martin. Where would you like me to send your lovely package today, Mr. Asshole?" he said into the mirror with a drunken giggle. He kept the lights dim, not wanting to see the streaks of white and gray clawing their way through his brown hair. A scruffy beard had started to sprout on his face. "Oh, you need it overnighted to Australia? Let me pull out my magic mail monkey and have it swim across the ocean for you today!" His head throbbed when he laughed, but he couldn't help himself.

Let's go live that dream today, since you couldn't complete your task last night. Martin winked at himself, the bags under his brown eyes remaining plump, having a slight regret at not pulling the trigger.

He maneuvered in the darkness to the kitchen to grab his lunchbox and left the apartment.

The outdoor air always helped eliminate the nausea that accompanied his daily hangover. To the east, the skyline glowed a magnificent purple and orange from the rising sun. Autumn had always been Martin's favorite season – that was, until his daughter went missing all those Septembers ago. Now autumn served as a reminder that life doesn't owe you an explanation. Bad shit happened to good people every day. Some rose, some crumpled. Martin liked to think he fell in the middle of the spectrum, functioning as a member of society, but having no interest in improving his life. *Just get me to the finish line already,* he often thought.

Hope kept him from pulling the trigger year after year. Hope that his daughter would return. Hope that his wife would come back and they could build a relationship for the twilight years of their lives. Hope that maybe one day, life would feel all right again. It couldn't always be this bad.

He and his mother had dinner together twice a week, each taking turns on choosing where to dine. His mother had always been a graceful soul, willing to open her heart to anyone in need. When she saw Martin struggle after Izzy's disappearance, and his resulting failed marriage, she convinced him to move into her basement until he could regain structure in his life.

Martin took joy in knowing his Tuesday evening would end with dinner with his mom. It was his turn to choose and he wanted nothing more than a juicy burger at the local joint, Roadhouse Diner. He might spend more time with his mother over the course of the week, with the anniversary of Izzy's disappearance looming on Sunday.

The morning dragged on as expected, but when lunch arrived he felt instant relief when he found the small break room deserted. The rusty microwave hummed in the corner while the stench of burnt popcorn filled the air.

Martin took the seat closest to the window with its breathtaking view of the parking lot for all of the mail trucks. He laid out his sandwich and chips before calling his mom.

"Hi, Marty," she greeted him warmly.

"Hey, Mom, how's it going today?"

"Oh, you know, just raked some leaves and made a pot of tea. Gonna be a long afternoon of soap operas."

"Of course, can't miss those. I just wanted to confirm that we're still good for tonight. I was thinking we could go to Roadhouse."

"Oh, perfect!" Her voice rose in excitement. "I just heard from Esther about a new antique shop that popped up a few blocks from the church. I don't remember hearing anything about it, but it's apparently open now. Do you mind if we stop by before dinner, since it's on the way?"

"I don't mind at all. I can pick you up at 5:30."

"Great, I'll be ready. See you then."

They hung up and Martin wondered what his mother's life was like. She spent her mornings in the yard, took a nap, and lazed the afternoons away on her recliner watching bad TV. Once a week she'd visit a thrift store or antique store with her friends in search of some rare find. Occasionally, she invited Martin to join her on these outings if her friends weren't able to go. He didn't mind keeping her company, but all these stores carried the same loads of useless shit and musty odors that reminded him of an attic.

Probably because all this shit is from someone's attic.

Regardless, he set his focus on the double cheeseburger with bacon awaiting him at the end of his day's journey.

4

Chapter 3

Martin's stomach growled as he pulled into his childhood driveway. He made it through another day, and thanks to the short week, tomorrow was already Wednesday.

His mother waited at the front door and stepped out of the light gray house as soon as he pulled up. Two patio chairs sat on the porch where Martin used to watch the sunset with his father as he spewed about baseball, the weather, and the mysteries of life. Many of his lessons came right from those two worn-down chairs, and Martin was glad his mother held on to them after making many renovations after his father's death. The front yard appeared leafless and immaculate. His father had always taken pride in a clean and green yard, and when he passed, his mother took the responsibilities in stride, claiming it made her feel close to her lost husband.

Martin watched his fragile mother wobble down the steps. She claimed to feel great despite her body starting to break down, and he had no reason to not take her word as she remained active, even as she was pushing 75. Her silver hair flowed graciously behind her as she cracked a warm smile in his direction. Underneath the wrinkles he could still see her youthful beauty. He remembered his mother being the most gorgeous woman he'd ever seen, and while time altered her outer appearance, he knew the woman from forty years ago was behind her gentle green eyes.

She pulled open the car door and plopped down in the passenger seat. "Marty! How are you?" she greeted him warmly, grinning ear-to-ear.

"I'm as good as can be," he said, forcing a matched enthusiasm.

This was the answer he reverted to whenever anyone asked him how he was doing, and it was true. He hated his life, but tried to make the best of the days while he counted down to his eventual death. That was the best he could offer the world.

"So what's this antique store we're going to?" Martin asked before his mother could dig into how he really felt on this dreadful week.

She clicked her seat belt and slouched back as Martin pulled back onto the road. "Oh, just a new store I heard about from Esther and Toni when we had lunch the other day. They told me it has an impressive collection of treasures. They walked out of there with a thousand dollars of stuff each."

A thousand dollars worth of shit, probably.

"I won't go spending all that," she continued. "I just like to look around. Maybe one day I'll see something that reminds me of my childhood or your father. Then I'll buy."

Martin nodded as she spoke, keeping his focus on the road. The church was only a five-minute drive, and this new store was supposedly a couple blocks from it.

"Well, I hope you find something you like, Mom. Don't keep us too late, though, I'm starving."

Smooth jazz poured out of the car speakers, his mom's favorite, and they hummed along until they pulled up to the store.

The building was a bland gray that blended in with the cloudy sky. Black, plain text lettered the front in a generic font: *WEALTH OF TIME*. Three panes of glass were centered below the lettering with the middle one serving as the only door.

"Has this building always been here?" Martin asked, unimpressed with the exterior.

His mother lowered her brow in thought. "I honestly don't know. In my sixty years living here, I can't say I've ever been in this part of the neighborhood."

They had passed the church and driven through a residential neighborhood for two blocks before spitting out into a random lot where the building stood.

"They certainly won't last long in this location. How is anyone supposed to find it?"

"We found it easily enough."

Martin wanted to tell his mom that wasn't the point, but let it slide as he sensed her growing excitement to get inside the store.

He parked, the lot empty with the exception of one other car, and stepped out to the brisk evening. The sun fought its way through the clouds before setting for the night, casting a hazy, orange glow.

A rusty sign hung next to the tall windows that read: *COME ON IN! WE'RE OPEN!*

Martin insisted this building had already existed, its exterior worn down from years of enduring the Colorado weather. A fresh coat of paint could make it look brand new.

He followed his mother as she climbed the three short steps and pulled open the door. A bell chimed as she crossed the threshold into the empty store.

The store stretched back into eternity. Martin craned his neck to see as far as possible and still couldn't find the back wall. The building hadn't looked this long from the outside, and his mind twisted in confusion. Obvious sections of furniture, music, kitchenware, china and ceramics, figurines, clocks, and jewelry separated the store.

Marilyn soaked in the inventory of old knick-knacks with wide eyes. "I've never seen a store so big. Not an antique store."

Her voice echoed, and she realized they were alone. "Anyone here?" she shouted.

A white head of hair popped up in the distance as an elderly man made his way down the never-ending aisle toward them. "Please come in!" His voice bounced off the walls. "Welcome."

He approached them and stuck out a bony hand with little white hairs curled around his knuckles. He smiled at Martin from his long, droopy face. The short white hair on his head matched that on his fingers. "Chris Speidel at your service, pleased to meet you fine folks." He shook their hands more aggressively than Martin anticipated. The old man's flesh felt cold as ice, as if he were holding a frozen drink for the last few minutes.

"I'm Martin Briar, and this is my mother, Marilyn." Martin spoke uneasily. He thought Chris's irises looked black at first glance, but realized they were dark brown after closer inspection.

"Glad to have you folks." He kissed Marilyn's hand when she offered it, causing redness to bloom in her cheeks. "What can I do for you kiddos today?"

"We were hoping to look around. I heard a new store was open in town, and I just love antique shops," Marilyn said as she held her kissed hand in front of her.

"Fair enough." Chris clapped his hands together. "Poke around. I have some great stuff you'll both enjoy. Do you like baseball, young man?" He turned to Martin.

"I haven't kept up much with it in recent years, but I used to be a big fan."

"Well, I have some very rare collectible cards. You can find them on a shelf near the dolls over there." Chris poked a skinny thumb in the direction of the wistful porcelain dolls that faced the front entrance.

"Thank you, I'll be sure to take a look."

"And you, young lady, is there anything in particular that you're looking for?" He offered what looked like a forced grin to Marilyn.

"Not really. If something grabs my eye then I'll take a closer look."

"With all due respect, madam, this is an antique shop. We are the keepers of time, the guardians of treasure, and the watchmen of memories. You should be looking for something to catch your *heart,* not your eye."

She blushed again, and Martin stood frozen in disbelief. *Is this how old people flirt?*

"But please have a look around. You can find me at the counter if you need any help at all." The old man winked at them and turned to head back to wherever he'd come from.

Martin locked eyes with his mother and they exchanged curious looks. "I suppose I'll go look at those baseball cards." Martin checked his watch. "Let's try to not be more than half an hour. I'm really hungry and have had that burger on my mind all day."

"Yes, of course." Her eyes remained locked on Chris as he disappeared into a row of shelves.

She stepped away from Martin, leaving him at the entrance as she walked to the china section and sifted through decades of old dishes.

Martin felt someone watching him and glanced around to see if any cameras were visible. Aside from the one pointing to the entrance, there were none that he could see, but the feeling wasn't a camera. He felt *eyes* on him. He shook the thought out of his mind and dragged his feet to the figurines section.

The shelves were lined with old collector's edition model cars, rare Barbie dolls and action figures, video games, and Pogs. Next to all of this rested a small wooden box with baseball cards lined up perfectly. He pulled the box off the shelf and cradled it in his arm like a football as he flipped through years of baseball lore.

Hank Aaron, Pete Rose, Cal Ripken, Ken Griffey Jr., Mickey Mantle. He paused on the Mantle card. *Isn't this card worth hundreds of thousands?* He pulled it out, examined its nearly mint condition. *Honus Wagner is the rare card, not Mantle.* He put the box back in its place and sighed as his stomach begged for food.

A quick glance around the store found his mother at the counter with Chris. She leaned in close to the store's owner, as if telling a secret, his snowy head nodding as she spoke. Martin shuffled his feet and cleared his throat as he approached. "We about ready for dinner, Mom?"

She turned and looked at her son with a stern face. "I may have found something, Marty."

On the counter was a thick gold ring with a large emerald in its center. They had been inspecting it up close.

16

"This ring looks identical to one my grandmother used to wear. She handed it down to my mom, and after she passed, we've never been able to find it. Part of me wonders if it's still on her finger."

She picked it up and held it up to the light, tears welling in her eyes. "Chris says it's valued at $7,000 and that he'll sell it for $5,000. I just don't know. That's still a bit out of my range."

"Five thousand is a steal, trust me. If you find this anywhere else, you'd likely find a price tag of ten grand on it."

Marilyn pursed her lips and Martin could read the frustration boiling behind her eyes. She wanted that ring. "I'll have to think about it. Will you honor that price if I come back in a couple of days?"

"Of course," Chris said, sliding the ring back into its felt case and snapping it shut with a coy smile. "I'll keep it off the floor for a couple days. You come let me know." He patted the case before putting it in a cupboard underneath an old cash register.

"Well, thank you, Chris. I appreciate that. I think my son here is hungry, so we should be on our way."

"Indeed. Enjoy your dinner. I'll see you both around, and it was a pleasure meeting you this evening."

Chris extended his fragile hand and shook with both of them before they left.

* * *

At dinner, Martin gauged his mother's interest in the ring.

"I'm convinced it's my grandmother's ring," she said, shaking her head. "I don't know how on earth it would end up in that gentleman's collection, but I felt something when I touched it. I don't know how to explain it."

"What if I pitch in and help you buy it?" Martin offered.

"That's very nice of you, Marty, but you can save your money. I can afford it — it's just a matter of if I really *want* it. I didn't want to make an emotional purchase. I just need some time to think it over. If I'm still thinking about it in a few days, then I'll go back and pick it up."

They finished their burgers that night with countless stories of Martin's great-grandmother. He heard the pain in his mom's voice. Some scars never healed, and losing a grandparent never became easier. He could attest to that.

I'm going back tomorrow to buy that ring.

5

Chapter 4

Martin returned to Wealth of Time the following evening. The must filled his lungs again as he strode toward the checkout counter where Chris read a raggedy paperback. He looked up from behind the small reading glasses perched on his nose.

"Good evening, young man. I thought I'd see your mother before you. Was there a baseball card you liked?"

"Hello. No. Although, you have an impressive collection. My card collecting days are behind me. If anything, I may bring you some cards to see if you'd be interested."

"I see. What can I do for you this evening?"

"I want to buy that ring my mom was looking at."

Chris dropped his book on the counter top, revealing an H.P. Lovecraft novel, and retrieved the ring box as if he had been expecting Martin to come in.

"I was thinking about this ring and my encounter with your mother. I'd like to sell it you for $2,000. That's what I paid for it, and I don't mind breaking even on it. Your mother was entranced. I believe it really is the long lost family heirloom."

Martin's jaw dropped. "Two thousand? That's impossible."

Chris grinned. "I'd give it you for free, but this is a business. Let's call it even and you can take her a nice surprise."

"I don't know what to say...thank you."

Martin pulled out his wallet and slid his credit card across the counter with a wavering hand. *This has to be a fake ring. No way this guy takes $5,000 off the listed price. He felt guilty trying to hustle my mom, and is trying to make up for it. She won't know the difference, and she'll never find out about this. As far as she knows, it's her grandmother's lost ring.*

"Your mom said this was her grandmother's ring?" Chris asked in a curious voice.

"Yes. My great-grandmother promised to leave it for my mom when she was only a teenager. You don't remember where you got it from?"

Chris scrunched his face. "Can't say I do. So much product comes in, and it's usually in bunches. Especially the jewelry, you should see how much I have that's not on display in the store – there's no room for it all." Chris chuckled gleefully as he spoke. "That is an interesting story about the ring, though. A mystery. What a small world if this is the actual ring, but we'll never know."

Martin nodded. He remembered how his mom had a whole box of jewelry set aside to one day leave for Izzy, her first and only granddaughter.

Chris wrapped the ring box in gilded gift-wrap with a bow tied neatly on top before pushing it across the counter to Martin. "Say, young man, what's bothering you?"

Martin looked into Chris's eyes and sensed the old man picking apart his emotions. "Nothing. I'm fine."

"I see pain behind your eyes. You do a bad job of hiding it."

Martin hated the shrewdness of older people; his mother was the same way. He looked down at the gift and fidgeted with it as he debated telling the old man what was on his mind. After a brief, awkward silence he decided to lay it all out there.

"This is a difficult week for me. This Sunday marks 22 years since I lost my daughter. Every day is a struggle, but this time of year is extra difficult."

"I'm sorry to hear that. May I ask what happened?" Chris leaned forward onto the counter and removed his reading glasses, his stale

20

breath now oozing into Martin's nose.

"I don't know. That's the hardest part. My wife got into a fight with my daughter that night. And when we woke up she was gone. We assume she ran away, but have no idea where or why. Part of me thinks she's dead. I know she wouldn't go this long without speaking to us. But maybe she's living in some exotic country, starting a new life."

"That must be a horrific burden to carry."

"It is. Two decades without any closure is a long time, and it never gets easier."

Chris sat upright and crossed his arms, shaking his head. "You know, I've dealt with some traumatic loss myself. I suppose you could call it the inverse of your situation. I lost both my parents when I was only seven years old."

Martin studied Chris who looked down as he spoke, wondering how such an event would have affected his long life. The man had to be at least seventy. "I'm sorry, that must have turned your world upside down."

"It's funny. When you're a kid you can pretty much go with the flow. All your worries are about who's gonna pick you up from school and who's gonna make your dinner. I think I went through the next five years of my life numb. I bounced around foster homes and schools, and it never hit me until I reached high school. That's when you need guidance most in life, and I had no one to turn to. I spent many days after school crying in the bathroom. It was the only place I had privacy. At home, I had to share a bedroom with three other boys, and crying was frowned upon. Everyone had a sad story – therefore no one felt bad about your problems."

"That's not fair."

"Might not be fair," Chris said matter-of-factly. "But that's how it goes. All you can do is try to make it to the next day and hope for the best."

"I know how that goes. That's been the last twenty years of my life." Martin felt for Chris, relating to the old man's tragedy.

"Sounds like we have a lot in common," Chris said with a slow shake of the head. He leaned over the counter to see the main entrance. A young couple browsed the store toward the front, but appeared empty-handed. "Say, how'd you like to come into my back room and see some rare things I've collected?"

Martin returned a puzzled look, unsure what prompted the random invitation. "Are you sure you want to leave the store unattended?" Martin asked as he nodded his head toward the young couple.

"Ahh, they'll be fine. He brought her here to try and prove his false sophistication. I see couples like that all the time. Some guys go to great lengths to get some these days. Back in my day, just being charming was enough."

Chris winked and raised his bushy eyebrows suggestively. "We'll just be a quick minute. Come."

Chris turned to the door behind his counter and pushed it open. More of that ancient odor oozed out of the back room.

Martin muddled cautiously around the counter and followed Chris into the darkness. Chris led them to an old wooden desk that sat beneath a hanging light fixture, its yellow glow illuminating only the desk, leaving the surroundings in an eerie blackness.

"In this business, you tend to come across things you maybe shouldn't. I feel like I've had more of this random luck than anyone else. I assumed it's to make up for all my shitty luck as a child." Chris opened a drawer on the desk and retrieved a flashlight. He clicked it on and pointed it to the wall behind Martin where the door had closed behind him.

A five-foot wide framed painting hung on the wall. The image portrayed thirteen men on a sailboat in the middle of a nasty storm. One glowing face looked familiar to Martin.

"This painting is called *Christ in the Storm on the Lake of Galilee*," Chris said. "It was painted by Rembrandt in 1633. Today it's worth almost five million dollars. It's been missing since 1990 from a major heist in Boston."

He lowered the flashlight to a short table flushed against the wall. Baseball cards spread across every inch of it, and Martin saw one staring at him that sent chills down his spine. He reached for it with a trembling hand.

"Ahhh, so you know about the rare Honus Wagner card." Chris grinned as he watched Martin. "That card is worth three million. In fact, it's the rarest trading card in history."

Martin held the card unsteadily in his hand, studying every inch of its orange background, Wagner's pasty face and neatly parted brown hair, all the way down to the detailing on his gray uniform that read *Pittsburgh* in brown lettering.

"This is the holy grail of baseball cards. Aren't there only a hundred of these left in the world?" Martin kept examining the card and wanted to pinch himself.

"Fifty seven still exist. Only 200 were printed to begin with." Chris leaned back in his creaky chair.

"I don't understand," Martin said, not wanting to put the card down. "How do you have these? And why don't you sell them? You're sitting on seven million from these two items alone. You would never have to work another day!"

Chris shrugged. "I suppose I'm a busybody. It's always been hard for me to relax and lounge. Besides, money is no issue for me. I don't *need* $7 million."

The mystery of this old man kept growing stranger as Martin learned more about him. Martin glimpsed around the room like a child in awe, even though most of it was left in darkness.

"Well, if you ever need someone to loan these cool things out to, just let me know. I can be that guy." Martin tried to lighten the mood.

"That's a generous offer, but I'll keep these under wraps. I trust you won't make any mention of what you saw in here, either?"

Martin nodded. "Of course not."

"Good. I have an oath to keep the secrets of time."

"Is there a reason this room is so dark? You developing photos in the back?" Martin sensed a shift in the mood and tried to make the old man laugh. It didn't work, and all he wanted was to get the hell out of this dark closet.

"I build things in here. Like I said, I'm the keeper of time, and I need to make sure I can preserve all parts of history."

Martin nodded slowly, not sure how to respond.

"Would you like to see?" Chris asked, raising the pitch in his voice. He grinned. "You might have an interest in what I'm working on in here."

"Okay, sure," Martin said, now trying to hide the fear in his wavering voice.

"Come!" Chris said and stood with a youthful spring in his legs.

Martin watched as Chris disappeared into the darkness, footsteps fading away before coming to a halt. A fluorescent light flickered to life, revealing a tall black countertop covered with beakers, piles of a sand-like substance, and a microscope.

"You're a mad scientist on the side?"

Chris walked behind the counter and pulled open a drawer. "Something like that," he snickered.

His skeletal fingers rose from the drawer with a small red pill pinched between his index finger and thumb. He placed the pill gently on the counter as Martin watched with cautious eyes.

"Martin. I feel like I can trust you. Quite frankly, it doesn't matter if you trust me back, but I believe I can be of service to you." Chris spoke with sharp enunciation on every word. "I'm going to tell you something. You're probably not going to believe me. Again, that doesn't matter, because what I tell you is true."

Martin subconsciously took a step backwards as he noticed a slightly crazed look appear in the old man's eyes.

"You see this pill?" he asked, holding up a small white pill pinched between his bony fingers. "If you swallow this pill, you'll fall asleep within minutes. When you wake up, you'll be in March of 1996, right here in Larkwood, Colorado. You'll be your current self in the flesh. You'll appear for everyone else to see, including your past self."

Martin gazed at Chris and wasn't sure if he should laugh or run out the door. He looked out the corner of his eye and noticed the door had disappeared. It was pure blackness where it had just been moments ago.

His legs froze and a lump formed in his throat. *What the fuck?*

"Relax," Chris said calmly. "I know this is a lot to take in, but hear me out. You can go back to 1996 and find out what happened to your daughter."

Martin remained frozen, but regained his ability to speak. "That's crazy. You're obviously making your own drugs back here. You should—"

"Get some mental help?" Chris completed Martin's sentence. *Where the hell is the door?*

"Now how would I know you would say that?" Chris spoke tauntingly, like a bully goading Martin on. "Perhaps, I took a peek into the future to see your reaction. Perhaps I already knew how you'd respond, and have an offer for you to give it a test run. Would you like to give it a try?"

"You're—"

"Crazy. Yes, yes, I know. And you're in denial. I have a pill that will take you back to this afternoon right when you got off work. I could've made you relive the work day, but that seemed a bit harsh." Chris checked his watch. "It's almost 7 P.M. If you take this pill, you'll return to four o'clock, just as you started your drive home. Like I mentioned, your current self returns to the past and is very much part of the world. You'll be here because when you fall back into the past, you'll awake where you took the pill. You can either wait around here until you arrive shortly after six to buy the ring, or you can take my car out back and meet yourself at home."

Martin gulped. His mind told him the old man was full of shit and it was time to leave. His gut, however, believed him, and his curiosity wanted to find out exactly what that pill could do.

After Martin remained silent, Chris said, "Tell me what you want to do. You can't leave without an answer, though. You can tell me no, and walk out that door and never see me again. You'll finish the rest of your life wondering what happened to your beautiful little girl. The unknowing will drive you mentally insane in your later years. I don't want to give away the spoiler, but it doesn't end well for you."

Chris strolled around the counter until he stood three feet in front of

Martin, still frozen.

"Or." He paused a brief moment. "You can take a look and try to get the closure your soul desperately needs."

Martin felt a sense of control start to return, his nerves settling. "If you know everything, why don't you just tell me?" he demanded.

"I do know everything. I can see everything from the past, present, and future. Knowing things and *doing* things are different, though. I can easily go back to the time of the Holocaust, but to do something to prevent it – that's out of my realm. I'm the keeper of time, not the changer of history. I study time and study people, but I'm not here to ruin or fix lives. History follows its course and I'm simply along for the ride. Think of it like the cameraman filming the lion hunting zebras in the jungle. He's observing, not getting involved. It's important to know your role and stay in your lane."

Chris stood close enough where Martin could smell the stale odor radiating from the old man's mouth.

"What's your angle? Even if all of this were true, why would you do this? You don't even know me."

"I like helping people."

"If this is all true, then why didn't you go back in time and stop your parents' death?"

Chris grinned like a politician expecting a tough question.

"You have to understand that there are rules when going back. It's not a free-for-all. I did go back to my parents' accident. Multiple times, in fact. What they say is true: things happen for a reason."

Martin stayed quiet, processing everything Chris had said.

"Well?" Chris persisted.

"What are these rules?" Martin asked.

"We can go over the rules if you decide to go back to 1996. For now, I just want you to see for yourself. There's not much you can damage in two hours, just make sure you don't get spotted by your past self. That can throw your life into limbo."

Martin took a final look for the door, and it still wasn't there. He realized he'd been trapped, perhaps intimidated, into taking this pill. Agreeing to these shenanigans seemed to be the only way out now.

What if it's just a sleeping pill and he tries to kill me or kidnap me? What if he has another secret room where he keeps his prisoners?

Chris studied him with a grin as wide as the Cheshire cat's.

"What if I say no?"

The grin melted into a frown. "Well, you can say no and leave this room and store and return to your life. But just know, the curiosity and regret will drive you into a frenzy. It can take quite a while until you can forget about this discussion."

Martin still hadn't moved despite having the feeling return to his legs. *Your life has already turned to shit. Say he does kill you in your sleep, then you get what you really want deep down: an end to it all. But say he's not lying, and this somehow works. Then you'll have the answer to a question you've been asking for two decades. I'd call it a low risk, high reward decision.*

Martin stared at Chris like a poker player, trying to see if he was bluffing or not. The old man smirked, as if he could hear Martin's thoughts out loud.

"Okay," Martin said confidently. "I'll try it."

The smirk widened again, reminding Martin of the villainous Joker from the *Batman* comics. "Fantastic!"

Chris hurried behind the counter and rummaged through his drawer until his fingers settled on a white pill. "This is the one! Follow me."

He dashed across the floor like a dancer and returned to his desk. He pulled out the squeaky chair and hung an arm out for Martin to take a seat.

"I don't have a bed in here or else I'd have you lay down. The chair will do just fine, though," Chris explained.

Martin stepped cautiously to the chair before sitting down, causing protesting creaks from the old wood. He plopped both arms on the armrests and watched Chris across the desk.

"Like I said, the rules are simple, at least for this quick journey: do not encounter your past self. Stay out of his sight, but feel free to hang

27

around and observe."

"When will I wake up?" Martin asked.

"I'm going to give you two pills. One will take you back in time, and the other will bring you back here. Keep the return pill in your pocket. Anything on your body will go with you when you go back in time. When you're ready to come back, just take the pill. Regardless of how long you stay in the past, only ten minutes will have passed here in the current world. Just make sure you come back before 7 P.M."

Martin nodded, still wanting to talk himself out of such nonsense, but it was too late. Chris placed the white pill on the desk. "This is to return. Put that in your pocket." Martin did as he was told. "And this is the one that will take you back to 4 P.M. Remember when you 'wake up' in the past, you'll be where your body currently occupies space, so you'll be in this room. I'll make sure the door's open."

Chris winked as he placed the new pill on the desk.

"You'll obviously see me when you go back. I'll know it's you. But as far as anyone else you interact with, they're going to assume you exist in the present time with them. Any questions?"

"Nope. Let's see what this is all about." Martin exuded a confident tone, but his heart pounded in anticipation to the point he could feel his fingertips throbbing against the wooden chair.

"Excellent. Feel free to roam around. You'll have two hours before your past self arrives to the store. Just stay out of your own way."

Martin picked up the pill and examined it under the hanging light. It was white and round, and felt no different than any other pill he'd ever taken. From his pinched fingers, he placed the pill in his mouth, letting it fill with saliva before swallowing. His heart pounded in his ears like distant drums.

Here goes nothing.

He closed his eyes and leaned his head back as he waited for what would come next.

6

Chapter 5

It only took a couple minutes for Martin to fall into a deep sleep. Blackness filled his mind temporarily while his body felt elevated by an invisible hand. His conscience remained alert as he waited anxiously in some sort of purgatory.

When the floating sensation stopped, his body jolted awake like it would after a nightmare. He sat in the same chair in the same dark room, only now the door he had longed for appeared, ajar with a stream of glowing light filling the darkness.

His body appeared intact as he studied his limbs and fingers. He stepped cautiously toward the door before pulling it all the way open. The bright lights from the store stung momentarily as his eyes adjusted. Once focused, he saw Chris sitting at the counter, reading his raggedy book. His frosty hair swirled in different directions as he kept his nose in the book, paying no attention to Martin.

"How do you feel?" Chris asked in an uninterested voice, startling Martin.

The old man didn't look up.

"Uh, fine, I guess. I don't feel any different. Should I?"

"Of course not. Nothing changes for you as long as you keep in mind the golden rule."

Chris flipped a page and continued his semi-ignoring of Martin. Martin looked around the store and saw the clock near the front entrance.

4:03. He could have just changed the clock. Doesn't make this real.

"If you're looking for proof," Chris said. "Then wait around two more minutes. An older lady will walk in and ask if I have any antique bookshelves. I'll point her in the right direction, she'll browse the two that I have, then she'll leave with a quick wave."

Martin didn't respond and walked around the store. He'd plan to see the old lady, but it still wouldn't prove anything. He could easily have paid some poor soul to come in and do exactly as asked.

Martin walked toward the entrance and looked outside where a car pulled in to the parking lot. The sun shone as bright as it did when Martin left the post office every day. *That's a nice touch, I wonder how the old man pulled off that illusion. The sun will be setting any minute now.*

The shiny sedan parked in the handicap parking space and a woman with a gray perm rose from the driver's seat and climbed the stairs, clinging to the handrail for support. She wore a large purse over her shoulder and moved with the fragility of someone with bad knees and hips.

She pulled open the store door and Martin froze where he stood, watching the woman with intense curiosity. She gave him a soft smile and walked past him to the counter where Chris had finally put his book down.

"Hello, ma'am, how can I help you today?" Chris said, sounding a bit scripted in Martin's opinion.

"Yes, I'm looking for an antique bookshelf. Do you happen to have any?" the old lady asked in a soft voice.

"I sure do. Have a couple right over there." Chris pointed in the direction, opposite Martin, and the woman wasted no time examining the bookshelves. Chris leaned over his counter and winked at Martin.

Okay, can still be a set up. This doesn't prove anything.

He struggled with his inner conscience, insisting this was all a well-planned sham, but believing deep down he would watch himself walk into the store in two hours. The thought made him nauseous.

Martin browsed a table of old, fine jewelry, but kept his eye on the woman. He could see her running fingers over the ancient wood, taking a mental picture of the shelves to imagine how they might look in her home. After a minute, she stepped away and headed for the exit. When she passed the counter she grinned and waved at Chris, who returned a grin.

"Thank you for stopping in," he said.

The bell chimed as the woman exited, and Chris gazed to Martin with a devilish smirk.

"I'm gonna go wander around outside. You said I can take your car?" Martin asked, not wanting to give Chris the satisfaction of acknowledging the events that just occurred.

"Yes, be my guest. Keys are in the glove box. It's the only car behind the store."

The smirk remained and Martin left the store with a newly found urgency. Surely it should have started cooling off by now, assuming it was still after seven, but the day remained hot.

You know this is really happening, he told himself. *Stop trying to resist. Go find whatever confirmation you need.*

He walked around the building and found a lone car parked, waiting for him. It was an old, blue Buick, much of the paint chipped away and giving way to brown rust.

"This guy sure lives a humble life for sitting on millions," Martin remarked before opening the driver's door. Despite its junky appearance, the interior was well kept, even smelling clean. He expected trash all over the floor, but there wasn't a single item in the car. He pulled open the glove box and found the key by itself.

The engine roared to life, stronger and in better shape then what Martin expected. The digital clock on the dashboard read *4:18.* "You pulled out all the stops. Great attention to detail."

Martin said these things to assure himself he wasn't going crazy, but the longer the sun didn't set, the more his doubt grew like a slowly inflating balloon. He drove out of the lot and left the Wealth of Time behind.

He drove in the direction of his apartment building, his mind racing out of control. The sun blinded him and he squinted as he weaved in and out of traffic.

What happens if I see myself? That would confirm this is either all real, or my friend at the store has been concocting some very powerful drugs.

It only took him five minutes to arrive to his apartment. He parked across the street from the main entrance and killed the engine. The clock read 4:24 as he drummed his fingers on the steering wheel, anxiously awaiting his past self's arrival.

He had stopped at the grocery store to stock up on more microwavable dinners and should arrive to the complex around 4:30. He faced the stop sign from which he should be turning, and held his breath every time a car pulled up to it.

When five more minutes passed and he still didn't see himself, his doubt and anticipation grew in sync. "Any minute now," he murmured beneath his breath. Then he saw the glimmering light from the hood of a small blue car pull up to the stop sign. Martin's heart dropped to his knees as he shifted in his seat.

"Please turn right, please turn right," Martin begged.

The car's left turn signal flicked on and started to turn his way.

"Fuck, fuck, fuck!" The car approached and he had no doubt it was his old Chevy sedan. Martin slouched in his seat, his eyes barely seeing over the dashboard. The car passed and he saw himself clear as day: chubby, scruffy beard, cigarette pinched between his lips. The car turned into the complex and drove around to the back where he always parked.

Martin's heart hammered against his rib cage, his fingers pulsing against the steering wheel he had clenched without realizing.

"What do I do?" he asked the empty car. "Do I go back to the old man? Take this pill now? Where will I wake up? *When* will I wake up?"

He started the engine, still unsure what he was going to do, but knowing he wanted to get the hell away from his past self.

He sped off and pulled into the gas station three blocks down.

Martin panted for breath as he surveyed the area for anyone he might know. Once he decided the coast was clear, he popped the pill in his mouth and gulped it down dry. With adrenaline flowing through his veins, he wondered if the pill would still put him to sleep.

When two minutes passed without a weary feeling, Martin panicked and reclined the driver's seat.

"Calm down. Relax. He told you this would work. You'll wake up from this bad trip. Drugs can't affect you forever."

He inhaled deeply. *There we go.* The world came in and out as his eyelids flickered in protest. It only took a few seconds before the world turned black and Martin returned to the floating sensation he had felt earlier.

7

Chapter 6

A sharp thud smacked Martin in the back as he jolted awake. He was back in the dark room inside Wealth of Time, his haggard breathing the only audible sound. The door was cracked open, letting in a lone beam of light. The light above him illuminated the desk, now clear of clutter.

"Have a nice visit?" Chris's voice carried from the corner where he kept his miniature laboratory. His slowly approaching footsteps shuffled along the ground as he returned to Martin's vision. The dim lighting revealed a sly grin that said *I told you so.* "Well?"

"That was very convincing," Martin said, trying to sound unimpressed.

"Oh, Martin, stop the act!" Chris giggled crazily as he spoke. "You're only lying to yourself at this point. There's nothing else I can do to prove to you that this is real."

"I believe it's real. I'm just refusing to accept it."

"Let's get out of this room. I sense it makes you anxious."

No shit.

Martin stood without hesitation and chased after the door before it mysteriously closed again. He swung the door open with aggression, adrenaline still pulsing throughout.

The store remained the same, although the sun finally started to set, causing an orange splash of light across the floor. Martin spotted the clock near the entrance and it read 7:14. His heart sunk as every part of him gave in to the reality of what had just happened. He could barely hear Chris speaking to him as the pounding in his ears echoed.

"Now stop playing around and tell me your thoughts." Chris egged him on like a child daring a friend.

"Well, it definitely felt real. I saw myself . . . completely freaked me out."

Chris nodded attentively, smirking.

"So do you want to go back to 1996?" Chris asked.

"This all seems so crazy. What am I supposed to do in 1996, play detective? I don't know what I'm doing."

Chris nodded as if he understood, but Martin could see the thoughts swimming behind his eyes.

"Well, you could start planning now and go back to 1996 with a strict plan. Or you can just go back and follow your daughter. Like I said, it would be March when you arrive, so you'd have six months to get situated before she goes missing."

Martin nodded. "Will you give me a glimpse into 1996 like you did tonight? I just want to know it's real."

"This is all legitimate. And no, I can't give you a glimpse, that's not how this works."

"Then I want to know how this works. Everything. What's in those pills? What's in this for you? Who are you?"

Chris raised a hand to silence the flustered man.

"I'll tell you what you *need* to know. The rules. One rule being that you can only do this once, and that's why I can't send you back for a peek into the past."

"But you just did!" Martin snapped.

"Yes, that was a three-hour time travel, has no effects. Going back twenty two years will certainly affect you."

"What do you mean affect me? What kind of drugs are in those pills?" Martin's voice rose to a near shout. He stood across the counter while Chris leaned back in his chair.

"These aren't drugs. The pills really do take you back in time, or forward, should you choose. But you don't seem like a guy who looks forward to the future. As for the effects, that leads to your other question of what I get out of this."

Chris stood up and leaned on the counter to look Martin straight in the eyes.

"This is serious business," he said. "I don't want any money from you. What I want in exchange is a part of you. During that brief moment when you feel like you're flying after taking the pill, you're in my domain. When you're in there, I can take from your soul as I please."

Martin narrowed his eyes on Chris, wanting to call a bluff, but remaining hesitant. "My soul?" he asked mockingly. "What are you? The Devil?"

Chris smirked. "I'm not the Devil. I'm the keeper of time, I've told you this already. Opportunities like this aren't free. All I ask for is a part of your soul."

"And what part of my soul will you be taking if I agree to this?" Martin played along. Every time the old man spoke, it seemed like a joke that was about to snowball out of control.

Chris pursed his lips and rubbed his head. "It may not seem like much to you, but I want to take your emotions."

Martin raised his eyebrows. "My emotions?"

"Yes. You'll keep your emotions when you go back to 1996. But when you return, you'll be emotionless. Apathetic. No more joy, no more anger. Just a wandering zombie."

"Bullshit," Martin said flatly. "You can't take my emotions, just like I can't move buildings with my mind. You're a goddamn liar! This prank is over."

Martin stormed away from the counter, stomping his feet toward the exit. Nighttime had finally arrived and darkness filled the void through the windows.

"Wait!" Chris shouted, and Martin stopped short of the exit. All he wanted was to leave this damn store behind and never come back, but that glimmer of opportunity proved too much to resist. "Come back and

I'll tell you everything you need to know." Chris spoke as if making a hard statement instead of the pleading he was actually doing.

Guy must be desperate for my "emotions."

Martin returned to the counter in a slow dragging of steps. "Tell me everything, and I'll consider your offer tonight. I'll need to sleep on it."

"Sure, sure," Chris said. "For starters, I'm not kidding about the exchange for the emotional part of your soul. You'll still be a fully functioning person, normal for the most part. But you won't be able to care for others, laugh at jokes, or cry at movies. Think of it as that emotional numbness you felt when your daughter went missing. Only this time it won't be numb, just normal."

"How does this all work? Am I really going back in time, or is it all a hallucination?"

Chris nodded. "It's very real, my friend. I'm not going to get into the science of time, but what happens when you take the pill is a sort of transportation. When you arrive in 1996, you'll still be yourself as you are now. Also, anything you have on your body goes with you, so play that to your advantage. If you want to take money with you, keep it in your pocket. Your money today can go a lot further in 1996. Gas was only a $1.30 back then.

"If you have money, great! If not, use your resources to find easy ways to make money. There's really no restrictions on what you can do except for running into yourself."

"And what happens if I run into my past self?" Martin asked, wondering this the entire time.

"Well, think about it. You essentially have two souls when you go back in time. If they meet . . . let's just say it's disastrous for you. You can end up in serious trouble, or worse."

"Okay, I'll stay out of my own way. What about my family and friends, can I talk to them?"

"Sure. If you think they'll recognize you somehow, wear a disguise. I don't know how different you look today compared to back then, so use your best judgment."

"What happens if I lose my pill to come back to present day?"

"Then you stay and live the rest of your life out in that time frame. If you die in there, you'll die here as well. So please stay alive, and don't ever lose that pill."

"Can't you come find me if I lose it?"

"Sure, but that pill is a one-way ticket. Each pill I make is unique, so it's practically impossible for me to replicate them."

"What happens if I change something? What if I take my daughter and run away?"

Chris paused to consider the question.

"Well, changing an event in history will obviously alter the course of the future. You might come back to a completely different life if you change anything. I always recommend to not change anything too drastically. The results could be catastrophic."

"How do you know this?"

"Martin, you're not the first person who has gone back in time. There have been thousands before you and will be thousands after. Every person has their reasons for going back. I've seen some nasty consequences result from someone getting in over their head while in the past. The terrorist attacks on September 11th were a direct result of someone trying to tinker with the past. Your trip back in time is meant to be mostly observatory. Sure, you'll leave a footprint and can effect minor changes, but a decision like running off with your daughter can end in disaster. Just remember that things happen for a reason, as the old saying goes."

"Why me? Why did you pick me for this?"

"Simple: you have something I want, and you have something in the past that demands answers. I don't go around offering this opportunity to random people."

Martin wanted to ask what Chris did with the supposed souls he takes, but figured that would lead down a rabbit hole he had no business in venturing.

"I want to think things over tonight. Can I come back tomorrow?"

"Of course."

"And no matter how long I'm in the past, when I take the pill to return only ten minutes will have passed?"

"Correct."

"I'll be back same time tomorrow."

Chris smirked. "See you then."

Martin jogged out of the store and found his car waiting under the moonlight. He drove home thinking about his daughter and where she was in the world.

8

Chapter 7

When Martin arrived home he wasted no time emptying a bottle of whiskey into a tall glass. His mind paced in frantic circles as he debated his next move. A sliver of skepticism remained, and he considered pretending that the whole thing never happened.

But it did. I really went back in time and saw myself.

He lay down on his couch as the room started to spin, his body tingling from the alcohol, and debated his own sanity.

Is this the boiling point? Have I finally reached it?

He wondered if a person could know when they've gone crazy, or if it was something only visible from the outside. This all could have been a nervous breakdown in anticipation of the upcoming weekend. Izzy was always on his mind during this week more than any other time of year. Maybe he was dreaming and would wake up tomorrow to jump back into his normal routine of hating his life.

But he knew better.

You can't get drunk in your dreams, and I'm very drunk.

Martin tossed and turned for the next hour on his couch. He usually had no issue passing out and snoring the night away, but his mind refused to shut down for the day. It demanded a decision on what would happen when the sun rose in the morning.

"Ten minutes," he whispered. "I could go in before work and still make it on time if all I lose is ten minutes."

He'd be spending at least six months in the past, depending on what he found. Six months in history to find out what happened to Izzy, all to come back to return to the post office like nothing had happened.

Every time he closed his eyes he saw Chris grinning, smirking, tempting him to go. *That guy is a demon,* Martin thought as he took one final swig to kill the last of the whiskey. *Ten minutes. No one will even know I was gone.*

He bolted upright and immediately regretted it as the blood and alcohol rushed to his head, causing the room to spin.

"I'm going," he declared. "I'm going. And if I die, then so be it."

Saying these words aloud provided him the confidence needed to take the gamble. He could either endure his life wondering what happened to Izzy, or he could take the chance to find out. How many people in his same situation would even debate the matter? It was a no-brainer and he couldn't believe it took him so long to arrive to the right decision. *I have to go. At this point, there's nothing for me to lose.*

Martin dragged himself into the kitchen to grab his laptop and a notepad. He rummaged through the cupboards for another bottle of whiskey, could only find vodka, and poured a glass of it mixed with orange juice before returning to the couch with all three items in hand.

The laptop wheezed to life and the screen's glow blasted his face with bluish light. Martin needed to return to 1996 with a plan. First and foremost, he needed a way to make money, and he liked the idea of sports betting. Sporting results were all recorded and could be found with a quick search. Finding an underground bookie in Larkwood, Colorado, in 1996, shouldn't be too difficult. He'd had some friends who got involved with the gambling ring around that time, and he often remembered them saying that the bookies would set a spread on any wager offered, including politics.

Martin noted down all the significant sporting events that would occur between March and September of 1996, and was delighted to find the results for the summer Olympics in Atlanta. *Maybe I can afford to go.*

Should I use an alias? He debated the matter. An alias was only helpful if he planned to immerse himself in the community and chat with people around town. Since the younger version of himself already existed in 1996, an alias wouldn't do much—he needed to focus on dodging familiar faces. A disguise might be a better investment to not raise any suspicion. Besides, using a fake name would only cause confusion, and flying under the radar would be much easier to achieve.

After a half hour he had a handful of pages with every sports score listed neatly by the event's date. With his income settled for the past, he shifted his focus to his personal whereabouts and life events in 1996.

He was obviously in Larkwood, but what was he doing?

Was 1996 when I had that data entry job?

Of course it was. He took a month off of work after Izzy went missing. They were accommodating of his situation and worked with him throughout the process. Some days he simply couldn't make it through, and they sent him home with no complaints.

Synergetix. That was the company.

He had started there at the beginning of the year and would be well into his first year of employment by the time 2018 Martin arrived in 1996. He drove an old station wagon to work every day with his sack lunch packed every morning by his beautiful wife. Life was truly as good as it had ever been in the first half of 1996, and the nostalgia made him excited to go back to those times.

They would have been in the only house they lived in as a family, having moved in shortly after Izzy's birth. Lela was a part-timer at the local daycare center, working most weekdays from noon through six. Martin's data entry job provided a big pay increase and they enjoyed eating out every weekend as part of their new, luxurious lifestyle.

He would need somewhere to live in 1996, preferably close to his old house to keep an eye on things. All he really needed was to be around in September to keep a close eye as the eventual day of doom approached. March through August could virtually be spent doing whatever he wished. There was no need for investigative work during that time frame, as life had been rather normal. The night Izzy went missing was a night he had to work late and arrived home to everyone in bed.

This was a particular point of initial interest for the police. A missing girl and a father who had to work late the same night smelled awfully suspicious, but a couple of calls to Synergetix was all it took to clear his name.

September 9, 1996, he remembered. The day life went down the shitter and never recovered. Tears streamed down Martin's face and dripped silently to the floor. The feelings from that morning had never left him. With every minute that passed, every shout of "IZZY!", hope had slowly dissipated and gave way to fear, panic, and sickness.

"These things don't really happen to people," he had said to Lela when they returned home after an hour in the neighborhood. "Izzy wouldn't run away."

"She's gone!" Lela had screamed. "She's gone!"

That was all she had been able to say on that day 22 years ago. Even when the police arrived, she kept saying it, trying to assure herself that it was real.

The police had poked around the house and yard looking for any clues, coming up empty-handed. They technically had to wait another day before issuing an Amber Alert, but they had started the process and paperwork in preparation for the following day.

Martin and Lela spent the rest of the day driving around town, going to Izzy's friends' houses, her school, and the rec center. Those were the only places she ever went outside of the house. When the sun started to set and they accepted that they weren't going to find their daughter, Lela burst into heavy tears in the car as they pulled up to their house.

"Why, Martin? Why did she leave us?"

I don't know. But I'm going to find out.

9

Chapter 8

When the sun rose the next morning, Martin's head throbbed as he rubbed his swollen eyes. The stench of alcohol seeped out of his pores, causing him to gag. He had fallen asleep on the couch, the stinging sun blazing through the living room window. His notepad was splayed on the ground with his chicken scratch notes. The digital clock on the stove informed him it was almost seven. He had just over an hour until he needed to report to the post office. *Plenty of time to clean up and visit Chris for a trip back to the 90's. Hopefully hangovers can't travel back in time with me.*

When he stood, the room spun violently around him and he collapsed back into the couch. *Fuck, I'm still drunk.* Martin belched and felt the alcohol sloshing around in his stomach as he stood again, this time with a hand on the couch's arm for support. He staggered to the kitchen like a zombie to fill a glass of water and swallow a handful of ibuprofen. His brain felt like an over-inflated balloon trying to burst against his skull. *Worst hangover ever?* he wondered. He'd had plenty—more than he could count in the last twenty years—but couldn't remember the last time he felt he might actually croak.

After chugging the water, he dragged himself to the bathroom to relieve his throbbing bladder and stared in the mirror. His hair was frazzled in every direction, his eyes were bloodshot, and his face looked a different shade, slightly gray.

"Damn, Marty. You are hung the *fuck* over," he said to himself in an attempt for a laugh, but his body and brain ached too much to appreciate the humor. He spent the next ten minutes splashing water on his face, putting eye drops in, and swishing mouthwash until the taste of alcohol finally vanished. He stared at himself with a stern expression when he was done. "We're gonna do this. We're gonna save Izzy. No more booze until she's found alive."

The brief pep talk provided a slight boost of energy, but his head still pounded in protest as he gathered his papers and dressed for the upcoming trip, sure to wear jeans and a plain t-shirt to blend in for his 1996 arrival. He stuffed the cash he kept hidden in a coffee can into his wallet and left the apartment in a hurry.

The sunlight sent a shockwave of pain from his eyes all the way down his spine when he stepped outside. When he pulled his car out to the street, he looked around in every direction, searching for some past or future version of himself who might be watching. There was no one, and his paranoia settled down. Every time he saw a person on the road, he wondered if they were really from this current time, or if they traveled back from the next century to see what life was like in 2018.

It only took a few minutes to arrive at Wealth of Time. If ten minutes were all that would pass during his adventure, he'd be in great shape to make it to work on time.

He'd never asked Chris if he would be at the store at 7 A.M., but figured it didn't really matter. Chris probably *knew* when Martin would arrive and would be waiting patiently behind his counter with that devilish smirk.

The storefront glowed under the clear sky as he pulled into the empty parking lot. The building seemed to pull at Martin with a magnetic force. Chills ran throughout his body, but he assumed those were remnants from his massive hangover.

"This is all for you, Izzy." Martin parked his car in the front row and looked through the store windows. The lights were on, and he knew Chris was waiting.

The usual chime greeted him, and the silence from the room soothed his throbbing head. He could only hear the sound of his own breathing and heart pounding in his ears.

"Good morning, Martin!" Chris's voice carried from the back of the store. "Come on over!"

The voice was distant, and Martin knew the old man was waiting in the back room. He took weary steps toward the counter to find the blackness of the open door. Chris sat at the desk, below the hanging light. With that smirk.

"Looks like you had a rough night," Chris said.

Martin wasn't sure if Chris had somehow "visited" him the night before, or if he truly looked like shit. Probably both.

"I'm doing this. For my daughter. Whatever it takes." Martin spoke as confidently as he could.

"Do you have everything you need? Money? Resources for future income? A plan?"

"Yep." Martin had all of the above except for an actual plan. He'd have enough time to get a grasp for how this time travel ordeal worked, but the plan was simple: observe his house from a distance and follow Izzy.

"Perfect. Now, six months is a long time. You'll likely reach a point where you forget all about your current life and get caught up in the midst of being in the past. It'll feel normal. Don't forget to come back. I'll be around to remind you."

"Where can I find you when I'm there?" Martin asked.

"You won't be able to find me. I'll find you, don't worry."

Martin stared at him silently, not pleased with the answer, but realizing there was nothing he could do about it. "Fine," he said like a defeated child.

"You sure you're ready?" Chris asked.

"Yes. Are you trying to talk me out of this now?"

"Of course not. This is a big deal. You're sacrificing a lot, but it will be worth it. Once you make a deal with me, there's no going back."

"Sure. I understand the risks. I'll be emotionless when I get back. No big deal."

Not like I've had emotions the last two decades, anyway.

"All right then, let's get started, shall we?"

Chris stood and extended a hand to his vacant chair. "Have a seat."

Sweat dripped down Martin's arms as his heart raced. The world seemed to vanish as he focused on the chair. It hadn't been an entire day since he sat in that same chair and traveled back in time two hours. He would sit in that chair again for ten minutes while he went back to 1996 to get the answers he had longed for his entire life.

Martin stepped behind the counter and into the old man's office. Chris remained frozen with his arm extended while Martin made his way to the desk. He stepped aside as Martin sat down, and hobbled to the dark corner where he kept his stash of pills.

Chris moved in the darkness, rummaging through drawers and talking to himself. Martin wondered how the hell the old man could know what he was grabbing, but decided probing him any further would only reveal truths he didn't really want to know.

"Shall we?" Chris asked as he emerged from the darkness with that fucking grin. Martin was ready to wipe the leer off the old man's face if he had to look at it any longer.

Martin waited in the chair, his trembling hands on the armrests, and watched as Chris placed two pills in front of him. This time they were light blue.

"Whenever you're ready," Chris said, the smirk gone.

Martin stared at the pills, grabbed one and slid it into his pocket. He wore jeans with deep pockets on purpose and would worry about stashing the pill securely when he arrived in the past.

"I'm arriving in March of 1996? In this same location?" he asked Chris, whose eyes had grown in excitement.

"Correct."

Martin thought back to this particular location, but his mind was too flustered to recall what the hell had been on this land.

It's time. Just go for it.

"See you in hell," Martin said to Chris and mimicked the grin he had grown so irritated of.

He popped the pill in his mouth and swallowed it in one motion.

No going back now.

"I'll see you in ten minutes!" Chris cried.

Ten minutes. 1996. Find Izzy. Don't encounter yourself.

He repeated these thoughts as he leaned back in the chair and felt all his worries melt away. The hangover faded, followed by his nerves settling. His eyes grew heavy as he fought the grip of sleep while bobbing his head. Then he slouched all the way back in the chair as darkness took control.

10

Chapter 9

Martin woke up in a deserted lot, lying flat on his back on a rough, dirt ground. His headache was gone, the alcohol absent from his breath, and overall he felt energetic and refreshed.

He hurried to his feet and regained his balance after the woozy sensation passed. Looking around, he wondered if he landed on a different planet. The dirt filled an entire open lot for the surrounding three blocks as far as he could see. A quiet neighborhood of one-level homes was to the south, separated from the lot by a stand of oak trees.

The sun beat down on him. It had to be at least 80 degrees as beads of sweat formed on his forehead. He felt nervous as he looked around and saw no signs of life.

"If this is 1996, the church will be in the same place," he reminded himself. He walked away from the neighborhood where the church would await three blocks to the north. Another neighborhood was at the north end of the lot where he could see actual homes, quiet and undisturbed in the warm day.

It has to be the middle of the day. He said I'd arrive in the same location, but not necessarily the same time.

Martin pulled his cell phone out and powered on the screen. Everything appeared to be properly functioning except for actual cell reception. And the time. He blinked his eyes and rubbed them to ensure he was seeing the time correctly as *00:00*.

"What the fuck?" he whispered, chills breaking out down his arms.

First matter of business is to confirm the date and time. Then I can plan from there.

A sliver of doubt remained within, but every instinct and voice of reason in Martin's mind assured him this was all real.

Even if this is a dream, or some sort of hallucination from the pills, I'm still here. At least, I think I'm here.

That was good enough for Martin and he walked to the north neighborhood, kicking up dust with each heavy step. A chain-link fence forced him to walk around the rows of houses instead of cutting through someone's backyard.

It took ten minutes to navigate around the neighborhood. The sun was straight above him and he figured the time was close to noon. When he passed the final house he saw civilization, and a wave of relief swept over him.

The dirt gave way to asphalt before changing to concrete on a sidewalk that ran along a paved road. The road stretched two blocks down and connected with a main road. "That should be 72nd, and the church should be one more block."

The church lot was surrounded by more trees, some bare, some green. *It's definitely March.* He paced faster toward the trees and crossed the street after another block. Cars zipped by on the main road ahead as he crossed into the trees, coming out the other side and seeing the building he was aiming for.

Martin skidded to an abrupt halt when he saw what remained of the church. The roof was collapsed and charred. Chunks of its once brick exterior lay scattered across the ground in messy piles of rubble. He could see inside the church where only the altar remained, also fried to a crisp.

"Holy shit," Martin said. "The fire of '96."

He thought back to this time when his mother had called him in a panic, sobbing uncontrollably into the phone.

"The church is gone!" she cried. "It's all gone!"

Martin didn't know how to respond at the time, and didn't know what to do in the present. The church would be repaired by December through tireless work from the parishioners and community. Izzy's memorial service was held there that month, two weeks after the reopening.

I forgot this happened.

All doubt vanished. His feet stood on ground from two decades earlier, and his lungs breathed air from a much simpler time in his life. There was no faking the burnt down church.

"It's 1996." He said this to make it *feel* real. His mind worked in overdrive to process the events of the last ten minutes, leaving him a bit lightheaded.

Snap out of it. What are you going to do now?

He reached into his pocket and brushed a finger over the pill, his return flight home. The idea of taking it crossed his mind. Why should a reckless alcoholic get the opportunity for time travel?

Without thinking about it, Martin started toward the church, feeling an urge to stand in the rubble. His mother had begged and pleaded for his help in rebuilding the church all those years ago, but between a packed work schedule and constant activities with Izzy, his free time was limited.

Martin stood at what used to be the church's main entrance and gawked at the collapsed doors. The smell of burnt wood oozed out of the piles of debris. The pews were buried underneath the roof. Stained-glass windows that once depicted each Station of the Cross lay shattered in ruins.

"Excuse me, sir, may I help you?" an older man's voice came from behind, causing Martin to jump and pivot around.

"Father Alfonso, you scared me," Martin said, not realizing his reflex reaction toward his former priest.

The old man squinted his eyes and put a hand over his brow to block the sun. "Martin Briar?"

Oh shit. Just run. Turn and run. Don't let him see you like this. How could I already fuck this up? I've only been in the past ten minutes and I'm about to blow my cover.

"Yes, Father, how are you? Long time since I've seen you." Martin forced every word out of his tense throat. *Play it cool, he may not notice anything different.*

"I'm doing just fine, aside from my church being a pile of ashes." The priest offered a soft grin. "How have you been? I haven't seen you around here in years. You look . . . different."

No shit. I'm 54 but you still think I'm 32.

"I've been good. Busy with the family and work."

"Too busy to give an hour to God each week?"

Martin looked to the dirt. *Fucking Catholic guilt.*

"I know I haven't been around, and I'm sorry. I rarely have a day off."

Father Alfonso spread a wide smile, revealing immaculate teeth. "I'm just kidding with you, lighten up, young man."

Young man? Have I not aged all this time?

Martin offered a shy grin, wanting to get as far away from this situation as possible. "I really should be going. I just wanted to come see this damage for myself."

"It's a shame. I expect I'll see you around on some of the repair crews?"

"I'll do what I can. I know my mom'll be here for sure."

"Bless her. Well you take care of yourself. Hope to see you around."

The old priest extended a fragile hand, which Martin shook quickly.

"Great seeing you, Father."

Martin turned away and strolled toward 72nd Avenue without looking back.

I'll certainly never come back here. Especially with how much my mom will be here to volunteer.

Bulky cars zoomed by Martin as he reached the main road. He paused to catch his breath and wipe the sweat dripping down his face. Two more miles west and he'd find himself in his old neighborhood where the 1996 version of himself lived with a happy wife and daughter.

With $3,000 stuffed into his wallet, Martin remembered he still had plenty to get done. If he planned to be around for six months, he'd need a car. This walking business had already grown old after traveling an entire six blocks. He'd need an apartment, preferably close to his old house.

For now, he needed a place to stay and knew of only a couple hotels in the Larkwood area, one near his old house. He could stay a night there and plan for the rest of the week. They'd also be able to tell him the exact date and time.

"I guess I need to buy a watch, too," he said as he looked at his phone still reading as *00:00*. He had pulled it out to call for a car through one of his apps, but forgot he had no service. And there was no such thing as ride sharing apps in the 90's—it was still wrong to get in cars with strangers, believe it or not. Since Larkwood was a smaller town, there weren't exactly any random taxis patrolling the area.

Motherfucker, two miles of walking it is, then.

Martin inhaled deeply, letting the fresh air fill his tarred lungs. Two miles wouldn't be too bad, and he thought of how a car became his top priority as he walked to the nearest hotel.

11

Chapter 10

The Sunset Dream Motel welcomed Martin as he huffed and puffed, his face flushed as red as a fire truck. Cramps throbbed in his calves and thighs from the hour-long, two-mile walk across town. His smoker's lungs couldn't handle the merciless abuse of fresh air and exercise.

There were no hotels in Larkwood. Martin had gone his entire life without realizing it was a town of all motels. Being a main hub for truckers, the motel room provided an uncomfortable bed, dirty bathroom, and a TV with terrible reception. The odor of cigarette smoke clung to the walls of the entire building. A couple of diesels were parked along the back of the building of the otherwise deserted motel.

"If you're looking for some fun during your stay, call this number," the front desk clerk told Martin after checking him in. He slid a paper the size of a business card across the counter with a phone number written in scribbly letters. "Hundred dollars for two hours, you won't find a better deal around here."

The clerk spoke with a twang to complement his mullet and handlebar mustache. The minty odor of chewing tobacco radiated from his breath.

"Thank you, I'll keep that in mind," Martin said.

"Glad to help. Name's Randy if ya need anything. I'll be here."

"Actually, Randy, can you tell me what the date is?"

"Today's March 18. You're not from around here, are you?"

"Thank you. And no, I'm not. Just passing through on a business trip."

"I see. Ya know, if you go about ten minutes south there's a hotel for business guys like you. If you want a more upscale place to stay."

"I'll be fine here. This is the perfect location."

"Suit yourself."

Randy pushed a key across the counter and wished Martin a good day.

Martin grabbed the key, left the office, and headed for his room six doors down. An old man sat passed out in a lawn chair in front of the room next to Martin's, cigarette still lit between his chubby fingers as smoke oozed into the air.

Martin's room welcomed him with the stench of cigarettes and bleach, causing an immediate migraine.

Maybe an apartment should be top priority.

He stared at his bed and wondered how many times a trucker brought his $50 per hour hooker for a night of romance at the Sunset Dream Motel. The number had to be higher than he wanted to know. Not wanting any disease to find its way into his bloodstream, Martin pulled the two extra pillows from the closet and laid them across the bed. It would be a long night sleeping on top of the pillows, but he considered it a minor inconvenience in the grand scheme of his journey.

He grabbed a pen and pad of paper from the nightstand and made a checklist for the rest of the week.

March 18, he thought. *Still don't know what day it is.*

He pulled out his cell phone and prayed the calendar application still worked. When he found it did, he scrolled for almost five minutes to 1996.

Today's Monday, March 18.

He scribbled this at the top of the notepad. The clock on the nightstand informed him it was also 11:37 A.M. He continued composing his checklist.

Apartment, car, watch, money, plan.

He circled the word *plan.*

What exactly am I gonna do for the next six months?

He debated continuing his 2018 lifestyle. Surely alcohol and tobacco were cheaper in 1996. More bang for his buck if he could get blacked out on twenty dollars.

Don't do it, he reminded himself. *You have a fresh start. No one here knows you. Except for your priest, apparently.*

The prospect of a job grew more appealing. He could make a little bit of money from work and gambling and take it all back to 2018.

I should have researched stocks. I still can. I'll know which ones hang around for the next two decades and have a pile of cash waiting when I return.

Martin wanted a quick nap. His mind felt like it had traveled on a twenty-hour flight across the world, but the sight of the bed with its stained sheets and comforter made him want to find an apartment instead.

He dropped the paper and pen and clicked on the TV. A fuzzy image came on, showing an old soap opera. The picture flickered constantly as Martin flipped through the channels in search of anything to watch that might distract his mind.

CNN came up and scrolled through the day's stock market prices, prompting him to grab his pen and write each price as fast as he could. Investing was a smarter choice than taking money from bookies. There would be no stockbrokers in Larkwood, so he'd need a car to get downtown.

With a short-term plan, Martin felt re-energized and ready to tackle his to-do list, leaving the motel in a hurry. The old man remained asleep and let out a hoarse belch between snores.

The sound of the highway behind the building roared with traffic, but the road in front remained deserted. His old house waited a short six blocks away, causing the temptation to swell as he debated taking a casual stroll down his old street.

Six months. Follow the checklist, he reminded himself.

From the motel, the nearest apartment complex should be two blocks north. It was the same building he lived in in 2018, and he vaguely remembered it opening in the mid-90's. With the leg cramps finally fading away, Martin started his journey north.

The sun didn't let up as the clock struck noon. Mid-March in Colorado meant there was still one more month of unpredictable weather that could swing an 80-degree day to a freezing blizzard the next day. It was the perfect day to sit on the balcony with a cigar and a glass of scotch. But Martin had no cigar or scotch, let alone a balcony. *Fuck this.*

Martin dragged himself the two blocks only to find an empty lot. "You're shitting me!" he shouted. Bushes and tumbleweed filled the landscape where his future residence would be built. "I could've sworn this was open by now." He rotated to check the rest of the area, seeing nothing but the houses in the neighborhood and no apartment building in sight. One more block north was the middle school where Izzy would be.

Martin's heart ached immediately at the thought. Here he was, one block away from his long-lost daughter, and all he wanted to do was barge into her classroom and hug her. Hug her and never let go. Take her from the school. Chris had cautioned against making drastic changes to the past. Surely kidnapping his daughter would change everything.

Stay patient. You'll see her soon enough.

Tears welled in his eyes. Just seeing her in person would be enough to call this a successful trip. One last hug and kiss on her forehead that he could hang on to for the rest of his life would suffice.

Go back to the motel. It's day one and you're already risking your cover. Finish your plan, then worry about seeing Izzy.

Martin swiveled around on his heel and dragged his feet in defeat back to the motel. His thighs protested the additional walking, but his mind stayed too consumed to notice. He closed his eyes while he trudged along the sidewalk, picturing Izzy with her round, green eyes, brace-filled smile, and childish giggle that echoed in his heart and mind.

The walk back to the motel felt shorter, thanks to his racing thoughts. He entered the lobby where Randy sat behind the front desk, a cigarette pursed between his lips as he watched *Seinfeld* on a small, portable television.

"What can I do ya for?" he asked, not looking away from the TV.

"I think I'm going to be in town much longer than I planned. Do you know where the nearest apartments are?"

Randy plucked the cigarette out of his mouth and turned his attention to Martin with a scrunched face.

"Couple miles east of here. Off 84th by the flea market."

"Perfect, thank you. Are you able to call me a cab by chance to take me there?"

"Yessir."

Randy snapped the phone off its cradle and turned the wheel on the rotary. Martin patted the cell phone in his pocket, thankful for how far technology had advanced through the new century.

While Randy ordered the taxi, Martin perused the lobby that he had ignored earlier. Pictures of diesel trucks decorated the wood-panel walls, fake plants stood in each corner of the room, and a table with magazines about guns and trucks was tucked along the back wall next to a raggedy water cooler. The ashtray on the table overflowed.

"Cab's here," Randy said, having already returned to his TV with the cigarette back between his crusty lips.

"Thank you, sir!" Martin replied as he crossed the lobby, excited to travel by vehicle.

The yellow cab waited outside the main entrance, smoke puttering from the exhaust pipe. The paint was chipped in scattered areas and the driver side taillight appeared busted in by a baseball bat.

Martin opened the door and plopped down behind the driver. A bald, black man greeted him. "Hey, mon. Where to?"

A small Jamaican flag hung from the rear-view mirror, just above his ID card that identified him as Clinton Green.

"Hello, I'm heading to the apartment complex by the flea market. I'm not sure of the name, but it's right off 84th."

"Got it," Clinton responded in a thick Jamaican accent. "Five minutes."

"Do you know the name?"

"Larkwood Suites."

"Thank you."

Martin looked out the window during the drive. He'd never realized how clean the town had become over time. Seeing it in the 90's again reminded him that it hadn't always been the safest of places to live. Broken-down cars were parked in front of run down houses. Graffiti decorated abandoned warehouses that blended into the city's skyline. A group of teenagers huddled in the warehouse's parking lot, smoking cigarettes while passing a brown bag around the circle.

Ahhh, Larkwood. You've changed, but you're still the same.

Seeing the city's transformation over the course of his life showed Martin that even the worst of situations could one day sprout a better future. In 2018, the same area had an outdoor strip mall with a restaurant, nail salon, and liquor store.

Driving through town felt like a trip through the history books. They passed the block where his mom lived, and he craned his neck for a view of her house. It stood with its beige exterior, not having changed one bit over the years. Seeing the house caused gooseflesh to break out across his arms. The trip started to feel more like a fucked-up vacation mixed with a sickening nostalgia.

What would happen if I visited my mom? What could that mean for my future self?

Martin knew he needed to suppress these thoughts before they snowballed out of control. Temptation to push the boundaries would surely keep pounding on the door.

"We here, mon." Clinton stared at Martin in the rear view. "Six dollars, please."

Fuck. All my money's in a single wad.

Martin didn't want to pull out a bundle of three thousand dollars in front of the cab driver. He was new in town and didn't need any locals murmuring about the new guy with all the cash. With a balled fist, he stuffed his hand into his pocket and wriggled his fingers to work out a lone bill from the wad, hoping it was bigger than a single.

Alexander Hamilton stared at him when he pulled his hand out and Martin handed the ten-dollar bill over without hesitation. "Have a good day, mon." Clinton watched Martin leave the cab with a quick head nod in return.

The cab drove off and Martin faced Larkwood Suites, an apartment complex he had a hard time remembering from any point in his life. It was tucked behind a neighborhood, away from the main roads. He had never ventured to this part of town and made a mental note to come back to this spot in 2018 to see if the building still stood.

The complex stood three stories tall with a brick exterior. Each window had an air conditioner visible from the outside, and many of them buzzed as they worked on the hot March day. The entrance had double doors that Martin pulled open, letting out a gush of cool air that felt marvelous on his sweating neck.

A wall of mailboxes, each marked with unit numbers, greeted him before passing through another set of doors into the main lobby. A vending machine hummed while its light flickered next to an open office door where Martin peered into in search of help.

A middle-age man sat behind a cluttered desk, his attention focused on the boxy computer monitor that took up nearly all of the space on his desk. The screen glowed on his face to highlight his thick, black mustache and wavy hair. A couple of crumbs clung to life on the bottom edge of his facial hair. Martin cleared his throat to get the man's attention.

"Oh, hello there. Is there something I can help you with?" The man's voice came out deeper than expected, and when he stood, Martin noticed bulging muscles stretching his polo shirt to its limits when he stuck out a hand to shake. "Vincent Mack. You're not from this complex, are you?"

"No, sir. I was actually hoping to see if you had any open units for rent."

"That I do. What's your name?"

"Martin Briar. I just got into town a few days ago and need somewhere to live. Been staying at the Sunset Dream Motel."

"Yikes. Are you a trucker?"

"No. I'm a writer. Just traveling around the country looking for new material." The lie came out naturally, and Martin decided to make this his story going forward.

"I didn't think so. You don't exactly look like the kinda guy who'd stay at the Sunset. Is it just yourself?"

"Yes."

"I have a studio unit that just opened up – I was actually putting together a flyer for it right now. 450 a month, includes water and electric."

450! Martin fought off a gasp. He had over six months' worth of rent, at that price, in his pocket. He could stay and not worry about a job.

"That should work fine," Martin said in his best expressionless voice.

"Awesome. I'll print out the contract for you to review. Will you have first and last month's rent?"

Buddy, I have all the rent.

"Yes."

"My man. Gimme ten minutes and I'll get you that contract. Bring it all back tomorrow and you got yourself a place to live."

"Thanks, Vincent, I appreciate you working with me on such short notice."

"Call me Vinny. And it's no problem."

Martin waited in the lobby while listening to the printer whoosh back and forth. This landlord didn't ask for any credit information, identification, or references. Life was simple in the 90's, and Martin celebrated by buying a 25-cent Coke from the vending machine.

12

Chapter 11

Vinny never asked for any of the standard background information that was common in 2018. Martin returned the following morning after a rough night of sleep at the motel. His neighbor apparently paid for a deluxe service from Randy's business card as screaming and moaning carried through the walls until 3 A.M.

Martin expected to live in a closet based on the tiny amount of rent due for his studio, but was surprised to find a spacious room when he entered. He walked into a full kitchen with his living room/bedroom combination behind the island counter, and a bathroom and closet in the far corner. The studio was roughly the size of his 2018 unit, and also had a balcony where he could continue his nightly traditions. A lemony scent filled the air, so Martin cracked open the window above his air conditioning unit to freshen the space.

The empty studio stared back at him, the white walls bare and demanding decorations. He'd need furniture. Sleeping on the floor for six months wouldn't suffice. A couch, bed, and some barstools were all he really needed. He could eat like a king every night if he wanted to go out and about. Downtown Denver was only a ten-minute drive in the 90's, before the constant rush hour that began after 2010.

Finding a car was his next objective now that he had shelter away from the hooker-loving truckers. As much as he wanted a flashy car, he knew he needed to blend in with his surroundings. Larkwood didn't exactly have BMWs rolling down the street.

Every time Martin had a thought pop into his mind he pulled out his phone to open Google, only to find it useless and disconnected. The Internet wasn't in homes at this point in time, and Martin realized he'd have to go to the library should he need to use a computer.

How did we function before the Internet? The thought of driving to the library to search for the nearest car dealership, then printing the directions to get there, seemed like an ancient practice.

The Yellow Pages! Vinny would have a copy in his office for the tenants to use.

Martin left his apartment and flew down the one flight of stairs to the lobby, where Vinny's office door stood open.

"Martin! There's not something wrong with the place, is there?" Vinny asked.

"No, not at all. I was actually looking for The Yellow Pages. Do you have one?"

"Of course."

Vinny swiveled in his chair and rummaged through a pile of papers on the desk behind him. He pulled out a thick yellow book heavy enough to knock a senior citizen unconscious and dropped it on the desk with a hard thud. "Here you go."

Martin flipped through the pages in the "C" section and appreciated the simpler times of life. If you truly wanted a piece of information, you had to go get it.

He arrived to a section labeled "Cars" and found a list of a couple dozen dealerships, mostly in Denver.

"Are there any car dealers you know of in Larkwood?" he asked Vinny.

"Yes. They might not be listed in there. Good buddy of mine runs a dealership on Quebec Street called Caracas. Tell him I sent you and he'll take good care of you."

Martin used the phone in the lobby to call a cab and only waited five minutes for its arrival, and another five to arrive to the dealership.

The dealership was a small building, no bigger than a fast food restaurant, with at least 100 cars surrounding it in the lot. A few clunkers were visible, but the front line showed some promise.

A scrawny man wasted no time meeting Martin on the lot when the cab departed.

"Hello there. Anything I can help you with today?" he asked in a squeaky voice and slight Latin accent. Martin studied the man's slicked back hair and the cheap jewelry adorning his wrists and neck.

"I'm in the market for a new car. Just need something reliable to get around town, nothing special." Martin watched the man's brown eyes bulge in excitement at the hot lead that just walked on to the lot.

"Yes, sir. My name's Antonio. Anything you need. Do you have a preference for American or foreign?"

"I don't. Just looking for the best deal."

"Of course. Come."

Martin followed Antonio, who darted around the corner of the building, and braced himself for the attempted screwing he was about to take from the car salesman. They passed a row of American makes, and headed deeper into European and Asian models.

Antonio, dressed in a cheap suit, stopped in front of an early 90's BMW. "This is one of the finest cars we have."

Martin studied the car and loved it, but a BMW was out of the question.

"I'll give you a great deal, yeah?" Antonio pressured as Martin remained silent. Antonio glanced at the information sheet on the driver's window. "Only 30,000 miles. Its price is $15,000, but I'll do ten for you. Yeah?"

Antonio nodded at the end of each sentence, finally receiving a smile back from Martin.

"I'm looking for something a bit more subtle. I wanna blend in, not be turning heads at every red light. I have $2,000 cash in my pocket. What can you give me for that?"

"Ahhh, yes, of course. I have just the thing." Antonio's skinny fingers clasped together as he led them away from the BMW and toward the back of the lot. He stopped in front of an old Buick and stretched a hand out to present it to Martin.

"1988. 120,000 miles."

"How much?"

"Two thousand."

"Bullshit." Martin stepped up to the information sheet and saw the price clearly listed at $1,600. "That's not what it says here. You trying to pull a fast one on me?"

Martin turned and walked away, not making it five steps before Antonio pleaded.

"Please, please. Sorry, sir. I made a mistake. I thought this was priced different."

Martin turned back to Antonio and saw the immediate regret on his face. He never planned on leaving; he had nowhere to go. Besides, he could negotiate an even better price now that he caught the salesman red-handed.

"So you'll give it to me for $1,000 then?" Martin asked.

Antonio looked to the sky as he made mental calculations. "I can do $1,200."

"Perfect." Martin played him like a fool.

"I'll draw up the paperwork." Antonio returned to the office building with his tail between his legs.

* * *

An hour later Martin pulled out of the dealership in his "new" Buick Regal, black paint chipped and fading, and bubbles about to burst from the poor tint job on all the windows. Now he felt like he fit into the Larkwood scene and knew no one would pay him any attention.

With wheels underneath, Martin felt ready to explore this 1996 version of the world more freely. He could even plan a road trip and visit the rest of the country. Perhaps a trip to the Olympics would be a reality after all.

He drove through town with the windows down, letting the air flow and ruffle his hair. The air conditioning was broken, so he had no other choice. He passed the pile of ashes that was once his church and sped through the intersection.

It's time. I just want to drive by.

It only took three minutes before he pulled into his former neighborhood. Cars lined the sidewalks as always; the residents never quite seemed to grasp the concept of a driveway.

The trees that normally shaded the block in the summer stood tall and leafless, and this allowed Martin to see his home the moment he turned on to Cherry Street. He coasted at a steady five miles per hour as he passed all of the familiar houses that were once his neighbors.

The nostalgia overflowed as he felt the effects of living in a different dimension.

There it is. The hairs on his arms stood at attention as he stopped the car across the street from his old house. The ranch home stood out with its light green siding and forest green trim. The lawn was still yellow but had clearly been aerated in preparation for the upcoming spring season.

The clock on the radio read 12:33, so he knew no one would be home, and pulled into the empty driveway. A squirrel stared at him from the front porch and darted away when he stepped out of the car. The house radiated its many memories as he walked around to the backyard to get out of sight from any nosy neighbors.

More yellowed grass stretched twenty yards to the back fence where thick bushes blocked the view of the neighbor's yard. A cement patio ran along the house with a basketball hoop at the far end. Martin had liked to come home from a long day and shoot around to release the tension, sometimes playing into the darkness if he arrived late from an overtime shift. He envisioned the younger version of himself, dribbling, shooting, and shouting as he worked to perfect his skills on the court.

A breeze swirled around and rattled the house's screen door, loose on its hinges, a small project that took him months to fix. He remembered how Lela curled into a ball beside him in bed the first night the door made constant banging sounds. She giggled when Martin inspected and returned with the cause of the noise. They had made their own banging sounds in the bed that night once the initial fear had worn off.

Martin walked up the two short steps to the door and pushed it closed, keeping his hand on its cool, metal surface. He wanted nothing more than to walk through that door and see his old home, smell its familiar scent, and bask in its charm.

The time will come. It's day two. Go home and plan out what you're going to do for the next six months.

A gust of wind whistled overhead, rocking the power lines and blowing his hair over his eyes. The screen door would have surely slammed against the house had he not been holding it. *Just one of the small things I'm preventing here in the past.*

Martin smirked joyfully before kissing the door and returning to his car. Tears welled in his eyes as he pulled out of the driveway to return to his "new" home.

13

Chapter 12

Martin spent the next three days planning the rest of his time in 1996. He only left the apartment to get food, basic furniture like a bed and couch, and more clothes to last him a couple weeks between loads of laundry. His cash supply had dwindled after the car purchase and rent, so the first task on his list was to establish some sort of income. He planned to place a couple of small bets with a local bookie and had a hunch Vinny could point him in the right direction. With his winnings, he'd reinvest into bigger bets with a more established bookie downtown. He calculated his cost of living to be $1,000 per month, including extra cash for entertainment. He loved movies and 1996 was a huge year with the releases of *Scream, Twister, Independence Day, and Mission Impossible.* Spending the summer in a movie theater sounded all right in his book. Unfortunately, alcohol wasn't allowed in theaters like it was in 2018, but he would manage.

I haven't had a real urge to drink since arriving. Martin figured he had simply been too distracted to go out of his way to the liquor store. Perhaps travelling through Chris's fucked-up time vortex killed his inner alcoholic. *Or maybe you just have hope again,* he thought. The drinking hadn't really begun until the reality sunk in that Izzy was never coming back.

Whenever he returned to life in 2018, he wanted things to be different. *No more binge drinking. Drink responsibly and stop before the world turns black.* What better time than the past to work on yourself? He also wanted to follow through with investing. He could arrive back in 2018 with a broker account loaded with millions, and tell the post office to go fuck themselves.

Until then, Martin's first matter of business on March 24 was to win money. It just so happened one of the many bets he had written down was taking place this evening. He went to see Vinny in his office.

Vinny was sipping a glass of scotch when Martin entered. His office hours on Sunday ran from nine to noon, and it was already eleven.

"Martin. Happy Sunday, my friend," Vinny said with a wide grin. Martin noticed the screen saver of bubbles bouncing around the computer monitor. "What can I do for ya today?"

"Good morning, Vinny. I was hoping to place a bet on a basketball game tonight, and wondered if you might know where I could do that."

"Ahhh, you're a betting man? What did you have in mind?"

"I have a hunch Toronto is gonna upset Chicago tonight."

Vinny gulped down the scotch and burst out in laughter. "That's a fool's bet!"

It was a fool's bet. Chicago sported a 60-7 record and was about to make NBA history as the best team ever. Toronto had only won 17 games compared to 49 losses. There was no reason for Chicago to lose this particular game other than an act of God, but Martin had it noted for a reason, knowing it would have a huge payout for betting on Toronto.

"I know it sounds crazy. I just think the Bulls are gonna go in there too laid-back. Toronto will be ready and surprise them."

"If you say so. Go see a buddy of mine, Delmar Graff, down at The Devil. You know where it is?"

"I sure do." The Devil still existed in 2018 and was the same old dive bar it had always been.

"Ask the bartender for Delmar. Tell him Vinny sent you."

"Got it, thanks."

"I'll pour you a glass after you lose this bet. I almost feel bad for ya."

"And I'll buy you a new bottle with all of my winnings."

Vinny threw his head back and howled as Martin left him to finish his scotch in peace. He could still hear his landlord laughing through the walls when he arrived to his car, and couldn't help but chuckle. Vinny must have thought Martin was a lunatic, but when he arrived tomorrow with a brand new bottle of scotch, he'd have a new friend for the next six months.

The drive to The Devil took a quick five minutes west from the complex, and Martin arrived to find it hadn't really changed in its two decades of existence. The pub was a small wooden building with neon lights in the windows advertising different beers. A white sign ran the length of the entrance with red letters that read *THE DEVIL*, a pitchfork on each end of the name.

Martin approached the front door, music booming behind its walls, and pulled it open to let the sound pour outside for a brief moment. It was Sunday morning, a few minutes before noon, and six men already sat around the bar with their beer mugs filled and their cigarettes burning. A smoky haze filled the bar and mixed with the stench of alcohol.

The bar was oval-shaped. In the center of the pub, a young black man worked his way around to serve each customer. No one paid any attention to Martin and sipped their beers as if they didn't notice a man from 2018 stroll into their haven. TVs surrounded the room, each showing various spring training baseball games from Florida that were underway. The bartender made brief eye contact with Martin before returning to pour a beer.

Martin sat at the end of the bar, his back facing the entrance.

Two older men sat to his left and carried on a conversation about the upcoming election between Bill Clinton and Bob Dole.

The bartender strolled over, staring Martin directly in the eyes.

"Good morning, sir. What can I get for you?" the young man asked. He was clearly college-age, likely working this job to pay his way through school.

Martin's mouth watered at the thought of a drink, but wanted to stay disciplined as long as he could. Deep down he knew he'd eventually give in, but for now he felt sharp and healthy, and intended to keep it that way.

"I'll just have a Coke. I actually came to meet with Delmar. Is he in?"

The bartender hesitated, confused as to why someone would come in to a bar at noon to order a soda, and then poured the Coke without any questions.

"Mr. Graff is in. I can have him come out to meet you." The young man avoided eye contact as he pushed the plastic cup across the bar.

"I'd appreciate that."

The bartender left without another word.

Martin pulled in his soda, suds bubbling over the edge, and took a long sip through the straw.

"Damn, this could use some Jack in it."

Keep your eye on the prize, his inner angel reminded. *You're here for a serious reason, not to get drunk.*

Martin watched the bartender cross to the other end of the bar and pick up a phone off its cradle, bobbing his head as he spoke. After hanging up, he returned to another customer and topped off a beer.

Martin sat back and watched baseball for the next ten minutes, wondering what to expect of this bookie he would soon meet.

* * *

A man dressed in dark jeans and a gray blazer strode from the back corner of the bar and approached the bartender. The two spoke, the bartender looked over his shoulder and nodded in Martin's direction, and the man waved him over.

Martin did a quick double take before hopping off his stool and walking around the bar. The two old men shouted at each other, one in clear favor of Clinton, the other adamant that Dole needed to bring America back to its roots.

"Delmar Graff at your service," the well-dressed man said, sticking a pudgy hand out. He was heavier up close than he had looked across the room.

"Mr. Graff, I'm Martin Briar. Vinny from the Larkwood Suites sent me here to meet you."

"Vinny!" Delmar barked in a scruffy voice. "I love that guy. Great businessman. So what can I help you with?"

"I was hoping to place a bet," Martin said in a lowered voice, despite the booming music, and wishing he had used an alias to meet with this obvious mobster.

"Let's go back to my office so we can actually hear each other," Delmar said as he put a hand on Martin's shoulder. Martin noticed a ring on each thick finger, gleaming through the indoor smog. Delmar turned and started toward a door that had a frosted glass window with *OFFICE* centered in neat lettering.

Delmar held the door open as Martin entered the office where a behemoth of a man in an all-black suit stood in the far corner watching a baseball game. He wore sunglasses above a perfectly groomed goatee, and had his hands crossed in front of him, gold rings on every finger. The man didn't budge as the two entered.

"Please, have a seat." Delmar crossed behind a desk in the crammed room. Martin thought it might have been a custodial closet at one point that had been redone as a fully functioning office space. The desk was cleared except for a stack of papers on its edge and a thick notebook in the middle with dozens of sticky notes protruding from its tattered edges. Martin shot uncomfortable glances toward the silent man in the corner. "Don't mind Hammer over there. He's my trusted adviser and personal banker."

Hammer? This guy is definitely a mobster. Martin's senses heightened at the thought and he wondered if this was a mistake.

"I do some bookmaking here. What did you have in mind?" Delmar asked, shifting the focus back to business.

"I was hoping to bet on the Toronto Raptors tonight."

72

Delmar nodded and flipped open the notebook on his desk, running a finger down multiple pages until he found what he wanted.

"I have Toronto as a 14 point underdog, I'll give you even odds on that."

Martin nodded as the bookie stared at him. There was no laughing like Vinny had done; this was serious business for all parties involved.

"I was actually hoping to bet on them straight up, no spread."

This caused a slight eyebrow raise from Delmar, but he remained composed otherwise. A straight bet meant that the Raptors would have to win the game outright and Martin would forfeit the 14-point cushion originally offered.

A fool's bet.

"How much were you wanting to bet?" Delmar asked as his finger paused on a different line in his notebook.

"Three hundred dollars."

Delmar looked at Hammer and nodded for him to come over.

Hammer took three steps sideways and craned his neck to see what his boss was pointing at. He took a moment, stood up straight, then nodded before returning to his corner.

"15 to 1 odds on that bet," Delmar said flatly.

Martin did quick math. *$4500. That'll cover some groceries.*

"Deal."

Delmar stuck his hand out and the men shook to solidify their wager.

"Tell me something," Delmar said in a softer voice. "You know something I don't? MJ not playing tonight?"

"No, sir. Just a hunch. The Bulls haven't lost to a bad team all year. It's bound to happen sooner or later."

"You better be right. If I find out Jordan or Pippen don't play tonight, I'll kill you."

Martin's heart froze. He had no fucking clue who played or didn't play in this game, but so help him God, Michael Jordan better suit up tonight.

Delmar watched as Martin's face turned pale. "I'm bustin' your balls, guy. Calm down!" The bookie threw his head back and cackled. Delmar walked around the desk and threw an arm around Martin's tense

73

shoulders. "You hang out here and watch the game tonight, I'll cover your tab. Least I can do since you'll be giving me free money." He laughed again before opening the door, letting the music return in all its glory.

The tension somewhat left Martin and he managed a grin as he stood. "Very good one, Mr. Graff. You had me going there for a minute."

"Go see Teddy at the bar. Tell him to put whatever you want on my tab."

Delmar smacked him on the back again as Martin walked out. The door closed behind him and he could only wonder what the bookie and his "banker" were saying about his crazy bet.

Of course I get an open bar when I'm not drinking. Maybe I'll just have one.

14

Chapter 13

Two drinks in, Martin started to feel the room spin. Did traveling through time reset his alcohol tolerance?

Stop right now, dammit, he demanded of himself. *Stop before this entire day gets out of control.*

Martin stopped after the two drinks and returned to sipping Cokes. It was ten past one when he swallowed the last remnants of whiskey. He had nothing to do for the remainder of his Sunday and decided to spend the day at the bar while he waited for his payday at the end of the night.

Teddy, the young bartender, kept his soda topped off and small talk to a minimum.

Martin didn't mind as he sat by himself all afternoon, enjoying the spring training game on the big screen between the Colorado Rockies and Seattle Mariners.

Smoke continued to fill the bar, prompting Martin to take a brief stroll outside for fresh air. The day ended up warm, low 70's and sunny, a perfect day to be drunk on the balcony.

"What am I doing?" Martin asked himself as he leaned on the building. He wondered if getting mixed up with a bookie was worth it. Delmar had joked about trouble if Jordan didn't play in the game, but was he really joking? Would he find himself behind the bar tonight with his kneecaps busted?

He desperately wanted another drink to settle his nerves. If Jordan didn't play, maybe then he'd get blackout drunk to numb his body for any potential beating that might come.

As the sun descended toward the mountains, Martin returned to the bustle inside the bar where the smoke, music, and loud chatter battered around his head. The afternoon baseball games were ending, and there was one more hour until tip off for the basketball game at five.

The lull between games gave Martin the opportunity to order a greasy burger with hopes of it settling his stomach. Placing this bet was the first big change he made in the past, and not knowing how it could affect the rest of his time in 1996 kept him on constant edge.

You shouldn't have come here. You could have gotten a job anywhere. For fuck's sake, you're from the future. Go invent Google or something no one's heard of yet!

His inner wise man was right. The world was his oyster with the knowledge he brought from the future, yet here he was fighting off alcohol in a hole-in-the-wall bar owned by a not-so-subtle mobster.

After a few minutes of sulking in his regret, Martin watched as the main TV above the bar switched to the Bulls and Raptors game, Delmar and Hammer walking out of the office in sync. The mobster pulled out the stool beside Martin and plopped down, placing his ring covered fingers on the bar top.

"Thought I'd join you for the tipoff," Delmar said with a smirk. Martin's faced turned pale immediately. "Don't worry, I'm not gonna sit here and watch the whole game with you. I'll come back toward the end if it's a close one."

"Sounds good to me," Martin said nervously.

Damn, I could really use a drink. His armpits soaked with perspiration as the pregame show concluded and the final commercial break came on before the start of the game. Michael Jordan came on to the screen, pushing an advertisement for Gatorade, and Martin's heart drummed as he waited to see Jordan come on for the actual game.

The commercials ended and the screen showed a bird's eye view of downtown Toronto where the game was taking place. The music continued to boom through the speakers, and Martin remembered how much he hated watching sports in a bar where he couldn't hear the game.

A young, dark woman came on the screen, speaking into a microphone while the players warmed up on the court behind her. The players cleared the court and headed toward their respective benches in anticipation of the tipoff.

Just show me Michael already. How have you not showed him yet?

The fact that they hadn't even shown a glimpse of the most famous athlete on the planet made him wonder if he was actually sitting out the game.

Finally, Michael Jordan stepped on to the court, adjusting his red shorts as he slapped hands with his opponents.

Thank Christ. Martin felt all the tension leave his body as he slouched in the barstool. Scottie Pippen also walked onto the hardwood and Martin knew the universe wasn't quite ready to fuck him over.

"You know you don't have a chance in this bet," Delmar leaned over.

Martin, feeling loose and relaxed, responded, "Just you watch. Bulls are on the end of a long road trip. They want to get to the playoffs already. It's the perfect combination for Toronto to come out and steal a win."

Martin had no idea if any of this was true, but played the year to his advantage. Delmar couldn't log on to Google to confirm the Bulls schedule and would have to take his word.

"We'll see. Here we go." Delmar chuckled then leaned back and crossed his hands behind his head.

Martin's pulse pounded in his head and he wondered why he was still nervous. The starting lineup was healthy for the Bulls, eliminating any suspicion from his off-the-wall bet. He knew the outcome, so why the rush of adrenaline?

The thrill of gambling had its same attraction even when the result was set in stone. Having the bookie rub elbows with you during the game added extra spice as well.

The Bulls started the game on a 14-2 run, and Martin could see Delmar nodding his head out of the corner of his eye.

"Well, at least you tried," the mobster said, taking a sip from a glass of beer. "I'll be back later," Delmar said and returned to his office, Hammer following behind like an obedient puppy.

"C'mon, Raptors," Martin said under his breath and finished the glass of Coke in front of him.

The crowd in the bar shifted from the day drinkers to a somewhat younger crowd coming in for pre-dinner drinks. Many sat around the outer tables, with a young couple getting cozy on the opposite side of the bar where Martin watched them out of the corner of his eye. The woman wore a tight, glittery dress that revealed every curve on her slender body.

Her date, a buff man in jeans and a dress shirt, leaned over and whispered in her ear. She giggled as she brushed a lazy hand on his back. The man kept his face hidden, but Martin could sense him staring across the bar in his direction.

Martin returned his attention to the game and was pleased to see the Raptors tighten the contest to a six-point deficit after the sloppy start. On the next commercial break, he watched as the couple had their tongues in each other's mouths for a few seconds before they stood and exited the bar, the young man keeping a steady eye on Martin as they crossed the room, sending chills down his back.

"Excuse me!" Martin shouted to the bartender as soon as the couple was gone. "I need a shot of Jameson, please."

The bartender nodded and brought the whiskey over within a minute.

He said I would lose my emotions, not my mind. Goddammit, Chris, what are you doing to me?

Martin leaned back in his bar stool and tried to focus on the game, eyes staring at the basketball game, but not watching. Somewhere in Toronto the Raptors led the Bulls by one point at halftime, but all Martin could think about was Chris.

15

Chapter 14

Three shots later Martin cut himself off. He basked in the pleasure of knowing Delmar was nervous. Toward the end of halftime, Hammer approached Martin at the bar and proposed an offer from his boss.

"We'll pay you out on half your odds right now," the gargantuan man said.

That's not a bad offer, Martin thought, but he knew the outcome of the game. At the moment, he would win $4500 should the Raptors hold on to their lead. Hammer's proposal was to pay $2250 right now and call the bet off. Martin had never heard of such a proposal in sports betting, but supposed bookies were constantly wheeling and dealing to stay in the black. *He's sweating back there. He thought the Bulls would already be winning by 30, which they should be.*

Martin stared down this first crossroads since arriving in 1996 and considered his cash flow, his kneecaps, and his overall future. Hammer breathed heavily beside him as every scenario ran through his mind.

"Well, do we have a deal?" Hammer insisted.

"I'll pass. It's tempting, believe me, but I wanna see the game through the end."

"Whatever you say, pal – it's your money lost," Hammer said in a final attempt to pressure Martin. The lackey wheezed as he turned and left. It likely made no difference to Hammer what Martin did; he still got paid the same.

The game resumed and people started to trickle out for dinner, leaving Martin alone at the bar. The alcohol finally numbed his mind, and his confidence burst through the roof. "Let's go Raptors!" he barked as they extended their lead over the Bulls to six points. The music that had boomed all day now felt like background noise as all of his attention focused on the game. Even with no volume, Martin felt like he was there, hearing the squeaks of sneakers on the court, the players shouting, and the roar of the crowd. He grew so entranced and didn't realize he was the only person in the entire bar once the third quarter ended.

The game tightened, and the Bulls took a four-point lead into the final quarter, prompting Delmar to come out of his cave.

The music cut to silence, leaving only the sound of the buzzing neon lights decorating the bar.

"Well, here we go," Delmar said calmly, approaching Martin at the bar with his hands clasped together. "Fourth quarter time. We all know this is when Jordan puts the nail in the coffin."

The game broadcast blared through the speakers, bringing with it the steady hum of a sold out arena on the TV.

"The Raptors are very much in this game going into the final period. I'll tell you, no one here saw this coming tonight," the color commentator said as the game returned from the commercial break.

Martin sensed that Delmar was genuinely enjoying this bet and poked back.

"Jordan's tired, tonight's not the night. Just wait and see."

Delmar clapped Martin on the back and kept his hand gripped tightly on Martin's shoulder. *All those fucking rings.*

The mobster released his grip and sat in the stool next to Martin. "Mind if I finish the game here with you? I'll help wipe up your tears when it's over." He chuckled hoarsely. Hammer wasn't in sight, possibly staying in the room to prepare the crow bar that would bash Martin's knees into tiny shards.

The final twelve minutes dragged, practically staying frozen in the moment. Martin watched every single second tick off the game clock and approach zero. The contest continued its back-and-forth, the teams trading buckets. At one point Delmar ordered a round of shots for the two of them when the Bulls pulled ahead by eight with six minutes left.

"You're done!" he shouted over the speakers. "It was close, but it's over!"

Clearly someone has never watched basketball. It only takes 90 seconds to score ten points.

"Eight points in six minutes, you're getting cocky now," Martin said calmly.

On queue, the Raptors roared back, leaving the game tied with 30 seconds remaining. The Bulls had the ball and prepared to inbound. Martin watched Delmar out of the corner of his eye. The mobster fell silent, rocking in his barstool as the game had become a virtual coin toss.

Even though he knew Toronto would win the game, Martin still sat on the edge of his seat because he didn't know *how* they would win.

The Bulls threw in the ball to Michael Jordan. He made a quick spin move and darted toward the rim, elevating an outstretched arm towards the basket. Doug Christie, a long-time role player in the league, came from behind and swatted the ball out of Jordan's hand. Jordan then fouled the Raptors' center, who had rebounded the ball, out of frustration.

"Holy fucking shit," Delmar muttered.

The Raptors made one free throw to take a one-point lead, but the Bulls had one more chance and sprinted down the court. The Raptors fell out of position and left Steve Kerr, a three-point shooting specialist, wide open as the clock winded down to three seconds. Jordan passed the ball to Kerr and the stadium held its collective breath as he lifted for the deep shot.

The ball hung in the air forever, and actually looked in line to go in by Martin's judgment. It came down and hit the back of the rim, bouncing out and falling to the ground as the stadium erupted in chaos.

"The Raptors win! The Raptors win!" the commentator screamed as the players jumped around like they had just won a championship.

Delmar slammed a fist down on the bar, causing the empty shot glasses to hop and rattle.

"You have got to be shitting me," Delmar said, and gestured to his bartender to cut the volume. Seconds later, the empty bar fell silent. "Well, congrats. I'm shocked at what I just watched."

That makes one of us.

Delmar stood from his stool and stuck out a hand to Martin. "I hope you'll give me a chance to win this back."

Like I'm ever showing my face here again.

"Of course. Next time I have a crazy hunch, I'll be sure to let you know." Martin winked at the mobster, his confidence soaring along with his alcohol levels. Delmar had ordered two more rounds of shots, and Martin now felt a familiar numbness in his lips and fingertips.

"Give me a few minutes to get your cash together," Delmar said before trudging away to his office. The heavy man seemed more disappointed than angry, and Martin suspected his knees would stay intact, at least for the time being.

The bar stayed silent as Martin watched the muted post game report where fans in Toronto danced outside the stadium. The win over the Bulls would serve as their best memory of an otherwise failure of a season.

Delmar returned moments later, a wad of cash wrapped in a white band. "Here you are. $4500 to spend on all sorts of fun things." He didn't stick the cash out toward Martin, instead holding it close to his body.

Martin stuck out an open hand, and Delmar forced himself to hand over the money. "Thank you for taking my bet. I'm new around here, so I'll definitely be back."

Not!

"I appreciate that," Delmar said softly, still a sliver of defeat lying beneath his attempted stern tone. "Don't go spending this all in one place."

"Of course not, I'll see you around." Martin stuffed the money into his back pocket and shuffled his feet backwards. Delmar held his ground and watched as the chubby man from the future inched toward the exit. The silence in the bar was deafening after a long day of constant noise.

Delmar didn't break his stare with Martin until he leaned into the exit door and a gush of fresh air blew through the doorway. In the dark lot, Martin ran to his car with a hand on his back pocket to keep the money from spilling out. Crickets chirped in the silent and abandoned parking lot. The lights from inside the bar provided a soft glow, but no actual visibility to its surroundings. He felt eyes watching him, but had no idea where they were hiding in the night.

Get in your car and get the hell out of here.

Martin reached the car and fumbled in his pockets for the cool metal of his keys. He unlocked the door and turned on the ignition in a swift motion. Toni Braxton came on the radio as Martin sped out of the parking lot to the main road. He drummed his fingers on the steering wheel and kept checking his rear-view mirror for anyone who might be following.

16

Chapter 15

The next morning brought a pounding headache, but a wad of cash lay on Martin's nightstand, and he knew he was set for the next few months. He had driven to his apartment with a constant eye on the rear view, but no headlights followed after leaving the bar the night before.

"What now?" he asked his apartment. With money in hand and nothing but free time ahead, Martin decided it was time to finally track down his daughter. Before doing so, he'd need to find a liquor store as he owed a bottle to his landlord.

He dressed quickly, knowing a day of fun awaited with more booze. And Izzy. Thinking of her, knowing he would see her, caused a tense heartache that wouldn't go away. So many years had passed where all he wanted was to kiss his daughter on the forehead and smell her sweet, innocent scent before bedtime. *I'm gonna save you, Izzy, if it's the last thing I do.*

Once he was dressed and swallowed a few sips of mouthwash, Martin headed back to his car to drive to the local liquor store. The store was a few blocks past The Devil, which he drove by with regret. The money was nice, but his inner guilt reminded him that he had won his small fortune by cheating the system. What would Delmar do if he knew the truth? He'd either kill him or hire him to set absurd lines for future games, assuming he believed it.

Speculation did no good in a stressful time, and he reminded himself to focus on the task at hand.

He pulled in to the liquor store parking lot, seeing only one other car at its opening time of ten in the morning. A homeless man sat on the ground, leaning against the store, snoring. Martin parked and closed the door quietly to not wake the passed out drunk. *We've all been there, brother.*

Neon lights hung in every window, but none had been turned on yet. The sign on the door had been flipped to say, "We're open, come in!"

The hobo tipped over and grunted, licking his dry lips in a sticky sound that made Martin queasy. Martin pushed the door open and walked in to a chime from above.

A young Asian man stood behind the counter and watched Martin cautiously as he strolled in for what would surely be the first of many visits.

"Hello," Martin greeted from across the floor as he searched for the scotch section.

The clerk nodded in response, maintaining an awkward amount of eye contact toward Martin.

"I'm looking for a high-end scotch for a friend. Do you have anything special?"

"Yes. Back there." The clerk spoke urgently and nodded toward the back corner of the store where a rack of bottles stood next to fridges full of beer.

"Thank you." Martin pivoted and walked to the back, sensing the man's eyes on him the entire way. A radio blared with a morning talk show, filling the store with background noise. When he arrived to the rack of scotch, Martin was surprised to find such a wide selection for a hole-in-the-wall liquor store in Larkwood. Not many in town had the resources to buy expensive bottles of booze, but there were four different options priced over $100 for him to choose from.

Vinny would've been pleased with any free bottle, but Martin wanted to make a stronger gesture than a friendly wager. He wanted his landlord to know he was a man of his word, and that he took care of his friends. Vinny's reaction to receiving such a fine bottle would also show Martin everything he needed to know about the man.

Martin settled on a bottle of Johnnie Walker Blue Label, a newer blend, for the time, from the iconic distiller. He held the bottle in two hands, admiring its perfection, and knowing he could never afford such a bottle in 2018. *You better pour me a glass, Vinny.*

He turned to return to the cashier and froze, his heart leaping up his throat.

The Asian man stood five feet away from him with a rifle pointed directly at his face. Martin saw the blackness in the barrel, death taunting him with its black eye.

"Whoa, man, I don't want any trouble," Martin said, trying to sound calm beneath his panicked surface.

"Who are you? What do you want from me?" the clerk asked, his lips trembling nervously.

Martin gulped, wondering what the hell he did to make this man think he needed to pull a rifle on him.

"Look, I think you have me mistaken for someone else. All I want is this bottle." Martin stuck the bottle in front of him, but the clerk kept the gun aimed at his face.

"Bullshit! Who sent you?"

"No one sent me. I live down the street. I'm new in town."

"That's exactly what a Road Runner would say."

Road Runner? What the fuck?

"Okay, can you please put the gun down? I have no idea what you're talking about."

The man refused, and Martin's heart tried to burst out of his chest. The adrenaline heightened his every sense as he caught the light reflecting off the man's shiny black hair, heard the buzzing of the lights above, and could smell the overall fear present in the room. The man's eye appeared magnified through the scope he looked through.

"Tell me what year you came from and what your business is here," the man demanded.

"Uh." The question smacked Martin with shock and confusion. "I'm sorry, what did you just ask?"

"You heard me just fine," the clerk barked, not budging his shotgun.

"How do you know?" Martin uttered in a soft whisper.

"Stop playing with me and tell me who sent you!" the clerk screamed, his hair ruffling as his body convulsed in rage.

"An old man named Chris sent me here. I'm from the year 2018." Martin decided to stop asking questions and cooperate with the crazed gunman.

The clerk lowered the shotgun from Martin's face, but kept it pointed to his chest. The rage behind the man's eyes softened as he cocked an eyebrow. "And *why* are you here? In this year? In this city?"

Martin hadn't realized his hands were raised in defense, so he lowered them to his sides. "I've always lived in this city, born and raised. My daughter went missing in 1996...was never found. I'm here to figure out what happened."

The clerk lowered the shotgun more as it now pointed to Martin's knees. "Prove that Chris sent you."

"How do I do that?"

"Tell me the name of his store."

"Wealth of Time," Martin said with complete confidence.

"How did he send you here?"

"With a pill."

"What's the painting hanging on the wall in his back office?"

Martin closed his eyes and imagined the painting. "I don't remember what he called it, but it was a sailboat in a storm with Jesus Christ."

The response satisfied the man and he lowered his gun all the way to the floor, loosening his tense shoulders in the process. "Okay, I believe you. What's your name?"

"Martin," he said, his heart rate dropping back to normal.

"How did you meet Chris?" the clerk asked, still sure to keep his distance.

"At his store. My mom loves antique shops and dragged me in there."

"How did you know to come find me here?"

Martin threw his hands in the air. "I don't know what you're talking about. I don't know who you are. I honestly came in here to buy this bottle. Can you please tell me what's going on?"

"Did Chris not tell you?"

"Tell me what? That there are people who know I'm from the future? No, he didn't."

Martin's earlier fear had now morphed into anger.

"Okay, okay. Come with me to the front. I don't want someone to walk in and see us like this."

The clerk turned and shuffled his feet back to the cashier's counter. Martin saw the homeless man still outside, falling deeper into sleep as the morning grew warmer. The clerk returned his shotgun underneath the counter and slapped his hands on top, leaning in to Martin who studied the miniature bottles that stretched the length of the front wall.

"Where to start?" the clerk said under his breath.

"You can tell me your name," Martin said.

"Ahh, yes, of course. My name is Calvin Yoshiki. I'm a political historian from the year 2076 and am here studying the re-election and impeachment process of President Clinton for references that we need in the future."

"2076? But that year hasn't happened yet. It's only 2018."

Calvin raised an eyebrow to Martin and rubbed his chin aggressively. "Chris really didn't tell you much on how any of this works, did he?"

"Apparently not. I don't know anything about 2076, or Road Runners, or why you know I'm not from here."

"Okay, okay. I can explain." Calvin repositioned himself to face the door while he spoke. "Time is always happening; we just live in our current times based on birth. Just because it's 2018 where you come from, doesn't mean 2076 isn't happening somewhere else. Every era in history and the future rests in its own dimension. Chris provides us the means to jump across these dimensions for our work."

"Okay, I understand the time travel portion, just didn't understand going to the future was an option."

"Yes, of course. You can go anywhere, but you must have a reason. He doesn't send you for vacation. You need a purpose."

"So who are the Road Runners, and why do you want to shoot them?"

"The Road Runners are evil bastards. They stole the potions from Chris and have been jumping through time trying to take over the world in every era of time. They will kill anyone who travels through time and doesn't join them on their mission."

"Why wouldn't Chris warn me of these people? How do you know who they are?"

"Look at me." Calvin stepped back and held his arms out.

"I don't see anything. You look like a normal guy to me."

And he did. Calvin was a twig of a man who would likely be toast against these Road Runners if not for his shotgun. Martin shrugged his shoulders.

"Look carefully. Stare at my arms."

Martin adjusted his focus, zeroing on the skinny arms that trembled slightly. A subtle, golden haze glowed from the man's skin.

Calvin saw the confusion fall over Martin's face and smiled. "You see it, yeah?"

"I think so. Are you glowing?"

"Yes! Exactly! Once you travel through time, your body emits the smallest amount of light. Something happens in the process that causes this, but everyone has it."

"You make it sound like there are a lot of people who travel through time."

"There are thousands of us. That's how I knew you were from another time."

Martin thought his eyes might be playing tricks on him; the glow wasn't visible unless he really focused on it. He held his own arm out and studied the same glow emitting from his skin.

"It's so hard to see," he said to himself.

"Yes, but in time you'll know how to look for it more easily."

"So what made you think I was one of these Road Runners?"

"Well, word is there are a couple in town. They usually like the finer things in life; they're very rich. So when you asked for an expensive bottle, I assumed you were one."

"Makes sense, but I can't be the only person to travel back in time and spend money. I might be poor in 2018, but with inflation, I'm rich now. I'm sure you're loaded with money, seeing how far from the future you've come."

"On the contrary, that's part of why I'm here. The year 2076 is ugly, my friend. We're on the verge of a dictatorship, and the economy is collapsing. We're studying the impeachment process, which is why I'm here."

"A dictatorship? In the United States? Impossible."

Calvin chuckled. "That's exactly what we all thought, but here we are, fighting for our democracy one day at a time. But we can have that conversation another time."

Martin nodded, not sure what to think. Fortunately, he'd be long gone by the year 2076.

"That'll be $126.98, please," Calvin said, placing the scotch in a brown paper bag. "You come find me if you need anything. We don't typically mingle, best to not be grouped together in case the Road Runners show up, but we do help each other. Don't be afraid to introduce yourself when you see another one of us."

"How do I know who the Road Runners are?"

"Oh, you'll know when you come across one," Calvin said and shot Martin a wink.

Well, that does me no good.

"It was great meeting you, Calvin. I honestly had no idea there were other people doing this."

"Pleasure's all mine. Best of luck finding your daughter. Come back any time if you need more booze, I'll give you a deal."

Martin had never heard more beautiful words spoken.

Chapter 16

With pieces of the puzzle finally falling in to place—granted, he hadn't been aware there was more to the puzzle—Martin returned to his apartment with a sense of accomplishment. Calvin had just taken him through Time Travel 101, and he now felt ready to take on whatever the past would throw his way.

Despite the information he had just learned, Martin felt relaxed, like he belonged in his current situation. He considered buying a gun to protect himself from the Road Runners, wondering if they would even bother a desperate father out on his own agenda. Martin felt relief knowing he was not alone in his time traveling adventure. Even if he never saw Calvin again, just knowing there were others out there made him feel less lonely on this journey.

He arrived to his complex and walked straight into Vinny's office where the landlord peered over a stack of documents. Martin kept the bottle hidden behind his back as he stepped into the office.

"Hey, Vinny."

Vinny looked up with droopy, tired eyes that quickly brightened up at the sight of his new tenant. "Mr. Martin! Quite the game last night. I saw the highlights. You were right, I can't believe it!"

"I know my basketball." Martin grinned and pulled the bottle out, dropping it on Vinny's desk. The landlord stared at it, and his eyes exploded once he realized the type of scotch. He grabbed it like a frantic child getting a new toy.

"Are you shitting me?" he whispered. "Where did you find this?"

"I have some connections," Martin said with a smirk.

"I've only ever heard of this scotch. It's like the fucking unicorn of scotches, but here it is on my desk! Holy shit!"

Vinny placed the bottle back on the desk and pushed it across to Martin.

"It's for you," Martin explained, realizing Vinny thought he was just showing off.

Vinny looked at the bottle, then to Martin with his giddy grin. "Get the fuck outta here," he said, revealing his inner Jersey accent that had remained hidden thus far. "Are you shitting me?"

"Not at all. I told you I'd get you a new bottle with my winnings. So there you go."

"And this is the bottle you decided to buy?" Vinny's eyes bulged.

"I won really big, what can I say?"

"Well get on over here and let's have a drink," Vinny said, standing to fetch a couple of glasses from his back cabinet.

"It's not even eleven yet, are you sure? I can come back later."

"I don't give a shit about the time when there's cause for celebration. Have a seat."

Martin obliged and sat down while Vinny popped the bottle open and filled two short glasses with the expensive liquor. Vinny pushed a glass toward Martin.

"Cheers," the landlord said while holding his glass in the air. "To the Bulls shitting the bed. God bless it."

The two men talked, Vinny suddenly interested in learning everything he could about his new tenant. Martin told of his faux life as a fiction writer traveling the country in search for new inspiration. He lied about having no wife, no family, no history, really. Vinny never asked about any past books he might have written, keeping the conversation fairly high level. Half an hour later, they both had finished their glass of scotch when Vinny offered to refill it.

"I'll have to pass on round two. This has me ready for a nap, I don't know about you."

"Guess you can't hold your liquor at this high altitude." Vinny chuckled as he slapped his desk. "Suit yourself, but know you're welcome any time for a drink."

"I appreciate that," Martin said and extended a hand to shake.

"You let me know if you ever need anything at all. You seem like a good guy, so just let me know."

Martin nodded before walking out of the office. Because of one ludicrous bet he now had a friend and a half in Vinny and Calvin, not to mention the knowledge gained about how this time travel business actually worked. He returned to his room and collapsed on to his bed, falling into an instant sleep with a wide grin slapped across his face.

* * *

Over the next six hours, Martin enjoyed the deepest sleep of his stay in 1996. When he woke, his mind felt clear and energetic, ready to tackle his next task.

"Dammit!" he barked when he checked his watch, realizing he had slept the whole day away. He had planned to see Izzy today, ideally after school during her walk home, but it would have to wait another day now. She would be at home already, doing her homework while Lela cooked dinner.

I can still drive by, maybe catch a random glimpse.

Martin needed no further convincing as he grabbed his keys and ran out the door. He drummed his fingers on the steering wheel as he mentally planned his route. The house was a mile west of The Devil, so he pulled out and drove in the same direction for the third trip in a row, admiring the fiery orange sky above the deep blue mountains as the sun began its evening descent.

Heavy traffic appeared on the road for the first time since he'd been in town. Everyone was on their way home after a long Monday's work, and Martin enjoyed the fact he wouldn't have to work one single day while he poked around in the past. Somewhere in 2018 his body lay asleep, an entire minute having passed, while he continued his search for his daughter. One day this would all end and he'd wake up to go back to the post office for another miserable day at work.

Until then, he needed a taste of his own past and turned onto his old block, pulling over immediately at the corner where he could see his home eight houses down. Two cars were parked in the driveway, both his and his wife's.

"We're all home together," he said to himself, a wave of emotions running through his body. He imagined the inside of the house: Lela cooking, Izzy at the table with books and notepads splayed all over, and himself at the sink washing dishes. That was the routine as long as Martin worked a day shift. That would change later in the summer when he moved to the graveyard shift.

He pulled the car back onto the street and coasted toward his old home, its light green exterior sending ripples of memories. The grass appeared freshly cut, likely for the first time that spring.

He pulled up directly in front of the house and gazed at it when the front door swung open suddenly, and he saw himself.

The man who he had once been, athletic build and chiseled jaw, locked eyes with the familiar looking face in the car. Martin floored the accelerator, tires screeching in the quiet neighborhood, and zoomed out of sight. A sharp pain struck the back of his head like someone had stabbed him with a chef's knife. The world spun around him as he approached the end of the block, nearly clipping a few cars parked along the sidewalks. He slammed on the brakes once out of sight and panted heavily as if he had just run a mile.

"What the fuck?!" he gasped, fighting for breath. His lungs felt like someone was squeezing them.

"I told you not to see yourself!" Chris's voice echoed in his mind, except it didn't feel like a memory, it felt like he was actually speaking in his head. "You'll survive this encounter, but be careful!"

The invisible hands released their grip from his lungs, and the imaginary knife pulled out of his head. Martin grabbed his chest and rubbed his skull simultaneously. "What the fuck?" he whispered.

This must be the price for seeing your past self.

Martin shook his head, unable to shake the intensity of what his body had just gone through. "Okay. So that's no bluff. Don't even look at my past self, got it."

He pulled back onto the road. Izzy would have to wait another day. He wouldn't approach her and would remain invisible with the many cars parked on the street. All he needed was to see her, to remember her presence. He could close his eyes any moment and see her face, hear her giggle, and smell her sweet scent. Feeling her presence, her soul, however, was not so straightforward. He couldn't picture the way she used to walk or the way her head bobbed when she spoke. These were the finer details that had faded as time passed.

Martin now knew exactly where the line was drawn in terms of interaction with his past self. He imagined the consequences would have been less severe had his young, handsome self not locked eyes with his uglier future version.

He drove back in the direction of his apartment, pulling into a restaurant parking lot. Dinner sounded like a good way to take his mind off things, perhaps a margarita, too. The Mexican restaurant, La Casa del Rey, had the lovely smells of grilled chicken and fresh tortillas oozing from its clay exterior. The sign in the front read "Bienvenidos, We're Open!"

His stomach growled at the thought of chips and salsa. The parking lot appeared packed for the dinner rush.

Martin killed the engine and strolled into the restaurant's lobby, ready to eat. A mariachi band played in the main dining room, their horns and guitars filling the air. A young boy who couldn't be older than twelve manned the host stand and greeted Martin with a warm smile.

"Good evening, sir," he said in a voice that cracked with the earliest signs of puberty. "Are you dining in tonight?"

"Yes, I am."

"I can get you a table, or you can find a spot at the bar if you'd like to not wait."

Now you're talking my language, kid.

"I'll try my luck at the bar. Thank you very much."

"Of course, just go through the dining room behind me and you'll see the bar on your left. Enjoy your dinner."

Martin nodded at the boy and followed the music into the dining room. Waiters ran frantically, serving the full tables, as dinner patrons carried on their conversations and enjoyed the ambiance. A waiter passed by Martin with a tray of sizzling fajitas, and he decided he would have that for dinner.

The bar had two vacant stools, front and center, facing a TV that hung above. Martin pushed his way through the crowd to claim his rightful spot. A young Mexican man tended the bar and wiped down the area in front of Martin as he sat.

"Good evening, sir," the bartender said, slipping a menu on the bar. "My name's Gio and I'll be taking care of you. Anything I can get you started to drink?"

"Yes, please. I'll have a glass of water and a margarita on the rocks."

See, you can be responsible, ordering the water. Your 2018 self would claim there was enough water in the ice cubes.

"House margarita?"

"Yeah, that'll be fine, thank you."

A waitress approached from behind Martin, reaching an arm over his shoulder with a loaded basket of tortilla chips followed by a bowl of salsa. He wasted no time diving in as he watched Gio create his margarita. The bar was also crowded, the empty seat next to Martin the only open spot, but Gio appeared to have everything under control as he moved quickly and with purpose from one customer to the next.

Martin received his drinks, ordered his fajitas, and leaned back to relax and watch the sports highlights running on the TV. The music and chatter had finally drowned into background noise when someone tapped Martin on the shoulder.

"Excuse me, is this seat taken?" a blond woman asked, pointing to the open stool.

"It's all yours," he replied, sitting up and shifting over to allow the woman room to squeeze into the tight fit between stools.

Once she situated in her seat, Martin glanced from the corner of his eye and admired the slender, smooth legs coming out of her skirt, and followed them all the way up to her porcelain face. Her hair draped over her face as she read the menu, blocking his awkward gawk. She wore a tight blouse that revealed the slightest of pudge on her belly. He studied her hands and noticed they lacked the softness of youth.

She sat back and pulled her hair behind her ears as she turned to Martin. "Are you here alone?" she asked in a gentle voice.

"I am," Martin responded in his best calm voice. Blood started to rush to an area he hadn't felt in years as she looked at him with big hazel eyes.

"Yeah, me too. Was a long day at work. Just wanted to come have a drink to unwind."

"I hear that. What do you do?"

"I teach eighth grade history. I love the kids, but goddamn, at their age it's constant teenage drama. My head hurts, especially on a Monday after a quiet weekend." She spoke with a smile that revealed perfect teeth beneath her red lipstick.

History? Check her skin for the glow.

Now that he was skeptical of everyone he met, he focused on her skin in search of the golden glow. No glow, just silky flesh he had a sudden urge to run his fingers over.

"That's very cool, I'm sure it's fulfilling."

"It has its ups and downs for sure, but I enjoy it."

"What was your name?"

"I'm so sorry. It's Sonya," she said as she stuck out a hand for a formal introduction. "Or Ms. Griffiths, if you ask my students." She chuckled at herself and Martin grinned.

"I'm Martin Briar."

"Briar? I thought you looked familiar. Does your daughter go to my school?"

Holy fucking shit. Still think that alias was a bad idea?

"Uhhh... I don't have a daughter. You must be mistaking me for someone else." Sweat formed around Martin's head as he felt the heat in the room suddenly rise. The combination of tequila, sexual arousal, and nearly being caught by the random woman at the bar proved too extreme.

"Oh," she said, brows furrowing as she looked down at the bar. "I must be mistaking you. I'm pretty sure there is a Briar girl at my school, but I'm sure anyone could have that name."

Martin gulped his water in relief. Sonya had damn near caught him in a complicated web of lies, but she fortunately blew it off.

"So what is it you do?"

Your lie won't work here. This isn't going to be a brief conversation.

"I work at the post office."

"How cool! The one here in town."

"No, actually in Denver, but I live here."

"Ah, I see. That's too bad, I'm at the post office at least once a week. Would be nice to see a friendly face for once."

"We're not all bad," Martin said, leaning in with a tipsy grin. The tequila started to kick in and ballooned his confidence. "So, is there a reason you're out alone? Or do you just insist on the quiet time?"

"My teacher friends don't really like going out. Well, at least on a Monday. It's not exactly quiet here, just feels good to be around normal functioning adults every once in a while."

"Do you have any family here?" Martin asked, really wanting to know if she had a significant other.

"My parents are down in the Springs, but that's it. I'm a lone child. Got a couple cousins out in California, but that's really it."

The sizzle of fajitas arrived to disrupt their conversation after Martin had forgotten he had ordered them. Steam filled the air in front of him as the sizzle slowly died down.

"That smells *so* good!" Sonya said, not having removed her eyes from his plate. "Makes me feel like I missed out since I ordered a boring enchilada."

"You can have a bite of mine." Martin shot her a soft grin.

"You don't need to do that. I'm gonna be going soon – I ordered mine to go. Didn't think I'd meet such great company tonight or I would've planned to stay." She chugged the rest of the mojito she had ordered and slammed the glass down on the bar. "Do you have a phone number?"

Martin's heart raced, realizing he didn't have any way to be contacted. "I actually haven't set one up yet. Just moved in a week ago and still have a lot to take care of."

"Oh, I see." Sonya paused and studied her fingers as an awkward silence hung between the two. "Well, how about this. Let's meet here next week. Same time, same place."

"Deal," Martin said quickly.

A waitress brought Sonya a white box with the enchilada inside.

"Great, it's a date. I'll see you next Monday, and next time I'm getting those fajitas."

Martin grinned. "Fajita date it is!"

She giggled as she stood from the stool and rubbed a hand along his back. "Have a good night, Martin." She disappeared into the crowded dining room and he watched her blond head bob toward the exit.

He returned to his dinner with a dumb smirk stuck on his face.

Did I just get hit on by someone way out of my league?

Her body language showed interest, and she did ask for his number. Meeting someone romantically had never occurred to Martin as a possibility when he prepared for his trip back in time. What could be better for a six-month stretch with nothing to do?

18

Chapter 17

The rest of the week proceeded with anxious anticipation. Martin couldn't remove Sonya from his mind for one second. The purpose of this trip was not to fall in love. While Sonya provided a great mental distraction, he needed to regroup and focus on his mission.

After the close call at his old house, he needed to plan for what should happen, what could happen, and the worst-case scenario, should Izzy see and approach him.

Staying in his car was critical. If she saw him, he would drive off again and hope to God his head wouldn't explode. Even though Chris had told him to not encounter his past self, he didn't want to chance bumping into anyone he might know. Chris apparently liked to leave out important details, so Martin would take caution with every action moving forward.

By Friday, Martin felt his plan was as close to perfection as possible. Every conceivable situation was addressed, scribbled down sloppily in a small notepad. He remembered seeing Calvin at the liquor store with a stuffed notebook and supposed everyone who bounced around time had to keep some sort of log and rules to keep their matters in line. Now he had his.

He kept his apartment free of booze, wanting to create his plans with a clear and focused mind. The temptation for a glass of whiskey always crept up, especially at night when he lay on his couch to watch TV, but anything that might compromise his mission could go and fuck itself.

After lunch he took a brief nap, setting his alarm for 2 P.M. When he woke, he slipped into his shoes and was out the door without a second thought. It was time to see Izzy.

* * *

School let out some time around three by his memory, so he wanted plenty of time to find a good hiding spot while he waited for the final bell to ring. He drove to Larkwood Middle School, a mere three blocks from his old house.

Martin arrived in a couple minutes, the brick school standing tall just as he remembered. Being the only middle school in town, he assumed Sonya was also inside the building.

Two school buses lined up in front of the school, meaning the final bell was indeed close to ringing. Martin found a spot under a tree across the street. He made a U-turn to face the direction where his daughter would walk, and slipped on a fedora and sunglasses.

He brought the latest edition of *Sports Illustrated Magazine* with Dennis Rodman on the cover, posing the question if he was the best rebounder ever. The pages flipped between his fingers, but his eyes remained glued to the school; he couldn't take a chance in missing Izzy walk out.

The clock on his dashboard read 2:32, and Martin put the magazine down to enjoy the beautiful day by rolling down his window for fresh air. This would also allow him to hear the bell ring.

He waited as cars passed and parents walked by. The air felt still, and Martin couldn't help but wonder if the past was somehow preparing for his secret encounter with his daughter. As the neighborhood fell eerily silent, the bell rang, echoing around the schoolyard and surrounding houses.

About twenty seconds passed before the school's front doors swung open and students poured out of the floodgates.

"Holy shit," Martin whispered to himself. Within a minute there were at least fifty students scattered around the entrance, some lining up for the bus, others walking back to the parking lot to meet their parents, and the rest walking off the schoolyard to cross the street where he waited.

He felt like a detective as he slouched in his seat, allowing only his eyes to see out of his rolled down window. Izzy would be one of the smaller girls to cross the street, having always been behind the curve in terms of size. When she was twelve she could have passed as nine by looking at her, but once she opened her mouth and let her wit and intelligence flow out, one might think she was actually sixteen.

Little boys and girls crossed the street, adamantly looking both ways before doing so. Giggles and screams bounced around as Martin narrowed his focus on the main crosswalk. It was half a block ahead of him, a clear view. When Izzy entered the crosswalk, he'd pull onto the road and drive behind her as she walked the three blocks home, following like a secret guardian.

Countless little people crossed the street as the crowd on the school's front lawn slowly died down.

"Where are you, Izzy?"

Both buses pulled away, and Martin's heart stopped mid-beat as his hands started to tremble. There she stood, backpack slung over her shoulders, hands crossed over a thick textbook in front of her chest, as beautiful as he remembered with her sandy hair tied in a ponytail that bobbed with each movement she made. She hugged another girl and started toward the crosswalk.

Martin wiped away the tears that streamed from his eyes. "Izzy," he mustered, a bowling ball lodged in his throat. Seeing her proved way more intense than anticipated; Martin couldn't stop his hands from shaking. His lips quivered as he could no longer hold back his emotions. The slow welling of tears burst into a flowing river down his face.

Twenty-two years.

He thought he'd never see her again, but there she was, crossing the street. Martin turned on the car through blurred vision. He slouched as the engine fired up, hoping it hadn't drawn any attention to himself, but Izzy crossed the street, oblivious that her father from the future had his eyes locked on her.

He pulled onto the street, coasted one block, and turned right to follow her, remaining roughly five houses behind her as she strolled through the neighborhood, ponytail swinging from left to right with each step.

Martin physically couldn't take his eyes off her. What was she thinking about on her walk home? Did she know her life would change in just a few months? Did she know her parents would never stop searching for her, even when the police had given up hope? Did she know just how much she was loved and adored?

He desperately wanted to run her down, squeeze her, kiss her face, and never let go. The past and future be damned, he wanted to hold his daughter right now. But the reminder from his prior encounter with himself kept him gun-shy from making any other moves.

Aside from the fact that he was looking at his daughter, the walk home was uneventful. She moved at a steady pace with her head down, not stopping to greet the dogs that ran up to her at the fences she passed, not looking at the cars that passed by. She'd always had that tunnel vision, an intense focus on the task at hand, and apparently walking home from school was treated no differently.

The walk took an entire five minutes as he watched her turn into the front yard and climb the porch steps to the door. He stopped before the car would be visible to his old house, not wanting to chance anything after such a beautiful moment of stalking. A wall of bushes that separated his house from his neighbor's provided the cover he needed. He could see her through the bushes, rummaging through her backpack for the house key.

No one's home.

The temptation to knock on the door swelled even more, but it was only day one.

"You're not here to kidnap your daughter. Father Time probably wouldn't like that too much." Martin had to constantly remind himself that he was only here to learn what happened. *And intervene when the time comes.*

She entered the front door and closed it behind her, leaving Martin to ponder what she was doing inside as he drove away, knowing himself and Lela would come down the block within the next hour.

19

Chapter 18

Martin spent his weekend unable to focus on anything, not that anything required serious attention to begin with. After finally seeing Izzy and knowing she was okay, he couldn't bear the thought of waiting in anticipation of her future disappearance. *There has to be a way to both prevent it* and *keep the time travel gods happy.*

He had already tested the boundaries, though by accident, in regards to encountering his past self. Now, he needed to know exactly how far he could get away with changing an event, ideally a drastic one, that didn't involve his past self or family. Larkwood wasn't exactly an eventful city, but Denver would surely have some tragedy he could try to prevent or alter. Martin pulled out his cell phone, praying by some miracle that it would work so he could research 1996, but it continued with a red X where his service bars should have been.

He thought back to all the tragedies he could remember from the 90's. The ones he remembered would have already happened by 1996. Then, as if someone had flipped on a light switch and slapped him across the face, he remembered what he had so closely followed in the final year of the decade: the Columbine High School shooting.

The shooting wouldn't occur until April of 1999, but the two shooters, who were seniors at the time of the shooting, would have been wrapping up their freshman year in the spring of 1996.

"Eric Harris and Dylan Klebold," Martin said to himself, sitting down on the couch. He had saved every newspaper article about the massacre in the months following it, wondering what could have turned two high school boys into such monsters. He remembered they had constructed bombs in their parents' garages while gradually building up an arsenal for the shooting. "Can I actually stop this from happening?"

There was no denying the effects the massacre had on society, seemingly kicking off what would become a normal part of American culture with bullied young men lashing out against innocent people.

I can get to these boys years before they may have even thought about shooting their classmates.

The thought sent chills up his spine. Who was he to try and stop what would be the deadliest school shooting for years to come? Would the past allow him to even contact these boys? He had no idea where to begin such a task. Should he talk to them, try to preach love and change their hearts? Should he just walk up to them in their garage one day after school and shoot them on the spot? That would certainly be the biggest attempted change to history, or the future, depending how you looked at it.

The chills gave way to twisting knots in his gut. Doubt shuffled its way into his mind. "I can't actually stop Columbine from happening."

Having skipped out on drinks all week, he poured a glass of whiskey to help settle his nerves. *Maybe this is my fate. To save Izzy and save all those innocent kids.*

He refilled his glass and chugged the booze to lull himself into a long Saturday nap. All he really wanted was someone to bounce these ideas off, but he'd have to keep them buried in his mind until he saw Chris again. *Come and find me, old man.*

* * *

Martin jumped out of bed on Monday morning. He had spent the rest of the weekend keeping his mind distracted with alcohol and fighting the urge to drive by his old house and see what his once happy family was doing. He also soaked in his responsibility as the man to stop a travesty across town, three years away. The fact that the event was so far out is what ultimately convinced him to move forward with it. He wouldn't be around in 1999 to see what eventually happened. When he returned to life in 2018, he could look up Columbine High School and see there was no tragedy that had ever occurred. He'd be the city's biggest hero without anyone knowing why. Living with a fulfilling secret like that seemed like a much needed addition to his dismal life in 2018. Chris could take his emotions and shove them up his ass. Martin would know he had done the right thing, and emotions wouldn't matter at that point.

Martin dressed quickly and left for the library. The library was one block from the church and he saw its pile of ashes dwindle as construction crews filled the lot. His mom was probably there helping, but he managed to push the thought of her out of mind.

He hadn't been to the library since he was a child, but it all looked the same from his memory: plain brown siding, dirty windows, and not an open spot in the tiny parking lot. He parked on the street and walked a block to the main entrance that welcomed him with the musty smell of old books.

The entrance opened to a wide, open floor, shelves of books to the right, tables in the middle, and three computers to the left where two elderly people occupied the machines. In front of the bookshelves stood a tall desk where a heavyset woman sat behind a computer screen, her eyes peering around behind pointed glasses. She smacked her red lips as she watched Martin approach her desk.

"Good morning," he said. "Do I need a library card to use the computers?"

"Yep," she replied in a snotty voice.

"Can I get one?"

"Yep. You got an ID?"

Martin paused. He did have an ID. From 2018. "What do you need an

ID for?"

"Need to verify your address."

Martin pulled out his wallet and held it open to the snarky librarian, keeping his thumb over the important dates on his driver's license, but allowing her to see his address, which was still in Larkwood.

"Thank you," she said flatly. "Give me five minutes and I'll have your new card ready. Feel free to grab the open computer. If you need to print anything, it'll be five cents per sheet."

"Thank you kindly," Martin said in the gentlest voice he could muster, hoping he could make this miserable woman's day a little better.

He crossed the library and sat down at the open computer. The elderly couple paid him no attention and continued clicking around on their screens. Martin opened the browser and punched Google into the web address. After thirty seconds of loading, the screen came back with an error message: THAT DOMAIN DOES NOT EXIST.

Oh, shit. Do I buy that domain? What could come of that?

The thought left his mind quickly, as he needed to gather all the information available for Columbine High School. He went to MapQuest instead, the main source for finding where to go at the time. The results came back and let him know that the school was 31 miles away, a 40-minute drive, and included turn-by-turn directions on how to get there. Martin printed these directions. There was no satellite imagery available, no way to view the school from the street. The technology of the future was something he had taken for granted as he realized his capability to research the school was limited.

He switched the browser to Yahoo, the new search engine that everyone was talking about since they could find any bit of information. *If you all only knew how obsolete Yahoo will become.*

Martin typed the school's name into the search bar and waited another minute for the results to come back. The elderly couple had left Martin alone to wait impatiently for the slow computer to work its magic.

The search returned exactly what he wanted: Columbine's official website. He clicked on it and found nothing but disappointment. The site had the school's name in big letters across the top banner, and *HOME OF THE REBELS!* Beneath. *That's it?* There was no menu, no pictures, nothing.

Jesus Christ. Martin had to remind himself that people were literally in the learning stages of building websites and using the Internet in general. The school's IT person, if such a position existed, likely threw together the most basic HTML knowledge he could find off Yahoo.

With zero information, aside from the directions, Martin called it quits, accepting defeat to the lost cause that was mid-90's Internet. He grabbed his directions from the printer next to the computers, dropped 15 cents into the change box, and visited his favorite librarian to pick up his card.

"Done already?" she asked, sliding over the card.

"Yeah, just needed to print some directions."

"Fine then, we'll see you next time."

"I look forward to it." Martin winked at her, yet she remained cold and stone-faced. *One day I will get you to smile.*

Martin left the library to return home and set an actual plan in stone. He also had a date later that night to prepare for.

* * *

Martin stopped to buy a telephone on his way home and would need to call the phone company to activate his line and get his new number. By his memory, phone numbers were still only seven digits, as there hadn't been a need for area codes quite yet. The nostalgia seemed to snowball a little more with each passing day as something always reminded him how simple and silly life used to be.

When he arrived home, Martin pulled out the notebooks he had also purchased at the store and flipped one open to its first, fresh page.

COLUMBINE, he wrote across the top and underlined with a jagged line. He wrote down everything he could remember off the top of his head:

-April 20, 1999

-Eric Harris and Dylan Klebold

-Pipe bombs and handguns

-Started in the cafeteria

-Ended in the library

-Both had parents who weren't around

-Both were bullied throughout high school

That was all he could piece together for the time being. With these few facts in front of him, he decided he had a few options as how to approach his heroic act. Would the right move be to try and stop the bullying? Help the kids feel more involved with their peers?

He'd have plenty of time to solidify his game plan. Later in the week he'd drive down to the school to see if he could even locate the two boys. It would likely require multiple visits to find them, then follow them, and learn their routine. They may have not even been friends yet during their freshman year, so he might have to follow them separately to see exactly what they did after school.

Martin closed his notebook and stuffed his papers neatly inside. He'd had enough of playing detective for the day, and began to prepare for his date with Sonya.

20

Chapter 19

The ambiance at La Casa del Rey was the exact same as last week. The mariachi band sang the same songs (they all sounded the same to Martin), the chatter echoed around in a way that made his head ring, and Gio poured drinks at the bar.

Martin shuffled through the crowded dining room to find a spot at the bar when he saw Sonya already sitting there with two full margaritas in front of her. Her back was to him, and he took the chance to admire her beauty. He was glad to have dressed nicely for the occasion, seeing as she wore a sparkly black dress that cut off mid-thigh to show off the legs that had driven him wild when they first met. Her hair curled down to her bare back, and Martin caught the scent of perfume as he approached her.

"I hope one of those is for me," he said.

She turned in her stool with a wide grin that showed her perfect teeth and gentle eyes. "It sure is. I was thinking we have a drink and get out of here. I know somewhere that's not so chaotic where we can actually converse without yelling."

"Works for me."

Sonya handed him his drink and he remained standing beside her, as no other seat was open at the bar. They talked about their weekends, Sonya having used hers to grade papers and catch up on sleep.

The small talk faded along with the margaritas. They both devoured a basket of chips and salsa before Martin waited for Sonya to suggest the next move.

"Let's go," she finally said after listening to one more song from the mariachi. She jumped off of the barstool and grabbed Martin's hand, pulling him through the crowded room toward the exit. The smells of food mixed with her trailing scent of fruity perfume.

Sonya didn't slow down as she barreled through the door, taking them back outside where the evening started to cool off.

"I like it here, don't get me wrong, but I thought we'd make this a more formal date," she said, continuing to walk to the parking lot. "I can drive."

Martin followed his spontaneous date to her car, a newer Toyota sedan with a bumper sticker that read: *IF YOU CAN READ THIS, THANK A TEACHER!*

"Sweet ride," he said casually as he closed the passenger door. "So, where are we going on this mystery date?"

"There's a restaurant right outside of Denver that one of my student's parents owns. He has a standing discount for any faculty from the school, and I like to take advantage from time to time."

"I see. I can drive us if you wanted to drop your car off at home."

"It's fine. I insist."

She giggled again, an innocent, charming sound that now combined with her scent in a mixture that made Martin's head spin, and his heart tingle.

Don't fall in love. That's not what you came here for. You're here for Izzy and nothing else.

"Martin?" she asked, interrupting his thoughts.

"Sorry, I zoned out for a minute."

"I asked if you like steak?"

"Yes, absolutely."

"Okay, good. Because we're going to a fancy steakhouse. Just wanted to make sure."

She popped in a cassette tape and they listened to a young Celine Dion during the rest of the drive across town.

* * *

They pulled up curbside to a valet parking attendant who greeted them with a warm smile. Martin grabbed her hand and led them toward the golden double doors that led to the stone building called Lavender.

Shrubbery decorated the outside of the building, purple neon lights running along the ground on the walkway into the entrance. Soft jazz greeted them as they stepped in to the lobby, where the host welcomed them from behind a tall stand.

"Welcome to Lavender," he said in his most formal voice to match his three-piece suit. "Do you have a reservation this evening?"

"Yes, sir," Sonya said. "It should be under Sonya Griffiths."

The man peered down a list with a keen eye and pursed lips until he found the name. "Perfect. Give us one minute to prepare your table, Ms. Griffiths."

"Cool-looking place," Martin observed as he looked around at the dim lighting and upscale art covering the walls.

"Yeah, don't think I'd ever be able to eat here if it wasn't for the discount. Ray takes such good care of us teachers."

"This way, folks," the host said, now holding two menus as he stepped out from behind his stand. He led them through the main dining room and to a back private room where a lone table awaited them, candles flickering in the center, two glasses filled with red wine in front of each seat.

The host pulled out a chair for Sonya and shuffled around the table to do the same for Martin, who thanked the man.

"Your server will be with you folks in just a minute. Have a pleasant dinner." He bowed out of the room hastily.

"So what's good here?" Martin asked.

"Everything," Sonya said. "I usually get a steak, but I've heard the seafood is great, too, if that's your thing. I'm not a fan of seafood in general."

"Neither am I."

"Well, then, no sushi dates for us!"

Martin chuckled and opened his menu, falling deep into the many options to choose from, and noting the hefty price tag with each item.

"Good evening, folks," a voice came from behind Martin, whose back faced the door. It sounded older and a bit too familiar for his liking. He looked up to Sonya and saw a wide grin on her face as she watched the approaching waiter. "How is the wine?"

The waiter stood at the side of the table, looking down at them from his dark eyes, his frosty hair standing out in the dim room. The man locked eyes with Martin, making him feel somewhat possessed.

"My name is Chris, and I'll be taking care of you folks tonight. Have we had a chance to look at the menu?"

"The wine is delicious, and I don't think we've decided on dinner yet," Sonya said.

"Very well," Chris said, turning to Martin. "Any questions, sir?"

Martin gazed up like the waiter was a planet in the night sky. His throat clenched as no words came out when he opened his mouth to speak.

Chris laughed. "Very well, sir. I know our menu can be a bit overwhelming. I'll come back in a couple minutes to check on you." The old man left the room as Martin's jaw hung open.

"What's wrong with you?" Sonya asked in a stern tone. "Are you okay?"

"I'm fine," he mustered. "I just . . . need a minute. Let me use the restroom and splash some water on my face. This room is hot, don't you think?"

"Okay?" Sonya's face scrunched into confusion.

Martin excused himself, stepped out of the private room, and followed a long hallway to the restrooms. He pushed open the swinging door and found Chris standing at the sink, hands under the faucet, an evil smirk on his face in the mirror.

"Martin, my friend! I knew you'd come find me here." Chris's voice returned to the more laid-back, eccentric version of itself that he had known.

"What are you doing here?" Martin asked.

"Take it easy. I'm here because you asked me to come. Did you not?"

Martin thought back to the other day when he had wished for Chris in his thoughts, but couldn't recall saying anything out loud.

"You don't have to say it out loud. I can hear your thoughts, my friend."

The statement sent a new wave of chills through Martin's body as he felt his arm hairs standing stiffly underneath his sleeves.

Martin studied the bathroom stalls, looking for feet beneath the doors.

"Don't worry, we're alone. You should get back to your date. You look to be doing just fine." Chris grinned as he turned off the faucet, and splashed his wet fingers into the sink.

"I asked for you for a reason. Why did you leave out so much information?"

"You talked to Calvin, yes? He's a good guy. I send all of you through time on a level playing field. I only inform you of the cardinal sin to not break." Chris smirked, staring into Martin's soul. "There are lots of little things to know, more than I could ever cover. It's best to learn as you go."

"So I'm supposed to just live each day like normal and hope some crazy Road Runner doesn't snipe me from a rooftop?"

Chris laughed. "You should worry about the Road Runners, but they're not as intense as Calvin might have you think. Yes, they have an evil agenda, but they don't just attack for no reason."

"How do you know all this? Do you have some master security cameras that you watch in your tiny room and get off to watching me struggle?"

Chris threw his head back and howled, his white hair dancing. "Of course not. I'm the keeper of time, I can jump around to wherever and whenever. If I wanted, I can know what you're going to do before you do."

Martin stood in silence and looked down to his feet.

"Look, I'm here to help if you need. I can't help you on your actual mission, but I'm here if you need to talk. For now, just go back to your date – she's starting to worry. Try to relax, everything will be fine. Enjoy the 90's. What a time to be alive!"

"I swear to God, if anything happens to me, I'll kill you."

"I'm sure you will," Chris mocked with a wink. "Now, I have a table to wait, I suggest we get back out there."

Chris shuffled past Martin, leaving him alone to stare in the mirror and wonder what the fuck he had gotten into.

"Be normal. Breathe. You have a beautiful date, go enjoy the night," he said to himself before stepping out.

He walked back down the long hall and returned to the private dining room where Sonya waited with a now empty glass of wine. A basket of bread had been placed in the middle and she started to apply butter to a slice.

"I'm so sorry. Can we just start over right now?"

"Sure," she said. "Is everything okay?"

"Yes. I've got so much going on, my mind has been in the clouds. I haven't been able to focus and give you all my attention, so I do apologize for that."

"No worries. Let's move on. I'm ready for dinner."

"Me too. I think I'm just gonna order the prime rib, something nice and heavy."

"That's what I was gonna get! I already ordered sides, so those should be out soon."

They dined and drank wine for the next two hours, falling into deep conversations about past relationships, family, and hopes for the future. Trust developed easily between the two as they swapped stories, a new waiter dropping in from time to time. Martin's mind tried to wonder where Chris had gone, but he maintained his focus on the beautiful woman across the table.

"Let's get out of here. Wanna have one more drink back at my place?"

Sonya asked after they paid the check.

"I'd love to," Martin said, his heart fluttering at the thought.

Maybe I'll save Izzy and just stay in 1996 after all.

21

Chapter 20

Martin hadn't made love to a woman in nearly ten years, settling for quiet evenings with bottles of whiskey and his reliable hands. He rarely sought women after finalizing the divorce with Lela, and had only had a fling with a low-rate stripper over a drunken weekend in Las Vegas. She was a classy lady who offered to share her cocaine before she took her clothes off in the one-star motel off the strip.

Sonya was a drastic improvement. There was no cocaine, just a glass of wine before she stepped out of the bathroom wearing lacy, black lingerie with a seductive smile. She led him into her bedroom where they spent the rest of the night together.

In the three weeks following, they had done this same routine at least five times a week, sometimes at his apartment, unable to keep their hands off each other. For Martin, it was more than sex; he felt a tingle in his soul that had fallen dormant. While he couldn't bring himself to call it love, he knew that's what it was. Falling in love could devastate his plans to save Izzy. If Sonya was present in his life every day, then how would he explain what he was up to without blowing his cover? Would Sonya even care? Or believe him?

She still had school every day, but summer break was fast approaching. As far as she knew, he had to drive downtown every day for work. He'd have to start spending the days outside of the house, and Columbine High

School would be a good place to start.

So, the answer is yes, Martin. You can have a relationship and *accomplish what you set out to do.*

As the final week of April began, Martin felt ready to jump in to his half-hearted plan. He wanted more information before driving all the way to Littleton, but it was simply unavailable thanks to the technological restrictions of the time. He really wished he could jump back to 2018, even for ten minutes, to gather needed information, but he'd have to approach this like a true detective.

On Monday, April 22, Martin jumped in his car with the printed directions to Columbine. His first task was to locate the two young boys who were still three years away from shooting their classmates. *Find them and follow them.*

Once he had an idea of their routines, he'd then decide what action to take in trying to stop them. Aside from stopping the massacre, Martin hoped to learn the boundaries of changing history. Because of this, he stopped at the liquor store first to have a brief chat with an old friend.

When he entered, Calvin greeted him with a warm smile. "Martin, how are you?"

"I'm doing good, how have you been, Calvin?"

"Very good, thank you. You need more of your fancy scotch?"

Martin laughed. "Not today. I actually ran into Chris, and he told me to come see you if I had any questions."

"Chris was here?"

"Well, not here, but a restaurant downtown. He said you're a great guy to come to with any questions, that you know a lot about how this all works."

"Yes. We need to keep these conversations quick, though."

"Understood. I really have one question today."

Calvin looked around the store to confirm they were alone. Apparently no one ever visited him in the mornings. "Okay, go ahead."

"I want to know about making changes to the past. Can it be done? How big of a change can you make?"

"I've never made big changes personally. But I do know of people who have attempted." Calvin spoke in a lowered, serious tone, keeping his eyes glued to the door where anyone could walk through.

"Attempted?"

"Yes, attempted. It's practically impossible to change a major historical event. The bigger the impact an event had on society, the more resistance you'll run into. I know a guy who traveled to 2001 to try and prevent the terror attacks of 9/11. His truck exploded the night of September 10 while he was driving to dinner, never to be seen again."

"Holy shit."

"Holy shit is right. However, saving your daughter shouldn't have too much resistance, as it wasn't something that directly impacted society as a whole. There will be some challenges, don't count it out, but I doubt it will be anything life-threatening."

"I've been toying around with the idea of stopping the Columbine shooting."

"Columbine? Can you refresh me what that was?"

"Major school shooting in 1999. The two shooters are currently freshmen at the high school."

"I see. Where I'm from—er, *when* I'm from—a lot has been removed from the history books. Censorship has skyrocketed under the admin-istration. That's why many of us have traveled back in time to rewrite history books for our safekeeping. It's like an underground Wikipedia we're trying to build."

"Oh, so you still have Wikipedia in the future?"

"Sure, but it's all censored. I guarantee you there's no trace of Columbine High School if I were to look it up. Anything negative toward the Second Amendment gets automatically censored."

"Damn, glad I'll be dead long before then."

"Yeah, it sure is an interesting time. To answer your question, though, I'd say you'll have to be the judge as to how big of an effect this shooting had on society. I'm not familiar with it myself."

"At the time, it was the deadliest school shooting ever. President

Clinton flew out here to deliver a speech. Personally, I consider it the shooting that sparked the hundreds that followed afterwards."

"Hundreds of shootings? I remember when I was younger, maybe around 2020 or so there were a few shootings, but they slowly started to fade. Then again, they could still be happening, we just never hear about them."

"I'm not gonna lie, I'm pretty intrigued to visit your future, just to see what the world is like."

"It's not pretty, believe me."

"What do you think I should do?" Martin asked, tossing his hands in the air.

"Why do you wanna do this? I thought you were here for your daughter. Seems silly to me to risk her life for anything else."

"I have a lot of time to kill between now and September. My daughter is in her routine; nothing changes between now and then."

"So you're bored and wanna change the world?"

"Not bored, I've just never had the opportunity to do good for the world. I've lived in a black hole since Izzy went missing and have run on autopilot for the last two decades of my life. But, here, I feel so *alive.* So alert and sharp. It would be a waste to sit around and watch baseball all summer."

Calvin nodded, a closed fist over his mouth. "It sounds to me like your mind is already made up. Just make sure you're careful, the past has a way of knowing what you're thinking, and will push back. I don't wanna hear about your car exploding while on a drive. I'd say if the president flew out here, then we're talking about a very big deal."

Martin nodded. "I'm just gonna follow these kids around and see what kind of opportunity there is."

"No harm in that. Just be ready for resistance. When you feel it, it's time to let off. You should probably get going now. We've been talking way too long. Try to stay away from here for at least another month if you can."

The way Calvin spoke made Martin wonder if someone was watching them. Surely Chris was, but there was no reason to fear the old man.

"Understood, thanks for your help again." Martin stuck out a hand to shake with Calvin. He left the liquor store behind and would never return, if he could help it.

22

Chapter 21

Martin arrived at Columbine High School forty minutes later. The directions took him on a couple of wrong turns, stranding him in the middle of an unfamiliar neighborhood. He had to resort to an old practice that had since gone out of style in the mid-twenty-first century: going into a gas station to ask for directions.

The attendant pointed him in the right direction and he pulled into the school parking lot two minutes later. He sat in the parking lot, facing the school's main entrance. The entrance was a wall of blue glass that reminded him of a shallow beach. Beige stone walls made up the rest of the school's exterior. Nostalgia filled Martin's tiny car as he stared at the building where hell would break loose and change the landscape of America for many years to come.

Maybe I shouldn't be here.

He sensed the magnitude of his side project and a natural doubt crept in.

"Don't be a chickenshit – you're here, just go look around. It's 1996, you can probably walk into the school and no one will pay you any attention."

Schools didn't have a reason for high security measures yet. The doors would be unlocked, there would be no security guard on duty, and there might not even be a sign-in sheet.

"Hi, I'm here to meet Eric Harris and Dylan Klebold so I can save your life," Martin said to the imaginary secretary.

He stepped out of the car and took a deep breath of fresh air. The grass on the front lawn was already a deep shade of green where a handful of students sat cross-legged with textbooks in their laps and composition books on the side. The school had to have housed at least 2,000 students based on its sheer massiveness.

We're not in Larkwood anymore, he thought, remembering his high school was lucky to even have patches of grass to sit on for mid-morning studying.

Martin glanced at his watch to see lunchtime would be right around the corner. He walked to up a young girl on the lawn, and she looked up at him from behind big glasses and flashed a smile full of braces.

"Hello," Martin said. "I just had a quick question."

"Good morning, sir," she replied warmly. "Are you looking for someone?"

"No. I'm actually just wondering about your school. My family has moved to town and I'm out and about today checking out the different campuses."

The girl stood up, brushed grass off her jeans, and stuck out a skinny arm to shake his hand. "Welcome to town. My name's Amy. I'm a junior here."

"Nice to meet you, Amy." Her overwhelming kindness caught him off-guard. "My name is Martin."

"What kind of questions did you have?"

"How big is your class?"

"I think we have a little over 400 students in my class."

"Are the classes separated? Like are freshman in one section of the school? Seniors in another?"

"For the most part. Classes are in different parts of the school, but our lockers are all separated by class, so everyone stays within their class for the most part during the day."

"I see. Do you know if the school offers any tours?"

"I think so. You should be able to go into the office and they can help you with that."

"Thank you, I think I'll do that. You've been very helpful, Amy."

"You're welcome."

The school's bell rang out across the lawn at noon, prompting everyone to return inside the building. Martin waited back until it appeared everyone had gone inside, and then he followed.

He stood in front of the school, watching dozens of students cross paths through the glass, and wondered if Eric and Dylan were in the mix. The thought sent chills up his back that he didn't notice.

Once the halls had cleared of traffic, Martin strolled to the building's double doors and pulled. The door didn't budge, shuddering in place as he kept pulling on it. His heart raced as he wondered if this was the past already pushing back at him. Schools didn't lock their front doors until *after* the shooting that changed the world.

The entryway was wide with three sets of double doors, so he shuffled down to another and pulled the door open with no resistance. He giggled at himself for panicking so quickly at one door being locked out of the six.

The hallway in front of him led straight back 100 feet before splitting into two separate directions. The walls were lined with blue lockers and a banner hung from the hallway's entry that read: *HOME OF THE REBELS!*

The main office was directly to Martin's right. He started toward the office when a cold hand tickled his back. He turned around to find no one. The hairs on his arms stood stiffly as he decided it was all in his head.

The secretary inside the office watched him through the doorway, and waved him to enter. "Hello, sir, is there something I can help you with?" she asked. The nameplate on her desk identified her as Ms. Helms, an older woman pushing sixty with curly gray hair and a bright smile that shined through her early wrinkles.

"Yes, ma'am, I was actually wondering if you do tours of the school?"

"We sure do. Is your child here?"

"Actually, he's not. My family is moving from out of state. My wife and son are still back at home while I get things started here, so it'll just be me for the tour."

Nice reaction, Marty. Looks like you do have a knack for this detective life.

"I see. If you want to have a seat I can find someone to show you around the school in a few minutes."

"Sounds good, thank you."

Martin sat in the row of chairs that ran along the office's wall. He could see into the empty hallway toward the exit that had played with his mind a couple minutes earlier.

The office walls were lined with portraits of the school's past principals. The photos all led to the back wall where an enlarged portrait of President Bill Clinton hung beside an American flag. A handful of offices were below these pictures, including the principal's office. The clock on the wall approached noon, ticking away in the silent office among the soft hum of computers.

Martin waited, not sure what to do. Normally, he'd pull out his phone and check his emails and social media accounts, but that was no longer an option in his current situation, so he fidgeted with his fingers and tried to erase the fact that some sort of force had brushed its coldness on his body when he entered the site of a future massacre.

"Excuse me, sir?" a voice interrupted his thoughts. A young woman stood in front of him who looked like she was maybe a day removed from college. "You're looking to tour the school?"

"I am, yes."

"Great! My name is Jessica, and I've been a teaching assistant here at the school all year. I'll be showing you around and I can answer any questions you might have."

"Terrific. My name is Martin Briar."

"I understand your son won't be able to make it in for a tour."

"Correct. He's still back home with my wife finishing up the packing."

"I see. Where are you all coming from?" Jessica asked in her cheery voice.

"California. I got a new job opportunity I couldn't pass up here."

"Very cool. Well, welcome to Colorado and welcome to Columbine High

School, we love to add to our growing community."

"Thank you. I've been very impressed with the town so far."

"Perfect, well follow me."

Martin followed her back into the main hallway where she stood with her hands clasped under her tiny bosom.

"So, this is the main entrance as you probably figured out. All of the administration is in the office should you ever need to meet with any one. Our school is two levels with the majority of the classrooms on the upper level. Down this hallway are most of the freshman lockers. Will your son be a freshman in the fall?"

"Yes," Martin lied.

"Terrific. So this is most likely where his locker will be, somewhere in this long hallway. If not, he'll be around the corner closer to the cafeteria, which we'll go take a look at now."

They walked down the freshman hallway, Martin knowing behind two of the locker doors was the property belonging to Eric and Dylan. He remembered they had both kept disturbing journals and couldn't help but wonder if those journals were already in the school building today.

Martin recognized the cafeteria when they reached the end of the hallway. White circular tables with blue chairs spread across the entirety of the room, dozens of students filling the room to eat. The view from the cafeteria faced the massive Rocky Mountains in the distance, and overlooked the soccer field where hundreds would flee when word broke of a shooting in the school.

He closed his eyes and remembered the images of the cafeteria he had seen on the news. Backpacks, books, and jackets were all left behind on the ground while abandoned food trays and drinks stayed on the tables, as if never touched. Two propane tanks had been placed around the cafeteria with hopes of blowing up that entire section of the school. Over 400 students were in the cafeteria at the time, but the bombs never detonated. Had those bombs gone off, the school would have surely been demolished and no longer exist in the future.

"Mr. Briar?"

He had gone so far off the deep end in his mind that Jessica's voice had droned into a cluster of noise in the cafeteria.

"Sorry, what did you say?"

"I asked if you had any questions so far."

"Oh, sorry. I do not, thank you."

"Great. If you'll follow me through the cafeteria, I can show you the few classrooms we have on the first floor."

She led them through the cafeteria where Martin couldn't help but stare out the window to the open soccer field. *If only you knew.*

Jessica guided them through a side door on the other end of the cafeteria, and when the door shut behind them, they stood in a short hallway in complete silence.

"Is that a soundproof door?" he asked.

"It is. Since we have lunch hours from 11 to 2, we don't want any of the noise to carry into this hall." More blue lockers lined the wall as they walked down and passed numerous classrooms in session. "These classrooms are home to our business and foreign language departments. So basically, any math class is over here, and then we offer Spanish, French, German, and Latin."

Martin looked around, hoping to see a glance of young Eric or Dylan somewhere. With the school's size, it would be a long shot tracking them down so easily.

Jessica kept strolling through the halls, and Martin followed as she pushed open a small door that led them back to the lobby at the main entrance. "Let's go upstairs."

Martin hadn't noticed the stairwell when he first entered, but it was directly to the right of the doorway and twisted upward to the second floor landing. Two long hallways stretched in opposite directions.

"Up here are the rest of the lockers. As you can see, the space spans all the way to the back of the school. The rest of the classrooms are up here, too. Language arts, science, the art studio, and the music room are all on this floor along with the library."

The library. He needed to see it—that's where all the drama occurred just before the boys turned their guns on themselves and called it a day.

"Let's go check out the east hall first and we can finish in the library," Jessica said, starting in that direction.

A knot twisted in Martin's stomach. He didn't know why he was so nervous. The library was a regular high school library. It hadn't seen any tragedy and it would be filled with students studying like any other day. He started to sweat and wiped it quickly off his forehead before Jessica could notice.

They walked down the hall toward the band room in what felt like slow motion. Martin suddenly felt lost in his mind, as if walking down a dark hallway by himself. He watched his body walk down the long hallway, having a true out-of-body experience.

Am I dying? Martin felt like he should be panicking, his heart should be pulsing, adrenaline should flood his body, but nothing happened. Everything felt numb. Jessica kept talking, probably creeped out by the strange father and wanting to end the tour as soon as possible. Her voice echoed in his mind, how it might sound when you could somewhat overhear a conversation through walls in a hotel room.

A sound filled his vacant head, reminding him of slithering snakes. "Get out," a voice whispered. "Get out. Get out."

As if shoved in the back, Martin returned to himself, feeling control over his body. He studied his hands as if he'd never seen them before.

"I'm sorry, Jessica. I'm feeling a bit off. I think I should leave."

"Oh. Are you sure? We're almost done."

"How much longer?"

"We can skip the classrooms and I can show you the library and gym before we wrap up."

Don't go to that library.

"Okay, I think I can manage." The temptation to see the library proved too strong for Martin, even in the midst of whatever was happening in his head.

Just go look, nothing bad will happen from looking at the library.

He wondered if a place could be haunted before a tragedy occurred, because walking through the halls of this storied school certainly felt like it.

"Can we just do the library and call it a day? Seen one gym, seen them all." He offered a forced chuckle, feeling normal again, but terrified of what had just happened to his senses.

"Oh, sure thing." She led them back down the hall, no longer speaking, and walking a bit faster than she had earlier in the tour.

Martin could see the library at the end of the hall, a set of wooden double doors leading into the infamous room where the two shooters killed most of their victims and themselves.

There was no further sense of an out-of-body experience as they approached the library.

"Here we are," Jessica said, the perkiness fading from her voice, as she pulled open the double doors.

They stepped in. And nothing happened.

He wasn't sure what he thought would happen, but life carried on as normal in the quiet library. Students huddled around the few computers available, while others claimed their territory at the many tables scattered about the room between the dozens of bookshelves.

"Anything in particular you wanted to see in the library?" Jessica asked, more relaxed.

"Nothing in particular. I'm just a believer that you can judge a lot about a school by its library, and I must say it's impressive."

"Well, thank you, Mr. Briar."

Martin peeked at his watch, wanting it to appear that he had somewhere else to be. "I really should get going, though. I've got some errands to run this afternoon, but I really appreciate you taking the time to show me around."

Jessica smiled, looking comfortable again. "It was my pleasure. I hope your family decides to join our community here."

Martin shook the girl's hand before they parted ways. He informed her he would find his way out of the school no problem, then deliberately took the longer route that passed through the freshman hallway.

23

Chapter 22

Martin thought of the high school as a historical landmark even though nothing had yet happened within its walls, aside from adolescent drama and education. He took a final pass through the freshman hallway in hopes of bumping into one of the boys, but the swarm of students when the lunch bell rang made it impossible.

The past flexed its muscles by toying with his mind. He still couldn't shake off the feeling that he had nearly fainted or died—he wasn't sure exactly what it was—and felt a stressful tension lingering in his chest.

Martin returned to his car and grabbed his notebook. He noted the resistance the past had pushed on him, comparing the sensation to possibly a stroke or heart attack. He mentioned the cold presence that lingered in the entryway and cafeteria. The past gave him no choice but to acknowledge its authority. Everything Calvin had told him was true, and he would need to tread carefully going forward. Maybe it was a good thing he didn't see one of the boys today.

Martin threw his notebook aside and inhaled deeply, his stomach gurgling anxiously.

This is bigger than you. You're messing with the wrong history. Go home and don't ever come back.

His subconscious had provided sound advice since he arrived in 1996, but he ignored it, believing there had to be a way to stop the shooting without getting himself killed.

After a ten-minute debate on what to do next, Martin fired up his engine and drove home. It had been at least a decade—in 2018's standards—since the Denver highways were clear of traffic in the middle of the day, and he enjoyed every second of driving 70 miles per hour on I-25. He powered on the radio and let the youthful sounds of the Spice Girls distract his mind. Izzy had loved the Spice Girls, and he remembered her dancing around the house with a hairbrush in hand as her imaginary microphone, singing her lungs out to every one of their hits.

"I can go back every day and try to find them on their way home. Can't go in to the school again, I'll become too suspicious."

This would require heavy detective work, but he had nothing better to do with his time. He'd like to follow Izzy home a few times a week to see her, but would have to treat that action with kid gloves to avoid being caught by her or an observant resident in the neighborhood.

The day had taken an emotional toll on Martin—it wasn't every day one encountered a supernatural force while traveling back in time. When he arrived back to his apartment, he snuck by Vinny's office, and went up to his unit for a glass of whiskey and to take a nap. Sonya would be over later for a dinner date, and he'd need his energy if she wanted another piece of Martin Briar for dessert.

* * *

Martin prepared dinner that night. They had been going out too often and wanted to save money, so they agreed to alternate cooking dinner at home throughout the week, and would eat out on the weekends.

Sonya arrived promptly at six as Martin put the finishing touches on the taco bar he had set up on the kitchen counter. She walked in to a margarita that lit up her face.

"It smells delicious!" she said, sitting on his couch with her drink and taking a deep inhale.

"Why, thank you. You *look* delicious," Martin crooned as he kissed the top of her head. Sonya never stopped showing off her toned legs, and he never stopped looking.

They caught up on each other's days, Martin lying about another long day at the post office, keeping the haunted high school in the back of his mind. He had gotten into the habit of telling these lies so much that he started to believe them. Every time the topic of work came up, he remembered, somewhere in 2018, he was asleep in Chris's office, waiting to be woken up to go in to work. The thought gave him the empty feeling you have on the final day of a long vacation.

With the table set, they sat down for dinner, Martin diving immediately into the juicy tacos he had spent the last hour preparing. After a couple of bites, he noticed Sonya poking around at her food, not having taken a bite yet. She maintained a smile, but Martin could see through it.

"Something wrong?" he asked.

She looked at him, her hazel eyes sparkling with natural beauty, a secret swimming behind them.

"Nothing is wrong. I've just got something on my mind is all."

Martin nodded, took a bite, and stared right back into her soul in an effort to hide how nervous he suddenly became. She remained silent and sipped the margarita.

"Are you gonna tell me or make me guess?"

She smiled, and it assured him that whatever was bothering her had nothing to do with him, at least in a negative sense.

"I suppose I have to tell you, or it's gonna eat at me for the next week." She paused, took another sip, and poked at the tacos again. "I want to tell you something, but I'm just afraid of how you'll react."

"You can tell me anything," he responded quickly and confidently.

"Okay, here it goes. I know we've only been seeing each other for a few weeks, but I feel like there's something between us."

Martin nodded and couldn't help but grin. Things were going very well. He'd never thought his first relationship in twenty years could feel so natural.

"At our age, I feel like it's okay to move quicker than normal. We're about halfway through life, probably more, so no point in taking things slow."

She paused for another sip, and Martin noticed the slightest tremble from her hand.

"I guess what I'm getting at . . . I wanted to ask you what you think about moving in together."

She grabbed her glass in sync with the words leaving her mouth and took a long swig as she watched Martin.

He sat back in his chair, one arm crossed, his free hand on his chin.

"Wow," he said, shocked.

"I knew it. It was too aggressive of me. Pretend I never said anything. Crazy thoughts, I know."

"Wait, wait, wait," Martin cut in. "I haven't even said anything. It *is* a fast move, but I agree with you. At this point in life we should both know what we want. We don't have to wait it out five years to be sure."

His eyebrows dropped in thought, scrunching his face into a shape that made him look closer to seventy years old.

"You know," Martin continued. "I haven't been able to get you out of my mind. I think about you when I wake up. I think about you when I go to sleep. Getting through a shitty workday has become so much easier knowing I get to see you at the end of it."

Sonya blushed, her entire face pink, as she took a giddy sip of margarita.

"So is that a yes?" she asked.

"I want to say yes, but have you thought about where would we live? Your place? My place? A whole new place?"

"I was thinking my place. My mortgage is low and I have plenty of space."

Martin nodded. "Okay. I just signed my lease, though, and I'm not sure I can get out of it."

"Aren't you friends with the landlord?"

"I wouldn't call us friends, but we get along just fine."

"It won't hurt to just ask him. Let him know the situation and he might be understanding."

"I can do that. I doubt he'll let me out of the lease for free, but maybe he'll work with me."

Sonya clapped her hands like a giggly teenage cheerleader. "I'm so excited. I was so scared you'd freak out and tell me to leave."

"Why would I do that?"

"I don't know. Some men are afraid of commitment, so I didn't know how you'd take it."

"Well, I'm certainly not afraid of commitment; I've been married before. It just didn't work out. I have feelings for you I can't deny. If anything, I'm relieved to know you feel the same way."

Sonya smirked and shot Martin an intense stare, suggesting that they get in bed right away.

"Well, since we're on the same page then, what do you say we put away these dishes and have some fun?" she asked him, refusing to break her gaze.

He pursed his lips and nodded as if in deep thought. "I suppose we could do that." He spoke in a serious tone, but couldn't keep the grin off his face, prompting a seductive giggle from his girlfriend.

They did the dishes as quickly as they had ever done. Sonya pulled him onto his bed and cut the lights. As they made love, a thought kept tugging at Martin, leaving him unable to focus.

If I live with Sonya, how am I supposed to pull off any of my plan without letting her know what this is all about? Is she the distraction sent by the past to hold me back?

These thoughts would keep him up late into the night as she snored softly on his chest. He ran gentle, steady fingers over her head while she slept, wondering if she was even real.

24

Chapter 23

After a brief internal debate of calling the move off, Martin decided to move forward with it. He *wanted* to move in with Sonya, that he never doubted, but his concern grew in regards to his actual purpose for being in 1996. He couldn't afford to compromise saving Izzy, so he would plan a fake work trip out of town during that dreaded week in September. He'd book a hotel nearby, preferably anywhere besides the Sunset Dream Motel, and keep an eye on all activity surrounding his old house. If he had to sleep in his car at the end of the block for the entire week, then so be it. He was here to keep his daughter safe and alive.

The Columbine mission could also continue. Martin wasn't expected home until six o'clock, leaving him plenty of time to scope the area surrounding the high school, follow the boys for a bit, and drive back across town for his now permanent dinner date with Sonya.

The conversation with Vinny had gone much easier than expected. His landlord gave zero pushback when asked if Martin could break his contract and move out as soon as possible.

"You're good people, Martin. For anyone else, I'd say no. Just promise to come see me from time to time."

"I can do that," Martin replied, wondering why things were falling into place without any resistance.

The two caught up for a few more minutes over a glass of scotch before

Martin returned to his apartment to tell Sonya the news. By May first, Martin could officially move out with nothing further owed to Vinny, and they could begin a life together.

Despite it being a cause for celebration, Martin lost a few nights of sleep after cementing his decision. Somewhere down the road he would be faced with the crossroads of either telling Sonya the truth or vanishing from her life without a word. Both options terrified him.

Telling her the truth could open numerous possibilities. She might believe him and wish him a good rest of his life in 2018. She could become enraged that he had knowingly dragged her along for six months after admitting they were both at no point in life to waste time on meaningless relationships. Or, and most likely, she would think him crazy for discussing anything like time travel and kick him to the curb.

These possibilities continued to pick away at his mind as they had since the decision was made three days earlier. While the unknowing bothered Martin, he needed to keep a clear mind to continue his work at Columbine. He also jotted new rules for himself in his spiral notebook regarding the project. If anything felt off about the situation, he vowed to turn around and leave. He'd already had close calls with that sense of vertigo that came with fucking with the past. He'd found the red line and couldn't afford to cross it so soon; if there were a time to do so, it would come in September when saving Izzy.

His racing thoughts kept him occupied during the entire drive to Columbine. The final bell would ring in twenty minutes, at 3:30, and all he wanted was to locate at least one of the boys to follow, and learn their daily after school routine.

He assumed they would exit from the main entrance, so he waited in the same parking lot he had parked during his first trip. Space was tight as many cars awaited their students, but he was able to squeeze into a spot that faced the doors. Then the fun part of waiting began.

Stakeouts weren't everything they made them out to be in movies. Martin grew bored within fifteen minutes of sitting in his car, staring at the same building, watching the kids who all looked the same pour out as they carried on their conversations and laughed with each other.

High school really is the easiest time of life. These kids have no idea what's waiting for them outside of these walls.

He watched some older kids walk out, wearing their blue and white letterman jackets, and felt silly for having always longed for one in high school. Those kids had always seemed so cool, but looking back on it, they were just assholes like everyone else.

Thirty minutes passed without any sight of Eric or Dylan. This part of the process was painful, and Martin didn't want to waste any more time. The boredom allowed him time to think of different ways to locate the boys, and he settled on a rather obvious solution that he should have thought of in the first place: the White Pages.

The White Pages was a directory of people, the past's version of Google searching someone's name to find their phone number and address. Before privacy had become such a major pain point in the new century, one could easily look up someone's name and know exactly where they lived and what number to call them on.

Pay phones! Martin had a grand revelation by remembering there should be phone books that hung at each pay phone around town. He left the school behind, no longer concerned with the crapshoot chance of finding the boys within the mob of students, and returned to the gas station around the corner, where he had stopped for directions the first time.

Most gas stations in 1996 had a payphone outside, and this location was no different. The pay phone stood in its hefty, silver box, a white book at least five inches thick dangling beneath from a chain. A suited man stood at the pay phone, talking with his hand over the mouthpiece, and looking around suspiciously. He briefly locked eyes with Martin before hanging up and returning to his white BMW and skidding out of the parking lot.

When the coast appeared clear, Martin strode to the pay phone and lifted the dangling phone book, flipping to the middle.

There will be too many Harrises listed. Klebold will be my best bet.

He flipped to the K section, running a finger down the page until he found what he needed: Thomas and Susan Klebold, the only Klebolds on the page.

"There you are." Martin pulled out his notepad and jotted the address; the phone rang out in a screaming, piercing chime.

Martin gazed around, seeing if someone nearby was expecting a call. No one was in sight, so he picked up the phone. "Hello?"

"You'll never get away with this," a raspy voice said, sending chills down Martin's spine.

"Who is this?" he demanded.

The phone clicked, filling his ear with the dial tone.

What the fuck?

Martin hung up and returned to his car, staring at the payphone through his windshield, wanting it to ring again.

"You'll never get away with this," he whispered to himself. He racked his mind for a familiarity in the voice, but could find nothing. Chris was never one to cower behind a disguise. *Could it be a Road Runner?*

Martin lacked the knowledge to know exactly how the Road Runners operated, but if anyone was trying to prevent the changing of a major historical event, they seemed the likely candidates.

He stepped back out of the car and went inside the gas station.

"Hello," the clerk welcomed him.

"Hi. I'm looking for maps of Denver, do you have any?"

"Yes, sir, in the magazine section." The clerk pointed to the row against the front window.

"Perfect, thank you." Martin hurried to the row, reminiscing over the old days of browsing the wide selection of magazines, books, and newspapers in the corner stores. Those times were long gone in 2018. At the end of the row was a rack of atlases and maps. Martin grabbed the one marked as Denver Metro Area, flipped through it to make sure Littleton was included, and took it to the counter.

"Is there somewhere in particular you're looking to find?" the clerk asked as he rung him up on the register.

"No, I'm just new to the area and seem to get lost every day."

"Fair enough. This map should get you around town just fine."

"Thank you," Martin said, grabbing his map and change before bolting out of the door. He'd normally contribute to meaningless chitchat, but he had pressing matters to tend, and apparently someone trying to stop him.

When he returned to his car, he thought, *Is this all worth it? I could get myself killed trying to stop these kids, and that's not what I'm here for.*

"It may not be what I came here to do, but I owe it to the world to at least try," he said out loud, backing out of the gas station and pulling onto the main road.

25

Chapter 24

The drive to the Klebold residence took longer than expected; they lived eight miles away from the high school, roughly the same distance it would take him to get from Larkwood to downtown Denver.

He followed the map carefully, turn by turn, as the quiet residential neighborhoods gave way to multi-level homes, before turning into open fields in the foothills of the Rocky Mountains. At first, Martin thought he had taken a wrong turn as he zigzagged through a stretch of green hills and thick trees, but when he finally saw Cougar Road appear on a street sign, his heart beat a little faster.

This is it.

He turned onto Cougar Road, immediately feeling out of place in his junker of a car. All of the homes on Cougar Road were hidden behind tall stands of trees, somewhere at the end of a private driveway that started from the main road and ended in the woods, out of sight. Each driveway had a black mailbox at the front with the street numbers in white lettering.

The homes were spaced hundreds of yards apart, providing plenty of privacy from neighbors. Martin drove another mile just to pass five different properties.

He came around a blind curve that opened up to more trees and the towering red rocks that were a staple in Colorado. He passed a small red barn when he saw the mailbox reading 8370, and pulled to the side of the road, directly across the barn that stood on the Klebold property.

Martin killed the engine and stepped out onto the dirt that served as an unofficial sidewalk along the road. Cicadas buzzed from the surrounding trees, echoing everywhere. He looked around, seeing nothing but green trees and more slanted red rock formations before stepping toward the Klebold driveway, to find it curved into more trees and vanished from sight.

Do I really want to go up this driveway? If someone's home or arrives home while I'm walking up, there's very few explanations as to why I'm here, in the middle of nowhere.

"I didn't come here for nothing," he said and started up the dirt driveway. *If anyone asks, I can say I got lost and my car broke down.*

The driveway twisted a quarter mile uphill, causing Martin to huff and puff, as he still hadn't been in any shape for the smallest of hikes. "At least it's all shaded," he remarked.

When he reached the top a few minutes later, his jaw dropped at the massive white house. The driveway turned back into pavement that spiraled into a roundabout in front of the garage. Behind the garage stood the house with gigantic windows that he could see through into the kitchen and dining room. A swimming pool and hot tub were to the side, behind an open space with a basketball hoop where young Dylan likely played.

"Holy shit." Martin had forgotten just how wealthy the Klebold family had been. Plenty of comfortable families lived in Littleton, but this private area of the city was clearly where the high rollers lived. He couldn't even see the entirety of the house from where he stood, but knew there was plenty of room for the boys to hide their stash of firearms that would accumulate in a couple of years.

This has to be where they filmed those tapes of them shooting their guns in the woods, he thought, admiring the surrounding foothills. Taking in the scenery, Martin quickly understood the ease the two boys would have had in keeping their plans a secret. Even if they chose to not hide their arsenal in the house, there would be plenty of spots around the property to keep everything under wraps. With no visible neighbors, they could have taken their time at their homemade shooting range, firing rounds that would surely be heard down the road, but no one would be able to pinpoint the exact location.

Martin stepped toward the house, planting his foot in a pool of mud six inches deep. "Motherfucker!" he barked, kicking his foot to shake it off.

One of the garage doors, about fifty feet in front of him, started to slide open, prompting Martin to pivot and dive into the trees. The garage's motor hummed softly as Martin positioned himself behind a tree stump to ensure he wasn't visible. He watched as a silver Mercedes backed out, circled the roundabout, and disappeared down the driveway, leaving a trail of dust in its tracks. A woman, presumably Dylan's mother, drove the car alone, but he couldn't make out any features aside from shoulder-length hair and a pearl necklace.

He saw no other cars inside the garage, leaving him alone at the Klebold residence. Martin tiptoed back to the driveway, the mud hardening on the skin around his ankle. Sensing his time was limited, he jogged to the main windows that overlooked the home's kitchen.

Everything appeared as pristine as he'd expected: polished marble countertops, wooden cupboards, and shiny black appliances—a standard luxury kitchen for the mid-90's. He put his face up to the glass for a better look, but could only see into the living room where a boxy big-screen TV faced a couch, and a gray cat stared back curiously before returning to its afternoon bathing session.

It's time to go. You've been here too long, Martin warned himself. He wanted to go around the house and see the rest of the property, but going any further would be too risky. *You have what you need for today. You know where the kid lives, and can follow him to and from school until you figure out what the hell you're gonna do.*

Martin surrendered and jogged back toward the driveway, skidding on his heels to keep from rolling down the hill like a boulder. As he left, he could feel the house pulling at him with a magnetic force, daring him to come back and have a look around.

"Just get out of here," he wheezed to himself, finally seeing the main road. "Go home."

Martin reached the bottom of the driveway and sighed in relief at the sight of his rust bucket waiting for him. Not a soul was present as he crossed the abandoned road. He sped off, eyes unable to look away from the house in the rear-view mirror until he rounded a corner and left it out of sight.

26

Chapter 25

Martin took the rest of the week off, wanting nothing more than to sit around and drink himself into tranquility. The Klebold house had a pull on him that didn't lift until he lay down on his couch, surrounded by a handful of moving boxes, that he felt at peace with the events of the prior two days.

He was set to move in two weeks, leaving him that much time to set a solid plan before Sonya would be around during all of his free time.

"This is never going to work," he said, pacing around his apartment. It was now Saturday afternoon, and he had spent the last hour reading over the notes he had taken on Columbine, trying to figure out what exactly to do next, and how the knowledge of the Klebold residence could be used.

First thing I need to do is meet the boys. I need to see how mentally stable they are as freshmen. It's four years until the massacre, so they may be completely normal and happy.

He briefly considered seeking employment at the school to be closer to them, but then he remembered that intense, death-like feeling he had experienced in the building.

I'll follow them until I learn their routine, then I'll approach them casually, ideally in public if possible.

The last thing he needed was to be the crazy fat guy who stalked teenage boys around a wealthy town. That would punch a quick ticket to the police station for questioning.

The police. I could tell the police what the boys plan to do. Leave an anonymous tip.

Martin scratched his head and rubbed his eyes in frustration. "It's too early. They haven't even considered getting a gun yet."

What about a private note to the school's principal? I could tell them the exact date of the shooting so they can be prepared.

"Still too early. Can be taken as an empty threat. Why would an educator in one of the best school districts in the state believe a secret note about an event that would happen three years later?"

Martin sensed his inner voice wanting him to drop the plan altogether, and deep down he knew the risk was too big to guarantee his own safety.

He sat on the couch and dropped his face into open palms. *You're here for Izzy. Not for Columbine. Izzy. Just forget about Columbine. Move in with your girlfriend, make love every night, and save Izzy in September. You don't owe the world a damn thing.*

"You're right."

The world could move on as planned. Even if he managed to prevent Columbine, there would just be another school shooting to take its place as the spark that changed the country.

"I still need to know my limits. I can't have any surprises in September when it comes time to save Izzy."

Martin poured himself a glass of whiskey and drank until he fell asleep.

* * *

The nap was the deepest Martin had slept in a few days. When he woke three hours later, he felt rejuvenated and ready to take on the world again. He decided he wouldn't completely put off the Columbine project, but rather have it on the back burner. There was only a month until summer break anyway, so he might as well wait until school started again in

August to track down the boys. The longer he waited, the closer they would be to their turning point that eventually pushed them over the edge. He could plan a couple of trips to the Klebold residence just to see if the boys might be around; he could even wander around the property from the backside, in hopes of finding their hideout in the woods.

He still had a persona to maintain. Sonya would expect to see him off in the mornings and return home around the same time as her. They could cook dinner together, watch TV, take showers, and fall asleep in each other's arms. The more normal he could make life in 1996 feel, the easier his mind could stay distracted from Columbine and focused on Izzy.

He'd spend the days at the library or wandering around downtown. Denver wouldn't be nearly as busy as it had become in 2018, and he could eat lunch in peace at the 16th Street Mall and watch the businessmen pass by with their hectic lives.

Sonya had given Martin a key to her house and told him to start moving things in whenever he felt ready. With three boxes ready to go, he loaded them into his car and headed to his home of the next five months.

"What the fuck am I going to tell Sonya in September?" he asked his empty car. He couldn't up and leave her with no word. Even in the past, he couldn't afford the kind of karma that would come with pulling the rug out from someone who actually loved him.

Why does she have to exist in 1996? Why couldn't I find her in 2018?

Sonya would be in her late 60's when he returned to 2018, over fifteen years older than him. Could two souls still love each other after going through time travel?

"I could bring her back. Anything on my body when I take the pill comes with me. I can have Izzy in one arm, Sonya in the other, and we'll all live happily ever after."

Or maybe she'll continue to fall deeper in love with you over the summer and she'll want to follow you into the future. Just take it one day at a time.

Martin smirked as he pulled into Sonya's empty driveway. It was a small ranch-style home with an unfinished basement, the perfect place to maintain a low-key lifestyle as he awaited the day he would save his daughter.

"Or maybe I save Izzy and stay."

No, Martin, that would be selfish. Rescue Izzy and return to the future. See where life will have taken you with her around. Don't forget how much you loved your life before she disappeared.

That much was true. He'd had a steady high-paying job where Lela didn't have to work. Izzy came home every night excited to see her parents and tell them about her day. Lela loved him just as much Sonya did now. Life had been perfect, and that's all he really wanted.

27

Chapter 26

On the first day of May, Martin stood in his apartment doorway, staring at the empty space. The sunlight filled the room much brighter than he recalled, as the studio no longer had a trace of his existence. The car was packed with the final few boxes, and all Martin had left to do was drop his key off with Vinny.

Vinny gave Martin a sad smile when he arrived in his office.

"You're out of here for good?" Vinny asked, disappointment in his voice.

"Afraid so. Thank you so much for everything these last couple of months, and for letting me leave like this."

Vinny put up a hand. "No need. You were a good resident, and a good guy. You're welcome here any time. But you go enjoy that girlfriend of yours, seems like a keeper."

"Thanks, Vinny. I'll stop by and see you, maybe we can grab dinner sometime."

"I'd love that." Vinny stood and shook Martin's hand, but they both knew the dinner invite was nothing more than a polite pleasantry. "I'll see you around, Martin."

Martin left the complex and looked up the brick building, appreciative of the stable home it had provided him when everything had felt uncertain upon his arrival.

He drove away, the next chapter of life waiting at Sonya's house, and had never felt so excited about the future. When he pulled into Sonya's driveway five minutes later, he felt at home for the first time in years. Sure, he had his apartment in 2018, but that had housed nothing but cheap booze and cheaper frozen dinners.

With Sonya he had a home: a clean house, home-cooked meals, decorations. And with him moving in, they now had a life together.

Despite all of the budding positivity, that nagging voice in the back of his mind kept reminding him that September wasn't that far away, and he'd be forced to make a difficult decision regarding Sonya.

Next month, you'll be halfway through this trip.

Six weeks had passed since he arrived at the empty lot and wandered by the burned down church. All it took was six weeks to build a life and fall in love. "The past is dangerous," he said as he stepped out of his car.

It was a Wednesday afternoon and Sonya was at school, leaving Martin the day to unpack and settle in to his new home. Birds sung in the pine trees that stood in the front lawn, stretching its shade over the driveway.

The perfectly groomed front yard had freshly cut grass and vibrant flowers that decorated the walkway to the front door. The porch was covered by the tree's shade where two rocking chairs sat around a table big enough to hold a couple cups of coffee. Martin had never seen a neighbor in the surrounding homes in his many visits to Sonya's house, yet today he spied an older couple across the street working in their garden. They waved, and he returned the gesture with a warm smile.

Martin went inside before unloading any of the boxes, wanting a glass of water to kick start the busy afternoon ahead. When he walked into the kitchen, he found a note on the counter.

Hey mister,

I'm so happy we're taking this next step in our relationship. I want to go have dinner where we first met to celebrate, then we can bring the party home.

Sonya

Martin folded the note and slipped it into his pocket with a grin on his face.

See, everything is going to be fine. You won't have any time to think about Columbine. Just need to figure out what to do during the days.

He could take some pretend time off from work to truly get settled in to the new house, maybe even tend to the garden and yard work.

How believable would it be if I "retired" from the post office right now?

Martin pondered this as he aimlessly unloaded the car and dropped the boxes into Sonya's guest room. Instead of fighting over closet space, he would use the guest room to store his clothes and any belongings. Over his six weeks in town, he hadn't accumulated much outside of some kitchenware and essential toiletries.

Once he unloaded the car, he lay down on the living room couch to do one thing he had missed dearly: watch TV. He flipped through the channels, not coming across much beside *Days of Our Lives*, *The Young and the Restless*, and a plethora of infomercials for guaranteed workout results and power washers, and eventually settled on reruns of *The Adventures of Batman and Robin*.

The afternoon dragged through two episodes when a knock came from the front door, startling Martin. He flailed as he rolled off the couch to rush to the door. He could make out the figure of a man through the blinds and figured it to be the neighbor across the street.

Martin pulled open the door, creaking at the hinges.

"Martin Briar! Hello, good sir," Chris said with a devilish smirk. "May I come in?"

Martin's eyes dashed around the neighborhood, again seeing no one else. "Hi?" The hairs on his back prickled in fear.

"You don't look excited to see me," Chris said with a cackle.

"Why are you here?"

"Why am I here? Why are *you* here?"

"I live here now."

"Shacking up with the locals, I see. Not a bad strategy, only five minutes away from your daughter's school."

"What do you want, Chris?"

"Relax, you shouldn't be so snippy. I'm here to let you know I won't be

151

around for the rest of your stay here in 1996. I have a matter to tend to: a civil war is breaking out in Africa in the year 2182."

"Okay, but what does that have to do with me?"

"Nothing, just thought you should know since you're new to this. There's going to be a day where you need me, but just know I won't be around. I'll see you back in 2018."

"What do you mean I'll need you?"

Chris grinned. "Just be careful with everything you do. Until then, take it easy, my friend."

Chris patted Martin on the shoulder before turning away and walking out of his life for the rest of his journey in the past.

His gooseflesh spread from his back to his arms and legs. The more he saw Chris, the less he trusted him.

The old man walked down the driveway and turned down the sidewalk.

Martin returned to his couch, arms trembling from a mixture of rage and fear.

"You can't throw me into the past with one rule, and then drop little hints like this. This is bullshit!"

Martin rummaged through Sonya's liquor cabinet, finding nothing but vodka and cheap tequila. He went into the guest room to find his bottle of whiskey, packed away in a box, and poured a glass to settle his nerves.

28

Chapter 27

Martin lied to Sonya about taking the rest of the week off from work. Thursday and Friday he unpacked all six of his boxes, setting things up where he wanted in the bathroom and kitchen, and filling the guest room closet with the clothes he had gathered since arriving in 1996.

They made passionate love during their first four nights living together. On Sunday, Martin examined himself in the mirror after stepping out of the shower and noticed he had lost weight. The reduced alcohol and constant exercise between the sheets did a miracle for his gut.

When Martin stepped out of the bathroom he found Sonya on the couch, folding a basket of laundry.

"I was gonna wash your uniforms for the week, but didn't see them anywhere. Are they packed still?" she asked him with a gentle smile.

Shit, he thought. He had never been one to cover all of his bases, and changing eras didn't fix that.

"We actually have a changing room down at the post office. They do our laundry for us."

"Wow. The *post office* does that?"

"Not many do," he continued. "But the ones in bigger cities will. The downtown post office is the place to be."

Martin's voice sounded fake to himself, but he kept a careful watch on Sonya, who apparently thought nothing of it.

"I see. That's pretty cool." Her hands kept folding while her eyes remained fixated on the VHS of *Romeo + Juliet* playing on the TV. If young Leonardo DiCaprio put her in the mood, then so be it. "I've been thinking," she continued. "With summer break coming up, maybe you can take some time off and we go on a trip?"

"I thought you teach summer school?" Martin asked.

"I do teach summer school, but it's only through the third week of June," she said, still not breaking her stare from young Leonardo. "We could plan for a trip in July."

"All right, did you have somewhere in mind?"

"I've always wanted to go to D.C. Have you ever been?"

Martin rarely went on trips for leisure, mostly passing by new cities on work trips where he spent ninety percent of his time in a hotel. His mom and dad took him on a trip to Disneyland when he was twelve, and he went to Cancun for a friend's bachelor party before he married Lela. Those were the only trips he'd ever gone on for fun; he and Lela never had the budget to take Izzy anywhere out-of-state.

"I've never been. How long would you wanna go for?"

"I was thinking maybe ten days, if you can get that much time off. Give us time to see the city and maybe spend some time in Baltimore, too."

"I should be able the make that work. I've accrued so much time off and never use it," he lied.

Sonya clapped giddily as she jumped from the couch, squealing as she ran to Martin. "I'm so excited! I'll call a travel agent and get everything arranged for us."

"Perfect. Our first trip together – I look forward to it."

Sonya kissed him, her lips moist as he tasted the bitterness of her lip balm.

"I love you," she said, wrapping her arms around his waist.

Martin grinned at her, looking into her eyes, knowing what all lay ahead. *I can't keep lying to you,* he thought.

"I love you, too," he said, and kissed her forehead.

* * *

As their relationship continued to evolve, they learned more about each other's past. Sonya could talk for hours, while Martin could only offer a few lines at a time to keep the conversation going. He decided to stick to his actual life history, finding no point in making things more difficult in his web of lies. When she asked him about his past marriage, he told her it was a matter he didn't like to discuss.

"Some things are best left in the past where they belong," he said. "It was a very dark time of life for me. I hope you can understand."

"I've had some nasty relationships myself, and I'll tell you all about them. I hope you'll confide in me one day." She always stroked a steady hand through his hair when they talked in bed.

"I do trust you. It's just one of those things I've pushed so far back in my mind, it's like it never happened. And I'd like to keep it that way."

"Alright. If you change your mind, I'm here and would love to listen."

Sonya lay her head on his bare chest, rising with each breath. "I just feel like I know you from somewhere," she said. "Do you ever feel that way?"

It's because you've probably seen my younger self passing around the school.

"I feel like I've known you forever. Hard to believe it's only been a few weeks."

"I know. They say time flies when you're having fun. I guess it's true."

They lay in bed that night listening to the gentle rustle of leaves outside as a soft breeze blew through the cracked open bedroom window. Sonya curled up into a ball beside Martin, an arm resting peacefully across his chest. She always fell asleep before him, he being the night owl, leaving his mind to ponder life.

Is this relationship even real? My reality is in 2018 where I'm out cold at a crazy old man's desk, probably from some fucked-up drug he gave me. Sonya might not even exist in my reality, but only in this dimension.

Martin had plenty of late nights thinking, but this was the first time he had stared at the beautiful sleeping woman and wondered what exactly her purpose was. The fact that she only existed in 1996, when he would have been in his thirties, suggested that her purpose was not to be the love of his life, but rather something else.

So, then – who are you?

Martin wanted desperately to travel back to the future to learn more about Sonya. A quick search online could pull up her information. She might even be on social media where he could see what she was up to in her older years; she would be seventy, assuming she hadn't passed away.

Would she remember me if I left her and visited her again in the future?

Martin supposed a visit to Calvin was in line, but didn't want to keep pestering his friend, or possible foe, from the future.

What if you can't save Izzy? His mind continued to wander, settling on a topic he had never considered. What if everything happened so fast that he couldn't react in time? *Would Chris actually set me up to fail?*

The thought made Martin question his own purpose. So many nights he had wanted to put his pistol in his mouth and pull the trigger. There would be no more sorrow, no more pain, no more lack of direction in his shitty, whiskey-chugging life. But every time he sat down to really consider it, his inner voice of reason whispered for him to wait, promising it would all be better one day.

It's still possible that Izzy is not why you were sent back in time. He could have baited you with her, but what if your real objective is to stop that shooting?

Martin closed his eyes and pictured all of those innocent, young faces they had shown on the news on April 20, 1999. He remembered wondering what he would do if he had to see Izzy's face on the news after such a tragedy.

"I would hunt down the shooters and make sure they never breathed again," he whispered in the silent bedroom. "And that's what I'm gonna do."

The faces of Eric Harris and Dylan Klebold spun around his head as he dozed to sleep.

I'm not letting you get away with it.

29

Chapter 28

A couple weeks passed, but the thought of confronting Eric and Dylan continued to throb in Martin's mind like a tumor.

You're doing this for Izzy. If you can stop this attack, you can certainly stop her disappearance.

He would wait for school to let out for summer break, and then stalk Dylan by hiding in the woods behind his mansion. If he could get Dylan alone, he'd tell him if he ever saw him talking to Eric Harris again, he would come back and slit his throat.

One thing Martin had learned over time, thanks to the several mass shootings every year, was that a lot of the shooters were nothing more than chickenshits. They might be frightening when they had time to plan their attacks on unsuspecting people, but they were no better equipped to handle a random confrontation than a child.

The plan surely wasn't a guarantee, but it would certainly throw a wrench into Dylan's life. Threatening a mass murderer three years before an attack would have to alter the track of history.

Maybe it would all backfire and the Columbine shooting would end up worse than it had originally. Maybe Dylan would kill himself before making the decision to harm his classmates. Martin had no choice but to at least try and hope for the best. Taking no action would lead to the same result, but making a move, even a small one, could change everything.

Sonya continued to work every day, leaving Martin at home to lounge around the house and get lost in his chaotic thoughts. Eric and Dylan remained front and center, with Izzy on the back burner. He had followed her home from school a couple more times. She giggled with friends and held her books between her skinny arms just like always. Her life was normal.

Martin had gone to the library to find Columbine High School's phone number and called them to find out when the last day of school was. May 23rd, and he marked it on his mental calendar. It was currently May 16th, leaving him another week until school would let out and Dylan had a whole summer to lounge around his castle. All the students in his class would have a summer full of fun at the swimming pools, day camps, and baseball parks, unaware their lives would be forever changed or ended just before their graduation in 1999.

I have to save them.

Martin no longer felt nervous when thinking about confronting the tall, scrawny high school student. He felt rejuvenated, like fate was on his side.

Every morning Martin got dressed along with Sonya, but he had the advantage of her needing to leave first, due at school at 7:30, while he didn't need to report to the "post office" until 9:00. Sonya didn't leave school until five in the afternoon, the same time Martin supposedly got off work. However, with his drive much further than Sonya's, he would cruise around, arriving home around 5:30 when expected. Often times Sonya stayed late and he'd still get home before her.

On this particular Friday, Martin headed to the liquor store, wanting to see Calvin, but to also buy a new bottle of whiskey. The weekend was upon him, after all. He pulled his car into the parking lot, noticing two other cars in the usually vacant lot. It was later than when he normally stopped by, almost noon, and he didn't think much of the extra visitors, only dreading that he might not get the chance to speak with Calvin.

As he stepped out and approached the entrance he noticed the neon lights were off. When he reached the door, he saw that none of the interior lights were turned on, either. Only the natural sunlight illuminated the store, seeping through the windows on the sunny day. Martin's heart skipped a beat as something immediately felt off. Even though he had only met with Calvin twice, he gathered that he was a man of habit and would never forget to turn on the lights.

Martin put his face to the door, tugging on the handle as it refused to budge. In front of the checkout counter, four men stood in a semicircle with their backs to Martin. As they wavered side to side, Martin caught a glimpse of Calvin tied to a chair with duct tape over his mouth and blood streaming from his forehead to chin.

Martin froze, unsure if he should distract the men or run and call for help. He mustered the strength to get out of sight and darted away from the door, peering through a side window instead. From here Martin would stay out of sight, obstructed behind a row of beer boxes, but he still had a clear view of Calvin.

They appeared to be in a discussion, the men bobbing their heads as they spoke, Calvin's eyes following their speech back and forth like a tennis match.

Are these the Road Runners? Martin wondered, now realizing this was not a robbery of any sort. Thieves made plans to get in and out as quickly as possible, not discuss dinner plans in front of the store's owner.

Each man wore a long gray pea coat, strange for a day expecting 85 degrees and sunshine. They had the collars flipped up to cover their faces, showing nothing but the tops of their heads, which all had identical black hair slicked to one side.

One of the men tossed his hands in the air before reaching inside his coat, and retrieved a black pistol. The two men beside him threw their hands up in protest, one even grabbing the gunman on his arm to plead with him. Calvin's eyes bulged in terror, his body trembling in fear.

The man appeared to have been talked off the ledge, lowering the pistol. There was a momentary pause where time felt frozen before the man whipped the pistol to Calvin's forehead and pulled the trigger, splattering blood droplets in every direction. Muffled through the glass, Martin heard the men shouting at each other. One shoved the gunman in the chest and sent the pistol in the air. Martin couldn't look away, trembling from the window and now fearing for his own life.

What the fuck?

The men remained in a circle, no one having moved and continuing their conversation above the dead liquor store owner, head split open and brains spilling out. Calvin's face had disappeared under a coat of blood.

The men all nodded in unison before turning toward the door. Martin used the adrenaline pumping in his system and dove around the corner, completely out of sight from the pea-coated terrorists. He heard the faint chime of the bell as the door swung open and one deep voice say, "Get it done with. Now!"

Three car doors opened and closed in near unison. Martin squatted, waiting for the fourth and final door to slam. When no sounds came after a few seconds, he tiptoed to the corner of the building and peeked a curious eye around to see what was going on.

Two men sat in the car furthest from Martin, on the far side of the entrance, while one man sat in the car next to it. They all had their eyes glued to the fourth man emptying a five gallon container of gasoline across the store's entryway.

"Hurry up, let's get out of here!" the man behind the wheel shouted through a rolled down window.

The gasoline man pulled a box of matches from his coat, and struck the tip to light a flame. He held the match to the box until the whole thing caught fire, and tossed it on the door. He dashed for the car, falling into the passenger seat as he tossed the gasoline container over his shoulder to the back seat.

"Let's go! Let's go!" the driver barked to the other car as they both fired up their engines and skidded out of the parking lot, leaving a trail of smoke from the burnt rubber.

Martin came out of hiding, gawking at the small flame that had already grown the height of his knee. The flame crackled violently, growing by the second, and spreading further across the building's façade. He pulled at the front door, wanting to save Calvin's corpse, but the handle was already scorched to the touch.

"God dammit!" Martin squealed, flailing his hand in the air. Realizing he couldn't save Calvin or the store, he jumped back into his car and burnt his own rubber. He kept his eyes on the store as he drove further, watching the flame grow in his rear-view mirror, knowing it would eventually swallow the entire building.

What the fuck is going on?

For the first time since Martin had traveled back in time, he felt genuinely terrified. If those men—who he assumed to be Road Runners—could murder a man and burn a building so quickly, what could they do to him? Calvin had been more prepared than he would ever be, watching every person that entered his store like a vulture ready to pounce.

I guess Chris was right: I need to be very careful.

30

Chapter 29

Martin watched the news every hour, sick to his stomach at the images of the roaring flames that devoured the liquor store. The firefighters arrived too late, showering flames that had grown too wide to contain. By the time the flames died down, the building was nothing but a pile of ashes. The news didn't report a body found in the rubble, and he could only assume Calvin had been completely cremated in the fire.

"That was my liquor store," Martin told Sonya. "I spoke with the owner numerous times; he was a good guy."

"I hope he was able to get out safely," she said.

"Yeah, me too." Martin could see Calvin in his mind, his brains spilling out of his skull from the gunshot wound. "I'm sure he did."

As more days passed, Martin managed to push the tragedy further back in his mind. Knowing what Calvin was working on, and seeing his end result made him wonder if those men were sent to prevent him from taking his knowledge back to the future, or if they were some figment of the past pushing back to make sure nothing changed in Calvin's future. The whole ordeal made Martin want to hide in his house until September. He even took his pill out of its hiding spot from the small zipper in his suitcase. He could swallow the pill and go back to normal, work at the post office, and go home afterwards to drink until he passed out, forgetting about the past and not worry about being hunted and killed.

Life wouldn't be any different if he called it quits right now and returned to 2018. Izzy would still be missing and the Columbine shooting would have still happened. The world was just fine without his interference.

You have to see this through. Going back now would just mean you've wasted two months of your life.

"Ten minutes. That's all this is costing me."

You don't actually believe that old man, do you? You're probably dead and trapped in some fucked-up purgatory.

"As slimy as he is, he's never actually lied about anything."

It happened much sooner than he had expected, but Martin wanted to see Chris immediately. He wanted to ask him how death worked: if he died in the past, what happened to his body in 2018? Who were those men? Why did they want Calvin?

Martin could only try to figure these things out on his own. Without Calvin or Chris, he was left to accept his questions would never be answered.

Just be cautious everywhere you go. You drove up to that liquor store without a care in the world. There could have been a gunman in the cars next to you when you pulled in, waiting to kill you. You've got to do better.

Every future move would be carefully planned. He needed a gun for protection, and would keep it on him whenever he left to fuck with the past. The past seemed to leave people alone so long as they stuck to a routine. Calvin must have been closing in on something, or else those men would have never showed up.

You can still stop Columbine, just take it slow and be ready for anything. The lives you save will thank you later. And so will Izzy.

* * *

Sonya had two more weeks of summer school. Once she was home for the summer, he'd have to leave the house every day and kill time while she thought he was at work.

For now, he sat in his car, fighting off nerves, remaining confident in his mission. He pulled out of his driveway, not knowing what could happen as he started his trip across town to Littleton. His plan was simple: park a half mile down the long road, out of sight from the Klebold house, and walk to the property in search of a workable path to the woods behind the home. Then wait.

It could be a day wasted, possibly a few days, but he had to stakeout and see if Dylan ever wandered into the woods, or at least step outside. If Dylan stayed inside all day, Martin would be left to peer through the windows from a distance.

During the drive he listened to the sports radio station where the two hosts discussed the upcoming summer Olympics, eagerly awaiting to see how the Dream Team would follow up their prior gold medal in basketball. Martin smirked, knowing the team would win again without any issues. The talk shifted to the Colorado Rockies down season a year after making the playoffs when Martin pulled into the discreet neighborhood. He twisted down Cougar Road and pulled off, driving no more than ten miles per hour to quietly approach the familiar red barn.

He squeezed the car into the tight space of dirt between the pavement and a ditch, and killed the engine, surprised he wasn't shitting his pants, considering how close he was to touching the past.

The day was already warming up and would be scorching by noon. Martin hadn't planned how long he would hide out in the woods, but with one water bottle, knew he wouldn't last too long.

Don't be such a pussy. You drove all this way. A little warm weather will not send you home.

With his reassurance, he stepped out of the car and took crunching steps toward the long driveway, roughly a quarter mile away.

A man in a Porsche drove by, but didn't look in Martin's direction. "Coast is clear," he said, not seeing another car in sight, and broke into a slight jog, slowing as he approached the driveway.

Everything appeared the same as his last visit, only this time he knew the future mass murderer had to be inside. High school kids rarely woke up before nine on summer break.

Martin hid in the trees, darting from spot to spot like a fox as he made his way closer to the house. When he reached the top of the driveway he worked his way around the left side of the house, seeing the swimming pool as he passed.

If Martin could know for certain he was alone with Dylan, he would approach him carefully. Surely the boy wouldn't do anything to him, but this wasn't exactly a neighborhood where a random stranger could get lost and need to ask for directions.

Martin worked toward the back of the house, which revealed nothing of significance: a couple of frosted windows suggested bathrooms, and another window was blinded shut. *It could be his bedroom. Back of the house, why not?*

The trees grew thicker behind the house, so much that Martin had to peer between multiple stumps for a clear view. He checked his watch to find the time as 8:15, and sat on the ground, sticks crunching beneath his heavy body. He thought back to when he was in high school and tried to remember what he did during summer break.

He'd wake up around nine, lie in bed for another half hour, then eventually make his way to the kitchen for breakfast. After that he'd lie on the couch and watch TV until lunchtime, which at that point he'd finally get dressed for the day. With a sandwich made, he'd go back to the couch where a crater formed from his ass, and sat there until the news came on, meaning his parents would be home shortly, prompting him to finally make his bed and pick up his room.

The good old days.

Hopefully Dylan was a bit more active and would go for an afternoon swim or hike. Martin heard gravel crunching from the other side of the house and his heart started to rattle his rib cage.

What the fuck?

Someone was pulling up to the house and Martin sprinted through the trees to get a view of the front door and garage. Adrenaline flushed his system when he saw a cop car parked in the roundabout, and he positioned himself behind a thick tree stump that hid his whole body.

A police officer stepped out of the squad car, taking a quick look around, before strutting up to the front door. He pounded on it with a hard fist, surely waking up anyone who might have still been asleep. The officer stood with his arms crossed as he waited.

The door swung inward and Martin saw the face that sent chills down his spine.

He'd only ever seen Dylan on the news, but knew him right away from his tall and lanky frame, long sandy hair, pale skin, and big nose. A face that would be etched forever in the history books. Martin hadn't expected anyone else to answer, but seeing the boy for the first time threw his mind into a whirlwind. Dylan wore a striped bathrobe, and his hair was frazzled wildly in every direction.

Rise and shine, he thought, now trying to focus his hearing on the conversation between Dylan and the officer. Martin was too far to hear anything, but could see the officer pointing toward the main road, where Dylan looked and nodded his head in acknowledgement.

Did that asshole in the Porsche call the cops on me?

He could imagine the conversation: the officer telling young Dylan to stay on the lookout for a suspicious man in the neighborhood, to not answer the door for anyone he didn't know, and to call the police if he saw anything out of the ordinary. Only in an uppity neighborhood like this would the police arrive ten minutes after a "poor" man was seen walking around.

Maybe I just wanted to go on a hike today. Is that illegal now?

The officer handed Dylan what looked like a business card before returning to his squad car. The shiny Ford Crown Victoria circled the roundabout and disappeared down the driveway, crunching gravel on its way out.

Martin remained frozen in the trees and watched Dylan close the door. "You're home alone," he whispered, knowing a parent would have answered the door under normal circumstances. His mind raced with possibilities and anticipation, yet his inner voice kept him in line.

Leave. The kid is probably on high alert. What else would the police have come to the house to discuss? The past is already pushing back, don't take any more chances.

Martin could feel the house pulling him, daring him to ring the doorbell and see what would happen. His cover had already been somewhat blown for the day, however, but a trip back tomorrow would have to suffice. He now had the knowledge that Dylan was indeed still asleep as of 8:30 by the looks of his dazed and groggy face when he opened the door. He could plan to come back closer to nine to start his stakeout in the woods, and hopefully go unnoticed by any passing vehicles.

As much as the decision pained him, Martin dashed through the trees back to the driveway. Once out of sight from the house, he stepped onto the gravel and walked at a brisk pace downhill. Panting for air by the time he reached the bottom, he looked around carefully in both directions to make sure there were no other cars, especially a police car.

Damn this day, he thought. *I had him right where I wanted: home alone. But now the whole town is on high alert because some rich asshole saw me walking on the road on his way to work.*

The past could go fuck itself, as far as Martin was concerned, and he continued to let his mind rage as he started on the quarter mile hike back to his car. *Hopefully they didn't tow me already.*

The sun beat down on him unforgivably, creating sweat beads around his neck that dripped down his back. He kept his head down as he walked, watching his shadow move with each step as gracefully as a dance partner. Birds sung tunes from high in the surrounding trees, and Martin caught a whiff of manure mixed in the freshness of the outdoors.

Only Colorado has city life and farm life within a mile of each other, he thought in an attempt to take his mind off the botched morning. When he rounded the corner of Cougar Road he felt instant relief at seeing his car parked exactly where he had left it, and started whistling now that he could relax, knowing he could get home without a visit to the car impound.

See, the past doesn't have to ruin everything. It just wasn't the right timing. Come back tomorrow, it'll happen when it's meant to be.

He strolled to his beaten up car, wondering if he should have purchased a luxury vehicle to fit in better in Littleton. But, that was all in hindsight now, and he'd have to make do with what he had.

He slapped the hood of the car, creating a hard thud that echoed and vibrated throughout the rest of the steel frame. "Ol' reliable," he cackled before pulling open the door, feeling an immediate heat wave escape like he had opened an over door instead. The temperature had to have risen at least fifteen more degrees during his quick ninety minutes away from the car. Maybe it was best he had to call off his plans for the day. The last thing he needed was to be passed out on the side of the road from dehydration. Ten Porsches, Mercedes, and BMWs would pass him before someone decided to help, then he'd have to explain to the Littleton police why he was stranded in the middle of an upper class neighborhood in his junk car.

Sorry, officer, I was looking for Arvada and took a wrong turn. And that's why I'm half an hour away from the nearest middle class town.

Surely that excuse would hold up – it was the 90's, after all, and no one had handheld gadgets yet that could direct them from point A to point B as efficiently as possible.

How did we ever survive? he wondered as he stared at the printed out directions on the passenger seat.

After a minute of letting the heat escape the car, he sat down behind the wheel and fired up the engine. He waited, the gentle vibrations of the engine relaxing his body as he sipped the final remnants from his water bottle.

I should find a pool. A pool and a frozen drink would go perfect right about now.

The clock on the dashboard read 9:53, leaving him plenty of time to get drunk and still sober up before arriving home after five. Saliva pooled in his mouth at the thought of a piña colada. He'd have to find a library first to see where might even offer booze in the middle of a weekday.

Maybe we can plan a trip to Vegas. I could get my drinks by the pool, and bet big money at the sportsbook without worrying about a bookie wanting to cut my dick off.

Martin's mind drifted into the fantasy that was Las Vegas as he put the car into gear. "Viva Las Vegas!" he shouted with a mad laugh.

Last time he left the Klebold residence the route took him another ten minutes away from the highway, so today he turned onto the road to make a U-turn to save time.

Martin didn't see the speeding semi-truck until it was too late. The truck boomed its intimidating horn as the tires screeched, smoke filling the air like a wildfire. Martin looked out the passenger side window to the sight of dormant headlights and a chrome grill with *Freightliner* inscribed across the top. For a moment, he wondered what would happen if he died in the past, then the truck slammed into his car, sending him tumbling like a boulder down the road as the windows shattered and the metal caved in.

After an eternity of rolling in the car, it came to a halt. Martin looked out his window and saw the asphalt from the road. The car was on its side. Drops of blood had splattered everywhere in the car, and he could feel the liquid oozing from his forehead. He tried to move his hands, move his legs, but nothing would respond.

Oh dear God, please no. Don't let this be happening.

His consciousness faded in and out, and all he could see in his mind was a laughing Chris. "I told you to be careful. You wanted to tango with the past, and this is what you get."

That old, evil smirk stayed in the front of his thoughts until blackness draped over, leaving Martin in a free falling sensation as the rest of the world turned dark.

31

Chapter 30

Sonya arrived home at 5:30 like most evenings, kicking off her shoes and changing into sweatpants to lounge around the house. Martin would be home in a few minutes, and she thought she just might have a drink with him. She had a rough day at school where two of her students broke into a fight in the middle of a lecture. Apparently, young Christopher stole a Gameboy from little Tyler, and Tyler didn't take it too well. Ah, summer school, where half the students genuinely need help and the other half are there to be kept off the streets. Sonya had caught a flying fist to her breast as she tried to break up the fight, and while it didn't hurt, it still put a funk on the rest of her day.

Once in her loungewear, she plopped down on the couch and cracked open a new romance book called *The Notebook.* She and some of the other teachers at school participated in a book club where they read one new release each month, usually a steamy romance to escape the daily grind of the booger-flicking and hormonal preteens.

She dove into the book, getting lost in the other world for a good half hour before realizing Martin still hadn't arrived. *Where could he be?* she wondered as she put in her bookmark and tossed the novel on the coffee table.

She crossed the room to the window overlooking the front yard and pulled back the shades to see if he was in the driveway or maybe coming down the street. He had always been prompt in coming home, but it was now 6:04, and he had never been home past six without giving her notice. He had talked about buying a pager, but hadn't got around to picking one up yet; that would have been handy in a moment like this and she'd be sure to remind him of that.

Maybe he stopped at the bar for a drink. We could have both had a rough day, we're usually in sync that way. Or maybe he's on to me.

She shook her head free of the silly thought and went to the kitchen to start dinner. She didn't have much energy and boiled water for spaghetti, her go-to meal when she didn't really want to cook. While the noodles cooked, she returned to her evening read, standing over the stove to stir the pasta every couple minutes. Surely Martin wouldn't be any later than seven, when they typically sat down for dinner.

The meal was ready by 6:26, and still no Martin, so she put some garlic bread in the oven to kill more time. Her lazy meal was turning into multiple courses now, and she grew more worried with each passing minute he didn't arrive.

What are you doing, Martin? This isn't funny—we have work to do.

"He's just at a bar having a few drinks I'm sure. Maybe he went out with some friends."

But he had never mentioned any friends. His daily recap of the day typically consisted of "Same shit, different day, how was yours?" She knew he didn't really going to work, but couldn't say for sure where he disappeared to during the middle of the day—those matters weren't important for what she needed to accomplish. Sonya scratched her head, debating what to do.

She could drive around to some of the local bars he liked to frequent, but if he had gone out downtown that would be a waste of time. The only friend he had ever mentioned was his old landlord. Maybe she would drive around just to see if his car was parked at any of the bars.

Just give him until seven before you do anything. Do you really want to appear so clingy and paranoid?

No, she certainly didn't want that and would wait at the kitchen table until seven before making any decisions. There could have been a long line at the gas station, or maybe he got a flat tire. Maybe he stopped to buy her flowers and dessert for later. There were hundreds of possibilities and not all of them had to involve him being at a bar.

What if he was in a car accident? She had kept this thought in the back of her mind as long as she could, but could no longer contain it. Martin had shown he was chaotic behind the wheel, but getting in an accident during rush hour would be difficult as the traffic coming north on I-25 was a sitting parking lot for the entirety of the drive. Not to mention how time itself may have been trying to throw her off her plans.

The oven dinged and she jolted out of her chair. She forgot about the bread and pulled it out immediately. The clock on the oven read 6:39 and she tried to keep her mind distracted. She could no longer wait and poured a glass of vodka, mixing in soda, and taking an aggressive sip.

Just as she had done this, headlights poured through the living room window and brought instant relief. "Thank God," she whispered, and pulled out two plates from the cupboard. *See, you were just overreacting. Everything's fine and now he's home to have dinner and hear about your shitty day.*

She started to set the table when a booming knock came from the front door. *Did he lose his house key?* She crossed the room and froze when she saw a bulky policeman standing on the other side of the door. Even though a curtain hung over the door's window, she could tell by the man's build and hat, and the crackling of a radio.

Oh, my God. No.

She pulled open the door, it creaking and groaning, dreading what waited on the other side.

The officer stood wide, broad shouldered, with his arms crossed. His name badge read *Rawlings,* and she could see the bad news swimming behind his brown eyes and stone face.

"Good evening, ma'am," he said, tipping his hat. His voice came out hoarse and he had to clear his throat. "Are you Sonya Griffiths?"

She wanted to tell him no, close the door, and crawl into her bed to pretend none of this was happening. *He can't be dead. He just can't.* A bulge formed in her throat that she had to force down before responding. Could she actually lose her job if Martin died? No such thing had ever happened before in her line of work.

"Yes, I am. Is everything okay?"

No, Sonya, everything is not okay. Martin is over 90 minutes late and there's a state trooper standing at your front door.

"I understand Martin Briar lives here with you, is that correct?"

Hearing the officer speak Martin's name sent an instant rush of blood into her belly. *Oh, no, this is bad.*

"Well, ma'am, I have some unfortunate news. Mr. Briar is currently in a coma in Littleton Adventist Hospital. He was in a nasty car accident involving a semi truck."

Her hands shot to her mouth as relief and panic both settled. Relief from knowing he wasn't dead, panic about the coma. Her hands started to tremble, and the officer noticed.

"From what we've been told, he'll make it out. The doctors aren't considering the coma to be life-threatening. There's also no timetable for when they expect him to come to, so it might be best for you to go to the hospital and speak with them yourself."

"You said he's in Littleton? What was he doing all the way out there?" she asked, running through any possibilities in her mind, but coming up with nothing.

"We were hoping you might know. We recovered his MapQuest directions in the car and found his starting point at his old apartment. We went there and spoke with the landlord who informed us that Martin had moved in with you not too long ago. Does the last name Klebold mean anything to you?"

"Klebold?" She paused and rummaged through her mind's filing cabinets of random knowledge. "It's not ringing a bell for me, sorry."

"That's strange, we reached out to their family and they don't know who he is, either. Hopefully he'll be able to tell us more when he wakes up. Do you know your way to the hospital in Littleton?"

"Yes, I should be able to find it. Will they let me visit him now, or do I have to wait until the morning?"

"You're good to go there now. Here's my card, let me know if you think of anything later on that might help."

Sonya took the card and forced a fake smile to the officer who tipped his hat, wished her a good evening, and left. She closed the door and thought deeply of any connection Martin might have had in Littleton, still unable to come up with anything. She'd have to go there first to speak with the doctors, make sure he was okay, and then try to get to the bottom of what he was doing in Littleton after work. Perhaps she did need to keep a closer eye on what he did upon leaving the house in the morning.

She rushed back to the kitchen, threw the pasta in a container before grabbing her keys and purse, and headed out.

It was now 7:15, the sun descending behind the mountains as Sonya drove, wondering what Martin had managed to figure out on his own.

32

Chapter 31

Sonya had never been to Littleton. The drive felt like an eternity, the thought of Martin lying comatose weighing down on her. After forty minutes on the road, she finally pulled up to Littleton Adventist Hospital.

The hospital stood four stories tall, its fluorescent lights glowing in the night sky. Within those walls was a man she loved. Anxiety had gnawed at her during the drive; she wanted to make sure he was okay, but at the same time wanted to shake him awake and demand answers.

Just go in there and make sure he's okay, because that's all that matters right now. Act natural and everything can return to normal.

With her courage finally built up, she stepped out of the car and walked toward the main entrance on a mission.

"Good evening," Sonya said, approaching a young nurse at the front desk. "I'm looking for Martin Briar. I believe he was admitted here today."

The nurse's eyebrows perched up. "Yes, Mrs. Briar, he's in our care. If you can have a seat for a moment, I'll have another nurse take you to his room."

Mrs. Briar, Sonya thought, not wanting to correct the nurse. *It does have a nice ring.*

The hospital was rather quiet, one family gathered in the main lobby where two kids ran circles around their seated mother and father. Sonya strode toward a seat and plopped herself down. A couple of vending machines hummed, and somewhere in the distance a radio talk show chattered softly.

Mrs. Briar, she thought again. She had ruled out marriage after she turned 45, believing at that point it was well too late to begin a family, so why bother with the formalities of signing a government document to seal a romantic relationship? Besides, there was no point in getting married while in her current line of work—she'd never get to spend quality time with a spouse.

The mere thought of a wedding, however, still sent a flutter to her chest, just as it had when she was 23 and madly in love with her college sweetheart. She had the dress, wedding colors, and songs all picked out in her head and knew exactly how her big day would play out to the finest details. That was until a year later when she walked in to her boyfriend's apartment to find him in the shower with another man. The shock had never really left, and she wasn't sure if she was more surprised that he was gay, or that he had cheated on her.

This incident had sparked a chain of trust issues that would haunt her in every following relationship. She could never fully submit her soul to another man, the sounds of her ex-soulmate moaning in the shower as the other man groped his crotch forever ringing in her head.

"At least this happened now instead of after you two got married." That's what all the women in her life had told her following the tragedy, as if they could relate.

Being cheated on was one thing. Living a lie was a whole new ballgame, and reality sunk in that five years of her life were wasted, a feeling that ate her alive from the inside. There was no lesson to be learned from the relationship; everything had become moot the second she learned her fiancé was living a double life.

Now she sat in the hospital, almost twice her age since that tragedy, wondering if this was the same thing playing out before her eyes. She didn't need to marry the guy, but needed to keep him along on this journey. Surely Martin would have a reason to be in Littleton; he didn't exactly take random cruises around the state. But could she believe his reason if it didn't sound truthful?

They had mentioned the Klebold family, but she had never heard of them. Did he meet a rich housewife at the post office who took a liking to him?

"Excuse me, ma'am," a nurse shouted from the door next to the reception desk. She was an older black woman, staring at Sonya with bulging brown eyes. "Follow me, ma'am."

The nurse pushed the door open as Sonya approached, allowing her to pass through to the main hallway that stretched to dozens of patient rooms.

"We're gonna take the elevator to the third floor. We have Mr. Briar stabilized, but the doctor will want a word with you."

"Is he still. . ."

"Yes, he's still comatose. The doctor will give you all of the details on his condition. Just to clarify, you're his only living relative, correct?"

There had clearly been some miscommunication between the Littleton police and the hospital as they all tried to piece together who exactly was Martin Briar.

"He has no living relatives that I know of. I'm his girlfriend; we live together in Larkwood."

Sonya thought she heard the nurse snicker at the mention of Larkwood, but brushed it off as the elevator doors spread apart in front of them. She followed and watched as she pushed the button for the third floor.

"No family at all?" the nurse asked. "That poor man. At least he has you to look out for him."

Sonya grinned. That was exactly the point. A man with no family had no reason to be held back for important work. He had his mother, sure, but that wasn't a concern after they had taken an extensive look into his life and past.

"He's right this way, ma'am," the nurse said as she led them out of the elevator and down another hallway. The third floor was even more deserted than the first, many of the lights dimmed and providing an eerie glow over the Intensive Care Unit.

The nurse stopped in front of door 317, poked her head in, and held out an open arm to guide Sonya into the room.

"Have a seat and the doctor will be with you in just a minute. You can even talk to Mr. Briar if you wish. They say people in comas will sometimes respond to a familiar voice. I'll leave you to it."

The nurse vanished as Sonya entered the room, lit by a lone lamp standing on the table next to Martin's bed. She hardly recognized him with the tubes running in and out of his body. A clear oxygen mask covered his face while other wires ran from his forehead to a nearby machine charting what she assumed was his brain activity; it was practically a flat line. An IV ran into his arm for hydration, and more wires appeared from his chest area to a heart monitor machine, beeping softly with each pulse.

Sonya remained frozen in the doorway and could tell, from a distance, that Martin's skin had turned a tint of yellow, making him appear as if he had aged another decade overnight.

When she mustered the courage to get closer, she approached her subject with trembling hands over her mouth, standing directly over him and looking into his closed eyes, wondering what he was doing lost in his own mind. His hair splayed out wildly beneath his head and she noticed more gray and white hairs than before.

"Oh, Martin," she whispered, running a hand along his arm. His index finger twitched when she touched him, causing her to recoil.

"That's perfectly normal," a squeaky voice said from behind. She turned to see an older man in a white lab coat. "Good evening, I'm Dr. Benjamin Lincoln."

The doctor stood short with a slight hunch in his back. He smiled warmly at Sonya as he stuck a hand out, short white hairs on his fingers that matched the curls on his head.

"Hello, Dr. Lincoln. My name is Sonya; I'm Martin's girlfriend."

"Pleased to meet you." Dr. Lincoln pulled out a pair of glasses from his coat pocket and slid them over his crooked nose. He turned in a swift motion to grab a file on the table next to the heart rate monitor. "Now, would you like to speak in here or in my office?"

Sonya turned back to Martin, seemingly gasping for every puff of air. "I'd like to stay in here if that's okay."

"Absolutely. Let's have a seat on the other side of Mr. Briar." Dr. Lincoln shuffled across the foot of the bed to the two chairs tucked in the corner beside the window overlooking the hospital's parking lot. Sonya followed and took her seat next to the doctor, who had already flipped open his folder and rummaged through a stack of papers. The anticipation had reached its peak and she couldn't stand to wait.

"Just tell me the news, doctor. I've been losing my mind the whole way over here."

He looked at Sonya with heavy blue eyes, but that smile never left his face. "Let me start by saying you're boyfriend here is very lucky. Did the police give you any details of what happened?"

"No, not really."

"Mr. Briar was in his car, in the middle of the road, I believe making a U-turn, when a diesel truck came flying around the corner and collided with him. The truck struck his car along the passenger side, which is good, and sent his car rolling three times over itself."

Dr. Lincoln paused and grabbed a tissue box for Sonya when he noticed the tears streaming down her cheeks.

"How exactly is this *lucky?*" she asked through her sobs.

"Well, if his car had been turned the other way, the impact would have hit him directly, and we wouldn't be having this conversation. It appears his head came into contact with the driver's side window as we found shards of glass in his skull and hair. If it had been anything else, say the steering wheel or the actual door, again, we wouldn't be having this conversation. His head broke the window and the impact was enough to put him into a coma."

"How serious is the coma?"

"Comas are always serious, but it appears this one is not fatal. I'd guess a week maximum until Mr. Briar wakes up. We've tried different therapies to get a response from his brain, with some success. I'd say

Mr. Briar is very much alert within his coma, whatever that might mean, we're not exactly sure."

"How can you know when he'll wake up?"

"It's not an exact science, nor is the technology to say for certain. All we can do is make an educated guess by comparing his brain's responsiveness to cases in the past. The way his mind is trending makes me think this is very much a short term coma."

"How will he be when he wakes up? Will he remember anything?"

"That we don't know. A majority of comatose patients will have struggles with short-term memory, often forgetting the event that may have put them in to the coma in the first place. But, every case is different, so it's a matter of waiting and seeing when the time comes."

Sonya shook her head, trying to absorb the information along with the intensity of the situation.

"Are there any other questions you might have?" Dr. Lincoln asked.

"What am I supposed to do while he's in the coma? Can I stay here with him?"

"There's honestly no need for that. I can say confidently that he will be fine. He suffered no damage to other organs, and it's just a matter of waiting. There's no chance for him to have any sort of relapse into a dangerous zone. He's stable and functioning as best as we could hope for. You can come visit whenever you wish, but know that we will call you as soon as he wakes up."

"Please do. I don't care if it's two in the morning."

"Of course, ma'am," he said with a grin. "If you have nothing else for me, I'll leave you alone with Mr. Briar. Talk to him. Touch him. It sparks responsiveness in the mind, and that's all we're looking for."

Dr. Lincoln patted Sonya on the shoulder before leaving her alone with Martin.

She turned back to him, a lifeless collection of tubing and wires, and could no longer hold back the floodgates swelling behind her eyes.

"Oh, Martin, please don't forget who I am," she cried, tears dripping onto his limp arm. "I need you. Everything depends on you." She imagined a world where she was fired from her job, exiled by her organization, and left with no choice but to return to her father and live a life of misery. The thought made her queasy.

She would stay beside him for another thirty minutes before her confidence returned and she was able to drive home, refusing to accept the thought of that alternate life.

33

Chapter 32

Martin knew he was in a dream, but could sense it wasn't an ordinary one. He felt awake within himself, like wandering through an endless fog of emptiness.

The scenery in this dream constantly changed. One moment he was walking through an empty town with cobblestone roads and ancient buildings lining the sidewalks. Then he'd free fall and land in a new place. Sometimes it was another deserted city, other times an empty room. This cycle continued for what felt an eternity, changing locations every few hours.

He currently stood in a dark, empty room, where a long bulb flickered on the ceiling, providing light no brighter than a single candle. Silence filled his head, piercing his mind as he could only hear the sound of his breathing.

"Hello?" he asked the room, his voice echoing into unknown depths. He couldn't make out any nearby walls as he paced around, his hands splayed in front of him in search of anything to make contact with.

He held his breath to better hear what he thought were voices whispering in the distance, but found it to be his voice still echoing faintly, as if traveling down a tunnel.

Martin had wandered at least thirty steps away from the flickering light, but the room felt no less dark than where he had stood previously.

The ground rumbled and he immediately knew a change of scenery was underway. He sat on the ground, having learned his lessons from the first two instances when he collapsed, out of balance and flailing. Since then, he sat every time the ground rumbled and waited for his arrival at the next unknown destination.

The ground became light, a floating sensation as he pictured himself flying on a magic carpet like Aladdin. If he could see the walls around him, he'd see them passing by in a blur, like riding a train and staring out the window. He wasn't sure if he was teleporting, falling, or flying, and he didn't care to find out.

Just sit down and enjoy the ride.

The rumbling of the ground beneath his ass settled into a soft vibration before halting completely upon his arrival.

The darkness of the prior room gave way to bright lights. When the gravity returned to normal, Martin stood on weary legs to explore his newest location: an empty library.

Shelves of books stretched as far as he could see. The librarian's desk stood thirty feet to his left, abandoned, a lone computer monitor turned on to a black screen with a digital clock bouncing around as a screensaver.

The silence didn't feel as thick in the library, not ringing in Martin's head. He looked up to see a second floor with more bookshelves and tables overlooking the first floor. The library felt familiar, but he couldn't quite piece it together.

He'd had that problem when he first arrived in this dream, struggling to remember the most basic things. A voice within told him he wasn't in a dream, that maybe he had died. And while he knew he wasn't in a regular dream, he couldn't muster the mind power to piece together what had actually happened. All he could do was explore the ever changing places around him.

Martin moved his legs that felt like bricks, dragging them closer toward the computer, the sensation like walking through two feet of mud as he forced his legs to move every inch forward.

"Psssst!" a voice whispered from behind, sending an instant chill down

Martin's spine. "Hey, mister."

The voice sounded adolescent, and Martin pivoted around to face it.

Two pale boys stood ten feet away. *How did they get there?* The library had rows of books in every direction, no exit in sight. The boys stood side-by-side, each holding a gun in hand.

The boy on the left had a long face, pointy noise, and short, spiked brown hair. A smirk revealed a charming countenance to go along with his light green eyes. The boy on the right was taller by at least six inches and had his flowing, sandy hair brushed back to reveal his green eyes. Both wore matching black trench coats that covered them from neck to ankle.

Eric Harris and Dylan Klebold. This is all a dream. They're not really standing in front of you.

Martin reminded himself of this fact as he looked from Eric's pump-action shotgun to Dylan's semiautomatic TEC-9.

"We *are* standing in front of you, dipshit!" Eric barked in a shrill voice.

Dylan smirked, nodding in gratitude. Both boys cradled their guns like babies in their arms, striking Martin as an odd pose. Martin accepted that anything was possible in his dreamscape, now knowing the future mass murderers could hear his thoughts.

"What can I do for you boys?" he asked, ignoring his trembling legs. An instinct told him this moment was critical to what he was doing, but he couldn't remember *what* exactly he was doing before arriving in the never-ending dream.

"You can mind your own fucking business," Dylan snarled, now raising his pistol in the air. "Long live the Trench Coat Mafia!" He pumped the pistol upward.

Eric howled at the ceiling like a rabid wolf. "Don't come near the school. Don't try and stop us. You'll pay if you do. I'll slit your throat and piss in your blood."

"Long live the Trench Coat Mafia!" Dylan shouted again, almost robotically.

Both boys studied Martin with hungry grins on their face, like a pair of lions about to pounce on a zebra. As if a light switched on in his mind, Martin remembered everything he had been working on before falling into this dream. The boys and the library had felt familiar because they *were* familiar. He had just stood in this very library within the last few weeks, and remembered his plans to try and stop the boys from slaughtering their schoolmates. Now, he wondered if this was a subconscious ploy to talk him out of it. The past seemed ruthless in preserving its history, and getting to someone through their dreams didn't seem too drastic for Father Time.

"Eric. Dylan," Martin said authoritatively, looking from boy to boy. "Let's talk this out. Why do you want to do this?"

Martin drew on his bomb threat training from years at the post office. If a bomb threat ever came in to the post office, either via phone or an in-person threat, they were instructed to ask the suspect "why are you doing this?" as the first question. In ninety-nine percent of bomb threat cases, the suspect was always equipped to answer "where is the bomb?" or "how much time until it goes off?" with a pre-scripted response already in mind. Asking the perpetrator their reasoning for their actions was the last thing on their mind, and he hoped to catch the boys off guard in the same way.

Eric smirked, turning to Dylan, who kept his own drunken grin fixed on Martin. "You know why we do this," Eric said calmly. "You saw it all over the news. Nobody at that goddamn school cares about us. They tease us. They think we're different, but we're the only ones truly grabbing life by the balls."

"Long live the Trench Coat Mafia!" Dylan shouted again, and Martin thought he saw saliva leaking from the corner of the boy's mouth.

"Dylan," Martin said. "Can you even say anything else?"

Dylan snickered, keeping a steady eye on the old man in front of him.

"You know, you're absolutely right," Martin continued. "I did watch all of the news reports, and read all the articles when they came out. It was a truly fascinating story. The first of its kind. If we only knew then the rest of the shootings that would follow your lead."

Eric threw his head back, cackling uncontrollably. "Yes! Yes! Yes! It's been a treat watching the others carry on our work. There's been so many, and there will be many more. They all will be taken care of by the Trench Coat Mafia."

Martin remembered the Trench Coat Mafia as nothing more than a group name for the less popular kids at Columbine. In the videos Eric and Dylan had filmed of their target practice in the woods, they made multiple references to the Trench Coat Mafia, and wore the same trench coats they had on during the massacre.

He remembered when those disturbing videos had leaked. They aired on the late night news, not wanting to risk any children coming across the footage in the old days before the internet made everything accessible. In the video, they had made multiple references to not only the Trench Coat Mafia, but also to the Nazi party, and Adolf Hitler. They worshiped Hitler, hailing his name numerous times in the video and in their notebooks that surfaced further down the road.

"I understand that life can be hard, especially in high school," Martin said, deciding to do what he could while he had both boys' attention.

"Save it, old man," Eric snapped. "We don't give a shit what you say. Everything is going to happen as planned."

"Yeah," Dylan finally said another word. "Tell someone who gives a fuck."

The boys chuckled at each other like they had shared an inside joke.

"You know, Dylan, Eric is only bringing you along because he's too scared to do this on his own. He doesn't actually care about you."

"Shut up!" Eric screamed, cocking his shotgun and raising it to Martin's face. "Shut the fuck up!"

"But it came out on the news, Eric. All the stories said you were a big loner. No friends. How sad. But you came up with this sick idea and brainwashed the only person who would give you the time of day. Dylan was a happy kid before he started spending time with you. Why bring him down?"

"Shut up, old man. I swear to God!" Eric shouted. Dylan stood by his

187

side, jaw hanging open in surprise as he watched the exchange.

"God? You don't believe in God, remember?" Martin responded calmly. "You shot a girl after she admitted believing in God."

"That did feel good. That Bible-thumping bitch," Eric said proudly, still aiming the shotgun at Martin.

"Was this all worth it? Killing each other after leaving such a mess behind. Too chickenshit to face the consequences?"

"You're just like the rest of them," Eric said. "You need a lesson in how to be nice to people. You walk around here with your rules and ethics, thinking you're better than everyone else."

"Do you know how stupid you sound saying you killed people because they weren't nice?" Martin asked.

"Go to hell, and stay away from our school."

Eric squeezed the trigger and the shotgun let out a booming sound, echoing across the empty library. The slug caught Martin square in the chest, spreading a burning sensation throughout his lungs.

Eric and Dylan both giggled as Martin collapsed in slow motion to the ground, hand clasped over the hole where the warmth of blood started to ooze.

"We told you to stay away," Dylan said, stepping up to Martin with his pistol aimed between his eyes. Martin had never stared down the barrel of a gun before, but seeing the small black hole of death created a strange sense of comfort as he knew what would come next.

I'm in a dream. I'm not really going to die. If he shoots me, I'll wake up. That's how this works. Martin reassured himself as a sliver of doubt crept in.

"No one remembers you two. Ten years down the road, after your shooting, your names are long gone and forgotten. I hope it's all worth it." Martin spoke with a forced smirk, *wanting* Dylan to pull the trigger so he could leave this endless nightmare.

"Long live the Trench Coat Mafia!" Dylan shouted, and shot Martin in the head.

34

Chapter 33

Martin jolted awake, glued to the bed beneath him by sweat, and looked slowly around the room to the sight of beeping monitors and dozens of wires and tubes running in and out of his body. He held up his hands to find an IV running into one and a pulse monitor clipped to his index finger on the other. Breathing felt as fresh as he had ever experienced, and he realized an oxygen mask was strapped around his head and clasped down over half of his face.

A chalkboard hung on the wall across the foot of his bed with his last name written in big, round lettering. It also showed his main doctor to be Dr. Lincoln and a list of the three nurses who likely took care of him.

Why am I in the hospital? He patted around his body, feeling for any sort of pain or missing limb. *Did I get attacked trying to save Izzy?* He squeezed his eyes shut and tried to gather his thoughts on what he had been doing, but all he could see was Eric and Dylan, laughing, taunting, and shooting him while they sung praises to the Trench Coat Mafia.

An older man dressed in a white lab coat strode into the room after a quick courtesy rap on the door.

"Mr. Briar," he said as he approached Martin's bedside. "Welcome back. I'm Dr. Lincoln, and I've been looking after you the past week."

Martin stared at him dumbfounded, and the doctor recognized this immediately.

"Mr. Briar, you've been in a coma for the last six days. You've been coming in and out of sleep for the last twelve hours, so we've been expecting you to wake up soon for good."

Coma? What the fuck?

"Do you remember what you were doing before you arrived here?" the doctor asked in a sympathetic voice.

Martin opened his mouth to speak, but felt his throat tighten with mucus. If he'd really been knocked out the last six days, his body likely wasn't functioning correctly.

He cleared his throat twice, lifted the oxygen mask off his face, and mustered out, "Water."

"Yes, of course."

The doctor spun around and filled a cup from the sink in the room's bathroom, returning with a wide grin. "This should do good for you. We'll get you some bottled water in a bit."

Martin grabbed the cup in a weak, shaky hand, and used all of his concentration to guide it to his mouth. When he took the first sip, he felt an instant clearing and soothing in his throat as the cool liquid went down.

"Much better. Thank you," Martin said. He curiously looked around the room more. "Where am I?"

"You're in Littleton, Colorado."

"Littleton?" Martin asked. "I'm not from Littleton."

"We know that. We were hoping you might remember what you were doing out here, so far from home or work?"

Martin closed his eyes and took a deep inhale, testing his lungs' capabilities without the oxygen mask. The last thing he could remember was having dinner with Sonya. But how long ago was that? Clearly something happened to put him in a coma. Why wasn't the doctor telling him?

"I'm sorry. I can't remember anything."

"What's the last thing you remember?" the doctor asked, now scribbling on a clipboard.

"I remember having dinner with my girlfriend. Is she okay?"

"Do you remember her name, Martin?" the doctor said, seemingly ignoring his statement about his last activity.

"Yes. Sonya."

The doctor nodded his head and continued writing notes. "Very good. I need to gauge your memory skills. It helps us know how badly the coma has affected your brain."

"Shouldn't all of these machines tell you that?" he asked, pointing a finger to one of the many wires taped to his forehead.

"Those tell us how your brain is doing physically. You suffered a concussion, but otherwise your brain is in good shape. You were very lucky."

Lucky enough to not know why the hell I'm in Littleton in a hospital bed?

"This will be a process, Mr. Briar. Just know that. There will be some basic things you probably can't remember off the top of your head. Things like names of people and places. That's common, and they will come back in good time. I want to make sure you're not suffering beyond that. Do you know where you live?"

"Larkwood. Born and raised."

"Good. Do you remember your mother's name?"

He opened his mouth, but paused before speaking. He had wanted to respond as a reflex. He could picture his mother, could describe her to the finest detail, but her name was coming up short in his mind.

"Don't worry. Perfectly normal. Do you know what year it is?"

Martin certainly hadn't forgotten that he had traveled back in time.

"1996."

Dr. Lincoln raised his eyebrows, apparently not expecting a correct answer.

"Do you know who the current president is?" the doctor asked.

"Bill Clinton," Martin said confidently, his voice finally feeling back its normal self.

"Very good. I'd say by these early tests that you've suffered mild memory loss. You're still very much aware of the current happenings.

Head trauma has some bizarre effects on the mind."

"Are you going to tell me what happened?"

"Yes. You were struck by a semi-truck."

"A semi? Where?"

Martin racked his mind, the memory refusing to come to the forefront.

"You were found in front of the Klebold residence in their private neighborhood," the doctor said, studious eyes on his patient.

The name Klebold must have been the trigger word as Martin's mind released a floodgate of memories. He could remember exactly what he was doing. He had just finished snooping around the Klebold house and saw Dylan answer the door for the police officer.

"Does that ring any bells?"

Martin stayed in his mind, tracking the events that had happened chronologically. After the cop left, he fled the scene, knowing the officer's visit had to do something with his rust bucket of a car being spotted on the side of the road in the glamorous neighborhood.

He scrunched his brow in thought. "I'm afraid I'm not remembering. You said the Klebold house?"

"Correct."

Martin tossed up his hands, feeling a slight tug from the tubes in them. "Sorry. That name doesn't sound familiar at all."

Martin made sure to stare the doctor in his eyes, not wanting any chance of him catching on to his lie.

"Don't stress. It will eventually come back to you. The police may still want to speak with you to get a statement on the accident. I believe the truck driver is in jail; semis are forbidden to drive through that neighborhood."

And they probably never do, until the past decides to push me out of the way.

Martin now understood what Chris had meant. Changing a historical event, whether for better or worse, wouldn't be straightforward. Columbine would have to proceed as history had planned, and the thought burned Martin inside. He'd come this far only to find himself in the hospital from a coma, and having nightmares about the two howling lunatics who would one day carry out their destiny.

Eric and Dylan win. I can't push any further than I already have. Anything more will get me killed. I need to recover and get ready for Izzy in September.

"I'm gonna let you relax for a bit. I'll have a nurse stop in later to get some of these tubes taken out, and I'll discuss the next steps with you at that time," Dr. Lincoln said. "Is there anything I can get for you right now?"

"I want to see Sonya."

"We're going to call her right now. Anything else?"

"No, doctor, thank you. I'm just going to try and think back to what happened."

"Don't push yourself. Your mind has undergone some drastic things in the last week. Try to clear your thoughts, I promise you'll recover just fine."

Dr. Lincoln offered a kind smile before leaving Martin alone.

Martin couldn't keep his mind clear as the doctor instructed. That had always been a tall task, but now with a week's worth of time unaccounted for, his mind worked overtime as he debated what to do when he got out of the hospital. One thought, however, tugged at him.

How the hell am I going to explain this to Sonya?

35

Chapter 34

Sonya hadn't felt such a conflict of emotions since the tragic shower situation. She wanted to barge into Martin's hospital room and put everything on the table. She could share her truth, and just maybe the rest of her mission could run smoothly. He was also being put to the test in his efforts to rescue his daughter, so she couldn't do anything to throw those plans off, either.

For now, she would only concern herself with his well-being. A lot depended on how the doctors said he was recovering, too. Dr. Lincoln had assured her it was a mild coma, one Martin should be able to recover completely from, but sometimes doctors were wrong. How could they know for sure until he woke up and they started running tests?

Sonya pulled in to the hospital's parking lot and shook her mind free of all the poisonous thoughts trying to form within.

"You're here for Martin. Everything else will take care of itself when the time's right," she said to herself.

The parking lot had changed, this her first time visiting in the morning. Hundreds of cars filled the lot, the sun glaring off the sea of metal. She squeezed through the rows of vehicles on her way to the hospital's main entrance where she took her first right to the elevators at the end of the hall and called for the third floor.

Will he even remember me? A hard enough rattle to his brain could have completely wiped her from his memory. It wouldn't be the most absurd thing to happen on this mission.

"Just shut up and go in there," she whispered to herself, walking down the third floor hallway on unsteady legs.

She reached his closed door and took a deep breath before pushing it open.

Martin lay where he had when she last visited, only this time his eyes were open and he turned his head to meet her stare. She hesitated, having an immediate thought that he didn't recognize her, but he cracked a gentle smile that revealed he was okay.

"Sonya," he said, extending a hand out. She stepped into the room and glided to his bedside, throwing herself onto him as tears of relief flowed. Her body convulsed beneath his arms and he started rubbing her back for a soothing effect that felt perfect.

"I didn't know where you were that night," she said, muffled into his arms. "I was so scared."

"I'm gonna be okay," he said, continuing to rub her back that had finally calmed down. "The doctors have had nothing but good things to say about my recovery."

"Where is Dr. Lincoln?" she asked, wanting to hear for herself.

"I don't know. He left after doing tests. There are some things I can't remember. Especially the accident."

"How do you not remember the accident?" she asked, sure to keep her voice calm. She stood up, staring into his eyes as he scratched his head.

Martin tossed his hands in the air. "I don't know. The doctor described the accident to me, but none of it sounds familiar. I don't even know what I was doing in Littleton. The whole day is like it's deleted from my brain."

"You don't know why you were in Littleton?" she snapped. Through all the shit she had going on in her mind, that was the one question she wanted to pin on him, and he came out and beat her to the punch, providing no information about his time in the affluent suburb. She wanted to call him a liar, but refrained, keeping her emotions in check.

And you thought there was an explanation. Your explanation was flushed down the coma toilet where all good explanations go.

"How are you feeling?" she asked, changing the subject before she spilled her guts. "Did nothing else get injured in the crash?"

He shook his head. "My ribs are a little sore, but the doctor said there's no damage, just some bruising."

"Did they say when you can go home?"

"He said I can likely go home tonight, pending some tests."

As if he heard them talking, Dr. Lincoln entered the room with a rapid knock on the door.

"Sonya," he said. "Glad to see you here. Martin was asking for you right away when he woke." The old doctor shuffled to Sonya's side and read the monitor next to the bed. "How are you feeling, Mr. Briar?"

"Much better. That food really helped."

"Perfect," the doctor said, and turned to Sonya. "We gave him his first solid meal since he's been in here. Eggs and toast – glad to see it's sitting well."

"Can you fill me in, Dr. Lincoln?"

"Of course. My apologies. Martin is doing better than we could have hoped. He's going to struggle a lot with his short term memory for the next couple months, so it's best for you to remain patient with him. He's going to forget basic things like where he put his car keys, or maybe what drawer utensils go in your kitchen. Nothing major or life threatening, but those little lapses in memory can be frustrating for you as his partner."

She nodded, feeling sympathy for the first time since arriving.

"Aside from that, there may be instances of long term memory showing some trouble, but nothing I suspect will last too long."

"And when will he be going home?" Sonya asked.

"Today. While comas are serious by nature, there's not really much else we can provide here at the hospital. As long as we feel a coma patient is coherent and can function normally, we'll release them. The best treatment is rest and relaxation, and you can do that at home just fine. The final tests will be for Martin to walk around and use the restroom on his own. Once he shows he can do that, he's free to go."

"And there's no treatment of any kind I need to worry about at home?" Sonya asked.

"Just keep the environment relaxed. I'd say for the first couple weeks, be there with Martin to assist with daily tasks. Do things like yardwork, cooking, and cleaning together. Really anything that distracts the mind is good for recovery."

This all sounded manageable for Sonya, but a realization also grew within like a slow burning flame: she would have to wait some time before prodding Martin for the truth. Not out of a courtesy for his recovering brain, but as a strategic move. Anything she threw his way in the coming weeks could be deflected by using his coma as an excuse. *Oh, you don't remember lying about your time in Littleton? How convenient for you and your damaged mind.*

She'd have to wait the couple of weeks as instructed by the doctor until Martin showed signs of a full recovery. There would be an eventual point in time where the coma seemed a distant memory, and that's when she would unleash her arsenal of inquiries. For now, and for the sake of her sanity, her main focus needed to be on Martin's recovery so she could one day get the answers she desired. She'd have to carry on as normal, knowing a showdown would eventually come.

"Well, what do you say, Martin? Wanna go for a walk around the halls?" Sonya asked, patting him on the legs. "Let's get you back home."

"We'll need a nurse for that, for an official evaluation, but you are more than welcome to join Mr. Briar on his walk when he feels ready."

"I'm ready, doc. I just wanna go home."

Martin sat up in his bed and swung his legs over the edge. All of the tubes from the last week had been removed earlier, after he woke. His body was again independent after a week of machines feeding him and shitting for him. His feet hit the ground with a heavy thud as he swayed to catch his balance.

"Easy, Mr. Briar," Dr. Lincoln said, putting a hand on Martin's shoulders. "Your body has been idle for a week, so you can't just jump off the bed and make a run for the exit. Let me call that nurse for you and she'll assist you through the halls."

Sonya had paid a visit to the library and researched treating comas. The nurses would have rotated his body over the week, changing the side he laid on to help prevent blood clots, among many other possible side effects. Standing so suddenly would have made the blood rush to his head, causing him to topple the way he had.

So, you're really gonna go through with this? Sonya's inner voice chimed in.

"C'mon, babe, let's take it slow and get out of here. The nurse will be here any minute."

Her mind was set on trapping Martin in his lies.

36

Chapter 35

The drive home was silent. A gentle rainfall had started, leaving the only sound as the drops hitting the windshield and the wipers screeching across to clear the view. Martin lay in the passenger seat, reclined, with a small stack of hospital papers on his stomach.

Sonya didn't speak, and Martin was fine with that. He needed to sort out his story and be able to cover his tracks; she would certainly have questions.

There's only one way out of this, he thought. *You have to tell her the truth. There's not a lie that can hide this anymore. No one has a clue what you were doing or why you were at the Klebold house. Just tell her.*

Martin toyed with the idea of spilling his deepest secret. Even a free thinker would need some convincing of time travel being true. This could go one of two drastic ways. She would either run for the hills and call the asylum on Martin, or take a leap of faith and believe him, being practically forced to join him on his adventure. No possible outcome existed where their life together could continue as normal. *Have fun at work today, I'm gonna go stop the 9/11 attacks this morning. Be home for dinner.*

He accepted the ultimatum that awaited, and wanted to rip the bandage off and get it over with. Was now the right time to bring up the matter? She had also gone through a lot in the past week, an emotional roller coaster surrounded by the unknowing. Was today, the most joyous day of the last week, really the best time to spring such news on her?

You can either tell her, or keep it a secret. Just know that if you wait long enough, she'll be the one asking the questions. Don't let her control where this conversation goes. This is all for Izzy – she'll understand once you explain.

Martin considered this. They may have not been dating long, but Martin knew Sonya well enough to anticipate the sea of questions floating behind her silent façade. She was curious about most things, and the topic of why he was in Littleton would surely be on the top of her list.

He would tell her when they arrived home; he didn't want her emotional while driving. Martin recognized the scenery outside of his window, knew they were back in Larkwood, but couldn't remember where or what her house looked like. It was like a blank spot on his internal map of the city, a Bermuda triangle of sorts when he tried to imagine the house's location. It terrified Martin that he couldn't remember where they lived. He could picture the apartment building and Vinny, his old house where Izzy would one day go missing from, but not his current residence.

Martin reached over the center panel and rubbed Sonya's arm, her soft skin gliding beneath his fingertips. "I love you," he said, prompting a flustered look of delight from the driver's seat.

She grinned at him, and he could see the pain and fear hiding behind her eyes. "I love you, too." She grabbed his hand and raised it to her lips for a quick kiss.

"How far are we?"

Her grin turned into a flat line. "We're about three minutes away. Do you not remember your hometown at all?"

"No, I do. It's just your house I can't remember. I remember my old apartment, the liquor store, our favorite restaurants. I just can't picture where the house is."

Sonya nodded, but remained quiet. She probably had no idea what to say to him. The doctor had spoken with Martin in private, letting him know that those close to him might appear to struggle with his recovery more than himself. The forgetfulness could wear down those who loved him. They could grow sick of having to repeat themselves and explain things a dozen times. But Martin believed Sonya to be a good-hearted person, even in the darkest times.

The car turned into a neighborhood and pulled into a driveway. Everything *felt* familiar, but Martin still couldn't piece it all together in his mind. It felt as if someone had dumped a 5,000 piece puzzle on the floor and left him no picture for guidance.

You're on your own. Sonya will try to help, but she's not lost in your head with you. She can't truly help without knowing what's going on. It's like calling for directions, but you don't where you are to begin with.

"Home sweet home," Sonya said, killing the engine. "Can I make you a soup?"

"That sounds delicious. The hospital food was nothing to write home about. And I only had one meal the whole time."

"Sounds lovely. Go lie down on the couch and I'll get something together. It's a perfect day to cuddle up and watch movies. How does that sound?"

"As long as you're there, it sounds heavenly."

Martin loved her, and should have known better than to get involved romantically with anyone while traveling to the past. Romance has a way of complicating even the simplest of plans. It didn't matter if she was sent to him as a gift from the past. The past would have to try a lot harder to keep him from his daughter come September.

Martin still hadn't regained his natural sense of time and checked the dashboard clock to find it was twenty minutes until five. The day had passed in a blur once Sonya arrived at the hospital, and he hadn't noticed, entranced by the chance to spend a day with her.

"Where's my car?" Martin asked. "Was it destroyed?"

Sonya nodded her head. "Your car was practically flattened. They found pieces of it 200 yards away from the accident."

She spoke in a wavering voice before collapsing into a new round of tears and heavy, painful sobs. "It's a miracle you're still alive. You should be dead."

Sonya threw herself across the center console and into Martin's arms that opened naturally for her. The sweet smell of her hair wasn't present as usual, and he figured that she had skipped a few showers while he lay in the hospital, his mind drifting to another dimension.

"I'm here."

"I love you," she said, giving him a half-hearted squeeze thanks to her awkward angle. "Can we please go inside?"

"Yes," Martin said, and he felt this was as good a transition as any. "Let's go sit down on the couch and talk. There's something I need to tell you."

Sonya recoiled and sat up stiffly in the driver's seat. "What do you mean?"

"I mean we need to have a talk."

"Those words are never good." She stared at him sternly, daring him to tell her bad news after the week she had just endured.

"It's not what you think. But it is about us and our future. Let's just go inside."

Sonya wasted no more time bickering in the car and swung her door open. Martin followed suit, only a bit slower. Sonya was already opening the house door when Martin closed the car door and shuffled around to meet her. He watched as she moved with a hell-bent purpose into the house, throwing her purse and keys on the table and nearly running to the living room. She reminded Martin of a kid being told it was finally time to open the presents at their birthday party, only he didn't sense the same kind of excitement.

Martin walked at his new, slow pace. Although it was temporary, it still frustrated him that his legs couldn't keep up with how fast his mind wanted them to move. And to think it wasn't even a direct result of the coma, but rather from lying in bed for an entire week.

He joined Sonya on the couch, her legs bouncing uncontrollably as she had her hands crossed in front of her face as if in prayer. Her eyes stared to the ground and ignored him when he sat down beside her.

Sonya had spent the last few days contemplating a way to force Martin to share his truth. She had the unique fortune of knowing everything about his life—even the things she had no way of knowing based on their time together. If he wanted to talk now, then she'd get what she needed. Putting him under pressure would also reveal more about his character. She jumped up from the couch and paced around the coffee table. "I'm not letting you do this," she said, an obvious hint of anger hiding behind her words.

"Let me do what?"

"Spill your guts and confess. No, sir. You must have hit your head pretty hard if you think I'm gonna let you sit there and be all saintly for making your confession before I caught you."

"Confession?" Martin said, more to himself. "Sonya, I'm not sure what you're talking about."

"Good, then let me explain for you." The boiling rage could no longer hide and was in full force with every motion she made. "I know everything. I know your lies, your secret life. Everything."

Martin's crippled mind raced in hundreds of directions, unable to make any sense of her words. The only way she could know that he had traveled through time would be if she had also traveled in time and knew what to look for. He examined her skin for the golden glow, but did not see anything.

"Tell me what you know, because you've lost me," Martin said calmly, hoping the composure would rub off on Sonya.

"Sure, Martin, if that's your real name," she said, sarcasm clinging to every word. "Let's see. For starters, I know you don't work at the post office. I called them to let them know about your accident. They said they've never heard of you, had no record of your employment. That's lie number one. I know you're married. How's Lela doing? That's lie number two. And I know that you and Lela have a daughter named Izzy. Because she goes to my school! What a shame that a sweet girl like that is stuck with a lying piece of shit father like you."

Martin sat stunned, eyes bulging at Sonya in a way that probably made him look guilty. He supposed if he hadn't just come out of a coma, she would likely be throwing things at him as she ranted.

Well, here it is, he thought. This *is the past pushing back.* This *is the past using Sonya to throw you off. You better explain yourself quickly before this woman goes in the kitchen for a knife to stab your fat, useless gut.*

Martin could sense the anger seeping from Sonya's pores, but remained calm himself as he knew she had it all mistaken.

"Are you going to say anything, liar?" she snarled. "Or can liars not speak when they've been caught?"

Martin shook his head and hoped for the best.

"I can actually explain all of this. But, I need you to sit down and really listen. This isn't at all what you think."

"Save it, Martin. What were you doing in Littleton? Fucking your rich housewife? Does she give you money when you're a good boy?"

The question caused a giggle to form in Martin's throat that he choked down.

"Sonya," he said, keeping a high level of composure. "I can explain."

She crossed her arms and cocked her head like a pissed off teenager. "Well, then start talking."

Martin patted the open space on the couch next to him, but Sonya didn't flinch and kept staring at him with hateful eyes.

"Okay, then," he said. "This is all going to sound crazy. Because it is. But it's all true, I need you to trust me, and you can ask me for any proof that you need."

He paused to stand Sonya, not wanting to talk up to Sonya the whole time.

"I'm not from here. I suppose that's the best way to put it. I'm from Larkwood, but I came here from the year 2018."

Martin paused again to read Sonya's expression that remained hot, but he could see the dials turning behind those hateful eyes.

"You're absolutely right about Lela and Izzy. In 1996, they are my wife and daughter. In September, Izzy will go missing and never be found again. That's why I'm here: to stop that from happening. Her disappearance led to the collapse of my marriage. If you go to my family's house right now, you'll probably see me, Lela, and Izzy all there together.

And I'll still be here. It's been made clear that I can't interact with my past self."

Martin noticed Sonya's arms loosen, but remained crossed.

"I've been here since March, tracking Izzy, and finding ways to kill time until the big day in September. I didn't plan to meet someone and fall in love. But, here we are. I'm not sure what I'm supposed to do about our relationship. I don't know what will happen when I go back. You could even come with me, I suppose, if you wanted."

Martin paused once more and let his words settle. Sonya's face morphed from anger to confusion as she scrunched her eyebrows.

"Martin, I think we need to get you back to the doctor. I think you hallucinated during your coma." She spoke with the slightest hint of fear in her voice.

"I wish I could take you to the future for a quick look to see for yourself, but that's not how it works."

"Well, I can't exactly ask you questions about the future, either – how would I ever know if you're telling the truth?"

Martin noticed her hands shaking, still likely flowing with the adrenaline of her outburst moments ago, but her voice had almost returned to normal, and that put him at ease.

She wants to believe me.

"Okay. I do have some minor things you could use as proof. I have a notebook of sporting outcomes that I use to bet and make money while I'm here. I can show you the outcomes, down to the exact score, and you can see for yourself."

"So you really don't work for the post office?"

"Well, I do in 2018. That's why I used it as a cover-up. It's easy for me to explain because I actually *do* work in a post office."

Sonya finally uncrossed her arms and let them fall to her sides. "I don't believe this. Time travel isn't real, and you know it."

Martin reached his arms out for her, expecting her to avoid them, but she didn't resist and let him squeeze her as if never wanting to be let go.

"I know this sounds impossible. I thought so, too. Sometimes I still wonder if this man in 2018 just drugged me and I'm on a hell of a trip. But it's been too long. No days have been skipped, and everything I know will happen *has* happened."

Sonya was silent, her heavy breathing the only sound filling the quiet house. She gently pushed her way out of his embrace and took a step back. "I think I need some time by myself to process this. I'm not asking you to leave or anything. I *want* to believe you, but I can't right now. It's too absurd to even consider. I want to see the proof you have, but part of me doesn't really want to - that would make it real."

"I understand. I damn near drank myself to death when I found out this was real. It's a lot to process, and only gets stranger the more you learn. So, what do you want me to do?"

"It doesn't matter. You need to rest and relax like the doctor said. I'm gonna go out, try to clear my mind if that's even possible at this point. I'll bring you some dinner later – just try to get better."

Martin wondered if she still thought this was a result of his head injury. It made sense for her to think that; he had never shown any signs of such chaotic thoughts before the accident, so it was a convenient enough of an excuse to use if she wanted to stay in denial.

"Okay, take your time. Don't be too late – I'd love to explain everything I know and answer any questions you have."

Martin stayed calm, wanting to show Sonya that he was perfectly fine and not delirious like she assumed.

Sonya nodded and turned for the kitchen where she swiped her keys off the table. She opened the front door, looked back at Martin with terrified eyes, and closed it behind her on the way out.

Martin returned to his spot on the couch, hearing the car outside turn on seconds later.

She'll come around, don't worry. Just give her some time.

Martin lay down, intent of falling asleep for a quick snooze, but knowing his racing thoughts would never allow it.

37

Chapter 36

Martin fell into a light sleep after all. He could only stare at the ceiling for so long before the fatigue kicked in. He slept for an hour and a half before Sonya's car pulled into the driveway. He sat up on the couch, neck sore from sleeping awkwardly. The clock read 7:38 P.M.

His stomach growled when Sonya swung the front door open, a bag of Taco Bell in hand, the smell of questionable ground beef slowly filling the house.

"Hey," she said flatly. "I brought us dinner."

"Thank you. How was it? Where did you go?"

She looked down and drew circles in the carpet with her toe. "I went to a park. There's one just outside of downtown that overlooks a lake and the mountains. It's somewhere I've always gone when I needed to sort things out."

Martin stood, expecting her to say more, but she didn't.

"What did you decide?"

She looked back down to her imaginary artwork and spoke just above a whisper. "I think I believe you."

Knowing he wasn't getting kicked to the asylum, Martin crossed the living room to her. He grabbed the bag of food, placed it on the counter, and grabbed her hands, one in each of his. Her head stayed down, but he could hear a soft sniffle.

"Sonya," he said. "Tell me what you're feeling."

She raised her head and had tears welled up in her eyes, bringing out her true hazel color, glistening majestically. He felt her staring into his soul and could feel her trying to enter it, as if she could lunge into his being.

"I love you, Martin. And I believe you."

He raised his thumbs gently to her face and wiped the tears out of her eyes.

"Thank you. I love you, too. More than I've ever loved any other woman."

"Before I went to the park, I went to your house. Well, your old house, I guess." Sonya spoke with uncertainty.

Martin felt an immediate pit fall through his stomach. If she went to his old house and interacted with his past self, she may have thrown a wrench into everything. If his past self met her, how would that affect him going forward? Martin still had a novel's worth of questions he wanted to ask Chris, but knew the old man was long gone.

"I only drove by, but I saw you mowing the lawn. It was clearly you, but younger. I wanted to stop and say something, but something inside me told me I shouldn't."

"That's good. I don't know what would've happened if you did."

"After I saw you, I felt like I had been knocked in the head. I felt dizzy and sick. It was like I was back in college and learned that the Vietnam War was a big hoax. It was just a sick feeling to learn something that you'd never guess in 100 years to be true."

"I know what you mean." Martin didn't understand the Vietnam reference, he was barely born when that all happened, but he could relate to the sensation of realizing that time travel was real and not something made up in the movies.

"So, I went to the park and tried to make sense of it all. I think I've come to accept it, but I still can't wrap my mind around it. I don't know how it's possible."

Just go for it. This might be your best shot.

"You can come back with me to the future. See for yourself," he said, caution clinging to each word. He watched Sonya for a reaction, but none came. She only nodded her head in a slow motion.

"I thought you might ask me that," she said. "I just don't know. Don't get me wrong, I'd love to go just for the experience."

She paused for an eternity, her head bobbing in thought.

"But at the same time it's terrifying. I don't know what the future's like. What if I'm not cut out for a world of flying cars and advanced technology?"

Martin chuckled. "There aren't flying cars. There are cars that can drive themselves, but nothing that flies yet."

"I just don't know, Martin. I feel like there's a thousand questions I need answered before I can even consider such a thing."

"I understand, I went through the same thing. Fortunately, I was given a sort of test run."

"So how does it work?" Sonya asked, her tone shifting to a curious one. "Is there a secret door you walk through and fall into another year?"

Martin sensed her list of a thousand questions was about to come. When dealing with this topic, he knew one question always led to another.

"No. It's actually a pill you swallow. Although, you wouldn't have to. There's only one pill left."

"Then how would I—"

"I would hold you. Anything that's attached to me will travel with me through time. I can show you my cell phone."

"Cell phone?"

"By 2018 just about everyone carries a portable phone with them. Mine doesn't work here in the past, so I can't show you all that it can do, but I have it."

Martin turned and hurried to the guest room where his belongings were. "I'll be right back."

A minute later he returned with a small rectangular piece of plastic clenched in his hand. Its shiny surface reflected the above lights as he held it out like an offering for Sonya.

She stared in curiosity, but hesitated touching it, like it was an alien species that had landed in her backyard.

"That thing's a phone?" she asked after a few minutes of studying it with only her eyes. "How? Where do you talk? Where do you listen?"

Martin grinned, her questions reminding him of his mother's reaction when they had bought her first cell phone some time in 2010. For a good two years she had called him at least once a week from her landline saying, "Marty, I don't know how to use this damn gizmo."

Martin held the phone at Sonya's eye level, on its side. "You speak into here and listen from here." His finger glided from the bottom of the phone to the top, pointing at small holes she had to squint to see.

"And that works? There's barely anything there."

"It works just fine. These phones also do more than make phone calls. You can send text messages if you don't feel like talking, play games, search the internet, update your calendar. All kinds of things."

"You're telling me you can walk around with the internet in your back pocket in 2018?"

The thought would have never occurred to someone in 1996, as the internet was barely accessible at the library.

"Oh, yeah. It happens even sooner than that. A little after 2000 is when everyone started getting cell phones. The internet part came a little later, but didn't take too long before everyone had it. Do you want to hold it?"

"Okay." Sonya finally reached out and grabbed the futuristic portal of knowledge from Martin's hand. She studied it, turning it as she held it up the light. "I just don't get how this little thing can do all that?"

"A cell phone is only the start. You should see the technology in the future – it only becomes more advanced every year."

"Don't get me wrong, this is cool, but it's not enough to convince me to go. What's the world like?"

Martin looked at Sonya, who still hadn't taken her eyes off the cell phone.

"Sonya. I need you to trust me when I tell you the world is fine. I'll be there with you every step of the way. I want you to come with me. Not just so you can see the future, but so we can continue our life together."

"What happens to my life here?"

Martin opened his mouth to speak, but snapped it shut when he realized he didn't actually know. The rules that applied to him for traveling to the past might not work for her since she wasn't taking the pill. He didn't know if her body would fall asleep for ten minutes and patiently await her return that might never come.

"I honestly don't know. For me, I'm asleep in 2018, and whenever I go back, only ten minutes will have passed. I'll actually need to go quit my job when I wake up."

Martin decided he didn't want to slog through life any more, regardless of what would end up happening with Izzy and Sonya. He felt a new sense of purpose in life and found he actually enjoyed being sober more than the constant state of drunkenness he had grown accustomed to.

"Why would you quit?" Sonya asked, pure curiosity in her voice.

Martin smirked. "Do you think traveling through time is something you can just do and go back to your normal life after it's all done? Pretend it never happened? My life will never be the same, and I think that's for the best. Don't worry, I'm going to make sure I have plenty of money ready to pick up when I arrive back."

The shock and worry that had physically consumed Sonya gave way to anticipation. Martin could see the dials turning in her head, digesting everything he said. He knew she would agree to visit, but not necessarily stay. A history teacher would never be able to resist a chance to see the future, no matter how absurd it might sound.

She pursed her lips and stared into Martin's soul.

"I'll go with you under one condition . . . and some other questions." Sonya spoke and her eyes seemed to follow the words out of her mouth, wondering if she could reach out and take them back.

"Of course. What's the condition?"

"You need to tell me what you were doing in Littleton. Did it have something to do with the future?"

Martin had witnessed a carousel of Sonya's emotions over the last few hours, and now saw one he hadn't yet seen: hope. Hope that whatever he responded with would be to her liking. Hope that whatever was in Littleton was part of some futuristic project she wouldn't understand. Martin offered a soft smile before delivering the good news.

"Yes, it did have to do with the future, but I clearly ran into problems. Do you know Columbine High School out in Littleton?"

She nodded. "I've heard of it, yeah. Huge school, virtually unlimited budget. What does a high school have to do with anything?"

Martin cleared his throat, knowing he needed to explain what would happen without scaring her out of joining him in 2018.

"In 1999, two seniors at the high school are going to take guns and homemade bombs to school and kill more than a dozen kids and teachers, and injure many more."

Sonya's mouth hung open and she slapped a hand to it.

"I figured since I'm already here in the past, I'd see if I can do anything to stop that from happening. You see, by 2018, America will have more mass shootings than any other countries combined. And it all started with the attacks at Columbine."

Martin watched as fear washed away the look of hope in Sonya's eyes. He remembered a time where shootings were still shocking to hear about, and he envied Sonya for still living in that era.

"Two students bring guns to school and shoot everyone?" Sonya asked. "I can't even imagine. What would I do if that happened in my classroom? I'm just a teacher."

"Exactly. It turns in to such a hot topic in the future that it literally polarizes everyone against each other and nothing gets resolved."

"Martin," she said, her brow furrowed in seriousness. "You have to stop it. You have to go back. I can help you."

Martin crossed his arms and nodded in appreciation. "That's nice of you, but I can't let you get involved. And I shouldn't stay involved, either. You see, one thing about traveling to the past is anything I try to change may resist. The day of the accident I was at one of the shooter's homes. I think I was close to having an encounter with him, and the past sent that semi-truck to stop me."

"There has to be something you can do, even without getting physically involved. What if you called the police? Or wrote a letter?"

"I thought about that. A letter would probably just get lost in the mail. And a phone call would never be taken seriously. If I called the Littleton police to report a crime that's going to happen in three years, they'll probably come and lock me up instead."

"I'll do it," Sonya demanded. "You can't tell me otherwise."

"Sonya—"

"Nope. I'm doing it. I'll take the chance and hand deliver a letter to the school's principal. If you want to help, you can watch out for me to make sure nothing happens."

Martin wanted to protest but recognized the determination on Sonya's face. Her mind was made up and there would be no talking her out of it. He could only hope she would forget about all of this and avoid a potentially deadly decision.

"Okay, we can discuss it more. I really need to explain more how the past will fight back."

"I don't care. Sometimes you have to do what's right, no matter what."

"Is this worth dying over? Because that could happen."

Sonya's look of determination gave an inch to doubt. She wanted to stay strong, but the notion of death may have planted the fear he hoped might change her mind.

"I'll think about it."

"Okay. Let's discuss it later. Is there anything else you had questions about?" Martin asked, pleading her to change the subject.

"Yeah. What's the date of this shooting?"

Chapter 37

Sonya wouldn't let it go, and after three days of constant nagging, Martin surrendered and agreed to let her deliver a letter to the school. She had even drafted a copy of the letter that she would take to the principal.

Sonya kept Martin company, watching many movies to pass the days while he remained a quasi-vegetable. He became fatigued easily, and one hour of each day, she helped him move around the house, refresh his memory on where things went, and if he was up to it, go for a relaxing walk around the neighborhood.

If there was one thing Martin remembered, it was why he fell in love with Sonya. She tended to him with a motherly touch he hadn't felt since he was a child. His heart still skipped madly every time she pressed her lips onto his.

She's the one, he thought. *I had to travel back in time to find the person I'm meant to love.*

She loved him so much, apparently, that she wanted to put her life on the line to carry out *his* goal of stopping the Columbine shootings. It had obviously struck a personal chord with her being a lifelong educator, but she might have obsessed a bit too much over the matter, bringing up the topic at every chance.

"We need to sit down and make a plan, and get this note delivered next week," Sonya said. "I already found out that their summer school is open one more week before they close down until the fall. You're going to be too consumed with saving Izzy by the time the next school year starts, so this needs to happen within the next seven days."

Sonya had practically hijacked the mission, telling Martin how things would play out. If he didn't like it, then she would just go on her own and enter the unknown battlefield without protection.

"Okay, Monday morning. Let's get it out of the way," Martin agreed reluctantly.

Monday morning had been the original date for their flight departure to their romantic getaway, but the doctor said it would be best if they wait another month or two as Martin needed to remain as stress free as possible.

Sonya was able to get most of their money back, and obliged to cancel the trip. She would, after all, be taking a different trip in September. One for the ages, you could say.

They spent a couple hours on Saturday crafting the final draft of the letter. It didn't say much, but Sonya was a perfectionist. It read:

Dear Sir,

I've come across some disturbing information that needs to be brought to your attention. Two of your students, Eric Harris and Dylan Klebold, are currently plotting a violent attack that will take place at Columbine High School. Their current plan to carry out this attack is April 20, 1999, when they will be in their final semester of high school.

Please do with this information as you wish, but know this is not an empty threat. You must consider this note with care to save future lives.

God bless,

A concerned citizen

Martin would have never been able to phrase such delicate information in the manner she had. Five simple sentences handwritten on a piece of notepad paper would stop one of the most horrific terrorist attacks in modern history, assuming they could deliver it without any problems.

There will be problems, Martin thought. *You weren't even doing anything when the truck hit you. And you think this time will be any easier?*

The thought wrung Martin's stomach like a rag. He had to be ready for anything, and also had to prepare Sonya to be ready. She didn't understand how aggressive the past would be, and he didn't want her to find out the hard way.

The plan they made was simple. She would drive, and Martin would ride shotgun to keep an eye on the road for the unexpected. She would enter the school with Martin following close behind, waiting outside to avoid being noticed again inside the school.

"And that's all we can plan for," he said, sipping a cup of tea. "As far as the unknown, I have no idea what'll happen. There could be another car accident, maybe the car will catch on fire. I just don't know. We have to be ready for anything, and you have to be ready to move at my command. If I say jump out of the car, you better swing that door open and jump like your life depends on it."

Sonya nodded silently, and Martin thought the severity of the task had finally settled in. She didn't do well with the unknown, but had committed too deep to back out now.

"Martin?" she asked, the slightest tremble escaping from her lips. "Do you think I might die?"

Remember, you don't know how the rules will apply to her. She's not the one traveling through time.

"Not likely," he said. "I think I'm still going to be the one at highest risk. When Monday comes, we need to move quickly and efficiently. We should plan to go during the peak of the morning rush hour. The slower we drive, the less likely for something to go wrong."

Sonya nodded. "Monday morning. I don't know if I'll be able to sleep between now and then."

"Of course you will – just try to keep your mind clear. You don't even know these kids or the severity of their attacks."

"That doesn't matter. I've agreed to do this, both as a sign of faith that I believe you, and to help keep the world a good place."

Sonya lay down on the couch and curled up beside Martin. He rubbed her up and down along her back while they both fell into a deep sleep.

* * *

They spent the rest of the weekend much how they had spent the entire week, dragging themselves around the house, not wanting to do much but stay rested for their eventful Monday morning. On Sunday, Martin decided to give grilling a shot once the sun started its descent and left them with a picture-perfect evening. He sipped a glass of neat whiskey while tending to two sizzling steaks. He couldn't remember what the different ways to cook steak were called, but knew they needed to have the slightest shade of pink in the middle to be considered finished and still juicy.

Sonya approached Martin from behind and placed her own glass of whiskey on the grill's side table. She slung her arms around Martin's waist and rocked back and forth with him as they stared out to the backyard. The grass had grown scraggly, but not too tall yet. Martin had always mowed on Sunday nights, but had taken the last two weeks off from that chore. Perhaps in another week he'd feel more up to managing machinery that could cut a limb off if used improperly.

"I love you," Sonya said from behind him, sounding almost hypnotized.

He put down the tongs and turned to her. "I love you, too."

"No, really. I've been thinking all weekend now. How could any of this have happened? How does life lead us where it does? This can't be some miraculous accident. The fact that you were sent here from 2018 and met me...it just can't be dumb luck."

Martin grinned and kissed her on the forehead. "I've thought the same thing since I arrived. I thought I was coming here for a sole purpose, but it turned out being three purposes: Izzy, Columbine, and you."

Sonya returned a grin as she looked into his eyes.

"I've tried to make sense of all of it," he said. "But all I can come up with is that it's some sort of fate—a cross-dimensional fate, at that. I've debated so long on when to tell you, knowing I would have to at some point. It means the world to me that you're going to join me."

He kissed her again, this time on the lips, and she returned the favor with a brief flash of deep passion.

"I'm terrified, you know," she said. "I'm terrified of tomorrow, I'm terrified of 2018, I'm terrified of the future in general. You don't know what happens beyond 2018. Unlike now, you could tell me everything that happens between now and then."

"I'm still here. You can ask me anything."

"I'd rather read the history books when I get to the future, and then I'll ask questions. The only thing I want to know is if we see a woman president by 2018."

Martin smirked. "Almost. Clinton's wife – Hilary – she loses in the 2016 election."

"Really?" Sonya's eyes bulged. "Lost to who?"

"That's a long story. Probably better for another day."

"So there *is* some hope for the future."

"Things aren't as bad as they might sound. Sure there's more violence in the future, but I've never felt in danger. I honestly think the violence is mostly the same, there's just more coverage of it with the internet and social media."

Sonya nodded silently, and Martin figured she had no idea what social media even meant.

"How will we know if what we're doing tomorrow will have worked?" she asked.

Martin took a sip and flipped the steaks, their sizzle slowly quieting as they came closer to completion.

"Well, we won't be here to find out for ourselves. We'll have to look it up when we get back to 2018. We can do a quick search on Columbine High School and see what shows up."

"It's that simple, huh?"

218

"It really is. You can find out literally anything you want to know. Not all the answers may be real, but you'll eventual learn how sort out what's fake or not."

"That needs to be the first thing we look up when he get back. Is the library close to your house?"

"We don't need to go to the library. Remember, it's all on my phone."

"Duh, right! How could I forget your portable encyclopedia? My apologies."

She grinned as she locked eyes with Martin, and he felt something he hadn't in the last two weeks: lust.

They hadn't lost their connection, but he was unable to perform physically grueling tasks. Now, he felt a familiar tingle in his crotch and an urge to kiss every inch of her body. If dinner went well, maybe he'd see what she thought about dessert in the bedroom.

39

Chapter 38

Monday morning, just before the sun poked above the horizon, Martin's nightmare of Eric and Dylan had recurred. Only this time there was no conversation, just the two boys laughing like rabid hyenas as they both lined up their firearms and shot Martin square in the chest. It was a quick dream, the kind you think back and realize had lasted only five seconds, but had felt like an eternity. The layers of evil that waited beneath their howling laughter sent chills down his spine both in dreamland and in his 1996 bed.

Sonya tossed and turned all night, likely facing demons of her own. He knew she had finally recognized that she had gone in too deep with this commitment, but would never admit it.

She had rolled out of bed shortly after 5 A.M., and Martin heard her rummaging around the kitchen, debated if he should join her, then rolled back to his side to try and steal another hour of sleep.

Their plan was to leave the house at eight, meaning they would hit the rush hour traffic toward downtown by 8:15 to have a slow trek the rest of the way to Littleton. There was a brief disagreement about the strategy to catch the rush hour. Sonya believed that more cars on the road increased the likelihood of something going wrong, while Martin argued something *would* go wrong regardless, so it would be best to drive as slow as possible. I-25 in the morning, between eight and nine was typically stop-and-go all the way to downtown. If something were to go wrong on the highway, they'd have plenty of time to react.

Martin ended up fidgeting for the next hour in bed, hearing the clatter of pots and pans from the kitchen, and the sizzle of what was either bacon or sausage cooking. Apparently Sonya was ready to get the day started.

The boys' laughter kept ringing out in his mind much like how the piercing blare of a fire alarm might echo even after it turned off. He forced the thoughts of the future day where all those innocent students were flashed across the screen to celebrate their lives that had ended too soon. He remembered all of the tears that were shed at the graduation ceremony a few weeks later, an event broadcasted by the local news stations.

Doing this replenished Martin's sense of purpose, and he finally jumped out of bed at six, ready to tackle the unknown challenges that lied ahead.

He dragged himself to the kitchen where Sonya stood over the stove, eggs cooking in a skillet, bacon *and* sausage in another, and the sweet smell of fresh bread oozing from the oven.

"Good morning, Chef Sonya," he said with as much comedic tone he could muster so early in the morning.

She jumped, startled, and turned to Martin with a nervous grin. "I couldn't really sleep, so figured we'd have a feast before setting out for the day."

Martin admired the gluttonous spread of food. "I'd say I'm sorry, but I'm not. This looks fantastic."

"Thank you," Sonya said quietly, her innocent smirk returning. "How did you sleep?"

"Not much better. Was hard to fall into a good, deep sleep."

He refused to tell her about the dream; she didn't need anything else to worry about.

"I know what you mean. When this is all done, I just wanna come back here and take a long nap."

"That sounds perfect," he said, hoping deep down that they would, in fact, make it back home. He still had a hunch that things would play out differently by having Sonya do the dirty work, but he couldn't gamble his caution away, either.

"Breakfast is ready," Sonya said, turning the dials off on the stove. "Would you like some vodka in your orange juice this morning?"

"More than you know."

Martin helped her set the table and serve the food. They sat down and enjoyed the meal with minimal conversation, the weight of their mission hanging heavily above their heads.

* * *

When they finished eating, they sat at the table staring at each other. Neither of them wanted to make the move to stand up because that would mean it was time to get the day officially started. If Sonya asked to stay home and watch movies all day, forget the simple task of delivering a letter to a high school almost an hour away, Martin would happily agree.

His entire body tensed up and his teeth chattered from time to time throughout breakfast.

This has got to be the most nervous I've ever been, he thought, unable to think of another time where he had felt more sick with anticipation. The thought of death kept jumping into his mind, hard to shake. *No one's dying today, stop worrying.*

The words sounded fake within his own head, and he stood up from the table, anxious to get the trip over with. "Let's head out," he said, mustering a confident voice. "Traffic will be starting to back up soon and we want to make sure we catch it."

Sonya nodded, and stood slowly, keeping her head down to her empty plate. Martin could only assume she felt the same way he did. He debated a final attempt of trying to talk her out of it, but knew she would never give in so late in the game.

"Let's go then," she said softly, passing the dishes to the sink and walking to the front door. "I'm driving, you're keeping watch. That hasn't changed."

They had known that was the plan, but it sounded to Martin that she spoke those words for her own comfort, needing to feel in control of something.

"Let's get this done. Then we can go have a big lunch later to celebrate." He offered a smile, but she didn't return it, grabbing her keys off the rack on the wall, and swinging the front door open.

Martin followed her outside to a perfect morning. Golden rays splashed across the front lawn, while dew from the prior night glistened in its glory. Birds chirped from the trees while Martin took a deep inhale of the pure, fresh morning air. His senses had seemed to strengthen since the coma, but it wasn't all the time. At times he could hear the slightest whisper, or smell a neighbor's cooking from down the block, while at other times food tasted bland, no matter how much seasoning he dumped on it. Today was a perfect day, and he wanted to enjoy every passing second of it.

Sonya was already in the car and had turned on the engine, giving it a minute to warm up. Martin broke out of his trance and joined her. *At what point does the past realize we're trying to change it?*

He had expected some sort of resistance to start the day, but was pleased to find nothing had happened yet.

"Are we ready?" Sonya asked, putting a shaky hand on the gear.

Martin noticed and grabbed it, squeezing it. "If you need a minute, just say so."

Sonya exhaled heavily. "I think I'm okay. I don't even know why I'm nervous. I think I just have your car accident in the back of my mind."

"That's why we're driving slow and being cautious. I wasn't ready last time. I had absolutely no awareness of my surroundings. Stay alert and everything will be fine."

She nodded her head rapidly and pulled the car onto the street. "I trust you. Let's go save some lives."

She drove quickly through the neighborhood, the freeway just minutes away.

40

Chapter 39

Sonya's knuckles turned white from her death-like grip on the steering wheel. Martin considered telling her to loosen up, but decided to let her cope with the stress as she saw fit. He had bigger issues to worry about, anyway.

The tension heightened whenever a car passed them by on the freeway. They were still a few minutes from where the traffic would logjam, so other drivers zoomed by them at 70 miles per hour compared to their leisurely 50.

Sonya drove in the far right lane and kept an eye glued on her driver's side mirror when a new car approached. Martin leaned over the center console each time for a clear look into the mirror, and studied the car, tracking its trajectory to make sure it wasn't headed for their back bumper.

When the car passed, his focus would then shift to the car's tires, watching them for any sudden movement that might cause the car to swerve into their lane.

These fifteen minutes of action felt like two hours of constant paranoia, and when they reached the outskirts of downtown, they both felt at ease at the sight of a sea of red brake lights. Cars honked and music blared as they joined the gathering of drivers on their way to start the work week.

Denver looked so young, Martin observed. There were less buildings than in 2018, less surroundings where the city would eventually grow, and Martin felt a tugging in his soul that he dismissed as nostalgia.

I'm downtown right now, he thought, recalling that he would've already been at work. He had worked on the 16th Street Mall as an underground parking garage attendant, and he needed to be there at four in the morning to welcome the early starters.

It's funny how irrelevant a job seems when you look back to it after many years had passed. Martin remembered busting his ass to receive a measly 50 dollar bonus each month.

Young and dumb, he thought. *And here you are. Back in the same year doing a mission that will probably get you and your lady killed. Why couldn't you have just gone to the beach with her like she wanted?*

He glanced over and saw Sonya's grip hadn't yet loosened on the steering wheel, but she otherwise appeared to have her emotions in check as she drove with a relaxed expression.

"Here we are," she said as the car came to a near stop to join the unofficial parade making its way through the city.

"All right," Martin said. "Let's keep our eyes open and alert. There could still be something that happens out of the blue."

Sonya nodded and let the car inch forward every few seconds.

Martin kept his stare out the windshield, observing every surrounding car and possible obstacle that could fall in their way. There was a pickup truck ten cars ahead with a refrigerator and various junk overflowing the cargo bed; he half expected something to spill out and block the road. To their left, a young mother in a rusty Chevy brushed makeup on her face in her rear-view mirror while a one-year-old baby screamed hysterically in the backseat.

With his bearings and surroundings covered, Martin leaned back in his seat and kept his vision wide, waiting for what the world would throw their way.

Five minutes passed with no activity, only moving one mile, and Martin wondered why it had moved slower than normal. He found his answer after another five minutes passed when they drove by the scene of a nasty accident.

The front half of an SUV was smashed flat like a soda can. The vehicle was flipped onto its roof in the middle of a pool of shattered glass and freckles of blood splayed across the road. The accident appeared near the end of its clean up phase, as there wasn't another car in sight. Police cars blocked off the shoulder and left lane, directing traffic into the right two lanes and creating a bottleneck of vehicles.

"Oh my God! Oh my God! Oh my God!" Sonya screamed and hyperventilated, squirming behind the wheel. "Martin, is this a sign?"

"No, it's not a sign. It's just an accident," he said, trying to lie to himself as well. *No shit, it's a sign. It's either a sign of what will happen or a warning of what* could *happen.* Martin didn't care for the particulars of the matter and his heart rate spiked. "It's okay. Just slow down a little, we're still doing great on time."

Sonya fell silent and kept her eyes glued to the cars ahead of her. She wouldn't break that stare if he told her Elvis Presley was in the back seat.

"Just keep going steady, nothing to worry about here," Martin said in his best soothing voice. The words must have bounced off her ears as she made no acknowledgement.

They continued in silence, and on high alert, through downtown.

* * *

When they reached the end of the traffic jam, and the road opened up to higher driving speeds, they both let out a long exhale. The sight of the pulverized car had created a palpable tension that neither of them wanted to discuss.

"We made it through that portion of the trip unscathed," Martin said cheerily. He had expected something to happen during the traffic jam – they were sitting ducks, after all. But nothing happened, and that fact made Martin even more uneasy. The unpredictability of the past drove him near insanity.

"What now?" Sonya asked.

"Now, we're only ten minutes away if we drive at full speed. I'll let you decide how you're feeling if you'd like to do that or not."

"I'll go exactly the speed limit," she said sternly, never breaking her concentration from the road. "Just tell me when to exit because I don't remember. My brain can't really focus right now on anything else besides driving this car."

"That's fine, that's all you need to worry about. We're almost there." Martin wanted to put a hand on her leg, but felt the radiating tension from her and decided to not distract her.

She accelerated the car to a steady 55 miles per hour, and they headed toward the Littleton exit, eight miles away.

* * *

Littleton had much less traffic clogging its roads when they arrived. The town was primarily residential and still growing into the bustling suburb Martin knew it as in 2018. Sonya drove steadily through the city, never going above the speed limit, keeping a constant eye on the rear-view mirror.

"I think we're gonna make it without any issues," Sonya said in a tone Martin couldn't tell was scared or happy. "Does that seem right to you?"

"It ain't over 'til it's over," Martin replied, using a quote his father had often told him, borrowed from some baseball player from his era.

"What's that supposed to mean?" Sonya questioned, focus unaffected.

"It means to not get excited until we actually arrive. I'm glad we made it this far, but there's still five more minutes to the school."

"Right," she said.

She continued to guide them through Littleton with Martin's directions. When they finally turned onto the block where the school became visible,

Martin noticed Sonya jolt in her seat.

"There it is! There it is!" she cried, like a little kid driving by a favorite amusement park.

Her sudden movement sent a wave of terror through Martin, and he giggled to release the tension.

"Where do I go? Where should I park?" He could hear the anticipation in her voice.

"Settle down, you need to stay focused. Go around the school and you'll see the main entrance. It has a parking lot right next to it."

"Sorry, I'm just super nervous right now. I can't even feel my legs. That feeling started in my stomach and spread."

"It's okay to be nervous. Nerves keep you alert."

Martin found himself calmer than he expected as Sonya drove the car around the school's massive campus, passing by the football, baseball, and soccer fields kept in pristine condition.

"This school clearly has money to spend," Sonya commented. "I wonder what the teachers get paid down here."

"Not enough to be killed," Martin said flatly, wanting to bring her back to reality. Her daydreams would sometimes take her on a tangent, and right now was not the time for such small talk.

Sonya pulled the car into its final destination where only two other cars filled the lot.

Perfect, Martin thought. *Less chance of someone remembering Sonya.*

Martin still felt a tingling doubt in his mind, dreading how this would all play out. Would the past make sure the letter got accidentally bumped into the trash can, hence explaining why they had encountered no resistance? Would the principal read the letter and dismiss it as a silly prank? This was, after all, in a time before school shootings were a part of everyday life. There wasn't any stock in such a wild threat. Would the school take the threat seriously and notify the authorities? What would the authorities do with a threat still three years away?

Probably laugh their asses off and toss the letter.

There were too many external factors for Martin's liking, but he had no choice. Getting too close to Dylan nearly cost him his life, and he'd have to finish this mission from the sidelines, cheering on his courageous girlfriend.

Sonya found a spot she liked and parked the car so it faced the school's main entrance. She killed the engine and rested her head on the steering wheel, taking deep breaths.

Martin reached a hand over and rubbed it down her back. "It's going to be okay. We've come this far. This is the easy part now."

Sonya nodded, her hair jiggling and hanging over her buried face. "Let's get it over with."

She looked up to him with terror-filled eyes, the color having rushed from her face. "I love you," Martin said. "Remember the plan for inside the school?"

"Yes. Walk in, go into the office, and tell them I have a letter for the principal. And make sure I see them deliver it to his desk."

"Perfect. Quick and easy."

Sonya nodded. "Letter?"

Martin pulled it out of the glove compartment and slid it into her trembling hand.

"Okay. Here goes nothing," Sonya said, and pushed open her door.

Martin watched as she walked confidently up to the school, not a shred of hesitation in her steps. She paused a moment when she reached the entrance, as if studying the door, then pulled it open and vanished inside.

* * *

The next two minutes felt like an eternity. The whole process should've taken maybe thirty seconds, in reality, but Martin gave her some cushion for any external factors. Maybe the receptionist wasn't at the desk. Maybe the principal was there and had struck up small talk with Sonya. Maybe Eric and Dylan were waiting with their guns and attacked everyone in the office.

Martin doubted the latter, but anything was possible, he supposed. The clock read as 9:27 when Sonya had stepped out of the car. If she wasn't back by 9:32, he would go inside and see what the hold up was.

He sat on the edge of his seat, leaning forward on the dashboard and never taking his eyes off the school's front doors. When he saw the door swing open it would signal success, or at least verify that nothing had gone fatally wrong. The clock crawled, teasing him: 9:29.

Martin drummed the dashboard with nervous fingers. *It's a simple letter drop off. Should be done by now.*

9:30.

Relax, knowing Sonya, she's probably exploring the school now, in shock of what a deep budget can do. If anything, she's probably asking for a transfer to teach here. Our next stop will be looking around the neighborhood for homes for sale. Maybe we can be neighbors with the Klebolds.

Martin shook his head. Sonya would be the one to strike up a conversation with the principal and probe about possible employment. She certainly had the charm and good looks to garner a middle-aged man's attention. Maybe she was already signing the contract to start teaching in the fall.

He chuckled under his breath and pushed open the car door.

9:31.

One more minute, and you're going in. Yessir, you can take that to the bank. Go in there ready to lay a smack down on anyone trying to hold Sonya host-

The door swung open and Sonya reappeared from its shadows, walking at the same pace she had entered. She kept her head down and gradually increased her pace as she got closer to the car. When she was thirty feet away she was practically jogging.

"Let's go! Let's go!" she squealed excitedly. "I did it! It's done!"

She dropped into the driver's seat, rocking the car, and fired up the engine with one fluid motion. "It was so easy!" She panted for breath, likely from the release of tension that had built up over the last hour.

"What took so long?" Martin asked.

"Nothing. There was no one there in the office. It was super quiet. I waited a couple minutes to see if anyone was going to show up, and when they didn't I went back to the principal's office—his door was open—and left the letter on his desk. Front and center where he won't miss it."

"That's perfect!" Martin cried, still hesitant to get too excited, knowing the past wouldn't let this slip by so easily.

"I know. It was like the perfect storm of events. Perfect timing for everything. I'm so excited!"

Sonya drove like normal again, throwing caution to the wind as she zigzagged through town in search of the freeway. "I can't believe how easy that whole trip was. It's like the past *wanted* us to deliver that letter."

"Right. Seems like it was the first easy thing the past has let me do."

"Let *me* do," she corrected him.

"Of course."

Martin and Sonya, two vigilantes traveling through time and saving the world one catastrophe at a time. I'm the brains, she's the muscle.

It would make for a silly movie, but maybe it could be their reality. He'd need to wait to find out to see if all this trouble was worth it. They wouldn't know until 1999 to see if the shooting had occurred or not, and still, it would actually be 2018 when he got the chance to look it up.

Martin leaned back in his seat, a sense of ease settling for the first time in many days. He gazed out the window, thinking of the next ten weeks ahead until his attempt to save his daughter.

41

Chapter 40

Martin and Sonya spent the next two weeks trying to return to normalcy. With her off for the summer, and Martin's secret out of the bag, they spent every waking moment together. Martin had a follow-up appointment where the doctor told him he was progressing as expected in his mental recovery.

His memory gradually returned, but he still had momentary lapses where he "spaced out" as the doctor explained, something that would likely stay with him forever. Dr. Lincoln suggested he do mental exercises to counter the forgetfulness, so Sonya bought him a stack of crossword puzzles, word searches, and new books to read for the summer.

"No TV until you've spent two hours in one of those books," she had told him.

Martin was never one for reading or any "mindless" activities, as he believed crossword puzzles were, but he also knew if he didn't take his rehabilitation seriously, he'd punch a quick ticket to the senior home with Alzheimer's in a few years.

I wonder if I'll still be affected when I return to 2018. Like when you die in a dream, it doesn't mean you die in real life. Time heals everything, right?

Time did heal Sonya's libido; she tried to jump his bones nearly every night. Martin typically agreed, but other nights he was too fatigued. Migraines struck some days, leaving him curled up on the couch with his hands grasping his head, trying to pull the pain out of his skull.

The only headaches he had previously were after nights of heavy drinking. Those held no comparison to the railroad stake drilled into his brain from the migraines. The doctor prescribed painkillers in anticipation of this, but they only dulled the pain to an uncomfortable throb.

These days were the worst. He couldn't go outside until nighttime, couldn't watch TV, couldn't *focus* on anything. Sonya cared for him, making sure he stayed hydrated and took as many naps as possible to get through the day.

In sickness and in health, Martin thought as Sonya felt more like his wife every passing day. Even on the worst of days, her grace sent a fluttering throughout his body, and he knew everything would work out for the best.

Since they had missed their planned trip, Sonya proposed a getaway to the mountains. She had a friend with a cabin willing to give them the place for a week. Martin gratefully accepted the invitation, needing a change of scenery after so much time trapped in the living room.

The day they left was a bad migraine day for Martin, so Sonya forced him to take a sleeping pill while she drove the two and a half hours to Snowmass Village. Martin resisted at first, but the urge to bang his head against the wall was the deciding factor in his agreement.

"I drove us across town with our lives on the line. I think I can handle a simple trip to the mountains," Sonya said as he swallowed the pills.

"I know. I'm sorry. I just hate feeling so helpless. You've done so much – everything for me. I just want to return the favor."

"It's only because I love you," she said with a grin. "And don't worry, you'll be returning the favor when you're back to your complete self. You're gonna cook me dinner and rub my feet every night for a month."

"I look forward to it."

Martin reclined his seat and dozed as Sonya drove out of the city.

* * *

Martin woke to the sound of crunching gravel beneath the tires as they pulled into a steep, uphill driveway. Rocks bigger than him lined the driveway, and tall trees swayed gently in the breeze. The cabin waited at the top of the hill, its faded exterior revealing that it had gone through plenty of seasons in the Rocky Mountains. The white garage door slid open, revealing two open spaces and a collection of cleaning supplies on a lone shelf.

"I've never had a garage in my life," Sonya commented. "Not growing up, not now. Let's see what the big fuss is." She parked the car with a childish grin.

"You're funny," Martin said, rubbing the sleep out of his eyes. His migraine had reduced to a minor throb, much more manageable to get through the day. "The only garage I ever had was used for storage when I was a kid, so I've never really parked in one either."

They parked and Sonya jumped out of the car, stretching after the long drive. Martin felt refreshed and ready to explore his new home for the next week.

"Leave the bags, let's go look around," Sonya said, her voice echoing in the garage.

Martin shuffled to the door he presumed led inside, and watched as Sonya jiggled the key before pushing it open. The exterior may have looked rundown, but the interior was immaculate and likely remodeled within the last few years. Hardwood floors gleamed, Southwestern art decorated the walls as they walked down a short hallway into the kitchen where granite counter tops and sparkling appliances awaited. The kitchen sink overlooked the mountains with a breathtaking view. The kitchen connected to the living room where an L-shaped couch was tucked into the corner, a throw rug in the center of the floor, and a TV above an idle fireplace.

"This is much bigger than it looks from the outside," Martin commented, noticing Sonya's bulging eyes as she studied every nook and cranny of the cabin.

"Yeah," she said thoughtlessly. "It has a basement. That's where the master bedroom is."

Martin remained in the kitchen while Sonya studied a rack of VHS movies in the living room. He looked out the window to the green mountains, admiring nature's beauty. The sight brought back that tug, tempting him to stay in 1996 and continue living his life without a concern of returning to 2018. He could even earn enough money to buy a place like this, and they could live happily ever after, watching the sun rise over the horizon every morning.

"I'm gonna go check out the basement," he said as Sonya made her way to the kitchen.

"Okay, I'll be right down. I wanna see what all's in this kitchen. We may need to run into town and get some groceries, but she told me there should be enough in the pantry for us."

Martin crossed into the living room where a side door opened to a staircase. The wooden steps creaked and groaned underneath his feet as they led him to the first carpeted area of the house.

The entire basement was the master bedroom. A king-sized bed was centered between two nightstands, facing the wall where a TV stood on top of a shelving unit with more VHS movies. The master bathroom was separated by a curtain serving as a door. Martin hurried across the room in the opposite direction, though, noticing a door that led outside to a deck.

He stepped onto the deck to find another amazing mountain view, this one facing west where they could watch the sunset. A hot tub was covered, but he could hear the water bubbling beneath the cover's surface. *Who is this friend you have, Sonya?*

"A good friend to keep around," a voice said from behind, causing Martin to jump. He automatically knew the voice and goosebumps immediately covered his flesh.

He turned to find Chris standing in the doorway. The old man leaned against the door jam with his arms crossed and that familiar evil grin.

"Are we going for a dip, Marty?" he asked in a menacing voice.

"Why are you here, Chris? You said you weren't coming back. Is the future too boring?"

As much as the old man terrified Martin, he still felt the confidence to be stern with him.

"Yes, yes, I know I said I was never coming back, but it sounds like you're in more desperate need than I anticipated."

"If you can jump through time, shouldn't you have already known you were going to need to come back?"

"I knew it was possible, but you could've always changed your mind. It's like how God knows what you're going to do before you do it, but he still gives you the free will to decide for yourself."

"Is this about Columbine? Are you upset I'm trying to stop it?"

"No, that is something we can discuss later, when you return. I love your ambition. I'm here because you've decided to stay here in the past and live out life like 2018 doesn't exist."

Martin watched Chris cautiously, not sure if he should respond.

"You can't stay here, Martin." Chris spoke like a scolding parent. "If you stay, then I don't get my payment. Did you forget about our agreement?"

"Of course not; I owe you my emotions."

Chris grinned, his face softening. "Precisely. I can't take that from you if you stay here. You have to return to your present time to settle your debts. If you don't, well, let's just say it's in your best interest to pay up."

The old man's eyebrows elevated above his evil smirk, a maniac expression that would haunt Martin forever. Chris wasn't bluffing.

"I'll return to 2018 after I save my daughter," Martin said, defeated. "I want to bring Sonya with me. How does this all affect her?"

"Yes, of course," Chris said, clapping his hands together in celebration. "It works like anything else. As long as she's making contact with you when you take the pill, she'll come with you."

"But how is it for her? Does she fall asleep with me? Does she get the glowing skin?"

"Look at you with all of your knowledge. I'm very proud of you, Marty. I honestly expected you to drink for six months, but you've made an honest man out of yourself."

"Answer my questions," Martin demanded, not giving a shit what the old man thought about his life choices.

"She'll be travelling through time as property—that's just how it works for anything or anyone who doesn't take the pill.

"So her body doesn't stay asleep here?"

"Nope. She gets a free ride with you. Like a buddy pass." Chris giggled at Martin. "But why would you want to bring her with you when you're gonna become an emotional dud? Surely she'll want nothing to do with you once you can't even fake a laugh."

"Leave," Martin barked, ready to choke the bastard. "Get out of here. Go back to wherever you came from."

Chris smirked, still leaning on the doorway. "Marty, my friend. It's a good thing we're friends, isn't it? We can have these heated discussions without worrying about breaking our bond. We go together like a fly and a frog's tongue." Chris stood stiffly, and Martin mirrored the action, noticing he had slouched. "I'll leave you alone. I just wanted to stop by and make sure you were still coming home. It's your first time working with me, so I thought I'd give you a warning. Be back in 2018 by October 1, or else I'll come looking for you."

Chris pointed at Martin with a skeletal finger, swirling it in a circular slow motion.

"Ta-ta for now. Give Sonya my best."

Chris pivoted and disappeared into the master bedroom. By the time Martin rushed in, he was already gone.

"Everything okay down there?" Sonya shouted from the top of the stairs.

"Yes!" Martin yelled back, pushing his fear away. "Just admiring the basement. There's a hot tub!"

His voice sounded normal to himself, and he hoped it projected that way.

"I'll be right down. Didn't bring a swimsuit – guess we'll have to get in naked."

Martin hadn't been naked in a hot tub with a woman since college. The thought started to excite him, but his mind remained stuck on Chris. He hated how easily the old man could show up and find him in the most intimate of places. He stared into the vast woods of the mountains, wondering where the secret eyes were that followed his every move.

Martin crossed the room to the foot of the stairs. "Can you bring me a glass of whiskey when you come down, please?"

"Coming right up!" she responded, her voice echoing down the stairwell.

Just have a drink and relax. You're in a beautiful cabin with your girlfriend. Make love to her in the hot tub like you were 20 again. Don't worry about that old fuck.

Martin repeated these thoughts on a loop, but no matter how hard he tried, he couldn't shake the image of that maniacal grin, secretive voice, and frosty white hair. He just wanted to go home and forget he had ever traveled back in time. 22 years had already passed without Izzy, so he'd have 20 more miserable years left to live should he return now, and could trim a few off with more cigarettes and whiskey.

He could explain to Sonya his decision, apologize for dragging her this far into his mess, and pop the pill before she could realize what was happening. Tears streamed down his face as he listened to his own doubtful thoughts.

"Suck it up," he said to himself. "You've come this far."

He pictured Izzy walking home from school, her ponytail swinging side to side, her smile showing both flashes of her youth and her pending womanhood.

I promise I'll save you.

42

Chapter 41

The scorching heat of July gave way to an even hotter August. Martin continued his mental rehabilitation, and found a helpful recovery in reading, helping him regain vocabulary skills. He gave *The Notebook* a try after hearing Sonya rave about it so much, and found he enjoyed the story, although he'd never admit it to a group of strangers.

"I've been thinking about the future," Sonya said one night at dinner. "What happens here? If I go away, will there be people wondering where I am? Or does my life just vanish?"

"Time just sort of stops," he said, not having a clue how it actually worked traveling *forward* in time.

"What happens if I die in the future?" she asked.

"Of course you're gonna die in the future. We all do." Martin offered a smile, but Sonya was in no mood for jokes.

"I'm being serious, Martin. If my life is in danger like yours is here, I just want to know what happens."

"You won't be in any danger. I promise." He reached across the table and embraced her hand, rubbing slow circles around her palm with his thumb. "When we arrive, I'll fill you in on everything you'll have missed. I could go over the major events, but it'll be helpful to have Google."

"Google?"

"Sorry. It's a website where you look up anything you ever wanted. It's like Yahoo, but a million times better."

Sonya nodded, grasping the simplest idea of the future internet juggernaut.

"You know," Martin said. "I was considering staying in 1996 with you. Just leaving my life behind in the future and seeing where it goes from here. I wanted you to know that you aren't the only one who made a difficult decision. I thought long and hard about it, but decided it's not best for me to stay in a world where I already exist. That alone is a high risk. And then there's Izzy. If I stay in 1996 and save her, that leaves her with two fathers and a world of confusion. I'd still have to watch her life from afar, and that's not what I want to do. I want to be *in* her life."

Sonya nodded. "I love you," she said. "That's the only reason I'm going with you. I'm terrified. Don't you know how scary this is?"

"Of course I do. I had to do it by myself coming here. I'm just glad I have someone to share the experience with now."

"I just want you to be happy. What happened to your daughter is disgusting. I couldn't imagine living another day if something like that happened to me. You deserve to keep her safe and return to a normal life with her."

"You're an amazing woman," he said. "I've never known anyone with such a big heart. I only hope I can make it up to you, and make your life everything you want it to be in the future."

"I know you will. I wouldn't take this leap if I didn't believe so. I've been having some weird dreams."

"What about?"

"This old man. He never says his name when I ask; he only smiles. But it's not a friendly smile; it's pure evil."

Martin nodded. He wouldn't let her know the truth about the man she had visions of. If she knew he was waiting for them in the future, she might reconsider going.

Oh, that old man? He's only the keeper of time, and sure, he's probably from hell and has dinner with Hitler every night, but he's a nice guy, don't you think?

Hopefully Chris wouldn't take his emotions immediately upon arrival in 2018. He wanted to enjoy at least a day with Sonya before his soul turned numb.

How you gonna explain that one to her, big guy? Thank her for leaving her life behind to join an old, emotionless postal worker in 2018? That should go over beautifully.

Martin knew he should've been upfront about what lay ahead, but he couldn't afford to let her change her mind. *She'll be fine. Everything can be explained. Just get her to 2018 and take it from there.*

"I want to talk about next month," Martin said. "Saving Izzy. I want your help. I know I had told you I needed to do this alone, but I've thought it over and feel it would be best to have another set of eyes. It's a small house, but I can only be in one area at once. What if I'm covering the front and she slips out the back? Or vice versa? I just want to have all my bases covered."

Martin caught himself speaking abnormally fast. *Nervous much? Did it finally occur to you that the big day is only four weeks away now? Time sure flies when you're comatose and forgetful.*

"I'm happy to help however you need me," she responded calmly. "What did you have in mind?"

"I haven't thought that far ahead, honestly, but perhaps I'll have you stakeout the area ahead of time. All we know is that Izzy goes missing at some point in the middle of night. Lela confirmed she checked on Izzy before going to sleep, and that was usually around ten; Izzy's bedtime was nine. So, I just want some eyes on the house in the hours leading up to then. It's too risky for me to hang out on the block, even from a distance. Maybe you can park a couple houses down and watch things. I really want to make sure no one is scoping the area ahead of time."

"And what will you be doing?"

"Probably pacing circles and trying to not puke my guts out. I'm going to show up when the sun goes down around eight. I need the darkness to blend in. I'll be dressed in all black and will hide in the shadows."

"Who knew you were such a ninja." Sonya made her attempt at humor, but now Martin was the one in no mood for jokes. "So what's your plan for Izzy? What will you do once she's safe?"

Martin nodded his head slowly, like a game show contestant who knew the answer for the big cash prize.

"Then we leave," he said flatly. He could tell Sonya was expecting a more elaborate response. "That's all there is to do. I can't risk her seeing me. All I can do is get back to 2018 as soon as possible and see how she is."

"And how will you go about finding her? Your life can completely change by her staying with you, and a lot can happen in 22 years."

"I'll be able to find her. You can find anyone in 2018 with the click of a mouse."

"I'll take your word. I just thought you'd have a better plan in place."

"I wish I did, too, but I just don't know how any of this works—travelling back into my present time, that is. Besides, I really do work at the post office in 2018 and can run an address search when I get back. I'm actually on my way to work when we return, so I'll probably go in and see what I can find before I quit my job."

"Why would you quit?" she asked like a disappointed mother. Martin waved two gentle hands at her to relax.

"I'm not going to need a job when we get back. I've done some investing and should have a small fortune waiting for me in 2018."

Martin had made a couple of trips to a small investment firm downtown and bought stocks he knew would grow by 2018. The stock broker had cautioned him against loading up on so much technology in his portfolio, but Martin insisted he knew what he was doing.

"We will be taken care of," Martin said. "Where do you want to live when we get back? Housing is through the roof, but we'll have enough money to live anywhere."

The words felt foreign leaving his lips. He never thought he'd get to say such a thing.

"I'd like to live in my same house," she said, distant as if her mind were already floating away to the future.

"I think we can manage that," Martin responded with a smirk.

He took joy in hearing Sonya speak about the future. While he knew she wouldn't back out this late, he wanted her to enter the journey with no hesitations. The more they spoke about the future, the more realistic it felt, even for Martin. His life in 2018 really did feel like 22 years ago instead of five months—or ten minutes.

He knew how the world was in 2018, that wouldn't change. But *his* life could wind up completely different. If Izzy was okay, there was a chance him and Lela would still be married. How was he supposed to bring the new love of his life home to meet his wife and daughter? If he tried to explain what really happened, Lela would call the mental asylum.

A lot can happen in 22 years. I just hope it's all for the best.

43

Chapter 42

School was back in session during the final week of August, and Sonya had returned two weeks prior to prepare for the upcoming year.

"I guess I know how my students feel during that final week of school now," she had said in regards to her pending departure from 1996. "It's hard to focus on anything. How are you holding up? We're just a few days away from the moment of truth, can you believe it?"

Believe it he could. A lot more had happened than he had budgeted for on this journey: falling in love and a coma at the top of the list. More importantly, Martin discovered a life as a new man where drinking was only done in celebration, not as a major part of his daily diet. His coma recovery also led him to discover that he enjoyed reading books, something he had never taken the time to do in his past life. It was hard to focus on such a task while in a constant state of inebriation.

He also reaffirmed something he had long believed: *Fuck crossword puzzles.*

The blank white squares on those bastards teased Martin every time he sat down to try and complete one. His mind simply didn't function in a way that could guess words from a vague clue.

Regardless of how things played out with Izzy in a couple of weeks, Martin knew life would be different when he returned to 2018. He'd have no need to work, he'd have Sonya by his side, and have actual hobbies that consisted of things besides passing out drunk in the living room while the TV flashed over his limp body all night.

No more hangovers. The feeling of waking up with a clear mind had been a big catalyst for Martin taking a new appreciation of his life.

All of these thoughts had flooded his mind, submerging from the depths of his psyche every time he glanced at the calendar and saw his date with destiny looming less than two weeks away. He fought to push them aside, dismiss them until they were needed.

This particular night was a Thursday, one more day until the school year's first weekend. Sonya had fallen into the groove of mindlessly telling stories about her students. She had made it clear that she wouldn't get too attached to them, considering she'd never see them again after another week and a half.

They had finished dinner and settled in to their new routine of Sonya doing the dishes while Martin picked up and swept the kitchen before sitting down together to watch the nightly news and sip glasses of tea.

See, this life won't be so bad in 2018. You basically have a wife again.

They would certainly need to pick up some new hobbies, seeing as neither of them would have to worry about going back to a job. He considered getting back into golf, something he hadn't done since before Izzy was born in 1984.

When they had finished their cleaning routine, Martin turned on the TV and adjusted the antennas for the clearest signal on Channel Nine before plopping down on the couch. Sonya joined him with the other part of their nightly routine: two glasses of steaming hot tea.

"I'm so tired," she said. "The first week of school is always the hardest." She swung her legs up on the couch and curled up on Martin's chest.

"It's only a couple weeks, then we're on to our new life together."

The news station played its familiar introductory jingle while graphics for channel nine danced across the screen. The channel's longtime anchorman, James Young, filled the screen with his typical stern expression to complement his strong jawbone and perfectly combed over gray hair.

"Good evening, Denver," he said in a booming voice. "We have tragic news out of Littleton that we want to cut right to."

The camera flashed to a school, and Sonya bolted upright on the couch, practically jumping off the edge.

"That's Columbine!" she shouted, pointing at the TV with a wagging finger. "That's Columbine!"

"A fire broke out today at Littleton's Columbine High School at 2:45, just a half hour before school was to let out for the day," James Young said. The screen showed different images of the high school they had just visited a few weeks earlier, charred and smoking like the bottom of a fire pit. There wasn't a trace of the building left. "Authorities are still looking for the cause of this enormous fire, but what we do know is that it started in the school's cafeteria and spread to the library. Since there was no one in the cafeteria at the time, it's unknown how long the fire had been burning before the alarms were set off, but by that time it was too late."

James Young choked up and fought for his next words.

"The flames completely engulfed the library, collapsing the second floor onto the first floor. So far, thirty six bodies have been discovered in the rubble in that section alone, with the count increasing by the hour. The fire spread from the library and took the rest of the school with it. Columbine High School is no more."

The words echoed as Martin felt a sharp pang in his stomach.

This is it. This is why you had no resistance that day. The past is toying with you now.

"Martin," Sonya said nervously. "Please tell me this was supposed to happen. Tell me this is part of history." She stood, gawking at the TV as she spoke to him, unable to break her stare from the gruesome images of charred skeletons and crying mothers. James Young's voice had all but drowned into background noise.

"It's not," Martin said through a clenched jaw. "This never happened."

"Well what are we supposed to do?" she demanded. "This is our fault, isn't it?"

She paced around the coffee table and sipped her tea with a trembling hand.

Martin raised his hand for her to calm down, feeling stuck to the couch. "I know this looks bad."

"Looks bad?" Sonya snapped. "I've never even heard of Columbine High School until you got here with your story from the future. Then I'm thrust into the school to leave a letter for the principal, and now the school is gone. It's a pile of fucking ashes, Martin!"

"I didn't know this would happen," Martin said, remaining calm. He had to. If he showed his true emotions that were running frantically around in a panic, Sonya might actually lose her mind. "This must be how the past pushed back. I'll bet the principal read that letter today, finally. And this is what happened. I'd bet money that the principal didn't survive."

"How do you know this?" Sonya asked. She was clearly upset, but didn't seem to be angry-more of a mixture of terror and concern, infused with some guilt. "There have been a lot of questions I've refrained from asking, mainly because I'm not sure I *want* to know the answers. But now I need some answers. How do you know how this all works?"

Sonya crossed her arms while she stared at Martin. He still couldn't move from the couch, the feeling in his legs having vanished.

"You know the dream you had about the old man?" he asked.

She nodded her head in quick jerky motions.

"Well," Martin continued. "I know that old man."

Sonya stood frozen, the only movement coming from her lips, which furled in disgust.

"You mean I've been having nightmares about this guy and you knew about him the whole time?" she asked.

"I'm sorry," Martin said. "I didn't want you to be afraid."

"Tell me who he is and what he as to do with all of this."

"I'll tell you what I know. His name is Chris, and he's the reason I can travel through time. He calls himself the keeper of time, but I think he's a demon – or maybe an angel – I'm not really sure. He's never done

247

or said anything evil, but I just get bad vibes. I met him right here in Larkwood in 2018 when he opened an antique store. I went in with my mom one day to look around and he lured me back to the store. When I went back a second time, alone, he took me into his back office where he has this lab of potions and powders, and that's where he makes these pills. He's visited me three times since coming to 1996, and he has all of the information. He's the one who warned me to never cross paths with my past self."

"But none of that explains about the past pushing back," Sonya barked. She had not calmed down one bit during his explanation.

"I'm pretty sure Chris led me to meet this other guy. Remember the liquor store that burned down a few months ago?"

Sonya nodded.

"The owner was also from the future. It's like Chris knew I would go into the liquor store and meet this owner. The owner was scared of me at first, but then explained many of the rules of living in the past."

"I used to go to that liquor store. You're telling me that sweet Asian man was from the future?" Sonya's words dripped with skepticism.

"Yes, and I watched him get murdered and the store get burned down. There are these people called Road Runners who travel through time and kill other time travelers. I'm still not clear what exactly their angle is, but they killed him and burned down the store."

Sonya shook her head, arms still crossed. "I don't know what to believe any more. I think I need a moment alone to think things over. This all sounded like a big joke and I've gone along with it. It's all become a bit more believable, and now this. All of these students dead and buried under the rubble of their own school. I can't even stomach the thought."

Martin pushed with all of his mental might and stood from the couch on wobbly legs. He jab stepped toward Sonya and extended his arms out for her, grabbing her around each arm.

"Sonya, please. I know this is crazy. I didn't want this any more than you, but this is what's happening now. All we can do is learn from it and be prepared for the next event."

"If you think I'm going anywhere near your past right now, you're out of your mind. I'd love to help you with your daughter, but I don't wanna see a worse outcome like this." She pointed at the TV as a lone tear streamed down her face.

"Sonya, let's relax and discuss this."

"I don't want to discuss anything!" she howled. "I don't want to risk my life. I don't want to risk others' lives. And I don't want to go to the future!"

Leave before you say anything that will permanently ruin your relationship.

Martin nodded and shuffled around Sonya, his legs stronger as he strode toward the front door.

"Where are you going?" she demanded.

"I think we both need a moment to cool off. I'm going on a walk."

"You shouldn't do that. You could forget your way home."

"I'll be fine. Just take a moment to calm down. I don't want to fight with you."

He left without another word and closed the door gently to not give any signal of anger. He wasn't angry, but rather anxious, and as he mindlessly walked through the neighborhood. One thought remained stuck to the front of his mind like a thumbtack on a corkboard: this is the past pushing back.

It had to be. He and Sonya had never fought. Not once. Now all the sudden she erupted into a ball of rage. Granted, she had every right to be upset, but to the point of screaming and cursing at him?

He tried to play down the thought, listing plenty of reasons why she could have snapped: her upcoming trip to the future, leaving her life behind forever, not knowing how life would be in 2018, and the start of the school year. Combine all of these factors with a spark like the Columbine news and you get one distraught girlfriend.

But Martin knew better. Sonya had a knack for keeping her emotions in check, something he had fallen in love with. This behavior wasn't like her at all. While she may have been stressed out, she still wouldn't act out in such an outrageous manner.

Be cautious. You've thought this from the start. The past will throw anything your way to throw you off your plan. You have less than two weeks until the big day. Be ready for anything.

Martin reached the end of the neighborhood and turned around to return home. Sonya was right about there being a chance of him getting lost, and that's why he walked a straight line and didn't venture down any new side roads. The sun descended, splashing a fiery glow across the quiet homes and lawns.

Somewhere a couple miles away Martin was watching the news while Izzy brushed her teeth and changed into her pajamas, unaware that their lives would be flipped upside down within a few days.

44

Chapter 43

Sonya's tension had blown over by the morning. When Martin returned from his stroll through the neighborhood, he found Sonya in bed already and decided to leave her alone for the night.

She apologized in the morning and claimed to have no idea where the sudden burst of anger had come from.

"I have so much on my mind; seeing that news about Columbine just set me off. Then knowing you were keeping the secret of that old man from me pissed me off even more. But I understand why you did it. I don't think it's made anything better now that I know who he is. Might have even made it worse, but that's my own fault for making you tell me. I think the less I know the better. Sometimes it's best to just be left in the dark about certain things."

"You're still having dreams about Chris?" Martin asked.

Sonya grimaced. "Please don't call him that, it makes him seem human. And yes, I am. It's not much of a dream, though. He just sort of stands there in the darkness with that evil smile, and stares at me like he's studying me under a microscope."

"That's really strange."

"I know. Do you think it's actually him? Like could he really be in my head and not just part of a dream?"

Martin shrugged. "Anything's possible with that guy."

Sonya shivered at the thought.

"Well, I need to get ready for school. I hope we can put this behind us. I still want to go to 2018."

"I love you," Martin said, and kissed her on the forehead.

* * *

When the calendar flipped to September over the weekend, Martin felt a calm settle over him that he hadn't felt since arriving in 1996, nearly six months ago. The sense of doom he had felt turned numb after several weeks, but now he felt it starting to lift completely. He had grown over the last six months and was ready to save his long lost daughter.

Sonya had highlighted the big day on the calendar with a big red circle, and every time Martin looked in the calendar's direction he felt that circle staring at him like the Devil's eye from a pit of darkness.

He had one more full week and weekend to make it through before encountering the reason for his trip to the past. Martin spent that final week ensuring he had the few things together that he wanted to bring back to 2018. His conscience pleaded to follow Izzy for the week, insisting he would be able to prevent the crisis ahead of time, but he knew better. The past would never make this task that straightforward. Izzy would be right where she always was like any other day: walking home from school by herself, her ponytail swinging with each step she took.

As he had vowed from the onset, much to his disgust, he had kept away from Izzy and his past self for nearly the entirety of his time in 1996. His one close encounter had been plenty to reassure him that he had made the right decision. Next Monday would change everything, as he and Sonya would keep a close watch on his old house from the time school let out.

Considering Izzy went missing in the middle of the night, everyone assumed she had sneaked out of the house. While Martin could stop her as soon as she stepped foot outside, he also needed answers after all these years. There were holes to fill in the timeline of events. He'd follow Izzy until her situation turned dire. Where did she go? Who did she meet with? What was she up to? Martin had a hard time over the past two decades wrapping his head around the fact that his innocent angel of a daughter may have been living a double life. Was this the first time she left the house in the middle of the night?

Find out after this brief commercial break, he thought, and chuckled nervously to himself. Just six months ago—or ten minutes—Martin had a pistol in his mouth after a lifetime full of sorrow and desperation. Now he had hope and a clear mind, and a healthy body that no longer begged to be put out of its misery. He'd never been the type to pray, and often questioned the existence of God, but on this particular Sunday night he thanked God for everything, especially Sonya. Maybe we sometimes get a second chance to right our wrongs, to love the right people. Martin didn't know for sure, but knew he would never take life for granted again.

As he dozed off to sleep later that night, Sonya curled into a ball with her back to him and he felt something he never thought he'd feel again: a full heart.

* * *

Over the course of the week, Martin kept his mind distant from the upcoming task. He didn't want to overthink anything, and preferred to make quick reactions when the time came. Sonya agreed to follow Izzy home from a distance that week, every day after school, just to make sure she wasn't being followed by anyone else. Each day the reports came back negative.

Meanwhile, Martin focused on books and word searches. The book of crossword puzzles had been thrown into a drawer where he'd hopefully never have to see them again. Word searches felt more therapeutic, and reading different stories took his mind to another world altogether. While these helped occupy his mind, he felt a constant, subtle tug on his brain.

Excuse me, Mr. Briar, just a gentle reminder that you'll be changing your life on Monday, his inner voice said, like a doctor's office calling to remind him of an important appointment coming up.

He could no longer deny the growing uncertainty and anxiety forming. Every day closer felt like a pending date with doom.

What if I fail? What if I've gone through all this for nothing? What if there's nothing I can actually do to stop this?

It was a realistic possibility he had managed to ignore this whole time, but with his date with destiny looming around the corner, it seemed a flood of every imaginable possibility had come rushing into his mind. He fully expected a hard fight from the past next Monday night and knew he might come close to encountering death again. But there's always a price to pay for something you longed for, right?

When Friday night arrived and Sonya was home for the weekend, Martin couldn't eat, sit still, nor focus on reading. He felt as useless as ever, wishing he could jump forward to Monday night already and get down to business.

Sonya had done a good job at killing his doubts about the situation and put his mind at ease. He had wanted to hold off on drinking in the days leading up September 9th, but happily enjoyed a glass of whiskey. It was the most relaxed he had felt all week, and he fell into a deep, dreamless sleep.

* * *

On Sunday, September 8th, Martin and Sonya spent the morning cooking a grand breakfast. Sonya had been quiet on Saturday as they wasted the day on the couch watching TV, even ordering pizza for dinner to avoid having to do anything.

This morning, though, Sonya had an extra wave of energy as she stood at the stove, dancing to the radio as she prepared bacon, eggs, and pancakes.

"If this is my last full day in my house. I'm gonna enjoy every second of it," she had told Martin when he entered the kitchen groggy-eyed and confused at the scene of her swaying hips at 7:30 in the morning.

He was glad that she seemed relaxed. Even Martin felt nervous about returning to 2018. Life really was simple in 1996. He could spend the days at work and come home to enjoy dinner and watch the news to see what happened in the world during the day.

Fuck you, Chris, he thought. *I could've had a great life here if you just left me alone.*

The thought of Chris forcing him back to 2018 triggered a tingle of hate for the old man. No one liked being told what to do, and Martin Briar was no exception.

After they devoured breakfast—Martin ate everything he could get his hands on thanks to his appetite returning—Sonya retreated into the bedroom to pack as many valuables as she could into an oversized gym bag.

"I've gotta pack my entire life into this one bag," she said, shaking her head as she stared around her bedroom.

"Don't worry about anything like clothes or stuff like that. We can replenish your wardrobe when we arrive—we'll need to, in fact, unless you want to look like you just arrived from the 90's."

"Oh, yeah? What do they wear in 2018, some sort of spacesuit?" she teased.

"Fashion doesn't change too much, I suppose. Although the young women seem to wear a lot less and show more skin. I wouldn't be opposed to you trying out that style if you really wanted."

He shot promiscuous eyebrows at her with a lewd wink.

"I'm sure you would like that. Tell me, are you the old man who always gets caught looking at the college girls?"

Martin cackled. "Of course not! I never get caught!"

Sonya burst into a cheery laughter and shook her head as she returned to her bag. "I'm not even sure what I should bring with me. I have some family heirlooms, but those would take up maybe ten percent of this bag."

"Then just take that. You don't need anything else. I came here with the clothes on my back and my cell phone in my pocket."

"Your alien phone that doesn't even work," Sonya teased. "I'm still convinced it's just a fancy Gameboy until you can prove otherwise."

They had plenty of discussions about the future's technology, most of which Sonya called "impossible." No, there couldn't be one device that made phone calls, took pictures, kept your schedule, *and* had games to play...and fit in the palm of your hand. She was in for quite the wake-up call in 2018.

"Just take what's important to you. Things can be replaced, but memories can't. So take any pictures, heirlooms, anything like that." Martin returned to a more serious tone. "No need to overthink it."

"Are you ready for tomorrow?" Sonya asked.

"Yeah, I feel good about it."

"No, Martin. I mean it. Are you *ready*?" She stared at him with crossed arms. "Our lives are going to change forever within the next 36 hours. I've come to terms with it; I feel like you haven't."

Martin didn't respond immediately and met her stare. Behind those eyes he had fallen in love with was a scared woman. Not scared in the sense of raw fear that made you want to hide in your room, but scared like a kid leaving for college for the first time. The fear of the unknown could cause even the most mentally strong person to crumble.

"I'm ready. All I've envisioned since I arrived here is bringing Izzy back home. It still doesn't feel real. I keep waiting to be woken up by my alarm, likely in a heavy sweat from all the booze I drank the night before, and realize this was all a dream. But I don't think that's going to happen."

Martin paused to gather more thoughts.

"I know I might die tomorrow. I've never thought about death before, not really, but now I can't help but wonder what it feels like to stop living. I know that's a realistic outcome, just like it was at Columbine. I know

I might lose you. What if the past doesn't let you come with me? This could be our last night together, and if it is, I promise I'll come find you in 2018. You'll be in your 70's, but I don't care. I want to be with you."

Tears welled in Sonya's eyes, and Martin figured she had never considered these possibilities.

"Don't cry. Remember we're in this together," Martin said, wiping the tears from her face. "I love you, and if you want to wait 22 years for me, I'll be there in 2018 looking for you."

He pulled her in and kissed her on the lips.

Sonya sobbed into his embrace, her body shuddering against his as they would spend the rest of the day together in minimal conversation, wanting nothing more than to enjoy each other's presence.

The reality had finally sunk in for both of them. Tomorrow would change them both. Forever.

45

Chapter 44

"Martin, get out of bed!" Lela Briar shouted, her voice brimming with fear. "Hurry!"

Having worked a swing shift the night before, Martin hadn't arrived home until two in the morning, and hadn't joined Lela in bed until just before three.

He shot upright in bed, cloudy-eyed and dazed, and swung his legs mindlessly over the edge. His eyes felt swollen and bloodshot as he swayed to catch his balance.

"MARTIN!" Lela shouted again, and this time he was cognizant to know she was calling from Izzy's room.

Martin always poked his head into his daughter's room when he arrived home in the middle of the night. This particular night he had checked on her and saw a lump in the middle of her bed. The fall nights were starting to get cold, so he figured she was just extra bundled up.

He stepped around his pile of clothes and shuffled around the foot of the bed. Izzy's room was across the hallway where he met Lela, pacing frantically around the bedroom. The sheets were tossed into a mess, the closet door open and appearing to have vomited all of their daughter's clothes.

"What happened in here?" Martin asked.

"Izzy's gone!" Lela shouted, her brown hair in a frazzled mess, sweat glistening on her forehead. "I've been looking for her for the last half hour. I checked the basement, the bathrooms, everything. Even outside, she's gone!"

"I'm sure there's a perfectly good explanation," Martin said. "She wouldn't just up and leave without a word."

"Martin! She's gone. She's not here. It's 6:30 A.M. and she doesn't need to leave for school for another hour." She stared at him with bulging blue eyes, fear swimming behind them like a terrified fish. Her slender body trembled in panic.

"I'm sure she headed over early. She loves school, remember?" Martin tried to stay calm, but hearing his own words made the situation seem less likely. Even students who enjoyed school didn't show up an hour early. Hell, the school wasn't even open yet. "Was her room like this when you got here? Or did you do this?"

"I did this. I thought she was under the blankets—that's how it looked—then I kept pulling them back and she wasn't here. Martin, what do we do?"

Lela's voice transformed from fear into hysterics in a matter of seconds. "This can't be happening to us. These things don't really happen, do they?"

Martin's heart tumbled through his chest and stomach. You always heard about kids going missing on the news, but never consider it a reality – your reality.

"Was she here when you got home?" Lela asked in between sobs.

Martin scrunched his face. "I don't know," he said reluctantly. "I checked, and saw the lump under the blankets, but I didn't come all the way in to know for sure. I never do in the middle of the night."

Lela's body heaved as she buried her face into her shaking hands.

"Relax. We still have places to check, and we can't jump to any conclusions yet." *More lies, keep it up, Marty.* "Call my mom, see if maybe she went there. If not, then call the police. I'm gonna drive down to the school and to some her friends' houses. She's gotta be at one of those places. She doesn't know anyone else."

"Then go, I'll call your mom."

Martin's mother lived two blocks away, and Izzy would often walk there to visit, although never so early in the morning. He hopped into his car and drove slowly through the neighborhood, checking both sides of the street for any sign of Izzy. A light fog settled in, limiting visibility. Martin arrived to Larkwood Middle School to find it abandoned, drove around the grounds for ten minutes in search of any clue, and then stopped by each of Izzy's friend's houses in the neighborhood. With each passing house and no sign of Izzy, Martin felt the pillars that held up his sanity dissolve one by one.

The school pulled at him like a magnetic force, so he returned for one more look.

The green mass that was the school's lawn grew bigger with each house passing in a blur. When Martin reached the school's block, he turned left and drove toward the main entrance, again feeling pulled to it, as if he were watching himself drive the car in an out-of-body experience. As he turned into the school's parking lot he saw Izzy standing at the school's main entrance, only the school wasn't Larkwood Middle School.

It was Columbine High School.

Martin parked and jumped out of the car in a swift motion, sprinting for his daughter. She stood still, facing his direction, with her head down. Izzy wore pajamas, a matching set with Ariel and Flounder from *Little Mermaid* spotted all around.

"Hi, Daddy," she said, looking up. "It's okay, Daddy. I'm okay."

Tears rolled down her soft face as Martin embraced her. She remained stiff in his grip. Martin squeezed, but felt no life in the girl. She had no scent, no warmth, but it was her; there was no denying her green eyes or her sweet voice.

"Daddy, go home. You can't save me. Even if you did, they will still take me. Here." She looked back to Columbine.

Martin took a step back. Was Izzy implying that if she lived she would've been killed in the Columbine attacks? How would Izzy have gone to Columbine? They were nowhere near the level of income to even consider moving to Littleton. A lot could change in a three-year span, and maybe the Briar family continued in an alternate universe where Izzy never went missing and they moved across town to where she would meet her eventual doom at her new school. But Martin thought it to be a long shot.

"Izzy," he said through a swollen throat. "What happened?"

"It was an accident, Daddy."

"What accident?" Martin squatted to meet Izzy's eyes.

Izzy sobbed, yet remained motionless as she stood in her pajamas.

"It was an accident. Please don't be mad, Daddy. I love you."

Izzy turned and started to walk toward the school.

"Izzy!" Martin shouted, his legs frozen. "IZZY!"

When she reached the entrance, she turned and looked over her shoulder, locking eyes with Martin. "I love you, Daddy." She pulled the door open and stepped into the school, letting the door glide shut behind her.

The force that kept Martin's feet stuck in the ground like concrete had lifted, and he tumbled forward, lunging for the door handles and clawing at them like a rabid cat.

"Izzy, come back!" he screamed, his face moist with sweat and tears. He pulled on the door handles, but none of them budged. Through the window was darkness. No hallways, no office, just a pit of blackness. He knew the doors wouldn't open, but kept yanking at them to the point he thought his shoulder might pop out of its socket.

"Izzy, please!"

* * *

Martin sprung awake, crying, sweating, and panting. He was in his bedroom, Sonya by his side, stirring from his jerky motions. The sheets were soaked with sweat and clung to his lower back like leeches.

"It's just a dream," he whispered. "Just a bad dream. It doesn't mean anything."

Like hell it doesn't mean anything. Why do you keep lying to yourself? You haven't once had a dream about Izzy since she went missing, and now this happens on the eve of your supposed rescuing her?

Martin brushed his thoughts aside. Dreams are nothing but a collection of subconscious thoughts. He knew this, as his mother was big into analyzing dreams, but she always reminded him of this simple fact.

There was no Izzy, no Larkwood Middle School posing as Columbine High School, no locked doors that led into darkness. Izzy was always on his mind, and being so close to the actual events that followed her disappearance, the details came back vividly from wherever they had lain dormant after all these years.

"Just a dream."

He looked over and was relieved to see he hadn't woken Sonya as she continued her light snoring. Today would be the longest day of her life and she needed to be as rested as a cat on a Sunday afternoon.

Was it a sign? he wondered. *What if Chris put that dream in my head?* Considering everything that had happened so far, it wouldn't be a stretch of the imagination for the old man to do such a thing. But why would he have given Martin this opportunity to come back in time only to be told to go back home when the time came? *Just a dream.*

Martin lay back down, the damp sheets now cold on his flesh as he stared into the darkness of the bedroom. *Today is the day your life changed forever. It's not the anniversary of the day where you drink a little more to bury the pain. It's the actual day and you're living in it. Save her life, save your life, and go back home.*

Martin would toss and turn for another two hours before falling into a light sleep. Shortly after, the sun rose from the eastern plains, cracking dawn on the morning of September 9th, 1996.

46

Chapter 45

Martin woke several hours later to find it was almost noon, sleeping while Sonya would have dressed and gotten ready for her final day at school. He panicked at first, worried that he had slept through something important, but relaxed once he remembered that he had nothing to do until that night.

One last day of waiting around.

He expected the suspense to kill him. What could he possibly do to make the day pass, knowing what awaited when the sun went down? The game plan was set: Sonya would follow Izzy home one final time to make sure she didn't venture off, come straight home to meet Martin for a dinner that would surely go untouched, then return to watch the Briar house until the sun went down and Martin would show up in his all-black camouflage for a front row seat to the big show.

Martin warned Sonya of a boring stakeout. Every report Lela had filed in those following days mentioned that Izzy had to have gone out in the middle of the night—she had kissed her goodnight just after nine before turning in for bed herself. All he could rely on now was Lela's word from 22 years earlier.

The one good thing about suffering such a tragedy was the ability to remember every single detail. He could practically recite Lela's police statements after all of these years and hundreds of bottles of whiskey.

When he finally got out of bed, a lump filled his body from his intestines up to his throat, and would stay there all day, thanks to the nerves that refused to settle down. This caused a lost appetite and a constant urge to sit on the toilet and pray for it all to end.

He didn't bother with breakfast or lunch, instead stepping outside with hopes of passing the time and taking his mind off the night ahead. Some flowers in Sonya's garden needed final tending before they would close up shop for the upcoming winter, so he poked around with some lilies to find that a whole twenty minutes had passed.

Is there anything left that I need to get done? Martin ran through a mental checklist of things he needed to have done before returning to 2018, and for the first time he welcomed the thought of returning home, not knowing if he could bear the stress of another day in the past.

Everything was in order. He had invested money to cover his life in 2018, and had his return pill ready in his pocket, buried deep in the bottom where it had no chance of wiggling out. He had decided it would be best to keep the pill on his body rather than leaving it at the house. There was a chance he would need to make a quick decision and take the pill, having no time to return home, but the original plan was to convene at home after saving Izzy and decide when they would want to make the trip into the future.

Martin returned inside to find his body randomly trembling and his teeth chattering. He couldn't recall ever being so nervous. He shuffled into the living room and threw himself on the couch.

Relax. This is what you came here for. Did you think the day wouldn't actually come?

The way his life was going before he had swallowed that pill, he thought he'd have a few weeks to live before dying from alcohol poisoning or a self-inflicted gunshot. He never expected the past to provide a cure for his escalating alcoholism.

What if I relapse in 2018?

He had considered this possibility before, but didn't know how much stock to put into it. Did the past really cure him? Or did he take advantage of a fresh start in a familiar era? He believed the latter. Besides, whatever happened tonight would change the course of his life in 2018. He could wake up and no longer have to go to the post office. Maybe he really did catch a break and would live in Littleton if his daughter had never disappeared. His own life could look unrecognizable, and the thought didn't help settle his nerves.

If everything went smoothly and he saved Izzy, returned to 2018 with Sonya, and no longer had an itch to drink every bottle of booze in sight, there was still Chris. What exactly did he mean by taking away Martin's ability to feel emotions?

If someone tells a joke, will I no longer laugh? If someone dies, will I no longer cry? What precisely does it mean and how severe will it be?

He feared becoming a zombie, a shell of his current self, for Sonya. He had an obligation to keep her happy and safe in 2018, and anything less than that would result in a lifetime of regret for her.

I'm gonna marry that woman when we get to 2018. And we'll have the most luxurious honeymoon.

While wedding bells would have to wait, Martin at least had something positive to look forward to, should everything go horribly wrong tonight. He still couldn't rid his mind of Izzy telling him to go home, and deep down felt it was a sign that he'd be right back at square one after tonight: clueless as to what had happened and left with another two decades of heartache that would tear apart his soul like a vulture on a dead animal's carcass.

Snap out of it. You'll only fail tonight if you keep having these negative thoughts. Get your shit together and be confident.

"Easier said than done." He never had soaring confidence, even before his life had taken a turn for the worst. His only confidence in 2018 came in knowing that a hangover awaited him in the morning if he dared drink another bottle of whiskey.

The thought of pouring what remained in Sonya's alcohol stash had crossed his mind—the nerves had taken full control, after all—but he couldn't push himself to put his entire mission at risk. What if he passed out on the couch while Sonya went on her stakeout, and he missed the whole thing?

Go one more night without it, and you can drink all you want tomorrow. A new life begins soon. One with money, and no job to go to. Just a full bank account and a woman who loves you, and hopefully, a daughter who thinks the world of you.

Martin pushed the negativity aside and tried to imagine a universe where he, Sonya, and Izzy all lived in 2018. A world where they could laugh over dinner for having pulled off the impossible and reflect back to this specific day as the moment that shaped all of their good fortune.

These thoughts settled his nerves a bit, although not completely. He had passed a good amount of time and didn't realize the clock on the wall read 2:45. Sonya would be off work within the next hour to follow Izzy home for the final time.

The time was finally here, and he just needed to hang on to his last shred of sanity for a few more hours.

47

Chapter 46

Sonya wished her students a great rest of their evenings. The 3:15 bell had struck within the last minute, and Ms. Griffiths had her class ready to head out immediately.

"Bye, kids," she said while they herded out of the room and into the traffic jam in the hallway. She loved her eighth graders and felt a pull in her chest at the thought of never seeing them again with their big glasses, pimply faces, and squeaky voices. This was all part of the job, however, and she had known this farce wouldn't go on forever.

Time for vacation? she thought. While the workday certainly had that final-day-before-vacation feel, she had to fight off the thought of what was actually happening within the next handful of hours. At home, Martin was probably a nervous wreck. She'd noticed how much more distant he seemed as this day had grown closer, and hoped it was just a matter of nerves building up to his big event.

If he's this nervous, should we really be trying to recruit him? She glanced at the clock with studious eyes. *3:20. It's time.*

Her classroom had actually emptied in five minutes, a new record. Normally a couple students would hang back to ask for help, or maybe a parent or two would drop in for a quick word. But today was her lucky day, despite a longing for something to stall her from leaving and officially moving to the next chapter of this mission.

She had parked on the rear side of the school this morning so she could easily slip out of her classroom's back door and remain uninterrupted en route to her car. She grabbed her purse and paused, looking over her classroom. Her students' artwork hung on the walls, giving the room a homey feel. In two short weeks of the new school year she had already formed a bond with her students. Her students loved her, and she loved them.

"Please don't be hurt when I'm gone," she said to the desks, and turned out the back door.

Some students ran around like uncaged animals on the open grass field between the school and the parking lot and she maneuvered her way through them like a native New Yorker pushing their way through Times Square.

She pulled her car around the building and found Izzy approaching the schoolyard's outer gate like clockwork. Izzy had apparently been a child of strict routine, going through the same exact motions every day in the way she packed her backpack and re-tied her shoes for her walk home.

Sonya crept down the road at a snail's pace as she waited for Izzy to cross the street. She kept close to the sidewalk and watched Izzy finally cross the street in her familiar pose with her hands crossed over her books and, this time, two pigtails bouncing behind her head with every step.

Sonya had gone through this same routine for the past week, but felt an extra flood of adrenaline today. What if something did happen right now? What if a creep in a van pulled in front of her and followed Izzy all the way home? It was only a two-block route and it would be impossible for an innocent child to be aware of a stalker. She had witnessed plenty of times how the past could throw plans completely out of whack, and hoped things ran smoothly so she could see what Martin was capable of tonght.

What exactly would you do if someone else got involved at this point?

Sonya had played out the scenario in her mind, and vowed to intervene should danger present itself. She kept a crow bar in her trunk and wouldn't hesitate to use it.

Sonya turned onto Cherry Street and kept a distance of five car lengths behind Izzy as she trudged down the sidewalk. Her eyes bounced from the rear view to the left and right sides of the road in search of anything out of the ordinary. There was nothing but cars parked on the street and lawns covered with the first layer of browning leaves.

Izzy strolled along at the same pace as any other day, minding her business, oblivious to the teacher trailing behind. Sonya had never actually spoken to Izzy, but had seen her around the hallways in between classes. She kept to herself for the most part, occasionally giggling with two other girls during lunch and recess.

By the time Izzy arrived home, Sonya's mind had drifted so far that she had to speed up to see the young girl step inside her house. She drove two houses down and waited for five minutes to see if anything would happen.

"Well, I guess that's that," she said into her empty car. So far, the day had gone according to plan. Izzy was home safe, undisturbed, and likely diving into her piles of homework. Sonya drove to the end of the block and took the long route home where she and Martin would sit down for a brief dinner before she'd return to watch the Briar house until nightfall.

* * *

When Sonya entered the house, tension mixed in the air with deafening silence.

"Martin?" she called. The smells of baked bread rushed to her nose, sweet and tempting, despite her lack of appetite.

From the doorway she could see the kitchen, living room, and a glimpse into their bedroom. He wasn't in any of them.

He wouldn't have made me dinner and left. Dear Sonya, I changed my mind and am going back to 2018 without you, she thought, then giggled nervously. She was in no mood to chase him down in the future.

"Martin, I'm home!" she shouted.

She dragged herself into the kitchen, where the bread scent was strongest, and felt an instant relief when she saw Martin's figure through the back window. He appeared to be rocking on one of the patio chairs, staring over the lawn that would be covered in blankets of snow in the coming months.

Sonya went outside and sat in the rocker next to Martin. He looked up to her and offered a warm smile.

"How was your day?" he asked, flat and distant.

"It was okay. How was yours?"

He rocked more before replying, and Sonya noticed how much of a shell he was of himself from just two weeks ago. He had lost a notable amount of weight, dark circles covered the spaces beneath his eyes, and thick streaks of gray had filled in across his scalp.

He traveled back 20 years only to age another 20 years. I'm really not sure if this is the guy we want?

"I've been losing my mind today," he said. "I've done so much thinking and I feel like I can't form another viable thought. I've never been so nervous for anything in my life."

She heard a tremble in his voice, but there was no visible sign of a pending cry, just the ragged expression of a man who has reached his breaking point.

"When I first got here I thought September 9th was so far away. It got here fast, and I know it'll pass just as quickly. Tomorrow will be here before I even realize it, and by then I'll know if my life stays the same or becomes what it was meant to be before all this shit happened."

Sonya wanted to suggest that maybe his life *had* become how it was meant to be. Martin stared at the ground as he spoke and was clearly riding his final train of thought.

"It's so hard going into this and not knowing what to expect. I need to be ready to react to anything. I don't know how many times I've imagined my own death today. I know that shouldn't be at the front of my mind, but it is. I have to acknowledge it as a real possibility."

He stopped talking and stared to the ground where a roly-poly crawled slowly along the concrete. Sonya didn't know what to say to address his fears of death, but knew she needed to give him some comfort if she wanted any chance of completing this mission.

"I can't imagine what you've gone through today, but just know that I'll be here every step of the way. You're not alone." She reached over and rubbed his arm, and felt a slight tremble coming from it.

"Thank you," he said. "You have no idea how incredible you are, and that makes you even more incredible."

"Izzy made it home okay," Sonya said, wanting to redirect the conversation. "No one followed her but me, and I saw her go inside and close the door."

Martin nodded as if he expected this information. "Perfect."

He stood from the rocker and put his hands on his hips as he stared into the distance.

"Let's go eat," he said. "I made your favorite meal."

By this he meant lasagna with baked bread, and she grinned at him.

"You know, you're pretty incredible yourself," she said.

Martin mustered a smile in return, through the thick layers of distraction that had taken control of his face.

"I sure hope I can be incredible tonight, for Isabel. I only get one chance to make this right."

"You'll be perfect, I have no doubt about it. Let's go eat so you can clear your mind. Maybe you can tell me more about the future?"

Martin nodded and followed her inside, where they would sit down for their final dinner of 1996.

48

Chapter 47

Martin changed his tune over dinner, and insisted that Sonya stay for an hour after he would arrive at his old house.

"I already know nothing significant happens until the middle of the night," he said. "The party doesn't start until after I show up, possibly well after I show up."

"What time do you think you'll get there?"

"The news said the sun will set at 7:18. I'll be there around 7:45, once it's officially dark." Martin spoke in between bites of lasagna. He ate like a starved stray dog hitting the jackpot with a tipped over dumpster full of food. After Sonya arrived home, his confidence skyrocketed. His senses were overloaded while he ate. He could hear every sound outside the house as if microphones were set up around the yard. Even the seasonings buried in the marinara sauce jumped onto his tongue.

I'm ready, he thought. *I'm not dying tonight, and Izzy will stay at that house if it's the last goddamned thing I do.*

After he did everything but lick the sauce remnants from his plate, Martin sat back in his chair, noting the clock that read 4:23, and grinned at Sonya.

"Are you ready?" he asked.

"I think so. I'm nervous, but kind of excited. I can't believe the time is finally here."

"I'm feeling good, too," Martin said. "I'm still incredibly nervous. Surprised I ate all of that, to tell you the truth, but I also feel focused."

"That's good," Sonya said as she finished her plate. She hadn't struggled with eating or sleeping as much as Martin had, having an ability to shove stressful thoughts aside and keep moving forward with her life. "I think I'm gonna head over there now. There's really no point in waiting around here. Even if nothing happens while I'm there, it'll still help pass the time. If I stay here I think I might go crazy."

If she wanted to go, Martin had no reason to stop her.

Sonya joined him at the head of the table and slung her arms around his waist. "I'll see you back here when it's all done."

Martin stood and nodded, pulling her into his embrace.

"Thank you for doing this. All of this. You could've said no. I can't wait to start our life together after tonight. It's going to be perfect."

Martin pulled her in tighter and inhaled the sweet scent of her shampoo.

"Don't do anything to put your life at risk," she said.

"Of course not. You either." Martin knew very well that if he saw an opportunity to save Izzy that would require his own life, he'd take it in a heartbeat. *Hopefully it doesn't come to that.*

"I love you," she said, planting a kiss on his lips. "I'll see you later."

Martin released Sonya from his arms and watched as she glided across the room, grabbed her keys and purse, and disappeared through the door with a quick glance over her shoulder.

Sonya was gone, leaving him three hours until he would start his walk through town. Even with a cloudy memory, he'd never forget the way "home" after all these years.

His past self would have just left for work a few minutes ago, giving Izzy a kiss on the head on his way out the door.

"I'll see you later," he had said, now wishing he could go back and never leave that night. *Why do bad things have to happen to good people?*

He could still taste the fruity smell from Izzy's hair on his lips after all these years, could see his final words to her hanging in the air, wishing he could grab them and have a second chance.

"Your second chance is tonight. Don't waste it," he said to the empty kitchen.

* * *

While Sonya watched the Briar residence from three houses down, Martin waited in their bedroom, dressed in black sweatpants and a black long-sleeve shirt, staring obsessively into the standing mirror that leaned against the wall. A black beanie and gloves rested on the bed to complete his stealthy attire. *I can't go out until it's dark; I look like a burglar.*

Martin studied the lines starting to fill his face and the streaks of silver in his hair.

When did I get so old? he wondered. *I've never felt better, and this is how my body thanks me?*

The damage was already done to his body, thanks to the past decade of drinking anything he could get his hands on. However, the man he saw in the mirror was a different one than he had known. The man in the mirror had gained hope, wisdom, and a refined willpower that would help him achieve what he set out to do. It was a man in love, both with his child and the woman he had met on this journey. True love can carry a man through any situation in life.

Remember, no matter what happens tonight, you still have Sonya and a future.

He longed for a life in 2018 with Sonya by his side and Izzy alive and well, but knew dreams didn't always come true. Sometimes reality wins.

Through the windows, the sting of brightness softened to an orange glow as dusk approached. The digital clock on the nightstand read 6:08, giving him less than an hour before he'd leave the house. Somewhere in 2018 he was snoring in a back office and would soon wake up to realize this whole thing was a horrible hallucination, or a reality he still struggled to grasp.

"This is real," he said to himself. "Dreams don't carry on this long, and they certainly don't stay in chronological order."

No days had been skipped aside from the coma. He had to wake up every day like anyone else and drag himself through the summer weeks as September loomed.

Well it's here now, my friend.

Martin patted the pill in his pocket, knowing home was just a swallow away. He stuffed the beanie and gloves into his back pockets and moved to the living room for his final few minutes.

* * *

At 6:58, Martin Briar walked out of the house. The sun glowed above the mountains and would begin its quick descent within the next few minutes.

Martin had planned his route and calculated the walk to his old house would take around 30 minutes. As he strolled through the neighborhood, he saw families at the dinner table, others doing the dishes, and some huddled around the TV as Monday Night Football started.

He remembered occasional nights when Izzy would sit on his lap and watch the games with him, asking a laundry list of questions. She had always been curious, even with matters she didn't actually care about, like football.

I'm coming for you, Izzy. And you can ask me all the questions you want.

The first hint of darkness took control of the sky and would swallow up the city by the time he arrived to his destination.

Martin reached the end of his neighborhood within twelve minutes, right on schedule, and crossed 80th Avenue to his old neighborhood where the houses were newer, maintained with well-manicured lawns and modern designs that gave every home a view of the mountains.

He remembered when he and Lela had moved into the neighborhood. It

275

was the peak of their relationship. Both had steadily paying jobs, and she was pregnant with the same child whose disappearance would destroy his life in the matter of one night.

The past could easily have placed Martin's mother on the front porch, smoking a cigarette and thereby throwing his entire night down the shitter, so he walked down the block one over from her house. He sensed the past wouldn't give him too much trouble and wasn't sure why – perhaps it was a hunch, or the eerie stillness in the air.

He passed Larkwood Middle School and found himself on the same route that Izzy took home every day, and imagined her walking by his side, head down, books in her embrace.

Dusk was officially upon Larkwood and the houses were no more than silhouettes against the sliver of orange that remained in the sky. Blackness filled in from the east, clawing its way to the Rocky Mountains on the west side of town. A few crickets chirped as Martin reached the corner of his old block.

He approached the stop sign where Cherry Street and 78th Avenue intersected and looked down the dark block. The night lacked moonlight as the street lights flickered on and wouldn't provide reliable light for the next half hour while they warmed up.

Martin kept to the west side of Cherry Street, where his house waited halfway down the block. He saw Sonya's car parked on the opposite side of the road, roughly three houses down from his, facing him.

Everything's in place and ready to go. Now, we wait.

Judging from the sky, total darkness was less than five minutes away. He'd wait until then before proceeding down the block, but prepared by slipping the black beanie over his head and making sure the gloves were snug over his hands.

He peered around to make sure no one was watching, and relaxed when realizing he was alone.

Down the block waited a new destiny and a second chance at life.

Who actually gets second chances in life? He trembled at the thought.

He started walking, taking the quietest steps he could manage, and headed toward whatever fate awaited him.

49

Chapter 48

Now that he stood in front of it, Martin remembered his house exactly as it was. It had an open front yard, half covered with leaves from the neighbor's massive oak tree that connected with a cement porch. Three windows spanned the front of the ranch-style home, with the front door centered between the first and second. Daylight would show the house's light green exterior, but the darkness made everything colorless.

Martin hid behind the scraggly bushes that separated his yard from the neighbor's driveway, peering around the lamppost that splashed a soft, yellow glow in the middle of the street. From the sidewalk he waved his arms in Sonya's direction, the car lights remaining off.

He turned his attention back to the house. From his initial assessment, hiding on the side of the house provided the best view of the front yard and driveway, *and* the flexibility to run to the backyard should he need to. An intruder would have a hard time sneaking in through the back where chain link fences would create noise and attention.

Martin cut across the front yard to the side of the house, scattered leaves crunching beneath his feet. The window above him belonged to Izzy's bedroom, allowing him to hear any encounter inside should it be loud enough. He crouched and felt devoured by the darkness.

I need to get comfortable; it's gonna be a few hours.

He wished he had his cell phone, but the battery had finally run out, even after remaining off for so long. The watch on his wrist had no glow; those were still a couple years away. If he really needed to know the time, he'd have to run into the middle of the street and check below the lamppost.

Rely on your instincts.

By his calculation it should only be 7:40, leaving him over an hour until Izzy would actually go to sleep. A thick curtain covered her window, blocking any potential for him to know if her light was turned on.

Martin peered back toward the street to see the car still parked. A car would drive by every few minutes, headlights filling Cherry Street, but not revealing the crouched man on the side of the Briar house. Each time one passed, Martin's heart raced with an extra boost of adrenaline.

It's not even eight yet, relax. Nothing happens until at least nine. Sit back, grab your popcorn, and wait for the show to start.

Martin did exactly this and sat on the ground, legs pulled to his chest as he curled into a ball like a roly-poly. And he waited.

* * *

Sonya watched from her car as the darkness fell over the city. Martin arrived next to lamppost, studied the exterior, and disappeared into the shadows along the side. He had waved at her, and she waved back, but the darkness concealed her gesture.

Don't worry about me – I'll be right here when you need me. We're all pulling for you.

The neighborhood felt still after the kids had returned inside at sunset. She tuned out the deafening silence in the car by whistling softly, knowing she also had a long, challenging night ahead before her life could resume to normal.

* * *

Sitting outside his old house had opened a floodgate of memories that Martin had to keep pushing aside to remain focused. He reminisced about the times he played with Izzy in the front yard, chasing her and pretending to be a dinosaur. Or other times they had played hide-and-seek on warm summer nights, and he had hidden in this same exact spot, watching his only child look around for him until she spotted him and called out, "I got you, Daddy!"

Life couldn't have been any more perfect.

Not knowing for sure how much time had passed, Martin figured it was at least close to 9 P.M. His ass felt like 1,000 ants were nibbling on it, so he stood up and stretched to get the blood flowing again. Any minute something could happen. He checked the backyard, found nothing out of the ordinary, and returned to his post when a car turned onto Cherry Street and crept at a snail's pace toward the house.

The headlights blinded Martin, leaving him no way to make out the car until it turned into the driveway. His heart tried to leap out of his throat, stomach churning, arms trembling as he realized this must be the person who ruined his life forever.

The car looked familiar, and it didn't register with Martin until the man parked and stepped out. He wore athletic pants and a zip-up windbreaker—another familiar look Martin recognized. A gold chain swung from his neck and illuminated the slightest gleam in the darkness.

Daniel?

His younger brother.

A world of confusion rained on Martin as he peeked around the corner. *What the hell is he doing here?*

Daniel loved Izzy, and she reciprocated his adoration. He was the fun uncle, taking her to amusement parks, museums, and random stops for ice cream during summer break.

How is Daniel involved in this night?

Martin couldn't recall a single police statement that mentioned his brother. Daniel walked up the front steps and rapped lightly on the door. It only took seconds for the screen door to fly open from Lela's skinny arm, and Daniel disappeared into the house.

Dear God, please don't tell me this is what I think it is.

Martin kept his neck craned to look around the corner.

Any minute Daniel is going to walk back out and drive home. He just stopped by for something, right?

After five minutes passed with no sign of the door opening, Martin leaned back against the house, panting like a thirsty dog in the middle of summer. Tension had built up that he hadn't realized until he released his clenched fist and his tight jaw. *Think, Martin. There could be one hundred other reasons that he's here.*

He thought back and tried to remember what was going on in Daniel's life. Was there something troubling him where he felt he could confide in Lela?

As best he could remember, life was pretty simple for Daniel in 1996. He would've been recently graduated from college, and had jumped right into a job. He had no romantic relationship from what Martin could recall.

He didn't need a relationship because he was fucking your wife.

Martin couldn't bring himself to accept the possibility of what might be going on inside the house while Izzy slept in her bedroom.

He had no choice but to confront it. His and Lela's bedroom was on the same side of the house he currently stood, only closer to the backyard. He dragged his feet to the spot below their bedroom window, his gut feeling like a wrung out rag. The nerves fled as his mind focused on the new task ahead.

Did this even really happen the first time around, or is the past just fucking with me to throw me off right now?

He gave the thought a whole second of consideration before dismissing it. The past had never done anything to psychologically mess with his plans, but rather did things like run him over with a semi-truck, or set liquor stores and high schools on fire. Whatever was going on between his brother and ex-wife inside the house was all part of the original story.

Martin looked up to the bedroom window. Lela hadn't put up a thick curtain as Izzy had, leaving flimsy blinds to fill the space. The room was black, not even the glow of a TV, but he could hear the faintest sound of a woman giggling. They were in the bedroom, not in the kitchen or living room having a discussion. In the fucking *bedroom.*

The soft laughter fell silent for a couple minutes before the sounds of moaning and groaning replaced it, followed by a pleasurable scream.

Jesus Christ, they didn't even try being quiet!

Martin felt his face flushing bright red, his temples pulsing with rage. His hands returned to white knuckled fists, shaking at his sides, as he fought off every urge to barge into the house and beat the living hell out of his brother.

How could they?

Martin stepped away, returning to his post below Izzy's window, thoughts from his past flooding his now distracted mind.

How long were they doing this? When did this start? Why did this start?

His and Lela's sex life was by no means lackluster. They had enjoyed each other at least three times a week, even when he started working the inconsistent hours. So why the hell did this come about?

Martin knew he should push these thoughts out of his mind—he tried, but failed—remembering he had come here to save his daughter, not learn about a lifetime of secrets that had remained buried underneath her disappearance.

Is this why Daniel moved away after the funeral? Did his guilt get the best of him and he couldn't bear to see us anymore?

Daniel had moved across the country to Delaware, citing a new job opportunity. At the time, it was positive news for a devastated family, but his phone calls became rare, and after two years, he simply stopped reaching out to the family. Their mother said Daniel would call her on occasion, but it was always out of the blue. Martin wondered if this was the real reason he left and broke off all communication. Even in 2018, with social media, Daniel Briar was nowhere to be found.

Just worry about Izzy.

The thought was easier said than done. He couldn't help but imagine the 1996 version of himself on his way home in a few hours, oblivious that his daughter was missing and his wife and brother had a quickie in his own bed.

He wanted to cry and scream at the same time.

Just worry about Izzy.

Martin peered back around the corner of the house, saw Sonya parked in her same spot, and wished he could go tell her the new developments.

Over the next twenty minutes Martin struggled to control his breathing and clear his mind. The night no longer felt still, but rather chaotic on Cherry Street. The crickets had silenced, leaving the only audible sounds to be his breathing and pounding heart. The temperature remained cool.

When the front door swung open, Martin almost missed it, too busy staring into the night sky, trying to piece his life together. Daniel stepped onto the porch, Lela joining him in her robe and slippers. She giggled as she ran a hand down his chest and stomach. Martin could hear their voices whispering to each other, but couldn't make out the actual words.

Lela planted a kiss on Daniel's lips before he hurried down the steps, jumped into his car, and left as abruptly as he had arrived. Still no sign of Izzy.

Lela returned inside as Martin watched the screen door glide shut.

He slid back to ground, relieved the adultery had passed, and allowed his mind to refocus on the task at hand. Just as his thoughts started to settle, Martin heard muffled shouting coming from inside the house—from Izzy's room specifically. He pressed his ear against the house, knowing he'd never be able to make out the words clearly, wishing more than ever to be a fly on the wall.

What he could hear was a back and forth between Lela and Izzy. Izzy's voice, though young and not fully developed, still projected. Lela responded with the same tone, only louder and approaching the level of a scream.

Is this what prompts this? Does Izzy run away after catching her mom in the act with her uncle? Why wouldn't she have just come to me and told me? Why run away from it all?

It pained Martin to think that his daughter might have carried this burden with her all of these years, feeling as if she had to leave her life behind because of the mistakes her mother made. *Why would she leave without saying goodbye? Was I that unavailable that she couldn't confide in me?*

Martin kept his ear pressed against the house like a burglar listening to a safe, patiently waiting for the click of the lock. As the doubts of his effectiveness as a parent continued to pour into his mind, he knew the next few minutes were the key to everything. The voices continued to rise but seemed more distant, likely having gone from Izzy's bedroom to the living room further down the hallway. He debated moving to the other side of the house, but decided to wait. He couldn't risk being caught in his own front yard at such a crucial time.

The sounds from Izzy's room had completely stopped, so he ran to the backside of the house and crept along the edge to see if the drama inside was continuing in a different part of the house.

For a moment he thought the shouting had ceased, but it picked up again, this time from the kitchen. The kitchen window overlooked the backyard, so Martin would need to stay put on the side of the house, especially with the backyard porch light turned on for when he would be arriving home later that morning.

Martin craned his neck and saw the kitchen light splashing across the backyard's grass. The voices remained muffled, covered further by a clatter of pots and pans.

Is Lela putting away the dishes while having this conversation with Izzy?

It wouldn't be the first time his ex-wife resorted to cleaning while in a rage. She used to claim that it helped clear her head.

The shouting reached another peak before abruptly stopping. It sounded as if Lela were screaming and was cut off mid-sentence.

Martin studied the window for any movement of shadows that would suggest the activity inside. There were none, and he pressed his head against the house to catch any sounds.

The bedrooms and kitchen had fallen into complete silence, as if no one were home, and Martin could only hear the sound of his own heart, pounding in his head like a distant drum.

This is it. The fight is over. Izzy must be in her bedroom packing up her things and getting ready to storm out of the house.

He knew it could take another hour or two before anything happened. Lela would need to go to sleep before Izzy made a run for it. She must have let herself out well after Lela fell asleep, but before Martin arrived home from work.

Martin squinted at his watch, but had no chance at reading the time as it remained consumed in the darkness. He calculated it to be around ten o'clock, but couldn't pin down a precise time. Daniel had come over just after nine, had his romp in the sheets with Lela, and was out before she could even brew the coffee. Then the shouting had started and lasted between ten to fifteen minutes.

If the timeline held true, it was certainly no earlier than ten, leaving him a four-hour window until his past self arrived home for the night.

Martin returned to the backyard and found the kitchen light turned off.

Strange, he thought, remembering Lela had always left an inside light on for Martin on the nights he worked late, but pitch-blackness came from the back of the house. Away from the street light, Martin could barely see his own hand in front of his face.

She wouldn't have gone to bed already, would she?

Lela had always needed time to cool off after an argument.

It doesn't matter. This speeds up the timeline, if anything. Stay here and wait for her to come out.

Martin knew Izzy would come out of the back door. They rarely used the front door since the driveway stretched to the backyard where Lela's car currently sat in the darkness. Besides, the front door creaked and groaned when opened, making a silent escape impossible.

He crouched, ready to pounce on Izzy the second she stepped outside, waiting like a vulture circling its prey, anticipating the perfect moment to swoop in and change destiny.

When five minutes passed, Martin remained frozen, both from shock and disbelief at what his eyes witnessed.

Lela swung open the screen door and ran down the porch steps to her car, unlocking the trunk, and flinging the door open.

With the house door and trunk wide open, Martin tried to piece it all together in a frantic attempt to make sense of what he didn't want to believe.

Don't you fucking do it, he thought as Lela returned into the dark pit of the house. *Please, God, don't let her fucking do this.*

He braced himself for what would come out of the door next, and when he saw it, his body fell into an instant state of numbness.

Lela appeared in the doorway, arms in front of her body as they held a white cloth draped over a limp body. Martin heard the faintest sob from his ex-wife as she dumped the body into the trunk and slammed the door shut. Lela returned to close the house door before dashing to the equipment shed in the back corner of the yard. She grabbed a shovel and sprinted back to the car.

She tossed the shovel into the backseat and fired up the engine and headlights, backing out of the driveway and leaving Martin alone in the darkness, still unable to process the horror of what he had just witnessed.

Lela killed her, he thought, lips quivering in unison with his now shaking body. *Two decades of wondering. And she fucking killed her.*

Martin turned back to the side of the house and vomited before making a run for Sonya, who was hopefully still waiting close by.

50

Chapter 49

Sonya already had the car running when Martin reached it. The adrenaline provided him a boost in speed he hadn't experienced since his high school days. He dove into the car just as Lela reached the end of the street, and turned right at the stop sign.

"Go!" he barked. "Follow her, and keep your lights off!"

Sonya obliged and swung the car around in a U-turn, tires screeching in the quiet night. Martin knew she had seen everything by the obvious shock in her bulging eyes and hanging jaw.

"Don't lose her!" he shouted as they reached the stop sign. Lela drove at a surprisingly normal pace as she crept away from the neighborhood, giving Sonya the perfect window of opportunity to catch up as a red light stopped her three blocks ahead.

"Stay 200 feet back, keep the lights off, and match her every move and pace from here on out." Martin felt like a movie director barking out his orders, knowing he had this one chance to follow Lela and see where she hid their daughter's body that would never be found.

Where would she go? he wondered as Sonya steadied the car two hundred feet behind Lela. They were the only two cars on the road, and it would likely stay that way for a while. Martin saw the clock on the dashboard reading 11:02, much later than he had mentally calculated.

I guess time flies when you're watching yourself get cheated on before your ex-wife kills your only kid.

The light turned green and Lela wasted no time crossing the intersection of Highway 85. Sonya kept her distance and followed as they drove through a dark service road with no street lights.

She only has four hours until I get home. She can't go too far. And if she's digging a hole, she needs to start right now.

The thought of the shovel sent a spark of rage through Martin. This meant Lela never thought twice about owning up to her crime, and had her mind set on taking care of the matter herself.

Sonya remained silent beside Martin, her eyes focused on the car ahead and waiting for Martin's next instruction.

Lela's brake lights filled the darkness, and they reminded Martin again of peering red eyes, much like the circle on the calendar in Sonya's kitchen.

Is that you, Chris? he thought, questioning his own sanity for a brief moment.

Lela turned right onto Dahlia Street, a quiet and scenic road that separated two lakes, but also connected Larkwood to the neighboring town of Grant. A thick fog blanketed the road and killed all visibility as Lela disappeared into the clouds. *The past can kiss my ass and take a seat in the back if it wants to try anything right now.*

Lela slowed down and flicked on her high beams, which actually made it harder to see as the light reflected off the fog, creating a virtual gray sheet of obstruction.

"Keep your lights off," Martin said calmly. "We can see her and that's all that matters. Get closer so we can follow her every move. This road is narrow and we could drive into a ditch."

Sonya nodded and closed the gap between her car and Lela. The fog provided them with coverage as they drove deeper in toward the lakes. She could pull up right behind the old Chevrolet and Lela would never know it.

Lela suddenly swerved to the right and slammed on her brakes. Sonya pulled up cautiously, stopping 100 feet behind as the fog lightened up just enough to see that distance.

"No, not here, Lela," Martin said absent-mindedly. "Not here dammit!"

"What is this place?" Sonya asked, speaking for the first time since they left the house.

"It's a lake we used to come to in the summers as a family," Martin said in a distant voice. "We'd have picnics and splash around in the water with Izzy. She always looked forward to it."

He fell into a deadly silence; Sonya nudged him to make sure he was okay.

"Now she's being buried here by her own mother."

Martin's bottom lip trembled as he spoke, and he sniffled to keep the tears and emotions inside.

"There's not even anything I can do to stop this," Martin said, slouching into the passenger seat as if it were swallowing him piece by piece. "She's already dead." The words came off his lips cold and surreal.

The amount of reality that had been dumped on Martin in the last two hours was the emotional equivalent of being buried alive, and he felt the suffocation of it just the same.

They watched as Lela jumped out of the car and popped the trunk open. Martin sat still, staring as if it weren't really happening. He shook his head as Lela struggled to lift Izzy's body out of the vehicle, a limp white arm falling below the sheet's coverage.

"Aren't you going to do something?" Sonya demanded, a stream of tears running down her face.

"There's nothing I can do," he said in a depressed voice. "Nothing at all. I just wasted the last six months thinking I had a chance at saving her. And she was going to end up dead before I even got the chance." He paused and looked down to his shaking hands. "I should've knocked on the door when I saw Daniel go inside. I should've done something then. This wouldn't have happened."

Sonya sat up stiffly in her seat and tossed her arms in the air. "You're telling me you're going to sit here and watch her throw your daughter in the lake? Are you fucking crazy? After all this, it ends with you sitting here in defeat?"

"What can I do?" he responded calmly. "I played out this scenario already. What do you think I've been doing for six months? I've thought every possibility all the way through to the end. I never gave this scenario much thought, but I did consider it."

Sonya stared at him with her mouth agape. Lela had carried the body and disappeared into the thick fog where the lake waited.

"What happens next is we go back to 2018, I tell the police that Izzy's body is in this lake, and then I confront Lela about it."

"Why? We could go find a payphone real quick and call the police. She can go to jail tonight. Why give her the chance to walk free like this?"

"Why wouldn't I give her two decades to sulk in her guilt? I'm sure she even reached a point where she thought she actually got away with it, that she would make it to her grave without having to confront anyone about it. I'm fine letting her live the next 22 years with that hope. I'll be there when it all comes crashing down, too. That's what I really want to see."

Martin spoke like a man possessed, keeping all emotion out of his voice, and even showed a hint of lunacy in his planning. He knew exactly how he wanted it to all play out when he returned to 2018, and he'd waste no time. It would be the early morning still, and he'd call in to work, letting them know he'd never come back, and then off to Lela's house where he would confront her and make her wish she had never tried to cover up her dirty actions.

For now, Martin only wanted to cry. And that's exactly what he did while Sonya begrudgingly turned the car around and drove back to her house. She didn't speak to him, and he didn't care why. He had an invisible dagger digging deep into his heart, twisting forcefully every time he closed his eyes and imagined Lela carrying their dead daughter through the house and dropping her in the trunk like groceries.

"Don't kill her, it's not worth it." Martin thought he had kept this in his mind, but had spoken it. Sonya looked at him, lips pursed while she drove.

Martin slouched further down in his chair, wanting to melt into a puddle of depression, and thought over the last six months.

I could've stopped this at any time. I could've picked her up after school today and told her I took the night off work to hang out with her. We could've gone to dinner and a movie, or fed the ducks at the park. I never imagined Lela doing this; she never acted guilty. Maybe all of the tears were the guilt. The guilt of knowing I would suffer forever because of what she did. The guilt of knowing I'd go my entire life without knowing the truth while she had to carry the burden.

Sonya pulled into her driveway five minutes later. "So what now?" she asked.

"Now we go to 2018."

51

Chapter 50

"I can't believe this is what happened," Martin said after they parked. "This wasn't supposed to happen. Izzy should be alive right now, sitting in the backseat."

Sonya pushed open her door with her shoulder and jumped out of the car. "Let's go," she demanded. "I know this is hard, but you're not done. I'm not letting you come all this way to stop here."

Martin watched her with puzzlement before following her into the house.

"I know this is fucked up," she continued, throwing her keys on the kitchen table and pacing around the living room. "I just watched it all happen, too. Let's get back to your time and make this right. Your ex-wife deserves to be locked in prison for the rest of her life, and you deserve closure."

Her determination radiated, providing Martin a temporary boost in confidence. "Are you sure you want to come with me? There's no ticket back."

"Martin Briar, for the hundredth time, I've made up my mind and I'm going. Please stop asking."

Martin nodded, and reached into his pockets to retrieve the small pill buried at the bottom. He held it an open palm like a wizard showing off an orb.

"Ten minutes and we'll go," Martin said. "I want you to make sure you have everything you want to take."

"Martin, my bag has been ready for the past week," she said, gesturing to the duffel bag that waited beside the living room couch. "I'm ready. Quit stalling and let's go."

There was no hesitation in her voice, no doubts or reservations. Just the sound of a woman ready to take the next adventure in life.

"Alright, let's go lay down in bed. Bring your bag." Martin found himself with an outbreak of nerves. He had his own reservations about going back to 2018. The world would be the same as he knew it, but how was he supposed to carry on after turning in Lela to the police. There would be news coverage of the cracked case after so many years. They would retrieve the body from the lake, and Martin would have to see the footage of it on a constant loop for weeks.

Reporters would hound him and throw him into the spotlight as the ex-husband of a monster. Sonya would need to remain under the radar for the beginning of the media circus. She didn't deserve such a chaotic welcoming to her new life.

These uncertainties came and went like a brief rainstorm when Sonya called out for him. "Martin, I'm ready." Her voice carried from the bedroom, and he realized he hadn't moved one step since they entered the house.

The pill rested in his sweaty palm, so Martin switched it to his other hand, worried it would disintegrate into its original powder form.

He shuffled into the bedroom to find Sonya lying down, her hands crossed above her belly, and her bag strap wrapped around her arm while the bag rested on the floor below. She looked as beautiful as ever, even through all the drama of the past few hours.

I wish we met when we were both younger, he thought. *Our life together would have been so perfect.*

"Are you ready?" Martin asked.

Sonya nodded, keeping her gaze to the ceiling fan that spun in silent rotations.

He lay down next to her as he had every night for the past few months. He rolled to his side to face her and held her hands in his. "I love you," he said. "Remember, we're going to wake up in a dark room, but I'll be there. Don't be afraid."

A tear trickled down her cheek and Martin brushed it away with a quick swipe.

He rolled to his back, keeping her hand in his, closed his eyes, and popped the pill into his mouth.

As he fell into a daze, he imagined Izzy, beautiful and young, running through the park with the serene laughter only a little girl could make.

It'll all be okay.

* * *

The trip back to 2018 lacked the falling sensation, and even though he had Sonya's hand squeezed in a death grip, it disappeared as soon at the darkness took over. He heard voices blurring by in a rush. *Is this the next 22 years of my life being fast-forwarded back to present time?* he wondered.

Instead of waking up in a deserted lot, Martin jolted awake in a chair, eyes shooting open to the familiar sight of Chris's back office. He panted for breath, a drizzle of sweat dripping down his back.

Where's Sonya?

He peered around the room, heart thudding against his ribs as he jumped from the chair on to wobbly legs.

"Sonya!" he shouted. "Sonya!"

"Relax, old friend," Chris said from the darkness before flicking on a light. "She's here, just in a bit of a daze from the trip. Give her a minute to wake up."

Chris stood in the laboratory section of his office and smirked while he spoke, crossing the room to meet Martin.

"How was your trip?" Chris asked how a casual friend might.

"Where's Sonya?" Martin demanded.

"She's asleep on the ground behind my lab. I took her over to make sure she was okay."

Martin thought he was dreaming. He could see Chris in front of him, grinning and talking, but had the hazy effect that often accompanied a deep sleep. He tried to move his legs forward but they remained frozen in place.

"Easy, my friend," Chris said. "I know you're excited, but we have a debt to settle, remember?"

"Bullshit!" Martin barked. "You set me up knowing what would happen. I never had a chance at saving Izzy."

"I never said you would," Chris said, getting right in front of Martin's face.

Martin observed the evil lurking behind the old man's eyes, and desired nothing more than to leave. "All I ever offered was the opportunity to go back in time. You picked the time and location. I made it happen. We had an agreement."

"You played me," Martin said, shaking his head as he sat back down. He had caught a glimpse of Sonya's legs splayed out on the ground behind the laboratory counter and had no choice but to accept that as satisfactory.

Chris cracked an evil smile and put an open hand to his chest. "I would never."

"So what now?" Martin asked. "You suck the soul out of me and I go around the rest of my life unable to feel anything?"

"That's an option yes. But I always like to make a counteroffer."

Chris sat down in the chair across the table, his joints cracking in symphony.

"The reason I tell you the parameters of our arrangement is because that is the minimum I will take in exchange for your trip through time. You see, I'm not quite human, as you've probably figured out."

"What are you?" Martin demanded.

Chris raised his finger. "Don't interrupt me. I ask the questions around here. What I am is irrelevant. What feeds me—what feeds my soul, rather—are human souls. Sometimes all of the soul, sometimes just a small piece. I'm no glutton."

"So taking emotions is some sick way you feed off people?"

"Perhaps *feed* was the wrong word. It's more like *fuel.*"

Martin shook his head in disgust. *Same difference, asshole.*

"That's not very nice, Marty, and I'm not an asshole. You see, I help people. I send people to times they never thought possible. I've sent people to the future and the past, all of them with good intent. All of them with plans on making their lives better. You met Calvin, right?"

Martin nodded slowly, remembering his tortured friend from the liquor store.

"I don't know how much he told you, but he was in 1996 from the future. He was researching how an impeachment process was carried out. Because where he's from, the history books have been erased and the good old United States is on the verge of a collapse from an authoritarian leader. Calvin worked for this future president undercover, and had high hopes in bringing him down."

"What happened to his body when he died? The one that was in his present time?"

"He died. What happened is what always happens when you die. You stop existing. I'm sure you've heard of people who go randomly missing. This is what happens."

"What does this have to do with *fueling* you?"

"It doesn't. You call me an asshole. I just want you to know whose side I'm on, and also understand that there's a price to pay for the gift I offer. Are you done with your questions, or can I proceed?"

Martin leaned back and crossed his arms, feeling more like himself, the jet-lagged sensation of traveling through two decades finally wearing off. "Go ahead," he said.

"You showed me something, Marty," Chris said, the smirk falling from his face. "You stretched your limits to try and stop Columbine. You showed a tremendous amount of courage. I don't know how you felt about it, but I believe there's a lot you can get accomplished if you had the opportunity to go wherever you wanted as you pleased."

The hairs stood at attention on Martin's arms.

"I can offer you that chance," Chris continued. "The chance to come and go as you please to different periods in time. You can use this for pleasure, research, or to make the world a better place. It doesn't matter to me."

Chris paused and Martin remained with his arms crossed over his chest.

"And what's in it for you?" Martin asked, skepticism nearly through the roof.

Chris smiled. "That, my friend, is the hard part for you. You'll get to keep your emotions, but I'll still need a payment in return, and it'll be something that keeps you up at night, wondering if you made the right choice."

Chris paused again, and Martin didn't sense that his old friend would elaborate.

"What the hell does that mean exactly?"

"I can't tell you. Think of it as a mystery box, a surprise."

"This doesn't sound like a fair trade."

"A fair trade? Marty, think of how long you can extend your life. You can go to any era in time and live there as long as you want, and it will still only be a whole ten minutes that passes here in your current life. You can virtually live forever."

Martin stared at the ground in deep thought.

Live forever? Just last week—in 2018—he would have laughed at the thought of living another day. But now with a fresh perspective and renewed energy, it seemed more like a second chance at life. The last 22 years had been a wash and passed by in one long, drunken blur. He thought back to 1996, watching Lela carry their dead daughter out of the house, and felt no urge to go through a similar disappointment again.

Martin shook his head, tears rolling down his face.

"You set me up. You made this bullshit offer to use it as leverage for a worse offer?"

"Not at all. Your original offer is still on the table. Why don't you take the rest of the day to think it over and let me know? I know you want to get out there and confront your ex-wife. Maybe that will give you some clarity. You know where to find me."

Chris appeared calm as always, despite having a snarling Martin in his face, and stuck out a hand to shake.

"Fuck you," Martin said and turned for the back of the room where Sonya was finally stirring.

"Make sure you come back tonight. You'd hate to see what happens if you ignore me. I'll be here all night."

Martin looked over his shoulder as he walked away and caught the devilish wink Chris shot his way.

"Sonya!" he shouted. "We need to go!" Martin knelt beside her and brushed a hand down her arm. She slow blinked as her eyes fought to stay closed, clearly enjoying the sleep.

"What happened?" she murmured. "Are we here?"

"Yes, we're both here and we're okay. But we need to go. I can explain." Martin pulled her arms and propped her up from the ground. She looked around the dim room and studied the counter where piles of different colored powders formed small mounds.

"What is this place?" she asked.

"I'll explain, but we need to go. We have a lot to get done."

He led her by the arm and toward the door that led out of the office and into the store where they found Chris sitting behind the checkout counter.

"Sonya, meet Chris. I'm sure you'll have a chance to catch up later." Martin spoke as they sped by Chris, who kept his smirk focused on them.

"Pleasure meeting you, Sonya," he called out before they reached the exit.

Martin expected the world to be completely different when they stepped outside the store, but felt an instant relief when he saw his car parked where he had left it.

"So this is 2018?" Sonya asked. "It doesn't look too different."

"You have no idea," Martin said, desperate to get off the property. "Let me charge my phone and I'll show you what the world is like. But first, I gotta pay a visit to Lela."

52

Chapter 51

Martin tried to organize his thoughts as he drove wildly through Larkwood, remaining silent as Sonya gawked out the window to the same city she had just left 22 years in the past.

"We have so much to do," Martin said, speaking more to himself. "I have so much to do. We have to go to Lela's, pick up the money I invested, and get you settled."

Don't forget your date with Chris so he can kill you from the inside.

Martin decided to not tell Sonya about the ultimatum Chris had given him. She needed to settle in before having such a bomb dropped on her.

What am I going to say to Lela? Do I just barge in and tell her I know she did it, and she better tell me everything? I could record our conversation if my phone's battery will hold up, and take it to the police.

He never thought he'd play a mental game of chess on how to get Lela to jail. They had remained cordial after the divorce. The divorce occurred more out of necessity than a desire. The pain cut too deep and neither of them had the energy to uplift each other, eventually fading away by seeking comfort through other means: Martin with alcohol, and Lela with food.

Their physical attraction had vanished. Martin supposed they both saw a piece of Izzy in each other, whether it was her eyes and smile from Lela, or her round nose and flat laugh from Martin. But now Martin knew the truth, maybe the attraction was gone because Lela had found it from someone else in his family.

Fucking bitch, he thought, and decided to lead in with that topic.

Martin turned on to Cherry Street and chills sprung up his back. He looked to Sonya who stiffened up once she realized where they were.

"Lela never moved out of the house?" she asked.

Martin shook his head.

"That's disgusting."

Martin snickered. "I never thought anything of it. But now, yes, it's very disgusting."

He pulled into the driveway, parking where his kid brother had all those years ago when he came over for a night cap.

"What do you want me to do? I'm not going in there with you," Sonya said, fidgeting in her seat in clear discomfort.

"Of course not. I want you to wait ten minutes and then call the cops. Tell them the address of this house, and that Lela Briar murdered Isabel Briar in 1996. Tell them to not cause a disturbance, that everything is under control inside the house. There's no need to barge in, Lela will hand herself over."

"How can you be so sure?"

"We were married for fifteen years; I know her."

Martin powered on his cell phone that had been plugged in to the center console. It had only reached a five percent charge, but would suffice for what he needed. He held it up for Sonya to see, and she studied it like a curious scientist.

"All you do is swipe your thumb across the screen like this to unlock it," he explained, brushing a quick stroke across the lock screen that showed a picture of a smiling Izzy. "Then just tap the green icon on the bottom left to open the dialer. The number is still 911—that much hasn't changed. Don't touch anything else for now. I'll show you what these things can do once this is all done."

He handed the phone over, and Sonya accepted it in two hands like it was the key to the city.

"Okay, I think I can do that," she said giddily.

"Perfect. Ten minutes. Don't worry if I come back out here or not before then, just make the call. There's a clock on the top right corner of the phone, go off that."

Sonya nodded before Martin leaned and kissed her cheek, causing a momentary blush.

"I'll see you in a bit."

Martin stepped out of his car and took a moment to stare at his old house, replaying that fateful night he had just witnessed a "few hours" ago.

He climbed up the steps and knocked on the door, expecting Lela to be awake by now. She didn't have to be at work until nine, and it wasn't quite eight o'clock yet.

The front door creaked open and Lela's face appeared, scrunched into a look of confusion. Her brown hair hung to her shoulders, and makeup attempted to cover the wrinkles starting to form on her forehead and chin. Familiar blue eyes bulged at the sight of her slim ex-husband. "Marty? What are you doing here?"

"Good morning, Lela, I hope I'm not catching you at a bad time," he said as she unlocked and pushed open the screen door for him.

"Not at all, come in."

Lela glanced at his car and saw Sonya, looking away quickly as if she wasn't supposed to have looked. "Is everything okay?"

Martin stepped inside the house for the first time in at least ten years. Everything was rearranged. The furniture had been updated with an L-shaped couch that spanned the entire wall, facing a massive flat screen TV mounted to the wall. *It's good to see these TVs again*, Martin noted.

"Actually, no, everything is not okay. I received a phone call from Daniel last night."

Martin paused to let the words sink into Lela's receptors, and he watched as her mind searched for the light switch. Lela was dressed for work in a matching purple blouse and dress slacks wrapped snugly around what was once a tight body that had filled in with rolls in recent years.

"Daniel," she said in amazement. "How long has it been? I didn't think any of us would hear from him ever again."

"That's what I thought. He's doing well, apparently still on the east coast and loving life."

"Well that's great to hear. Is everything okay, though? Why did you come here to tell me that?"

"I think we should sit down."

"Okay?" Lela said hesitantly, and crossed the room into the kitchen that had also been updated with stainless steel appliances and granite counter tops. A square dinner table stood in the center of the room and Lela pulled out a seat as Martin followed, taking the seat across from her. The morning light struggled to claw its way into the west facing kitchen, leaving them in a dim setting. "What's going on?" she asked, a slight trace of fear in her voice.

Does a guilty conscience last all these years? Probably never thought you'd hear Daniel's name again, did you?

"Lela, we have a major problem. Daniel told me everything."

She stared at him, eyebrows scrunched, and he wasn't sure if she was playing dumb or truly confused.

"Told you everything about what?"

Her voice cracked on the word *what,* and he knew she was playing dumb.

"He told me about the night of September 9th, 1996. He told me about him coming over here. Fucking you and leaving. All before Izzy went missing."

Lela's face turned ghastly pale as she wiggled in her seat. She remained silent and looked down to the table.

"There's no point in denying it. I should congratulate you. I never knew. You would have gotten away with it, had he never told me. Do you have anything to say?"

Lela looked up to him with tear-filled eyes. Hearing the date of September 9th, 1996 spoken out loud always made Martin cry as well, regardless of the situation. Lela was no different.

"I'm sorry," she mustered through a clenched throat. "I'm sorry I did it, and that you had to find out this way."

"Did you know that's why he moved away? He felt so much guilt once Izzy went missing, that he felt partially responsible. Can you believe that? He didn't even do anything but slide in between your slutty legs."

"Martin, please," Lela said, now sobbing. "I didn't want to hurt you. I was just home alone every night. I couldn't take the loneliness any more. Daniel was in the same boat. We never planned on this happening. He came over one night to see Izzy, and after she went to bed things escalated."

She looked down to the table, shame taking hold of her face as tears and mucus dripped from her nose.

Let's go get her, Martin thought, and placed his hand on top of hers.

"Lela, I can forgive you. This was so far in the past. I'll admit when I first found out I was ready to kill both of you. But so much has happened since then, there's no point. You haven't had any contact with Daniel since then?"

She shook her head.

At least there's that. Maybe he really did leave because of the guilt.

Lela looked up and stared at him with watery eyes. Somewhere behind her deceiving and murderous eyes was the girl he fell in love with in high school. Lela Morgan, one of the coolest girls in school who had a line of guys around the building, begging to go on dates with her. The girl he used to watch dance in the car to the radio, using his hand as a microphone as she belted out lyrics at the top of her lungs.

He couldn't believe that same girl would end up as a child murderer. And not just any murderer, but one who thought she could actually get away with it.

"What happened after he left that night?" Martin asked once Lela's sobs had finally ceased.

"What do you mean?" she asked.

"I mean what happened when he left? What did you do? Watch TV? Go to bed? Surely something happened, time didn't just stop."

Time felt like it had stopped when he watched from the backyard as Lela carried their dead daughter to the trunk, and he knew she would have felt the same during that moment. Tragedy has a way of freezing time for those involved, leaving the rest of the world irrelevant.

"Well, I went to bed, I don't know. That was a long time ago."

"You don't know what you did after you *fucked* my brother?"

"No."

"Are you sure there wasn't anyone in the house that night who caught you and was upset by it?" Martin slammed a fist on the table that caused Lela to jolt in her seat. "Are you sure, Lela?"

He fought every urge to call her a murdering cunt, knowing it would be best to lead her into her confession.

"Martin, what's this about?" she asked, sitting upright, clearly trying to hide how nervous she was being put under the spotlight. "How do you expect me to remember such a detail from over twenty years ago?"

"A detail? So carrying our dead daughter's body out to your trunk in the middle of the night is a small detail now?"

Her eyes nearly exploded from their sockets in a look that said *how the fuck do you know that?*

"What?" she asked.

"Stop playing stupid. I know what happened that night. I know everything. So you might as well tell me the truth."

He paused and studied her face, watching her try to calculate a way out of the accusations and running into road blocks at every turn. The more she realized she was caught, the more her face drooped in despair.

At least two minutes passed with them staring at each other, silently arguing over who would say the next word.

It was Lela. "I don't know what you want me to say."

"I just want to know what happened, and why it happened."

Lela sniffled and rubbed her face in frustration.

"It was an accident."

There's the confession.

"I never meant to do it, Marty, you have to believe me. I would never kill our little girl."

"But you did." Gone was the urge to cry or scream. Composure took over his emotions as he sat across from Lela like an interrogating detective.

Lela, on the other hand, had melted into a puddle of tears and repeatedly wiped the moisture off her face every few seconds.

"She caught me and your brother that night," Lela continued through sobs. "She caught us, and that's when everything came crumbling down."

Martin wanted to question the timing of events, remembering neither of them had appeared in any rush when Daniel left the house, but didn't want to tip his hand quite yet.

"It turned into a huge argument. Izzy insisted she was going to wait up all night for you to get home and tell you what happened. I begged her not to, promised that I would tell you myself—and I was going to."

Lela paused and ran through the events in her mind. The sobs were slowing, but had formed a thick layer of mucus between her nose and lips.

"We were arguing in her room after your brother left, and that's when I left for the kitchen. I wanted to take my mind off everything, so started doing the dishes from dinner. I thought she would have dropped the argument, but she ran into the kitchen and kept yelling at me."

Lela's lips quivered uncontrollably as the mucus dripped to the kitchen table in a neat puddle.

"She called me the worst mom on the planet. She told me to burn in hell." Lela paused, mustering the courage to say the next thing. "She told me that you and her would live a happy life together without me. That neither of you needed me."

The heavy flow of tears returned, only this time silently.

"I couldn't handle her saying those things to me. I know what I did was wrong, but she wouldn't stop, so I threw the pan I was washing at her and it hit her square in the head, on her temple."

Lela stared to the spot in the kitchen where Martin presumed Izzy had stood that night.

"She collapsed right away and I rushed over to help her, but she wasn't breathing. I tried CPR, I punched at her chest, but nothing was working. I felt her skin turning cold, and I knew it was too late. Whatever I did killed her immediately." Lela looked into Martin's eyes for the first time since her confession had begun. "I didn't want to kill her. I didn't even want to hurt her. It was a freak accident."

Martin cleared his throat before speaking. "We have to get her body out of the lake. She deserves to be buried properly."

Lela shook her head. "No, Marty, please. If we do that, they're going to send me away forever."

Martin nodded. "I know." The police would be close by now. "Don't you think you've gone long enough living out this lie? I mean, had you come clean about it at the time, you'd probably be out of prison by now. You could've cleaned up the rest of your life and lived out the rest of your days with a somewhat clear conscience. Now you'll have to think about this every day until you die."

"Marty, please. Please don't do this." Her words dripped with desperation, but her voice showed the defeat of a woman who knew she was going to prison.

"I've already done it. The police are outside."

New tears streamed down her face. "Marty, I'm so sorry. I loved our family and I fucked it all up. There hasn't been a day that's gone by where I haven't thought about the three of us together again. I'm so sorry."

Martin stood and shuffled around the table to Lela who buried her face into her hands. "I love you, Lela. That never stopped. I even forgive you for cheating on me with my brother. But you've ruined my life. I lost every motivation to live since Izzy died. I've been a zombie for the last 22 years all thanks to you. I've almost killed myself, and I will *never* forgive you for killing Izzy."

He leaned over and kissed her on the back of her head. The once love of his life, who had turned into an accidental murderer, fell silent when a thundering knock came from the front door.

Martin glanced over his shoulder and saw two police officers.

"It's time, Lela," he said. "Should I let them in?"

With her head still down, she nodded in a quick, jerky motion.

Martin smiled. When he set out to save Izzy six months ago, he never imagined this adventure would end with Lela confessing to murder and being taken into custody. Then again, he didn't have any idea what to expect.

"Just think of this as payback for getting away with this for so long," Martin said as he walked toward the front door.

He opened the door to find the officers waiting patiently, nodded at them, and stepped aside. "She's right in there," he said, pointing to the kitchen where she still sat with her face buried.

Martin returned to his car where Sonya gawked out of the window. Even though a sick feeling continued to gnaw at his insides, he felt relief knowing justice would finally be served to Izzy's killer. She'd never be back, and he had accepted this fact over ten years ago, but the closure felt as perfect as a frozen drink on the beach. He no longer had to wonder what happened to his daughter, wonder if she was still alive somewhere, or worry about her killer or kidnapper causing her any further harm.

With one final matter to settle, Martin was ready to move on with his life for the first time since 1996.

53

Chapter 52

Martin couldn't keep the smirk off his face as they drove back to the Wealth of Time.

"She's going away for a very long time," he said. "A very long time."

"Are you okay?" Sonya asked. "I mean this all happened so fast. Last night you found out about all of this, and this morning you confronted your wife who confessed to it all."

"I feel great. Don't get me wrong, this is not the outcome I wanted. I thought I was going to save Izzy and bring her back home. It's going to take some time for this all to really sink in. Hell, I'm still trying to process the fact that I actually traveled through time *and* was able to bring you back with me. Nothing about these last six months feels real yet, and who knows if it ever will."

"I definitely understand that."

"I have to go see Chris right now. I have a matter to settle with him, and I think it's best if you stay in the car again. Then I promise I'll show you all that 2018 has to offer."

Sonya kept quiet as she stared out the window and Martin left her to soak in the surroundings, hoping she would open up to him again at some point. There was a definite adjustment period to accept the fact that you traveled to another era in time, and Martin understood this. Sonya might be distant for a few days, possibly weeks, but he'd be there when she was ready to immerse herself in the times.

How bad could it even be? he thought ahead to his meeting with Chris. *I've already lost my daughter, and lived through it twice.*

He knew better than to doubt Chris's ability to destroy him, whether emotionally or mentally, but Martin felt on top of the world and ready to take on whatever the old man threw his way.

"I don't like the vibes I get from this old man," Sonya said when they pulled up to the store. "I told you he was in my nightmares."

"Well, I can't say anything about him being in your dreams, but Chris is a pleasant man. I wouldn't worry about anything."

The words felt fake coming out of Martin's mouth and he hoped Sonya didn't notice.

"If he's so pleasant why can't I come in with you?"

She got you there.

"I just need to speak with him in private. Remember, it's not everyone who gets offered this opportunity to time travel. There are sensitivities to consider."

Sonya stared into the store, ignoring him, and Martin assumed she didn't find that answer acceptable.

"You know what. Come in with me. Look around his store for something you might like. He and I can talk in the back."

She perked up at this. "Okay. Deal."

"Let's head in."

Martin stood from the car and couldn't believe that only an hour had passed since they arrived back in 2018. That one hour was all it took to bring Izzy justice and put his mind at ease from all the sick doubts and thoughts that had plagued it for more than two decades.

They faced the storefront together, hands held. Thick gray clouds filled the entire sky to create an unsettling gloom over the city, and the air came to a standstill.

"Everything will be fine," Martin said, both to reassure Sonya, but also himself.

Sonya led by taking the first step up the small three stairs to the entrance, and Martin reluctantly followed, realizing he wasn't as ready as he had believed to encounter Chris with his new proposal.

Sonya wasted no time and pulled them both into the store, the bell chiming from the entrance.

The store was deserted, as it seemed to be more often than not, and Chris sat behind the cash register reading a copy of *Dracula*.

"Ah! Martin and Sonya, please come in."

Martin's blood froze at the sound of his voice, and he assumed Sonya's did, too, as she stopped halfway between steps.

"Good morning, Chris," Martin mustered through a tense jaw, receiving back that smirk that could haunt a grown man's dreams for months.

"A great morning it is. I take it everything went well where you just came from?"

Martin started to walk again, and now he pulled Sonya along. "Yes, I would say things went as best they could, considering the circumstances."

"That's what I love hearing. Happy endings!"

Chris clutched his gut and cackled like a loon.

"Let's cut the bullshit, Chris. Can we talk in your office?" Martin asked.

"It would be my pleasure." Chris hopped down from the stool he sat on and extended an arm toward his back office, the door already open and inviting anyone who dared enter its darkness.

"Stay here, look around," Martin said, turning to Sonya. She nodded in return, but he could practically smell the fear oozing from her. *Bet you wish you would've stayed in the car now, right?*

He released her hand and turned to Chris who stood like a statue with his arm out, patiently waiting for Martin to enter his office so he could feast on his soul.

"Everything's on sale today," Chris said to Sonya. "Pick anything you like and I'll give you a great deal." He winked before disappearing into the office and closing the door behind them.

"That's quite the lovely lady you have there, Marty," Chris said as he worked his way around to his desk. "Have a seat."

Martin sat down across from where he had just slept over an hour ago during his journey back in time.

"What's the deal you want to offer me? I need details." Martin sat back and crossed his arms, ready to enter negotiations, despite knowing Chris could get whatever he wanted at this point.

Chris leaned back in his creaky chair and propped his feet up on the desk. "Do you know what the strongest human emotion is, Marty?"

Martin shook his head quickly.

"It's pain," Chris said flatly. "Pain drives you humans. If you think about it, you carry out your life to avoid pain. Pain is scary and no one wants to confront it on any given day. When a human experiences pain, they release so much negative energy into world. So much that I can practically grab it with my hand like it was a floating piece of paper in the wind."

"What are you getting at?" Martin asked, arms staying crossed to show he wasn't interested in the sentimental speech.

"Relax, old friend. It's all part of the offer. You see, my original offer is still on the table. You can agree to hand over your ability to feel emotion. It won't affect you quite as badly as you think, but you can forget about things like joy, pleasure, and happiness. But at the same time, you'll also never feel pain, sadness, or grief again. I think it's a fair trade."

Martin gestured at the old man to get on with it, growing impatient as the seconds passed.

Chris ignored Martin in a clear reminder of who was in charge.

"The alternative offer I want to make you has two main components. One being a Juice that you can take to travel through time as you wish. No questions asked. Think of it as a permanent round-trip ticket. In exchange, you will experience pain that I can feast on. Not a physical pain, but an emotional and mental pain, and it will come when you least expect it. I can't tell you what the experience will be, as I don't even know. It's one of those matters I carry out when the time feels right. So, if you think you can handle it, if you can live through terrible pain once more, then you'll be able to continue life with your emotions intact, and the ability to travel anywhere in time."

Chris stopped and crossed his hands behind his head as he stared at Martin.

"So what'll it be, my old friend?" he asked.

Martin uncrossed his arms and sat forward in his seat.

"I need you to answer my questions about time travel before I can consider this," Martin said. "I want to know the rules. I want to know who the Road Runners are and what they're trying to do. I want to know why you decide to randomly show up."

For the first time Chris had no deceiving grin to offer, but rather a flat expression of thought.

"Well, Marty, there are hundreds of little rules that you will experience for yourself. I'm not going to cover those with you. I gave you the golden rule to live by, and perhaps I can share more if you accept. As far as the Road Runners, those are a group of people trying to take control of the world. They're dangerous and shouldn't be trusted."

"Then how did they get access to travel through time?"

"They weren't always bad, Martin. They received access just like you are now, and made decisions for the worst. This ability comes with great responsibility, and some people just can't handle it. Perhaps it's my own fault for bad judgement, but that's what they say about hindsight, right?"

"What's your angle with all of this?" Martin asked. "Why not hold on to this ability for yourself? Why do you share it, and what do you want out of it?"

Chris leaned forward in his chair, the smirk returning.

"I've told you already what I want out of it. I need to feed myself, and I feed off human emotions. I've always had this ability. I've been around throughout the existence of time, you see. It's like I live in the same world as you all, but not really. I've lived in all of the worlds, and it gets lonely. That's why I started to share this gift with others, so there could be other people in my world."

Martin locked eyes with the old man and thought for a moment that he could see the thousands of years of history brimming behind those gentle, blue eyes. Maybe he was telling truth. He'd never know, but he was sold on the opportunity.

I've lived through time-travelling, and how sweet it was.

He thought of the bank account waiting for him, loaded with money from his investments made in the past, thought of meeting Sonya and having his life changed forever. A lot of good had come from time travel.

"If I agree to this, what happens next?" he asked, prompting a slow nod from Chris.

"It's quite simple," Chris said. "You go home today with your Juice, and continue living life. There's really no strings attached aside from the pain I'll bring to your soul."

"What about Sonya? Can she have the Juice?"

"She can drink it but nothing will happen. It's created specially for you. She can always travel with you the same way. So, tell me, Marty, do we have a deal?"

Martin sat in silence. *How bad can the pain be? I've been to hell and back. Me and Sonya can see the world.*

He wouldn't have given two shits about having life experiences before his journey into the past, but now it felt as if a thousand doors of possibilities opened in unison.

"Deal," Martin said, and stuck out his hand instinctively. Chris grabbed it quickly, and Martin felt the coldness of the old man's flesh.

"I'm happy to hear that. Please, let me grab your Juice so you can get out of here. I'm sure you have lots planned with your beautiful lady."

Chris skipped across the office and disappeared into the dark corner where his laboratory waited. The sounds of glass bottles clanging against each other echoed around the room before Chris let out a grunt followed by, "I found you!"

He appeared in front of Martin in chilling quickness with a glass canteen filled with purple liquid held out in front of him.

"Here you go, old friend. 128 ounces of the finest time-traveling Juice your soul can buy. All you need is a single drop on your tongue and it works the same way as the pills."

"How do I choose where to go?" Martin asked as he grabbed the heavy bottle of purple liquid.

"Simply think about it. You'll be transported to the same location of your current body, though. So if you want to visit, say, ancient Rome, you'll need to first travel to Rome and then take the Juice. When you fall asleep and wake up, you'll be rubbing elbows with Julius Caesar himself!"

Martin studied the bottle that felt no different than an over-size bottle of wine.

"So this is it? I'm free to go and wait for some tragic thing to happen to me?"

"Don't bother waiting. It will happen when you least expect it."

"Will I still see you around?" Martin asked, knowing he never planned to come back to this godawful store again.

"I'll drop by from time to time. But don't worry about me, get out of here. The world is yours!"

Martin nodded toward Chris and gripped the bottle tightly in both hands. Outside the office door waited the world in 2018 as he knew it, with a woman he loved, and a life that had finally moved on after his daughter's tragic murder by his ex-wife.

More adventures waited outside the walls of the Wealth of Time, along with a lurking shadow in his soul that waited for life-altering pain.

Martin left the back office for the final time and didn't look back. He grabbed Sonya from a nearby aisle and they departed the store as quickly as they had arrived. A long future waited ahead for them, and he had never been so eager to start the rest of forever, with her by his side.

II

Warm Souls

Wealth of Time Series, Book #2

54

Warm Souls Cover

BOOK TWO OF THE WEALTH OF TIME SERIES

WARM SOULS

ANDRE GONZALEZ

55

Chapter 1

It had rained every single day since they pulled Isabelle Briar's remains from the lake. Martin had shed tears as he watched the dive crew jump into the water in search of his long-lost daughter. An hour later, they emerged with a pile of bones and Martin's heart sunk as the gray skies cried heavy tears over the small town of Larkwood, Colorado.

His ex-wife, Lela, had already been taken into custody by the local police. Martin was forced to watch old pictures of his family flash by on the news and internet. The story was all anyone talked about, and he soon refused to show his face in public—especially with his new girlfriend nearby, who didn't need the harassment of the limelight during her first week in 2018.

In 2018, news stories were posted online for viewers to watch at their leisure. These same stories were shared to social media for the entire world to watch, judge, and even leave their opinions in the form of a comment.

There were thousands of thoughts and prayers for Izzy, and this touched Martin as he scrolled through the comments. There were even dozens for Martin directly, people trying to step into his shoes and imagine their spouse murdering their child. But, as always on the internet, ugly, cruel people also crawled out of their dark corners and accused Martin of being a neglectful husband. Why wasn't he home that night?

Was he out at the bars? Having an affair?

Get fucking real, he thought, reading these ludicrous theories. He wondered why people bothered reading articles online if they were only going to form their own story.

Despite the trolls, the overall support from the online community helped Martin through a difficult week. So did Sonya.

Sonya had learned over their six months together in 1996 how to handle Martin's emotions: when to insert herself into the situation, when to back off and give him space. This particular week was a balanced mixture.

Martin's cell phone rang constantly from relatives and friends all around the country. Sonya still gawked in amazement every time he spoke into the tiny device.

"What can I do for you?" she had asked the night after the body recovery.

"Just *be* here. Please don't stress about doing anything. We can order takeout for every meal, I really don't care. Just being by my side is all I can ask from you right now."

Seeing Izzy's bones pulled from the water had fucked with his mind; part of him had expected her body to still be somewhat intact.

"Unfortunately, people litter this lake, making it more acidic," a member from the forensics team had told him. "That accelerates the decomposition process."

Martin had spoken with a handful of forensic team members, and each of them spoke in the same tone: flat and emotionless.

He thought of these events as he stared at the casket, its perfect black gloss still glimmering on the gloomy day. The prior night was the rosary service at the church, an event he still couldn't remember. Before arriving to the cemetery was the funeral service at the same church, also a fuzzy memory. All he could do was stare at the coffin and allow the burden of regret to settle on his soul.

Sure, he received the closure he had sought by learning what exactly had happened to his daughter after 22 years of wondering. But what he really wanted was one final hug, one last kiss on her forehead, a final whiff of her scent to hold in his lungs and heart forever.

He never encountered her when he had traveled to 1996, always keeping a safe distance to watch her from afar like a guardian angel, terrified to tinker with the past before learning how it worked. Only guardian angels weren't supposed to stand helplessly outside the house while the one they protected was murdered inside.

Thinking of those few minutes of hell made him clench his fists and tremble with rage. Chris, the old man, the keeper of time or whatever the fuck he was, had knowingly set him up for failure. There was no situation where Martin could have barged into the house and saved the day; he had no reason to believe that Izzy's demise would come from inside.

God damn it all.

The priest droned on in the background as Martin kept his eyes fixed on the casket. His daughter was in there, never able to laugh or sing again. Martin's mother sat on his right, hugging his arm. A gathering of roughly fifty friends and family came to show their support for Martin and Izzy. When the story became widespread news, Martin was asked if the funeral would be open to the public, which he promptly rejected.

The priest finally stopped speaking and many of the guests visited Martin in the front row to offer him hugs and handshakes, wishing him the best in his recovery. He mindlessly returned the hugs and mumbled a quick thanks as people moved down the line.

After fifteen minutes the cemetery had cleared out, leaving Martin alone with Sonya and his mother. The funeral director prepared to lower Izzy into the earth. He didn't want to watch, but felt comfort in knowing where she was.

"Do you feel up to grab some coffee?" his mother, Marilyn, asked. "My treat."

"Sure." Martin just wanted to leave the cemetery.

They all walked slowly to the car, Marilyn struggling up a slight hill to the parking lot. Sonya handled the driving on this emotional day and took them to the nearest coffee shop in a silent car ride.

When they arrived, Martin grabbed a table while Sonya and his mother went to order the drinks. They had gotten along well despite just meeting a few days ago. Marilyn hadn't asked where they had met in the midst of all the commotion, and he was glad because they hadn't yet discussed a story to tell people when asked that very question.

They joined Martin at the table.

"Martin, I need to tell you something," Marilyn said, a sudden shift in her already solemn tone. "I know this isn't the best day, but it really can't wait any longer."

"Mom, what's wrong?" he asked, a pit forming in his stomach.

She forced a smile as she stared down to her coffee cup, running a finger nervously around the brim.

"I've been diagnosed with Alzheimer's."

Martin's jaw dropped and Sonya seemed to shrink into herself. Welcome to 2018 with Martin Briar, where kids get buried and mothers contract deadly diseases.

Chris, he immediately thought. *That motherfucker.* He'd been waiting for something bad to happen; the old man had told him it would when he least expected it.

"I. . . I don't know what to say," Martin replied.

"There's nothing to say," Marilyn said flatly. "It's not in the early stages, either. The doctors said I have two to four years to live, and that the symptoms will start progressing any day now."

Not realizing he had any more left, tears formed in Martin's eyes. "Have you already been suffering?"

His mother, who seemed to have aged twenty years in the last five minutes, nodded gently as a tear rolled down her cheek. "I've been forgetful with silly things: where I put my keys, what I was looking for in the kitchen. I didn't think anything of it until I got in the car to go to church and couldn't remember which way to go."

The church was only a mile from her house, the same one he had seen burnt to ashes on his trip to 1996.

"Mom, I'm so sorry."

"I know. And I wanted to tell you before I get any worse. I don't know when that will be. My mind still feels clear, and I don't know what exactly it's going to do."

She fell silent. They all knew how this would progress and eventually end.

"I've made arrangements with a senior home that specializes in Alzheimer's. It's just over in Grant."

Martin shook his head aggressively. "No. I'm not letting you go to that home."

"Marty, it's okay. You'll be able to visit—it's only a fifteen-minute drive."

Martin's face had turned bright red as tears and mucus flowed from his eyes and nose, pooling together on his chin.

"No. I'm not gonna let you rot away in a home while you forget every detail about your life. You can stay with me."

"Marty, there's no room for me in your apartment—"

"I'm moving," he interrupted. "I've come into some money and am going to buy a house."

He wasn't lying, but he also wasn't sure exactly how much money was waiting for him in his investment account, either. That would have to go on the to-do list for tomorrow.

"Money from what?" his mother asked.

"I've done some investing, and things have exploded for me."

"You never mentioned this."

It felt like it had been six months since they last met for dinner after their quick trip to the mysterious store, the *Wealth of Time*, which it had been for Martin, but in reality it had only been a week. Martin didn't keep much from his mother, so her surprise was warranted in this scenario.

"It sort of took off over night. Caught me by surprise as well."

"Well that's great news, Marty. I still don't want to burden you. The toll this disease can take on the family shouldn't be questioned."

"I know it'll be hard, but I'm going to step away from my job. I've come into that much money."

He didn't know if this was for certain. Yes, there should be a good sum of money to at least live off for a couple of years. It was also possible that his investments changed the route of history and saw the companies flop. Maybe he would have to go back to his miserable job at the post office, but his bad fortune had to turn around at some point.

"You're living with me, Mom. You don't have a say in the matter."

He almost said *us*, but caught himself. His mother wouldn't have an issue with Martin and Sonya living together, but he wanted to avoid the topic at the moment.

"I love you, Marty. That's the main thing I wanted to tell you now before I forget who you are."

She resumed crying as if she flipped on a switch.

"Why would you say that?"

"Because it's going to happen. I've accepted it. I've taken all the pictures of you and your brother, and your father. I wrote on the back of every single one who is in the picture and who they are in relation to me. I don't want to forget, but as you said, I don't have a say in the matter. I love you, Marty, and I'm proud of you. I knew one day you'd be able to get your life back on track after Izzy, and it looks like that's starting to happen."

She shot a quick wink to Sonya that made her blush.

"I love you, too," Martin said. "Now let's get out of here. We need to get ready to move."

56

Chapter 2

The gray clouds disappeared the next morning, and the sun shone into Martin's apartment for the first time since he arrived back in 2018. The heavens knew the gloom was necessary, and with Izzy now properly buried, the world returned to normal.

It was Friday, and Martin refused to wait until Monday to learn what waited in his investment account. Waking up in his apartment without a hangover was a new sensation, but having Sonya cuddled up next to him was something he wouldn't trade for all the alcohol in the world.

His feet hit the ground at six o'clock and he wasted no time making a quick breakfast. He had slept like a log the night before and felt ready to tackle the day ahead. Butterflies flapped wildly in his stomach as he pondered the prospect of becoming rich in the next few hours.

He didn't expect it to happen so quickly, but Martin already felt at peace with Izzy's burial. After so many years, it was only natural for the brain to accept her death, no matter how hard the heart refused to believe it. The news of his mother's Alzheimer's also helped overshadow some of the emotion, as did the pending excitement of what would soon happen at the investment center. The past few days had been an abstract painting of emotions.

Sonya joined him in the kitchen a few minutes later, her hair a frazzled mess, but still beautiful with its subtle streaks of silver mixed in with gold.

"Good morning," Martin greeted her as he flipped an egg in the skillet.

"You seem awfully chipper today," she replied with a wide smile.

"I'm hoping today's a great day. Do you care to join me downtown this morning? You can explore since it's changed so much since you've last seen it, then we can grab lunch when I'm done with the investment people."

"I'd love to. I've always enjoyed downtown—can't wait to see what it's like now."

"Perfect, I'm planning on leaving here at eight to head down."

"Works for me," she said, crossing the room with her silk nightgown flowing behind. She had visited the local department stores to rebuild her wardrobe while Martin spent hours at the police station to conclude Izzy's decades-old case.

She wrapped her arms around Martin's waist from behind and rested her head on his shoulder. "Are you sure you're doing okay? This whole week has been absolutely crazy. I can't imagine what you're going through."

Martin nodded, keeping his concentration on the stovetop. "I'm doing okay. I'm sure this will be a process. Some days will be good, and others will be bad. Yesterday was extremely difficult, but I hope to leave it in the past. All I can do is look forward and control what I can."

Sonya kissed his back before setting the table. "I'm glad to hear the positive outlook. I'm here for you on the good days and bad, don't forget it."

They sat down for breakfast, laughter and life filling the apartment for possibly the first time ever.

* * *

Martin debated wearing a suit, but settled for slacks and a polo. There was no dress code to enter the investment center, but he needed to look the part of a wealthy man stopping by to pick up his funds.

During the drive downtown, they found themselves on the same stretch of highway they had driven during their mission to Columbine High School in 1996. That memory felt like it really had happened two decades ago, and Sonya never acknowledged it after seeing the entire school in flames on the nightly news.

Within thirty minutes they parked in a garage underground from the Sixteenth Street Mall, an outdoor mall spanning a mile long through the heart of downtown Denver.

Businessmen and women filled the sidewalks on their way to work in one of the many skyscrapers. Sonya gawked at the city that had nearly doubled in size from what she remembered in 1996.

"When did Denver become so big?" she asked, more to herself.

"Don't get lost this morning," Martin said as he led them toward the investment firm.

They crossed one block before reaching the sparkling golden sign that read: THOMAS AND LEONARD INVESTMENTS.

"Well, this is it. I have no idea how long this will take, maybe an hour. Go grab some coffee and walk the mall, I'm sure everything has changed since you've last been here."

"Yeah, you could say that," she replied, admiring the buildings that kissed the clouds.

"Meet me here in, say, one hour. If I'm not here, just come back every half hour. We really need to get you a cell phone. That will make this all easier. If you find a phone store, maybe take a look. Tell the sales people you're just browsing, otherwise they'll harass you into a $1,000 phone."

"A thousand dollars for a *phone*?" she gasped.

"Yeah, you'd be surprised. Does that all sound like a plan?"

"Yes. I'll even find a spot for lunch."

Martin pecked her on the lips and entered the building.

He had chosen to invest with this firm simply because he knew it still existed in 2018. Many firms had gone under during the recession in 2008, but he remembered the massive golden sign on the mall, inviting those with the deepest pockets to enter its doors.

Their offices were on the lower level of an eight-story building, and the gold theme continued all the way inside with golden walls, chandeliers, and a fish tank in the lobby's floor.

This place is obnoxious.

"How may I help you, sir?" a young African-American man asked from behind the front desk.

"I was hoping to withdraw some funds from my account today. Is there someone available to help?"

"Certainly," the man replied, typing on his keyboard and splitting his stare between the screen and Martin. "Give me one moment to track someone down for you."

"Thank you."

Martin took a seat in one of the heavily cushioned lounge chairs in the lobby. A door— with a golden handle, of course—was the only other thing visible aside from expensive artwork hanging on the walls.

The door opened and another man appeared, much older than the enthusiastic kid behind the front desk. He locked eyes with Martin and started toward him with a hand extended, his perfectly tailored suit moving precisely with each step.

"Good morning, sir," he said in a most formal voice. "I understand you're looking to draw funds today?"

"Yes, sir," Martin replied, shaking the man's firm hand.

"Perfect, I can assist. What is your name?"

"Martin Briar."

"Oh," the man said abruptly, and scrunched his brow. "Please come this way, Mr. Briar."

Martin met the man's puzzled face and his heart drummed a bit faster. *Do they know something about me? Why would he look at me like that?*

"My name is Edward Clarence. Let's get situated in my office and we can discuss your account."

"Okay." Martin's nerves throbbed in his fingertips as his palms started to moisten.

He followed the man, whose pointy features reminded him of a weasel, through the door and into the silent office space where finance professionals moved millions of dollars every day for their clients. Behind the door was a long hallway that branched into other hallways. Offices lined the hall, each with a name painstakingly etched on the glass doors. The work spaces resembled the prestigious lobby with polished oak desks, golden nameplates, and more abstract art on the walls.

They walked three doors down, and to the left entered the office of Edward Clarence.

"Please have a seat, Mr. Briar. I'll be right back."

Martin situated himself in the chair, less comfortable than the loungers in the lobby.

Edward returned a couple minutes later with a stern-faced woman in a pantsuit.

"Mr. Briar, this is our vice president, Karen Grabble."

"Good morning, Mr. Briar, it's a pleasure to meet you," Karen said as she sat behind Edward's desk and logged into the computer

"Likewise."

Karen had bright red lipstick and curly black hair tucked behind her ears. Martin imagined she had been attractive in her twenties, but life in the finance world had clearly taken its toll on her in the way of wrinkles and bags under her brown eyes.

"Mr. Briar, I'm here because we have some questions," she said, crossing her hands on the desk as she stared at him. Edward had closed the door and stood awkwardly in the corner of the room.

"Is there a problem?" Martin asked, fighting to keep his voice calm.

"Not a problem, just some curiosity. We've been trying to get in touch with you for the past few years with no success."

"What exactly were you trying to get in touch with me about?" He tried to play it off cool and felt like he was succeeding.

"Well, sir, you made some investments in 1996 and haven't touched your account one single time since. As your balance grew, this caught our attention and we wanted to reach out to make sure you were okay. We even searched through death records to make sure we hadn't missed something."

"I'm sorry about that," Martin said in a forced voice of gratitude. "I've been out of the country for the last few years. I honestly forgot about this account until recently, and that's why I'm here today."

Karen stared into his eyes, clearly trying to fight back the urge to say something.

"Very well," she said. "How much were you hoping to withdraw today?"

"I don't even know what my balance is. Could you tell me that?"

"Of course."

She turned to the computer and drummed on the keyboard.

Martin had invested $30,000 in 1996 into various technology and health companies that he knew still existed in 2018.

Please be a million. A million would be so perfect.

Karen continued on the keyboard, and Martin wondered if she was dragging out the process for whatever reason. She seemed like the kind of lady who got hers kicks from pissing off people.

"I show your current balance as $12,750,000."

Holy. Fucking. Shit.

"Excuse me?" Martin asked, his heart going from a rabid, caged animal to a frozen snowman in the matter of one second.

"Twelve point seven five million, sir."

How the hell did this happen? I'm not rich. I'm filthy *rich.*

The tension in his body had reached its peak and Martin wasn't sure if he should laugh or cry all the way to the bank. He could buy his new house and car and never have to work a day again.

"That's a lot more than I was expecting," he said with the slightest waver in his voice.

Karen stared at him, unimpressed.

"Can I withdraw all of it?" he asked.

The vice president scrunched her eyes at the screen, as if looking for some loophole that would not allow this random bum off the streets to take home $12 million. She pursed her lips tighter with each scroll down the screen.

"Yes, you can. Please know that we take a 1% cut from all withdrawals."

"Not a problem. I appreciate you taking the time to track me down."

Martin knew they were hoping he would turn up deceased at some point. There were no beneficiaries listed on the account and all of that money would have become their own.

"Please give us a few minutes to cut you a check. Is there anything else we can do for you today?"

"No, just the withdrawal will do. Thank you, you've been a great help." He hoped she could sense the sarcasm in his voice, but her poker face left him clueless.

She offered a quick grin that likely hurt her face before standing and leaving the office.

"Well, that was interesting," Edward said as he returned to his rightful spot behind his desk, and they both let out relieved laughter.

Edward made small talk with their famous client while they waited for the check to be delivered.

Twelve million dollars, Martin thought. *I'm gonna marry Sonya.*

57

Chapter 3

Martin stepped outside to find Sonya pacing circles outside the investment firm. She stopped when she saw him and jogged over.

"How did it go?" she asked.

"We need to get to a bank right now," he said. He had folded the check and slid it into his pocket, not removing his hand from the pocket in the process.

"What happened?"

Martin looked over his shoulders in both directions and whispered. "Twelve million dollars."

Sonya's eyes bulged. "You're shitting me."

"I'm not, let's go right now, my bank has a branch on the mall."

He walked as she followed along his side.

"Martin, what on earth are you going to do with all of that?"

He walked faster.

"I have no idea. Apparently I'm buying a house for all of us to live in. Maybe I can buy us each a house on the same block." He chuckled. "I'm still shaking from when they handed me the check."

"We need to sit down and budget this money. I don't want you blowing through it all before Christmas—that can happen."

"That's not gonna happen. I'm gonna put it in savings while I figure out what I'm gonna do. I really do want to buy a house. My apartment is miserable and harbors lots of bad memories. That's all I really want. I suppose we can travel the world."

"Travel the world or travel through time?"

"I told you to not bring that up yet."

"We could do both. Travel through time and see the world. Imagine the Renaissance Era. We could live like royalty."

Martin had hidden his canteen of the Juice in the back of his liquor cabinet. He explained to Sonya the terror he felt wielding so much power, and the guilt of knowing he had caused his mother's Alzheimer's due to his selfish decision. He could have taken the original offer and lived the rest of his life like an emotionless zombie. Instead he would spend every night crying as his mother forgot the face of her own son.

How's that for a fair trade?

The bottle was stored away in hopes of being forgotten. As soon as Martin had arrived home with it he immediately regretted his decision, overwhelmed to know he could go to any time. He could visit the triceratops that used to roam Denver, or go to the year 3000 and get struck by a flying car, assuming the world still existed.

Having a history buff for a girlfriend didn't help, either. She wanted to live out her life's work: witness the construction of the pyramids, be a fly on the wall during the Civil War, and a whole list of things he'd never have a desire to do.

All he wanted was to get the check deposited, and if it didn't bounce, know that this wasn't a dream.

Still, the Juice pulsed in his mind like the heart beat from Poe's *Tell-Tale Heart.* It tugged at him with a mystical force, begging him to drink it and go on a new adventure.

Who do you want to go try to save today? it asked. *Fall into my trap where you are most vulnerable. Remember Columbine? Do you want to try to stop 9/11 next? Maybe the Oklahoma City bombing? We can have a grand time.*

They reached the bank, deposited the check—in which the teller did a double take at the figure—and were back on the mall within five minutes after what ended up a non-climactic encounter. He'd obviously never deposited millions of dollars, and didn't know what to expect, soon learning it was treated like any other transaction.

"Let's go eat lunch," he said as the first wave of relief took over. "I need a drink."

* * *

"Our life is going to change forever," Martin said as he took his first sip from the Jack and Coke delivered to their table. Sonya had decided on the first restaurant she spotted with an outdoor patio, a concept rare to find in 1996, but standard in 2018.

"Outdoor patios and rooftop decks are all over the city now," he explained to her.

The restaurant was deserted as the lunch rush was still an hour away at noon.

"I want to make one thing clear, Martin: all of this money is yours. I don't expect a penny of it. If I need to get a job to help contribute, then I'm happy to see what the teaching world has to offer here."

Martin threw his head back and bellowed laughter.

"Sonya, I just deposited a check for an amount I can't even wrap my mind around. I'm not working another day in my life, and neither are you. All we need to figure is out how we can stretch this to last for the activities we want to do."

Sonya stirred the straw in her soda and smiled. "Marty, you really don't need to be so generous."

"How can I justify wiping my ass with hundred dollar bills while you go work some job for twelve dollars an hour?"

She giggled, and Martin used the moment to soak in her beauty as the sunlight glowed on her face and lit up her blue eyes.

"Well, thank you. I'll help you with whatever you need, even taking care of your mom."

The topic was still sensitive, and Martin winced at her words.

"So how does this magic juice work?" she asked, knowing she needed to change the topic immediately.

Martin chuckled. "Magic juice? I guess we can call it that. Apparently it works just like the pills, only I have a lot more of it than one pill for each trip. Chris said all I have to do is think about where I want to go—er, *when* I want to go—and drink the Juice. Then I fall asleep and wake up where I want to be."

"Do I still get to come along?"

Martin nodded as the waitress returned with their food. "Yes. That works the same way. As long you're touching me, you'll come along for the ride."

Tell her now, before it's too late.

Martin could still hear Chris telling him that Sonya continued to age regardless of how much time they spent in the past, compared to him, who wouldn't age until he returned to his present time in 2018. She went through time as a form of property, apparently having her own set of rules.

"You should know something," he said.

She looked up to him curiously as she took a bite of her sandwich.

"I love you."

She chewed with a smile, mumbling that she loved him back. He couldn't tell her, not with the obvious look of joy on her face. She already had enough on her plate with trying to figure out life in 2018, and he couldn't justify adding more to her well-hidden stress levels.

"So tell me," he said. "If you could go to any era in time, where would you go?"

Sonya stared to the table and took a sip of her drink.

"Honestly, I would go back to the 20's."

"What's in the 20's?"

"My grandfather," she replied coldly. "He's always been a mystery in my family, but it's my family's fault. They shunned him. I don't know why."

"Really? Your grandmother never mentioned anything?"

Sonya shook her head. "Nope. She was the one who started the rule about never speaking his name. I don't even *know* my grandfather's name. That's how bad it is."

"What *do* you know?"

She shrugged. "I've heard that he was an English spy, captured and persecuted by the United States. I've heard he was an outlaw on the run, robbing banks for the Irish mob. I've also heard he went crazy and was admitted into the asylum. I have no idea which of them is true, but I'd love to find out."

"How would we go about finding him if we don't know his name or what he looks like?"

"My grandma has a storage unit. It was filled with all of her things when she passed. I'm convinced there has to be a trace of my grandpa in there."

Martin nodded. "Well, if you can get strong research together on how we can go about finding him, I'll go with you to the 20's."

"Really?" Sonya slapped her hand on the table, rattling the silverware and glasses in unison.

"Well, jeez, if you're that excited, how can I say no?"

"Martin, this is huge. I'll start researching tomorrow. You have no idea what this means to me." Sonya stood and crossed the table to give Martin a kiss.

"The Roaring Twenties," he said. "Do you know how far our money will stretch in that era? Twelve million is like a billion dollars in those days. We can live like actual gods."

"Martin, we're not taking all of that money. Are you trying to get us killed? We can't just show up out of nowhere as a random rich couple."

"We can tell everyone we come from oil in Texas and wanted to escape to a more laid-back city like Denver."

"No, that's not happening. That was a time of not just the mafia, but also bandits running rampant. You could shoot someone in the middle of the street and get away with it because there wasn't the technology to track down a murderer like there is today. If we show up with all that money we'll be robbed and murdered within two months. Word gets around fast, especially about new people in town."

"Okay, okay. You're scared of the gangsters and cowboys. Fine, we don't bring the money, just enough to get by on. But I need you to have a complete plan. I went back to 1996 without a clue what I was doing, and it was absolutely painful at moments trying to figure things out on the fly."

"I can do that." Sonya couldn't contain the overflowing joy brimming in her voice.

They ate their lunch, making plans to buy Sonya a cell phone as soon as they finished. And lingerie.

58

Chapter 4

Martin stood outside the Adams County Courthouse on Monday, angst and excitement brewing. The weekend passed in a blur as he and Sonya spent Saturday and Sunday looking at houses with a realtor.

Today, however, wasn't about him, Sonya, nor their future home. It was about justice. Lela Briar had her scheduled arraignment. The news channels had touched on her story throughout the week, with one legal analyst suggesting her team of attorneys plead guilty to save the taxpayers time and money. She had already confessed, and there was no use in trying to fight it with an insanity plea. The entire city knew she had done it, and insanity would be impossible to prove twenty-two years after the fact.

Despite the dozens of opinions swirling around, no one had any insight as to what would actually happen. The final piece of Martin's closure was to see Lela locked behind bars for the rest of her life. *The cherry on top,* he thought, reminiscing on the night he had witnessed his wife toss their deceased daughter into the lake like a fish.

Rumors spread that Lela had made a request to attend Izzy's funeral, but the judge promptly shut it down. True or not, it was an idea that disgusted Martin. A murderer who went to the funeral of their victim was a new level of twisted.

Martin entered the courtroom and hid in the back row of the gallery. He had spoken to her for the last time at her kitchen table when she confessed to ruining their lives. How she lived with such a dark secret for more than two decades was beyond his comprehension. Maybe she was psychotic, after all.

"All rise for the Honorable Ernesto Garcia!" the bailiff shouted from the corner of the room. A tall, lanky man of brown complexion appeared from the secret door behind the judge's bench.

"Thank you, you may be seated," he said in a booming voice that could strike fear into the bravest men. "Please bring in the defendant."

A side door swung open to reveal Lela, her orange jumpsuit baggy over her thin body, handcuffs snug around her wrists. Her hair was tied into a messy bun, something she had always done when in a hurry. Black bags hung below her eyes.

A police officer led Lela across the courtroom to her position at the defense table where two attorneys nodded to her.

"Will the defendant please stand."

Martin watched as the judge spoke in a tone that tolerated no bullshit.

Lela rose from her seat and kept her head down as the judge prepared a stack of papers.

"Lela Briar, the state of Colorado hereby charges you with murder in the second degree of Isabel Briar. Do you have a plea offer today?"

Lela broke into hysterical sobbing. Martin believed she hadn't meant to kill Izzy. It was an innocent affair that turned for the worse when she was called out by their daughter. Maybe she hadn't done so well over these last twenty-two years after all.

Lela's attorney, an older man in a basic suit, stood beside her, handed her a tissue and spoke on the defendant's behalf.

"Your Honor, we plead not guilty to the charges," he said. Groans and murmurs waved through the gallery as Martin sat frozen and attentive.

"Are you planning to enter an insanity defense?" the judge asked, scribbling furiously on a sheet of paper.

"No, Your Honor," the attorney replied while Lela continued to wipe at her face. "We are willing to plead guilty to a charge of manslaughter."

The district attorney who sat across the aisle from Lela and her team jumped out of his chair. "We will need a couple of days to discuss, your Honor." He was a large man with muscles that filled in his suit, certainly not a man you'd want to cross on a bad day.

The judge nodded while keeping his focus on the notes he was writing.

"We will reconvene on Wednesday," Judge Garcia said. "If the state would like to revise its charges to manslaughter, this will need to be decided by then. There will be no extensions. Court is dismissed."

The judge banged his gavel and disappeared.

Martin stayed to watch Lela, the one-time love of his life. She had finally stopped crying, but kept her head down, nodding as her attorney leaned over and whispered to her.

Martin had brushed up on Colorado law and knew the plea for manslaughter was nothing but a desperate attempt at a shorter sentence—six years maximum compared to twelve years for second-degree murder. Lela would unfortunately have no path to life in prison or the death penalty, as those were punishments strictly applied to first-degree murder. The district attorney had assured he'd pursue the harshest punishment available.

Lela was taken out of the courtroom by the same police officer who helped her in. Martin left, hoping she'd get the maximum twelve years.

* * *

When Martin returned home, Sonya sat at the kitchen table with a laptop open and papers spread messily across the table. He had shown her how to use the modern computer and the new (to her) search engine called Google.

"What are you up to?" he asked, knowing damn well what she was looking for.

"I found him," she said. "I actually found him."

"How?"

"I came across a website that lets you track down your family tree. All it asked was for certain information on at least two prior relatives. I was able to give three: my mom, dad, and my grandmother. Then it shows the info it has. All it gave me was a name and a date of birth, but I've been trying to dig more with it."

"What was his name?"

"Charles Heston. It was confirmed through the marriage certificate from when he married my grandma in 1912. I just can't find much else. No death certificate, no mention of him being an outlaw, mental patient, or any of the other wild stories I've been told."

"Is it possible that all of the stories are false?"

Sonya nodded slowly. "It is. My mom claimed my grandmother never told her anything about my grandpa. Most of the stories I overheard were between my mom and her cousins speculating when I was little. Even the storage bin full of documents might just be another myth."

Martin slung his arms over her shoulders, embracing her warmth. "Look, I know how badly you want to find out the truth about your grandfather, but you've got to understand it may not be easy, even with the Internet."

"I know that. I've kept my expectations low and tried to not get overexcited when I found his name. But that's more than I've ever known about him. I just know somewhere—or someone—has the answers."

"You know, in all this time we've been together, you've never once mentioned your family, aside from the fact that your mother died when you were young. What do you know about your dad?"

Sonya closed the laptop and stood from the chair to meet Martin at eye level. "I think of myself as a pretty open book, but when it comes to my family history, I'd rather not talk about it. My father was a bad man, and I'll leave it at that. I loved everyone else in my family very much, except for him."

"And there's no one that would still be alive today? Or even back in 1996?"

"I'm sure I have some distant cousins somewhere, but everyone else passed on. After my mom died, my dad obviously raised me. Let's just say I moved out of the house on my sixteenth birthday because I couldn't take it anymore."

"I'm sorry you had to go through that by yourself." Martin pulled her in, wanting to provide the comfort she deserved. "Whatever you want to do, we'll do it. Just say the word."

They stood in silence for a moment before Sonya spoke. "I want to meet my grandfather. Even if I don't tell him who I am. I want to meet him and know who he really was."

"We can do that."

"And I don't want you to ever bring my dad up again. I'll talk about him when the time feels right, if there is such thing."

"Of course. I certainly understand that feeling."

Sonya hesitated as if she wanted to say something, so Martin nodded to her to continue.

A lone tear rolled down her cheek. "One last thing," she said. "Please don't make me see that old man ever again. I've had nightmares about him. I need him out of my head."

Martin tensed up at the mention of Chris, but calmly said, "Don't worry. We'll never see him again."

59

Chapter 5

"First you give my mom Alzheimer's, and now you're fucking with Sonya's mind." Martin spoke to himself as he sped through town for a return visit to the Wealth of Time store. "You're gonna tell me everything I need to know, then I'm gonna choke the life out of you."

He laughed nervously as he passed the church, only two blocks away from the antique store that was tearing apart his life. The memories sent chills down his back as he recalled his brief encounter with the priest at the burned down church in 1996.

He turned into the Wealth of Time's parking lot and felt the world fall silent as the blood froze in his veins.

The building was gone. Not gone like the church, which had been a pile of rubble, but gone like it had never existed. It wasn't a matter of Chris closing down shop and moving out, leaving a vacant building. There was no building, just an open field as if there had never been anything constructed on this specific plot of land. Tall grass sprouted from cracks in the random patches of concrete.

"What the fuck?!" Martin screamed, driving further into the deserted lot. "You motherfucker!"

A figure appeared to be walking toward the empty lot from the surrounding neighborhood. It could have been someone out for an afternoon stroll, but Martin sensed the person was headed straight for him, even from a quarter of a mile away. He put the car in park and waited.

He's definitely coming here, Martin thought as the figure drew closer, and was able to make out that it was a man. He took confident steps like he was on a mission and had no time to waste. He was dressed in jeans and a t-shirt, and puffed on a cigarette.

Martin stepped out of his car, compelled to encounter the man.

"Mr. Briar?" the man shouted, now fifty yards away. Martin could make out black wavy hair slicked back with lots of grease.

"Who wants to know?" Martin asked, now regretting leaving the comfort of his car.

The man popped the cigarette between his teeth and grinned as he took the final steps to reach Martin.

"Mr. Briar, my name is Mario Webster. Chris told me you'd be here today, sorry I'm late."

What the hell is going on?

"You're probably wondering where the store went. Chris likes to move it shortly after giving someone new the Juice."

"Who are you?"

Mario grinned again and flicked the cigarette away after a final puff.

"I suppose you could call me a travelling secretary of sorts. Chris isn't able to be in multiple places at once, even though it seems like he always is." Mario chuckled at himself.

Martin debated trusting this random stranger, but who else would know exactly where he would be?

"Why are you here?" Martin asked.

"Well, Chris knew you needed to speak with him, but he's unavailable. I guess you could say I'm filling in for him."

"Do you know things?"

Mario smirked. "I know *everything.*"

"Good, because I came here for answers. Everything has been fucked up since I got back."

"Well, that was part of your agreement, was it not?" Mario asked mockingly. "For something bad to happen in exchange of the Juice. Chris feasts on emotional pain, and that's what he's getting from you."

"How can he get it if he can't even show his face?"

"He has his ways."

Within a matter of seconds, Mario morphed from a friendly person into a face Martin wanted to punch. How dare this man come to Martin and spew nonsense.

"I just need answers before I even consider taking a sip of that Juice."

"That's funny, because we know you've already made up your mind. Going back to the Roaring Twenties? One of my favorite times."

Martin dismissed the comment. Chris had always shown the capability to know what he was thinking and didn't want to get into it with this new messenger.

"So what is it you want to know? I'm not as secretive as Chris, I promise. He gets his kicks watching people figure things out on their own."

"When I take my girlfriend with me, what happens to her in the current world?"

Mario's grin returned, as if he expected the question.

"Well, she's already left her current world, so she disappeared."

"Can we go back to 1996? What would happen?"

"You can go to any time you want. When you take a person through time as an object, they completely vanish. Their body travels through time, leaving no trace in their past. You know the missing person reports, right? Grown men and women who go randomly missing and we wonder how on Earth someone with a family and friends can just vanish. This is how."

"But no one knows she's here besides my mom."

"Well then, you have nothing to worry about. You can come and go as you please with her, since she's essentially unaccounted for in 2018."

Martin stared Mario in the eyes and noticed that they looked black. Yet, behind that grin, he sensed a secret.

"What is it you're not telling me?"

"You're good, Mr. Briar," Mario said, chuckling. "Very good indeed. Chris was right about you being a perfect fit."

"A fit for what?"

"For the Juice. You see, we don't just give this stuff to any random Joe off the street. People are carefully scouted and observed for years. We chose you because you have a hunger to make things right. Even in your darkest days, Chris saw the light in you, knew you'd be the perfect candidate to do big things."

"Then why does he travel to the future to watch wars like it's a spectator sport?"

"You have to understand there a billion things happening at once for Chris. Like I said, he can't be everywhere. Besides, he doesn't get in the way of the world. He lets life carry on as it would normally. No interference."

"Except for giving my mom Alzheimer's, right?"

Mario's grin vanished into pursed lips.

"You made an agreement. Don't try to make us feel bad about what that agreement led to. You were warned it would be painful, and you haven't even experienced the truly painful part yet."

"What else can you tell me?"

"I can tell you to stay cautious everywhere you go—and with everyone you meet. The Road Runners are out in full force and will stop at nothing to get every glowing person they can find."

Martin had forgotten about the subtle, golden glow that radiated from the skin of those who had been blessed with time travel. He studied Mario's arm and saw it immediately.

"No matter what era you decide to travel to, or even what part of the world you go to, for that matter, it's imperative that you remain alert for the Road Runners. They have grown considerably with their brainwashing of innocent time travelers."

Martin remembered watching them burn down the liquor store in 1996 and murdering his acquaintance, Calvin Yoshiki. He didn't need an explanation on why they should be avoided.

"And how can I tell if someone is a Road Runner?" Martin asked.

"You can't. That's the problem. They'll approach you to strike up a bond, because hey, you're both time travelers, and why shouldn't you be friends? If you fall into that trap, it's already too late. They'll poison your mind."

"Why do they do this?"

"They want to rule the world. I think they're just evil people trying to stop others from doing good during their travels. Your friend, Calvin, did nothing wrong. You met him—he was doing research to try to make his present time a better place. And they came and wiped him off the map. It's best for you to simply not get close to any other time travelers should you meet them. They are spread all throughout time: past, present, and future, as well as all around the globe."

"You guys ask me to avoid people, but sometimes I need information and I never know where to find you."

"You know enough now, my friend. Just stay out of the way of the Road Runners. Go do what you need to do and keep a low profile. The more exposed you are to the public, the easier they'll find you."

"How can I find you?" Martin asked.

Mario's grin returned. "We'll find you, Martin. We're all over the place, and we'll know when you're truly in need."

Martin nodded and extended a hand. "Thank you for all your honesty."

Maybe these people aren't as bad as I thought.

"The pleasure is all mine, Mr. Briar," Mario said as he returned the handshake. His flesh was cold and clammy. "We'll see you around."

Mario turned and walked with his same confident pace back toward the neighborhood, disappearing as quickly as he had arrived.

Martin watched the sun glowing orange above the blue mountains. He had never felt so small in the world.

60

Chapter 6

On Wednesday, Martin returned to the courthouse for the prosecution's decision. Things could progress quickly depending on what occurred today, and he needed to be the first to know.

The gallery was filled with more people than the initial hearing on Monday, likely due to the press coverage received in the two days since. The silence deafened the room when Lela entered, shortly followed by Judge Garcia.

The orange jumpsuit looked good on her. It had been hard at first to see his former wife in such a predicament, but she had asked for it. Everything would have been handled much differently had she come clean on that fateful night. It was the cover up that irked him into having such vengeful thoughts and wishes. She would have gotten away with it had Martin never met Chris. Maybe there was some good that came out of this situation that otherwise grew more regrettable every day.

"How will the prosecution proceed?" Judge Garcia asked in his intimidating voice.

The district attorney stood and brushed off his suit. "Your Honor, the state would like to drop the charge of murder, and press a charge of manslaughter against Lela Briar."

Lela's defense attorney nodded as if he expected the decision.

"And does the defense have a plea to this charge?" Judge Garcia asked.

The defense attorney stood. "Your Honor, we plead guilty to the charges of manslaughter."

"Very well. Court will be in recess until this afternoon when we will convene for a formal sentencing. Please note this will strictly be handled by the court. There will be no testimony or jury required since the plea is guilty, so no need for the attorneys to prepare any statements."

The judge banged the gavel and chatter immediately erupted like a busy high school cafeteria. Martin stayed in his seat and wouldn't leave until he knew Lela's fate.

* * *

They kicked everyone out of the courtroom for the four-hour break, so Martin had called Sonya to inform her of the news. She wouldn't let her new cell phone go more than two minutes without checking it, even though he was the only one who had its number.

Martin had lunch in the court's cafeteria, sure to keep his head down to avoid harassment from any reporters who might be in the crowd, before court resumed and he settled into his seat in the back row.

"Will the defendant please rise?" Judge Garcia boomed.

Lela stood in slow motion, bracing herself. Martin saw her hands shaking from across the room and knew the rest of her body trembled beneath the baggy jumpsuit. Lela wouldn't last in prison, where there were no manicures and pedicures available. She had a feisty personality but lacked the toughness to survive against women who would be twice as strong as her.

Will you be having such angry thoughts if she actually gets killed in prison? Martin asked himself. Even prisoners didn't take kindly to inmates who had harmed children, leaving a high probability that Lela would, in fact, face some dark days ahead.

"Ms. Briar—" Martin shuddered as he heard the judge address Lela by her married name, which she clung onto after all of this. "After reviewing previous rulings, I've decided to impose the maximum sentence of six years in prison. In addition, you will be forced to pay a fine of $500,000 and have four years of probation upon your release. If I could add more years I would, but the law doesn't allow me to do so. No one who kills a child should be allowed to see the light of day. Our bailiff will assist you with some clerical matters before you begin your sentence. Now please leave my courtroom."

The judge rose from his bench with a snarl and exited to his chambers. He must have been having a rough week, or he genuinely hated Lela, which was fine with Martin. He smiled to himself in the back row and stood to exit.

"Mr. Briar! Martin!" a woman's voice shouted as soon as he stepped out of the courtroom into the main hallway. It was a reporter, one he recognized from TV on one of the local news stations. "Mr. Briar, may I have a word?"

Almost made it out, he thought as the short woman ran to him with a microphone in hand.

"Alright," he said flatly.

"Thank you, Mr. Briar. I'm Dani Fisher with Channel Nine." She stuck the microphone in his face, and he remembered her as the field reporter for the evening broadcast. She seemed to always be trotting around town, her skinny frame and short hair always in someone's business. Seeing her up close reminded Martin of a raccoon the way she stared at him with such desperation above her tiny nose. "Mr. Briar, what did you think of the sentencing?"

"I would've liked to see a longer sentence. I thought the DA was going to pursue second-degree murder no matter what. Apparently he has more important things to tend to."

Martin had learned the art of giving short responses after being interviewed numerous times in the days following Izzy's recovery from the lake.

"Are you happy to see your ex-wife go to prison?"

"I'm happy to see justice delivered, but still wish it could be longer."

"Will you move back into your old home now that she'll be in prison?"

"Absolutely not. That home is where my daughter was killed. I have no interest in going there for any reason."

"Will you visit your ex-wife in prison?"

What kind of stupid questions are these?

"Of course not. I've made my peace with her already and have nothing further to say."

"What's next for you?"

"I'm going to live my life in peace and try to put all of this behind me."

More reporters gathered around with microphones and recorders held out to catch a statement from the defendant's ex-husband. He felt like a celebrity with the bright camera lights blinding him.

"Are you going to stay in Larkwood?"

"I haven't decided yet. I'm currently in the market for a new home."

"Who was the woman you were holding hands with at the funeral?"

"My—" Martin caught himself before saying *girlfriend.* The press would have a field day if they knew he took a new woman to sit with him at his daughter's funeral while Lela sat in a jail cell. "She was a relative. No more questions, please."

Cameras snapped and reporters barked various questions in what sounded like group mumble. He had no interest discussing his personal life with any of these people and perhaps had already said too much. The fact that they had seen Sonya disturbed him, and knowing that they had been hiding at the funeral—whether from a distance or blending in with the crowd, he'd never know—disgusted him. He pushed his way through the mob like a running back trying to plow through a defensive wall as they all shouted one last desperate attempt. Martin kept his head down and darted toward the exit.

His cell phone buzzed in his pocket.

"Hi, Mom," he said.

"Marty, I just saw you on the TV, wanted to make sure you're okay."

"I'm fine. These reporters are like bloodhounds. Hopefully that was the last time I ever have to deal with them."

"You looked good on there. Are you happy with how it turned out?"

"It's the best we could have asked for given the situation. I wish the DA would have put up more of a fight for the murder charges instead of jumping for the plea."

"It's probably for the best. This way it doesn't have to be dragged out for a trial and everyone can get back to their lives, especially you. Did I ever mention that I never liked Lela? Always thought there was something off about her."

Martin chuckled, the tension starting to leave his face. "Yes, Mom, you've mentioned it hundreds of times since we got divorced."

"Okay, good, just wanted to make sure you knew."

Martin wrapped up the call with his mom and wanted to leave this whole situation behind. It was ugly business, being reminded about Izzy's murder on a daily basis. Perhaps his mom was right about there not being a full trial. That would only lead to hearing testimony and details about the day that ruined his life. All he wanted was to pretend it had never happened.

61

Chapter 7

"I want two things done within the next couple of weeks," Martin said to Sonya when he arrived home from the courthouse. "We need to have a new house picked and ready to move into, and a concrete plan for what we're going to do in the past. And when we're done with our business in the past, I need a vacation, and one that doesn't involve following people around. I need a beach and an unlimited supply of frozen drinks."

Sonya had not removed herself from the laptop aside from eating and bathing.

"Well, do you wanna help me do research then?" she asked. "I've been on this computer all day and can't find anything on my grandfather."

"You need a break from the research. How about we look at houses for a little bit? Help clear your mind. Daydream about our future home. Then jump back into your research with a clear mind."

Sonya nodded and kept clicking the mouse.

"I don't know anything about real estate in 2018. All of these prices look outrageous to me, but I also don't know if it's normal."

"It's normal. Houses don't cost $100,000 like they used to. Those same houses are probably selling for $300,000 today. Remember, we have a lot of money now. We won't be outbid."

"I know, but a million dollars for a house is absolutely wild."

"Then wild it is. I don't really care at this point. I just want the house that I'm going to live in for the rest of my life."

"Martin, some big mansion isn't going to magically change your life."

"I know that, but I need a change. I'm literally getting a second chance at life and a fresh start. I want to build a life with you. Is that not what you came here for?"

"Of course it is."

"Well then, find some houses where we can do that. I'm not expecting a mansion, but I don't want another apartment, either."

"Okay, you've made your point. I'll look at houses."

Martin wanted to tell her about the press, but decided to leave her out of the drama. They were all obnoxious maggots, as far as he was concerned, and he didn't want to frighten her by revealing that they had seen her at the funeral. She had enough on her plate.

* * *

Sonya had arranged three house tours and one open house visit the following day. She had apparently thrown her reservations to the wind as the houses were in wealthy areas like Cherry Creek, Washington Park, and even one in their old stomping ground in Littleton.

How ironic if we end up the Klebold family's neighbors, Martin thought, the idea actually giving him goosebumps instead of a laugh.

Each house was beautiful by its own right. The one in Cherry Creek faced the Rocky Mountains straight on and had the most up-to-date appliances and interior. It was truly the house of a filthy rich person. The house in Washington Park was historic, probably built in the early 1900's, but had its own natural beauty that no modern home could compete with. And lastly, the home in Littleton and soon-to-be winner of Martin and Sonya's brief house hunting adventure, was the biggest of the three, yet the lowest priced. The tri-level home had seven bedrooms, five bathrooms, walk-in closets, and a finished basement that opened to a beautiful backyard complete with a basketball court and swimming pool.

Martin watched her as they walked through the house, her eyes growing bigger with each new room and section of the house they explored. He wanted a home they could live in until Father Time took them from the world, and they found it, but thinking about the future made Martin's stomach churn in guilt.

You have to tell her, he thought. *She has to know that she won't stop aging like you. If you go back to the 20's and live there for even a year, that's one more year she'll be older while you remain frozen at 54.*

Martin shook the thoughts out of his head, living in the moment instead of dwelling on the future.

"I think we should live here," Martin said when they finished the tour. "I think we should buy this house right now."

Sonya couldn't keep the wide grin off her face and jumped toward Martin, into his embrace. "I never imagined living in a place like this. It's magical. There's so much room for all of us."

The house provided plenty of distractions to keep Marilyn's mind occupied as she clung to every last memory that tried to flee her ailing mind.

"It's perfect," Martin said. He called his realtor and asked for the paperwork to be drawn up for an offer of $1.2 million.

* * *

Not even Martin had realized how quickly the real estate process now moved. The offer was sent and accepted within an hour, and they already had a move-in date set for two weeks after inspections and other tasks were complete. His realtor assured him this was the norm, seeing as he hadn't purchased real estate since his and Lela's house almost thirty years ago when it took months to complete the process.

Martin only needed two days to pack up his tiny apartment. Sonya had tried to make it a sentimental event—he had lived there for eight years—but all he could really remember were the late nights drinking on the patio, drinking on the couch, drinking in the kitchen, and even drinking in his bed. The apartment walls had witnessed Martin at rock bottom, and he wanted to take none of those memories with him into his new home.

His mother's house required a lot more assistance. She had lived there over forty years, and the process was indeed sentimental as they helped pack up memories that had lasted a lifetime.

Cleaning out his mother's closet, Martin found a dusty, worn-down shoe box filled with decades-old family pictures. Seeing portraits of him and his brother playing in the backyard made his stomach churn.

This is all because of you, he thought, the images of Daniel slithering into his house where Lela waited to take him to bed playing in his mind. Martin had never taken the time to reflect on this specific incident, considering what happened a few minutes afterward, but the sight of his brother filled his soul with a hot rage.

"Thank God you're out of our lives," Martin said, staring at the portrait of him and his brother at age eleven and nine, their thigh-high shorts showing all the leg scrapes and bruises that accompanied childhood. He packed the box away and continued digging through the closet where he came across a chest that housed all sorts of mementos from his late father: handwritten letters, post cards, and random gifts from the various places he had visited.

Martin lacked memories of his father. His old man had worked in both the military and later as a traveling salesman for one of the most successful nutritional companies in the country.

"Your father just can't stand to be home. He doesn't believe in home," his mother had told him and his brother when they were teenagers. "He loves you very much, and insists he does this so you can live a comfortable life, but we all know he needs to be on the road, living out of a suitcase in a different city every night. I think your father wishes he were a rock star."

Marilyn had never told them about the drug addiction he fought, or the dozens of women he had slept with, but Martin had grown to suspect these things after having more adult conversations with his mother. He sensed that she hated the man, but didn't want to say anything to tarnish his reputation as the head of the family. She had shouldered a lot of pain when the boys were teenagers in need of a man to guide them, and essentially raised them on her own.

Looking back, Martin wouldn't have it play out any differently. Marilyn Briar was the hardest working person he knew, and her constant display of fighting through every day is likely what kept him alive during the barrage of suicidal thoughts in the years following Izzy's death.

Martin didn't even cry when his father passed away. At the funeral, it felt more like a distant relative lying in the casket instead of the man responsible for giving him life. He had so many questions he wanted to ask his mother about him, but always held back, noting the obvious pain that swelled behind her eyes every time his father's name was mentioned.

He imagined a family running through the halls of his new, massive house. Kids gathering around the dining room table for dinner every night. It was the best way he could imagine what kind of home it truly was. And it was perfect, everything he could have asked for thirty years ago. But today, Sonya was beyond her child-bearing days.

There would be no kids to fill the bedrooms, no family gatherings to fill the living room, but it was a home, and exactly the start of a new life he needed with Sonya.

62

Chapter 8

When October arrived so did the moving trucks, ready to pack up both Martin's and Marilyn's lives and move them across town to Littleton, Colorado. Martin never thought he'd have the opportunity to pay for professional movers, and took great pride in watching them haul loads of boxes without him having to touch a damn thing.

"As soon as we get unpacked and settled in I want to sit down and make a clear plan. We need an exact date for when we'll be going back, along with where we want to try to live, and what our story will be for anyone who asks. We also need an escape plan in case we get spotted by those Road Runners."

Martin explained this to Sonya in his empty apartment as the movers took the last box out and journeyed two blocks down to his mother's house that would take a lot more than the twenty-five minutes needed to pack up his tiny apartment.

"I'm having a hard time finding anything on my grandfather," she said. "But I'm pretty sure he's still in Denver in 1919. It was never mentioned that he went—or was sent—anywhere else."

"There's got to be something we can at least follow as a lead. We'll find it."

Martin and Sonya left his apartment for the final time and drove to his mom's house.

When they arrived a couple of minutes later, they found Marilyn sitting outside on the front porch crying as the movers ran in and out of her house with boxes and furniture.

"What's wrong, Mom?" Martin asked, hurrying over to her. "Did the movers break something?"

"No," she sobbed. "My mind is the only thing that's broken. It's starting to get worse. I was on the phone with a friend and she asked where we're moving to, and I couldn't remember. I still can't remember. You've told me a dozen times and I just don't know."

Marilyn rubbed her forehead in frustration as if trying to press the thoughts back into her skull.

"Mom, it's okay. Don't put so much pressure on yourself. We're moving to Littleton."

"Littleton. That's right."

Martin could see the light in her mind turn on as she remembered. The fact that there was still a light in her head was a good sign.

Marilyn leaned in to Martin and whispered. "I'm so sorry, dear, but I've forgotten your girlfriend's name. I think she's too new for me to remember."

"That's okay. Her name is Sonya."

"Sonya, okay... that's a pretty name."

There was no look of remembrance to this information.

Sonya hung back a few steps away from the porch, leaving a path for the movers.

"Mom, I'm going to buy you some puzzle books. Things like crosswords, word searches, and those hard Sudoku ones you like. You need to try and do these every day. They say it helps slow the decline of Alzheimer's. So does reading, so I'll get you a library card when we move so you can stock up as many books as you need."

"Thank you, that's very kind."

Marilyn's tears slowed down, her son comforting her with a strong embrace. Sonya served them all a glass of lemonade as they watched the movers pack away the rest of the house over the next two hours.

* * *

The movers finished unloading everything into the new house by four in the afternoon. Martin ran to his new liquor store, sure to introduce himself to the staff, and bought an expensive bottle of wine, something he rarely drank but knew Sonya and his mom would enjoy.

Sonya ordered pizza for dinner and they all sat on their new deck overlooking the Rocky Mountains, drinking merrily and stuffing their bellies. Life was perfect and Martin looked forward to plenty more evenings just like this one.

Marilyn pulled him aside after dinner, while Sonya cleaned up, and thanked him for letting her move in with them.

"It's going to be ugly, and if it gets too hard, feel free to admit me into a special home—"

"Mom, I'm not doing that; stop with that nonsense. You dedicated your life to me; this is the least I can do."

Martin kissed her goodnight and watched her disappear down the long hallway to her new bedroom suite, complete with its own bathroom and small living room to lounge in.

When he returned to the kitchen, Sonya put away the final dish.

"Are you ready?" he asked.

"Ready for what?"

"To plan our trip."

"Already?"

"I want to move quickly, possibly even leave tomorrow. I have an idea to help my mom with her disease, but I want to do this first."

For Martin the math was simple. He could leave tomorrow—or even tonight—spend a few months in 1919, and only ten minutes will have passed in 2018. Then he could travel to the future in search of an Alzheimer's cure—there had to be one.

All that would see only twenty minutes pass, even if he spent ten years in the future seeking a cure. He'd leave Sonya behind for the trip to the future, unsure of how long he'd need to stay. He wanted them to spend their lives in the new home they just bought, not in some unknown future.

"Take out the laptop, so I can dig into your grandfather's past. There's gotta be something we can use."

Sonya obliged and put the laptop on the dining room table.

"What all have you searched for?"

"Just his name."

"Sonya, you're never going to find anything that way. You have to be more specific."

He wanted to tell her she had been wasting her time, but having such a powerful search engine was a new concept for her, so he let it slide.

"Google will give you whatever you want, so you've got to give it more details. Let me show you."

Martin opened the search engine and typed in *Charles Heston.*

"Look at how ridiculous this is. It pulled 1.5 million results in half a second. It even tells you that."

He pointed to the small gray print that showed these statistics as Sonya peered over his shoulder.

"You're not going to find anything that way. It's a virtual needle in a haystack. This entire first page is all about an old actor named *Charlton* Heston, and I'm sure there are hundreds of pages all about him."

"I'm so sorry, Marty, I didn't know. I was going to click through all of these pages until I found something."

"It's okay. Let's see what happens when we narrow our search terms."

Martin entered *Charles Heston Colorado* and hit the enter key.

"There we go, only 330,000 results came back by adding that one word—a bit more manageable. Let's try others."

Martin opened multiple tabs and Sonya watched as if he were performing a magic trick.

"You said there were theories that he was an outlaw, a spy, and a mental asylum patient?"

"Those are the rumors I know of."

"Let's try those."

Martin entered *Charles Heston spy, Charles Heston outlaw, Charles Heston mental asylum* into each of the tabs.

"Still a lot of results on Charlton Heston, but these should be easier to skim through and find something that might stand out."

Martin clicked around as Sonya pulled up a seat beside him. He clicked through the numerous tabs, adding *Colorado* to each search term for the best results. Sonya remained silent as she kept up with his fast scrolling down the pages.

After ten minutes of silence, Martin exclaimed, "Here we go!"

He clicked on a link and waited anxiously for the page to load.

An old newspaper clipping from *The Denver Post* filled the screen. The article's image was a mugshot of man with a deranged appearance: bulging eyes, wild hair, and a wide grin as he held the letter board in his fingers.

HESTON, CHARLES

10 14 1919

They both studied the letter board and looked from it to the man's face.

"It fits the time frame. What does the article say?"

Martin read aloud.

"Denver, Colorado. A suspected English spy, Charles Heston, has finally been captured after a four year run from the law. Mr. Heston is suspected to have lived multiple lives across the country under different aliases. He has fathered children with at least four known wives around the country. His most recent wife, Maryanne Heston (nee. Bowman) reported her husband to the local authorities after learning of his secret identity. He is set to stand trial in December and is pleading an insanity defense."

"Maryanne Bowman. That's my grandmother. I never knew her as Heston, and now I know why."

"Sounds like *all* of the rumors you heard were true. He really was an English spy, and an outlaw on the run. And I'll bet he somehow won his insanity plea and got sentenced to an asylum."

"I can't believe I'm related to this man," Sonya said, holding her hand to her open mouth. "Four different families that they know of. What a scumbag."

"So what exactly do you want to do if we go back to 1919?"

"Oh, we're going. And I'd love to stab him in the dick."

Martin giggled. Sonya rarely showed an angry side, but when she did, made sure it counted.

"I need more than that before I can agree to go. This doesn't need to be some game of revenge."

"I can get revenge without getting my hands dirty. What if we're the ones who turn him in? We can go back, live in the city for a while, and spill all the facts to the police. Then we can be there to watch him get arrested, and even stay for his trial and see what happens. I think back then the asylum was a harsher punishment than going to prison."

Martin tried to put himself in her shoes and thought if that was worth the trip one hundred years back in time. He didn't enjoy the thought of having to follow people around, but what else would ever be an option when traveling through time? If they wanted to change a part of the past, there would always be a need to follow someone.

After the botched attempt of saving Izzy's life, this proposed trip seemed tame in comparison. Besides, it was only ten minutes to him, and he could live like a king in that era.

"Okay, let's go. If he gets arrested in October, maybe we should plan to get there in August or September, what do you think?" Martin asked.

Sonya stared at the screen blankly, clearly concentrating on her thoughts and not the computer.

"Let's say early September. Do you get to decide which day we arrive?"

"I honestly don't know. All he told me was to think of the time I want to go to and drop the Juice on my tongue. I suppose I can think of a certain date and see what happens."

"Let's say September first. It could take a couple weeks to find him, then we can figure out how to get him to confess."

"Okay, that's fine. Now where should we plan to live? What's our story for 'moving' to Denver in 1919?"

"We don't need to explain anything to anyone. If anyone feels the desire to ask, tell them the truth: you're a postal worker."

"I don't know if that's going to work in this era. People know each other. They know who their postman is. It's not like today where you'd never know if the Pope was dropping off your mail."

Sonya nodded. "You can always say you're a writer covering stories in Denver for Colorado Springs. Who says you have to be from a different state?"

"I like the writer angle, but I'm still gonna go with a different state. I don't want to risk anything. We could meet someone from Colorado Springs, and they could throw all sorts of doubt our way. I'll pick some remote place like New Hampshire. What are the odds of meeting someone from there? I never have." Sonya shrugged. "I don't know much about the landscape in 1919, but I think we should stay in a central place near the capitol. If we get spotted by the Road Runners, it's easier to lose them in a crowded space instead of a secluded one."

"Makes sense. How are we supposed to know what these people look like?"

Martin had never told her about the golden glow around his skin, figuring it was best to not have her in a constant paranoid state of staring at everyone's skin. He didn't even know if she'd be able to see it since she wasn't a time traveler.

"We don't have a way of knowing for sure," he said. "All they warned me was that they will try to be overly kind to try and lure us in. So it's important to be careful who you become friends with. In fact, it's best if we don't really become friends with anyone. I'm not saying to not speak to anyone, but we have to be careful about accepting invitations for dinner and things like that."

Sonya crossed her arms, clearly unsatisfied with the terms, but Martin had rules to uphold if they didn't want to end up in the wrong hands.

"It's not as thorough as a plan as I would've liked, but there's only so much we can prepare for. We'll have to take another day when we arrive and really set something in place. I say we leave tomorrow."

"I've been thinking about the money," Sonya said dismissively. "We can't take any with us because the bills won't look the same. Did you even think of that?"

Martin's brow drooped immediately at the thought. No, he hadn't thought of that, and she was absolutely right. The currency was different in 2018 compared to 1919, and that was something they would surely consider counterfeiting and throw them in prison for.

"Is there anywhere we can get old currency?" Martin asked, nodding to the computer.

"Not for an even exchange. Those old bills are rarely seen in circulation any more. It would have been easier to get some in 1996, but I've looked it up already and you can only find them from collectors. And they don't even have that much for us to take."

Martin nodded. "Well, I was hoping to not have to do it again, but it works. Betting on sports is how I made all of my money in 1996. I already knew the results because I looked them up and made bets with bookies when I was visiting."

"Well, we're gonna need something. We can get jobs that pay like twenty cents an hour."

Martin laughed. "No, we're not going to do that. Besides, that puts us at a greater risk by encountering more people. It's too risky."

"And dealing with bookies isn't risky?" Sonya snapped at him.

"It is in a different way, but that's usually only when you lose and don't pay up. I think I'll play it much differently this time, lose some bets on purpose to keep them less suspicious. In 1996 I was so excited to win sure money that I wasn't thinking straight. The bookies were getting very suspicious after I won a couple of questionable bets."

"If you think it's safe, then I don't see why not."

"Perfect. I'll do some research on games to bet on, and tomorrow you can go buy at least one of those older bills for us to take. We'll need something when we arrive to stay in a hotel for a couple of days until we can get everything figured out."

"Tomorrow? You sounded like you were ready to leave first thing in the morning."

"I'd like to, and we still can. We should probably head to bed for the night, we need to bless our new bedroom, if you know what I mean."

"Martin Briar," she gasped. "Your *mother* is in this house."

"Yeah, on a different floor on the opposite side."

Sonya smirked as she grabbed his hand and pulled him away from the kitchen table. Life felt normal, and the thought of traveling back in time one hundred years was the furthest thing from their minds when they made love that night.

63

Chapter 9

The night dragged for Sonya. She had no problem falling asleep, but wished she never had. Her mind brewed a horrendous barrage of nightmares and dark thoughts on the eve of their trip to 1919.

Her first dream sequence took her to Colorado Springs, to the cemetery where her mother was buried. Only instead of a green, welcoming cemetery, the grass was dead, the trees bare and black as if charred by a fire, crows cawing from high up on the charcoal branches.

All of the tombstones lay flat on the ground between dead flowers. Except for one.

She walked slowly, the lifeless grass crunching with each step, and as she approached the only visible tombstone, she smelled the lingering odor of smoke.

Am I in hell? she thought as the crows laughed in chaotic unison.

"You're not in hell. *I* am," her mother's voice cackled from the tombstone.

"Mom?"

"Yes, Sonya. I hope you're happy. You sat by while your father killed me. Did you think I'd forget?"

A hand appeared atop the tombstone, fingers splayed out like a high-five, only the hand had gray skin, and random spots of flesh missing to reveal the bone underneath. It grasped the top of the stone, blending in with its grayness, before the rest of the body to which it was attached appeared.

The corpse had the characteristics of Sonya's mother: high cheek bones, round nose, and eye brows stuck in a furrow. Her once brown hair was now thin streaks of white on a mostly bald head. The gray face drooped as if it might fall off the skull like a perfectly cooked rack of ribs. There were no eyes in the sockets, just two black holes that stared into Sonya's soul.

Sonya tried to speak, but her throat clenched shut with tension. She tried to turn and run, but her knees locked, and her eyes refused to look away from her dead mother.

The corpse put both hands on top of the tombstone and glared down to it. It was cracked down the middle, splitting the text that read: *In memory of a most loving mother, Gloria.*

The corpse managed a grin through the loose flesh, revealing yellow and black teeth. "You see that?" the voice croaked. "A most loving mother."

Sonya remained frozen, heart thudding against her chest like a trapped person banging desperately on a locked door.

"I spent all those years raising you to be a woman, only to watch you stand aside while your father killed me. You didn't even flinch! Tell me, *Sonya*, was it worth it?"

"Mom, I'm sorry!" she managed to shout with a sharp crack in her voice, tears pouring down her face.

"All I get is a 'sorry'? Why don't you come give your mother a kiss?"

The corpse reached out its arms, and this time the flabby flesh *did* fall to the ground in a *gloop!* sound that pushed Sonya to the brink of vomiting. Her mother smooched her lips before laughing like a madwoman.

The ground trembled, causing the crows to flap away and return to their depths in hell. The tombstone completed its collapse by splitting down the middle and falling to each side, and Sonya's mother remained standing, howling at the skies turning black, making everything invisible.

The tension left Sonya's body as the world changed in front of her, even though she couldn't see it happening. It reminded her of a stage play when the crew would hurry and change the set during a brief moment of darkness. When the ground settled, she heard nothing but her heart pounding in her ears. Sweat formed heavy beads on her back, but she didn't notice; all she wanted was to wake up.

"She's over there," a voice whispered from behind, and she whipped around to see nothing but more blackness. "Sonya," it whispered again, then more whispering voices joined a chorus repeating her name, echoing in the silence. "Don't be afraid. Don't be afraid."

The whispering grew louder, and she became convinced all of the voices were somehow coming from within her head.

"Don't be afraid. Don't be afraid."

The voices repeated this a dozen times before fading back into silence.

"Sonya," an older man's voice came from behind her. She turned around to a flash light pointed right at her, blinding her as her arms shot up to shield her eyes. "It's me."

It was the old man from the antique store and she broke into immediate goose flesh at the sound of his voice.

"Get away from me!"

The flashlight turned upward to reveal the old man's grinning face and blue eyes staring at her. "Now, now, Sonya. I need Martin. If you dare take him from me, you'll have hell to pay! I'm in no mood for negotiations. Leave him alone. You'd disappear in the night if you knew what's best for both of you."

"You don't control us!" she barked, rage brimming to her surface. "You have no right to interfere with my life, or Martin's life."

"I would never violate our agreement, but I have to defend what is rightfully mine. You've gotten away with so much, but it ends here. Leave Briar to me."

Chris giggled, eventually howling as the world rumbled like an earthquake. A black cloud swirled around Chris, making him invisible as darkness spread across the skies.

Sonya looked up and shrieked.

* * *

She didn't wake up screaming, but the sheets clung to her sweaty back. Her heart thumped in her ears as she panted for breath like she had just run a marathon.

Martin snored next to her, undisturbed by her quick trip to hell and back. He had no clock on the nightstand, so she checked her cell phone to find it was only 11:30. She hadn't been asleep for two hours and it felt like a whole two days had passed.

Everything had moved so quickly from the time Martin asked her to join him in the future. *Too* quickly. It had all been part of the plan, but not expected several months ahead of schedule. It would all work out, regardless. They always made adjustments on the fly.

On a personal front, it became clear what she needed to do before going back in time with Martin.

I need to visit my mom's grave.

She would drive to Colorado Springs in the morning, but for now had to find a way to fall back asleep. She stared at the ceiling, listening to the steady whooshing sound of the ceiling fan, unable to close her eyes, fearful of all of her regrets and guilt waiting on the other side of her eyelids.

64

Chapter 10

The next morning Sonya rolled out of bed at eight o'clock. She had played around on her cell phone to research her English spy grandfather, but came up with nothing further.

By the time she stepped foot on the ground, Martin was already five pages deep in a small notebook of baseball scores from the 1919 season. He hadn't mentioned what awaited after they returned from this trip, but it was definitely driving the urgency in him to complete every task promptly.

She had volunteered to go buy the rare currency to use when they traveled back. Colorado Springs was about an hour away from Littleton, but she could make it in good time and be back before lunch with a clear mind and a crisp hundred dollar bill.

She dressed quickly and quietly, not wanting to draw any attention, and when she strolled to the living room, Martin was writing in his notebook with the laptop on his legs.

"How's it going?" she asked.

"Good. I completely forgot 1919 was the year of the Black Sox scandal."

Sonya stared at him blankly, having no idea what he was talking about.

"The Chicago White Sox were the best team in baseball, one of the best teams in the game's history. They were paid off by the mob to throw the World Series and let Cincinnati win. They were huge favorites, so the payoffs for anyone who bet on the Reds were enormous. What I'll do is make some decent money off the games during the end of the regular season, of course losing some on purpose, before placing a big bet on the Reds to win the World Series. Why not stock up on this old currency while we can? In case we decide to come back for a luxurious vacation one day."

"I think after this we'll definitely need a vacation. So what's the plan for today?"

Martin put the laptop aside and stood from the couch, looking over his shoulder to the hallway toward his mother's room.

"I think we should leave after lunchtime. Make sure my mom is fed and content, maybe have her relax with a movie."

Sonya nodded. "Okay. That'll work. I need to go buy this currency."

"Do you want me to go with you?" he asked.

"No, that's okay. You stay here and make final preparations. I know where I'm going. I couldn't sleep last night, so stayed up exploring the map on my phone. It's pretty cool how you can drop yourself into the middle of the street and get an up close view of everything."

"Is everything okay? Are you nervous about this trip?" he asked.

She was nervous, but for reasons she could never explain to him.

"I'm a little nervous. My grandfather was always spoken about like an old myth, on the rare instances he was actually mentioned. It's like he was Santa Claus, and all I ever wanted was to know him. I'm still in shock by what we learned last night."

"Yeah, I can imagine," Martin said, crossing the room to embrace her. His scent was bitter, but she had grown to love it. She wanted desperately to tell him the truth she had kept buried since meeting him. She was the best at her job, but had never made the mistake of developing real feelings toward one of her subjects. Daydreams had started popping into her head during their summer together in 1996. She toyed with the idea of running away with him, having him dump his special Juice down the drain and run off to a remote island with his millions. But there was no escaping her life. They would find her and force her to return.

"Well, I really should get going if we want to stay on schedule. I'll be back in a bit. Is there anything else I should get while I'm out?"

"No, I think we're all set. I'll order the lunch, so don't worry about it."

She kissed him, a faint taste of milk from his bowl of cereal still on his lips.

"I love you," she said, meaning the words for the first time.

* * *

The drive to Colorado Springs had light traffic and she made it there in fifty minutes, leaving her ten minutes ahead of schedule. She turned into St. Michael's Cemetery, underneath a stunning archway decorated with sculptures of angels and flowers. Cemeteries always created a sick feeling within her, a grim reminder of what the finish line looks like, no matter how far away it may seem. A directory stood near the entrance. This was a map of the multiple loops and plot numbers. Beside the map was a bundle of laminated pages with the listings of every name currently resting within the grounds, alphabetized by last name.

Even though it had been years since her last visit, she still knew the way, driving directly to loop B. Her arms trembled when she stepped out, and her legs felt like giving out if any more nerves built up within them.

She spotted the tombstone from forty feet away and enjoyed instant relief when she saw it had no crack down its center. The only damage was a couple of chips around the edges that likely came from years of weather.

Sonya stopped in front of the grave and studied the rest of the stone. The same quote was inscribed from her dreams, and this gave her a brief moment of goosebumps before she fell to her knees. She wept uncontrollably, tears sinking into the soil below. What always made her sick—and perhaps hesitant for visiting and getting her final closure—was knowing her mother's body wasn't actually buried in the ground, instead sunken to the bottom of some river across town. Maybe that's why she had a different connection with Martin, considering his daughter had also been tossed in a body of water just like her mother. The gravestone was merely a tribute to a life lost too soon, a dirty throbbing secret that only her and her father knew about.

How many others have visited you, Mom? she wondered. Their family in Denver was scarce, only a couple of cousins that she could think of. Everyone else lived out of state. There was a good chance Sonya was the first visitor to this grave since the funeral ceremony in 1952.

"I'm so sorry, Mom," she cried. "I should've said something."

"You can always go back and save her," a familiar voice said from behind.

Sonya pivoted around, ready to swing at the old man, but decided it best to not cause a scene in the middle of a cemetery.

"What are you doing here?" she asked, her sorrow vanishing and giving way to an instant rage.

"Why such anger toward me?" he asked, cracking that fucking grin.

"Anger? You *disgust* me. I don't know what kind of game you're playing, but you better cut the shit out. Martin seems to believe you and your thugs, but I'll get the upper hand. I always do."

"You have it all wrong. We have a deal, you and I, and you've not been following it. You're supposed to leave my recruits alone, but you've only been helping yourself to all of them. I haven't been too upset and have let you continue living your free life, but I can't help but surprise you like that night at the restaurant. You and Martin were having such a lovely evening until I showed up as your waiter, it's too bad."

"I get it, you get to play God and think you control everything and everyone you give your nasty Juice to. We're getting very close to creating our own juice, so we won't even need to steal your mindless recruits."

"That's not very nice, dear. You only see the surface of people, and that's your problem. Sure there are plenty of duds, but every now and then I get to meet someone like Martin. My knowledge goes beyond that of time. You can learn a lot about people when you have the capability of going through time and seeing the person they once were. A person's formative years are so crucial."

"You don't know what you're talking about."

"Angelina, dear, I always know what I'm talking about."

"Fuck you—don't call me that!"

Chris winced at her shouting, but his grin remained. "My, my. You should know such attitude is frowned upon in 1919. If you act like this they'll have eyes on you around town."

Sonya gave up. She couldn't stand arguing with this old piece of shit. "Crawl back into your hole and don't ever show your face to either of us again. And don't send your goons, either."

Chris winced again. "Mario would not like to hear such hateful talk from a lady. I'll be sure to let him know you called him a goon. Don't let the Road Runners eat you alive, it might hurt."

Chris blew her a kiss and turned to leave the cemetery.

Sonya had forgotten where she was or what she was doing. She turned to the gravestone, rage boiling to the top of her head. "I'm sorry, Mom."

She left the cemetery with no closure.

65

Chapter 11

Martin packed the notebook into a briefcase. He also put on a suit, realizing no one in 1919 walked around in jeans and a t-shirt. The world was still very much formal and he'd suggest for Sonya to wear one of his mother's older dresses to help her fit in with the times.

He started to wonder what was taking her so long when she finally rolled into the long driveway. The garage hummed as she pulled in and he met her at the entrance, splaying his arms out to act like a 1920's entertainer.

"Everything okay?" Martin asked after she parked and got out. "What took so long?"

"I drove to Colorado Springs first."

"The Springs? What for?"

"I had a dream about my mom last night, and I figured I should go visit her grave before we go back into the past."

"Are you okay? You didn't have to go alone—I would've joined if you asked."

"I'm fine. I needed to go by myself. I had my moment there, but now I'm ready for our trip." She stopped and examined his attire. "Why are you wearing that?" she asked with a grin.

Martin laughed. "It's my outfit for the 20's. What do you think?"

He spun in a circle to model his three-piece suit.

"I think I like it. I've never seen you in a suit before. We might just have to stay in the past if this is what you're gonna wear every day."

"Very funny. It's your turn. My mom has some outfits you can wear."

"I'm not wearing your mom's clothes, that's absurd."

"You wanna show up in 1919 like this? Wearing sweatpants and a baggy t-shirt? They'll think you're homeless or a cheap hooker."

"Well, good thing we need money, right?" Sonya said with a hearty laugh.

"Sonya Griffiths, cracking a joke? I never thought I'd see the day."

"Well my mind is all messed up right now, so you're getting a weird version of me today, sorry."

"Oh, no, it's fine. No need to apologize, but you really should change. At least wear a long dress if you have one."

"I have exactly one."

"Perfect. We'll need to blend in, not a good idea to stick out on our first day. All the men wear suits when they go out and about, and the women wear long dresses. No skin."

"What time are we trying to leave?"

"My mom already ate. I think she's in her room working on a crossword puzzle. So I was thinking we can have lunch, then get out of here."

"Okay, that works."

Martin had fought nerves all weekend, but speaking about the trip in such a nonchalant manner helped relax him. He still hadn't retrieved the bottle of Juice from the basement bar, uneasy at the thought of drinking it.

Sonya disappeared to their bedroom, leaving Martin at the top of the basement stairwell.

Just grab it and bring it up, no need to stall at this point.

Martin ran with his brief moment of inner courage and walked down the stairs with his head held high. It was just a bottle of liquid, what was there to even be afraid of?

The bar stood in the back corner of the basement, overlooking the large party space. Cabinets lined the wall, and he pulled one open to rummage through the alcohol, bottles clinking together as he reached into the back. He could feel the Juice's presence in the cabinet, and when his fingers found the bottle they clenched it, pulling reluctantly to bring it back into the open.

I wonder what happens if someone else drinks it? he thought. Knowing Chris, it would probably cause the person an eternity of emotional pain for him to feast on.

With the bottle in hand, Martin studied its contents—purple liquid flowing, tempting with its secrets—for a brief moment before running back up the stairs. His appetite for lunch had vanished, but he needed to force something down.

Just one drop on your tongue, he remembered Chris explaining. *Just like taking medicine. Nothing to it.*

His reassurance carried him to the top of the stairs where Sonya had settled at the kitchen table for lunch. Martin had ordered Chinese takeout and immediately regretted not getting something even heavier like barbecue. The kitchen smelled of fried rice and egg rolls as Martin placed the bottle on the table with a heavy thud.

"Are we taking that with us?" Sonya asked.

"Well, you want to be able to come back, right?"

"Duh. But we shouldn't take that whole bottle. It could break, and then what? Pray to your beloved Chris to come save you?" She said this with a visible amount of sarcasm. "We either need to move it to a plastic bottle that won't break, or take a small amount in a container. Do you have a flask?"

"What do you think?"

"Of course, silly question. I'd say fill a flask with it, and that can be your travel container. That way it can't be damaged, and we just need to worry about keeping it in a safe place."

"Do you think the Road Runners will try to steal it?" Martin asked.

Sonya glared at him for bringing up the mysterious people they were supposed to blindly run from.

"No, I'm not worried about the Road Runners. I'm worried about people thinking this is some kind of moonshine. Remember, we're entering the era of Prohibition, and people will pay a premium for alcohol. They'll also steal it if they think they can get away with it."

"Prohibition, huh? Not cool."

"You'll live. And we'll find a speakeasy—it's not like alcohol just vanished from the world."

"What a time to be alive. Let me get the flask, I might as well bring another with booze – maybe we can sell it for a few bucks."

"Not your worst idea."

Martin left the bottle with Sonya and ran back downstairs to get his flasks, returning a couple minutes later with one empty and another filled to its brim with whiskey.

"Were you gonna eat?" Sonya asked him.

"Oh, yeah. I should."

"Eat real quick and I'll fill the flask."

Martin obliged, forcing the food down his throat as he watched Sonya fill the silver flask.

"So this is it? You just take a swig of this stuff and off we go?"

Martin nodded. "Not even a swig. A drop."

"One drop? This stuff will last you forever. Literally."

"I know, it's like a lifetime supply in that bottle. Are you stalling?" Martin asked, and Sonya looked to him with big eyes and raised eyebrows.

"No. Why?"

"Well, you've taken the lid on and off from that bottle at least ten times now. You're either stalling or nervous."

Sonya looked to her hands as if they had betrayed her. They had indeed been fidgeting with the bottle. "Maybe I'm just nervous."

"Well, it's time. Everything is ready upstairs. I figured we'd just lay down in bed and I'll take my drop."

Martin rose, threw the empty takeout boxes in the trash, and started for their bedroom upstairs, grabbing the bottle in a tight fist. He was also nervous, but wouldn't tell Sonya since she was having her own doubts. It wasn't the traveling that made him antsy, but the barrage of warnings from Chris and his team. Why wouldn't they just tell them specifically what to look out for, instead of these vague statements?

Chris had issued no warnings when Martin first swallowed the pill to return to 1996. Instead, he let him know the only rule was to not encounter his past self. And when he had, by accident, Martin had felt like his head might explode right off his neck.

It was important to follow Chris's advice, but fair to remain skeptical about his motivations. All they could trust was his word, but now they had a little more knowledge for this journey back in time.

Martin entered the bedroom where his briefcase waited on the bed. Sonya lay down, her blue dress splayed in every direction.

"Ready?"

Sonya nodded silently, thoughts clearly plaguing her mind.

"Alright, I'll see you on the other side."

Martin twisted the lid off of the bottle and held it to his lips.

"Bottoms up," he said, sticking his tongue out and letting the drop fall on his tongue. It had no flavor, might as well have been water, but it did tingle his tongue while his lips instantly turned numb.

Martin placed the bottle on his nightstand and slid onto the bed, his briefcase clutched in his left hand, and Sonya's hand in his right. His mind started to spin from a strong sense of fatigue as he stared at the ceiling and thought, *September 1, 1919. September 1, 1919.*

He repeated this like a child counting imaginary sheep to fall asleep. Within seconds, blackness took over and he was falling.

66

Chapter 12

"We should've done this from a hotel room downtown," Martin said as he sat up on the dirt. Sonya joined him in staring at the open space that stretched into eternity.

In 1919, Littleton was nothing more than a small town. The area where their 2018 house stood was in the middle of a dirt field. Homes wouldn't be developed for another seventy years. There were no roads or buildings in sight. A journey to Denver proved challenging since they had no car and no way of calling a ride from their phones. They were alone, left to scrap for resources on their own.

"We should probably start walking," Martin said. "There's gotta be civilization around here. I think downtown Littleton is six miles away from our house. We should start there."

They used the mountains as their compass, knowing they were always to the west.

"Six miles will take three hours for us to walk," Sonya said. "There has to be a better way."

"Yeah, it's called running, and I don't exactly want to do that in this suit."

Martin judged it to be roughly the same time of day as when they had left 2018, shortly after noon.

"We'll get into town around dinnertime, find somewhere to eat, then call a cab to take us downtown," he said.

Sonya shook her head, clearly not pleased with their current situation. If they had gone to a hotel downtown, they'd already be there to settle in right away.

"Do you wanna tell me what happened in your dreams?" he asked as they dragged their feet through the dirt.

"Not really. I don't wanna relive it anymore. It has a lot to do with my past haunting me, and I'll leave it at that."

Martin sighed, wishing she'd open up about the nightmares so he could help, but if she wanted to hold that burden for herself, then he couldn't stop her. Now that they were in 1919, Martin decided it was time to tell her the truth.

"Can I tell you something?" he asked nervously.

Sonya walked with her head down to spot the random holes and bumps that might cause a broken ankle.

"Sure." Her voice came out depressed, and he debated if this was actually the right time.

"There's a bit of information I recently learned about you and traveling through time."

Her head perked up like a dog who just heard a whistle in the distance. "What? From your friend Mario?"

Martin nodded. "Yes, from Mario, and he's not my friend. He told me that you'll continue to age as you travel through time. There's no stopping of aging for you. So if we stay here for ten years, you'll be in your sixties both here and when we return to 2018."

Sonya shrugged. "Are there people who don't age?"

Oh, boy.

She stared at him, eyes burning his face to get a read.

"Martin," she said calmly. "Are you telling me that you don't age when you travel through time?"

He nodded slowly, refusing to show any emotion. They kept walking and she remained silent, Martin growing increasingly uncomfortable with each step they took.

384

"So?" he finally asked after ten minutes.

"So what? Do you want me to congratulate you?" She made zero effort to hide her sarcasm.

"No, of course not. I just want to know what you think."

"I think we need to hurry up and *not* spend ten years here. It's not really fair, but I guess I was aging regardless, either way, right? Have fun watching me grow old."

"Sonya, I didn't tell you this to upset you. I didn't even know about this until Mario mentioned it. It was already too late by then. We were here—well, in 2018—already."

She waved her hands in the air. "It's fine. Nothing we can do about it now. Stop worrying so we can get out of here and go back our lives."

"We're here for you—I just wanted to make sure all the facts were out on the table."

"Yes, Martin, I know what we're here for, thank you. I still plan on handling that, then we can leave."

Martin fell silent. They continued walking, having covered at least a half-mile since they arrived. There was still no sight of life anywhere, and the thought made Martin uneasy. These weren't quite the Wild West days, but the scenery reminded him of an old Western movie. There was actual tumbleweed blowing along the ground, dirt kicked into their faces from the random spurts of wind, and surely people riding around on horses somewhere. They just needed to find them.

* * *

Four hours later they finally saw a building on the horizon. As they approached it, they saw even more and realized it was the beginning of a neighborhood. Small houses lined up neatly next to each other, all ranch-style, as multi-level homes still weren't a concept at this point in time. Even though they were both exhausted after hours of walking on rough terrain, they sped up at the sight of life.

"Thank God," Sonya muttered under her breath. Their discussion earlier had taken a back seat and they were able to converse about their plans of this particular trip, and ideas Sonya had to spruce up the new home when they returned to 2018. Martin still sensed a sort of resentment from Sonya, but she didn't exactly make it obvious.

Martin's mind remained occupied with a trip to the future to find medicine for his mother. It probably wasn't fair to Sonya to be so distracted with that thought when they had business to tend to here in 1919, but he couldn't help himself.

He had every intention on taking his special, solo trip once they arrived back to 2018. It would only be a quick ten minute nap as far as Sonya was concerned.

Back with the Alzheimer's cure before dinner is even served. Martin smiled at the thought.

Aside from that trip, he didn't have much of an interest to travel to another time without her. It was becoming their pastime, but Martin would like the solo trip to the future to truly learn all of the rules and nuances of time travel. He suspected there were thousands of small details he didn't know, and would probably never know, no matter how hard he researched.

* * *

Forty-five minutes later they reached the neighborhood where all of the houses looked similar: two wide windows with a door in the center, brick exterior, and green lawns all covered by generous shade from the many trees that lined the block. The leaves were starting to fall and peppered yellow and orange marks across the grass.

"Honey, we're home," Martin said with a small cackle to himself.

"This definitely looks like early suburban life. There were no suburbs until the car was invented—people would never make it to work on time—so it's safe to assume anyone who lives here has a car, which means they have money." Sonya spoke in her history teacher voice, poised and informative. He could listen to her talk all day. She had a way of lulling him into a deep comfort regardless of what she was talking about.

Martin had brushed up on the era on Wikipedia. Aside from Prohibition beginning, women were in the middle of fighting for their rights to vote, World War I had ended the prior summer, and the worst Depression the country would ever see loomed around the corner in the next decade. And somewhere on the other side of the country Babe Ruth was smacking home runs at a rate that made people believe he was superhuman. Maybe he was also from the future and came back to become the first celebrity athlete.

"Should we knock on someone's door? Ask to use their phone for a cab?" Sonya asked.

"No, of course not," Martin said. "We look like shit. We're covered in dust and dirt, and I'm pretty sure I stepped in horseshit. We can't go into some stranger's house like this."

The neighborhood was quiet. All of the men would have been at work downtown while the women stayed home with the kids. School would be in session, so many of the women likely spent their days cleaning the house and preparing a massive dinner for the family to chow down whenever Dad got home from work.

Life was simple, and while he didn't agree with the gender-specific roles of the era, it kept the chaos to a minimum, something that had all but vanished in the new century.

"If there's a neighborhood here, then there's got to be a restaurant nearby. Or even a small grocery store. Something." Martin spoke as if he knew the area well, but had no idea where he was in relation to modern-day Littleton.

"We can go for a little bit more, but we'll have to stop at some point. We're not walking all the way to Denver," Sonya said, her voice a bit more hopeful than before.

It only took them ten more minutes before they found what was downtown Littleton, a block of shops and restaurants.

"The promised land!" Martin shouted, giggling at the sight. Sweat dripped down his back, his shirt clinging to his back while his kneecaps burned like they were on fire.

They settled on a restaurant called The Cottage, a small diner with a window table that faced the main road. There were a couple of families walking around the town, but it remained rather quiet.

They entered and were given the window seat, relieved to have survived the first half of the day in 1919.

67

Chapter 13

The owner of The Cottage was a short Italian immigrant named Milo. He had lived in the United States for forty years, moving with his parents from Italy when he was a teenager in 1882. Life was hard when he had arrived during his developmental years, trying to fit in with American kids in high school, all while learning English and the new culture.

It was a culture shock in every sense, and when the American kids started calling him names like wop and spaghetti slurper, Milo would return home to cry in his room until dinner was served. He had hated it, and after six months had decided that taking his life would be more bearable than facing the racial slurs thrown his way all day by the American assholes.

One cold night, Milo ventured down to the railroad and lay on the tracks. It would probably hurt, might even make his eyeballs gush out of their sockets, he supposed, but it would be quick and over without a second thought.

That's when the old man had approached him.

"You don't need to do this, Milo," he told him. "You can be anything in this country, didn't they tell you that?"

Milo had refused to get off the tracks and spoke from his lying position.

"It's a lie!" he cried. "You can be anything if you're an *American*. They hate everyone else."

"I don't think that's true now. You're in the land of opportunity, my friend. That's why your parents chose to come here."

"No," Milo snapped back. "They came here so we didn't get killed. It's no longer safe at our home. I wish they picked somewhere else."

"Milo, what would you say if you had the opportunity to go back and change everything? Would you do it?"

The old man's voice was cold, yet filled with temptation.

"Yes. I'd change it all. I'd take my chance in Sicily, or maybe just move north where it wasn't so bad."

"I see. What if I could give you that opportunity?"

At this, Milo sat up, but it was too dark to make out any of the man's features besides his white hair, the color of snow.

"Who are you?" Milo asked.

"I'm Chris."

"How did you find me here?"

"I was out for a walk. Beautiful evening, don't you think?"

"What do you want from me?"

Chris grinned, his white teeth revealed in the dark pit that was his face.

"I only want to help. Call me crazy, but anyone lying on the train tracks isn't having a good day. So tell me, Milo: do you want my help?"

Milo's mind had raced with so many thoughts that it didn't occur to him until this moment that he never gave his name to the old man. His arms and back broke into chills at the realization.

"I can give you opportunity, both in this country, or back at home should you choose," Chris said.

"What kind of opportunity?"

"If you get off those tracks and come with me, I'll show you. All I ask is that you trust me. A train will be here in twenty minutes, so I suggest you decide quickly."

Milo stayed on the tracks and dropped his head. "Okay," he mumbled. "Where are we going?"

"I have a store. I do all of my work from there—I even sleep there. I can show you what I'm working on. If you think it's a fit for you, then great. If not, you can leave, but at least I kept you off the tracks, right?"

Milo thought about the kids calling him a wop. "Sure, I guess."

Milo went with the old man that night and never looked back.

* * *

After reminiscing on that cold night in 1882, Milo smiled when the couple walked into his restaurant. Chris had asked him to keep a close ear on their conversation, wanting to know their plans for the year 1919.

Milo greeted them as he would any customer. The woman was beautiful with glowing skin and a heart-melting smile. The man was nothing special and his suit looked like he pulled it from a dumpster in the alley. He must have had money to land a lady like the one in the flowing blue dress.

"Good evening, you two, and welcome to The Cottage," Milo said as he approached their table, a gentle smile greeting them. "I haven't seen you around before, are you new to town?"

The man nodded while his lady friend stared at him nervously.

"Yes we are. My wife and I just moved here from Texas and we're checking out the area for a place to live," the man said.

"Oh? Well, in that case, welcome to Colorado," Milo replied, a most distant Italian accent buried in his speech. "Do you nice folks know what you'll be having for supper?"

"I think so," the woman said.

How strange the woman speaks in public. What kind of man would allow this? Milo thought. Women never spoke unless directly asked what they were ordering. These people must certainly be from the scary future where women voted for who ran the country. What were they going to ask for next, to *work* in the government?

"I'll have the turkey sandwich," she said, ordering first in a power move that made Milo question every bit of the man's dignity.

"And I'll have the burger, with a soup on the side," the weak man said.

Milo stared at them both, debated calling out the man, but decided to not make a scene. Chris had made it clear to not be memorable to the couple from the future.

"Perfect, I'll get those orders started for you right away."

Milo left them for the kitchen to prepare their meals. The entryway to the kitchen allowed for the restaurant's sounds to carry in with perfect clarity. Milo used this to his advantage, often times being the only one working, as he could hear when a customer needed something or had a complaint. He could beat them to the punch, making him appear like a spectacular waiter who deserved the best of tips.

Today, however, the acoustics allowed him to spy on the couple. Milo had met plenty of people from Texas, and these two didn't have one trait of a Texan. He didn't appreciate the obvious lie.

As he threw the burger and turkey on the grill, Milo took a step back to soften the sizzling sound and focus on the couple's conversation. They were the only ones in the restaurant, so he could hear them as if sitting at the table beside them.

"This is a cute place," the woman said.

"Yeah it's nice. Do you think he's a Road Runner?" the man asked.

Road Runner? Milo thought. *Why would they think I'm one of those assholes?*

"Martin, you can't go around assuming everyone is a Road Runner. You're paranoid."

"We just need to eat as fast as we can and get to Denver. Something's not right about this place."

The woman sighed. "Is this how our entire trip is going to be? You living in fear of everything and everyone?"

"No. I have my reasons for my suspicions. Just trust me."

Milo heard frustration in Martin's voice. They sat in silence for the next few minutes, so Milo peeked around the corner to see what they were doing. The woman was staring out the window while Martin fidgeted with his silverware.

Milo flipped the meat and filled two glasses of water.

"Here you are, folks," he said as he stepped back into the dining area. "Your supper should be ready in a few minutes." He placed the waters on the table and watched them with the curiosity of a child. "What are you folks doing after dinner tonight? Any big plans?"

"I think we're gonna head downtown to find a place to stay. That's where we want to live, and need to start looking at places tomorrow." The man spoke as the woman turned her attention to Milo. Even though she had spoken out of turn, Milo felt a kindness radiating from her, something rare for people from the future.

"And what do you do for work?" Milo asked, knowing the man wouldn't have likely prepared an answer.

"I'm an author," Martin responded quickly.

"Oh? Anything I would know?"

Milo hadn't touched a book in years, but wanted to play along.

"Probably not. I write children's books. For young kids just learning how to read."

Perhaps you're smarter than you look, Milo thought as Martin seemed to have an answer ready for any question.

"What part of Texas are you from?"

"Dallas," Martin said confidently.

"Ahhh, the big city. No wonder you want to live in Denver."

Martin nodded as a bell chimed from the kitchen.

"Ah! Appears your dinner is ready. Let me get it all together for you nice folks."

Milo disappeared into the kitchen and listened.

"What are you doing?" the woman asked in a hushed and hurried voice.

"I'm saving us."

"We never agreed on a final plan for our backstory. I hope you're remembering everything you're saying because you'll need to repeat it to anyone else we meet."

"I know that. We're doing fine, stop worrying."

Now the man seemed to have control of the conversation.

393

Milo put their food on plates and returned to the table where he interrupted an apparent stare down between the couple.

"*Buon appétito!*" he said cheerily as he slid the plates in front of his customers. "Is there anything else I can get you?"

"Not right now, thank you," the woman said.

Milo nodded and let himself back into the kitchen.

The couple remained silent as they ate, not speaking one word to each other until the food was gone. Milo debated calling Chris, but didn't have much to offer.

When he cleared their table, the man asked, "May I use your telephone?"

Milo had expected the question, and knew Chris wanted him to do anything to slow the couple down.

"I'd say yes, but my telephone has been out of service for the last week, I'm afraid. It takes a while to get someone out this way and take a look."

"Is there anywhere around here that might have a phone to use?" Martin asked.

"Most places will be closing down for the day in the next few minutes. I'm the only one who stays open past six in case anyone wants to have a late dinner."

Milo knew about the payphone two blocks further down Main Street, but it intentionally slipped his mind in the moment.

The woman looked at Martin in an unsettled way and Milo knew he had thrown off their plans. "I suggest you folks get going and start asking around before everyone turns in." Milo grinned at them as he dropped off their bill.

The man rummaged through his pockets and retrieved a crisp twenty dollar bill.

Wow, they are good, Milo thought, the currency one of the small details people usually overlooked. Whenever the snobby people from the future came into his diner and tried to spend their futuristic money with gigantic faces on them, Milo took great pleasure in calling the police on them for attempting to pay with counterfeit money. Watching them squirm as they were questioned, and lie about receiving the money from the local bank, brought warmth to Milo's soul.

But not these two. They were on top of their shit and likely had every fine detail accounted for. It explained why Chris was so insistent on keeping the man on their side. Milo would never mention it to the old man, but he had been making some highly questionable mistakes in who he was giving the Juice to. Granted, Milo didn't get to meet anywhere close to all of the newcomers, but the dozen he had met in the last five years have been complete busts and traitors. He wondered if the Road Runners' sales pitch had improved in recent times because it never used to be so simple for people to disobey Chris and change their allegiance.

This was all beyond his knowledge and paygrade to worry about such things, but he wondered nonetheless.

The couple tossed the money on the table and stood from the booth.

"You folks have a pleasant evening, and come back and see me sometime."

"Will do," the man lied, and they left the restaurant in a hurry.

Milo gathered the money and studied it, admiring its crispness, before flipping the sign on the door to Closed and going to his back office to call Chris.

68

Chapter 14

"I think he was one of them," Martin said as they hurried down the sidewalk.

"One of who?" Sonya asked, her arm interlocked with Martin's.

"Road Runners. I think our waiter was one."

Martin didn't want to share the knowledge of the glow he had seen on the man's skin, but might have to if danger kept presenting itself.

"He was friendly," Martin continued. "Chris said to look out for people who are overly friendly, trying to trap you in their trust."

"Oh my God, Martin, stop it with the nonsense. I don't give a shit what Chris says. He's a delusional old man."

"I'm just saying we need to be cautious."

"Of *friendly* people? Are you shitting me?"

"Can I ask you something?"

Martin knew Sonya hated being asked if she could be asked a question. *Just ask the damn question!* she would yell, but she only nodded this time.

He rolled up his sleeve and stuck his arm out in front of her. "Do you see anything?"

She examined his arm, clueless as to what she should be looking for. "Looks like your arm. Do we really have time for this?"

"Look closer. Really look. Do you see a glow?"

Sonya put her face a couple of inches from his arm and squinted, turning her head in different directions.

"Martin, are you feeling okay?"

He could see his glow as clear as daylight, but he knew what he was looking for.

"So you don't see anything?"

"No, all I see is your arm. What are you getting at?"

"Look, I know that waiter was at least another time traveler. Those of us who are have a glow to our skin. I guess you could call it a side effect. He had the glow, and I'm sure he saw mine. That's why when he started acting too friendly, I knew we had to get out. I've never been so uncomfortable during a meal."

Sonya stared at him blankly.

"Your skin isn't glowing, and neither was that man's, so what do you want me to believe? I'm looking at your arm as closely as I can."

"I don't know if you're able to see it. I don't know how any of this works. I just know that I can see the glow on myself and others. I learned of this in 1996 from the liquor store owner."

"The guy who was killed in that fire? He was a time traveler?" Sonya's voice had risen.

"He was. And he was a good guy, doing research to help save his future. He taught me a couple of details about time travel, the glowing skin being a main one. He also warned me about the Road Runners, said they were after him. Then I watched them murder him and burn his store to the ground. So, yes, I believe Chris when he says they should be avoided, and you should too."

"Just so I'm clear, the Road Runners really are bad and you can tell when someone is a time traveler, but I can't?"

Martin nodded as he stared at the ground in deep thought. "That's why it's important we keep a low profile. We just don't know what to expect from the Road Runners. I'm pretty sure our waiter was one, or else he would have acknowledged my glowing skin, right? I don't know their game except for that they'll act nice to lure you into trusting them. Was he supposed to let us go so easily tonight? Is he going to pop up again later, maybe run into us on 'accident?' It's best we don't speak with anyone unless we have to."

Sonya nodded, staring at Martin with her seductive eyes that had never lost their pull on him. He only hoped she would put her negativity toward Chris aside and realize what they were dealing with. The old man pissed him off plenty, too, but it was clear he didn't want any unintended harm to befall Martin.

"We really need to get downtown," Martin whispered, and started walking again.

The sun approached the mountains, casting orange across the sky. They'd only have another ninety minutes at best before the darkness would creep in.

After walking two more blocks, Sonya spotted their way out.

"There it is! Look!" she cried out, pointing like an anxious child to a toy on the store shelf.

Martin followed her finger to the glass phone booth that he had passed over just moments ago, mistaking it for a store kiosk of some sort. It stood right below a high arching sign that read WELCOME TO DOWNTOWN LITTLETON.

They locked eyes with each other, grins forcing their way onto their faces, and ran to the phone booth. Martin pulled open the door and they both squeezed inside. Martin couldn't recall having ever seen an actual phone booth. There had been plenty of payphones downtown, even a couple still in 2018, but never an actual glass box to stand in for privacy.

He pulled the phone from the cradle, popped in a nickel, and turned the rotary dial to zero.

The phone rang twice before a woman's voice answered. "How may I direct your call today?"

"Yes!" Martin said, excitement nearly leaping out of his throat. "I need a taxi to come to downtown Littleton."

"One moment, sir, and I'll connect you with a cab company."

The phone cut to silence with subtle clicking sounds. Martin thought the operator might have accidentally hung up, but was relieved at the sound of the phone ringing again.

"Thank you for calling Denver Taxi, my name is Chris, how can I help you?" a man's voice greeted him.

Martin froze.

"Hello? Is someone there?" the man asked.

"I'm sorry, yes," Martin snapped out of it, realizing it wasn't *the* Chris that kept his girlfriend up at night. "I need a taxi in downtown Littleton as soon as possible."

"And your final destination?"

"We'll be going to downtown Denver, looking for a hotel."

"Okay. I'll have a driver head out now. He should be there in thirty minutes. Your total trip should cost around two dollars. Meet him on Main Street right on the corner of the strip mall."

"We're already there."

"Perfect. We'll be there shortly. Have a good evening."

Martin hung up and found Sonya hanging on to every word after doubting they would make it out of Littleton tonight.

* * *

Dozens of cars drove by while they waited. The men working downtown would have finally made their way home. Martin watched in amazement as the clunky boxes of steel passed by them.

Sonya sat on the sidewalk, citing soreness in her knees from the long walk all day. She planned to take a warm bubble bath whenever they checked in to a hotel.

The sun had set for good when the taxi arrived, an all-black box that looked like a hybrid of a future Jeep and the past's horse-drawn carriages. There was no sign on the roof indicating its purpose, but when the lights flashed at them they knew it was for them.

Martin led them to the car and opened the door for Sonya to slide in first. They settled in the squeaky leather seats.

"Good evening," the driver said, turning to look over his shoulder at his new passengers.

Martin immediately examined the man's skin, not seeing any glow.

"Good evening, sir," Martin said.

"My name's Thomas. How do you do?"

"We're doing well. I'm Martin, and this is my wife, Sonya."

"Ma'am," Thomas said to Sonya with a nod.

Thomas looked like he couldn't have been much older than twenty-one. His face was youthful, glowing, and his brown hair slicked back with plenty of grease.

"Where can I take y'all tonight?" he asked.

"We were hoping you could tell us," Martin replied. "We want to stay downtown, but don't know any hotels. Is there anywhere you recommend?"

Thomas drove away from Main Street and stared at Martin in the rear view with a thoughtful expression. "What kind of hotel you looking for? I know the fancy ones, the average ones, and the ones where you can take a street lady into. I've seen it all since I started driving this taxicab two years ago."

"How about a fancy one?"

Thomas nodded. "Sure. The fanciest are the Oxford and the Brown Palace. The Brown Palace is where the rich and famous stay. President Taft stayed there a few years ago when he was in town."

Martin should've remembered these two options, seeing as both hotels remained in operation in 2018, still welcoming the high-class members of society.

"Let's do the Brown Palace then," Martin said.

"Alrighty," Thomas said as he led them through the outskirts of Littleton.

Martin noticed the engine's steady puttering and thought back to the BMW he wanted to buy in 2018. It was going to happen, dammit. After all the shit he had endured in 1996, the least he could do was splurge some of the money he had wisely invested.

"You folks new to the Denver area?" Thomas asked as they approached an on-ramp for the freeway.

Sonya stared at Martin, deferring to him to keep their fake story going.

"Yes, we just arrived here from Dallas," Martin said.

"Dallas, huh? I've heard that's a good place." Thomas spoke in an emotionless voice that made Martin wonder if the young man was depressed or just bored.

"Yeah, we heard Denver is a fun place, and wanted to see it for ourselves. How long have you lived here?"

"I've lived in Colorado my whole life. Grew up on the eastern side of the state. My papa runs a ranch, but I wanted to go to school and got the chance here in the city. He wasn't happy that I didn't wanna continue the ranch life with him, but my mama talked some sense into him."

"What are you going to school for?"

"Business. I don't know what I wanna do, just that I wanna work for myself. Like Mr. Brown, the owner of the hotel you're staying at—he owns everything in this city. I just started my senior year, so we'll see how it goes when I graduate in May."

"Well, good luck to you."

"Thank you, sir."

Martin stared out his window at the blackness of the night. There were no neighborhoods, no commercial buildings to provide the glow of a city at night.

"How often do you drive?" Martin asked, breaking a prolonged silence.

"I drive five days a week—or should I say nights. Wednesday through Sunday. During the week I drive from six 'til midnight. Saturday I go until two, but that's prob'ly gonna change when Prohibition goes live—no more drunks to pick up. And Sunday I drive from lunch 'til dinner time, an early night for me."

"And are you mostly in Denver?"

"Yep, I'm only in Denver. Only time I'm not is when someone requests a ride elsewhere, but that's not too often."

"We may need some rides around town in the next couple months. Would we be able to request you?"

Thomas nodded, staring from the rear view to the road with quick flicks of his eyes.

"Yessir. Just ask for me when you call, if it's during those hours. If I'm available, I'd be happy to give y'all a ride."

"I'll keep that in mind. Thank you."

"My pleasure."

Martin sunk deeper into his seat, relieved. Thomas had passed his first test and didn't realize it as they drove closer to downtown. The young cab driver didn't ask what they were in town for, why they would need rides, or why they insisted on having him. It was simple yes and no answers with the kid, and Martin appreciated it. They now had a local with plenty of knowledge of the geography and happenings in Denver. He didn't know how often they would need him, if at all, but it was a tremendous resource to have in their back pocket.

Buildings appeared in the near distance, many of them lit and glowing a soft golden light to contrast the black night. It was nothing like downtown in the next century, but it was downtown Denver just the same. And they had finally arrived.

69

Chapter 15

The Brown Palace looked no different from how Martin remembered it in 2018. He had never been inside the luxurious hotel, but the exterior apparently went undisturbed over its century of existence. Its brick facade towered eight stories tall, one of the bigger buildings in town at the time. The street-level windows provided a glimpse into a packed bar of patrons—mostly men—enjoying the last days of alcohol before the government took it all away. Signs on the building advertised a spa, along with times for serving tea throughout the week. Martin felt like he was trapped within an old black and white photo of the historic hotel.

Thomas had dropped them at the main entrance, but they walked down the block to get a feel for the area and their bearings, wanting to know exactly how much had changed since they were last downtown to collect Martin's millions of dollars in 2018.

Sonya gawked at the building. "I've been here before, but look how pristine the building looks in this era. All of the future chaos of downtown is gone, and this is clearly the place where the highest class people hang out."

"Well, this is where we're going to be tonight and maybe the rest of the week."

"I just can't believe I'm going to stay at the Brown Palace when it's still a new hotel in the city."

The same street names were in place, but downtown was still in its early years and lacked the towering skyscrapers and constant bustle of a major city. A few homeless people rummaged through trash cans on the deserted sidewalks. One in particular walked by them mumbling to himself about a spaceship landing on his brain. Apparently, some things never changed.

They completed a lap around the hotel and Martin remembered a bit of history he had learned about the Brown Palace. There was supposedly an underground tunnel that ran from the hotel to a brothel across the street. This gave the upper-class businessmen a chance to sneak over and live out their wild fantasies. Rumor had it that even Presidents who stayed here took advantage of the secret tunnel. Martin recognized the whore house right when he saw it, a two-level house directly across the street. All the lights were off, every drape closed, and the front door had its window covered up, too.

Martin would confirm if this longstanding rumor was true on his own time.

"Shall we?" Martin asked when they arrived back to the entrance, a set of heavy double doors with shiny golden handles.

"Please, I'm exhausted."

Martin leaned into the bulky door as the hotel's lobby welcomed them with the soft tune of a piano in the background. Chairs and tables filled the open space ahead with hotel guests enjoying a late dinner as the pianist played from the corner of the room, his fingers gliding like angels over the keys. Granite walls towered over them, lanterns hanging on each pillar. They looked up to see the square shape of the lobby stretch to the hotel's ceiling, the hallways for the eight levels of rooms appearing maze-like from the bottom.

Across the lobby Martin spotted the front desk, and led them to it, slightly embarrassed at their raggedy appearance as everyone in the dining area was dressed in pristine suits and dresses while they sipped expensive champagne and ate steak and lobster dinners.

A tall man with thin complexion and pale features stood behind the counter dressed in a black-and-white suit and a top hat. He smiled at them as they approached.

"Good evening, and welcome to the Brown Palace," the man said in a stern voice. "Do you have a reservation?"

"No. We were hoping you might have a room open."

The man looked Martin up-and-down, not bothering to hide the disgust in his eyes. His eyes jumped to Sonya and made the same judgmental path along her dirty clothes. The man, whose name badge read *Carson*, sniffed and looked down to the guest book on his desk.

"I'm afraid we have no open rooms," Carson said after a few moments. He looked at Martin blankly.

"Are you sure about that?" Martin asked.

"Certainly."

Don't cause a scene, but don't be pushed around, either.

"Well, sir, I think you're lying."

"I most certainly am not lying."

"You're assuming I don't have money because of the way we look. You're making a mistake."

Sonya tugged on Martin's arm. "Let's just go."

"No, we're not going."

Martin rarely caused a fuss, but felt compelled in the heat of the moment. His legs were practically numb after walking all day, even after dinner and the long cab ride. All he wanted was a drink and a hot shower, and if this skinny asshole behind the counter was trying to stop him, then he was going to hear about it.

"Sir, money is not the issue. I have no rooms to offer."

"Is there a manager I can speak with?"

Carson scoffed and turned away, disappearing into a back room behind the desk.

"What happened to keeping a low profile?" Sonya muttered under her breath.

"I'm not putting up with this guy's bullshit," Martin said, emphasizing *bullshit* so the word would carry into the room where Carson had gone.

405

Three minutes passed and Martin wondered if Carson was simply hiding in the back and waiting for them to leave. As someone who used to spend eight hours in the same spot on the couch, drinking and smoking, Martin welcomed the challenge.

Two more minutes passed before another man walked out of the office and approached the desk, a wide grin revealing polished teeth.

"Good evening, folks, what seems to be the problem?" the man asked. He stood eye level with Martin, and appeared slightly younger than Carson. He wore the same suit as every other staff member in the hotel.

"I feel judged by the gentleman who was just helping us. I just want a room for my wife and I. We've had a long day if you can't tell—that's why we're a mess."

Martin pulled his wallet out and rummaged through it, slapping a crisp hundred dollar bill on the counter.

The manager's eyes bulged at the sight of Mr. Franklin staring at him with his usual pursed lips.

"Like I explained, I have money. I'm sorry I don't *look* like the rest of your guests right now, but I just need a room so we can clean up and stay in town for a few days."

Martin felt Sonya's leg bouncing beside him, and nudged her to stop.

The manager flipped through the book, searching for anything that Carson may have missed.

"What is your name, sir?" he asked casually, as if there had been no issue at all.

"Martin Briar."

"Mr. Briar, we can make arrangements for you to stay as long as you'd like. I do apologize for any inconvenience so far."

Martin wished he could laugh in Carson's face. *That* would cause a scene. He had always fantasized about being rich, having that rare opportunity to push his way through any situation with the power of a dollar, acting entitled, knowing the world owed him everything because of what was stashed in his pockets. And it worked. And he liked it.

Martin never thought money would change him, but then again, he never had money like he did now in 1919.

The manager completed checking them in to a room and handed over a pair of two brass keys that jingled. "You'll be in room 619. It will be $30 per night, but I'll waive the first night for the trouble we've caused you today."

"Thank you," Martin said in his best *I'm-rich-and-entitled* voice.

"Please let us know if you need anything at all during your stay."

Martin took the keys, grabbed Sonya by the waist and left the front desk with a quick nod. They rode the classic elevator to the sixth floor—stairs weren't an option for their exhausted legs—and proceeded down a narrow hallway to room 619. Old Western paintings decorated the hallway, as they passed them in a blur, gaining speed as they approached their room door.

Martin jiggled the key into the lock and twisted until he heard a click. The door creaked open to the room already lit up from a floor lamp in the far corner. Their legs were useless as Martin's knees tingled from the throbbing pain. Without saying a word to each other, all stress had disappeared as they stepped into the room, relieved to have made it to the end of the day that seemed to never end.

70

Chapter 16

"I'm not gonna lie, I could go for a shower right now," Sonya said when they entered the hotel room. "I'm pretty sure my brain is running on fumes, but I am *not* getting into that comfy bed covered in dirt and sweat."

"I agree, but I just need a second to lie down," Martin replied, lunging for the bed and splaying across the comforter decorated with a pattern of large, obnoxious flowers. The curtains over the windows had a matching design that made Martin feel like he had indeed traveled back one hundred years. He took a moment to admire the repeating hexagonal pattern running along the carpet, and the small cushioned chair and ottoman that appeared to be for someone half his size. "How about you get started and I'll join you in a bit?"

"I've heard that one before," Sonya said, rolling her eyes. "I'm gonna get out of the shower and you'll be snoring in that same spot."

Snoring never sounded so appealing, the ultimate sign of a heavy sleep in Martin's opinion.

"Whatever you say. I just need five minutes," Martin mumbled, already feeling sleep's tight grip around his mental throat.

Sonya wandered into the bathroom, closed the door, and had the water running within seconds as Martin rolled on his back and stared at the ceiling.

Here we are again, he thought. *Back in the past with no clue how this will turn out.*

A knock banged from the door, causing Martin to jump off the bed and stumble to catch his already wavering balance. *Did they forget to give us something at check-in?*

There were no peepholes in 1919, just a solid door to leave the surprise of who stood on the other side. But with Sonya in the shower, and Martin alone for at least the next fifteen minutes, he already knew who was knocking. The very thought of the old man sent fresh adrenaline throughout his veins, even with his body fatigued beyond belief.

Martin pulled open the door.

"Fancy finding you here," Chris said, grinning in his usual black suit.

The quickest way to get rid of him, Martin had learned, was to listen and do whatever he asked.

"What do you want, Chris?" Martin asked, trying to sound authoritative, but too tired to make it believable.

"I heard you were staying here. A good friend of mine owns the hotel, and told me he spotted you checking in."

"You're friends with Mr. Brown?" Martin asked, raising an eyebrow.

"Certainly. Mr. Brown chose to use his Juice to create businesses in sites that will thrive in the future. He's made billions throughout time and all around the globe. The savviest man I know."

"So why are you here?" Martin asked again.

"I know you had a long trip today, so I'll make it brief. May I come in?" Martin stepped aside and let the old man enter.

Chris plopped down on the chair next to the window, and grabbed his chin before he spoke. "I have some news about the Road Runners. It appears they've made you a top priority.

"The Road Runners know you're in this year and plan on hunting you down," Chris continued. "That's why I'm here—to warn you."

"And what exactly am I supposed to do about it?" Martin asked.

"Do exactly as I told you. Be aware of anyone trying to be extra kind. You can look for the glow, but they keep it concealed with long sleeves, gloves, and anything that will help cover their skin. Some have even found a way to conceal the glow. I'd advise you don't go out at night. That's the only time they'll snatch you off the street. During the day is when they'll try to lure you with smooth talk or something that seems innocent. If you know you've encountered one, it's important that you lose them. Change locations because they'll be following you all over town until they find the right moment to take you."

"What do they want from me?"

Chris shrugged.

"They think you'll betray me and join them. It's unfortunately something they've succeeded at in recent months. You don't have any plans on joining them, do you?"

"Of course not. After I've seen them in action at Calvin's store, and all the stories I've heard, why would anyone want to join them?"

Martin had a list of questions to ask about the Road Runners, but the quick burst of adrenaline had already worn off. His eyes felt like boulders in his face trying to pull his head down to a pillow.

He didn't need a reminder about how dangerous the Road Runners were. The old liquor store in 1996 was probably still smoking. His old friend, Calvin, would have turned into a pile of ashes within minutes.

"I wanted to warn you about the severity of which they will be following you," Chris continued. "I have my own people around town keeping an eye on you, as well. For security. If they notice any Road Runners tailing you, they'll be quick to interject. These encounters can turn violent quickly. But we have to do whatever we need to defend ourselves and what we stand for."

"And what exactly is it that you stand for?" Martin asked, his body refusing interest, but his mind demanding answers.

Chris stood and paced around the room, stopping to stare at the bathroom door where the steady sound of running water continued.

"We encourage a free world where people can roam through history and make the world a better place."

"And making those same people sell you their souls in exchange?" Martin hadn't expected to be quick on the draw with a snarky comment.

"There's a price to pay for everything," Chris said calmly, as if he'd heard this hundreds of times. "Even those who wish to do good in the world have to pay. Nothing comes free."

Martin could have continued his argument with the old man about the morality of his "fees", but had no energy to do so.

"You always come here and tell me to be aware of these people, but you never seem to give me any advice on what to do if I encounter one," Martin said. The room started to spin and he wanted to go to bed. Why couldn't have Chris come in the morning?

"There's not much you can do besides run," Chris said. "Keep in mind these people don't have any special powers—aside from the Juice, if you consider it a power. If you hide, they have to find you like anyone else would."

"So I can fight them off?"

Chris waved a hand at Martin. "I wouldn't take any chances. The ones they send out to hunt people are highly skilled in combat and stealth. Ninjas, essentially."

"Why do they exist?" Martin was finally getting answers. If Chris wanted to talk, then why send him away? He'd been waiting forever to learn this information. "If you're the keeper of time, then how did these people end up with the power?"

Chris nodded. "I gave them the same Juice as you. There was a time when they were good and wanted to make the world a better place. Sometimes power corrupts people. A handful of them revolted, upset by the price they had to pay to obtain the Juice. They made it their number one goal to get revenge on me."

"They want to kill you?"

"Kill me?" Chris chuckled. "That would be nice. They'd love to *torture* me. Pick me apart limb by limb. The funny thing is they'll never catch me. I have people all over watching. I know where the Road Runners are in different parts of the world and in different eras of time. They've grown into quite the organization, I must say. There are thousands of them, all trying to recruit people to join their angry cause. But I have an army.

They're no match for me."

"If you have so much manpower, why not just wipe them out?"

Chris chuckled, a sound that sent chills down Martin's spine as the clock ticked away on the wall, approaching midnight. "Despite what you think about me, I don't just go around killing people. I'd like to capture the Road Runners and speak with them, try to get them to see things the way they did before their brain was corrupted by their bitter counterparts. We've only killed when pushed to those limits."

Martin took two steps forward and stood directly in front of Chris, staring into his deep blue eyes, wanting to see his soul, if there was one. The old man reeked of stale cologne that nearly made Martin gag.

"Is there a problem?" Chris asked, his familiar grin returning.

Maybe it was the irritability, but Martin had an urge to choke the old man and save the Road Runners some time. He'd had enough of the random visits and vague explanations. *Why did I ever accept this bullshit?* he wondered. *Why didn't I just say no and continue on with my shitty life? I would've pulled the trigger eventually and ended it all so easily.*

He thought back to his mother, sitting in their new house in 2018, her mind slowly fading into the darkness of dementia. It was her idea to go into the antique store—she would never pass one up. That one decision led to all of this. If Martin would have just waited in the car that day, would he be in this current mess? Sure, he had Sonya now, the brightest light in his life since Izzy, but was it worth it if they both ended up dead in an unknown place, far away from their current lives?

"What will they do if they catch us?" Martin asked, his last question.

"They'll try to convince you to join their group, that's always their main objective. They'll give you some time, too. They'll work hard to convince you. You could call them the world's best salesmen, because they sure do convert many."

Chris paused and cleared his throat.

"And if you don't agree to join their pact, they'll kill you."

Martin chuckled, slap-happy by this point in the night. "I suppose that's a bold strategy."

"You won't be laughing when they catch you. You need to take this seriously."

"I *need* to go to bed."

Chris sighed. "Very well. Just know that if you think you're being followed, it's because you are. We'll have our eyes on you, for protection. Carry on with your business and stay alert. Even though we're close, we may not necessarily be fast enough."

"Gee, your guys must have trained under JFK's Secret Service detail."

Chris shook his head. "It's your funeral. I'll see you around."

The old man pivoted and left the room, shutting the door quietly behind him.

Martin lay on the bed, the water still running in the bathroom. As he dozed, he imagined the world as it must have truly been: thousands of people all with a special ability to travel through time, jumping from century to century as effortlessly as boarding a bus.

There was a war of sorts between Chris's people and the Road Runners. A war that had gone on for how long? A few months? Years? Thousands of years? Martin could have asked questions for the next six hours if he had the energy. Was everyone who got sucked into the world of time travel forced to pick a side in this war, or were some neutral and allowed to carry on with their business? He wanted to stay neutral and not involved. If they wanted to protect him, then that was their choice. He was here to help Sonya quickly so he could plan a trip to the future to save his mother's ailing brain.

71

Chapter 17

They woke at noon, groggy and needing more sleep. Yesterday was filled with an absurd amount of exercise and stress. Martin faintly remembered hosting Chris in the room a few hours ago, the encounter feeling more like several weeks in the past. Part of him wondered if it was a dream. Even if it was, everything Chris had told him was still true, and he'd be sure to not let Sonya know about the special visit.

"I think we missed breakfast," Sonya said with a loud moan and stretch. They stayed under the sheets, their bodies aching everywhere. "I've never been so tired in my life."

"I wouldn't mind a relaxing day, honestly," Martin said. "What is the plan regarding your grandfather? What did you find in your research?"

"Not too much. Looks like they were in Kansas before coming to Denver. They should be getting here sometime within the next two weeks."

"Then why don't we go to Kansas and find them?"

Martin wanted to get as far away from Denver as possible after Chris's warning, but knew better than to come out and say it.

"We're not going to Kansas. Why would we put ourselves in the line of danger? They had guns, and they used them."

Martin felt sick. A long journey awaited trying to find someone by sheer luck, wandering around town until they either bumped into them, or met someone who knew them. How easy it must have been for criminals to stay on the run in these old days.

"Then what should we do today?" Martin asked, ready to concede.

Sonya shrugged. "I think we should walk around town and learn our surroundings. We also need to find a place to stay, unless we're staying here the whole time?"

Martin had forgotten about his encounter with the man at the check-in desk the night before. That felt like five years ago, not twelve hours.

"For now, I think it's best if we move locations every few days. We can stay here a couple more days then move to another hotel. I don't think a permanent place of residence is a good idea anymore. Just in case there are Road Runners following us."

Sonya rolled her eyes. "You're so paranoid, but I still love you."

They had discussed buying property in downtown, and selling it when they returned to 2018 for ten times the price. Martin supposed they still could, but his bigger concern was dodging the Road Runners, not adding to the millions of dollars that awaited him in 2018.

"We still need clothes, toiletries, food," Sonya said. "There's a lot to get done."

"Then let me wash off and get ready."

Their dirty clothes piled on the ground at the foot of the bed, covered in dust and sweat from their prior day's journey. Yes, they definitely needed a new wardrobe, especially in a time where everyone left their home dressed up. The last thing they needed was to look like hobos as they explored the city. Although, wouldn't that be an even better disguise?

"I'll call down for some breakfast," Sonya said. "Or lunch. Whatever they're serving now. Go get in the shower."

Martin rose from the bed, undressed, and disappeared into the bathroom.

* * *

Two hours and two gourmet chicken sandwiches later they stood outside the hotel.

"It really doesn't look much different," Martin said of the area. "Just no tall buildings."

The Brown Palace was one of the taller buildings at the moment, a few years before skyscrapers would start to go up and take over every corner of the city.

Men in suits filled the sidewalks and crossed the streets. Cars motored by at a snail's pace. It was definitely the middle of a workday in Denver, and the sensation made Martin nostalgic for 1996 when he had worked downtown every day, right before life went down the shitter.

They crossed the street to the next block of buildings, passing everything from restaurants, butcher shops, clothing, and grocery stores. Everything they needed was within a one block radius.

The best part was how few people there were. Traffic was scarce compared to what they were used to, but the narrow roads and slow vehicles caused more jams. That and the lack of traffic lights. Every intersection had stop signs to control the flow of traffic.

"Well, I know my way around the area," Martin said with a proud grin. "Everything is the same, just smaller, or different businesses in the buildings."

"Alright, smart one, but we need to buy things and find where we're going to move next. What other hotels are around here?"

"The only other old hotels I can think of are on the other end of Sixteenth Street—maybe a 20-minute walk from here. There might be others closer that I don't know about."

"Is the Oxford around in this year?"

"Great idea, it should be." Martin led the way, heading south two blocks to reach Sixteenth Street—still decades away from becoming an outdoor shopping mall—and soaking in the area once they arrived. To the east stood the state capitol, appearing the exact same with the exception of its future golden dome appearing more bronze in the old century. To the west, the street ran a mile into the distance, lined with more shops and office buildings.

A man dressed in raggedy clothes hobbled toward them. Dirt and grime covered his skin and he revealed yellowing teeth as he grinned; only it wasn't a friendly grin.

"You people don't belong here," he barked. "Go back where you came from!"

Martin looked down to the hunchbacked man, and immediately clenched his fist, ready to swing if the hobo tried to make a move.

Sonya took a step back and grabbed Martin's arm.

"We're just out for the day. Carry on," Martin said, remaining frozen. He had encountered plenty of the homeless population when he had worked downtown. They always asked for money or food, or stared awkwardly as he passed by, but never did one approach him directly with their seemingly random blurting of words.

"If you knew what was good for you, you'd turn around and never come back," the man said, not breaking his intense stare toward Martin. He pivoted and limped down the sidewalk, mumbling to himself, "If I could leave I would. This idiot has no idea."

Martin and Sonya sighed in relief. "Looks like the bums haven't changed much," he said, getting a nervous chuckle from her.

"Shall we?" she asked, taking back her spot at his side, keeping her arm intertwined with his.

They walked down Sixteenth Street and Martin pointed out all of the buildings that he knew still existed in 2018. The 1919 version had a much homier feel with the classic setup of the business on the ground level, and living quarters on the second floor. The entire mile-long walk was filled with these small businesses. It felt more like a small town instead of the capital city of the Centennial State. All of the structures were built from bricks or stones, no hints of the glass skyscrapers that would become the norm in the next century.

After 20 minutes of walking and window shopping, they reached Wynkoop Street where the local Union Station welcomed floods of travelers. In 1919 traveling by train was still common enough to make the station a bustling area. It stood in all its glory with a couple stores across the street and dirt lots along its sides.

They turned north onto Wynkoop and walked one more block to the Oxford Hotel, Denver's other famous landmark hotel. It lacked the glamour of the Brown Palace with less golden decorations and virtually zero curb appeal, but when they entered, they found an upscale world of fine chandeliers, polished oak floors, and more suited men pacing around frantically on their day's mission.

"What do you think?" Martin asked.

"It looks nice," Sonya said, admiring the lobby.

He crossed the lobby that had a U-shape of couches facing a fireplace in the wall, and met a tall man at the check-in counter, again dressed in a three-piece suit and white gloves.

"How may I assist you, sir?" the man asked in a faint European accent.

"Just curious about your room rates for a stay of about a week. Possibly checking in tomorrow."

The man flipped open a notebook and ran a thin finger down the page.

"One night's stay is thirty dollars. We're currently having a special, though. You can get two nights free if you take a free tour of the hotel and recommend us as a place to stay to your friends and family."

"A tour?" Martin asked. "What exactly do we see on the tour?"

Martin had only toured the Stanley Hotel in Estes Park, but that place was infested with ghosts. He didn't realize regular hotels had special tours.

"We like to show you all of the hotel so you can speak of it with more detail. We meet here in the lobby at four o'clock, then go down to the basement and work our way up to the Presidential Suite."

The man spoke in an uninterested voice, as if he had made this same pitch 54 times already today. Perhaps this was the past's version of sitting through a timeshare presentation. No one actually wanted to buy anything, just give us the free shit already!

"So if we come to the tour, do we have to book our free nights right away?" Martin asked.

"No. You can use them whenever you'd like within a month."

He turned to ask Sonya what she thought, but she was too busy studying the art that hung on the walls, likely suffering from an intense case of sensory overload from getting to live in the past.

"I'll have to check with my wife and get back with you," he said. "But we'll probably be here at four for the tour."

The man scoffed, likely at the suggestion that Martin had to run an idea by his wife. "Certainly."

Martin left the appalled man and joined Sonya across the room, now staring deep into the whipping flames in the fireplace.

"So are we staying here?" Sonya asked casually, still lost in the flames.

"I think so. They invited us to a hotel tour at four today for two nights free."

"Sounds riveting."

"Is everything okay?" Martin asked. "You've seemed out of it since we got here. Are you nervous about finding your grandparents?"

"Not so much. I think I'm just tired still. Yesterday took a lot out of me. I'm getting too old for this."

Martin understood, as did his sore joints. Maybe on this trip into the past he would focus on eating right and staying in shape. His trip into 1996 saw him give up drinking, at least by his standards, so why not try another self-improvement on this go round?

"We only have another 40 minutes until the tour starts," he said, checking his watch. "Anything you want to see around here? Union Station?"

"I just want to sit down, honestly. Want to grab a drink at the bar?"

"We might as well, before they take all the alcohol away," Martin said, still baffled that the government would soon make alcohol illegal. The law of the land, and a complete pile of horseshit. As if removing alcohol would somehow create world peace.

They found the bar on the other side of the fireplace and sat down for their final drink together.

72

Chapter 18

"Are we going or not?" Sonya asked, slurping down the last of her martini. The drink had brought her back to life, putting a smile on her face and the temptation in her eyes.

Martin downed two doubles of whiskey and felt ready to conquer the old century, only he dragged his feet for the upcoming tour.

The clock behind the bar read three minutes till four, and all he wanted was to stay at the bar and drink until midnight. The booze numbed his aches and he didn't want the sensation to fade. Sonya still wore the long dress she had brought, but he followed the outline of her legs underneath, having a sudden urge to run his hands along her bare skin. A quick romp under the sheets would have everyone feeling normal again.

"How about we go back to our hotel?" Martin proposed. "Forget about this place. We can come back any time."

Sonya giggled. "We're already here. Let's just get it over with. How long could it even be?"

"Okay, then, let's go before they start without us."

Martin slapped a five dollar bill down on the bar top and helped Sonya out of her stool.

A small group of people gathered in the hotel lobby. There were four men and one woman huddled around the man who had worked behind the front desk. He met Martin's eyes and waved them over.

"Good evening, folks," the man said. "My name is David, and I'll be guiding you throughout the hotel. This tour should take us approximately 45 minutes. We'll start here in the lobby, then go down to the basement to work our way back up to the Presidential Suite. The suite is currently vacant so we'll be able to take a look around."

David's tone had completely changed from earlier when he was a grumpy check-in worker. A new wave of energy spewed from his mouth as he explained the hotel's brief history.

Martin felt an instant relief when seeing they wouldn't be alone on the tour. *We can all suffer together.*

"Where is everyone in town from?" David asked the group.

"New York," one man said.

"We're from Philadelphia," the other man said for himself and the woman.

"Chicago."

"Atlanta."

"We're from Texas," Martin said.

David nodded. "Welcome to Denver. We're not nearly as big as any of the places you're all from, but we hope to be one day. For now, we're a major destination for people traveling from the east coast to California. That's what caused this hotel and many others around town to open. There are currently more hotels than houses in downtown Denver, to give you an idea of the surrounding landscape. The Oxford Hotel is proud to be the first hotel that opened for business in Denver in 1890. We opened here due to our close proximity to Union Station, where ninety percent of travelers arrive."

David continued with more history about the hotel, its founder, explanations of the artwork on the walls, and anything that could be used in a trivia game later.

File it right next to all the other useless knowledge in your head.

After five minutes of random facts, David led the group to the elevator. They shuffled into the small cage and David manually slid the cast iron gate closed. *Elevators sure have come a long way,* Martin thought. The ancient elevator hummed and clattered to life, the sounds of a million tiny mechanisms grinding in unison as they lowered to the basement level.

David pulled the gate open and led them into the gloomy basement. The luxury of the main lobby gave way to concrete walls, dim lighting, and pallets with boxes full of hotel equipment.

They stood in an open space, but a hallway stretched further into the distance to what appeared to be small offices.

"Here we are," David said excitedly. "The heart and soul of the hotel. Down here we have a furnace, power generators, freezers, and storage for everything from food to towels. The room we're in is obviously storage, as you can tell from all of the boxes. The basement is also home to all of the executive offices. There was simply no room in the main building for offices. If you'll follow me, we can take a quick stroll down the hallway to see the offices."

David led the group, Martin and Sonya directly behind him. For feeling like a dungeon when they entered the basement, the row of offices had a more normal appearance. They passed open doors that showed quick snap shots of hotel executives' lives: family portraits, calendars, inspirational posters. Their desks were wide, or maybe only appeared so from the lack of technology. There were no phones, keyboards, or any of the clutter common in 2018, simply stacks of paper where all work had to be manually completed.

"This is our main conference room," David said as they reached the end of the hall, stepping into the largest room of the underground. A chalkboard hung on the wall and overlooked an oval-shaped table with chairs around it.

"We try to use the hotel's conference room on the second floor whenever possible, but sometimes we'll have meetings down here. Please come in."

The tour group filled the room as David crossed to the chalkboard. Martin never heard the door close behind him, let alone the click of it being locked by one of the tour members.

Two of the men remained in front of the door like bouncers.

"That was too easy, Martin," David said with a grin. "Sonya, I thought you said he was smarter than this."

Martin stood at the table and looked from David to Sonya, clueless.

"He *is* smarter than this. Apparently hotel tours are his weakness," Sonya said, and the rest of the group erupted in laughter.

Martin spun around to find everyone looking at him, laughing as if there was an inside joke they all knew about.

"What is this? What's going on?" Martin asked, a waver in his voice. He saw the closed door and the two men guarding it. His gut wrenched and his heart beat a little faster.

"Please, have a seat, Martin, we're not here to hurt you," David said in a gentle voice.

"I demand you tell me what's going on. And open that door!"

David shook his head. "That door is staying closed until we have a little talk. Will you please sit down?"

Martin locked eyes with Sonya, who immediately looked away.

"Sonya, what is this? What the *hell* is going on?"

Everyone had taken a step back and watched Martin, including Sonya.

"If you sit down, David will explain everything," she said.

Martin obliged, realizing whatever the hell was happening wouldn't proceed until he sat at the damn table.

"Thank you," David said. "Tell me, Martin, what do you know about the Road Runners?"

Holy fucking shit. This is it. We're dead. Did they already threaten her? Did she save herself by turning me in?

Martin's mouth hung open, his eyes bulging as he scanned the room and realized he had been ambushed by Road Runners. They were all in on the secret.

"Wait," Martin said. "How do you know about the Road Runners?"

Martin knew they were Road Runners, but needed to stall. For what, he didn't know. For an obvious death, he presumed. Death in the Oxford Hotel basement, where not a soul would hear his screams. In a few years he'd be a ghost haunting these same halls on a future tour.

He was too flustered to notice that everyone in the room, except for Sonya, had their bodies mostly covered. The men wore suits and gloves on their hands. The other woman wore a dress that ran from her neck to the floor. Martin wanted to see glowing skin, but they all hid it so well. If he could get up close to one of their faces he'd likely see the faintest hint of the golden glow.

"Martin, we *are* the Road Runners," David said. "Well, not just us. There's thousands of us. But we are part of the team, and we wanted to talk with you about joining us."

Martin thought back to Chris warning him about this exact moment. *They'll do anything once they you have you in their possession. There's no getting out.* He would need to play along, maybe even agree to join, then run away in the middle of the night. Would they follow him if he returned to 2018? Would they find him if he constantly stayed on the run, jumping from year to year? Or would they let him go? Why go through the hassle to get someone who clearly wants no part of your club?

Martin's heart pounded ferociously in his throat as he fought to steady his trembling hands.

"Okay," he said, gulping. "What do you need to tell me?"

What kind of stupid question is that? Get your shit together if you wanna get out of here alive.

"I asked you first," David replied. "What do you know about the Road Runners?"

Martin looked around the room, all eyes staring back in anxious anticipation. Sonya still refused to make eye contact. *What did you get us into?*

"Okay," Martin said. He was outnumbered and could only talk his way out of this situation. "All I know is what I've been told by Chris. I assume you know who that is."

The whole room laughed, David nodding with a cheesy smile. "Oh, yeah, we know him. Let's hear what he told you about us."

"Well, he's always told me to be on the lookout. That you're dangerous and will go to any extremes to recruit someone to join the Road Runners."

How the fuck did I get into this mess already? Martin felt surprisingly calm once he started talking. Maybe they weren't as bad as Chris made them out. They had all shared a laugh twice already. Then again, psychotic people laugh, too.

"He told me to stay on the run, to avoid being captured. He told me there is a war between you and him. He also said you were all responsible for killing Calvin in 1996 by burning down his liquor store."

David smirked at this last part and nodded. "Well, it sounds like Chris has fed you a lot of bullshit. I expected as much. We're used to it. Who knows the last time he's told the truth?"

Martin watched Sonya nod to herself, and he could take no more. "Sonya, tell me what's going on. Right now."

All eyes in the room turned to Martin's girlfriend.

"I'm sorry, Martin," she said. "I know this is hard; I was just doing my job."

"Doing what job?" Martin demanded. The truth was knocking on his door, but he refused to answer it.

"My job was to get you here. I'm sorry." She spoke flatly and stared into space. "I'm a recruiter for the Road Runners."

Martin watched these words hang in the air as all eyes returned their focus to him. The room fell silent as he processed this disturbing truth. If the room wasn't full of strangers, he likely would have allowed himself to vomit all over the table. After a minute, he finally spoke. "So our entire time together has been one big lie? The night we met at the bar, you already knew what the next six months held?"

"All I knew was that you would be there and I needed you to fall in love with me. I didn't know how anything would turn out, especially your coma. We would have never let that happen if we knew about it."

"So the entire time I thought I was keeping this life and death secret about time travel, and you already knew."

Sonya shrugged and remained silent.

Falling in love with Sonya became the highlight of his trip to 1996, especially after he failed to save Izzy. Sonya, his first true love since Lela, turned out to be a hoax.

"So it was all a lie?" he asked. "The story about your grandparents. Us. All of it?"

Sonya nodded.

"Well, good for you. You must be quite the professional. You don't even seem bothered."

"Of course I'm bothered," she snapped. "This is a dirty job and this particular part is never easy. But we can always move past it."

"Wow, so I'm not even the first schmuck to fall for this trap. I'm honored. Thank you for toying with my life and ruining everything."

Martin wanted to leave these people behind and go home to 2018. Hopefully his bar was stocked, because long nights of drinking awaited.

David spoke. "Look, Martin, there's a lot to process here. And we fully intend on giving you time to decide, but there are some things you need to know before you leave here today."

Martin stared at the table, trying to listen to David as his mind pieced together the lies from his 1996 life.

"Chris is probably the stupidest person you'll ever meet," David continued. "He finds people at their weakest and talks them into trying his pills. At that point, it's too late to turn back. No one who gets a taste of time travel is simply going to walk away from the opportunity to right a wrong in the past. He's got that much figured out, I'll give him that. He really does feed on people's emotions. He loves sorrow and fear, and tries to create that when he exchanges the bottle of Juice."

"If Chris is so bad, then why doesn't he just keep the Juice for himself and leave people emotionally scarred?" Martin asked. "He has no reason to hand it over unless he was honest."

"It's all a big game to him," David said. "He loves destroying people and watching them try to fix everything. He's sick. But this is where he gets stupid, you see. He gives the Juice out to so many people and never questions their loyalty. They enter this realm of time travel thinking it's going to be some constant life adventure, not that they'll be forced to

426

choose a side in this war. He doesn't see the big picture that continually ruining people's lives leads to them seeking revenge. That's where we come in since there are so many of us working to kill him."

"Why kill him?" Martin asked. "Why not strip him of his powers, take his pills and potions away?"

David sat down in the seat across Martin, the tension fading with each question.

"We need to kill him. He's trying to infiltrate each era of history, one country at a time. He takes his knowledge from both the past and future and uses it to manipulate the world."

Martin recalled when Chris had mentioned he was tending to a war in Africa. Had he caused the war?

"What about Calvin?" Martin asked.

David nodded. "We did kill him. He was working for Chris and plotting an attack on us."

"So you shot him and burned his store to the ground?"

David sighed. "This is a war, Martin. It's not pretty. Our people have died. Their people have died. We're fighting for a world of prosperity. Do you know how much good can be done with this gift we have?"

Martin wanted to trust these Road Runners, but they had tricked and lured him into a fake hotel tour. Sonya manipulated him and played him like a fiddle. They might preach about all the good they do, but their tactics were simply off the mark.

"Who's to say Chris isn't doing good? Why are you so convinced you're the only ones doing good?" Martin asked, a hint of rage suppressed in his voice.

"Martin," David said sternly. "We've been following Chris for years. Hundreds of years, or even thousands. It's hard to tell time for sure when you're constantly jumping around. We have people in his inner circle, learning more and more. We know what he's planning. We know he's not human and can't be killed through traditional means. He's very complex, and all we want to do is overthrow him before we live in a world of darkness."

"Then why not capture him?" Martin asked. "If you already have your people surrounding him, tie him up and bring him here."

David shook his head. "It would never happen. He constantly has two dozen people watching him. It's impossible to get him. He rolls deep with security—has more protection than the president. Even if we did manage to capture him, all that does is put a target on our back. It would be a manhunt around the clock until they found him."

Martin understood and nodded. "Why do you need me? I don't have any special skills."

"We need everyone we can get. We're setting up eyes all around the world, all throughout time, watching, learning. The more coverage we get, the closer we get to cracking the code on how to take him down. Like I mentioned, we don't expect you to make a decision right now, but we do expect you to make the right one in due time. You can always find me here at this hotel if you decide to stick around. Should you choose to go back to 2018, you can find a gentleman named Adrian in this same hotel. He'll know who you are. How about you take a week to think matters over and get back to us?"

Martin sat silently, staring at his twiddling thumbs. The Road Runners were as good as advertised. They made a flawless sales pitch on why he should join them, but something whispered in the depths of his mind to hold off. Give it the full time to think over—his mind currently consumed with what the fuck had happened with Sonya.

"Okay, I'll get back to you guys by next week. Not sure if I plan on staying here or not, though." Martin spoke confidently and maintained relentless eye contact with David.

"We appreciate that, Martin. We'll see you upstairs and act like we're finishing the tour so you can leave here without any suspicion."

David slapped the table and stood, everyone in the room shifting toward the door. Martin rose and followed suit. One of the large men who had stood guard pulled open the door and stepped into the hallway.

A pistol fired and the man collapsed to the ground into a pool of his own blood. Everyone froze in place, still safe inside the conference room.

"Well, well, well," a familiar voice said from the hallway.

"It's *him*!" David whispered loud enough for everyone to hear. They all drew guns from their waists, cocking them in a harmonic unison, and pointing them at the door.

The fallen man twitched on the ground as the footsteps grew louder and Chris appeared in the doorway, grinning with his hands held high in the air.

"Oh no, please don't shoot me," he mocked.

"What do you want?" David demanded.

Chris ignored him, looking around the room and nodding his head to everyone who pointed a gun his way. "Sonya, my dear, always a pleasure to see you." He turned his attention to David, who had taken a step in front of the defenseless Martin. "I'm here for Martin. I'm no longer sitting back and watching as you gouge my people. Time to take action. You can hand him over and we leave peacefully, or I can have my crew of twenty men come in and take him by force, leaving you all here in an orgy of death. How does that sound?"

David held his ground, but didn't say anything, locked in a staredown with the old man.

"I'll go," Martin said. "No need for people to die because of me." He stepped around David and patted him on the back in a gesture of faith as he passed.

"How noble of you," Chris said. "I thought for sure they would have already brainwashed you about how evil I am."

"Chris, these people are full of shit," Martin said. Chris howled maniacally at this, grabbing his gut.

"That they are. Let's get out of here."

Chris turned and left the room. Martin looked back to David and nodded quickly before following. He looked to Sonya, who stared back with a blank expression.

It's over, Martin. She's gone. You've been conned. Just leave.

So he left without a word.

73

Chapter 19

Chris really did have twenty men in the hallway. Two of them had made a quick disposal of the dead body and rejoined the group by the time Chris and Martin stepped out of the conference room.

"Is everything ready?" Chris asked.

"Yes, sir," a short man squeaked from the group.

"Perfect, let's gather round," Chris said. The group huddled around the old man and Martin watched from two paces behind, unsure what to do. He glanced back and saw David peeking out of the door, but not stepping fully into the hallway as a handful of Chris's men still had their guns pointed in his direction.

"Martin, your Juice," Chris said, pulling Martin's flask from his inner coat pocket. Martin stared at it in amazement. "This is what I really went over for last night. Just wanted to see where you were hiding it so we could bring it to you today." Chris returned to the huddle and stepped aside to allow space for Martin. "Now, everyone, let's return to the main headquarters."

The men nodded and pulled their own flasks from their jackets, taking quick swigs of the Juice and promptly lying down on the ground.

Chris put his face in front of Martin's. "Go to the year 1981. Follow us outside and be ready to hop on the bus picking us up. We'll be going to a private jet to take us to our headquarters. Go to 1981 right now or I'll come back and slit your throat."

Martin had dozens of questions, but Chris quickly lay down, closed his eyes, and fell into an immediate sleep as his soul presumably traveled to 1981. He looked around, considered a trip back to 2018 instead, and immediately rejected it. Now was not the time to get cute with the old man.

Martin twisted the top off of his flask, took a sip, and lay down, thinking repeatedly of 1981. The familiar dizziness filled his head as he closed his eyes and slipped into unconsciousness.

1981, he thought a final time before falling asleep in 1919.

* * *

Martin promptly woke up in the same spot, as did the rest of the men who had fallen asleep in a big circle around him in the Oxford Hotel's basement. They were all on their feet by the time Martin arrived.

"Okay, we're all here," Chris said once Martin opened his eyes. "Let's head up to the bus."

Chris pulled Martin up by the arm as Martin shook his head to clear the fog that accompanied a heavy sleep.

The hallway they had arrived in appeared the exact same as the one they had left, newer lights in the ceiling the only visible upgrade.

"Take the stairs," Chris demanded. "Quickly."

The men formed a single-file line and marched toward a door at the end of the hallway, past the conference room where the Road Runners had just held Martin hostage 60 years in the past, or two minutes ago, depending how you viewed it.

Martin, not knowing what the hell was going on, joined the back of the line, Chris rounding out the group behind him.

Boots clapped along the concrete ground, echoing throughout the hall as the line of men disappeared into the stairwell. Once in the stairwell, the sound reflected louder in the tighter space, like a marching band squeezed into a public bathroom.

They climbed one flight to reach the main level, just next to the main entrance, where they swiftly poured out of the hotel and back onto 18th Street. Martin followed and was relieved to see numerous skyscrapers in the city. They had certainly reached 1981 as Union Station also appeared in its more modernized version with neon lighting on its exterior.

"Around the corner!" a man from the group shouted as they slowed to a powerwalk.

The sidewalks were empty of foot traffic, suggesting it must have been the middle of a workday. It only became crowded during the lunch hour and after 3 P.M. when people started leaving for home.

They walked the direction opposite of Union Station and turned right at the next intersection where a small black bus waited. It reminded Martin of the kind that would eventually become commonly used as party buses, only this one lacked the flashing lights and built in ice chests full of beer bottles.

An older man with a white beard and a black fedora craned his neck as the group filed onto the bus. He had a cranky expression, his face scrunched into years of fatigue.

"We're all here," Chris said as they filled the bus. "Let's move!"

He clapped his hands excitedly.

Martin sensed they were being followed based on the urgency with which Chris barked his orders. After learning firsthand what the Road Runners' main objective was, he didn't exactly feel safe sitting in a bus full of Chris and his men. What if they tried to bomb it? Surely they would sacrifice Martin's life if it meant wiping Chris and twenty of his goons off the planet.

He shook the violent images that filled his head and stared out the window as he plopped down in a seat near the front. Chris had sat directly behind the driver and they appeared to be catching up on the day's activities.

Martin watched as the city passed by his window. Everything had changed since 1919, both in the buildings and the few people he saw out for an afternoon stroll. Gone were the days of everyone dressed in suits and magnificent gowns. Now people wore jeans, mullets, and carried boom boxes over their shoulders. *We're definitely in the 80's.*

The bus rumbled through the city, reaching the freeway within five minutes and revving up to a much higher speed. The men remained silent, keeping to themselves and looking out their windows. Martin hadn't noticed earlier that they were all wearing sunglasses and long pea coats, looking like a group of mobsters on their way to a fancy dinner.

Chris leaned back in his seat and Martin took the chance to move up one row to speak with him, sliding in beside the old man.

"I know you have questions," Chris said. "You always do."

"Can you blame me?" Martin replied. "You like to leave all of the details out when we speak."

Chris smirked. "I literally warned you last night about the Road Runners, and you still managed to get captured within 24 hours. You're not the sharpest knife in the drawer, my friend. A hotel tour? Really?"

"They told me you're trying to rule the world. Is that true?"

Chris sighed. "These people will say anything to recruit and brainwash. I'm not trying to rule the world. I'm part of a coalition trying to make the world a better place. I have counterparts on each continent. I'm in charge of tying to gain control over North America, as my counterparts are trying to take control of their continents."

Sounds an awful lot like trying to rule the world, Martin thought.

Chris laughed. "We're not trying to rule the world."

Shit. Martin forgot that Chris could hear his thoughts.

"If we wanted to rule the world," Chris continued. "We would've done that already. It's as easy as manipulating some governments and running them from the inside. In a sense, that's what we're trying to do, but not in the evil ways it may sound."

"So you're glorified lobbyists?"

Chris nodded. "You could say that. We definitely have the funds to lobby for anything we desire."

The bus rattled as it slowed, turning off the highway. They had driven ten minutes east of downtown and arrived to Stapleton, a small neighborhood only known for its airport in 1981.

"We're here, gentlemen," Chris announced, standing and facing the rest of the crew. "Remember to get on the plane quickly. Dinner will be served."

The bus turned into the airport grounds and drove around a small building to the back where private hangars awaited, each with private jets lined up neatly beside each other.

"You have your own jet?" Martin asked. "I thought you could go wherever you want – why waste your time flying?"

Chris chuckled. "Martin, please. I'm not Harry Potter. I can go to any *time* I want. If I need to go somewhere else in the world, I still have to physically travel there."

"Where are we going?" he asked.

"Our headquarters are in Alaska," Chris said.

"Alaska?"

"Yes. It's a perfect hideaway. And it's not just Alaska; it's northern Alaska, practically on a glacier. No one ever thinks of going there, or even *wants* to go there. I'm pretty sure your Road Runner friends know about it, though, and I believe they've set up a similar type of hideout nearby."

The bus came to a complete stop at the last hangar, and the doors swung open.

"Let's go, gentlemen!" Chris commanded, leading the way out.

Martin followed him into the hangar where they approached a luxurious private jet with glossy blue and red exterior, appearing freshly waxed. There were no words, logos, or anything that could identify the plane as belonging to anyone in particular.

Chris approached the stairs that led up to the jet and walked up without any hesitation. He looked over his shoulder and waved to his group of confidants below, still making their way across the hangar.

Martin followed, his legs trembling with each step, not sure what the hell he was getting into. *I don't belong with this group of people. They all carry guns and sit in silence, taking orders from Chris like he's the goddamn president. I just want to explore, not get caught in the middle of this stupid war.*

Martin entered the jet to find a world of luxury. It was clearly from the future, not 1981, as flat screen TVs hung on the walls, oak tables decorated the lounge, and wide, cushioned recliners were the only options for sitting. Laptops and tablets were piled neatly on the tables, and Martin longed for a return to 2018. It felt like a mere pit stop between the trips to 1996 and 1919, and now 1981.

Where is my true self? he wondered. When he left for 1919, his body was asleep in his bedroom in 2018. But when he jumped from 1919 to 1981, what happened then? Could he fall seven dimensions like that movie *Inception?*

And what the fuck happened with Sonya? *Is she really a Road Runner? Or is this all some big joke?*

His chest felt like it had taken a bullet in the heart, the blood of his pain spreading throughout his body. His mind waited in a state of shock for the truth to reveal itself, and he found himself unable to focus his thoughts on anything aside from his six months of life with Sonya in 1996.

You're stunned. That's what this is. Just like the morning you realized Izzy was gone, and just like the night you accepted that she was never coming back. Stunned.

If she really was a Road Runner, then all of their time spent together had to have been part of some epic plan to get him to join their team. What other explanation was there for them to all end up in a hotel basement together?

She played you. Your wife fucked your brother, and your new girlfriend only dragged you along to fight on her team. Now here you are, on an airplane with a madman, and your life no longer in your own hands.

Whatever was happening, he'd have to wait for answers. The rest of the crew piled into the jet, conversation a low murmur among them all. Chris grabbed a recliner in the main lounge and ordered a meal from a young waiter who had appeared out of nowhere.

Martin approached the old man.

"Chris, I'd like to know what's going on," he said calmly, even though he wanted to burst with a flood of questions.

Chris looked up to Martin and rolled his eyes. "My god, Marty, can you ever just sit down and relax? All you ever want to do is ask questions. I've told you we're going to our headquarters. We'll have a meeting when we get there to discuss our next steps. Now find a spot and shut up. You're on a fully equipped, private jet with anything you can imagine. Order dinner, have a drink, I don't care. Just leave me alone."

"Sorry."

Martin left Chris and found a lone recliner looking out a window. The old man had really snapped at him, making him feel like a disciplined child sitting in timeout. He didn't know if he should mingle with the men in pea coats and sunglasses, and decided to keep to himself.

Everyone had settled in their spots as the airplane rumbled to life. The lights dimmed, and many of the men removed their sunglasses and slid sleeping masks over their eyes. Martin wanted to sleep, exhausted from the day's events, but his mind wouldn't allow it.

Something had felt off since Chris and his gang arrived. Were they really there to rescue him from the Road Runners? He sensed that more was at stake. Why did both sides show such an interest in a middle-aged, out-of-shape man with no skills aside from chugging beer and whiskey? Martin only had to take a quick look around to see that he was the only one who didn't belong with the rest of the group.

All of the men seemed like programmed robots, rarely speaking to each other, obediently doing exactly as Chris demanded. Nothing about them seemed realistic except for the fact that they *looked* like humans.

Could Chris be trying to brainwash me and turn me into one of them?

Martin lay back in his recliner, his brain torn between sleep and a desire to keep his eyes open. The latter won, and he watched Chris for the entire duration of the six-hour flight. The old man eventually fell asleep after finishing his steak dinner.

What are you really *up to?*

74

Chapter 20

Six hours later the plane landed in the small town of Barrow, Alaska. The pilot announced their arrival, but Martin had no idea where to find the city on a map. Chris explained it was the northernmost tip of the state with a shore that touched the Arctic Ocean. The city had an airport with a small neighborhood practically on the landing strip.

The jet's door opened and they filed out, Martin gawking at the Arctic Ocean in his immediate view, glaciers floating like giant ice cubes. He had never seen a glacier, or iceberg, or whatever the hell they were called.

Giant chunks of ice.

He immediately shivered, as the town was known for high temperatures in the mid-30s. The heatwaves of summer might push the thermometer to 45 on a good day.

The airport was smaller than the one they had left in Stapleton, a lone office building standing at the end of the airstrip, with only one hangar that housed two other jets.

Another bus waited for them, and they wasted no time crossing the tarmac to enter it.

"Welcome home, gentlemen," Chris said proudly once everyone had settled into the bus. "We have some long days ahead of us, so tonight will be a relaxing night. If you didn't eat on the plane—which it didn't look like anyone did—get a good dinner tonight and sit back, watch a movie, read a book—whatever you do to unwind. Tonight we will all return to the current time in 2018. Tomorrow we'll start planning to get another of our own back, just like we rescued Martin today."

Chris looked down to Martin, who sat in the row behind him again, and winked.

One of our own? Martin thought, then immediately shut down his mind since he was close to Chris. He hadn't declared an allegiance to any side in this fight, and didn't intend to. He just wanted to go home, dump his bottle of Juice down the drain, and pretend none of this had ever happened. No 1996, no witnessing Izzy's death, no Sonya. None of it.

You can't do that now, remember? his mind cut back in. *Your mother now has dementia because of you, or did you forget already? Are you really going to leave her to rot away in her own mind? Let her talk to you like a complete stranger?*

The bus ride had only lasted ten minutes when they turned onto a dirt road for another mile and pulled up to a mansion that looked as large as the White House. The dirt road gave way to cobblestone and led them to a wide roundabout in front of the house. A thin layer of snow covered what would have been a lawn. The mansion was made of dark stone, reminding Martin of a medieval castle. Two rows of a dozen windows lined the front, all of equal size.

"What is this place?" Martin asked when the bus came to a complete stop.

Chris looked over his shoulder with his usual grin. "My house. Our headquarters. *Chateau de Chris.* Whatever you want to call it. It's where you'll be living for the next few weeks while we figure out what to do."

"Do with what?"

"With the Road Runners. We'll have plenty of time tomorrow to discuss. Tonight is all about relaxing. I know that's a difficult concept for you, but give it a try. You might even smile for once."

Martin couldn't take any more of Chris's snide remarks. No, he didn't want to relax. He had lost his daughter, his mother, his girlfriend, his life as he knew it. If things could go back to the way they were, drinking into oblivion every night, eating his pistol once a year, then he could relax. Routine brought him the calm he desired, not being kidnapped and flown to the fucking North Pole.

The bus door slid open, and the robotic men all stood and filled the aisle, waiting for Chris to lead the way. It became more apparent with each passing second that these men were incapable of thinking for themselves. They simply followed Chris around all day and did as they were told.

Chris rose, bones cracking and popping, and led the parade to the mansion.

The house had no exterior decorations, a plain fortress on a private lot, far from the town that was already off the map. They reached the entrance, a lone wooden door, and Chris pulled it open, leading the crew inside.

The interior was something out of a movie, and certainly didn't fit in this small town. They walked into an entryway with a spiral staircase that led up one level and down another. A kitchen was to the left, and a lounge area to the right. A crystal chandelier hung above them, illuminating the room with abstract paintings as decorations.

Martin stood frozen as the men all made their way up the stairs to the second floor. He looked up to the skylight windows that provided a glimpse of the gray sky.

"Shall we?" Chris asked once the men had cleared out, leaving them in silence, the only audible sound a fireplace crackling somewhere around the corner. "Quite the scare the Road Runners gave you back there."

Chris crossed his arms and waited for Martin to respond.

"Yeah. They didn't seem too evil. In fact, they were gonna let me walk out before you showed up."

"Oh, please. They only play nice to try and trick you into trusting them. How can you trust a group who sent Sonya to trap you?"

Martin had tried to push Sonya out of his mind, wanting to forget the fact that she had been playing him like a used piano since they first met. All of the lovemaking, late-night talks, and romantic dinners had been a lie to land him in a basement conference room with the Road Runners.

"I'd rather not talk about that," Martin said.

"Understood. Let me show you around." Chris raised his arms as if soaking in his surroundings. "This house is four levels. We're on the main level. Kitchen, lounge, laundry – pretty much any of your basic needs. Food is always stocked and nothing is off limits on this floor. Make yourself at home."

He shuffled to the stairwell. "Downstairs is the basement and some-where you'll never need to go. We have an entire team down there con-ducting research throughout history and the future, creating databases and algorithms, and a bunch of other things I don't really understand until they summarize it in a weekly report for me."

Martin joined Chris at the stairwell and looked down to a pit of darkness. Chris pointed up.

"Upstairs has two more floors. The top floor is all bedrooms. The second floor has more bedrooms along with meeting spaces and my main office—well, more of an office and bedroom combo. It's where you'll usually find me."

"I take it I have one of these bedrooms?"

"Of course. You'll be on the second floor. I've already stocked your closet with winter clothes, or else you'll freeze to death in this city. The highs are usually in the 30s, but the nights get as low as 20 below. You'll want to stay inside, but don't worry, our lounge has a fully stocked bar."

"Sounds like quite the bachelor pad."

Chris cackled. "It certainly is. Any questions?"

Martin wasn't given much of a tour but more of an explanation of the layout. He'd have to explore on his own apparently, although it seemed there wasn't much to look at beyond the main level.

"Yes. Are your men okay? They seem a bit . . . out of it."

"Ahhh, yes. They're just fine. You see, traveling through time in rapid succession is very draining on the mind. Me and my men had just jumped around ten different decades looking for you. We have eyes all over. There were lots of false tips claiming to have seen you. The guys are just drained and need to sleep. That's why they slept on the flight and will probably sleep right through lunchtime tomorrow."

Martin nodded. "I'm pretty tired myself. I didn't get any sleep on the plane."

Chris grinned and started up the stairs. "Follow me, I'll show you to your room."

Martin followed up the spiral staircase, looking over the edge to the basement, nothing but a black pit of death. He felt the perfectly human urge to go where forbidden. What was really down there?

They reached the second floor landing and Martin looked both ways down a hallway that stretched far into the distance.

"This way is all the bedrooms," Chris said, pointing to the left. "The other side is my office and other meeting rooms. If the doors are open to a meeting room you're more than welcome to use the space. If closed, you need stay out. There can be highly confidential meetings taking place."

"Understood," Martin said, inching further into the hallway.

"Now, follow me." Chris turned left and led the way down the hall, stopping at a door only three from the end. The old man rummaged in his pocket and pulled out a small silver key. "This is for you. All bedrooms are complete with queen-sized beds, bathrooms, dining rooms, and satellite TV. If there's anything else you wish to have, just let me know and I'll see what we can do."

"Thanks." Martin didn't know what else to say, and now that the excitement of being kidnapped twice had worn off, his head spun in fatigue.

"I'll leave you to it. Come find me if you need anything today. I'll introduce you to our house assistant tomorrow. He'll be the one you can go to anytime for anything. Have a nice nap."

Chris nodded and turned, strolling down the hall and disappearing into a door on the opposite end.

Martin jiggled his key in the door and pushed it open to a breathtaking view. Past the bed and mounted flat screen TV was a window overlooking a blanket of whiteness. This mansion was hidden in the middle of an open field with the ground covered in at least two inches of snow as far as he could see. Having lived his entire life in Colorado, he couldn't recall ever seeing an area of land so flat. Snow-capped trees completed the landscape that looked like a Bob Ross painting.

He sat on the foot of his bed, wondering how Chris managed life this far from civilization. Within seconds, Martin's body and mind gave way as he sprawled across the bed, staring at the ceiling, falling in to a heavy slumber.

75

Chapter 21

"I think we need to send him to the basement," Chris said. He sat in his dim office, the curtains drawn, and his trusted confidant, Duane, across the desk. Chris kept a tight inner circle, but Duane was the only one he could tell anything.

Duane had been there since day one, always curious and willing to test new theories in the past or future, willing to do anything short of risking his life. It was the sort of loyalty that money couldn't buy, and Chris needed that. Everyone else closest to him had lucrative incomes, leaving him to wonder if they remained obedient because of the money or if they truly believed in their work.

Duane nodded, his wavy brown hair jiggling slightly. He snapped his round-framed glasses off his face and rubbed tired, brown eyes. "If you say so."

"Do you not agree?" Chris asked. Duane rarely disagreed with him, so when he did, he knew there was a good reason.

"We've reached an unfortunate point in this war, Chris," Duane said, standing up. He was of average height and build, and always wore a fine suit. "We're at a crossroads. Right now we have fifty Road Runners in our basement."

"There's room for fifty more," Chris added.

"No. Listen. We've reached a point where there's so many people

444

traveling through time that they make friends and develop relationships. They bond. They become important to each other. When someone goes missing, they all know about it. They make plans to find their friends. We have reason to believe the Road Runners have increased their surveillance and are implanting location chips into their people. Just to find you."

"What are you getting at?" Chris had heard enough and wanted to get to the point.

"We can't keep taking people and stashing them in the basement. It's going to get us caught at some point."

"My soldiers are highly trained and won't make mistakes."

"It's not about mistakes. One day we're not gonna be fast enough when we take someone. You didn't know it, but someone had followed you out the hotel when you took Briar. They were on foot and couldn't follow once you got on the bus, but it's one step closer. Next time, there will be someone ready in a car to follow you. I wish you'd stop snatching people every time you get a hunch. But at this point, I think it's best for you to let Briar go. Put him on a flight back to Denver, and wish him the best. We can only hope he won't run off to the Road Runners, but we are getting crushed in that department anyway. They're 200,000 strong now."

"And we're 1,000,000. You worry too much."

"They were only 50,000 two years ago and we were at 600,000. You tell me if you like the direction of that trend."

Chris leaned back in his seat. Duane loved to discuss numbers and strategy like he was a general in charge of a war. While he appreciated the information, Chris believed in bold approaches to problems.

"So then we should kill everyone in the basement. Briar, too."

Duane shook his head. "You're not understanding. That's not going to do anything but keep the search alive. We have two options: release them slowly back into the world, or kill them and publicly dispose of their bodies so the Road Runners know it's one their own."

Chris grinned. "Now you're talking my language."

"That doesn't mean it's the best option. That only leaves more clues behind. You know how advanced science becomes in the future; leaving a corpse behind puts us at a high risk of being caught."

"Fine. I'll think it over. But Briar needs to go. He slept with Sonya, and I can't forgive that."

"*You* need to let that go. Your daughter has slept with *numerous* people to trap them. She's gone, Chris. A full-blooded Road Runner, probably because you act so goddamn selfish all the time."

"Selfish?" Chris sat forward, hands in the air. "I give people my Gift. I let them share it with others and spread the joy. And you call me selfish?"

Chris knew Duane didn't have the energy to stay in arguments for too long, and rejoiced when his friend sat back down.

"You know what I mean, and I'll just leave it at that. You drove Sonya out of your life. No one else did."

"You know, Duane, you've told me that plenty of times before. I don't need a constant reminder of how things played out. If I need your opinion on my past, I'll ask you for it. Otherwise, I'd appreciate if you'd stick to business."

"What are you gonna do, Chris? Fire me? Kill me? Throw me in the basement? I don't like bringing these things up, but sometimes you go off the rails and I need to mention it."

Chris glared across the desk. "You've always been good to me, and I'd never do such a thing to you. You just need to stay in your lane. Now if you wouldn't mind leaving me be, I need a moment alone."

Duane sighed and let himself out of the office.

Chris crossed his hands on his desk and plopped his head down. He couldn't take any more arguing. He had lots of meetings lined up over the next few days, and even more difficult decisions to make.

He needed to interview Martin, see where he stood with matters before making the rash decision of sending him to the basement. A quick visit to the basement was in line as well. It had been a couple of months since Chris had stopped by to visit his enemies.

Chris rose from his seat and paced circles around the office, hoping he wouldn't have to send another lost cause to the basement. Martin didn't seem infected by the Road Runners; he did follow them this far, after all, without any protest, murder attempts, or acts of violence like others before him.

Martin was a perfect citizen, and Chris had no reason to suspect he was working with the Road Runners, but something felt off. The way Sonya had played him surely left him scarred and hurt. There are fewer things more frightening than a person with nothing to lose.

Chris left his office space and crossed to his bedroom at the opposite end. He sat on his bed and pulled open the nightstand drawer to retrieve a photo.

His fingers trembled with the picture of the young girl smiling with her father. She was his world, and it showed in his eyes – youthful, sparkling, and excited for the future.

"Angelina," Chris said, brushing two fingers over the portrait. "Where did we go so wrong?"

He thought back to what felt like thousands of years ago when Angelina was a little girl, many years away from changing her name to Sonya. Time became jumbled when constantly traveling through it, so much that Chris often forgot where he came from. Seeing the picture always returned him to memory lane, and the perfect life he once had.

For now, he needed to stop by the basement and see his daughter's goons.

He placed the old portrait back in the nightstand and rose from the bed, crossing to a small door in the corner. Chris enjoyed having his own private elevator to get from floor to floor. At his age, the stairs took too much of a toll on his body. But he would take them in the presence of company, to show that he had no weakness.

He called the elevator with a quick push of the button on the wall and pulled open the door as it arrived. The car stood seven feet tall and was wide enough for two people to stand comfortably. Chris never let anyone besides Duane ride along with him, and even that was on rare occasions; he liked to have these stolen moments to himself.

He stepped into the elevator, pushed the B on the panel, and watched his office disappear from sight as he went down two levels to the dark basement. The elevator opened to a pitch-black corner of the basement; he liked to surprise his prisoners and never wanted them to know when he arrived.

He stepped out and turned the dark corner into the open space.

Everything he had told Martin about the basement was a lie. It wasn't some elaborate research center with dozens of men working toward a greater good. It was a prison for captured Road Runners.

The room stretched the length and width of a football field. Tape decorated the concrete ground, forming three by three foot squares, appearing like a life-sized chess board. Each prisoner was assigned a square, and only 50 of the 100 available spaces were occupied. Chris dreamed of filling the basement with desperate Road Runners.

Chris believed in killing only as a last resort. Road Runners held useful knowledge about their plot to overthrow him, and he wanted to gather all of the information possible. Perhaps the basement was a research center of sorts, after all.

Each square had a steel hook bolted into the ground and a shackle running from it to each prisoner's ankle. The shackles allowed them to reach the edge of their squares, nothing more, nothing less. Prisoners were given three meals a day, and had to relieve their bowels in whatever corner of their squares that they chose. One pillow and one blanket were provided after dinnertime.

The basement was usually silent, the forty plus men and handful of women all sitting in their squares, knowing they were hidden and wiped off the map.

"No one will ever find you where we are," Chris would tell them each upon arrival to the dark and dank room. "Ninety nine percent of the population can't even find this place on a map."

He loved teasing them with this line, watching all hope flee from their eyes.

The lighting in the basement was as bright as a movie theater. The prisoners could all see each other, but not well enough to know who was who. With plenty of vacant spaces, Chris had the prisoners kept at least three squares apart to avoid any sort of plotting, not that there was a way to escape the shackles.

Road Runners were still a smart bunch—loyal, too—and he couldn't afford to have them brainstorming with each other.

When Chris emerged from the darkness all fifty prisoners stood up and started howling and screaming at him, making him feel like an infamous athlete stepping onto the field. He loved being hated by his enemies. Loved having them trapped as his prisoners. Sometimes when they screamed, he'd get an erection, about the only thing that aroused him any more at his ripe old age.

Not today, though. Today was a matter of business, not pleasure, in his visit to the basement.

I really should take away their ability to speak, he thought as the screaming grew louder.

Chris waved his hands in a shushing gesture. "Good evening, everybody," he shouted so the prisoners in the back could hear him. "Does anyone have information on Martin Briar?"

The prisoners looked around the room at each other, shrugging their shoulders.

"He is possibly one of you. I may grant a release for anyone who can provide information on Mr. Briar."

"I know some things," a voice shouted from the middle of the room. The voice came from square number 37, Terry Brooks, a short, thin man in his late 40's.

"Ah, Mr. Brooks. Perhaps today is your lucky day," Chris said with a grin. "I'll see to it that a guard brings you to a conference room so we can have a little talk about Mr. Briar. Our new arrival is sleeping, so plan to be moved in the next five minutes. As for the rest of you, have a pleasant night."

Chris bowed his head before turning back for the hidden elevator. The screams erupted again as he strolled away, and this time a slight amount of blood rushed to his crotch.

You're all mine. Forever.

He disappeared into the shadows to return to his office.

76

Chapter 22

Terry Brooks had lived a luxurious life as a Road Runner. He had millions in the bank and a huge Victorian house for him and his wife, settling comfortably in the year 2030. He had worked as a recruiter for the Road Runners before getting captured by Chris's people, and every day sitting in that shithole basement reminded him of the bad decision that had landed him there.

He knew better than to pursue new arrivals right away. They were always fresh arrivals from the University of Bullshit, taught exclusively by the crazy old man. The Road Runners may have passed the old man in terms of a long-term strategy, but Chris grew wiser by the day. They needed to be careful to not lose any of the valuable ground they had gained. This was still Chris's world, and they were only living in it until he one day croaked.

Terry had climbed high in the ranks, attending quarterly meetings with the Forerunners, the leadership group who overlooked the entirety of the Road Runners. He had received heavy pressure to increase recruits, and Terry promised to deliver. He had worked with Sonya on the plan to land Martin Briar, a prized target for the organization to acquire.

Martin still didn't know it, but he just might hold the key to taking down Chris. Terry wondered if Chris knew this, but if so, why have a discussion about the matter with another Road Runner? Why not just throw Martin in the basement and toss his key into the Arctic Ocean?

Yes, Terry knew where he was on the map, and yes, the Road Runners knew about the headquarters. Infiltrating the headquarters was another story. Guards covered the premises in a blanket of force and intimidation. Chris deserved credit for having an army of savage men ready to kill anything or anyone who posed a threat.

Bombing the mansion had been briefly discussed and promptly dismissed, no one wanting to take responsibility for the blood of 50 Road Runners, even if it was for the greater good.

"Brooks!" a voice barked from one of the mindless guards who hovered over the prisoners like a hawk. "On your knees, hands behind your head!"

Terry did as ordered, knowing any single disobeyed command could result in a bullet in the skull. He had seen a handful of friends go out this way, and it was never a pleasant sight.

A rifle jammed against his spine as he knelt with his trembling hands on the back of his head.

Just remember, you're more important than Briar. The Forerunners need you, not Briar.

"On your feet!" the voice shouted.

Terry couldn't see them, but knew at least two other guards hid in the shadows, guns pointed directly at his head. The shackles around his ankles jingled as someone worked their way around the ground with a set of keys clanging with every movement. Within seconds, the pressure around his ankles released, and he was free to walk outside of his tiny square.

"Try anything cute and you'll be dead," the deep voice said from behind.

"Understood," Terry responded in a wavering voice.

"Hopkins!" The voice returned to a shout. "Let's move!"

Hopkins must have been one of the guards hiding in the shadows. A tall, muscular man emerged from the darkness with a mean grin, and stepped in front of Terry who had to look up to meet the man's eyes.

All of these motherfuckers look the same. Giant cavemen with no mind of their own.

"Follow me and put these on," Hopkins said, clicking on a flashlight to illuminate the path ahead while handing over a pair of thick sunglasses.

"What are these for?"

"You've been sitting in the dark for months. If you don't wear those, you'll go blind the second you step out of the basement."

Terry marched at the same pace as Hopkins, still aware of the rifle directly behind him. He only knew the basement as darkness, nothing visible from the confines of his square, so seeing the rest of the room, albeit limited by a flashlight, was a rare treat.

If I get sent back here, I'll at least know a way out if I can ever break free of the shackles.

The freedom of his legs gliding across the floor reminded him of his old life, where such tasks didn't need to be taken for granted.

They reached a wall where Hopkins pushed forward, swinging open a door to a well-lit stairwell. Terry recognized it as the main spiral staircase from when he had arrived at this hellhole of a mansion over eight months ago.

Eight months, he reminisced. Eight months of eating slop, shitting where he slept, and praying for his fellow Road Runners to break him and his friends out.

"Up we go," Hopkins said with a glance over the shoulder. "No funny business on the stairs or we'll kill you."

I already know that, asshole.

They moved single-file up the stairs, the mystery rifleman trailing behind, patiently waiting for any sudden movement from Terry. They reached the main landing where he saw the house's front door before continuing up to the second floor. So far everything had looked the same from when Terry arrived. Now he approached new territory.

On the second floor, which equaled the basement in eerie silence, he saw a hallway that stretched from his left to his right. Hardwood floors with elongated throw rugs provided a path to dozens of doors on either side of the hallway. Pictures lined the gray walls further down the hall, but Terry couldn't make out their images from a distance.

The rifle nudged him in the back, bringing him back to reality.

"This way," Hopkins said, and turned to the right where there were fewer doors. He led them to the end of the hallway where the last door stood ajar. Hopkins entered the room where Chris sat behind a massive oak desk.

"Ah, Terry Brooks, how are you my old friend?" Chris asked with an evil grin.

Terry fought every urge to rant about their inhumane treatment in the basement, and to let him know that the Road Runners would take great pleasure in slitting his throat. But, he remembered Chris could read his thoughts and likely didn't give a shit what Terry thought about the living conditions in the basement. This was war, after all.

"I'm doing just fine," Terry said with as much sternness as he could muster. He glanced around the room and admired the lavish lifestyle that Chris had lived. Flat screen TVs lined the walls, a grandfather clock stood in the corner, its pendulum swinging back and forth as each second passed. A canteen of scotch called out to Terry from a table behind Chris's desk.

"Care for a drink?" the old man asked.

As much as he wanted one, Terry didn't trust anything from Chris. He knew too much of the old man's history and how he always surrounded people with temptation.

"No thanks, I just want to leave this place," Terry said.

Chris snickered. "Have a seat, Terry, we have a lot to discuss." He gestured to the chair across the desk. Hopkins stood in the doorway, now equipped with a rifle of his own. Chris nodded to him and Hopkins closed the door, remaining on the outside.

"Now that we have some privacy, Terry, you know I can't just let you go. You're too important to the Road Runners and will just run back and tell them everything about this place."

"We already know about this place."

"Yes, of course, but no one knows what goes on inside this house. I've kept a tight lid, and observations can only be made from the outside. I doubt your people know about the basement."

"We do." Terry bluffed. "But you don't have to worry about me, Chris. I'll live my life in exile. Won't even be that hard if the Road Runners don't know I'm free. You can drop me anywhere in the world and I'll live out my life there. Just get me out of this house."

Chris smirked as he looked down to his crossed hands on the desk. "I'll see what we can arrange. But first, you need to tell me everything you know about Martin Briar. What's the Road Runners' angle in using him? I know him well and don't exactly see him as your typical type of foot soldier."

Terry nodded. "I agree. I actually fought against his recruitment, but our team insists he has a talent."

"A *talent*?"

"I honestly don't know the details. It's been kept under a tight lid. I think only Commander Strike and her inner-circle know about it. But they seem to think he has some special skill."

"Have you met this guy?" Chris asked, sitting up and chuckling. "There isn't much special about him. The guy is a dud, but I'm intrigued at knowing he holds some value for the Road Runners. You're sure you don't know what they love about him?"

"Afraid not, sir. I only know he's highly valued, and it's a secret."

Chris stood up and paced to his window, gazing out to the snowy landscape, stroking his chin. "This is interesting. I suppose I need to make him as comfortable as possible here, really sell him on this life with the Revolution." Terry didn't know if he should respond, so remained silent. "It would be a shame to see him pushed away where you dirty pigs would likely swoop him right up."

"That is probably what will happen, yes."

"Perfect. That's all I needed to know. You can go now."

Terry gulped down the spit that had formed in his mouth. "What do you mean?"

Chris grinned. "I mean you can leave this house. You've provided me plenty of information and have revealed a new secret weapon. You just better do as promised and not return to the Road Runners. If you do, I'll kill you myself."

"I don't know what to say . . . thank you."

"I'm not as bad as you people think. I'll always be fair when possible, and I'm certainly a man of my word. Hopkins will see you outside."

As a reflex, Terry stuck out his hand to shake with Chris, instantly realizing he didn't owe an ounce of gratitude to the scheming old man who had held him hostage. But mercy was mercy, and all Terry could see in his near-sighted vision was freedom.

"Best of luck," Chris said as the men locked hands. "Hopkins!"

The door creaked open, and Terry's old friend from the basement showed himself with his usual stern, dead expression.

"Please see Mr. Brooks out of the house. He is free to go." Chris gave one final grin to Terry before Hopkins entered the room to lead him out.

"Follow me, Mr. Brooks," Hopkins said in a deep baritone.

Terry followed him back down the hallway, descended the spiral staircase to the main floor, and to the front door that had a half dozen locks for Hopkins to tinker with before pulling it open.

Terry saw the outdoors for the first time in months, and the sight sent an instant flutter to his chest.

Time to get the fuck out of here.

"Thank you," Terry said to Hopkins as he passed him in the doorway and took his first steps into freedom.

The crisp air filled his lungs as the orange sun fought to provide heat on a cold day. He'd need a jacket and some thicker clothes, but he'd have time. Besides, the Road Runners kept a secret hideout nearby. Surely they would have some extra clothes for him.

Not knowing which way to go, Terry started for the stand of trees 100 yards in front of him. He'd walk a straight line until he found a city or a road, or the Arctic Ocean. The snow crunched beneath each step as the pine trees ahead swayed in the breeze.

Wait till everyone hears about the basement, he thought, his pace increasing with each step.

Terry looked over his shoulder and stopped in his tracks. The house, now 100 yards behind him, had somewhat shrunk in his vision, but he could still see Hopkins standing on the front porch, a rifle cocked and aimed in his direction.

"No!" Terry shrieked in unison with the rifle's explosion on the otherwise silent day.

For that brief half of a second, Terry swore he saw the bullet fly out from the muzzle. Before he could blink, it struck him square in the forehead, and he collapsed to the ground.

77

Chapter 23

"Holy shit!" Martin panted under his breath. He watched the entire thing unfold, at least from the moment the man started walking across the open field toward the trees. From his window, he could barely make out the guard standing on the porch with the rifle now slung over his shoulder.

He couldn't take his eyes off the dead body, lying limp at the base of a pine tree, face down in the snow. *Who was that? Why was he walking out there? And why did they shoot him? Did he try to escape?*

Without having seen the rest of the mansion, Martin sensed something off about the place. The way the guards all worked together—and all looked the same—he couldn't help but feel a bit like a prisoner. If he wanted to go out for an evening walk, could he? If he asked to borrow a vehicle to drive into town, would they allow such a request?

Regardless of what they allowed him to do, Martin settled on one new priority: getting out of the mansion.

After having an afternoon to sleep and meditate on the last twelve hours of his life, he decided that anything involving Chris led to no good. Sure, the old man and his army of clones had busted him out of the trap set by the Road Runners, but were the Road Runners really the bad ones in this war? How was Martin supposed to know?

The Road Runners had caused him no harm, and didn't so much as suggest they would. Hell, he had apparently lived with one for six months in 1996 with no sign of danger. So what exactly was their angle?

Something is going on behind the scenes much bigger than you, he told himself. *You're wanted by both sides in this conflict.*

"But why?" he said to his empty bedroom. Since arriving and taking a quick nap, Martin had studied the bedroom further to find it was set up like a hotel room: private bathroom, fridge, closet, ironing board, and the TV mounted to the wall. Landscape paintings hung on the beige walls, showing a glimpse into his Colorado life with a cabin in the snowy mountains.

Martin's internal alarm sounded off, demanding he leave the mansion. His door wasn't locked, and he could wander down the hallway, but he still felt a resistance. His gut told him to remain and wait. How hard could it be to walk out of the mansion? Even if he escaped, he had at least a mile to the main road that led back to town; he couldn't even spot it from his elevated bedroom window.

Stay, the voice in his head said.

A knock came from the door, startling him as he jumped away from the window. *Do they have cameras in here? How would they know I'm awake?*

Martin considered this, knowing Chris could have any sort of technology from the future implanted in his room. The paintings could have cameras in them the size of a needle tip, and there could be microphones as small as ants propped anywhere in the room for listening. And there was still Chris's ability to hear his thoughts. Did he have the range to do such a thing simply by being in the same house?

Clear your mind right now.

Another knock echoed around the room, this time louder and harder.

"I'm coming!" Martin shouted, irritated, as he dragged his feet across the carpet.

He pulled open the door to find a grinning Chris. "May I come in?"

Martin stepped aside and allowed the old man into his room, keeping his mind clear of any thoughts.

"Did I wake you?" Chris asked as he crossed the room to study the portrait on the wall.

459

"No, I just woke up a few minutes ago."

"Very good. I wanted to see how you're holding up. Today was pure chaos, especially for you."

Martin nodded as Chris turned his attention to him, and closed the door to lean against it.

"I'm doing fine. Glad you got there when you did. I don't know what would have happened if you never showed up. How did you know?"

"When you arrived in 1919, you were being followed from the moment you made it downtown. We followed the Road Runners who were trailing you. This war has progressed to a point where they are becoming a viable threat. They've been poaching people I've given the Juice to by promising a lavish life. A life safe and free from me, like I'm some sort of monster. What these people don't realize is that they can get their dream lives all on their own. How much money did you have waiting in your bank account when you arrived home after your journey to 1996?"

"Millions."

"Exactly. That's because you're smart and a forward thinker. The Road Runners try to plant doubt about me and the success people can find while traveling through time, then they insert themselves as the only solution. It's gross, but I suppose all is fair in love and war, right?"

Martin nodded, continually fighting off the urge to think about his encounter with the Road Runners. "That is true."

Chris smiled as he crossed the room toward the window, and gazed into the landscape where Terry Brooks had just been shot dead like an elk in the woods. "How are you liking the place so far?"

Chris had his back to Martin, and this caused Martin to release the tension in his shoulders that he hadn't realized existed. "My room is nice, very modern, but that's all I've seen. Am I allowed into the rest of the house?" He asked this like a curious child.

Chris chuckled before turning back around to face Martin. "Of course. This can be your home for as long as you'd like, so get yourself acclimated. You're by no means obliged to stay here, but keep in mind the Road Runners are looking for you, so it's not exactly safe out there at the moment. In here, you'll have the highest level of security. No one gets into this house unless I say so."

"I thought you can't die by traditional means. You don't even eat food, right? So why have so much security?"

Chris locked eyes with Martin and sent chills up his spine. "The security isn't for me, old friend. I'll be just fine. It's for the secrets buried in the walls of the house. If the Road Runners were ever to get ahold of the information that lies within this house, the war would be over in ten minutes."

These words hung in the air as Martin tried to process them. "The secrets of time?"

Chris nodded. "Among other things, yes. Now, I don't want you to get hung up on this. Everything is fine and safe in this house, including you. Feel free to wander around, it's really just the main floor. This floor is all bedrooms, and the basement is locked and off limits."

"What about outside? I can't stay cooped up in the house all day."

"Impressive, Martin. You wouldn't have said that a few months ago when you spent every day drunk in your apartment with no idea what time it was."

"Even then I would go out to my balcony for some air," Martin responded with obvious sass in his voice.

"You can go wherever you want, Marty. You're not a prisoner here. I just wanted to make sure you weren't kidnapped or killed. You're encouraged to stay for your own safety, but you can do as you please."

It was rare when Chris called him Marty, but he hated it the same every time. That was a nickname from his mother and for use by close family and friends only.

"I'll leave you to it," Chris said. "Let me know if there's anything at all you need. Consider this your home for the time being."

"Will do. Have a good night."

Chris crossed the room and left, closing the door gently behind him.

Martin sat on his bed and had an instant urge to plan a way off the property. Chris clearly had a lax approach for keeping him in the house, and he needed to take advantage of that before anything changed.

"Do I move tonight?" he whispered to himself. He grabbed the remote off the nightstand and turned on the TV, letting it play as background noise so he could continue to speak to himself. "There's something going on that no one is telling me. Why would Chris want to keep me safe? He just offered me everything he said the Road Runners offer to lure people: a lavish life and protection."

Martin's leg bounced wildly on the bed and he focused to make it stop. "Why am I nervous? He essentially invited me to leave. Maybe he's counting on me loving the mansion. I can't afford to explore it and fall into a trap of comfort. I need to move tonight."

A quick pep talk to himself was all it took for him to decide he would flee the mansion at night. He had no idea what kind of surveillance was on the property, but moving in the darkness was always an advantage. If any of the guards followed him, he'd lose them in the woods. Since Chris clearly wanted to keep him alive, he dismissed the possibility of being shot. If they had wanted him dead, it would be done by now.

Martin jumped off the bed and rummaged through the closet. There was one coat, a couple pairs of sweatpants, and three shirts. They all looked slightly small for him, but would manage as he needed all the layers possible for his escape in the North Pole.

"I need to move fast into the woods. The trees will give cover so I can run to the main road." His senses had been heightened during the drive over as he kept track of every move the van made.

His stomach growled when he checked the clock that read 4:03.

"Don't go into that kitchen. Everything in this house is designed to trap you into staying." Martin kept whispering to himself, pacing around the room. Once the adrenaline kicked in, he'd forget all about his hunger.

His curiosity throbbed, begging to see the rest of this luxurious mansion that made his new house look like a shack. He pulled open the door and stuck his head out.

The long hallway stretched into the distance, but no one was visible. All of the doors were closed, much like a hotel, and he realized that was exactly what this hideout was designed to feel like: half hotel, half home, with the kitchen and who knows what else on the main floor.

"Act casual, pretend you're exploring the house and see how far you can get without being seen."

He stepped into the hallway, slight creaking beneath his feet from the hardwood floor, and glided the door shut with steady hands.

"Just act normal."

Instead of tiptoeing down the hall like he wanted, he broke into his usual stride and walked toward the stairs. When he reached the steps that led to the main floor, he noticed an open door at the end of the hallway, light spilling out in a yellow sheet.

The incoherent mumble of voices came from the open door, and Martin took the softest steps he could manage toward the voices. He stopped within ten feet of the room once he could hear the voices clearly. One belonged to Chris, the other to a man he didn't recognize.

"Did you dispose of the body?" Chris asked.

"Yes, we moved it into the woods. Will let the animals have some easy dinner."

Both men chuckled. They had to be talking about the person who he just watched get shot. Would Martin's fate end the same way if he tried leaving?

After the laughter faded, Martin heard the soft clink ice made in a glass when you took a drink.

"So what's the word on Briar?" the unidentified man asked.

Martin's adrenaline exploded at the mention of his name.

"I don't know what to think. Terry says the Road Runners have a secret about him—I think he was talking out of his ass to try and get out of here. Briar doesn't seem like anything special. Was there anything you noticed in your research?"

"Interesting. Nothing at all from my end." the man responded with an elevated pitch in his voice.

"I figured as much. I just want to create an environment so that he doesn't want to leave us—pretty much gave him free reign here around

463

the property. I highly doubt he'll bother trying to find his way home, but we'll help him once he's ready. If anything, we'll just brainwash him and make him another soldier for us."

The men roared laughter one final time as Martin turned and shuffled down the hallway. "I'm getting the fuck out of here tonight," he whispered as he approached his door.

He returned to his room and slammed the door shut in a panic, collapsing to the ground, heart trying to burst through his rib cage. He gasped for air as adrenaline flowed through his veins.

His eavesdropping just confirmed two things: there was definitely something bigger at play that involved him, and he would be leaving the mansion as soon as the sun disappeared.

78

Chapter 24

Martin forgot the daylight situation was all fucked up in Alaska. He was also fortunate. Had he arrived two months earlier, they would've still been in their cycle of 24-hour sunlight. They were still a couple of months from around the clock darkness, so he had to settle for the sunset that arrived shortly after 8 P.M.

He wanted to kill time like a normal person, pacing circles, flipping through the TV channels, reading books that were tucked away in the nightstand drawers. He even spent a good half hour gazing out the window, trying to plot his exact path when he escaped the house.

None of it mattered.

A constant paranoia tickled his every thought, waiting for Chris to barge into the room with his guards to take him down to the basement. The basement had to be either a prison or a slave ring, he decided, and he had no plans on finding out which it was.

The adrenaline from his eavesdropping had given way to a twisting knot of stress in his gut. Every instinct in his body told him that if he didn't leave tonight, he never would.

When eight o'clock finally rolled around, the sun disappeared behind the horizon, leaving an orange glow to collide with the swarming deep blue sky. Waiting for the sun to set reminded him of that fateful night when he had gone back to rescue Izzy. He had stared out the window in the same manner, contemplating what happened next. The old Martin would have had a panic attack and drank every drop of alcohol in sight. But enough adventure had made him numb to the sensation of the unknown. Minus the bubble guts, he was ready to take on the next mission.

Martin slipped into the tight sweatpants and pulled the extra shirts over his current clothes. The jacket zipped up with no problem, despite him feeling that his body might burst through all the layers.

"Are these clothes for children?" he asked, and let out a nervous giggle. Within fifteen minutes the orange glow outside had vanished, leaving a purple splash that would soon melt into complete darkness. "It's time."

He checked himself in the mirror and found that he looked rather normal despite the three layers of clothing. Wearing the baggiest layer on the exterior made it rather simple to achieve. He certainly *looked* like he would be going out for an extended walk around town, but would tell anyone he might run into that he only wanted to explore the property.

Martin drew a deep inhale before crossing the room to exit. He left the light turned on, wanting to give the appearance that he was still in his room, and pulled open the door. The hallway remained empty.

Does anyone here ever leave their room?

He started down the hallway and took the stairs down to the main level. The mansion's front door was the first thing to greet him. Voices carried from another room, presumably the kitchen from the sounds of silverware clashing with dishes. Laughter broke out, making Martin jump, but the voices carried on in their murmur of conversation.

Don't just stand there, get out of the house and run!

Martin studied the door before stepping up to it. There were four dead bolts and two chain locks scattered around the doorframe.

Clearly no one is supposed to get into this place.

"Or out of it," he whispered, and lunged for the door, twisting at the locks until the final one clicked. He grabbed the knob with a shaking hand and pulled open the door.

A cold rush of air burst through while one of the men stood guard on the front porch, pacing back and forth with a rifle slung over his shoulder.

The man, who stood equal in height with Martin, swiveled around on his heels and met Martin's gaze.

"Good evening," Martin said, heart drumming wildly.

The man nodded. He was bundled up in a puffy red jacket so that only the tip of his nose showed, matching the shade of the jacket, and he studied Martin with curious blue eyes.

"Hello," the man said, robotically.

"I was hoping to do some hunting later this week, and wanted to look around the property. Don't mind me."

Martin took a confident step off the porch and had started toward the woods before the man stopped him. "Wait."

Martin froze, convinced a bullet was coming his way. *Please let it end quick.* He turned back to the goon and was relieved to see the rifle still perched on his shoulder and not pointed at him.

"The best spots for hunting are behind the house. You're going toward the main road, there's nothing there."

Martin almost burst into laughter. Not only did the guard not want to shoot him, he even gave directions during his escape.

"Oh, thank you," Martin said, and started toward the back of the house, the frozen snow crunching beneath each confident step. "Just around this way?"

The man nodded, and kept his gaze to the woods in the distance.

"Thank you. Have a great night."

Once Martin rounded the corner of the house and confirmed the guard was no longer in sight, he broke into a sprint toward the woods on the backside of the house. It hadn't felt cold until he started running, the falling temperatures biting at his bare face as his feet crunched the snow below. As long as he kept moving, the cold wouldn't get the best of him. Lacking gloves, he stuffed his hands into the jacket pockets for relief.

It only took him thirty seconds to arrive to the outer trees that housed the rest of the woods. Once the mansion was far enough, looking like a regular-sized house in the distance, he stopped and dropped to his knees, huffing and puffing, gasping for the cold air that felt like icicles filling his air pipe.

"Oh my God," he wheezed. "I'm too old for this shit."

After a couple minutes, he gathered himself and rose to his feet. The guard had confirmed the direction of the main road, and Martin started walking through the trees in that general direction. He had the cover of the trees, and no one from the mansion would be able to see him as he worked his way through the darkness.

He debated taking a swig of the Juice to return to 2018 right now, but had no clue how different the world would be at that precise time in Barrow, Alaska. He had to work with what he had and focus on getting out of the city. It would only be a matter of time until Chris realized he was missing, at which point he'd travel back a few minutes—or hours, hopefully—to track down Martin. He and his soldiers would be on his trail within a day, so he couldn't afford to waste a moment.

He had run a lot further than he thought. It took him five minutes to weave through the trees and get back into position on the front side of the house. The guard remained on the front porch, continuing the circular pacing in his best effort to stay warm. What a boring job. Who would ever find a hideout in the middle of nowhere?

With the guard to his back, Martin continued into the woods at a brisk pace. Stumps, logs, and sticks attempted to trip him, so he focused on each step to avoid falling.

Doubt remained stuck on his mind like a bug on a windshield. What if the guard had led him into a trap? They surely couldn't be too dumb if Chris had chosen them for protection. What if there was no world beyond the woods, and it was a ploy? Chris had mastered time travel, and creating an enclosed, fake world wouldn't be too difficult considering the access he had to future technology. Chris wouldn't agree to let him wander around the property if there really was a way out, would he?

As Martin progressed through the woods, he kept his hands in front, anticipating an invisible force field that would surely bounce him back to the mansion where Chris would howl laughter. Then he'd be off to the basement.

He continued for ten more minutes, the mansion completely out of sight, nothing but tall, skinny trees in every direction. The moonlight provided just enough of a glow for Martin to see the trees in front of him, but beyond that was pure blackness. He hadn't realized how much light the mansion had provided when he first left, and now felt lost.

Maniacal laughter echoed throughout the woods, carried by the soft breeze that brushed the tops of the trees.

From the mansion? Martin wondered. At his pace he'd be close to a mile away from the house. *No way a laugh would carry that far.*

The laughing continued, swirling around Martin's head to the point he had to stop walking. *It's just the wind howling, keep going. You can't stop.*

He held his breath, planted his feet in the ground, and listened.

The sound continued, steady and uninterrupted.

That's not wind. It's a real laugh. Like a madman.

The thought sent chills down Martin's back that not even the stinging cold had accomplished. The trees continued to sway from fifty feet above, the leaves rustling as they provided Martin cover from the moonlight.

He remained frozen as the sound of sticks crunching on the ground grew louder behind.

Fuck, they're already on to me.

He peered through the trees, squinting to make out any shape in the darkness. The crunching approached him from directly behind and stopped.

Martin spun around and shouted, "AAAAHHHHHH!"

He swung fists into the air and collapsed to the ground when he saw nothing there. His heart pounded in his head as adrenaline tried to burst out of his eyeballs.

"What the fuck?" he panted as he pulled himself back up, brushing off the snow clung to his coat.

You've been in the woods for 20 whole minutes and are already losing your mind. Keep going.

Alone in nature, Martin continued toward where he believed the main road awaited. His mind kept returning to Izzy, now buried peacefully in the cemetery in 2018 Denver. Her disappearance led to this exact moment, and he felt her presence beside him, assuring him it would all be okay. The parent was supposed to console the child, but perhaps the roles switched when the child became an angel.

He closed his eyes and imagined her soft, gentle voice. "Go, Daddy. You can make it."

Her voice was no longer in his imagination; he *felt* her speaking in his head.

"Go, Daddy. Run!"

Martin obliged and pulled himself up, immediately breaking into a sprint despite his legs protesting and his tar-filled lungs begging for mercy.

The road was closer than he realized. After three minutes of running, leaping, and dodging through the trees, asphalt greeted Martin's feet, its unexpectedly even surface nearly causing him to tumble after his escape from the rocky terrain of the woods.

With the trees separated by the road, the moonlight provided a mystic glow. Martin looked both ways, each direction winding into more darkness, unsure which way to go. He ran to his left for no reason other than following his gut instinct that told him which way was north.

Martin didn't run for too long—his legs and chest grateful—when he stopped at the sight of approaching headlights a quarter mile up the road, but moving with rapid speed as they drove along the twisted street.

Hide.

Martin took two long lunges and dove off the road, tumbling into the woods where branches and rocks scraped his hands as he rolled to a stop. He momentarily lost his bearings as he brushed the debris and snow off his clothes, but found them again when the car's engine roared like a lion in the still night.

He hid behind a tree, hands on his knees, panting for breath, the freezing air stinging his lungs with each inhale while his vision blurred in and out of focus.

Relax, it could just be a car driving by.

He wanted to believe this, but knew better. With the events that had transpired in the last half hour, it surely wasn't a coincidence that some asshole was driving 70 miles per hour in the middle of nowhere.

Martin crouched, studying the headlights that grew closer with each passing millisecond. With the car roughly 100 yards away, he could make it out as a four-door sedan, a dark color, possibly black or navy.

The brakes slammed, splashing red light on the road and trees behind it. Smoke rose from the screeching tires, complemented by the stench of burnt rubber. The car had stopped directly in line with Martin, no more that thirty feet from where he hid behind a tree trunk, as if the driver knew exactly where he was.

It's gotta be Chris. Who else would know how to find you when you're lost?

The car's engine puttered, blowing gray clouds of exhaust. The world felt still. *Too* still. As much as his mind was stuck in a panic, Martin noticed the trees no longer swayed. Silence filled the air, thick enough to cut into with a plastic knife, his breathing and drumming heartbeat the only audible sounds within his conscience.

"Martin!" a voice whispered loudly from the car.

His blood froze as a new layer of goosebumps broke out on his back and legs.

They're certainly here for you. No mistaking that now, big guy.

Martin didn't recognize the voice, and because of that, stayed behind the tree, praying to God that the mystery car would drive off and mind their own business.

"Martin!" the voice called, louder. A man's voice.

It's not Chris. Sounds too young.

"Martin, I know you're there. Come get in the car. I'm with the Road Runners."

He had no way out of this. They called him out by name and were shouting directly to the tree he hid behind. He had two options: to get in the car on a blind leap of faith, or sprint back into the woods where he would further become lost, unequipped for an overnight stay in the blistering cold.

Could it be Chris's men posing as Road Runners? Why would they take that approach? Martin had never done so much as hinted that he trusted the Road Runners. He willingly fled their capture with no second thoughts.

But you've been thinking about them more. The Road Runners are the good guys in this war.

"Martin! Get in the fucking car or you're gonna freeze to death!" the man barked, impatience dripping from each word.

No more energy or willpower was coming. Running was off the table of options, leaving one obvious, but hesitant choice.

Martin stepped out from the tree, hands raised in the air like he was under arrest.

"Quit dicking around and get in the car!"

A young man hung out the passenger window, someone Martin had never seen before.

Martin crawled up the slope back to the road, thighs burning and demanding a rest as they wobbled beneath him.

"Hurry!" the man called, returning to his hushed tone.

Martin approached the car, doubt swirling, and pulled open the back-seat door.

"Get in," the driver said. He appeared a similar age as Martin, suggested by the gray streaks in his goatee. Piercing blue eyes studied Martin as he lunged into the car.

The passenger who had been shouting rotated in his seat and craned his neck to look at Martin. He was as young as his voice had sounded, fresh out of college by Martin's guess.

"Out for an evening stroll, Martin?" the young one asked, blinking his brown eyes that surely charmed the ladies at the university.

"Who are you guys?" Martin asked, still catching his breath as the tension of the last thirty seconds started to wane. After all the urgency they had thrown his way, the men seemed content sitting in the middle of the road as they got to know each other.

"We're with the Road Runners," the older man said. "My name is Bill

Jordan, and my partner here is Julian Caruso. We're sorry to meet you under such stressful circumstances."

"How did you know where I was? We're in the middle of nowhere."

"Yeah, this place is a fucking dump," Julian said, head still craned awkwardly. He gawked at Martin as if the two men had stumbled across Sasquatch sitting in their backseat. They had a calming presence, and Martin leaned back as if he had jumped into a car with friends.

"Seriously," Martin said. "How did you find me?"

Bill chuckled, his small double chin jiggling as his shoulders trembled with delight. "Finding you was the easy part. How the hell did you get out of that place? That's the question we've been dying to ask."

Martin furrowed his brow and scratched his cheek. *What's going on?*

His stomach dropped, not out of angst, but more out of frustration at the growing sense that he was some minor cog in the vast time travel world.

"I walked out," Martin said, unsure what sort of explanation the men wanted.

Both men threw their heads back and howled like lunatics.

Martin watched them and wished he could be anywhere else besides the backseat of this car. Were they here to rescue him or make fun of him?

"That's a good one, Martin," Bill said. "Tell us. Did you have to fight off Chris's bodyguards? Or were you just faster than them?"

"I told you. I walked out of the house, then ran through the woods."

Now it was Bill and Julian's turn to stare at each other, confused. "You mean you weren't locked away?" Julian asked.

"No. I was in my own private bedroom, kind of like a hotel."

"What a fucking moron," Julian murmured under his breath.

"Excuse me?" Martin demanded.

"Not you. Chris. He's a complete moron. I'll never understand how he rose to power, but I suppose we should be grateful he's calling the shots. He just handed you to us on a silver platter."

"I'm not on either side of this. I just wanna go home and dump my

Juice down the drain."

Bill shook his head. "You're way beyond that point, my friend. You're in this war whether you like it or not. And I think you already know what side the good guys are on."

Martin still hadn't had any true exposure to the happenings of this supposed war, but it was obvious that the Road Runners had a much less aggressive approach, at least in terms of dealing with him.

"What if I refuse?" Martin asked nonchalantly.

Bill and Julian exchanged glances again, speaking to each other through mere eye twitches. They may have been different in age, but it was impossible to know how long someone had actually existed in this time travelling ordeal.

"We'll let you speak with the Commander about that," Julian said.

"The Commander? Who is that? And when will that be?"

"Right now, and she's the leader of the Road Runners in North America," Julian said. "She flew up here as soon as we told her you were captured."

"She's waiting," Bill said before turning his attention back to the steering wheel. "It's time to go."

Bill made a U-turn and drove along the dark road. Martin slouched, trying to relax, but remained ready for what would come next.

There's definitely something they want from me.

79

Chapter 25

The drive lasted ten minutes, and all three men remained silent for the duration. The small chat ended, and Martin sensed the tension weighing down on the car.

"We're here," Bill said, but Martin only saw darkness through the windows. They had pulled off the road half a mile ago and were still in the middle of nothingness.

Martin's heartbeat had calmed since the two Road Runners picked him up. He didn't sense any danger, just unease of the unknown.

Bill killed the engine and stepped out of the car, prompting Julian and Martin to follow suit. Sticks and rocks greeted their feet as they trudged along a small path that had been cleared of snow toward a small structure, no bigger than an outhouse.

The leader of the Road Runners hangs out in a shitter all day?

Bill led the way and pulled open the creaky wooden door. There was no toilet, just a four by four slab of concrete. "We all fit, let's go." He stepped in, Julian and Martin following into the cramped, dark space.

Julian rummaged his fingers along the blacked out wall, the clicking sound of buttons being pushed as the only audible noise over the three men's hoarse breathing.

"The Commander is excited to meet you," Bill said, this time with a chipper voice.

Julian pulled the door shut as a loud humming sound filled the outhouse, the ground rumbling beneath them.

"Nothing to worry about," Julian said after seeing Martin's bulging eyes. "Just a different kind of elevator."

The ground lightened as the concrete descended at a snail's pace into the earth. The darkness concealed everything until they reached their destination where two dozen people were scattered across a room that stretched back at least two hundred feet.

They all sat at desks in the open space, computer monitors glowing, keyboards clattering, attention focused on their tasks at hand. A bell let out one shrill ring as the elevator came to a complete stop, and all heads turned to Martin.

He stood behind Bill and Julian, but felt the stares burn right through them. A blanket of silence fell over the room as the three men stepped off the elevator.

"Commander Strike, he's here!" a giddy voice from the back called. "He's here!" The squeaky man was near hysterics, running across the back of the room like he had just remembered a meeting he was late for.

"Everyone back to work," Bill barked with authority. "Nothing to see here. Move along."

The two dozen heads held their ground for a couple more seconds before ducking back into their computers.

"This way," Julian instructed, leading them to the left.

Bill's and Julian's boots clapped and echoed along the concrete ground as they passed the area of desks that formed a large rectangle across the room. Above the desks hung 100-inch TV screens that lined the length of the room. Some showed images of people and places, others showed maps with different colored dots splayed about. Every section of the office had at least one person with a close eye on the screens.

"This is our headquarters," Julian said.

"*One* of our headquarters," Bill corrected.

"Just because it's not as glamorous as some of our other locations, doesn't mean it's not our *main* headquarters. We have other places around the world, but since this is where all of our studies on Chris are conducted, it's considered the most important headquarters."

Julian explained this as if he had built the place himself, and Bill grunted as they reached the middle part of the room. Martin hadn't noticed the offices that lined the perimeter.

All of the private offices appeared roughly the same size, big enough for a desk, a corner plant, and two chairs for visitors to sit. Only one office stood out as special, and that was the door they stood outside of. It was also the only door that had frosted glass, keeping any wandering eyes from seeing inside.

Bill rapped on the door with a balled fist.

"Come in," a woman's voice called.

Bill pushed open the door and stepped in first, keeping Julian and Martin at a distance.

"Good evening, Commander Strike," Bill said. "Glad to see you made it in so soon."

"I hopped on the jet right away. Is everything okay with Mr. Briar? Were you followed?"

"Yes, and no," Bill said proudly. "I have him right here, and he has loads of questions."

"Thank you, Bill. I owe you and Julian. Have Mr. Briar come in and leave us in private, please."

"Absolutely." Bill bowed out of the room and held up an arm to welcome Martin. "Commander Strike is ready to see you."

Martin stepped into the doorway and locked eyes with a blue-eyed, light-skinned woman who greeted him with a warm smile. Her red hair was pulled back into a ponytail, revealing early wrinkles that had formed on her temples. Martin judged her to be in her mid-forties as her face lit up with a flash of youth.

"Mr. Briar," she said, standing and crossing the room with an extended hand. "It's such an honor to meet you. I'm Commander Strike."

He shook her hand and admired its smooth texture. She was dressed casually for someone who was called Commander—jeans and a sweater—but she apparently just got off a plane. And they were in Alaska.

"Nice to meet you," Martin responded, unsure of a certain protocol for greeting the leader of the Road Runners.

"Please have a seat. We have lots to discuss." She was tall, almost six feet, and walked with her shoulders held high and a swagger that dared someone to mess with her.

Martin obliged and stepped all the way into the office. Strike had the same set up of a desk and two chairs, but also had a sofa along the front wall with portraits of men and women covering every inch of space, monitors in every ceiling corner, and another side door that led to either a bathroom or closet. There was also a table along the back wall, and Martin couldn't help but notice the bottle of scotch standing unattended with two glasses at its side. The days of heavy drinking were long gone, but he still drooled at the sight of scotch. Who was this lady, anyway? Tall, strong, in charge, and a scotch drinker. Maybe his next love interest?

Fuck that. No more time-traveling women.

The wounds still hadn't closed from Sonya, mainly because he hadn't had any time to grieve, let alone process what the hell happened. He'd been running for his life ever since the Road Runners dropped the bomb that Sonya had been a ploy to lure him into their possession. Maybe Strike would have some answers.

She situated herself in her wide, cushioned chair that was clearly out of place for a typical office setting, appearing more like a black throne. "I can't tell you how excited I am to meet you."

"Thank you?" Martin responded.

"I know you have plenty of questions. It's been brought to my attention that you don't even know the extent of your abilities. You won't leave this office with any more questions; I can guarantee you that much."

"I just want to know what's going on."

Commander Strike chuckled. "You're invaluable." Martin stared into Commander Strike's eyes, as if the truth would magically jump out. "You have a rare gift, Martin. Something even more rare than the capability to travel through time."

She paused, looking for a reaction, but Martin gave none.

"You're what we call a Warm Soul. Beyond time travel, there are others with different abilities. There are some who can freeze time. And on the flip side of that, there are others who can *resist* the freezing of time."

Martin's eyebrows elevated to his hairline. "What do you mean by freezing time?"

"When time is frozen, everything comes to a complete standstill. You can be in the middle of a run through the park, and be frozen mid-stride. We could freeze in the middle of this conversation, and the thing is, we would never know it—well, *I* would never know it. *You* would."

If Martin scrunched his face any more it would fall off his skull. "Are you saying I'm immune to this?"

Commander Strike nodded, her ponytail bobbing joyfully.

"Wouldn't I have noticed that everyone around me was frozen?" Martin asked.

"Not necessarily. This isn't something that happens often. There are only a handful of people in the world who can freeze time, and even less who can resist."

"Why me? What did I do?"

"That's one question I wish I could answer. We don't have any knowledge on how this actually works. As far as we know, it's all random. We've conducted studies on those who can resist frozen time, and have found no similarities across subjects."

Martin squirmed in his seat, uncomfortable that he had such a unique ability. His dreams of going home to a normal life were shot. Although, maybe he could leverage this situation for his personal gain. Strike hadn't said it yet, but he had something they wanted. He stared blankly across the table. "So what is it exactly you want from me?"

"We want you to be a Road Runner. To fight on the right side of history."

She let her words hang in the air, pressuring Martin to speak next after a few awkward seconds of silence.

"How do I know you're on the right side?"

Commander Strike stood from her desk and paced along the back wall, rubbing the bottle of scotch as if debating to pour a glass or drink straight from the bottle.

"Tell me everything Chris has told you about his plans." She tossed her hands in the air. "Go ahead."

"Well, he never tells me much. He told me some of the rules for time—"

"I don't care about that. Tell me about *his* plans for the future."

"I can't say he's told me anything. He's mentioned that he has counterparts on every continent. . .but that might have been the Road Runners who told me that before Chris came and busted me out of the hotel. Today has been an absolute blur."

"That's exactly my point. I can tell you everything about our plans as the Road Runners, where we've been and where we're going."

"I'm listening."

"Our main reason for existence is to keep Chris and his friends from ruling the world. It is true that he has counterparts on every continent, even Antarctica. And they're all as equally bought in to their mission of taking over the world. It's why they're on each continent. They're slowly manipulating every country's government to the point where they have rule over those countries by planting their own people in positions of power."

"So, they're like the New World Order?"

"You could say that, except this is real. Their movement is called The Future Revolution, and they call themselves the Revolters. They're real, and they're powerful. They travel throughout time to learn what can make each government fall, and how to manipulate people into believing what they're selling."

"Which is?"

"No different than anyone else who makes empty promises: a better world, a better future. Every action they make, every word that is spoken, has a direct purpose behind it with a specific goal at the end. Their end goal is to rule a world where there are no people who can think for themselves, and it's frightening. They're succeeding, in fact. But that's the beauty of there *not* being linear time—we can always inflict change in any era and save the future from itself."

"Is there a point in time where you see an end to this war?"

She crossed her arms and frowned. "There's not necessarily a time where the war ends, but there's a time where it becomes obvious that The Future Revolution rules a majority of the world. What year is it in your current time? 1995?"

"No, 1996 is what I traveled back to, to save my daughter. I'm from 2018."

She nodded as if she should've known this. "The takeover has already begun by 2018. The world is going mad by then. It's one of our main eras of focus."

"And you want me to help stop it from happening?"

"Yes. We're just not sure how yet. We have so much to learn about time freezing that we won't put you in a situation that we don't understand ourselves. One thing I can promise you is that every decision is made methodically and we never put a Road Runner's life at risk. Unlike Chris, who rotates through his soldiers like it's World War One all over again."

Martin processed this information with care. Aside from their encounter in his mansion bedroom, Chris had never discussed plans of any sort, and left many answers vague. Martin had always sensed the old man was hiding something, even back when they had first met.

"Be honest with yourself, and with me," Strike continued. "What has Chris done for you? Did he deceive you into a better life by granting you time travel? Hurt your family? Try to lure you into comfort with a luxurious life?"

Martin looked to the floor and nodded. "He's done all of that."

"That's what he's done to all of us, one by one. Every Road Runner received their Juice through Chris—there's no other way, although we're getting closer to reverse engineering it. The point is, you're not alone, and it's why we believe so strongly in our mission of taking him down. There are people who will fall for anything and get sucked into Chris's tricks. The rest of us become Road Runners." Martin smiled at that last line, the ultimate sales pitch. "I'm not going to stand here and make you empty promises for agreeing to join us. We're not going to deposit $100 million dollars into your bank account in exchange for your soul. Any dipshit with the Juice can find a way to make easy money. We believe in helping each other build a life that you can be proud of—whatever that means to you."

"I like everything you've said, but I really need to think things over. I didn't ask to be sucked into this, and I'm honestly not interested in joining a war that never ends. I have a sick mom at home—thanks to Chris—and I just want to be with her."

"I'm not going to argue with that. We can get you on a plane back to Denver in 2018 within the next hour. All I ask is that you give this serious consideration. And keep one thing in mind: you're never going to be able to watch from the sidelines. Without us, Chris will come after you and make you his prisoner. And if you reject us, we don't really have the resources to protect you. As much as you hate to hear it, you're going to need to pick a side, or one will be picked for you, and it will never be us who force the matter."

Martin's heart beat a little faster. He didn't know for sure if the Road Runners truly would leave him in peace, but he had no problem believing that Chris wouldn't.

"I'll consider this. You have my word. But I really do want to get home to my mom."

Commander Strike nodded and smiled. "Alright, then. I'll have Bill and Julian take you to our private jet. Do you know where the Chop House is in Denver?"

"The restaurant? Yeah."

"When you make your decision, go to the parking garage behind the restaurant. Go to the stairwell and go as low as you can and wait. I'll have someone meet you there so we can discuss your decision."

Chills broke out down Martin's back. *How big is this underground network? It's like an entire society living in another world.*

"Okay. I can do that."

"Perfect. I look forward to seeing you again. I'll grab Bill and Julian and let them know the plan. We'll be in touch."

Commander Strike left Martin alone in the office, leaving him in silence to ponder what the rest of his life would now look like.

80

Chapter 26

Commander Strike followed her word. She left Martin alone in her office for ten minutes before Bill came knocking to retrieve him.

"Jet's being fueled and will be ready when we get there. Any last questions for the Commander before we leave?"

Martin shook his head.

"Alright then, let's head out." Bill gestured for him to stand.

When Martin stepped out of the office, a few of the Road Runners tried to sneak a peek at him. They made it less obvious than when he had arrived, but they all eventually caught a glimpse of their secret weapon.

Julian waited in front of the elevator, pacing back and forth like a guard.

"Let's get Mr. Briar back home," Bill said.

The three stepped into the elevator, and stood in the same positions as when they had arrived. "Pretty cool place, huh?" Julian asked as the elevator door cut off the view of the underground headquarters.

"Yeah. It's crazy to know this is all going on."

"You should see some of our other locations: swimming pools, racquet-ball courts, all kinds of amenities. It's hard to get those kind of things all the way up here in Santa's land. Besides, the Commander doesn't think we should be playing when we're so close to Chris. That's really the only reason for this location, to follow his every move."

"Was his mansion on one of those screens?"

Bill laughed. "One of those screens? Try half of those screens. We watch that house like a hawk."

"Have you ever seen the inside?"

"No. We're hoping you'll tell us about it later. Whether you join us or not." Bill said this last line in a *how-dare-you-consider-rejecting-us* tone.

"How many Road Runners are trapped in that house?" Martin asked.

"At least fifty. We want to know about the basement..."

"I didn't get to see it—wasn't exactly exploring the place—but I think that's where they're all being kept."

"We sent in some people, undercover, to try and learn about the inside of the place. They were all volunteers, but Chris snuffed them out as liars and we've never seen them again. We just assumed they were dead. We've recently implanted tracker devices into Road Runners—for reasons like this."

"But no one volunteers to go into that house any more," Julian cut in. "If we could get just one person to go, we could know for sure if our people are being kept prisoner or being killed. But it sounds like you may have the answer to that question."

Martin shook his head as the elevator door opened back into the outhouse on ground level. "But I don't. I just know about the existence of the basement. All he told me was that the basement is where they conduct research that spans all eras of time. No idea what that actually means."

The men stepped back into the freezing Alaskan air where the car they had arrived in waited. Bill returned to his position behind the wheel as they all filed into the car.

"We'd love to sit down with you sometime and draw all of this out. If we even had a rough sketch of what the inside of the house looks like, it might be a game changer."

"If you guys have such intense surveillance on the house, why don't you just shoot Chris when he steps outside?"

Julian giggled. "If it was that easy, we would. He's not mortal. All of us *are*, even all of those who work for him are, too. But he's not. We've shot him, square in the head. He just plucks the bullet out of his skull like it

485

was an annoying hair and laughs."

"And this is why we have so many eyes on him. There has to be a way to kill him, we just don't know it yet."

Martin slouched in the backseat. As open and honest as the Road Runners had been, it sounded as if they were still light-years behind Chris. There were too many questions unanswered. How would they ever win a war that way? The sales pitch back in Commander Strike's office suddenly felt unstable, a cheap attempt to get Martin to join their circus of the unknown. Their entire operation was built around killing a man who, quite possibly, couldn't be killed.

They drove in silence for the next ten minutes, Julian occasionally whistling a tune.

"We're here," Bill announced as they turned into the hangar. Most were empty as they drove to the far end where a small blue jet waited.

"Are you guys coming with me?" Martin asked.

"Afraid not. We have lots to do here. You're going to have a relaxing flight back to Denver. Be sure to take your Juice *after* you land to get back to 2018."

"We'll leave you here, but go check in with the pilot. I believe Wendell will be flying you tonight. He's a great guy."

"We'll see you at another time hopefully," Julian said.

Both men reached a hand over the center console and Martin shook each. "It was great meeting you guys, thanks for rescuing me."

"The pleasure is all ours," Bill said. "Best of luck with your decision."

Martin left the car and strode to the jet where a portable staircase welcomed him, much like it had on Chris's plane.

I could get used to this life.

A young African-American man stood at the top of the steps and waved. "Come on up."

Martin climbed the steps, feeling he should have luggage, but remembering his suitcase and belongings were in 2018, and somewhere in 1919 was a briefcase in an abandoned room at the Brown Palace.

Sonya, Goddamnit.

After checking in with his mom when he arrived home, his next priority would be an intense crying session. Or maybe a fit of rage. He could visit the shooting range to blow off some steam. He couldn't fault Sonya for what she had done, but he didn't have to accept it, either.

"Good evening, Mr. Briar, how are you today?" the man asked, sticking out a hand. "My name is Wendell and I'll be flying you to Denver."

"I've had better days, Wendell, but I'm doing well."

Wendell patted Martin on the back as he stepped into the plane. "Well, we can certainly help make things better. I have a full bar, and a decent-sized menu."

The plane was half the size as Chris's, but still housed plenty of luxury. It wasn't built to carry two dozen Revolters, but rather a half dozen Road Runners as six reclining chairs graced the sides along the windows. Toward the back was the bathroom next to the aforementioned bar, sleek trim lighting around its edges.

"Get comfortable. It's a five-hour flight." Wendell checked his watch. He dressed like any other pilot Martin had encountered. "We should be landing in Denver at 5:30 A.M. local time."

"What time is it now?"

Martin had left his watch at the Brown Palace and his cell phone in 2018. It could have been 3 A.M. for all he knew.

"It's 10:30 here in Alaska, and I get the sense they're going to have a late night at the headquarters. Commander Strike sounded excited and flustered. No one gets any sleep when that happens. Anyway, we'll get going shortly. It's just me, you, and Leanna. She'll be tending to you if you need anything. She's also a certified pilot, so can take over if I have a heart attack."

Wendell howled at this, too young to worry about a heart attack. The pilot pushed a button on the wall that closed the plane's door, and worked his way into the cockpit.

Just one drink before bed. Lots to do tomorrow.

Martin crossed the open space and sat in the front row seat furthest from the door. Within minutes they rumbled along the jet way, and elevated into the night sky. He never meet Leanna, as he fell asleep three minutes after take-off.

81

Chapter 27

Martin didn't wake when the plane landed, and if Wendell hadn't poked him back into consciousness, he might have slept for the next ten hours. His nap in the mansion felt like decades ago as his body demanded every second of shuteye.

But he was now back in Denver, and somewhat back to reality—whatever that meant anymore.

Wendell had opened the plane's door where a new flight of stairs waited.

"Thanks for the flight," Martin said, groggy and bleary-eyed.

"The pleasure is all mine, sir," Wendell said as he stood by the door waiting for Martin to deplane. "Happy to fly a friend of the Commander any time."

Martin wished Wendell a good night and descended the stairs. They were in the middle of nowhere, creating a brief spark of panic that vanished as soon as he remembered it was still 1981.

Downtown Denver glowed in the distance. "Home sweet home."

Martin was back on his own. No one waiting for him. No Sonya. No Izzy. Judging by the distance to downtown, he was maybe a ten-minute drive west of town, putting him somewhere in or near the city of Lakewood.

He remembered he was originally asleep in 2018, having bounced all around the world and throughout time. When he sipped his Juice to return to 2018, he would wake up in his bed in his brand new house where he and Sonya had lain next to each other to take what was supposed to be an adventure into the past.

She was probably already gone. Or never left with him to begin with.

Bed. Your bed. That does sound lovely.

Martin sat on the concrete ground, a lone landing strip in the middle of an open field, and pulled the flask from his back pocket. One rule he had learned on this journey was to never let his Juice out of sight.

He twisted off the cap, and held up the flask to toast the Road Runners' jet.

"Off we go," he said, taking a small sip, and thinking about his present time in 2018.

He lay on his back and stared at the stars, crickets chirping all around him as he dozed.

* * *

From his recollection, they had left 2018 shortly after lunch, but when he woke, it was five in the evening.

I returned and stayed asleep. That's how tired I am.

His brain finally felt refreshed, however, and the sensation made him ready to tackle the world.

Sonya was gone, the outline of her body sunk into the comforter where she had lain.

At least you know she was real, and that you haven't truly lost your mind.

"Lost my mind? No. Lost my life again? Yes."

Martin rolled off the bed and looked around his room as if it were a foreign place. Everything reeked of Sonya. She had decorated the house. From the stupid throw pillows, to the porcelain figurines that stood on the wall shelves. She had done it, not him. Martin would have a blank, empty room with a nightstand and bed if he had his way.

How long until the Road Runners come knocking on the front door? Maybe another hour? How long until Chris shows up? That desperate lunatic.

Even without knowing an exact timeline for the next day of his life, Martin sensed the urgency in his upcoming actions. He decided to do what should have been done in the first place when Chris made the initial proposal of time travel: ask his mom for advice.

He had been too afraid of how she might judge him for bringing up such a bizarre topic, but he was well beyond that point now. He'd seen too much shit for anyone to even try arguing with him about his sanity. You can stare out the window to the world, but do you really know what's happening behind each closed door?

His mom might resist at first, but she had no proof. No grounds to call him crazy. And the best part is that she would still offer him advice whether or not she believed his story.

"I only have a few more months to save her mind." Martin needed to say this out loud to remind himself where he was and what he was doing. The Alzheimer's still gnawed at his mom's brain like ants on fallen crumbs. If the Road Runners expected him to join their team, they better damn well understand that saving her mind was his number one priority over anything else. Anyone else with an agenda for what he should do with his gift could go right ahead and fuck themselves.

He studied himself in the mirror above his dresser. Dark bags hung below his bloodshot eyes. More gray hair had filled in since he last checked. *Nothing like aging five years in ten minutes.* Apparently, the reward of not aging in the past didn't apply to the common side effects of stress. At this rate, he'd be sixty going on ninety if they thrust him into the middle of a war.

Nothing lasts forever, especially your brown hair, his mother once told him shortly after Izzy's disappearance brought his first gray hairs at the age of 32.

Martin left the bedroom, refusing to waste another second, and went downstairs to the main level where his mother stood in the kitchen, stirring something in a pot on the stove.

She turned and smiled, the wrinkles on her face seeming to have multiplied over the past few days. She brushed her silver hair behind an ear and said, "Sleepy much?"

"You could say that. What are you making?"

"I *was* going to make some pasta, but we don't have any. I could've sworn I saw some in the pantry the other day."

"Don't worry about it, we can order some takeout."

Marilyn scoffed at this. "Restaurants can't make dinner as good as me. Besides, there'll be a day where you can't enjoy my cooking anymore."

"Mom, you don't have to say things like that."

She raised a hand. "It's fine. I've prayed on this and accept my fate. I still have at least five years until things get horrible. I'll be out of your way by then. You don't have to care for me as this reaches its peak."

A tear rolled down Martin's cheek. The last day had been emotional enough without his mother talking about her dementia plans.

"Mom, that's not happening. I need to talk to you about something important."

"Okay, what's on your mind?"

"I think we should sit down—this may take a while."

"Where's Sonya?"

"That's part of this."

Her bony hands shot to her mouth as she shook her head. "Oh, Marty, please don't tell me she left."

"It's not what you think. Please. Let's sit at the table."

Marilyn hobbled to the table where Martin had already pulled out a chair.

"I think this will be best if you just let me talk. Don't ask any questions until I'm done, or else we'll be here for eight hours."

Marilyn obliged, and Martin began.

He started from the beginning when they had first met Chris at the Wealth of Time store in Larkwood. He told her how he went back the next day to buy the ring she had sworn was her grandmother's—a ring he never ended up taking due to the distraction that followed. From that point on, life had been nothing but adventure with Sonya, Izzy, Road

Runners, and now the people known as Revolters. Martin explained every detail from the night Izzy was killed, all the way up to the last few hours when he had met Commander Strike.

His mother nodded throughout the one way conversation, eyes bulging at some parts, mouth frowning at others. When Martin finished, she stared at him blankly, like Jesus Christ himself had just told her his entire life story.

"Do you think I'm crazy?" Martin asked.

Marilyn scratched her head and scrunched her face. "I don't know. It's one hell of a story, that's for sure. You were never one for creative endeavors, so I don't know what would compel you to make this all up. I suppose being dumped by a beautiful girl is a good excuse, but there are far too many details."

"Everything I said is true. Believe me, I know it's absurd. There are still times where I don't think it's real. I can leave to a different time whenever I please, and that's what I really wanted to talk to you about first. But I need to know that you actually believe this is all real."

"I'm not ready to call it real, but I'm even further from calling it fake."

"I'll take it."

"Well then, what exactly is it that you want to discuss?"

"Two things. First, I plan to travel into the future to get medicine for you."

"Impossible."

"None of this is possible, but it is. And the best part is I can go into the future to find your medicine and be back here in the next ten minutes, even if I have to spend 20 years in the future looking for it. It doesn't change what happens here in our current time."

Martin leaned back and studied his mother. She looked at the kitchen table as if expecting it to speak to her, growing disappointed that it didn't.

"How do you know a medicine from the future can cure what I already have?"

"Why wouldn't it? It's medicine for Alzheimer's. Even still, why wouldn't you want to at least find out?"

"What's the other thing you wanted to discuss?" Marilyn asked, dismissing the medicine topic.

The sudden change caught Martin off guard and he hesitated with his mouth hung open.

"This war," he said. "I've all but been told that I'm going to be forced to be a part of it. With this gift I have, they consider me too valuable to let me live my life like a normal person."

"Why not just hide in another country?"

"These people are all over the world. And they can find me even when I don't know where I am. It's like they have eyes on every corner of the globe."

"What side would you join in this war?"

"The Road Runners. I've experienced both sides and it seems they're the good guys. Chris is a lunatic con man who will say anything to get his way."

"It sounds like a unique opportunity. I think you should seize it and run with it."

Martin bolted upright, planting his elbows on the table. "Wh-what do you mean? There's a good chance I could die."

"No shit, son. Guess what? There's a hundred percent chance you're going to die one day. No one gets out of this thing alive."

"Where is this coming from?" Martin never knew his mother to have such a careless attitude on life. Caution had always been her forte, anything to avoid a bad situation.

"I've spent my whole life being held back by myself. Always afraid to take a chance at anything, playing it safe so I could make it to the finish line. But these last couple of months have taught me that was a huge mistake. They say you shouldn't die with regret, but I think everyone who plays it safe will die with regret. There were so many things I wanted to do—even had the chance to do—but never did."

"Like what?"

"I could sit here all day and tell you, but that's not the point. The point is you have an opportunity to change the world. To actually make this shitty place better, and all you can think about is me. Why bring this cure back just for me? Why not bring it back for everyone?"

"Mom, I'm not worried about everyone."

"And that's why the world has changed so much. We all get so caught up in our own lives that we forget the stranger on the bus is probably going through a similar hell as us. I'm not asking you to save the world, but I'm urging you to consider it—whatever it may mean to you."

Martin leaned back again, and now he studied the table. When he had run through this conversation in his mind, he thought he and his mother would be packing a bag to go live in an exotic place where no one could find them. Instead, she was talking him into not only joining the Road Runners, but to enjoy it and make a difference.

A couple more tears rolled down his cheek. "Mom, I can't leave you to go fight bad guys that I just learned about."

"Yes you can. Don't make an excuse. Once you let go of excuses, you open your heart to a whole new world. Besides, you said you'll only be gone for ten minutes no matter how long you spend in the other world."

Martin had never heard it referred to as the "other world," but that's exactly what it was: another existence that was taking place without anyone's knowledge from the present time. He looked up to the ceiling, hoping a reasonable response would fall from the sky.

"You can look for all the excuses you want up there," she said. "But just know this. No matter what you decide, you're going to look back to this exact moment as the one that shaped the rest of your life. You just need to decide if you want this moment to look glorious or regrettable."

Martin nodded. "I love you, Mom. Your energy and courage after all that has happened is so admirable. I'm gonna fight this war so we can kill Chris, *and* I'm coming back with the cure for Alzheimer's. I want you to stop talking about death; you're going to live another thirty years, and we can stay in this house for all of it."

Tears streamed down both of their faces as they stared at each other with glossy eyes.

"And I'm proud of you, Marty. I know your life has been pure darkness since Izzy died, but you still found a way to turn it around after all these years. Do this in her honor, let her know her daddy's a hero."

"I do everything for her."

"Good. So what are we ordering for takeout?"

They both wiped their eyes and laughed into the empty house.

82

Chapter 28

Martin's excitement grew the more he thought about joining the Road Runners. His mother was right—this was a once-in-a-lifetime opportunity at a new life. Izzy was gone, Sonya was gone, and his mother gave her blessing to pursue this. He had no reason to say no, and couldn't stop his legs from bouncing while they sat through dinner at a local Italian restaurant.

He warned her that if he died in the past or future, he would die in his sleep in 2018. She could sit by his side for a mere ten minutes, and wait for him to either wake up or stop breathing.

His gut churned at the thought of driving downtown to meet with the 2018 Road Runners. Would the Commander be there? Did they already know what he was thinking, like Chris? They could have had eyes on his house and heard the entire conversation with his mother, already making arrangements for his arrival.

Regardless of what the Road Runners had planned, Martin rode the energy of his personal renaissance. He imagined killing Chris, not knowing exactly how since the old man was immune to bullets and blades. He closed his eyes and pictured himself hoisted in the air by other Road Runners, hundreds of them chanting his name, because dammit, he was the secret weapon. And the hero.

Martin grew nauseous while he drove his mom home after dinner. "I don't know what's going to happen, but I'll make sure they let me come home before sending me anywhere else."

"Not necessary. Let this be our goodbye. And if I never see you again, just know that I love you."

Neither had any more tears to shed, but Martin had every intent on returning home before officially jumping into a war.

"I love you, Mom. Do you want me to help you inside?"

"No. I can see it in your eyes. You're ready. Don't waste another minute. Go wherever you're going, and start your new life. I'll be here."

She leaned over the center console and kissed him on the forehead before pushing open the car door.

"I love you, too," she said before she closed the door. She looked over her shoulder, eyes wet.

Martin watched her wobble to the front door and had a brief flash of memories from his childhood, his mother prominent in every one. She had always been there to guide him through life, and he would be forever grateful for the final lesson she had given, pushing him into a whole new world.

He pulled out of the driveway, the sun starting its descent. Darkness would swallow the city by the time he arrived downtown, so he flicked on his headlights and drove out of his neighborhood, passing the other large houses, imagining the lives that carried on as normal inside their walls, oblivious to the thousands of people battling across the spectrum of time for the betterment of the world.

Carry on, everyone. I'll be back. I promise.

* * *

The drive downtown took Martin just under thirty minutes. He paused when he reached the Chop House, a two-level steakhouse where Denver's finest gathered to dine. The building hid behind Coors Field, but glowed elegantly in the night, its red neon letters sure to draw the attention of any passersby.

He passed two valet workers, and drove to the back where a separate, public garage awaited.

The garage's bright lights splashed across the road in front of him. He pulled in, took a ticket, and drove toward the corner stairwell. It was a quiet evening, so he had no issue finding a spot.

Martin parked with the stairwell door in his rear view and waited a moment in his car. He wondered if they were already watching him from underground, then cracked his knuckles and stepped out of the car.

The garage remained deserted as he strode toward the stairwell, eyes bouncing from corner to corner. He pulled open the door to the stinging stench of urine soaked into the metal steps where numerous homeless spent their nights off the streets. He briefly reminisced on kicking the bums out of his parking garage way back when he had managed one in 1993.

Those good 'ol days when you had a family and life seemed perfect.

Martin immediately shook the nostalgia from his mind as he descended the stairs, his footsteps thudding and echoing. The garage was a small one, only two levels into the earth, so Martin reached the bottom landing within a minute.

He stood at the door that entered back into the garage and found it abandoned. Surely no one would drive so low when there were dozens of spots on the ground level, and probably a hundred more on the level above.

These Road Runners sure do find the best hiding spots.

"You also never thought this was real," he said aloud, no longer worried about eavesdroppers.

Five minutes passed as he waited at the bottom of the stairs. The dim lighting proved why a homeless person would choose this location as their overnight hotel. It was just warm enough for comfort, and just dim enough for a good sleep. Not to mention the privacy provided when the garage was barely in use.

Did they tell me the right spot?

As if his thoughts could be heard, footsteps came from the top of the stairwell, thudding with each heavy step, vibrating the entire building with it. Martin's heart thumped harder, anticipating the encounter that would change his life.

What if it's just a bum ready for bed?

But it wasn't.

It was Bill.

"How did you get here so fast?" Martin asked, trying to do quick math in his head that ruled Bill's appearance as an impossibility.

"We have more than one jet."

"Why didn't you just ride with me?"

"Commander Strike wanted you to have a moment alone to gather your thoughts. We all had a good laugh when you fell asleep right away." Bill chuckled to himself.

"I wouldn't have minded. If she would've just asked, I'd have told her I planned on sleeping."

Bill raised a hand. "It's no worries, we have jets all over the world and can refuel them for incredibly cheap in the past. She wanted a familiar face when you arrived, and asked for me to come right away in case you made a quick decision, which it appears you have."

Bill's old face cracked into a warm grin.

"Yes. I had a long talk with my mother, and spent time reflecting on what I want. I'm ready to discuss terms."

"Glad to hear. Let's go meet the Lead Runner here in Denver—he's been anxious since the Commander got on the phone with him after you left Alaska. You drove, right?"

"Yeah."

"Good, you can drive us over."

"I thought this is where we're supposed to be."

Bill looked up and around, examining his dim surroundings. "This is a parking garage."

He slapped Martin on the back and cackled. "This is just our meeting place—we don't actually conduct our business in a parking garage."

But you do out of an outhouse basement?

"We have some office space about ten minutes away, walking. But I'm tired. So you can drive us there in 2 minutes. Let's go."

Martin noticed the droop in Bill's eyes. The old man was probably ready to relax for the evening after having found the Road Runner's most prized person. Then Commander Strike sent him on a five-hour flight across the country to meet with that same man. He led the way to his car and drove to the office building that really was two minutes away. On the exterior, a sign hung on the brick building to welcome them to Centennial Marketing. The windows provided a view into the office where unattended computer monitors glowed in the darkness.

"There's a parking space up front just for this building. Take it."

Martin obliged and wiggled into the tight space.

"You conduct all of this business out in the open like this? Anyone could just walk in."

"Oh, Martin, we're not dumb like Chris and his obnoxious storefronts. This really is a marketing company, operated by us. There's a staircase in the far back of the building, behind the manager's office, where no one from the public would even be able to get to."

Martin nodded. "Another basement hideout?"

"*Always* a basement hideout. Being underground doesn't allow things like our cell phones or other electronics to be detected. It's the safest way to conceal what we do, and it's worked forever." Bill opened his door and stepped out, prompting Martin to do the same.

Martin gathered his surroundings, and found they were only three blocks south of the Chop House, and one away from the Oxford Hotel that seemed to live three hundred years in the past.

Bill climbed up the three short steps to the office building, wiggled a key in the lock, and pushed open the door with a steady *swoosh.*

Martin joined him inside and let the door close, the lock clicking shut immediately. Bill had already worked his way through most of the office and was toward the end of the long hallway. "Let's go, Martin, lots to do."

Martin walked faster to keep up and joined Bill outside of a door that had *MANAGER* written in big letters.

"Right through here."

Bill pushed open the door to a standard office: desk, computer, filing cabinets with papers bursting out. He crossed the messy room and tapped on a cabinet along the back wall. A vibration rattled the ground as the sound of a humming motor filled the silence. The cabinet slid aside, revealing a dark hole that led into the ground.

"This way," Bill said, dropping a foot into the darkness. As he did, a light flickered to life, illuminating the path below. The steps and walls were all made of stone, lined with modern fluorescent lights that appeared out of place.

Bill started down the stairs, boots clapping and echoing just as they had in the parking garage moments ago.

Martin followed, taking careful steps, expecting the ancient stone to suddenly crumble beneath his shoes. No such thing happened, and he reached the bottom landing to find a whole other world.

The layout was similar to the one he had seen in Alaska, with desks spread across the middle of the floor as TVs hung on the walls. This location had an aquarium in the ground, a billiards table in the back, glowing glass refrigerators, and sofas in an area that appeared to be a lounge.

"Whoa," Martin said, glancing around the room. No one froze to gawk at him like he was a rare species. At least forty men and women kept their focus on their computer screens, some appearing more relaxed than others as they watched movies instead of tracking down Revolters.

"Welcome to our Denver office," Bill said, looking around the room in search of someone. "I've only been here a couple of times—I go where the Commander goes, usually. Tarik runs Denver. I just don't see him anywhere."

On cue, a man no older than 40 raised his hand in the furthest corner of the room and started jogging toward them. Bill waved back and they waited.

"Good evening, gentlemen," he said, sticking out a hand. "Martin, I'm Tarik. We'll be working closely together since I oversee our Denver operations. I understand you're a native of the city?"

"I am."

"Fantastic. Beautiful city. I'm originally from Egypt, but moved here ten years ago on assignment from the Commander."

Martin couldn't help but examine Tarik. His new Egyptian ally had brown skin, buzzed black hair, and muscles that would rip his t-shirt apart if he did so much as sneeze. He had all the appearances of a military man, even down to the cargo pants that hung loosely around his waist.

"Shall we step into my office?" Tarik asked.

Bill nodded and they followed Tarik around the corner into an office that looked no different than the Commander's, only this one had no bottle of scotch. Hard to justify alcohol when you had to maintain muscles strong enough to rip a head off a body.

Tarik guided them in as he closed the door behind. "Commander Strike gave me her blessing to accept your response and negotiate on her behalf." He crossed the office and sat down in his well-cushioned chair across from Bill and Martin. "Let's get right to it. We want you, Martin, and are willing to work with you to ensure you'll join the Road Runners."

Martin nodded and folded his hands on his lap. "I'm interested in joining. But I do have a condition."

"Let's hear it." Tarik watched Martin with studious, brown eyes.

"My mom has Alzheimer's disease, recently diagnosed. It's my understanding that there's a cure for it in the future. No matter what I get tasked to do with the Road Runners, I want it known that my main priority is to get this medicine to my mom as soon as possible."

"Did Chris tell you there's a cure?"

"Yes," he lied, relying on faith that there would be such thing.

"Hmmm. I'm not sure that there is, but I'm happy to look into it for you. I caution against traveling to the future alone—it's a truly dangerous time."

Martin's stomach sunk at this news. "Well, what can I do? This is kind of a deal breaker. I *need* that medicine."

"Look, I don't know how far in the future we may need to go to find this. Just because I don't know off the top of my head if it exists or not, doesn't make it definitive. I can look. I'll even look tonight. If it's real, it's yours."

"Thank you. I'd like to know soon. Tonight preferably."

"Consider it done. And what do you plan to do if the medicine isn't real? Surely, you can't just go home and forget all about this."

"I can, and I will. That's all I care about. Your war has gone on for years; I highly doubt I'm the secret ingredient."

"You'd be surprised. But before I get into that, I want to make sure there's nothing else you want to discuss."

"Sonya—I want to see her."

"What for exactly?"

"I never got closure. I just want to leave her knowing nothing was held back."

Tarik squirmed in his seat. "I'm afraid we can't accommodate that request."

"Why not? She's a Road Runner. It should be pretty straightforward to arrange a meeting with all of your fancy jets."

"It's not the logistics we can't handle. You see, Sonya is actually a part of your mission should you join us. And we can't have you seeing her before we give the green light."

"Part of my mission? How?"

"You're going to kill her."

83

Chapter 29

Martin sat in silence for the next three minutes, staring from Tarik, to the ceiling, to the floor. Tarik let his words sink in while Martin fidgeted in his chair like a student in detention. Bill remained quiet, as he had throughout the entire exchange, staring at the walls, likely praying someone would let him out of the office.

"I'm sorry," Martin finally said. "Did you say you want me to *kill* Sonya?"

Tarik nodded with his hands folded beneath his chin.

"Absolutely not. Are you crazy?"

Martin fought his urge to jump across the desk and choke this meathead. It wouldn't end well going up against such a strong man, but one should never underestimate the power of a fit of rage.

Tarik raised a finger. "Trust me when I tell you this was not *why* we wanted to bring you on board, but a unique opportunity has arisen because of it. We've also never killed any of our own, but some new and critical intel has shown this as a likely way of killing Chris."

"So killing Sonya is a way to kill Chris? Do you know how stupid that sounds?"

"I know how stupid it sounds to someone who doesn't know how this all works, yes. But there is evidence – overwhelming evidence – that this will work. Killing Chris will end the war in North America."

Martin shook his head, his lips pursed.

"You're right, Martin," Tarik continued. "This war has gone on for too long. We've exhausted thousands of options, tried hundreds of tactics, all to no avail. This option has been debated dozens of times in the last two weeks, and both sides feel strongly."

"What side are you on?"

"I'm against it." Tarik paused and looked down.

"But...?"

"But it should work. Is taking one life worth the millions that can be saved? I used to say no, but having been to the future and seeing what becomes of this world, it's hard to argue against trying anything to prevent it."

"It can't be that bad."

"Oh, it's not bad. It's fucking *horrifying*. It's not a world you want to live in, or have anyone live in. It's hell on Earth."

"Why does Sonya have to die?"

"Sonya is Chris's daughter."

Martin opened his mouth and closed it, and then scrunched his face into pure confusion. "I'm sorry, did you say his *daughter*?"

"I'm afraid so. We'll have plenty of time to go into the history, but Chris tied his soul to her. As long as she lives, he remains invincible."

"There's no such thing as tying your soul to something," Martin said flatly, frustration bubbling beneath every word.

"Right, just like there's no such thing as time travel, or freezing time. Open your mind, Martin, this is all real."

"What does it mean?"

"It means that if Sonya is alive, Chris is immortal. If she's dead, he becomes a regular human being just like you and me. Bullets can actually puncture his lungs, his skull can explode. None of that is possible as long as Sonya's still breathing."

"Does she know that his soul is tied to her?"

"Yes. He told her when she was a teenager. The funny part is she pretends to not know about it anymore, probably for good reason."

"So that you won't kill her to end the war."

"Exactly. She doesn't know that we've had teams putting in heavy research on Chris's earlier days before he became a Revolter and master of time. It's been grueling espionage, especially with the amount of eyes Chris keeps on him and his property—he always has. We've got to a point, though, where we found this to be true. We overheard the conversation between him and Sonya when he admitted what he had done. The planting of his soul has no bearing on her, other than making her a prime target for anyone wanting to take down Chris."

"So if I kill her, you guys kill Chris?"

"At the very next moment we get, yes."

"Why do *I* have to do it?"

"We think she's on to us. There have been some half-hearted attempts at a quiet execution—we don't want the community to know that we're willing to kill our own. It goes against our values."

"Then why do it?"

"I'm not going over this again. We need to save the world from itself, and this has become the main option. Believe me, we love Sonya. She's been a factor in every major decision for the Road Runners. And now she still is. The ultimate sacrifice."

"Again, why me?" Martin was growing sick of Tarik beating around the bush. Bill continued staring into space.

"She has never spoken of anyone like she does about you." This statement sent an instant flutter to Martin's chest. "We believe she'll let you close enough to actually pull this off. She'll let her guard down. We think she has feelings for you. We tried to get her to admit it, but she refuses every time. But we sense it."

"You want to use her love for me to kill her." Martin said this more for himself to process, his guts twisting like a rung out dishrag. *She loves me and they want me to kill her. I love her, too.* "I can't do that. It's absurd, and I'm not a killer."

"We thought you'd say that. We really need you to look at the big picture. If you want to join me on a trip to the future to see how bad it will get, I'm happy to do that. Again, this is our last resort. Even the people who voted in favor of this are against the thought of having to kill Sonya. But we have no choice."

"I'm not killing the only person I've loved in the last 20 years. Even if it was all a lie."

Tarik stood up. "Let's take a break. Commander Strike is on her way and should be here in the next hour. We can reconvene at that time and you can discuss any further concerns with her. How does that sound?"

"That's fine with me. I'm still interested in being a Road Runner—I just can't go through with this specifically."

"Understood. Feel free to relax in our lounge, and we'll have someone come grab you when Commander Strike gets here."

Tarik pulled open the office door and gestured for Bill and Martin to leave.

* * *

Bill parted ways with Martin when they stepped out, telling him to take time alone to think. One thing had become clear about the Road Runners: they truly didn't believe in forcing the issue. In their eyes, they had the most prized possession of the war in Martin, and yet no one had done more than try to persuade him into joining the cause. Chris hadn't even had a direct conversation with Martin and already had plans to make him a robotic soldier if he didn't oblige.

Martin crossed the main floor, where the mood was relaxed compared to the tension inside Tarik's office. Still, no one so much as looked up at him. Everyone remained deep into their computer screens, and some had even pulled out beds from under their desks and prepared for a night's sleep.

Do these people live here? he wondered, and would ask the Commander when she arrived.

Martin went to the lounge and plopped down on a sofa. Refrigerators hummed in the background as the soft murmur of voices faded into distant whispers from the office floor. He wanted to lie down, but decided it wouldn't look good for their savior to take a nap while everyone else worked diligently.

He thought back to his talk with his mom, wondering if she would have given the same advice if she knew killing was part of the job.

How am I even supposed to kill Sonya? This is barbaric. If they want to do it so badly, they should do it themselves. They can hide out so well around the world, surely they can cover up a simple murder.

Martin buried his face into his palms, clammy with sweat, and prayed for a way out of this situation. Maybe the calling for a new life was reserved for those with ambition. He would still be content running off to an exotic country and spending his money and life there until the end. He wouldn't live into this supposedly scary future, and no longer had a child who would, either. None of this was his problem.

I can give them some of my blood so they can run tests on what makes me so special, but I don't need to be a part of this. I'm not going to get a desk in this office and sleep under it for a war that has no end. This is all a sucker's bet. They claim that leaving isn't an option, but it always is.

He thought about how Chris had randomly shown up at the cabin when he and Sonya had left town for a few days after the coma. Chris had been the furthest thing from his mind, yet he still showed up, uninvited and in the middle of the mountains.

You know he'll find you. He probably already knows where you are. The Road Runners aren't the only ones in this war. He has ways of finding people, too.

Martin felt queasy and fought off nervous belches that tried to make their way up. He suffered a mild out-of-body experience when everyone in the room stood up and faced the entrance.

"Good evening, everyone," a woman's voice called, prompting Martin to stand and see the Commander across the room. "I want to thank you all for the hard work you've been putting in. We're getting closer. Believe in what you're doing every day, because every small step that each of you make leads to one huge leap for the Road Runners."

The room broke into brief applause as Commander Strike bowed her head and worked her way across the room to Tarik's office where she closed the door behind her.

Everyone settled back into their places and Martin sat back down on the sofa, debating if he should rummage through the cupboards for a snack.

He had no time, as Bill started toward him from one of the side offices. He waved a hand and grinned. "They're ready for you."

"Already? She just got here."

"Tarik briefed her over the phone on her way. Things move quickly in this organization; don't be surprised if you're already thrown into the middle of things tomorrow, should you still agree to join us."

"What should I do, Bill? Am I crazy for not wanting to kill Sonya to end the war?"

"Not at all. This has been a polarizing topic for us. The topic was put up to a vote for all Road Runners in a position of leadership, minus those who work directly with Sonya. Across the world, we had 600 total votes cast. 301 came back in favor of killing Sonya, 299 against. I don't think Commander Strike has slept in four days. She's a huge fan of Sonya—once had talks with her about moving into a higher position in her office. But, she's a bigger fan of ending this war. This decision has been eating away at her. I don't think anything can happen that will change her mind at this point."

"You're not helping me."

"I'm not trying to sway you one way or another. This is a heavy decision and I'm glad I'm not in your shoes. You have to decide what's best for you. But I suggest you get in that room before the Commander gets impatient."

Martin nodded and shook hands with Bill. "Thanks for everything."

Bill bowed his head in appreciation and Martin pivoted to return to Tarik's office. The door was cracked and he pushed it open to find Tarik standing in the corner of the room while Commander Strike sat behind the desk, hands folded beneath her chin.

"Hello again, Martin. How are you doing?" she asked with a gentle smile. Now that Bill had mentioned it, he noticed slight bags under her eyes.

"I've had better days, that's for sure."

"I know this has been a lot thrown your way, and I hope we can still reach an agreement on you joining us."

Martin nodded as he sat down in the seat across the desk. "I can't kill Sonya."

"I know. But we need you to. Hear me out. We believe Sonya is on to us. We tried poisoning her drink, and she conveniently knocked it off the table to look like an accident. She has stopped contacting some of her closest friends within the organization. All of her trust has vanished, and that's on me. We have someone slipping her information; there's no way she could have figured this out on her own. We've kept her duties the same as always, kept her security detail consistent, but she still knows."

"Not surprising. It sounds like there are some strong opinions on the matter."

Commander Strike nodded. "I know. I must have changed my mind at least a hundred times. But it's what needs to be done. It's one life against millions; it's really a no-brainer."

"It's not. Because Road Runners aren't monsters—I've gathered that much in the last day. You are good-hearted, well-intentioned people. You're the complete opposite of Chris. He would've had Sonya dead within five minutes of learning this information, if the roles were reversed."

Bill had said she wouldn't change her mind, but Martin felt obliged to at least try. He watched the wrenching decision swim behind her exhausted eyes.

"I appreciate the input. It means a lot coming from someone who is still technically an outsider, but the decision is made and we want to discuss it with you."

"I've already talked about it with Tarik."

Tarik nodded from the corner, arms crossed with a foot planted on the wall for support.

"We haven't discussed *how* you would go about this. We've considered multiple ways of carrying this out. We don't want anything vicious done to Sonya. It needs to be a painless death. We're not asking you to shoot her in the head or anything like that. We have three options prepared: more poison for a drink, an injection, and a letter."

"A letter?"

"It's covered in a poisonous powder—from the future. Our plan is to equip you with all three options when you go to meet Sonya. Each one will affect her in the same way. These poisons are designed to make the receiver fall asleep, and eventually slow down the heart rate until it stops. She won't feel anything painful this way."

It's like putting an animal down.

"Why the three options?"

"We want to give you flexibility. The plan is to have you meet with Sonya, spend some time with her and catch up."

"Catch up? It's only been a few hours since she even left me."

"Yes, but she left you with a laundry list of questions. I heard about the meeting in the Oxford Hotel basement. They said you were completely stunned, and I don't blame you."

"Do you guys always trick people like this?"

"Not always, but it's Sonya's role with us. She's even passed up promotions to continue doing it. She loves being in the field."

Martin thought back to that day at the cabin again. Sonya was upstairs when Chris had stopped by for his visit. They were that close to each other and she didn't even know it. What would she have done if she came downstairs and saw her father chatting with Martin on the balcony?

"It just feels like I'm being used at this point. All this effort to get me to join so I can kill Sonya. If I do, then the war ends. Then what?"

"Then you're a hero, and the world is saved. There will be a recovery effort that takes place. A lot of damage has been done at certain points in time that we'll need to evaluate how to fix. But we'll have the ease of knowing there will be no more attacks."

"Just because Chris dies, you think the Revolters will give up?"

"The Revolters are a lost cause without him. If Chris dies, so does their vision. He recruits weak-willed people who require guidance. Sure, there'll be a few who give it a try and attack us, but the majority will go into hiding. Because if Chris doesn't survive, how can they expect to?"

Martin looked in the Commander's direction, but not at her. He looked *through* her, into a future where he was considered a hero. A secret hero that the whole world wouldn't know about, just the Road Runners and Revolters. A hero in a second world that existed not by imagination, but underground, working every day to keep the world safe.

"It's not everyday someone gets an opportunity like this," Strike said. "We have a unique opportunity to give ourselves—humanity—a second chance at life by fixing things. One thing I've learned is that none of that matters. What happens in your current life is what will forever shape you. Even if you had managed to save your daughter, your soul remains forever scarred by her disappearance. That alone dictated the next twenty years of your life." Martin nodded. She was good. "Now you're here at the ultimate crossroads. You can go back to your life and spend the rest of your days on the run from Chris. Or you can be the one who ends him once and for all, so no one ever has to be running again."

"I want to know something. If I kill Sonya and Chris never steps foot outside of his house, will you blow up that mansion knowing there are at least fifty Road Runners being held captive underneath it?" Martin drew on his knowledge from the brief conversations he had with Julian and Bill.

"You're a forward thinker, and that's how I know you'll do big things for us, even after the war. To answer your question, no, we would not put those 50 lives at risk. There are ways to get to him even if he hides in the house."

Martin nodded, imagining himself slipping poison into Sonya's drink while she cooked dinner for him. He longed for his old life with her and wished it could've been real. He'd happily spend the rest of his life on the run if she was by his side.

He leaned back in his seat, relaxed for the first time in hours, and grinned at the Commander who watched him with anxious eyes.

"I'm in."

84

Chapter 30

Martin had no plans to kill Sonya, but the Road Runners didn't need to know that. All they cared about was that he *agreed* to go through with it. Who was to say he couldn't have a change of heart at the last minute?

Just get me in with the Road Runners and I can explore other options from there.

He had no clue the magnitude of their resources. There had to be a different option. Road Runners only murdered Revolters, not other Road Runners.

"I don't have to sleep in this office, do I?" Martin asked after Tarik had pulled a bottle of whiskey from his desk drawer. Turns out the Commander and her trusted leaders weren't so different after all.

Commander Strike threw her head back and laughed, an obvious wave of relaxation spreading over her like a wildfire. "Of course not. The folks in this office are researchers and watchers. We have eyes all over the world in offices just like this. They know that living here is part of the job when they accept it. A lot of these people come from lives destroyed by Chris. They feel they have no other purpose than to eat, breathe, and sleep Chris until he's pronounced dead."

"So what will I be doing?"

"You're on a special assignment in the field. We have even more people in the field than in offices, physically following Revolters in an effort to find their hideouts, among other tasks, of course."

Like killing your own?

"So what happens now?" Martin asked.

"Well, something new that we've been doing: injecting a tracking device into your body."

Martin's grin turned into an immediate frown.

"It's not so we can keep an eye on you, it's more to know if you're still alive and well. And if you're in danger, where you are exactly."

"Why is this new?"

"We decided once people started getting taken into Chris's house that we needed a way to check on them. We had no way of knowing if they were alive or not, making a decision difficult about what to do with the house. We still don't know, actually, as the only one who had a tracker was shot the same day you escaped."

"I watched that from my window." Martin remembered that moment, thinking he'd never make it out of the house.

"Yeah, we had to watch it, too. Had a car on the way to pick him up, but Chris never really meant to let him go. You know, you're not the first person to escape from his mansion."

"Is that so?"

"We've watched five of our own make a run from that house, all who were shot. We don't know if Chris just let them out to a hopeless escape, or if they actually broke out and were caught. That's another reason we want everyone to have tracking devices—it just helps us gain more information. "

"Makes sense. After I get my tracker, then what?"

Commander Strike was beating around the information he wanted.

"We're all gonna rest tonight. Tomorrow morning we'll implant your tracking device, provide you with the poisons and the information about Sonya, and you'll be on your way. We'd like to see her dead tomorrow night, if possible. We already have heavily-armed crews surrounding Chris from a distance. Sonya has a tracking device already, so we'll know the moment she dies. Their deaths will nearly be in sync."

"That's pretty aggressive. Won't I need time to regain trust with her before trying to slip anything to her?"

Martin's plan was to stall once he was with Sonya, maybe find a way to warn her. It sounded as if the entire Road Runner community would be watching this play out like the Super Bowl. A death party. Can Martin pull off the impossible and save the world? Bring your chips and dips and find out, this Wednesday at six!

The thought sent a shiver down his back.

"We've been complacent enough, especially under past leadership. I don't believe in waiting things out. We have a mission, and it's time to complete it."

The smile left her face as she spoke sternly. Commander Strike was this close to achieving their biggest goal and wouldn't risk it so Martin could have small talk with Sonya.

"Now let's all get some sleep. I know I'm running on fumes and you probably are too, Tarik."

Tarik nodded, tipping his glass to finish the last of his whiskey.

"We have extra beds here, or you can go home and come back in the morning. It doesn't matter to me, just know you'll need to be here by seven."

Martin pulled out his cellphone (oh, how he had missed it) and saw the time as 12:30. It was already Wednesday morning.

"I'll just stay here." There was no point in driving home to toss and turn in his bed for five hours when he could just do that here. His mom wouldn't even be awake, and he had said his final goodbyes, just in case.

"Perfect. We'll get you a private room. Welcome to the team."

Commander Strike rose and stuck out a hand that Martin grabbed firmly.

This is really happening. I'm a Road Runner.

The nightcap in Tarik's office must have helped Martin fall into a deep sleep, because his mind still raced despite his body falling into a limp pile of flesh on the mattress. It turns out all of the offices doubled as bedrooms where beds pulled out of the wall, and the temperature adjusted to a perfect 70 degrees on the thermostat.

Martin fell asleep thinking about Sonya and the life they had made in 1996. It was perfect, and he wished he could've stayed. With his new knowledge of her, he knew that was impossible. No matter how long they would've carried out their lives together, it still would end with him joining the Road Runners. That was her job, and she was damn good at it.

He remembered when they played house—cooking dinner, doing dishes, and making love multiple times a week. It was a glimpse into the life that could have been if Izzy never died. Izzy always thought her dad was a hero, and now she could look down from heaven and see for herself.

I'm here because of you, and I need to see it through.

The thought of joining the Road Runners and taking on a mission of killing Sonya didn't worry him. Not knowing what his life would look like, say, in the next 48 hours, terrified him. He could wind up a hero just as well as dead. He was officially in a war now, and all is fair in love and war, right?

Except for when you use your love to kill someone for the war. Martin reflected—something he had lacked the time to do—on what he had accomplished during his first trip into the past.

Nothing. Not a goddamn thing. Izzy is still dead. Columbine ended up worse. I almost died. And I fell in love with a girl who was only trying to recruit me to this shit show.

Martin cried in his dark room, tears streaming from his face and soaking into his pillow. The fear of failing again, on such a grand stage, made him sick just thinking about it. Izzy, Sonya, and his mother all spun around in his head. His old life was gone, and forward was the only direction to go.

85

Chapter 31

Martin had set the alarm on his cell phone for 6:30 A.M. His brain itched with fatigue as his bleary eyes opened. He had made a point to not look at the clock while he tossed and rolled all night—that only made it worse. By his mental calculation, he had slept a total of two sporadic hours throughout the night.

He told himself that he could go through with whatever the Road Runners asked of him, but the thought of killing anyone kept him awake.

The next 24 hours would be spent on autopilot, and he preferred it that way. The excitement had worn off, the determination vanished, leaving him a sulking pool of regret.

I never asked for any of this.

Martin pulled himself up from the bed on wobbly legs. His mind protested having to do anything as a long day awaited. *They expect me to have this mission done tonight? I'm gonna need a nap. Maybe I'll take some of this poison and enjoy the ride. They said it doesn't hurt.*

He shook his head clear of the thoughts, knowing that was just the exhaustion speaking.

"Get off your ass and be the hero. For Izzy. She led you here."

Martin's pep talks to himself usually worked, but they fell on deaf ears this time. He crossed the room to examine himself in a mirror on the wall. His hair flew in every direction, eyes bloodshot and puffy. *I look how I feel.*

A knock banged on the door, startling him, and he crossed the room to open it.

"Good morning, Sunshine," Bill said, chipper with a cup of coffee in his hand. "I heard you're officially part of the gang now. Welcome."

"Thanks, Bill."

"Rough night? You look like a pile of shit that got run over by a semi-truck."

Martin chuckled. "You know, I've been hit by a semi before, and I'd have to agree with you."

Bill laughed and slapped Martin on the shoulder. "I know this has been a lot, but hopefully today goes quickly and smoothly for you."

Martin nodded, unsure what to say. Quick and smooth was the last thing on his mind. He preferred it to be dragged out and avoidable.

"I came to make sure you were awake and ready. Commander Strike is expecting you in Tarik's office at seven sharp."

"Yeah, I'm just about ready. I'll be there."

"Great, have fun. I won't be in there, have a couple matters to tend to, but wanted to wish you good luck."

"Thanks again for everything. Maybe we can grab a drink after this is all done."

"I'll hold you to it."

Bill patted Martin on the shoulder one final time before turning toward another office down the hall.

Martin closed the door and returned to the mirror, patting his hair down with a quick spit on his fingers.

"You can do this—whatever *this* is."

He felt more alert, but couldn't ignore the tingling in his head that demanded sleep. It would have to wait. His cell phone chimed to let him know it was now 6:55.

He took one last look at the man who had overcome so much since 1996. Bouts of depression, alcoholism, and numerous suicide attempts weren't enough to bring him down. *And neither will this.* He smiled to himself before leaving his room to meet Tarik and Commander Strike.

Walking down the hallway felt like an eternity as he passed each door with increasing stress. When he reached Tarik's door he paused, knowing a new life waited on the other side.

"Come in!" the Commander called without him knocking.

She's good.

Martin pushed the door open and found Commander Strike with Tarik in their same positions as the night before. She had her hands folded on the desk, and Tarik fidgeted in the corner with a small syringe.

"Good morning, Martin," she greeted. "We had a team prepare a plan for you overnight. I reviewed it earlier this morning and have signed off on it. All we need to do is get you set up with your tracking device and you'll be ready to head back to 1996."

"I'm going back to 1996?" Martin asked, a sudden tremble taking control of his arms.

"Yes, that's where Sonya lives."

She played you, Marty. Played you good. All that talk about leaving her life behind. It was all an act.

"She's still in her same house?"

Commander Strike nodded.

The house he thought they had turned into a home together. How many other men had she laid a similar trap for throughout history?

"Here's the report." She slid a file across the desk with a sturdy finger. "It's only two pages. You can read it here, but you can't take it with you—can't have any trace of this mission when you go."

Martin grabbed the file and flipped it open. It contained instructions on the proper way to dispense of the poisons along with random information about Sonya's house and neighborhood, should he have to get involved in a foot chase. It had a clipped picture of her, not smiling and staring blankly at the camera.

"This is pretty standard stuff, especially since you lived in that house. The poisons are pretty straightforward," Strike explained, glaring across the desk

"I don't see my condition listed in here."

"What condition?"

"About getting a cure for Alzheimer's in the future, to bring back to my mom."

"This isn't a contract of any sorts, it's just a mission report."

"I want it in writing somewhere."

Martin spoke sharply and returned a hard gaze into Commander Strike's eyes.

She nodded and held out an open palm. "Okay, pass it here."

Martin handed it over and watched her flip a page and start scribbling notes. She passed it back.

"An effort to find a cure?" he asked. "I *need* the cure."

"Martin, we don't know if there's such thing. As soon as this mission is done, we'll get people on it right away. I'm not going to put it into writing that there's a cure because I don't know that for sure."

Martin rubbed his eyes, the puffiness starting to shrink.

"I need this. Just as badly as you want Chris dead."

"You need this *because* of Chris. Don't forget that."

Martin nodded. "Fair enough."

Commander Strike turned to Tarik, who stepped to the middle of the room with the syringe held out. It looked like a regular shot you'd get at the doctor's office.

"I have your tracking device right here," Tarik said. "I'll inject this into your arm, and within 15 minutes the device will cling to a muscle and expand to the size of a dime. You won't feel a thing."

"That's what everyone says around here."

"Are you ready?"

"Let's get it over with." Martin rolled up his sleeve and held out his pasty arm.

Tarik stepped up and pulled the cap off the syringe, swiftly inserting it into Martin's flesh and pushing down on the lever.

"All done," he said with a grin as he pulled the needle out. "Not a drop of blood."

Martin checked his arm and saw nothing.

"Now we can officially say, welcome to the Road Runners." Commander Strike had a stupid grin on her face that wouldn't leave for the next hour. "You'll be leaving shortly. The poison is being prepared as we speak."

Martin thought he felt a bubble burst within his arm, but chalked it up to his imagination.

There's no hiding now. These people can find you wherever you are.

The thought was comforting and terrifying at the same time.

A knock banged on the door.

"Come in," Tarik barked.

A weaselly man with glasses poked his head in. "The project is ready."

Martin looked from the weasel to Commander Strike.

"Thank you," she said.

The weasel left as quickly as he had arrived.

"That's the poison," she said to Martin. "You're all set."

His gut dropped to his knees. He thought he'd have more time to stall, but clearly the universe wanted to get this over with as well.

"Are you ready?" she asked.

Martin nodded, avoiding eye contact.

Fuck no, I'm not ready to kill Sonya.

He'd been a Road Runner for less than a minute and was already thrust into the war. *She did say they move fast.*

"Where do you want to lie down before you drink your Juice?"

"Shouldn't I go to Larkwood?"

"You can go wherever. We'll give you a ride in 1996 if you need it."

Martin crossed his arms. "I'll just do it here. Can I do that?"

"Of course. This was still a hub back then, so someone will be here to take you to Sonya's house. We'll make sure the arrangements are made."

She nodded to Tarik, who promptly left the office.

"I want to wish you luck, and thank you in advance for the service you're doing." Commander Strike stood and crossed the desk to meet Martin. He rose and grabbed her hand to shake. "I know this is hard, but it should be rather straightforward. I don't foresee any complications if you act normal and keep your poisons hidden."

"Where is the poison?"

"Your driver will have it for you." She checked her watch. "You should get going. We'll be watching both of your tracking devices from here. As soon as we see Sonya has died, we'll move on Chris immediately. We already have five snipers surrounding his mansion."

Martin nodded and left the office, pulling his flask from his back pocket. He looked over his shoulder and saw Commander Strike still standing in Tarik's office, her arms crossed and her face scrunched into heavy anticipation.

He strode down the hall, and this time people stared at him. Those he made eye contact with gave quick nods as he passed. *They have my back. I wonder how much they know.* Martin returned the nods and even some smiles until he reached the office that had doubled as his bedroom the night before.

He took a sip of the Juice and started thinking about 1996 as he lay down on the bed. Within minutes, his mind drifted out of 2018 and started its journey to another world.

86

Chapter 32

Martin jolted awake on the floor and sat up, finding the room to be nothing but a storage closet as boxes lined the walls.

He stood and pulled open the door to find the office set up in the same manner, only with less people.

"Mr. Briar!" a man shouted from the desk in front of Martin. "Welcome to 1996. My name is Brett McBath." The man rounded his desk and met Martin in the aisle. "I'll be driving you to Larkwood."

"Thank you, Brett, nice to meet you."

"The honor is all mine, sir. It's not every day you get to meet a real-life hero. When they asked for someone to drive you, I couldn't resist the opportunity."

Brett spoke in jittery phrases and fidgeted with his fingers. Something about his eyes looked familiar to Martin, and after another glance, he recognized him as the weasel man from 2018. He would be 22 years younger in this current encounter.

"Thank you." Martin didn't know what else to say. He'd never experienced any sort of popularity throughout his life, and being called a hero certainly pushed him out of his comfort zone.

"Shall we get going then?" Brett gazed at Martin with blue eyes, and Martin saw the shock and awe swimming behind that stare.

"Yes." Brett's excitement rubbed off on Martin, making him determined to carry out this mission.

See, there are other people who are behind this. It'll be fine.

"Follow me." Brett walked away and took Martin down the familiar path to the stairwell that led to the marketing office above. The flat screen computer monitors had been replaced by boxy tanks that hummed and buzzed.

"No one gets into this office until 10 A.M." Brett checked his watch. "It's only 8:30."

He led them outside the building where a black sports car waited for them.

"You drive a Mustang?" Martin asked.

"Yeah." Brett laughed nervously. "I figured why not. I can drive any car in the world and I've always loved Mustangs."

"Nice. I like them, too."

They sat down in the car and Brett roared the engine to life, the vibrations rocking both of them.

"We shouldn't have any traffic right now, can get you to Sonya's house in a little more than ten minutes."

Ten minutes. The thought drained all the blood from Martin's stomach and chest. Ten minutes stood between him and a difficult decision. The more he weighed it, the more he considered actually going through with it. The glimpse into life as a hero appealed, but did he really want that for the rest of his time on Earth?

You couldn't save Izzy, but you can save others. Don't let her death go in vain.

"Are you nervous?" Brett asked. "I know I'd be nervous—actually I think I *am* nervous. For you. I have that feeling like there's a boiling pot of water in my stomach. You ever get that?"

"All the time."

"Oh, before I forget." Brett reached into the backseat and pulled a duffel bag that he dropped on Martin's lap. "This is your stuff. It's meant to look like you packed for this trip. There's some clothes, toiletries, and books. The special letter is tucked inside a book in an envelope, and the small jar and syringe with the poison are in the middle of the toiletries bag. It's all stored safely for you to touch, so don't worry about hurting yourself. Which one do you think you're gonna use?" Brett asked like an excited child asking to go out for ice cream.

"I don't know yet, I'll need to get a feel for the situation."

They drove off, weaving north through downtown toward Larkwood, where destiny awaited.

"I can't believe I'm driving the man who will end the war."

Brett kept his eyes fixed on the road, but Martin could still sense the emotion about to burst beneath his driver's surface.

"I appreciate your excitement, but if you don't mind, I'd like a few moments of silence to myself."

"Gotta get in the zone? I can dig it. Pretend I'm not here."

Brett hummed to himself, perhaps trying to make himself disappear. Anything for Martin, right?

Martin leaned back in his seat and closed his eyes.

What the hell am I going to say to her?

He tried to imagine how this would all play out. She would either send him away, refusing to explain herself, or she could invite him in, tell him why things played out the way they did. He assumed the latter, at least based on the person he thought she was.

His emotions would try to reveal themselves, and he'd need to hide them. Sonya had always shown an ability to read him, and if he seemed distraught at the thought of having to kill her, she would definitely sniff it out.

"We're here," Brett said.

Martin opened his eyes to the familiar neighborhood. The houses all looked the same on the quiet block. Brett had pulled to the side as they faced Sonya's house at the opposite end of the road.

"I was instructed to leave you here and let you walk the rest of the way. They don't want Sonya seeing any car she might recognize."

"Thank you, I appreciate the ride."

"No. Thank *you*, Mr. Briar. Can you feel it in the air? The world is about to change forever."

Martin felt nothing in the air aside from the typical smog. "Glad I can help."

"Help? You're a living legend."

"Thank you." Martin shook Brett's hand and wondered how long it would be until his new friend washed it. It wasn't everyday you got to shake hands with a living legend. He stepped out the car, anxious to get away from his groupie, and slung the duffel bag over his shoulder.

He may have not sensed a shift in the air, but there was a definite change in his stomach. The urge to vomit had risen to his throat as his fingers turned slick with sweat. He started walking down the sidewalk on weak legs, trying to clear his mind and relieve the stress that throbbed on every inch of his being.

Brett had left—surprisingly—making Martin the only person standing outside on this pleasant Friday morning. His arms trembled and his vision blurred in and out of focus while his heart thumped like a rabbit's foot. When he was three houses away, he collapsed to the ground and vomited on the sidewalk, looking around as he wiped his mouth clear of any remnants. He could hear Chris laughing all the way from Alaska, daring him to carry this out.

Get your ass up and go.

Martin wondered if the past would push back on this mission. They hadn't mentioned anything in his brief preparation. Wasn't he about to embark on not only changing the past, but also completely alter the fabric of time? Perhaps killing Sonya wasn't the big event that the past was waiting for, but rather Chris's death. That is what would officially throw the world into a chaotic limbo.

Martin pulled himself back to his feet, convinced the world wasn't stopping him, only himself. He dragged his legs to Sonya's house, its green lawn welcoming him to his past memories. He stood at the driveway and remembered all of the good times they had together.

He remembered the long drive home from the hospital after he woke from his coma. They had sat in the driveway as Martin debated revealing the truth to Sonya—a truth she had known all along. He shook his head and walked up to the door, a sliver of confidence finally working its way into his psyche. He knew she was inside, waiting for him.

When he approached the door, it swung open and Sonya stood there, eyes bulging.

"I've been expecting you," she said. "Come in."

87

Chapter 33

Sonya was as beautiful as ever. Even though he had just seen her two days ago, it felt more like five years.

"Are you just gonna stand there, or do you want to come in?" she asked with a grin.

He stepped into the doorway and let the screen door fall shut behind him as he entered the kitchen. The house was immaculate as always, and the smell of bacon and sausage oozed from the stove. He looked around the house for any sign of another man living there.

"Sit down, relax." She left him in the doorway to turn off the stove. "So, what are you doing here?"

She leaned against the counter and watched Martin with a careful eye as he sat at the kitchen table.

"These last two days have been hell," he said. His stomach bubbled with anxiety; he could feel her studying him, waiting for him to make a move. *She has to know.*

"You could say that. We went through all of this trouble to get you in private, and that piece of shit had to barge in and take you. How did you get here?"

"I escaped from Chris's house. I ran until I found civilization, and took the next flight out of that place."

"I see." She crossed her arms, all but saying that she didn't believe a word coming out of his mouth.

"Look, Sonya. I came here because I need closure. I thought we were about to start the rest of our lives together, then all of this shit happened."

His nerves settled; speaking the truth had that effect.

"I was just doing my job. I don't enjoy the disappointment that comes at the end of my missions, but it's part of it. There's not really a way around it."

"I don't care what anyone says. I know what I felt. We had something real. You wouldn't have dragged me along for six months if you didn't feel the same. You could've lured me into a trap at any time."

"You wouldn't leave without Izzy. I wasn't going to bother."

"Did you know Izzy's outcome all along?"

Sonya bowed and let her blond hair hang over her face.

"Jesus Christ, Sonya. Are you fucking kidding me? You sat with me through all that planning knowing how it was going to end. Is that why you stayed parked across the street that night?"

She looked up and brushed her hair back, nodding. "I'm sorry, Martin. You shouldn't have come here. You're not supposed to know these things."

"So both you and Chris knew the outcome and let me wander around, pretending to be a superhero. You really are your father's daughter."

"Don't call him my father!"

"Is he not?"

"Yes, he's my father, but that's not the point. He ruined my life."

"Is that why you ruin other people's lives now? Needed a way to get revenge on the system?"

"It's not like that."

"How does it feel to be living a lie?"

"I don't live a lie. *You're* the one living a lie. You were gonna just jump into a new life and pretend that your past never happened. I have to live with my past every day, so don't feed me your bullshit."

They sat in silence for a minute, both looking to the ground and avoiding eye contact. Martin's legs bounced uncontrollably under the table.

"I saw the look in your eyes at the hospital," Martin said. "There was a genuine care and concern, and I saw the woman I loved."

"I was just doing my job, checking on you. We needed you alive."

"I'll always love you. I don't care what you say. I know it was real, and if you want to keep lying to yourself that it wasn't, then that's on your conscience."

"Martin, if I could love you I would. Being with me will keep you in the line of danger for the rest of your life. If you escaped from Chris already, he'll kill you the next chance he gets."

"I don't think he will. I can take this chance with you—I have nothing to lose."

"He will. I've seen it plenty of times to know. He has zero heart, especially once he considers you a traitor."

"I'm a traitor because I didn't want to stay a prisoner in his house?"

"Yep. That's how he thinks."

"Regardless, I'll do anything. If it means risking my life, then so be it."

"Drop the act, Martin. I know why you're really here."

"What do you mean?"

"Don't play dumb with me." Sonya turned to the counter, pulled open a drawer, and retrieved a black pistol. She cocked it before aiming at Martin.

"Whoa, take it easy, Sonya. I don't know what you think, but it isn't this." Martin slowly raised his hands in the air.

"I'm not surprised about this grand scheme. I *am* surprised that you actually agreed to it. What's in that duffel bag over there?" Sonya nodded to the bag Martin had dropped on the ground by the front door. "Gonna spike my drink? Were you gonna propose a toast to us and watch me die?"

"Sonya, it's not what you think."

"It's exactly what I think. Did you know I've been with the Road Runners for more than 30 years? I joined them the day after I graduated high school and ran away from my dad's house. There's a lot you don't know, but you just barge in here thinking you can kill me. I've been to hell and back, and I'm not leaving this world on anyone's terms but my own."

"Sonya, I have no intention of killing you."

"I can't believe you. I hope you understand." The pistol wavered in her hand and Martin watched her debate pulling the trigger. "I've been waiting for this day. As soon as Chris took you from the hotel and they sent me home, told me to not worry about it. I knew something was going on. They *never* take anyone off of a mission until it's complete."

"How did you know?"

"I have many friends. I've been here forever—there are people more loyal to me than to the Road Runners, even in the highest of positions."

Martin wondered if Bill might have slipped Sonya the secret. He had said he was against it, and seemed to have also been a lifelong Road Runner. Commander Strike shouldn't have told a soul about this plan, but the burden of such a secret could crush even the strongest-minded person.

"I don't know what you want me to say," Martin said. "I came here to talk, honestly. Yes, I have poisons in my bag that they asked me to slip you, but I'd never be able to."

"I know you're probably telling the truth, but I can't take any chances. I hope you understand."

"Sonya—"

The pistol fired, its explosion echoing throughout the house. She had lowered it from his face to his legs.

A piercing, burning sensation immediately filled his left thigh, the warmth of blood soaking into his pants.

"Motherfucker!" he screamed, grimacing and squeezing his leg.

"I'm sorry, Martin," she said, and pulled the trigger again.

His right knee exploded, blood splattering across the tile floor like an abstract painting. Martin collapsed from the chair, sliding to the ground in his own pool of blood.

She had shot each leg, and he couldn't so much as wiggle his toes.

"If one day we can put all of this behind us, then I'd be open to giving life with you another chance. But odds are you'll never see me again. None of you will."

"Sonya," Martin gasped. The adrenaline rush had numbed his legs, but he still couldn't move them, let alone stand up.

"Don't follow me. Just let me go."

She tucked the pistol into the back of her pants and hurried out of the kitchen. Martin lay face-down and dragged himself with a half-assed army crawl, dark red smearing behind him in a messy trail.

Sonya had gone into her bedroom as Martin crawled through the living room. "Sonya!" he shouted. "Sonya, help me!" His entire bottom half had turned numb, and his arms became Jell-O as they trembled with each forced movement.

When he finally reached the bedroom doorway two minutes later, he found the room deserted.

"Sonya?"

A glass bottle of green liquid lay on the ground, a puddle forming around it. Next to the puddle was another pool of blood with what looked to be a chunk of flesh and a dime-sized microchip floating on the surface.

"Nooooooo!" Martin cried, rolling to his back.

She's gone. Forever.

She had drunk her Juice and vanished. Even though he hadn't seen one, Martin knew the chip was her tracking device that she would've cut out of her arm.

You've seen her for the last time. She has no way back. Wherever she went, she's staying there forever.

Martin kept his gaze to the ceiling, the same one he had looked at so many mornings, waking up next to Sonya, and wondering if life could get any better. Those memories were from another lifetime and he'd never get them back. A lone tear rolled down his cheek and splashed on the ground, mixing in with the stream of blood that had followed him from the kitchen.

I'm never going to be a hero, he thought, and then fainted.

88

Chapter 34

Across the spectrum of time, Commander Strike watched from the Denver office with the rest of the Road Runners gathered around in the bullpen. The technology of the tracking devices allowed the host person to be watched regardless of what year they were in. All attention was focused on the screen showing the devices for both Martin and Sonya.

Martin had arrived five minutes ago to Sonya's house, and Commander Strike announced to the entire room what was going on.

"Attention all. Today is the day. Our very own Martin Briar is currently in Sonya's house in 1996. There has been a plan in the making to assassinate Sonya Griffiths. Her death will open the opportunity for us to make a final, fatal move on Chris. We currently have snipers hiding in the woods around his property in Alaska, and have received confirmation that he's inside the house."

People gasped while others shouted in protest.

Commander Strike raised her hands and waited for the bickering to settle down.

"I need you all to keep a tight lid on this information. I'm trusting you with this secret since we'll be watching the outcome from here."

She nodded to a young woman who sat behind a control panel.

The master screen, a 120-inch wide monitor, flickered to life and showed a map of Larkwood. The young woman clicked around until the screen zoomed in on a satellite image of Sonya's house where they saw the roof and her car parked in the driveway.

Two green dots flashed within the image of the roof, one labeled as S. Griffiths and the other as M. Briar.

"I want you all to know this decision was not easy. We debated heavily on how to approach this, but ultimately decided to move forward with sacrificing Sonya to end this war."

Murmurs spread across the room like wildfire as people turned to each other. Mention of ending the war was rare and never taken lightly. Everyone had fallen into such a daily groove that they sometimes forgot there was a possibility for an end to it all—it just never felt like it would actually arrive.

"You heard me correctly. To make a long story short, if Sonya dies, Chris becomes mortal and we can kill him through regular means."

"Are you saying the war can end today?" someone shouted from the back.

"Yes, it can, and it will."

The murmur grew into a nervous chatter as people broke into conversation about the news.

"This is a day that will live forever in history. On this screen we'll be watching Sonya. When her sensor turns from green to red, Chris will officially be a mortal human being. I have my phone ready to make the call to Alaska where the snipers will be instructed to shoot him at first sight."

More chatter.

"This might take some time—I honestly don't know. I hope Mr. Briar can carry out this mission within the next few hours, but I suspect he'll take his time. They do have a past together, so we're unsure how exactly that will factor in to their current encounter."

Everyone had abandoned their desks and gathered in the center of the room to watch the main screen that hung high on the wall. Commander Strike crossed the aisle and joined the rest of the team, excitement and anticipation in the air like a thick fog.

Rarely nervous, Commander Strike's stomach spun in wild cartwheels. Tarik and Bill joined her among the crowd of Road Runners anxiously waiting to see if their years of hard work would finally yield the result that had become a Holy Grail.

The screen zoomed in further, showing only the outline of the house, cutting off the front and back yards along with the surrounding neighbors. All eyes were drawn to the two flashing green lights that stood inches apart on the screen, not moving.

"They're obviously talking," Tarik said to the room. "This is good. We were somewhat worried that Sonya would run off as soon as she saw Martin, but that doesn't appear to be the case."

The Commander nodded, also pleased with this information.

Ten minutes passed and neither of the green dots moved from their place on the screen.

"Are we sure it's working?" someone asked from the crowd of two dozen people.

The woman behind the control panel clicked a few buttons and said, "Everything is working just fine."

"They're in her kitchen," Tarik commented. "I've been to her house before."

"Give it a moment," Strike said. "They certainly have some catching up to do, and it appears Sonya is agreeing to it."

What if he's telling her to make a run for it? Commander Strike wondered. It was possible, but made no sense. They both had tracking devices and couldn't actually hide anywhere. *He wouldn't do that. He has no reason to be disloyal after a day. What could she be saying to him, though?*

Those watching the screen started to squirm as they stood and watched absolutely nothing happen. It reminded Commander Strike of watching TV coverage of election night in the United States. There was always great stress and impatience as to how the night would end, but getting to that point was flat-out boring.

Please don't converse all day.

Most wars didn't end with some dramatic climax, but rather quietly through negotiation behind closed doors. When she was elected as the new Commander, she avoided any sort of promise to ending the war, and leaned on guarantees to take another step closer. The Road Runners had grown tone-deaf to repeated promises from leaders who vowed to end the war under their watch, so she built a platform on community and teamwork to advance the team's knowledge on the Revolters that would ideally lead to knowledge on how to kill Chris. She had achieved this, though by accident. Then again, she believed if you remained diligent and put in the hard work, your chances of getting lucky increased.

The tension faded by the second, and the green dots remained frozen in place. She looked down and rubbed her eyes, frustrated at the prospect of waiting an entire day to find out if she would place the phone call to change the world.

"She's moving!" someone shouted, sarcastically. Whispers spread through the crowd as they watched Sonya's green dot move across the screen, leaving Martin in the same place in the kitchen.

The Commander's eyes darted back to the screen and waited in antic-ipation. *It could be nothing, she could just be going to the bathroom.* She considered this likely since Martin had stayed in place. It clearly wasn't a heated argument or both dots would show as flailing across the screen.

"She's in her bedroom," Tarik said, calm and stern.

"He's moving, too!" someone shouted from the back.

"No he's not," responded another.

Everyone squinted in unison as they tried to figure out what was happening on the screen. Sonya's green dot flashed in her bedroom, while Martin's moved like a sloth toward her.

"Whatever he's doing he's approaching her slowly," Tarik said, eyes bulging. "Is he sneaking up on her?"

The commotion had Commander Strike's heart ready to leap out of her throat. *This is it, he's going in for the kill.*

As Martin's greet dot continued to inch closer to the bedroom, Sonya's green dot remained still.

An eternity of five whole seconds passed before Sonya's dot turned into a pulsing red on the screen.

He did it. It's done. He must have handed her the letter and she took it to her room to read.

He still wasn't quite within proximity to have injected her with a syringe, and never was close enough to have slipped anything into her drink.

What should have been an eruption of applause was met with deadly silence. Sonya had just been killed, and all eyes in the room turned to Commander Strike in eerie unity.

She pulled her phone from her pocket, fingers trembling as she dialed the number to the Alaska headquarters. While the phone rang, she wondered what her legacy would look like after her term ended. She had over a year left, plenty of time to conclude the war and let it snowball into a legacy as the greatest Commander in the history of the Road Runners. Office buildings would be named after her where a new generation of Road Runners could work on something besides cracking the code of how to defeat Chris.

"Hello, Commander," Julian answered 3,000 miles away.

"It's time."

89

Chapter 35

Andrei Morozov sat on the top of a tree, a thick and sturdy branch nestled between his legs, and his rifle perched to aim at Chris's mansion that glowed in the dawn of a new day in Alaska.

Andrei had gained fame within the Road Runners as their best soldier. Killing 319 Revolters earned that sort of respect. At least 300 of his kills had been achieved in his native Russia, but as word spread from the United States that an opportunity was on the horizon to take down Chris, he couldn't reject the offer to board the next plane to Alaska.

No one took their job as a sniper more seriously than Andrei. He committed to a rigorous workout routine, diet, and hundreds of hours educating himself on the Revolters. When he woke up in the morning, he imagined shooting Revolters. Same thing when he went to sleep at night, and likely during his dreams that he never remembered.

It was easy for Andrei to dedicate his life in such a dramatic manner. When the Revolters blew up a village in 2008 that took the lives of his mother, grandmother, and two sisters, he had no choice but to seek refuge with the Road Runners.

Now he was here, ten years after the fact and loving every moment of life as a Road Runner. They supported him in anything he needed, which wasn't much. All he asked for was a house to be built on the same land that had been destroyed. The village remained deserted, so he lived alone on the northern coast of Russia, hunting animals and fishing. And immersing himself in shooting practice, 300 rounds a day, delivered fresh at the beginning of every week from the Road Runners.

The leaders of the European branch of Road Runners knew how to get ahold of him: a quick helicopter ride from Moscow. He would never be anywhere else unless they had authorized him to go hunting for Revolters.

When word arrived that he was requested in Alaska, he had his bag packed and was on the return helicopter ride to Moscow within thirty minutes. From there he boarded a jet and arrived at the Alaskan headquarters in five hours.

He spent three weeks getting familiar with the area. The climate was no different from where he lived, but he needed to know the grounds surrounding Chris's mansion like the back of his hand.

It all led to him on this specific tree that he had picked out last week as the prime location to land a clean shot on Chris the moment he stepped onto his front porch.

He led a squad of five other snipers, all surrounding different corners of the property in case Chris tried to run from a different exit.

"When the time comes, he shouldn't actually know that he's mortal. We're gambling on an eight-hour window until he learns he's mortal again. He'll feel things like physical hunger and fatigue." Commander Strike had informed him of the plan when he arrived, and by all accounts it made sense. When it came down to it, all Andrei cared about was if his slug would indeed kill the main leader of the Revolters. And there was only one way to find out.

None of these past events stuck in his mind as he currently sat in the tree. His senses heightened, and his eyes focused on the house through his scope. Andrei drew long, heavy breaths, an exercise he had learned to keep his heart rate down when sniping enemies from hiding spots.

He had watched the grounds since his arrival in hopes of learning a daily routine Chris might have, but nothing was an exact science. Between six and eight in the morning, Chris would step outside to get into his van and leave. Andrei didn't care where he went. He wasn't in this business to follow people, but rather learn their schedules and execute them when the time came.

Chris would then return between ten and noon, typically having been gone for two hours each time. Beyond that knowledge was a crapshoot. Some days Chris would leave again in the afternoon or night, other times he'd never come back outside until the following morning.

It was 6:15 in the morning when Andrei had last checked his watch, and he waited for the voice in his ear to buzz through and give the order. If they could authorize it within the next fifteen minutes, Andrei knew Chris would be dead within the next 90 minutes.

You can take that to the bank. After the morgue, of course.

All week, the other Road Runners who were assigned to this mission had discussed it like middle school children excited for summer break. They were happy just to be a part of history, and didn't take the necessary preparations as seriously as Andrei expected for such a delicate mission.

None of it mattered—he was assigned the prime shooting location. The only reason Chris would go out a different door was if he knew something was going on. Andrei knew the cameras on the mansion didn't reach this far into the woods, so no one had a reason to alert Chris of any foul play taking place outside.

Carry on as normal, my friend.

Now was the waiting game. Andrei had an earpiece as a direct line of communication to Julian back at the headquarters. He didn't like Julian, thought he was too book smart for such a high position of power as the Commander's number two.

The earpiece finally crackled to life and Julian's squeaky voice echoed in his head.

"Andrei, it's time. I repeat, it's time. You have the green light."

The voice left his ear, leaving the silence and steady breeze as the only audible sounds. Somewhere under his three layers of jackets was a small microphone that the other snipers could hear him through.

"Gentlemen, we're all set. Fire on first sight, and kill anything that tries to get in the way."

Andrei grinned as he lowered his head down to look through the scope.

* * *

Forty minutes passed before there was any movement from the house, but when it came, Andrei sat ready with his finger on the trigger and his scope focused on the mansion's front door.

Come to Daddy, he thought, still keeping his breathing under control despite the sudden realization that he was about to become an international hero among the Road Runners. They would ask him to speak at events, to offer his training services to the others who trained for combat. He would decline all of this, jumping right back into his daily routine of exercising, eating, and sleeping until the war was officially declared over.

Until then, there was no point in resting on his laurels; that was a surefire way to get killed.

These thoughts briefly rushed through his mind before the front door opened and the familiar white hair of Chris appeared. He was surrounded by his usual posse of four guards. They all checked the surroundings in search of anything out of the ordinary.

Andrei wondered why they did this if Chris was supposedly immortal. Perhaps it was for their own good and not necessarily for their leader.

He drew one final deep breath and held it in his lungs, a ritual he had done every time before lining up a long distance shot. From the tree to the front door was just under 600 yards, a range he was comfortable shooting within, but still required more concentration than most shots. He had to factor the wind, altitude, temperature, and weight of the slug to project the perfect shot. Fortunately, for him and the rest of the world watching, the altitude, temperature, and ammunition were nearly identical to his set up in Russia. The only difference, as it could change any given day, was the wind.

The breeze had been steady, no more than ten miles per hour, but there had been instances where it stopped altogether. He had maybe ten seconds to calculate all of this data as Chris strolled from the front steps to his van.

Under five miles per hour, he thought as he zeroed on Chris's head. *Almost no breeze, but not quite nothing.*

He still hadn't exhaled, now with the perfect shot aligned.

Pull, he thought, squeezing the trigger and exhaling in unison.

Chris's guards whipped their guns out at the crack of the sniper rifle, but it was too late. Chris had been struck in the head and his body fell to the ground four steps shy of the van.

The Revolters started shooting blindly into the trees, clearly unsure of where the kill shot came from. They were shouting, but the sounds were nothing but gibberish by the time they reached Andrei.

He lowered his jaw back into his jacket and spoke into his microphone. "Take them all out."

Andrei had a clear shot and took down one of the guards. Four other shots fired within the next ten seconds, and each Revolter had fallen face down onto the cold ground.

"Nice work, men," Andrei said.

Somewhere underground, all around the world, Road Runners were screaming and shouting at the TVs. If they could riot in the streets to celebrate, they would. But no one else in society would know what was going on.

Andrei sat up and looked outside of his scope for the first time in thirty minutes. The dead bodies splayed across the front of the house were the ultimate badge of honor as he admired their stillness in the cold day.

He squinted at the sight of something his brain wouldn't allow him to believe.

Chris's frosty head sat up in the middle of the dead bodies, prompting Andrei to lower his eye back into the scope.

"Don't celebrate quite yet, men. He's back."

Through the scope, Andrei watched Chris sit up, take a quick look around, then turn his head directly in his direction with a wide grin.

The old man raised a stiff hand and waved to Andrei as he stood. He reached for his head with his scrawny fingers, worked around the side, and plucked the slug out as if it were an annoying hair. Chris examined it between two fingers before flicking it aside and returning another grin and wave to Andrei more than 1,500 feet away.

Andrei felt something he couldn't recall having ever experienced: goose flesh. Chris locked eyes with him through the scope, freezing him from pulling the trigger again. The others on his team apparently didn't have the same problem as they all fired their rifles in near unison.

Five bullets tore through Chris's head and chest, prompting a maniacal laugh from the crazy old man in the otherwise silent morning.

"What the fuck?" Andrei whispered, still trying to gain control back of his own mind. He'd never imagined such a thing to be possible, but he had once thought the same thing about time travel.

Chris plucked the rest of the slugs out of his body and head, flicking them aside like pocket lint, and turned back into the mansion. Heavy steel walls rose from the ground and swallowed the mansion, securing the house in a virtual bulletproof fort.

"What's going on out there?" Julian crackled from Andrei's earpiece.

"I have no idea. We just shot him six times and he walked back into the house."

Silence filled the airwaves as he assumed Julian was in a panic, on the phone with Commander Strike. Any celebrations that might have begun would've already ceased. Chris lived on, and the Road Runners now had a new list of questions as to why.

90

Chapter 36

"What do you mean he's *not dead*?" Commander Strike asked into the phone. She had slipped back into Tarik's office after watching the previous moments unfold.

She had watched the live feed that had cut out moments after Chris had risen from the ground, but hearing the confirmation from Alaska made it real.

"He's in his house and has barricaded himself," Julian explained. He had been the one to cut the live feed that was showing around the world.

"How is this possible?" Commander Strike demanded.

"There are two possibilities," Julian replied calmly. "Either our theory was wrong, which I don't believe is likely, or Sonya isn't actually dead."

"She's dead. She's still flashing red and hasn't moved in 20 minutes. Are you suggesting our tracking device technology is faulty?"

"The equipment is fine. We need to get someone to Sonya's house right away. Something's not right. Briar hasn't moved either and is still next to Sonya. He wouldn't just be lying next to her dead body."

"He might. He was deeply in love with her."

"I'm just suggesting someone goes there to see what exactly happened. Something's not right, and we need to have an answer ready for the people. They all saw Chris rise before I cut the feed. Although, many might have missed it due to celebrating. I know I almost did."

"I'll go myself. Me and Tarik. I'll call you when we get there."

"Be careful, Commander. Sonya is very wise and knows her neighborhood better than anyone. It could be a trap."

"I'll be fine."

Commander Strike hung up and rubbed her temples. "How the fuck is this happening?"

This was supposed to be a day of celebration, a future holiday for all Road Runners. As of now, it was nothing but another botched assassination attempt. Chris was alive and hiding in his house now, with dozens of Road Runners trapped in his basement. He might never come out, or maybe was already jumping to another era in time to plan his next move.

Strike slammed her fist on Tarik's desk, sending pens and paper clips out of place as they hopped around the oak. "Fuck!"

Tarik knocked and entered. "Commander, it's a dark mood out here. I think you should say something."

"I have nothing to say. You and I are going to Sonya's house. Now."

Strike crossed the office and forced Tarik aside, stepping into the bullpen where two dozen pairs of eyes all locked on her. She froze, and debated storming out of the building or addressing the crowd. She had never shown her frustrated side, and even though this was a justifiable moment, decided to keep her cool facade.

"Hello, everyone. As you saw, our mission has failed. We're not sure why, but I'm going out right now with Tarik to get to the bottom of this. Please save your questions, as I honestly don't have an answer. We hope to know more when we return."

The silence that hung in the room could have been cut with a plastic spoon. The hype had vanished, leaving behind a world of terrified and confused Road Runners. For nearly all of them, taking down Chris was their life's work. To have the illusion of having worked so hard, and come this far, only to see it all fail before their eyes was a gut check none had been prepared for.

Killing Chris had always seemed as likely as winning the lottery, and they understood that. But when Commander Strike informed them that it was finally a real possibility, a sense of fate settled across the room, and hope came out in full force.

I failed these people. I should've never said anything, and carried on like it was a normal day.

The thought was pure fantasy. People would have known something was going on the moment she arrived at the Denver office unannounced. It wasn't every day that the leader came down from Alaska to meet a new recruit. The rumors would've swirled and prompted her to address them anyway.

No one asked questions as she walked to the exit with Tarik chasing behind. She felt all of them watch her as she fought to bury the stress beneath her confident countenance.

She stormed up the stairs without a plan, hoping and assuming Tarik had a way to get them to Larkwood.

"I'll drive," Tarik said from behind as he joined her outside. Somewhere in 1996 Brett McBath would be returning to the same parking space after dropping off Martin Briar at Sonya's house. But on this cool day in 2018, an all-black Tesla sat in the spot, ready for their trip across town.

Commander Strike didn't hesitate as she walked straight to the passenger door and let herself in. If Tarik couldn't sense the urgency right now, then maybe she needed to find a new leader for the Denver headquarters.

He must have sensed it as he ran down the steps from the building and threw himself behind the wheel, clicking the remote to start the engine that quietly hummed to life.

"You know what's funny," Tarik said, buckling his seat belt. "They call these the cars of the future. You and I have seen the future, and the cars are nothing like this."

He chuckled as he put the car in gear and pulled onto the road. Commander Strike didn't laugh, although she did find the comment ironic. It also reminded her of how grim the future was, thanks to Chris. *Why didn't he just die?*

She clenched her jaw and shook her head. Everyone had executed their part to perfection. Even Martin, who she had half expected to back out at the last minute.

"How long to get there?" she asked.

"Should be ten minutes, assuming there's no traffic."

There was none, they had that much going for them, at least. She didn't even look out the window as they drove to Larkwood in silence, keeping her stare to the ground, sulking in confusion.

When they pulled in to Sonya's neighborhood, she asked Tarik, "Do you have a gun?"

"I keep one in the trunk. Why? Are you thinking we'll need it?"

"I don't think so. But Julian was warning me, like I should be ready for something to happen. Do we know if Martin has moved yet?"

"He hadn't when we left. I don't know if he has since then."

"Whatever happens inside that house, we need to leave with an answer, and we need to get back to work. Chris will be killing our people by tomorrow, and we need to have something prepared to tell the community."

"You mean to tell the world. The whole world was watching. People woke up in the middle of the night on the other side of the globe just to see history."

"Well, they saw it alright."

Tarik parked the car at the curb, blocking the driveway. He killed the engine and they both stared at the house as if it were a rare bird. Commander Strike noted the homey feeling from the front yard, with its green lawn, big tree, and front porch with two rocking chairs. A long time ago she had a life just like this, but hadn't been back since becoming Commander and constantly traveling the world to kill bad guys.

Those memories would have to stay buried in the past with her dead husband.

"Let's jump back to 1996 and go in. Is someone watching us?" she asked, referring to someone within the organization keeping an eye on their tracking devices.

"Commander, someone is *always* watching you. Even on the rare days you sleep."

"Very funny."

"It's true. So yes, you're being watched. I have no idea about me."

"As long as one of us is being watched then we'll be okay. Let's go."

Strike pushed open her door and went to the trunk where Tarik opened the door for her to get the pistol he kept concealed. Tarik joined her as she sat down on the sidewalk, unscrewing the lid off of her flask. They both took a quick swig of their Juice. After having taken thousands of trips through time, the process became as seamless as tying shoelaces. They briefly fell asleep and woke up in 1996 within one minute.

Without a word, Strike stood, dusted herself off, and walked up the driveway to knock on the door with a balled fist.

"Sonya, are you home?" she called. *Of course she's not home, because she's dead, remember?*

She knocked again, hoping for Martin to come answer, but didn't want to call out his name just in case Sonya was alive and hiding. She couldn't have her know that Martin was sent by the Road Runners.

They waited a minute, knocking a couple more times, before Commander Strike turned to Tarik and shrugged.

"Try the door," he whispered, creating a stealthy mood.

Strike nodded before turning the knob and pushing the door open with ease.

"Sonya?" she called again as she took her first step inside the house and froze.

The house appeared empty, but the splatters of blood on the kitchen floor and walls made her stop. She cocked the pistol and held it out in front of her body.

"Sonya, is everything okay?"

This wasn't supposed to be a bloody mess.

Her eyes followed the trail of blood that started at the kitchen table and smeared its way across the house, to the bedroom where the door stood wide open, and she watched the blood turn into it and out of sight.

"Is any one here?" she barked, thinking Martin better damn well respond.

Silence filled the house, the only sound being the hardwood floor creaking beneath her feet. Tarik had stepped into the doorway and couldn't take his eyes off the apparent massacre in the kitchen.

A thousand thoughts rushed Strike's mind as she now accepted the possibility of Sonya being alive. She could've killed Martin. Maybe the system was glitching because they were so close to each other. Sonya could be hiding in the bedroom over Martin's dead body, waiting for the next Road Runner to show up and try to end her life.

"If anyone is in this house, speak now, or consider yourself at risk of being shot."

Strike's voiced echoed and returned to her with no response. She turned to Tarik, his eyes bulging from their sockets as the realization sunk in that something terrible had happened just minutes ago. The terrifying part was not knowing what awaited in the bedroom.

"Commander," Tarik whispered urgently. "Shouldn't I go in first?"

Strike almost laughed. Only Tarik would pull out an official procedure in a time like this. Yes, it was written that if a dangerous situation should arise, the Commander is last to act, sending in others to the potential danger first. This was obviously done for the sake of keeping leadership in tact, but now wasn't the time to pull out the rule book.

"This is my mess," she spoke in her normal voice, not believing there was any living person in the house. "I'm going in first. I don't sense any danger."

Tarik glared to the blood splatters to say *are you shitting me?* with his eyes.

Commander Strike turned back to the bedroom and took gentle steps toward it, pistol as far out as her arms would stretch.

When she was within two steps of the bedroom, she leapt across the doorway and into the room, pistol jerking from left to right as if she had expected someone to jump out and attack her.

"Martin," she said, seeing their newest member flat on his back, eyes closed, blood seeping from his legs. "Martin!"

Holy shit, he's dead. She killed him. But where is she?

She lowered the pistol, deciding Sonya wasn't in the house. Why would she hide when she could be in the 1400's already? "Tarik, get in here."

He had watched from the living room and let out a long sigh when the Commander called him in. He joined her, and immediately dropped to a knee to examine Martin.

"He's still alive," he said. "His breathing is fine."

Tarik poked Martin on the face, and snapped his fingers right next to his ears. "He's unconscious. If all of this blood belongs to him, he's suffered a pretty heavy loss. I see a bullet wound on both legs. One in the kneecap—that could've hurt enough to make him faint."

At first glance, Commander Strike thought the liquid on the other side of Martin was more blood, but with her nerves settling down, she recognized the green liquid for what it was after seeing it next to the spilled, empty bottle.

"Tarik, is that what I think it is?"

He was still hunkered over Martin and pivoted on his knee to examine the mess behind him.

"Oh, my God," he said, clapping a hand to his mouth. "She cut it out."

"Cut what out?"

"Her tracking device."

Tarik reached into the pool of liquid and plucked a small item that Commander Strike had originally thought was the bottle cap.

"Do you know how bad this would hurt?" he cried. "Never mind the cutting open of your own arm, but these devices *attach* to the muscle—it's how they stay in place. It wouldn't have just plucked out like a hair; she would've experienced excruciating pain."

"I don't care about her pain. Where the hell is she?"

Strike paced around the room, looking for the ultimate truth in this mystery. Every time traveler, whether a Road Runner or a Revolter, was guaranteed to have two things: a bottle of their Juice, and a small flask to carry that same Juice when traveling. There was no other way.

Sonya's bottle was on the floor, its liquid mixed with blood and no longer useful. Finding the flask—or not—would decide everything from this point forward.

Commander Strike rummaged through Sonya's dresser before moving to her night stand. Tarik watched her bounce around the room like an alcoholic searching for the private stash they hid from themselves.

"Fuck!" she barked from the nightstand, and sat down on the bed with a silver and blue flask clenched in her grip. She shook her head, looking at the flask like it was fake.

"What does this mean?" Tarik asked, knowing very well what it meant, but not sure what else to say in the spur of the moment.

"She's gone and not coming back. She has no way back." The life had left her voice as she debated lying all the way down on Sonya's bed and crying. How could they have been so close to ending this war, to only end up even further from a solution?

"Commander, if she drank one final drink of her Juice and left, where is her body? Shouldn't her body be lying here on the ground while she traveled to wherever she went?"

"She doesn't go by the same rules as us. Only her and Chris have the ability to travel without leaving their bodies behind. Their bodies travel *through* the dimensions of time. I guess it's a perk of being related to Chris."

"She can run, Commander, but we have eyes all over. We can alert everyone we have. At this point, we have to treat Sonya as an outlaw. She needs to be arrested on sight, and if she tries to run, then she needs to be shot."

This much was true, but it was the last thing Commander Strike wanted to authorize. *So fucking close. Sonya was expecting Martin.*

There was no other explanation as to why she would've shot Martin in both of his legs before fleeing to another time with no return trip home.

"Tarik, we can't tell anyone about what happened or what our next move is. I think someone has been leaking information to Sonya from the inside."

91

Chapter 37

Martin woke up in what looked like a hospital room; only it had no windows, no TV, and no beeping machines. There was a closed door with frosted glass, and he assumed he was back in the Road Runners' office, hopefully still in Denver, and hopefully back in 2018.

His bleary vision came in and out of focus as he looked down at his own body. White bandages were wrapped around both of his legs like a mummy. He tried to move his legs, but an instant blast of pain ruptured from his knee at the slightest movement.

Then he remembered what happened, which he was thankful for after once having woken up in a hospital and *not* remembering how he had arrived.

"Sonya," he croaked. *Did she really shoot me in both legs to escape? Did she actually consider me that dangerous that she felt she had to flee? If she would've just asked, I'd have just turned around and pretended to not notice.*

The door swung open and Bill appeared in the doorway. "Good morning, Sunshine." He turned back into the hall and shouted, "Let the Commander know Martin is awake."

Bill trudged into the room and approached Martin's bedside. "That's quite the beating your legs took. The doctor said it'll be six weeks until you can get out of those casts. I've never had a mummy friend before, so I'm not sure what to expect."

Bill let out a hoarse chuckle as he slapped a hand on Martin's chest. Martin couldn't help but grin in response.

"What happened? What year am I in? Did we find Sonya?"

Bill shook his head, his eyes drooping. "You're back in 2018, and I'm afraid not. She's as good as dead, the way I see it. She took off to some other time and has no way of returning; she left her Juice. For all we know, she's hiding out a million years ago with a group of triceratops. I'm sure we'll come across her eventually, but something tells me she's had this escape plan brewing for a while. She'll be hidden really good."

"Bill, I wasn't even doing anything. I wasn't even going to try and kill her, but she came out of nowhere and shot me before she left."

"Yeah, I understand. She has no idea who to trust right now. Can you blame her?"

"It just seemed drastic. We were literally talking in her kitchen, about our past, when she pulled a gun out of the drawer and started shooting."

"Well, at least you're fine. She spared your life, don't forget that. She could've shot you anywhere, but chose your legs. She's no dummy; that was intentional."

"I suppose. So what happens next?"

"Commander Strike will be in to get you up to speed. You have a long road to recovery ahead, my friend."

"There's not some magic medicine from the future that heals my legs in 24 hours?"

Bill laughed. "What exactly do you think the future is like? There's no magic."

Says one time traveler to another.

A rapid knock came from the door as Commander Strike entered, dressed in a sweater and jeans. The bags under her eyes had darkened to a deeper shade.

"Haven't you two become the best of friends," she commented.

"Martin here is the brother I never had," Bill said.

"Very good. Do you mind giving us a moment in private?"

"Sure thing, Commander." Bill patted Martin on the shoulder before leaving the room. Strike took slow strides to the foot of the bed.

"How are you feeling?" she asked.

"Well, it appears I can't walk, so I've had better days."

"Your legs are going to be fine. You'll have about a month in those casts, then will be walking within a couple weeks of that. You might have a limp, but we won't know until you actually start walking."

"Lovely, hobbling gets all the ladies."

Commander Strike giggled. "So what happened in there?"

"A paranoid woman shot me in the legs and vanished into dust."

"We know that much. How did it play out?"

Martin recounted the story from the moment he entered Sonya's house up until he crawled into her bedroom and fainted.

"Did it seem like she knew what you were up to?"

"She knew everything. She called it out, even told me where the poison was in the duffel bag."

"I was afraid so. We've already begun investigating to see who was leaking information to Sonya. We're starting with everyone in this office since she had the closest relationships with people here."

"What's the word on Chris?"

The Commander pursed her lips at the mention of his name. "We don't know. His house is still barricaded. No one has gone in or out in the last 16 hours. We're worried he might have a secret way out, an underground tunnel of sorts. We have eyes on that place and all around Alaska, waiting for him to make a move."

"That's kind of scary."

"Don't mention it. We've had to tell the people that everything is under control, that we know exactly where Chris is."

"So what happens next? I know I'm not of much help at the moment..."

"We're officially back to the drawing board. We need a plan for finding Sonya, but that's more like the needle in a haystack. I guess we're just hoping to get lucky and stumble across her."

"One thing she made clear is that no one was going to end her life on their terms."

"Well, now that the secret's officially out, we can't exactly back off. We don't know if she'll go into hiding or possible retaliate. It's not to our benefit to assume one way or the other. If we can at least locate her and know where she is, we can figure it out from there."

"Exactly how far in time can you travel?"

"As far as you can think. If the year actually exists in the past, you can go to it. Same for the future. If you can't go to the year, then you'll just wake back up in your present day."

"Are you saying you know when the world ends?"

"It's not for a long time, but we can discuss that another time. I need to know that you're still with us."

"Of course."

"I hoped so. Some would go running for the hills after going through what just happened to you. "

"I'm committed to this cause, maybe even more now. I still want what we agreed upon. I have to save my mom."

Commander Strike sighed. "I've been expecting you to bring that up. I have looked into the matter. The cure exists in the future, but it's not easy to obtain."

"I'll get it. Whatever it takes."

Commander Strike shook her head, causing some hair to fall over her face. "It's not what you think. The medicine is being held in secret by the government."

"Why would they keep it a secret?"

"You'll understand when you see this government—there's no interest in caring for people. It's all about money. Only the richest citizens have access to the medical secrets."

"Aren't we all rich? Can't we just buy some?"

"It's not a matter of only money. Every person who receives this medicine has to be vetted by the government. They hook you up to a lie detector—and this is an advanced one—and ask you about your loyalty to the Revolution. If they find you're loyal, they'll let you buy it. If not, they send you off, or might even execute you depending on your answers to their questions."

"The Revolters take control of the country?"

"Yes, that's why we have an urgency to end the war. We've seen the future with them in charge, and it's not a world anyone should have to live in."

"I've already lived through hell way before I met Chris. I'm not scared of a little danger."

"I knew I wouldn't be able to talk you out of this. We'll make arrangements for you to go as soon your legs are healed. As you'll need to be mobile. There aren't any more accommodations for handicapped people in the future."

"Why aren't you pushing back harder on this?"

"We owe you—*I* owe you," she said, crossing her arms. "I didn't think the situation we were sending you into would have any danger. You're not even trained to be in the field as a Road Runner, and clearly you should have been. I rushed into this decision and it almost got you killed. I have to live with that."

"There was no time to waste."

"There was plenty of time. We had eyes on Sonya. She wasn't going to move until we approached. She was waiting for us to make her escape."

"One thing I've learned since time traveling is to not dwell on past decisions. It's over, and I'm alive. You're not doing anyone any good by looking back. It's time to plan for what's next."

She nodded, appreciative of the comment. "Oh, I've been thinking about what comes next. Now that I know you're committed to the Road Runners, what do you think about taking a position in the field—after we get your mom's medicine, of course?"

"What kind of position?"

"I don't know yet. You would have to go through field training; it's a boot camp of sorts. From there, we'll have a better assessment of your strengths and weaknesses. But there are all kinds of roles you can take on, and we still haven't figured out how to use your special gift to our advantage."

Martin had forgotten all about being "warm." Perhaps he'd get to trail blaze a whole new role. "As long as I don't have to sit in there all day, I'll take anything." He nodded to the door where the dozens of desk workers waited on the other side.

"Don't worry, the office workers also go through a rigorous education program. Two years, seven days a week, if that interests you?"

"Nope."

Commander Strike laughed. "We'll get you a ride home so you can recover from the comfort of your own house. We'll come check in with you in a few weeks and see about your rehab schedule. Then we can plan from there."

They wrapped up their conversation with some small talk, and Martin couldn't stop grinning, despite the pain and drama he had just endured. He felt part of something bigger than himself for the first time in his life. The stress that Chris had created by leaving so many questions unaddressed had washed away. The Road Runners would support him in anything he needed going forward, and they proved that by staying true to their word on helping him obtain the cure for Marilyn's disease.

The future, which sounded like a dystopian nightmare by everyone who had traveled there, awaited Martin and his next adventure. He already knew the road ahead would bring more unforeseen twists, but he finally had control over his life, knowing what he wanted. And as he lay down, staring at the ceiling and pondering what his life would look like in the next six months, one thought played over and over that kept his spirits high.

I'm a Road Runner.

III

Bad Faith

Wealth of Time Series, Book #3

92

Bad Faith Cover

BOOK THREE OF THE WEALTH OF TIME SERIES

BAD FAITH

ANDRE GONZALEZ

93

Chapter 1

Martin Briar sprawled in the mud, a generous gash oozing blood over his exhausted legs, his arms screaming in protest, sweat rolling down his mud-caked face, his entire body numb with pain.

"Pain is weakness leaving your body!" Staff Master Collins had barked at least 200 times over the past two months in his sharp, intimidating growl. Martin particularly enjoyed when the belligerent staff master would drop to the ground as he completed his 150th push-up, shouting that same line in his face while demanding fifty more.

Martin had put on a few pounds during his twelve-week recovery and rehab from Sonya blasting his legs into uselessness, but the Road Runner Training Program was simply a nice way of phrasing "boot camp." With the calendar flipping to 2019, Martin shed all of the extra weight, and for the first time since his twenties, sported actual muscles.

"I'm too old for this shit," he had muttered under his breath on the first day, wondering how the hell he'd make it to the finish line. Staff Master Collins had promised to destroy the body and psyche of all those in attendance, a group of Martin and six others recently recruited to join the Road Runners. Only one had dropped out after the first week, leaving the rest to form a bond and push each other through the ten-week program.

"You people don't know true hell," Staff Master Collins had calmly explained one day after training ended. He stood exactly six feet tall, with muscles bulging from every centimeter of his dark-skinned body, a heavy brow line keeping his face in a constant frown. *Even his muscles have muscles,* Martin noted before the first day of training.

Collins liked to give his version of motivational speeches at the end of each day, always while the group panted for breath, hands on knees as they listened. "I've been to hell and fought the demons. You need to be strong, mentally and physically, because they will try to break you."

Part of the program was learning to survive. Each trainee was given a specific amount of water to drink each day, decided by their weight and age to determine the bare minimum needed to not faint during the rigorous workout.

"What happens if you travel into the future and get captured by the Revolters? Do you think they're going to give you a bottle of water? Maybe order a pizza and fix a soft bed for you? Hell *no!*" Whenever Collins shouted, spit flew from his mouth in messy droplets.

"These people will leave you to starve, leave you to thirst, and leave you to die. If they don't kill you right away, they'll take you hostage, wait until you can barely stand up, then beat you to death because you're defenseless and can't even lift your hand to wipe your ass! Do you understand, Briar?"

Martin nodded at the crazy bald man two inches from his face, bulging brown eyes burning into his spirit.

"Good. Especially you, Briar." Collins paused and crossed his arms, taking a step back from Martin. He lowered his voice and continued. "They want you bad, Briar. You're not the kind of man they'll kill at first chance—they will torture you. They want that sweet, sweet gift you have, and if they have to rip it out of your organs, then that's what they'll do."

This moment ten weeks ago had forced Martin to dedicate his life to the training program. He didn't know if the things Collins said were true, but he did know Chris wanted him, whether out of revenge for fleeing, or for being a Warm Soul.

Today was day 70, the final day of the training program, as Martin lay in the mud. They expected him to maintain his new figure, and he had every intent of doing so. Martin felt the best he ever had in his life. He slept better, ate better, was never tired, and no longer craved alcohol. He was now a middle-aged man with a chiseled physique and the skills to murder a man with his bare hands.

"Everybody up!" Collins grumbled, intentionally kicking mud in the faces of those slow to rise. Despite the cramping spread across his entire body, Martin jumped to his feet within two seconds. His mental strength had developed even more than his body, in his opinion. "To the rifles!"

The group of three men and two women dragged themselves out of the mud pit where they had just completed a twenty-minute round of army crawling. At least the rifles didn't require any further physical strength, but rather mental will.

A gazebo housed the rifles one hundred feet away. Martin ran to it, grabbing his rifle and a bandolier to sling over his shoulder. Every day ended with a quick session on the shooting range.

"Start us off, Briar," Collins shouted. They all had to watch each other shoot, a way to practice in the spotlight.

"Learn to shoot under any circumstance. There will be times you feel like you're dying, maybe you *are* dying, but you have to shoot on. Kill every last Revolter until you no longer can." Another inspirational line from Staff Master Collins.

Martin obliged and took his post. Ten rubber dummies stood across the open field, ranging from fifty to five hundred yards in distance. He focused on his breathing, inhaling deeply through his nose and exhaling steadily out of his mouth. He dropped his head to see into his scope and started firing.

He shot the first nine in rapid succession, his hands gliding from side to side as each dummy rocked in its place. The tenth and final shot required extra concentration as it stood 500 yards away. He'd heard the stories of Andrei Morozov's long distance shot on Chris in Alaska. Even though the shot didn't end up deadly, it was still touted as the greatest shot in the history of the Road Runners. Martin had the opportunity to meet Andrei at the beginning of their training program and received a few tips from the pro, including the breathing technique used when lining up the long distance shots.

He drew his breath and fired the shot, watching the dummy's head rock back. His fellow trainees ruptured into applause at witnessing his performance. Maybe once a week someone would have a perfect outing and hit all ten targets; this week was Martin's turn.

"Nice shooting, Briar," Collins said in the closest tone he had to a normal voice.

Martin stepped back and joined the rest of his team, who all offered slaps on the back and fist bumps for his stellar performance.

"Can I have a word with you?" Collins asked as the next trainee stepped up with their rifle.

"Sure."

They dropped back a safe distance where their voices couldn't be overheard by the others. Collins spoke in a low voice, just above a whisper. "They want me to report back what I think your best role would be. Now, by the looks of it, you have all the tools of a front line soldier. That would mean you'd barge into Revolter hideouts and kill everyone in sight, help with ambushes, and kick ass in general. But I get the sense that doesn't really excite you—you don't have the killer mentality that most soldiers have."

Martin nodded. "I'll go wherever I'm needed."

"Get off your high horse, Briar. Just tell me what you want to do."

"I honestly don't care. I just want to get this medicine for my mom. Whatever happens after that I'm fine with. I do want to kill Chris."

"Well, get in line. We already had a task force assigned to kill him, and they failed."

"The mission failed; they did not. Andrei landed that shot."

"Precisely. You may not have all the knowledge of someone who's been with the organization for years, but I feel you have the smarts to figure out a way. Combine that with your Warm Soul, and you might be the person who brings down Chris."

Martin had never thought of himself as smart. He got by in high school, never went to college, and bounced around jobs as a mid-level manager for various companies. Now with the Road Runners, more and more people had been praising his thinking ability, when all he thought he was doing was giving honest feedback.

"I don't even know what my ability means—I've never even seen it in action."

"There'll be a special session for you with some of our scientists. I think you'll be heading there the day after tomorrow."

"Can't wait."

"Don't be a smart-ass, Briar, I'm trying to help you."

"I know, and I appreciate it." Collins had never shown his compassionate side, and Martin wasn't sure what to do with it as the others in his group howled and cheered for each other on the shooting range. "I have my sights set on one thing at a time, and for me, it's getting that medicine."

"I respect that, but you can't lose sight of the future. Especially around here – you have to be ten steps ahead."

The two men stood in silence as an ugly gray cloud moved above them.

"I know. Honestly, I'll trust your recommendation for whatever position you think is best."

"I only recommend, but Commander Strike has the final say. She's checked in with me every day about your progress."

"What have you told her?"

"I told her there's something burning inside you, something that's pushing you to do the impossible." Collins paused and kicked the dirt with his heavy boot. "I'll be honest with you, this program is not meant for fifty-year-old men. It's designed for kids in their twenties, in their physical prime—like them." He nodded to the rest of the trainees. "I didn't think you'd make it past day one, but you've proven all of us wrong. That's how I know there's something driving you; I've never seen a transition like yours."

The Road Runners had put Martin through a rigorous rehab for his legs before starting the training program with Collins. Through that, he felt a motivation to not let Sonya's cowardly actions define the rest of his life. They thought he'd have a new limp after coming out of his cast—he didn't. They said his knee would never bend the same way again, leaving him no flexibility—they were wrong. The weakness in his shot knee tried to creep up at times, but he followed the rehab program to the last detail. The Road Runners' doctors may have not had medicine from the future, but they had knowledge from it, and applied it to his rehab to make his legs stronger than before.

"I appreciate the compliment, and I'm sure Commander Strike will have a talk with me before deciding anything. I assume a lot will depend on how these tests go with the scientists."

"I suspect that, too. Either way, it's food for thought. If you ever need to talk about things, just let me know. I'll be here."

Collins stuck out a hand for Martin to shake. He had never shown his human side, and by doing so, showed Martin how highly the Road Runners thought of him. Collins thanked him for working so hard over the last ten weeks and wished him the best in whatever he'd end up doing for the organization.

An hour later, Martin was officially free to return home after living on the training base for the last ten weeks. Granted, it was only ninety minutes away from his house—and had all the luxurious accommodations he'd come to expect of anything hosted by the Road Runners—but he wanted to sleep in his own bed and see his mother in person instead of the brief phone calls they had at night.

He'd have to drag himself to the car to begin his long drive, but the prospect was enough to spark a new wave of energy as he left the hardest chapter of his time as a Road Runner in the rear view mirror.

94

Chapter 2

Martin's stay at home would be short-lived. During his drive, Commander Strike called to inform him that the group of international scientists
had arrived in Denver and were expecting Martin in the office first thing
the next morning.

He agreed to arrive at eight, citing a night of deep sleep that awaited him.
The Commander was also flying in to witness the experiment, hoping to
learn of a breakthrough in how Martin could best be utilized.

Martin didn't know what to expect of a gift that was foreign to even
himself. They claimed he had remained mobile while the world was
frozen through earlier tests, but he had no recollection of this happening.

During the rest of his drive home, soaking in the breathtaking nature
of the Rocky Mountains, Martin reflected on his life. He never imagined
ending up an integral part of a secret society trying to stop another secret
society from taking over the world. Only, the Revolters couldn't be too
big of a secret if they end up rising to power in the future.

Thinking about the future made him uneasy. Was it really as bad as
everyone claimed? People tended to make things a bigger deal than they
actually were.

*It can't be too bad if they're sending others with me. Why put Road Runners
at risk to save my mom?*

As the sun set, casting an orange glow across the horizon, Martin tried to push the future from his mind to think about the past. Even though he had a fresh take on life, he still felt the same inside: helpless and desperate for the end.

Sure, he had a lot going for him, but he was back to square one with no Izzy, no Sonya, and a future where his mother's brain would slowly but surely deplete, unless he secured a miracle medicine in the future.

Not exactly winning at life, Martin thought most nights before falling asleep. His body had undergone a transformation, but he had no use for it. Part of him hoped to join the front line soldiers just to increase his chances of being killed.

"You can't die," he said to his empty car. "There's a woman who needs you. She brought you into this world, and now she needs you."

A tear rolled down his face as he sped down the freeway.

* * *

The next morning's sunrise came quicker than expected. Martin had arrived home late after stopping at a diner for a burger, finally strolling in to his house at ten and immediately going to bed, his body drained.

His mom was already asleep, and was still snoozing when he woke—she'd been sleeping a solid ten hours each night since moving in, and that apparently hadn't changed while he was away.

Martin dressed and was out the door by 7:15, leaving him just enough time to get from Littleton to downtown Denver by eight.

When he arrived to the office, he made his way through the main level that served as their front as a marketing company. Martin nodded at the many familiar faces as he crossed toward the stairs and descended to where the Road Runners conducted their official business.

The basement was filled, as usual, with the brains of the operations scattered about, sitting at their desks and watching monitors that changed every second. Tarik's office was immediately to Martin's left, its door open with a handful of people packed inside.

Martin assumed these to be the scientists and knocked on the wall to get their attention.

Tarik and Commander Strike both stood behind the desk, while the group of four scientists all turned in unison. Two men and two women, all young and fair-skinned, watched Martin in amazement.

"Good morning, Martin," Commander Strike welcomed him, taking a sip from her coffee mug. "Thanks again for coming in so soon after completing your training. I'd like you to meet the team – please introduce yourselves."

A short woman stepped to Martin with a hand extended. She had piercing blue eyes that complemented her strawberry hair and wide smile. "I'm Megan Privvy. We've heard so much about you."

"Nice to meet you."

"I'm Steffan Privvy," said the man behind Megan, who sported equally good looks with his chiseled brow and jaw, and wavy brown hair.

"That's my husband," Megan said. "We met studying time travel thirty years ago and have been together ever since, still studying."

Thirty years? They don't even look thirty years old.

Martin grinned at them and shook Steffan's hand. Thirty years could mean a variety of things when discussing time travel.

"And I'm Leigh Covington," the other woman said. She appeared slightly older than the rest, perhaps in her mid-30's, and lacked the natural warmth that Megan had radiated. Leigh had long brown hair that framed her high cheekbones.

Martin shook her hand and turned to the final man on the right.

"I'm Brigham Kelley," the man said in a strong British accent.

"Nice meeting you all," Martin said to the circle.

"Our scientists come from Europe," Commander Strike said. "Their advances in medicine in the future are way beyond what we have in the future, and they're actually accessible."

"Why didn't you just have them bring the Alzheimer's cure instead of sending me into the future?"

"We don't actually have that cure, Mr. Briar," Brigham said. "I'll be staying here while you go on your mission to get it. We're interested in studying it and replicating the medicine, if possible." Brigham adjusted his glasses as he spoke, his black hair spiked in every direction.

"So I need to get more than just for my mom?" Martin asked, puffing out his chest to show off his new strength. He felt much older than everyone else in the room, being the only one with streaks of gray on his head and early wrinkles forming below his eyes.

"Yes," Commander Strike said. "We figured since you'll already be there, we can use the opportunity to get some for ourselves and rightfully distribute it in different times throughout the past."

"Fair enough."

"We can discuss those details later. I know these fine folks are excited to start the experiment with you, and I don't want to waste any of their time. Shall we?"

The scientists nodded and filed out of the room, strolling by Martin with wide grins. Commander Strike and Tarik joined the back of the procession and followed behind with Martin.

"What are they going to do to me?" Martin asked Strike.

"It's not much," she replied, brushing a hand through her blond hair. "They're going to draw some blood to examine in their labs, run some tests on your brain, and film you with time frozen to see how the experience is for you."

"They can freeze time?"

"Steffan can. It's why he's in this group, trying to figure out how someone could resist it."

"Does that mean he's also warm?"

"Sort of. Anyone who can freeze time is warm, but not everyone who is warm can freeze time. The latter is more rare, which is why we need to figure it out."

"And use this to kill Chris?"

"Exactly. Imagine a scenario where all of his guards are frozen while we send in someone like you to kill him."

Martin knew they wanted to use his ability to their advantage in the war, but having him be the one to personally kill Chris? Yes, he wanted the old bastard dead, but he couldn't even kill Sonya. How was he supposed to become the biggest hero in Road Runner history?

They went to a conference room in the back of the office—the largest one they had—where a camera stood on a tripod along the front wall. The room had been cleared of the tables and chairs that normally filled it, leaving a lone table pushed into the corner, out of sight from the camera. Chairs were positioned for each person, seven in total.

The scientists filed in, taking their seats around the table, leaving the middle chair open. "Please sit here, Martin," Megan said.

Martin obliged, all eyes studying him.

"Today will be fairly simple," Steffan said. "We're going to run some tests, and then you and I will go for a little spin in the frozen world, right in this room. I expect we'll be done within an hour, not counting the frozen time, but that doesn't count anyway."

Steffan spoke to Martin as if he already understood how this worked, so he offered an obligatory nod in return.

Tarik and Commander Strike sat on the ends of the rectangular table, clearly here to observe, as they lacked the pens and notepads like everyone else.

"Let's begin," Leigh said, plopping a briefcase on the table and flipping its latches in one fluid motion. Wires jumped out, which she pushed aside. "First, we're going to take some blood from you. We'll study it back at home to see what our machines say." She pulled a syringe from the briefcase along with four empty vials, each three inches in length.

"Go right ahead," Martin said, sticking his arm out and pulling his sleeve up to his shoulder.

The others took out papers and scribbled notes while Leigh drew the blood. Strike and Tarik looked around, possibly bored, possibly anxious. Martin couldn't tell for sure. Having his blood drawn had always made Martin a bit woozy, and this time was no exception. Tarik recognized this and left the room to bring back bottles of water for everyone.

As soon as she packed away the full vials, Leigh pulled the wires in front of her and separated them from the tangled mess they had formed. She flattened them across the table, creating what looked like a tree with bare branches spreading out. She stood, wires in hand, and shuffled behind Martin. "You can stay seated. I'm going to strap these to your head so we can measure your brain activity before, during, and after time is frozen."

Martin noticed a slight elevation in her voice as she spoke this final line. Her fingers danced around his head, pushing down in random places as she pressed the wires into position. All of the wires converged at the base of his neck and twisted into a thick bundle that connected to a small black box.

"What does that thing do?" Martin asked after Leigh had sat down.

"That records everything going on with your brainwaves. The technology is the same in terms of *how* we measure, all that's different is where that data is stored and sent. We have a laboratory full of scientists back in Europe waiting for this data to be transmitted so they can start analyzing. The video feed you'll be on with Steffan will also be sent their way as soon as we wrap up today."

"And when will you analyze it? I assume you're the best if you came all this way."

"We're boarding the jet immediately after we wrap up here today, except for Brigham, of course. He'll be staying back for the medicine. As soon as we arrive home, we'll join our teams and analyze all of this data."

"This is a huge deal, Martin," Strike cut in. "This is the first test of this kind. We once had a chance to draw blood from an enemy who we learned was warm, but he died before we could run him through an experiment like this. We have no expectations, only hopes of learning something new."

Martin nodded. *So I'm the lab rat for Warm Souls. Be sure to put that in my obituary.*

"I see," he said. "Why haven't you just studied Steffan, then?"

"We have. He's not actually warm—just someone who can freeze time—so we didn't learn anything valuable from his tests."

"How do you know I can't freeze time?"

"Can you freeze time, Martin?"

"Well, I don't think so."

"That's how we know. It's not an ability that lies dormant."

Steffan nodded and stood up. "It's more like a sixth sense, you could say. Enough with the questions. Let's start!"

Megan strolled to the tripod, pushed a button on the camera and stood in front of the lens to speak. "Today is Monday, February 4, 2019. We're in Denver, Colorado, at the Road Runner offices with Commander Strike, Tarik Sadi, Steffan Privvy, Leigh Covington, Brigham Kelly, and myself, Megan Privvy. Our test subject is Martin Briar, who we have confirmed is a Warm Soul. Blood samples have been drawn, and the pre-examination tests are complete on his brain activity." She checked her watch. "I have a current time of 8:52 a.m., Mountain Standard Time."

Megan returned to her seat and gestured to Steffan to begin.

"Martin, please stand and go to the back of the room," Steffan said, his voice turning suddenly serious. "And take the black box with you."

Martin rose, a slight tremble working through his legs as he grabbed the box off the table. A palpable tension hung in the air as everyone inched forward in their seats, watching Martin cross the room. He stopped about forty feet away from the group of scientists and the tripod.

"You're good there," Steffan shouted. "I'll commence the freezing of time on my count of three. You will all be frozen, except for myself and Mr. Briar. You will not realize you're frozen, as your current perception of time will be temporarily halted until I unfreeze it. Since I'll be in direct contact with the camera, it will roll and capture our interaction. Are we all ready?"

He looked down the table of his colleagues, and each returned a silent nod, still not breaking their stares from Martin in the distance.

"Okay. On my count. Three . . . two . . . one."

95

Chapter 3

Martin expected a rumble of some sort, but apparently the freezing of time was as uneventful as the passing of regular time. He watched Steffan place his hands on his head, eyes shut, giving his entire concentration to the task of stopping time in its tracks.

No rumble. Just the blank stares of three scientists and two leaders of the Road Runners.

Steffan put his hands down and stood, slightly wobbling.

"How are you feeling?" Steffan shouted across the room.

"I'm fine," Martin replied. "What am I supposed to do?"

They could have been playing a prank on him by how fake they all appeared, looking like a panel of gawking judges on one of those shitty televised talent contests.

"Walk this way," Steffan said, coming out from behind the table. He positioned himself in the camera's view and turned to speak to it. "I can confirm that time is frozen. My colleagues are sitting at the table, unable to move. As you can see, Mr. Briar is mobile." He looked over his shoulder as Martin approached.

Martin took cautious steps, feeling like he had magically stepped into a photograph. Even though the others were in the room, it seemed more that he and Steffan were the only two people in the world. Gooseflesh broke across his body at the thought. He reached Steffan's side and joined the scientist in front of the camera.

"Martin, how are feeling?"

"I told you I feel fine."

"I need you to elaborate. Are there any kinds of side effects you're experiencing? Light-headedness, dizziness, wooziness?"

"No. I feel completely normal. How I always do."

"I see doubt in your eyes."

Martin pursed his lips, his brows furrowed at Steffan's accusatory tone. "This is hard to imagine as real, but I thought the same thing about time travel when I first experienced it."

"Is your memory still intact? Do you know where you are, what you're doing here, et cetera?"

"Yes. I'm in Denver, at the Road Runners' office, and we're testing my warmth."

"Very good. I want to take the camera out to the office, and perhaps out of the building. Martin, I want you to go out and interact however you see fit. Let's take these wires off your head so you can roam more freely."

Martin looked at Steffan with a cocked brow as he reached over and started tugging the wires off, stashing them next to the black box on the table.

"It's fine," Steffan assured him, and grabbed the camera from the tripod. He held it in a shaky hand and gestured for Martin to exit the conference room. "We'll put them back on when we return."

Martin shuffled by his frozen colleagues, reminding him of those wax museums where you can hang out with Elvis and Michael Jackson, only these were people he actually knew. And they definitely weren't wax.

As he passed them, he swore Tarik's eyes followed him, but chalked it up to paranoia. The pictures of Jesus Christ in his mom's old house had the same effect and always made him walk a little faster down the hallway. He did the same thing now and leapt toward the door, pulling it open to reveal the rest of the office.

Martin stopped in the doorway.

The office looked exactly the same: monitors flashing, Road Runners at their desks, knee-deep in work. But no one was moving, and a deafening silence blanketed the room. Martin's heart raced a tad quicker at the sight.

"It's okay, go ahead," Steffan said from behind, camera held high to record Martin's first interaction with the frozen world.

The scene reminded Martin of a haunted house around Halloween time. They often had several characters set up that looked fake, but there was always one who was real, waiting to jump out and scare the shit out of you. He waited for someone to make a sudden head turn and send him running back to the conference room, but it never happened. Everyone sat or stood exactly as they were.

"Did they know they were going to be frozen?" Martin asked over his shoulder, refusing to break his gaze ahead.

"No. There's no need to tell someone they're being frozen. They don't realize it, and when I unfreeze them, they just continue with what they were doing, unaware they ever stopped."

Martin stayed against the wall as he shuffled toward the kitchen. A man had apparently been speaking with a woman, pouring a cup of coffee from the pot, the brown liquid frozen in mid-air.

"So this is all normal?" Martin asked.

"Sure is. Pretty cool, don't you think?"

Martin didn't think it was cool, but rather disturbing.

"How many people have this power to freeze time?"

"Twenty-three that we know of for sure."

"And how many are warm like me?"

"You are the fourth known instance of someone being warm *without* the capability of freezing time."

"I still don't understand how the abilities are different."

"Those who can freeze time remain mobile when *they* perform the action. If someone else freezes time, that same person is not immune. If a Revolter were to freeze time, I'd be frozen right along with everyone else, unlike how I'm mobile now because *I* caused this."

"Doesn't this seem kind of dangerous? Does Chris have the ability to do this?"

Steffan nodded and shrugged his shoulders. "We don't believe he can freeze time, but he can certainly resist the freeze. It has its frightening parts, but that's why we're trying to figure this all out."

"How did you do it—freeze time?"

"It's hard to explain. It's sort of a telekinetic power, I guess. I have to completely concentrate on it until it happens."

"And you were born with it?"

"I dunno. It didn't start until I was in college. Fortunately, that's when I met Megan, and she was already a Road Runner."

"Right. You guys said you've been together for 30 years?"

Steffan cackled. "Yeah, that always gets a good reaction from people because we're both only 27. We met in 1987. I became a Road Runner, and we've been traveling through time ever since, never aging."

"So you never go back to your original time?"

"Rarely. We both lost our families to Victor—he's Chris's counterpart in Europe—so we don't have any reason to go back. We've built a life together trying to keep the world safe and wouldn't have it any other way. So, yes, it can be scary knowing this capability even exists for our enemies to use, but we suspect they're also figuring out how to use it to their advantage. I know Victor once made an attempt to assassinate our leader, Commander Blair, by freezing time, but failed because he is also warm—one of the four that we know of."

"Who are the other two?"

"One is a Revolter in Africa, and the other is an ex-Revolter who now lives in the middle of a forest in China. We tried recruiting him, but he swears to a life of neutrality and doesn't want to be bothered. He sleeps with guns in both hands, waiting for anyone to try and tell him otherwise. And there's also Chris, but we don't count him, for obvious reasons."

"So I'm the only one in the U.S. that has this ability?"

"You're the only one on this side of the ocean that is warm. That's why Chris won't stop until he gets you. Your ability is something he's only ever heard of."

"But isn't he hiding?"

Steffan snorted laughter. "Please. He's probably in Denver as we speak. I'm not convinced one bit that he's still in his house. He probably froze time and walked out the front door. And now everyone is in a panic. There's an infinite number of places to hide if you're Chris, and his silly mansion is at the bottom of that list. Enough with all of this talk – let's go for a walk outside."

Martin didn't realize how long they had been talking, and had no way of knowing for sure, either, as the clocks on the wall remained still, not ticking the day away. They had an entire conversation in the middle of the silent office, their words falling on literal deaf ears.

Steffan pushed by Martin and led them to the stairs. They went up, crossed through the marketing office that held a similar scene of employees mid-conversation, and rushed out the building.

A short flight of four stairs descended from the building to the sidewalk below, but Martin stayed at the top, keeping his back to the building as if it protected him. The scene outside reminded him of zombie apocalypse films where the roads were filled with cars, either abandoned or occupied by corpses.

Vehicles always lined the streets for metered parking downtown, but seeing dozens of cars in the middle of the road, drivers staring out the windshield, was both chilling and surreal.

"What the fuck?" Martin whispered under his breath, as Steffan jumped down the steps and ran into the middle of the street.

"Isn't it fun?" he shouted, twirling the camera in circles to capture the frozen world. A group of pedestrians, clearly all downtown office workers, filled the sidewalk. Some had their cell phones to their ears or held in front of them as they looked down. Others had grins on their faces as they enjoyed the fresh air. "Come down here!"

This is your reality now, Martin thought before going down the steps with the caution of tiptoeing through a minefield. The back of his mind still waited for one of these frozen people to jump at him.

When he reached the sidewalk, Martin looked up to a flock of birds frozen in flight, their dark V-shape contrasting against the bright blue sky. The nearest tree on the sidewalk stood slightly tilted, and he could only assume there was a strong morning breeze blowing its way through town.

"Wanna play hide-and-seek?" Steffan called from across the street, a cheesy grin on his face as he ducked behind a car.

The air was silent, so Martin heard him cackling like a teenage boy telling dirty jokes. As uptight as everyone in the Road Runners seemed, it was refreshing to see one of them enjoy life with childlike wonder. Steffan may have been alive for 50 years (or however the hell he calculated it), but he knew how to bask in the small pleasures in life.

I wonder how often this guy freezes time and goes playing in the middle of the street.

The thought of Steffan dancing in the middle of the cobblestone roads in Europe forced a grin.

"I'm not gonna come find you," he shouted back. "But you're right, this is pretty cool."

Martin approached a car in the middle of the road, noticing the driver through the rolled down window. It was an older man with a cigarette pinched between his lips, his left hand on the wheel, and his right hand on the radio dial, the gray clouds frozen still from the orange embers on the cigarette's tip. He debated plucking the cigarette from the man's mouth, but couldn't find the courage to do it. All of the people looked eerily dead with their lifeless stares and eyes that never blinked.

But they also looked so alive. This wasn't a zombie apocalypse; these were people on their way around town.

Steffan came out from behind the car, grin still splattered across his face, camera pointing at Martin. "So what do you think?"

"It's definitely weird, but I can see why you like to have so much fun with it."

"Yeah, I suppose it's like any great gift. It can be used for good and fun, but others will use it for evil and selfish reasons."

"I can see that. So what exactly are we trying to figure out here?"

Steffan flipped the lid over the camera. "I don't know, man. It's a total shitshow. All of the Forerunners are losing their mind over Chris. They don't know if he's home plotting some great massacre, or hiding in an underground tunnel waiting for the search to die down. They've done some digging—literally—around the mansion, but have come up empty. And now they have you to consider, and everyone has an opinion on how to best utilize your skill. Commander Blair wants to send you into Chris's house with loaded guns and shoot everything in sight while it's all frozen. Commander Guang—from Asia—wants us to freeze time and have you infiltrate the Revolters' hideouts one by one and take whatever information you can gather. And Commander Strike is clueless. I think she's still losing sleep over the whole Sonya debacle. Maybe we should have just frozen time and let you slip that poison into her drink. She would've never known you were there."

"Why didn't you suggest that?"

"I did. I spoke with Julian while he was out in Europe for a trip. He thought it was brilliant and said he'd take the idea to Commander Strike. I never heard anything back, so figured she vetoed it, or he never told her."

"I don't see how she could veto that. She made the choice to move forward with the assassination, and never presented that as an option."

Steffan looked around as if one of the frozen people might be eavesdropping. "Look. Between you and me, Commander Strike isn't exactly the best fit for her position."

Martin's eyebrows shot all the way up to his slowly receding hairline.

"Don't get me wrong, she's an incredible woman, confident most the time. But when it comes to difficult decisions, she's extremely indecisive. It's like she waits for someone to make a choice for her, or wait for matters to play themselves out. You haven't been in the closed-door meetings since we arrived. She has no input, just defers to Tarik and lets him guide the discussion."

"Interesting. I don't get that impression at all."

"Of course not. She's charming and can radiate her authority over those who don't know better. You should hear the way she's perceived over in Europe."

"How's that?"

"Let's just say when news broke out about your gift—keep in mind, the first of your kind on this side of the pond—almost all of leadership started making jokes about how Strike would blunder the situation. We were all watching the footage of Chris getting shot by Andrei. We all saw him rise like he had only been punched in the chest. But we all had a feeling, in the back of our heads, that there wasn't going to be a different outcome. No way Strike would ever be the one to end Chris."

"Is that why you all came out here together?"

Steffan nodded, brushing a hand over his chin. "I'm afraid so. There are plenty of capable scientists here who could conduct this experiment, but we were afraid Strike would try to lead the way with them. With us, she's happy to take a back seat since we're the visitors who came all the way from Europe. She doesn't want to do anything to step on our toes and warrant an angry call from Commander Blair."

"So then what's really the plan?"

"We're going to keep running experiments. We want to know *why* you are able to resist time freezing, but I'll be honest, I think it's sheer luck. There's nothing concrete that stands out about you compared to this old man smoking his cigarette." He gestured to Martin's friend playing with the radio. "Commander Strike has one year left of her term. We're going to try and wait her out and hope that someone more decisive can get elected and set a plan in stone."

Martin crossed his arms and stroked his chin. "I didn't realize this was so political."

"Oh yeah, more than you know. All of our leaders are elected by the people, for the people. Everyone is on a one-term, two-year limit to ensure ideas are kept fresh. That alone cuts all the nonsense out of the politics; no one really bothers campaigning extensively for such a short term and never has to worry about re-election."

"Are you ever going to run?"

"Nah, it's not for me. I like conducting my research and contributing to the big picture that way." Steffan looked around again at the frozen cars in the middle of the road. "We should head back in. Not nice leaving everyone frozen while we have all the fun."

Steffan howled laughter to the sky and turned to go back up the stairs to their office.

Martin followed, still trying to figure out how all of this Road Runner business worked. Apparently, Commander Strike wasn't taken seriously by her peers, something he'd need to keep in mind in his future interactions with her.

96

Chapter 4

Returning inside, Steffan had unfrozen time as they walked back down the stairs to the office. The bustling floor of Road Runners remained oblivious that they had just been frozen, and continued with their work as normal, paying no attention to Martin and Steffan as they strolled back to the conference room.

The scientists asked Martin what he thought of the experiment, hanging to his every word as he explained the experience. They had a brief chat about the next steps, which included them all returning to Europe to analyze the data and review the video footage. Aside from Brigham, they all wished Martin safe travels into the future, and offered him a place to stay should he ever end up in Europe. They left with hugs and handshakes before departing.

Strike, Tarik, and Martin returned to Tarik's office, where the space felt welcoming again with the large crowd gone. Brigham posted up in another office down the hall to work on research.

"We need to swear you in under our official oath," Commander Strike said as they settled in. "If you plan to go to the future with other Road Runners, you need be an official member of this organization."

Martin agreed to the terms, and mentally pushed away all of the negativity Steffan had said about Strike. Was she really as clueless as he made her sound? From his personal experience, she seemed a savvy leader with all the traits of a demanding presence and powerful voice that one would expect of her position.

Maybe she was different in certain situations, but that didn't have to discount the work she had already done. She *did* authorize the mission that would've killed Chris; it wasn't her fault Sonya was already three steps ahead of everyone else.

"When should I expect to leave for the future?" Martin asked when Strike closed the office door.

"As soon as you're ready," Tarik said, sitting down behind his desk, his brown eyes studying Martin.

"Let's execute this oath, and you can head there right now if you want," Strike said, remaining by the door. "Please stand and face me, and hold your right hand over your heart."

Martin obliged, standing in the middle of the room like a schoolboy ready to recite the Pledge of Allegiance.

"Please answer my questions," Strike said. "Do you, Martin Briar, vow to uphold the integrity of the Road Runners by never putting yourself above the greater good for your own personal reasons?"

"I do."

"Do you swear to use your abilities for the improvement of the world, and not for the collapse of modern society as we know it?"

"I do."

"Do you vow to kill Chris Speidel, should the opportunity ever present itself?"

"I do."

"Do you vow to do as instructed by the Road Runners, no matter how difficult the task?"

"I do."

"Last, and most importantly, do you vow to keep the secrets of our operations from anyone outside of the organization, with the exception of immediate, household family?"

"I do."

"Perfect. With that said, welcome—officially—to the Road Runners.

You are now cleared to go on missions on our behalf." Strike stuck out a hand to officially seal his membership with the team.

"Thank you."

"Normally we have a small celebration, but we can postpone that until you come back," Tarik said. "Now that you're ready, let's discuss the year 2064."

Tarik gazed at Strike as she crossed the room to stand beside him.

"Martin," she said. "I need you to understand that everything we've mentioned about the future is not an exaggeration—it's a dangerous time. We suggest you always cover as much skin as possible. Wear gloves, hats, scarves, whatever you need to make sure no one can see the glow of your skin. They will shoot any known Road Runner without hesitation. We suspect they have orders to not kill you, seeing as Chris wants you to himself, but we can't afford to assume that is completely true."

"Why is it so dangerous?" Martin asked, sitting on the edge of his chair.

"Between now and 2064, Revolters infiltrate the government, both locally and nationally. They spark fear into their supporters. Fear of anyone not like them."

"Fear of who?"

"Poor people, minorities, handicapped people. Basically anyone who isn't rich or prominent in society. Every government program that was designed to assist those in need has been erased by 2064. The country basically runs on the wealthy and leaves the rest to kill each other in the streets; they literally deliver crates of guns to the middle of these poor neighborhoods just so everyone can shoot each other."

"That's sick."

"It's a war zone. You need to always be wary of your surroundings. If you walk down the wrong block, and they recognize you as an outsider, they'll jump you and likely kill you for your wallet. No police patrol these areas; no one cares."

"You're going to give me something to protect myself, right?"

"Yes. Protection is always provided. We'll give you a handgun to travel with, but when you get there you'll want to head over to one of our weapons warehouses—they're in discreet locations just like our offices. You can go there any time for more ammunition or if you want a new weapon."

"I'd recommend the most powerful gun they have," Tarik said. "In the areas that do have police, you'll see them with fully automatic Uzis."

"Don't have any run-ins with the police," Strike said. "They will throw you in jail for any reason, and if you have to face a judge, you're toast. The legal system has also been overtaken by Revolters—they actually started there before moving to the political stage."

"So what *can* I do?"

"We'll have someone with experience in the future lead you. Save any specific questions for them, as they'll have a more concrete answer."

"Okay. I get it, but are we going to talk about an actual plan for getting the medicine?"

Strike looked to Tarik, who returned an uneasy stare.

"We don't really make plans for missions this far into the future. Plans require research, which require Road Runners to spend time in that era," Tarik said.

"We don't send Road Runners to any time period after 2050 unless they specifically request it," Strike said, a hint of irritation floating beneath her voice.

"So then who's coming with me?" Martin asked.

"We put out an offer for volunteers. There are still plenty of Road Runners who *want* to conduct research in the future and know the risks associated with it."

"You'll be fine, Martin," Tarik said. "You'll be with a group of experienced Road Runners who are prepared for this mission. Stay aware of your surroundings, confirm your decisions before doing anything, and you'll make it."

"What if Chris finds me?"

Strike paced around the desk and faced the door, her back to Martin and Tarik as she seemed to look for words to fall out of the sky. "I don't want you to worry about Chris. We have our eyes on him. He's in his mansion.

If we think you're in any danger, we'll send word for your return."

Martin remained silent, remembering everything Steffan had told him about how no one actually knew where Chris was. He thought he heard doubt in Strike's voice, but chalked it up to the new knowledge he had just learned.

"I'll have to trust you on that. Is it possible he's hiding in the future if we have no presence there?"

"He's in his mansion," Strike snapped.

Martin knew Chris could time travel through simple mind power—the old man had admitted as much. But was Strike in so much denial that she thought everyone else was too dumb to know that as well? Her adamance frustrated Martin, so he dropped the topic before he said anything he might regret. Besides, he didn't have any proof of Steffan's claims. When did trusting gossip ever work out for anyone?

"When will I get to meet the people I'm traveling with?" Martin asked.

"They're in town already. Whenever you're ready to go, we'll call them all in for a brief meeting and you'll be on your way. We have very specific instructions about traveling into the future, and we need to make sure everyone is on the same page. For safety reasons, of course."

"Well, I'm ready. I have nothing else to wait for."

Strike looked to Tarik with her eyebrows raised, tossing her blond hair behind her head before returning her gaze to Martin. "Look, Martin. We know you're anxious to get there, but we really need to advise you to tie up loose ends here at home. Do you even have a written will for all the money you have? Have you said goodbye to your mother?"

"I don't see how that's any of your business."

"It's not our business, but we've witnessed enough instances to know that these types of matters should be addressed before going into the 2060's."

"It's like you're going off to war," Tarik chimed in, his fingers rapping nervously on his desk. "This isn't some glory trip back to the 1920's to experience prohibition and try all the underground moonshine. There is no glory in the future, and you'll see that within five minutes of arriving."

"And we're not saying you'll get killed," Strike added. "But you should understand that the odds of that will increase dramatically."

Martin's fingers started to fiddle on his leg. All *he* wanted to do was get the medicine and come home. And all *they* wanted to do was provide him a never-ending list of reasons to not go. *My mind is made up, people. I'm not backing out.*

They watched him juggle his thoughts, face scrunched into what probably appeared as confusion, but was actually anxiety trying to blow through his head.

"I don't want my mom to worry. I've already told her I'm going to get this cure for her. Why is this such a concern for you?"

"Because if she doesn't know, then it falls on us to deliver the news. We're adamant about providing support to the family members of our team. In a distant way, they're a part of us."

Martin imagined a world where he dies in 2064, leaving his mother alone to care for herself while her mind fades to darkness. The final days of her life would be spent in a confined room, staring at the walls, having no memory of her son, her family, her life. She would've lived an entire life—a full life—only to have no recollection of any of it by the time the reaper came to escort her to the abyss.

"Give me three hours," Martin said. "I'll go home, and I'll be back here in three hours. I don't want to waste another second."

"We can do that," Strike said. "We'll place the calls to those joining you on this trip and make sure we're all ready to meet here."

"Thank you. I'll see you then."

Martin stood and left Strike and Tarik in the office without another word.

97

Chapter 5

Martin pulled into his driveway half an hour later and scrambled into the house. His mom lay on the living room couch, a romantic comedy playing on the TV.

"Marty," she said, jolting up, clearly startled. "I didn't know when I'd see you again. Are you already back from your special trip?" Martin watched his mother stand, her body frail and thin, her left arm twitching as she dragged her feet toward him. She still managed a smile, though, and he recognized the beauty he'd always remember her for.

"Sit down, Mom," he said, meeting her and helping her back to the couch.

Her mind had already taken a turn for the worse by the time Martin checked in to the Road Runners' training program. He had told her where he was going and that it was all so he could get her medicine. He explained this numerous times, as she forgot everyday leading up to his departure. She was still functional, simply an extremely forgetful mind. He had no plans of stopping home until he had the medicine in hand, but here he was having to explain himself once more.

"Not yet. I'm leaving in a couple hours."

"Oh. Did you forget something?"

Martin feared she hadn't even realized ten weeks had passed since they last saw each other. She spoke relaxed, as if he had just left the house this morning.

"Not really. I just wanted to come back and say goodbye. Everyone has assured me that this is a dangerous trip and that I should come say goodbye in case anything happens to me."

Tears immediately welled in her eyes, giving them a glossy coat over their redness. "Marty, if I'm the only reason you're doing this, then please don't. It's not worth it."

"You're worth it; I don't need any other reason."

"Marty, I'll be fine. There are medications that slow the process down."

"All that does is drag out the inevitable, Mom. I can't sit by and watch you fade, knowing I could've done something to stop it. I'm going, and I didn't come here for a discussion about it."

The tears that had pooled in her eyes now streamed down her face in moist trails. "Can I tell you something, Marty?"

He nodded and sat down next to her on the couch.

"You sound just like . . . " she continued.

"Like who?"

"Your father."

Martin's heart skipped a beat; she had rarely spoken of his father since his death.

"How do you mean?"

"He had that same look in his eyes that you have now. Now that you've lost weight, you *look* like him."

As blank of a mind as she had shown over the past weeks during their phone conversations, a new tone took over as she spoke about her late husband. In it, Martin heard years of familiarity, as if his father was someone her mind would never forget, no matter how bad the Alzheimer's advanced. Her voice came out confident and strong.

"Mom, I don't understand why you're saying all this. Dad's been gone for over forty years and you've never told me anything about him."

"There's plenty I can tell you, but none of it matters anymore. Your dad was two different people. There was the man I fell in love with, and the man I didn't know. I have a confession that you should probably know before I forget it all."

Martin subconsciously sat on the couch next to Marilyn and inched closer to her, a fruity stench oozing from her freshly washed hair. "What is it?" The thought of traveling into the future now seemed so distant. His mother had wrapped him in the claws of a story he thought he'd never hear.

"Your father didn't die from a heart attack, Marty. The truth is, I don't have any idea what happened to him."

"Wh-what do you mean? Is he still alive?" Martin's throat suddenly felt as if it were being clenched shut by a heavy fist.

Marilyn shrugged. "He could be. I have no idea. But what you said, Marty, is the same thing he said to me before he left forever."

"What did I say?" he asked in a defensive voice.

"The medicine. The last time I saw your father, I had a bad cold: runny nose, fever, all the bad you can think of. He insisted to go out and get me some medicine. I argued with him for a bit, but I didn't have the energy. So, he left. Off to get me medicine, and I never saw him again."

Martin's jaw hung open. "I don't understand. Why did you tell us he had a heart attack?"

"I couldn't bring myself to admit the truth, especially at your young age. I battled a lot of demons in those following days. I felt like a complete failure for marrying someone who would just walk out on his family like that. I figured pretending he had died was easier to explain. If I didn't, it would have been nothing but a life of questions and doubt for all of us."

Martin sat back, not quite slouching into the soft couch, but needing a moment to gather himself. The truth, a lifelong truth, hit him on the head with the force of a speeding diesel truck.

"I'm sorry, Mom, I can't handle this right now. I really do have to get your medicine, and I *will* be back."

Martin stood, hot anger filling his gut that he wasn't sure was directed toward his mother or his father. The new revelation made him dizzy with confusion, and somewhere in the deepest, most intimate fibers of his being, he already knew he wanted to travel back to this particular night of his father abandoning the family, and learn what exactly happened.

Yeah, and we all saw how well that turned out this last time.

He shook the idea out of his head, the thought overwhelming his already flustered mind.

"Do what you need to do," Marilyn said. "But if you claim this could be the last time we speak to each other, I just thought you should know the truth."

With tears welling in his eyes, Martin leaned toward his mother. "I love you, Mom. And this truth doesn't change anything. You raised me and I'm happy with how my life turned out." These last words were ones he never thought he'd hear leave his lips. While he had suffered incomparable pain throughout his life, he had no regrets. "Now. I'm leaving, I'm getting your medicine, and I'll be back here within two hours at the latest."

Marilyn nodded, keeping her lips pursed as Martin kissed her one final time on the forehead before turning and walking out of the house.

When he closed the front door, he stood on the top step of the porch and ran a hand down the smooth stone walls that lined the mansion's main entrance. He had his new life waiting for him right here in 2019, and it would always be there. All he wanted was to make sure that his mother would be there with him, too.

98

Chapter 6

Martin drove like a maniac, weaving through the traffic that had formed during his quick hour at home. He had intended to draft a document to serve as his last will and testament should he die on this trip, but didn't foresee this elephant of a revelation being dropped on his head by his mother.

He thought back to the morning of his childhood when his mother had sat at the kitchen table in their small ranch home, crying with stacks of papers spread out across the table.

When he and his brother had entered the kitchen, she sat them down and told them their father had suffered a heart attack in the middle of the night. She hadn't mentioned that he was dead, forcing Martin to ask the dreaded question.

Marilyn had refused to say it aloud, only nodding her head in confirmation, and now it all made sense knowing it was a lie. It ended up as the main turning point in Martin's life, losing his father as a child just starting middle school, but his mother had stepped up in a heroic way, ensuring nothing skipped a beat in their household.

He watched the sky and prayed this mission would end within a day. He had no desire to study the future and see what a shithole the world would one day become. *Just give me the medicine and get me the fuck back.*

When he arrived to the office, Martin parked and waited in the car.

His stomach throbbed with anxiety, and his legs turned to mush as they bounced beneath the steering wheel. He hadn't felt nerves like this since his first trip to 1996. A sense that death was waiting for him on the other side of this trip had swelled within. Death or failure now seemed more plausible than success and a happy life.

For the first time, Martin considered turning around and dumping the Juice down the sink. The Road Runners certainly moved with an uncanny urgency, a trait that was already rubbing off on Martin, and kept pushing him into rushed decisions.

You were already thinking of the next mission after this. You're hooked. And since when? What happened to the old Martin who was content with a glass of whisky and a cigar?

"He died when Izzy was murdered and thrown into the lake," Martin said, pushing open the car door and stumbling onto the sidewalk. He faced the building with his hands on his hips, as if he were about to enter the old Colosseum for battle. "Just take it one day at a time. One hour at a time. And everything will be okay."

He entered the building and marched to the back of the office where the stairs led down to his upcoming fate.

* * *

Strike and Tarik were gathered in Tarik's office, the door open as they carried on with an apparently casual conversation. Tarik saw Martin and waved him in. No one in the office paid him any attention.

"Well, that was quick," Strike said, standing up to meet Martin at the doorway. "Your team is here, in the main conference room. Let's head down and meet them."

She pushed by Martin and led them to the conference room where he had just experienced his first freezing of time with Steffan a couple hours ago. When they entered, the room was restored to its typical setup of scattered tables and chairs.

A group of three men gathered around a table beside the entryway, the same area where the scientists had sat while Steffan and Martin danced around on camera.

The three men turned their heads in unison as the group entered the room, and Martin was taken back by a massive dark-skinned man who stood and approached them.

His bald head gleamed under the lighting, and Martin noticed a horrific scar that ran from the man's left eye to his jaw. He towered over Martin, standing damn close to seven feet tall, and stuck out an arm that looked bigger than Martin's entire torso. "You must be Martin," he said, gripping Martin's hand. "I've heard a lot about you and your training. Impressive for an older man coming off an injury like yours."

Is this gigantic man actually complimenting my physical abilities? Martin thought the man could easily pick him up and chuck him across the room like a sack of potatoes.

"My name's Gerald. Gerald Holmes."

"Nice to meet you, Gerald. I'm not sure what you mean about training. I don't think I did anything that remarkable."

"I'm good friends with Staff Master Collins. Don't underestimate how well you did. He raved about you and your dedication. Working hard is ninety percent of the battle."

"I'll take your word for it."

"Gerald here is the one I mentioned who has been to the future before," Strike added.

"That's where I got my scar, but we can talk about that later."

"He'll sort of be the one in charge since he knows his way around and knows what to expect."

Sort of?

Now Martin picked apart every word spoken by Commander Strike. Her last statement sounded unsure of herself, revealed her to be lacking confidence in her decisions. Wasn't she supposed to be in charge of everything? If she wanted Gerald to lead this mission, then she should just say it.

The two others had gathered behind Gerald, hidden behind his massive frame that reminded Martin of poor John Coffey from *The Green Mile.*

"Brigham?" Martin asked, seeing a familiar face. "You're coming with us now?"

The scientist nodded. "I figured why not take advantage? We never really get out and study in the real world. I'm terrified and excited."

The other man, who stood eye-level with Martin and boasted a slight potbelly, stepped to the front. "I'm Webster Baldwin, but you can call me Web. Or Baldy. Doesn't really matter to me." Webster had ruffled black hair and droopy brown eyes that looked depressed.

"Web is our brains," Gerald said. "He'll be the one suggesting our best courses of action, as he has studied the geography of the area."

"I know the places to avoid, the places to relax, and the secret ways into places we shouldn't be," Web added. "Think of me as working in the background to keep us all safe. On that note, shall we begin?"

Martin's stomach drained of all fluids as he looked at this group of men he'd be going into the future with. Someone thought it was a good idea to incorporate Martin and Gerald as equals, at least in terms of fieldwork.

This has to be a mistake, Martin thought. Sure, he had felt accomplished throughout training, even strong and confident, but how would this work with him being Gerald's right-hand man in a gunfight with Revolters? He had the skills to hit a target when there was no pressure aside from a handful of people watching, but to be thrust into the nastiest part of this war with no prior experience seemed ludicrous. He expected to be going with a whole team of Geralds.

This has *to be a mistake. A clerical error.*

"Yes, let's gather around and get started," Strike said, and everyone returned to the table.

"Commander Strike?" Martin asked. "Can I have a word with you?"

She nodded. "One moment, everyone," she said to the group, and pulled open the door to step outside the conference room. When the door clicked shut, she asked, "Is everything all right?"

"Yeah, I'm fine. I'm trying to understand this team I'm going with. It seems Gerald is the only one who's physically capable of . . . battling Revolters."

Strike scrunched her face in confusion. "This is a standard squad that we send into the future: two combat-savvy Road Runners, and two scientists or researchers."

"I'm the other combat person?"

"Do you not think you are?"

"Well, no."

"Martin," she sighed, her blue eyes swimming back and forth. "I don't know why you think so lowly of yourself. Have you not looked in the mirror lately? You are just as physically capable as Gerald. You're not even going into war—this is more a stealth type of mission—but you still need to be strong and agile, which you are."

The truth was Martin hadn't looked in the mirror for quite some time. Sure, he'd catch a glance in the morning when brushing his teeth and washing his face, but he no longer examined himself, terrified to see more gray hairs and wrinkles than he'd like to acknowledge.

"It just seems weird to me that you make the future sound like this horrific place and want to send in Gerald with three people who probably shouldn't be there."

"You wouldn't be going if you didn't pass your training." Strike crossed her arms and furrowed her brow. "You do remember this is *your* mission, right? *You* asked me for this as a favor. I warned against it, but *you* insisted. What were you expecting, for us to just go do this for you?"

"Well, no. I—"

She raised a finger, once again flashing her authority that Martin had originally known. Like Steffan said, she was a great leader in one-on-one situations. "I don't want to hear another word about this, Martin. I put this mission together for you as a thank-you for almost dying in the Sonya debacle. I'm not undoing it." She kept her finger raised while her stern words hung in the air for a few seconds. "Now, can we go back in there and discuss this mission with the rest of the team?"

Martin nodded and followed Commander Strike back into the conference room.

99

Chapter 7

"Let's get to business," Strike barked as she stormed into the room, Martin trailing behind.

Everyone was seated and looked down to the table as they sensed an immediate shift in Strike's mood. Martin sat between Tarik and Brigham.

"Gerald," Strike said, nodding to him.

Gerald had a notebook that he flipped open and ran a finger down.

"Okay, lots to cover," Gerald said in his booming voice. "To start, we'll be driving over to the location of our weapons warehouse and transporting from there. The building is located in Watkins, about a thirty-minute drive east of downtown in the plains. It's underground and will be considered the safest place to return should you come into trouble in 2064."

"Is there something wrong with this office in 2064?" Brigham asked.

"Yes, it doesn't exist." Gerald said this matter-of-fact. "It was raided and eventually bombed by the Revolters when they learned it was a Road Runner office. I think that happened in 2048." Gerald looked into the air as if he were reliving the event.

Strike glared across the table to Martin.

"Now as far as the actual mission," Gerald continued. "We know the medicine is housed at three separate hospitals in the city. Web, you'll need to find which hospital is the best one for us to try and take it from.

The meds are stored in the basement of each facility, with two armed guards at each door. The guards are Revolters—not hospital staff—so we'll also need to figure out how to get by them without causing any gunfire—they will shoot any of us on sight if they find out we're Road Runners. On that note, special attire will be provided when we arrive to help us blend in around town."

"How are we getting around?" Brigham asked.

"We have a car, but need to be wary of where we park it, because it can be stolen if we have to leave it in a shady place. Minor detail, but plan to do a good amount of walking once in town."

Gerald referred to his notebook before speaking again.

"One thing to note is that you will always be on camera once you step outside. Cameras cover every inch of space—this government likes to watch its people closely. There are areas that even have hidden microphones, so it's imperative to not speak about any Road Runner business out loud, or anything negative about the New Age Revolution, for that matter. If the microphones pick up any key words, there will be a squad of Revolters hunting you down. Is that understood?"

Everyone nodded, shifting in their seats.

What the fuck kind of world is this? Martin wondered.

"To further build off this," Gerald continued. "If we're out in public, avoid striking up conversations with random people. The Revolters go undercover to talk with people in coffee shops, grocery stores, wherever, in an attempt to learn of their political leanings. They'll try to get you to admit you don't like the current administration. If you say anything along these lines, they'll either arrest you or shoot you, depending on the severity of what you say. It's best to just not say anything. The right of free speech has been replaced by the right of silence."

Brigham and Web both nodded excitedly at the revelation. While it terrified Martin, they clearly wanted to learn more.

"Is it President Poe who's running the country in 2064?" Web asked.

"Yes. President Poe. And it's an election year, so the crazies are out even more than normal. President Poe is running for his fifth term in

2064, and he'll easily win. He was elected in 2048 under the official political party known as The Revolution. Halfway through his second term, Revolters had taken control of the Supreme Court, the House, and the Senate. He had zero resistance to abolishing the Twenty-Second Amendment and has been in power ever since."

Brigham and Web went from nodding to scribbling notes in their own notepads.

"Question," Martin said, not sure if he was allowed to speak up. "Are there any *good* people in the future?"

Strike smirked as Gerald answered. "Of course. There are Road Runners, and there are lots of people who stayed after the Revolters came into power. They just can't speak of any of it. There are even people who appear to be hardcore Revolters, but it's just an act to survive."

"How do we know who's who?"

"We don't. That's why you don't talk to anyone about it."

"The future sounds like pure chaos," Brigham said, running his fingers in circles over the table.

"That's a good way of putting it," Gerald said.

"Where are we staying?" Brigham asked.

"Just outside downtown. I'm not allowed into the city because I'm black, unless I were to go undercover as a janitor. We'll figure those details out later."

"Isn't outside of the city dangerous?" Martin asked, not fully processing Gerald's previous statement.

"Yes, but as long as we stick together, we'll be fine. People don't really mess with me, and if you're with me, they'll leave you alone, too. Never go out by yourself, especially at night. Does anyone have any questions?"

Everyone shook their heads as Commander Strike stood up. "I don't have a question, but I'd like to say something."

Gerald nodded at her to continue.

"I want you all to know that Sonya was spotted last night in 2064, and she's apparently under the protection of the Revolters. We believe this is purely a coincidence that she's in this year, but we may have a new

605

mission for you when you arrive. Research is still being conducted, and we've commissioned a team of scouts to the area for the sake of tracking her down. She's in downtown Denver and will likely never step foot outside of it."

"Are you talking about having us hunt her down?" Martin asked.

Strike stared at Gerald as she responded, sure to avoid Martin's eyes. "It's possible, but I can't confirm that yet. It depends what information our team comes back with. If it's plausible to capture or kill her, we may have your squad carry out that mission."

"Commander Strike," Gerald cut in. "I don't know if this is the best squad for such a task."

"It's not. But you'll be there. Don't worry, we won't put you into a position for failure. If we decide to move forward with a new mission, it'll be one that fits within your qualifications."

Silence hung in the room as Gerald wrote in his notebook, a frown on his face that clearly showed his displeasure with the news.

"You will all do great," Strike finally said. "I wouldn't have brought this up if I felt differently."

The rest nodded, but Martin remained still. He wondered if this was a desperate ploy to right her wrongs from the previous botched attempt. Would the highest ranking official of the Road Runners really put four of her own people at risk for the sake of correcting a mistake?

A day ago Martin wouldn't have believed it to be true, but now knowing how political everything functioned behind the scenes, he saw no reason to doubt it.

"I know we'll do just fine," Gerald said. Tarik had stayed quiet throughout the meeting, examining his fingers and nodding on cue when appropriate. "We have one final matter of business, and that is our weapons to travel with."

Gerald nodded to Tarik, who pulled out a briefcase and set it on the table, flipping the latches to swing open the lid and reveal four black pistols. Tarik grabbed each pistol and slid them across the table to the four men.

"These are your pistols," Gerald explained. "We're only taking these with us in case something happens during our transfer into 2064."

"I thought we were transferring to and from our weapons warehouse," Brigham said.

"We are. It's just better to be safe than sorry. You never know what will happen in the future. Now, with these in your possession, we're ready to go to 2064. Are there any more questions?"

Everyone looked around the table, realizing there was no turning back.

"I'll get the car ready," Gerald said, and left the room.

100

Chapter 8

Chris sat in his office and clicked through the different camera angles on his computer screen. While they hadn't approached his house in a week, they still watched him from the woods.

"Cocksucking Road Runners," he said, knowing they'd go away soon. How productive was it for them to spend six hours each day staring at his barricaded mansion? It had been particularly entertaining when they tried knocking down the barricade. They tried sledgehammers, drills, and even dynamite. Outside of that effort, it had remained an uneventful series of days that seemed to run on the same loop.

The barricade was designed to withstand any form of attack. When his team designed it with a stronger steel from the future, the lead engineer had told Chris, "They asked what happens when an unstoppable force meets an immovable object. Well, this here is the immovable object, and I'd hate to see what happens to anyone trying to move it."

They had laughed about this during the test run when they ran a bulldozer into the steel, and howled when it simply rolled its way up the house before tipping onto its back.

He wished they would've tried more, but what could you expect from the lazy Road Runners? With one click of a button he could raise the barricades and expose his house for all to see again, but that would take all the fun out of the game. He knew Commander Strike was having fits trying to figure out where he was, when in reality he hadn't left the place for one second.

If they truly thought I was hiding here, they'd keep coming back and trying to find a way in.

This exact situation was planned for. Food lined the pantry, enough for an entire two months to supply the twenty-five Revolters and fifty prisoners. Five Revolters were dead, meaning they had a couple extra days of supplies.

Chris had no plan. He could've gone to another time, but knew there were thousands of eyes on the lookout. Duane, his closest confidant, had advised the same approach as soon as the barricades had gone up. "This will all blow over," he said.

Duane remained in the mansion with the other Revolters who were fortunate enough to not get shot down by the Road Runners hiding in the trees. He visited with Chris at least three times a day in his office, ensuring the old man had kept what remained of his sanity intact. It had been a week and a half that they were trapped in the house, and while no one had quite yet cracked under the pressure of cabin fever, Duane informed Chris that the general mood was growing antsy among the Revolters.

"You've brainwashed them into machines who love to get work done, and right now they can't. They have pent-up energy that will need to be released." Duane had reluctantly explained this a day before, creating a new problem that Chris didn't have the energy for at the moment.

He slept on the matter and decided to open the mansion in the next five days to let his soldiers out to perform their duties. They'd be ready for whatever Road Runners awaited in the woods, and the more rabid they became with anxiety, the better chances they'd have at killing some of them.

Chris leaned back in his chair, hands crossed behind his snowy head, and watched the monitor that showed the mansion's front entrance. A small black figure appeared in the distance, and Chris bolted upright. He watched it grow bigger as it walked through the open field toward the mansion. His finger dashed across the desk and planted on the small intercom button.

"Duane, to my office please."

Chris rapped his fingers on the shiny oak desk, watching the figure grow bigger with each step it took. When the barricades had first gone up, the Road Runners sent over some of their people to study the unbreakable steel. But a week had passed since they last sent anyone, leaving Chris to wonder who would come knocking on the door after so long.

The office door swung open to reveal Duane, dressed in his usual stay-at-home attire of sweatpants and a baggy hoodie. "Everything okay?" he asked, closing the door behind him, and running a hand through his flowing black hair, his gray eyes bloodshot with fatigue.

"I think so. We appear to have a visitor. Have you checked the cameras?"

"Not in a few hours. What's going on?"

Chris pointed to his screen and waited for Duane to come around the desk for a look.

The figure was still 100 yards away, but close enough to see its hands held up in a typical "don't shoot" position.

"Who's that?" Duane asked, eyes bulging at the screen.

"I'd assume it's one of our friends, but why come back after so many days?"

"They could know you're still here."

"How?"

"Because you're not anywhere else."

"Don't be a smart-ass."

"It's true. They're not exactly stupid. You do know their entire purpose now is to kill you—they don't care about anything else."

The figure reached the front steps, hands still held in the air. The presumed Road Runner on their front porch was dressed for the weather: a heavy jacket, a thick knit cap, and a neck cover that hid their face up to a pair of ski goggles. The person waved a hand, while keeping the other elevated and still.

"Do they want to talk to us?" Duane asked.

"I'd assume so."

The figure twirled in a slow-motion circle to show that they had no weapons on them. Even if they had, their current attire would make it extremely difficult to pull out a gun and start shooting, especially with the thick mittens over their hands.

"What do you want to do?" Duane asked.

"We can talk to them from here, right? Without having to drop the barricade?"

Duane nodded, as if he should've remembered this. The design had been constructed over two decades ago, and it was impossible to remember all of its features, especially with this being their first time using it.

"Hold on!" Chris shouted at the screen, as if the person could hear him.

Duane ran to the nearest cabinet and rummaged through files of paperwork. He muttered to himself as he flipped through them, pulling out a handbook the size of an old encyclopedia. He flipped open the book and ran a finger up and down the pages until he found what they needed.

The visitor remained a statue with both hands in the air.

"Do you have a headset?" Duane asked. "The kind with the microphone attached."

"Of course." Chris opened a desk drawer and pulled out the headset he used to place calls with his counterparts around the world.

Duane explained what Chris needed to click on the screen, within the security system software.

As soon as the connection was made, the crackle of white noise mixed with wind filled Chris's ears. He looked up to Duane and nodded.

"Now you just talk," Duane explained.

"Hello?" Chris said, not moving his eye from the monitor.

"Chris!" a man's voice cried out, youthful in its tone. "Chris, I just want to talk with you. I have no weapons, just need a word."

The volume was loud enough in the headset that Duane could hear the response.

"Who are you?"

The man lowered his arms, probably exhausted from holding them up for so long.

"I'd rather not say my name, but I am a Road Runner."

"Obviously you're a Road Runner. I must say it's pretty brave of you to come this close with no protection. I can have you shot dead in seconds."

"I know that, sir. But I don't know how else to show you that I'm here for a peaceful visit. Can I come in to speak with you?"

Duane frowned and shook his head so hard Chris thought it might fly off.

"No," Chris said. "We can't let you in here, I'm sure you understand."

"That's fine," the Road Runner said. "This will have to do. I have a proposition for you."

Chris looked to Duane with his eyebrows raised. Duane twirled a finger in a gesture that said *keep him talking.*

"Let's hear it," Chris said coldly.

"We know you have our people held hostage in your basement," the Road Runner said. "We also know we're reaching a crossroads in this war. I can give you something valuable to us, if you release those you're holding hostage."

"Spit it out already. Tell me what you're offering." Chris rose from his seat and subconsciously slammed his fists on the desk.

"I can give you our leader."

Chris sat back down and rubbed his forehead. Duane returned to his studious frown as both men stared at the monitor in shock.

"Are you referring to Strike?" Chris asked, sitting forward.

"The one and only," the Road Runner said, and Chris was sure he heard a smile in the man's voice.

"What's your angle?" Chris asked. "I thought you people were sworn to loyalty."

"My angle is simple: I want our people back. And we are loyal. I'm loyal to the Road Runners and everything we stand for. That doesn't mean I need to be loyal to Commander Strike."

A traitor? Chris wondered. In all of his time learning about the Road Runners and their rapid growth, he'd never heard of such betrayal. He supposed it was only a matter of time before corruption worked its way into their system. The more people you involve in an organization, the more likely it becomes a bad apple will find its way into the pack.

"What do you think?" the man outside asked.

"Part of me doesn't believe you. This could be a bluff."

"I know you're a man of your word. And I assure you I am as well. A gentleman's agreement is all I'm proposing."

"How can I believe you when you won't even tell me your name?" Chris felt he was losing control of the conversation, causing a bubble of frustration to inflate.

"Who I am doesn't matter. I don't want you to think we're friends—I just want to make what I think is a fair trade. I have access to Commander Strike's schedule and can let you know exactly where she'll be at any given time."

Chris looked to Duane, who had remained a statue with his brows furrowed and his hand cupped over his chin, keeping his stare to the floor as if the secret of life were written down there.

"I need a minute," Chris said. "Don't go away."

He removed the headset and dropped it on the desk. Duane finally looked up, looking like someone had just shot his mother.

"What do we do?" Chris whispered.

Duane shrugged before saying, "Part of me believes him—scratch that, I *do* believe him. I just can't figure out *why* he's doing this, and that's what's keeping me skeptical."

"It seems too good to be true, right? We just hand over these 50 useless prisoners we have, and we get Strike in return? Does this guy even know the possibilities that arise from us having Strike?"

"I know that, and that's why I'm trying to think of any advantage they could gain from having the prisoners back. They don't have any knowledge of our operations and have only seen the front entrance and basement of this house."

"Do you think he's just trying to get the barricades down? Maybe planning an attack that way?"

"Possible, but not necessary for him to come here and make this offer. They could've just waited for that to happen—we'll have to drop the barricades eventually, and I'm sure they know that."

"Then what the hell is he really up to?"

"I can't say, but I think we should do it. I'm trying to think of the worst thing that could happen by us releasing these prisoners, and it simply doesn't hold a flame to what we'd be gaining by having Strike in our possession. You should accept this offer."

Chris watched the screen, the Road Runner standing patiently in the cold, awaiting an answer to a question bizarre in every shape and form. He grabbed the headset and slipped it back over his head.

"I accept your offer," he said. The man on the screen showed no emotion to the response. "To keep this honest, I'll agree to release half of the prisoners before we receive Strike, and the rest after she's in our control. Can we agree on that?" The man didn't move, and Chris adjusted his headset to make sure his voice was carrying outside. "Did you hear me?"

"I heard you. I'm thinking," the Road Runner snapped.

He stood in silence for what felt like an eternity as Chris watched the speck on the screen ponder his decision. The man had come this far and risked his life to make this offer; there was no way he was leaving without some sort of agreement.

"I can agree to those terms," he finally responded. "As soon as I see the first group of people released, we'll need a couple days to make sure they're healthy—we don't want any damaged goods. If everything checks out fine, I'll be back the following day with Strike's schedule and can help you plan a way to capture her. When can I expect to see my people freed?"

"I'd rather not share that information with you. I still don't trust something about this situation, and I'm not going to tell you when my barricade will be down. It'll be done within the next three days, but you need to ensure me you'll have your men in the trees back down."

"I can ensure that if you do the same. I don't want to see another dead Road Runner on the edge of your property as soon as you let them go. If you do that, I promise you'll stay hiding in that shell of yours forever."

"Deal," Chris snapped. He hadn't considered doing such a thing—Strike was too valuable of an asset to risk.

"Perfect. Like I said, when we get our men back, give me forty-eight hours to return. I can't guarantee a certain time. Would it be okay if I have to come back in the middle of the night?"

"Fine with me."

"Perfect. I'll see you soon."

The Road Runner turned and disappeared back to the woods where he had come from.

"Well, this just got interesting," Duane commented.

"Yes, indeed," Chris said. "Very interesting."

He watched the monitor as the man shrunk to a small black dot in the distance before disappearing for good.

101

Chapter 9

Martin crunched into the back seat of the crowded car as Gerald drove them out of downtown Denver, heading east to the town of Watkins.

Gerald had tried to keep the mood light with small talk, but when no one responded, it became clear that all of their minds were elsewhere, likely wondering what the future had in store.

While the anxiety stabbed Martin in the gut, his mind kept wandering to his mother. On the other side of this trip was a better life. A life with no Alzheimer's. A life with no worries. And hopefully, a life with no more war. He decided that when he returned, he wanted no more of the Road Runners, Revolters, Chris, or any of the bullshit that came with his magical liquid. He'd dump that shit down the drain and never look back, and if Commander Strike couldn't respect that, then she was full of shit about how accepting the Road Runners were.

The sun reached its peak and beat down on the world. Martin thought about Lela and what she might be doing on this beautiful day. Even though she was behind bars, she had managed to remain in the forefront of his mind at the most random of times. She had, after all, hurled the frying pan that changed both of their lives forever. Would things have played out differently if she confessed to the accident from the beginning? Absolutely.

But she didn't. And now they were in their current situations of a prison with bars and a prison of time travel and war.

When they reached the freeway and Gerald sped up to 70 miles per hour, Martin glanced around at his peers, wondering what kinds of journeys had brought them to this point in time. Every Road Runner he met had joined the organization out of a hunger for revenge on Chris. Somewhere along the path, the old man had wreaked havoc on their lives, pushing them to think they had no choice but to dedicate their lives to finding a way to end him.

These men in the car seemed completely content with their lives. But Martin also knew how easy it was to fake a smile when the pain became buried deeper in the past with each passing year. Odds were that these men had an equally painful story that drove them forward, but were they as committed as they appeared on the surface? Or did they each have a selfish motive, like Martin?

The engine hummed as they moved along I-70 and Martin pondered. Perhaps they'd all bond and develop a brotherhood during this trip. If they did, they'd surely get to know each other's stories.

The car pulled off the freeway, taking the exit for Watkins. Gerald led them down a frontage road that twisted into the middle of nowhere. "We're here," he called out. Everyone looked around at the open fields that stretched to the horizon.

"You sure about that?" Brigham asked, a giggle caught in his throat.

Gerald grinned as he turned around in his seat. "Positive."

The rest of the men shot puzzled looks at each other.

"You do know there's nothing here, right?" Brigham asked.

Gerald pulled the car to the side of the road and stopped it completely, dirt, tall grass, and tumbleweed the only things visible.

"We set up different warehouses throughout time. In this era, this is just an open field. But, in 2064, this is home of the Road Runners. Let's all take our sip of Juice to 2064, think of the current day and time, and I'll see you on the other side."

Gerald pulled out his flask and took a quick swig, leaning back in his seat to wait for the trip into the future.

Everyone else pulled out their flasks and twisted the caps off.

"Cheers," Brigham said, and took an amount that looked more like a gulp than a drop on the tongue.

Martin nodded to Web and they took their sips in unison. There was less fear doing this act with others. Each time before—except for the time Chris had busted him out of the Oxford Hotel—Martin had gone at it alone, always wondering where he'd wake up, and if somehow his soul would get lost in the shuffle of time and never return to his body. This time, however, he sipped his Juice with confidence, knowing exactly where he'd be waking up and who would be there to join him.

The car fell silent as everyone waited for the brief two minutes to pass before their bodies dozed off to sleep.

Martin leaned his head against the window and gazed at the year 2019—his year, his current life. He wondered if he'd ever see it again and said a quick prayer to whoever wanted to listen to his helpless soul.

Little did any of them know, the Road Runners were striking a deal with Chris in Alaska that would flip the organization forever.

Martin woke up last, the others already standing outside of the car and admiring their new surroundings. The open field was now a five-level apartment building, possibly abandoned by the look of its deteriorating brick façade, busted out windows, and random ivy running up and down the exterior.

Martin stepped out of the car to join his group. The building they stood in front of was part of a community of similar buildings, all equally destroyed.

"What happened to this place?" Brigham asked.

Gerald sighed as he gazed at the building. "A complete massacre. In 2055, President Poe called for a cleansing of the country, calling for all pure Revolters to extinguish the slime of any one who wasn't one of them. It was a call to action that every Revolter pounced on. You should understand that many Road Runners and non-Revolters all moved far away from the city to places just like this. They built new communities, started their own schooling systems, and even their own political systems with elected leaders. The people lived in peace and remained out of sight from the Revolters, but unfortunately, not out of mind." Web nodded to himself as if he'd heard this story before. "When the Revolters got word that everyone they had pushed out of the city were thriving without them, the leadership grew scared. They felt if a group of people could create a new life so quickly, that they could one day grow into a force big enough to overthrow them."

Gerald paused and looked to the building as if it were supplying him with its history.

"So what happened?" Brigham asked.

"Genocide," Gerald said, rubbing his face. "A cold-blooded slaughter of innocent lives."

They all gawked at Gerald, unsure if they wanted to know more details. He continued anyway.

"We didn't know it was coming—we didn't exactly watch the Revolters' news channels. They wanted us to live separately from them, so that's what we did. We minded our business, and assumed they would mind their own. April 15, 2055 was the day. Thousands of these monsters piled into their trucks with their automatic guns and boxes of ammunition. They started downtown, shooting anyone who wasn't a Revolter, setting buildings on fire, running kids over with their trucks."

"Wait," Martin cut in. "Were you there?"

Martin noticed the story didn't sound like a historical recounting, but rather a personal one.

Gerald nodded and rubbed the scar on his face. "That's where this came from. I was living outside of Chicago at the time—after living in the city my whole life before being forced out. So I don't know exactly what happened here at this Denver location, but I'm sure it wasn't too different from what happened in my experience. It was around four in the afternoon when word started to spread about what was happening downtown. We watched in shock as the city we loved was destroyed. We didn't realize at the time that it was going on all around the country, we thought it was just in Chicago. Have any of you actually seen a loved one get killed?"

Martin nodded, thinking back to the night he had watched Lela carry their dead daughter to the trunk, causing a shudder to run up his back. Everyone else shook their heads.

"I've seen the aftermath of a loved one's murder, but not the actual event," Web said.

"I watched my best friend get beat up by three men, doused in gasoline, and set on fire," Gerald continued. "On live television. It was horrific watching these grown men laugh at what they had done. Right when we thought the worst of it was over, they got back in their trucks and drove out of the city. Helicopters followed the scene as it led to the outskirts where most of us lived. The only news stations that had the cameras were the Revolters' channels, so we watched and listened as they cheered on what they called a 'cleansing' of the country."

"How many survived?" Brigham asked.

Gerald shook his head and shrugged. "We don't know. After these attacks, many fled the country or went into hiding. Some went undercover as Revolters just to stay alive. There are 80 million people unaccounted for since these attacks, and we suspect 60-70 million of those were killed."

Gerald paused and let the astronomical number hang in the air.

"That's almost a fifth of the county's 2019 population," Web added.

"2019, yes," Gerald said. "But by 2055, there was already an exodus of about 100 million people that happened after Poe's third election. So at the time, the murders account for roughly thirty percent of the population."

"Jesus Christ," Brigham said, a hand covering his mouth.

"Jesus had nothing to do with it."

"How did you survive?"

"Pure luck. Right place at the right time—or the wrong time, I suppose. I was at work when all of this started. That's where I was watching the news when I saw the trucks leaving the city. They blew out my office's windows, and I caught a chunk of glass in my face. I didn't have time to worry and raced home to my family, only to find they had already beat me there."

A tear glistened as it streamed down his dark face, following the trail of the scar.

"When I got home, everyone was dead. We lived on a quiet block of one-story houses, big backyards. When I turned into the neighborhood I knew there was no chance. Every house I drove by was shredded by bullets. Bodies were in front lawns, blood was pouring from the driveways into the street like a river. I saw one of the trucks speed off when I reached my driveway. All of my windows were shattered and there were probably a thousand bullet holes in my house."

"You don't need to continue this story," Martin said, eyes filled with tears. They all knew what came next.

"I do. I don't talk about it enough. When I went inside, I found my wife and two sons in the kitchen. My wife had her arms over them, but it didn't matter. There were just too many bullets for her to have stopped it. My boys were eight and ten."

Gerald paused, his lips quivering, arms trembling, and buried his face into his hands.

Martin stepped to him and embraced the man nearly twice his size. "I lost a child, too," he said, sobbing. "I know how hard this is."

His words felt empty when they left his mouth, but he didn't know what else to say. He knew from firsthand experience that there wasn't actually anything one *could* say to a grieving parent. The pain never leaves, and every passing day comes with a growing numbness that eventually turns your soul into stone.

They had clearly forgotten what they came to do, standing outside the tattered building that surely had its own, similar story to tell. Martin looked up its five levels and thought about all of the families that had once lived in it. Families that came home after long days at school and work, ready to relax and enjoy each other's company for the evening. Families that had already survived hell, but still held on to a thread of hope for a better world.

It was clear why Gerald was here. There is nothing more frightening than a person who has lost everything. Martin was glad to be by his side for what was sure to be meaningful work. Hearing Gerald's story showed Martin that this mission went beyond his selfish need for a medical cure. He belonged to an organization that strove to save itself from a looming apocalypse, an extinction of their very existence. Because if they didn't, the world as they knew would further dwindle into a dystopia. A world that Martin was now in, with nothing to hold on to but the past.

102

Chapter 10

Chris didn't sleep all night—not that he needed to. He spent another two hours in his office after the mysterious Road Runner had left, watching his screen and hoping by some long shot that the man would come back. He wanted to make the deal immediately, having an epiphany that he shouldn't waste any more time. What would his counterparts around the world think if he had hesitated on the opportunity to have Strike in their possession? That was something they had drooled about for years. Opportunity literally came knocking on the door, and Chris told it to come back later.

Duane had left him alone, as he did require sleep to function as a mortal being. "We can discuss this in the morning," he had said in regards to devising a plan for when to release the twenty-five prisoners to guarantee Strike's exact location.

It was morning now, and Chris was ready. He'd still have to wait two days to get Strike, and that was two days too many. It had been decades since he last had a morning routine of eating breakfast and getting ready for the day ahead, so he wasn't sure when might be a good time to page Duane to continue their discussion. Not that he needed approval from anyone; Chris respected Duane's perspective on every matter that arose. He was a wise man with an ability to spot the vulnerabilities in any decision, a gift Chris never took for granted.

When the clock struck seven, Chris pushed the intercom button and called for Duane. He drummed his fingers on his desk for the next five minutes as he waited, thinking about the prospect of Strike sitting in this very office across from him, forced to spill the Road Runners' secrets or suffer a most painful torture.

A steady rumble of footsteps came from the hallway, and Duane finally barged into the room, dressed and wide-eyed. "You were up all night, weren't you?" he asked Chris after a quick glance around the office.

"Why sleep if it's not necessary?"

"You know, you could probably lure more people into our group if you offered them the ability to stay fully functioning without sleep. I know I'd kill for an extra eight hours a day."

"The world doesn't need people out and about any more than they already are. I love the silence at night. That's not what we're here to discuss anyway, stop distracting."

Duane nodded and gestured for Chris to continue. "So what did you come up with?"

"I want to release those prisoners today. Right now. Tell me why I shouldn't."

Duane sat down in the chair across from Chris's desk with his face scrunched. "You know, I've thought this over and I can't come up with any logic for one time being better than another. This entire thing is riding on a mutual trust that has no backbone, so the playbook is out the window."

"Do you think they're bluffing?"

"It's possible, but not likely. Even if we released half of the prisoners and they backed out of their end of the deal, what good would that do them?"

"We'd kill the rest to send a message."

"And I'm sure they know that. It sounds like there's turmoil within the Road Runners, or at the very least, someone pushing their own agenda."

"I find it interesting that this happened *after* our friend Martin decided to join them with his special gift. Maybe they can't agree on how to use him?"

"That seems most likely. Here they are thinking they've struck the key to the war, but they don't know what exactly to do with him. That's the kind of situation that can cause friction in an instant."

"Now, do we think Strike will even talk? None of these other bastards do."

"Well, we don't torture them aside from making them live in a three foot space. With Strike, we'll break out the big guns. She'll talk. No amount of loyalty can withstand the pain we'll bring onto her. It might take time, but she'll crack."

"I'd hate to release these people for nothing."

"It's a risk, but we have to trust ourselves in getting Strike to talk. If she really wants to die as a martyr with all of their secrets intact, then good on her. But we won't actually kill her if that's what she's hoping for. We'll show her death, but not let her meet it."

Duane chuckled at this, looking to the ceiling with a crazed look of a man who didn't get much sleep.

"Well, it sounds like the decision is made," Chris said. "Let's release twenty-five prisoners right now. Can you head down to arrange it?"

"I can't. That approval has to come from you directly. You made that rule."

"Ahh, yes. Okay then, you start preparing to drop the barricade. I want every soldier in this house armed and ready when it drops. We still have enough to cover every side of the house. When it drops, we'll give the prisoners thirty seconds to get out of the house, then I want it back up immediately."

"Perfect, I'll get on it."

Chris nodded and stood from his desk, shuffling across the office to his private elevator. He whistled while he waited, and entered the elevator car with a wide grin as he watched Duane slide in behind his desk. A sliver of doubt still tugged at his mind. *There has to be something bigger at play.*

Chris had taken a quick peek into the future last night, but saw nothing of substance. Most times the future didn't reveal itself, especially when a decision was up in the air much like his. He now had to live in the moment and trust his instincts that rarely led him wrong.

The elevator stopped on the basement floor, opening to its usual darkness and dank smell of solidarity. The room had always remained fairly quiet, only erupting into chaos whenever Chris decided to show his face.

The basement was designed so the outer perimeter was left in complete darkness, leaving guards the ability to roam the area without being seen. The center of the floor, where the Road Runners were held hostage, was illuminated by the soft glow of overhead lighting, done to force the prisoners' eyes to adjust to the dim light. Should they ever escape, stepping outside would blind them as a result. Chris had forgotten about this detail until he stepped foot out of the elevator. The visiting Road Runner had made it clear they didn't want any of their people damaged upon their return.

The perimeter lighting was turned on, something that had become the norm after the prisoners and guards had grown tolerable of each other. The guards had no need to hide from the prisoners, not that they ever needed to since the Road Runners were chained to the ground, but it helped maintain the peace at first. Once the Road Runners realized they were never going to be released, they accepted their fate and tried to make the best of the situation by befriending the guards and sharing stories with those closest in proximity.

Chris couldn't deny that the Road Runners had a knack for making the best of any situation. They marched forward—emotionally—as the days, weeks, and months all eventually formed into one big, hellish blur.

He cut the perimeter lights with a flick of the switch, not wanting to be seen on this brief visit, and worked his way around the walls to where the guards always sat. Some murmurs spread throughout the room, but there was nowhere near the fuss that would have risen had the prisoners seen Chris.

"Is that you, boss?" a wary voice called out to Chris.

"Yes. Sorry if I scared you. Can we have a word in private?"

"Certainly."

In the darkness, Chris listened as the guard pushed open a door, hinges creaking before thudding against the inside of a small office. Chris followed the sound of the guard's footsteps and closed the door behind him, causing an automatic light to flicker on above. This light was slightly brighter than the one that shone above the prisoners, but still dim compared to what Chris was used to in his personal office.

"Everything okay, boss?" the guard asked, his droopy face making no attempt to hide the exhaustion. His name tag read *Wheeler*, and the young man had a strong jaw and wavy brown hair, but also fear that Chris could smell oozing from his pores.

Chris knew many of the guards were having a tough time after the massacre of their teammates outside the mansion. Some suffered from survivor's guilt, others from a growing paranoia that they were next. Chris understood their minds had already been fucked beyond repair thanks to him, so their overreactions were understandable.

"Everything is just dandy," Chris said. "We've just come into a situation where I need to release twenty-five of these fine Road Runners as soon as possible."

The guard's face scrunched as the words processed.

"Twenty-five? Who?"

"It doesn't matter. If everything goes according to plan, they'll all be released in the next few days."

The guard looked around the room as if someone was going to jump out and tell him it was a prank.

"Am I still going to have a job?"

"Of course," Chris chuckled. "It won't be down here, but we'll have lots to do. Don't even worry about such a thing."

"What do I tell the prisoners? They'll have questions—especially the ones not leaving today."

"Tell them they're being moved to another location, and leave it at that. Tell them that's all you know."

"That *is* all I know."

"Easy enough, then. How long do you think it'll take to have them rounded up and ready to go upstairs?"

The guard checked his watch. "Half an hour."

"Works for me. Myself or Duane will meet you upstairs in half an hour to fill in the Road Runners on what they need to do. I'll send down some help for you to get everyone together."

"Thank you, boss."

Chris clapped a hand on Wheeler's shoulder and winked at him. He loved when he saw his rigorous brainwashing in action. The guard asked no questions that didn't pertain to his job, and responded respectfully to Chris by calling him "boss." When it felt like the world was crumbling all around, it was refreshing to know he still had thousands of soldiers and Revolters below him, all working toward one common goal of making the world a better place.

"Thank you, young man. I appreciate everything you do for us." Chris patted him one more time, the guard now grinning and wide-eyed from the compliment.

He turned and pushed the door open, the light immediately turning off as they stepped out to the perimeter and watched the prisoners sitting or lying on the floor, oblivious that they were about to have their lives altered once again.

And so is mine, Chris thought, a smirk smacked on his face. He strolled down the dark hallway to return to the elevator, knowing that the next forty-eight hours would bring change he'd never imagined possible. As soon as he stepped in the elevator, all of the lights in the basement blasted on, causing moans and screams from the prisoners as their eyes made the adjustment to normal lighting.

"I need twenty-five of you to stand up right now and put your hands behind your back," the guard shouted. "We're going for a little walk upstairs."

103

Chapter 11

"Ladies and gentlemen," Chris said to the group of twenty-five Road Runners standing in the mansion's entryway. "Today, you'll be released. Don't ask why—it's none of your business. In five minutes I'll unlock this door and you're free to go. Your people are somewhat expecting your release, so they may or may not be around to assist you. From here you'll want to head north, which is straight out this door. There's nothing south or on the back side of the mansion, so don't bother."

The group of Road Runners looked around at each other, not sure if they should believe the Revolters' main leader.

Chris smiled to himself. "I hope there are no hard feelings. We did what we had to in the name of war." A sudden tension rose to the surface after he said this, but still no one said anything. They probably wanted to rip his head right from his shoulders, but they all had their hands cuffed behind their backs. "I want you to form a single file line. When the door opens, you'll step outside one-by-one, have your handcuffs removed, and be free to go. Don't try anything cute; we have guards all around this place who won't hesitate to shoot. Any questions?"

Nothing but blank stares.

"Perfect." Chris rotated and started to unlock the numerous bolts and chains that kept the front door sealed. The shell of the barricade remained, but Duane waited upstairs for the official word to drop it. Chris turned back to the small crowd. "We only have five minutes to get you all out of here, so form your line now and move quickly. If you don't make it out, it'll be your own fault."

The Road Runners looked at each other one final time before wiggling around in the crowded space, forming a sloppy line that curved around the room.

Chris nodded to a guard standing on the stairwell that led upstairs. The guard returned the nod and disappeared upward.

Thirty seconds later, a humming sound filled the house, much like a mechanical motor. Darkness had filled the windows, giving the appearance of night time, but daylight slowly seeped through the gaps in the house, filling it with a golden glow that provided a sense of life compared to the dungeon they had all been living in. Some of them winced at the sunlight.

"We've tried readjusting your eyes as best we could, but they're probably not back to normal quite yet. You may need to wander outside with your hands over your eyes. Don't try to be a hero, you can go blind if you take in too much light right away. There is a pretty heavy overcast today, so it shouldn't be too bad."

The humming motor stopped, and Chris felt like a sitting duck with no protection around his house. The Road Runners could have ten thousand of their troops waiting to storm the property, and there would be nothing they could do to stop them. His heart raced at the thought.

"Let's move!" he barked to the Road Runners, all craning their necks for a view of the world they thought they'd never see again.

The two guards who had stood by the front door worked their way outside, the first Road Runner in line following.

"Goodbye. Come again," Chris joked, more to calm himself down.

They filed out as instructed, stepping onto the porch, turning their backs for the guards to uncuff them, and jumping down the steps to freedom. Some broke into sprints, others wandered aimlessly like they had just woken up in Jurassic Park. Only a handful looked back at the mansion, and when they did, they turned and ran like it was an evil force trying to claw them back in.

When the final Road Runner stepped outside, Chris nodded to the guard who had reappeared on the stairs, prompting him to vanish once more into the abyss where Duane waited for the next command. The two outside guards stepped back in and Chris slammed the door shut, cutting off the view of the Road Runners dashing across the open field toward the woods.

"Goodbye, old friends," Chris said with a smirk. "Now we wait."

The humming motor kicked back on, leaving Chris and his guards to watch the brief glimpse of daylight slowly vanish and return the house to its dark mood and dim lighting.

"Thank you, gentlemen," he said, and climbed up the stairs to return to his office.

Duane still sat behind his desk and stood up when Chris stepped into the room.

"I'd say that went pretty smoothly," Chris said with a wide grin. "No complications, no surprises. Just an easy release of Road Runners back into the wild where they can try to spread their nonsense."

Duane laughed as Chris sat down, turning his attention to the monitor. Almost all of the Road Runners had already vanished from sight, minus a couple who were taking their sweet time crossing the open field. They had taken his word, as not one of them ventured to the back of the house. In a different scenario, he would've led them to their deaths, but there was a price to pay for obtaining someone as valuable as Commander Strike.

"I was thinking more about what happens next," Duane said, crossing his hands on his lap. "This could be a Trojan horse type of play they're making."

"How do you figure?"

"Well, they now have twenty-five Road Runners who know their way around the basement. They're offering their leader to us on a silver platter. What if their plan is to turn around and use those prisoners to attack us at the exact moment we capture Strike?"

Chris scratched his head and leaned back in his chair. "Do you really think that's what they're up to?"

"No, but I'm thinking of every possibility, and this one seemed realistic."

The two men sat in silence, sizing up the possibility of an ambush.

"Why now?" Chris asked. "We've had their prisoners for almost a year. Why wait until they've failed an attack on me and after the barricade has gone up?"

Duane shrugged. "There are hundreds of reasons we can talk ourselves out of the possibility, but that doesn't make the reasons for it any less important. They see you as the key to this war. Even if they can't kill you, if they *have* you, the war can't go on. We don't have a chain of command like they do, and they know that. The Revolution would have no leadership in North America if you vanished."

Chris nodded, stroking his face with a nervous hand. "Well then, I guess we should plan for the best and prepare for the worst. When we go to get Strike, I want every soldier in this house with us, armed and ready for any surprises."

Duane nodded. "What about the house? We can't leave it abandoned."

"We have before when we all go out on a journey together."

"That was before this. What happens if we return to a burned down house. We've certainly burned down plenty of theirs."

"Fine. Then you stay here and put the barricade back up after we leave. Don't talk with anyone who tries to come by."

"I can do that."

"Good. Now we just have to wait for our friend to come back with the information we need. Now's a good time to fill in our soldiers on what to expect in the next few days. Stress to them that this a highly secret operation we're taking on, and to not mutter a word about it, even to each other. Doing so will result in immediate death."

"I'll handle it."

"Thank you. Now, I want to know more before we capture Strike. What *do* we know about their chain of command? Who could be calling the shots?"

"I know Strike's number two is a younger guy named Julian. He's been by her side since she came into power. Then there's an older man, Bill. He's been a Road Runner forever."

"Ahh yes, I remember Bill and Julian. Looking back, I can't say I'm surprised they joined those fools. It's always the ones who ask the most questions that end up leaving me. Just like Briar. I swear the guy was going to have a panic attack if I didn't answer his thousands of questions."

"Sounds like we should revamp our recruiting process, then."

"That's for another time. Tell me what you know about Bill and Julian."

"I spoke with our team in Europe, and they let me in on a little secret."

Chris's eyebrows raised to the top of his head.

"It appears that Road Runner leadership in Europe, Asia, and Africa is not at all pleased with Strike. They're all making plans for after her term ends."

"Fascinating. Do you think this deal is coming from across the ocean, then?"

"It's very likely, and that's why I'm not buying the theory of an ambush. I think the Road Runners don't want Strike anymore and see her as trade bait. They may be known for their loyalty, but that shouldn't discount their ability as strategists. They really do put the greater good of their organization over any individual."

"Do you know what this means?" Chris asked, standing on excited legs. "This means—and I know it's a long shot—that we can maybe convince Strike into joining us."

Duane shook head in a jerky motion. "She would never."

"Oh, she might. If she finds out that her own people turned her over to us. Don't underestimate the tug of revenge in someone who's been betrayed. I've seen it play out numerous times. Why do you think so many people leave us for the Road Runners? They feel a sense of betrayal, even though I let them know the terms of our deal well before anything bad happens in their life."

"Why would we want her if her own people don't?"

"If she commits to us, we'll have access to all of their secrets. Where the hideouts are, what their plans are, whatever we want to know, we'll have an answer to. We may need to reconsider our plans of torturing her, and instead plan to court her. Make her feel welcome. Sooner or later, she'll have that dreaded realization that the Road Runners were nothing but a huge lie. And we'll be here, ready with open arms."

"How was she when she first met you?"

"I'm actually not the one who gave her the Juice. She's originally from Europe and joined from there."

"We should try to find out her backstory. If we're going to court her, it's best to know what's been driving her."

"We can inquire, but don't get your hopes up. Our European friends don't distribute the Juice the same way we do here. We try to tempt people who have suffered in their past, and they like to hand it out like it's a charitable cause. They use it for fun and historical research. I'd guess half of Europe has access."

"How do they get away with it? Keeping it a secret?"

"It's not a big deal to them. They don't treat it as this mystic gift like we do here. It's almost like it's a right, not a privilege."

Duane stared blankly at Chris, shaking his head after a moment of silence passed.

"Good for them, I suppose," Duane said. "I guess we'll have to wait and find out for ourselves how she really is behind closed doors."

Chris nodded and turned his attention back to the computer monitor, watching the now open field, abandoned by all of the released Road Runners, knowing his world would change within the next two days.

104

Chapter 12

After sharing sob stories, they entered the abandoned building with heavy hearts. Even inside, deep in its halls, bullet holes peppered the walls, along with random splatters of dried blood. Martin half-expected the odor of dead bodies, but the place had been cleaned out of any human remains. Gerald mentioned how, in Chicago, the Revolters had stacked all the corpses in an open field and set them on fire, claiming mass cremation as the best option. The handfuls that had survived watched their friends and family burn like logs on television. Gone were the Road Runner networks, leaving only channels run by the Revolters, who praised the attacks and the cremations as a huge success for cleansing the soul of America.

Martin tried to not think of this horrific imagery as he walked through the apartment building, but could still hear the helpless screams crying out from the walls.

There was no power to the building, or to the neighborhood, for that matter. Gerald led them down the main hallway, having only the soft glow of daylight that broke through the shattered windows at the ends of the hall. Doors lined the hallway, former entryways into family life and innocence. Cracks zigzagged down the walls, weaving between the craters formed by bullets. The musty smell of abandonment filled their lungs as they reached the back of the hallway where the fire exit stood across from a closed door that concealed a stairwell.

"This way," Gerald called, his boots clicking on the tiled floor, echoing throughout the building. Martin's paranoia kept him looking over his shoulder, positive they were being too loud and would be found by a group of passing Revolters with nothing better to do. But they never came, and they never would. Their work had already been done here, and Gerald assured them that the Revolters mainly stayed in their upscale neighborhoods in or around downtown. The war was won, as far as they were concerned, and they no longer believed any group of surviving people to be a threat. Yet, when a Road Runner did appear, they simply shot them dead without question.

Gerald swung open the stairwell door, and led them into a dark pit where they had to rely on the sounds of his obnoxious boots to lead the way. When the door shut behind Brigham, who was at the back of the line, the stairway fell into pitch-blackness. Martin waved his hand in front of his face and couldn't see a damn thing. It reminded him of following Lela through the fog that fateful night when she decided to dump Izzy's body into the lake.

Fucking bitch.

They all clopped down the stairs until bottlenecking and bumping into each other as Gerald stopped to knock on what sounded like a steel door. Someone let out a nervous laugh after they had all fallen into each other like dominoes.

Martin's paranoia vanished. No Revolter would go out of their way to step into the darkness and climb all the way down these stairs. It was a perfect hideout for the Road Runners, something he realized they excelled in creating.

"What's going on?" Brigham whispered from the back.

"He's coming," Gerald said. "Just give him a minute."

A few seconds later they heard the rattle of chains and the clunking of bolts as someone on the other side unlocked the door, swinging it open to stinging lights that filled a basement the size of two football fields.

A young pale man with long, wavy brown hair to his shoulders greeted them with a smile. "Welcome, gentlemen," he said in a nasally voice. "Come on in."

Gerald stepped in first, shaking the man's hand and admiring the walls that stretched into the distance, every inch of them covered with guns of all sizes. Webster stepped in next, followed by Martin and Brigham.

"Holy shit," Brigham said. "How many guns are in this place?"

Not only were the walls completely smothered with firearms, there were dozens of tables spread across the room displaying more guns, bombs, swords, and knives. It looked like a trade show for all things weaponry.

"We have over 10,000 firearms, ranging from muskets to fully automatics, and even bazookas. More than 3,000 explosives, and 2,000 blades." The man explained this proudly with his hands on his hips.

"Gentlemen, meet Ralph," Gerald said. "The craziest son of a bitch I've ever known."

Ralph threw his head back, revealing a bulging Adam's apple on his skinny throat, and cackled to the ceiling. "He only says that because I sleep in this room."

"You could sleep in any room in this building, but you choose the one that could blow up the entire state," Gerald joked back, the comic relief spreading its gracious arms around the men.

"If it's gonna blow up the state, what does it matter where I sleep?"

Gerald burst into laughter, a welcoming sight from the behemoth.

"In all seriousness," Ralph said. "I'm here for you guys. Anything you need, I have it and can tell you exactly where it is."

"We'll be making a plan first. Do you still have some office space we can use, or did you fill that room with guns, too?"

"Funny. No, it's still a conference room, and it's all yours. I haven't had too many visitors lately, so make yourselves at home."

"Let's meet in the conference room in five minutes," Gerald said to the group. "It's that door along the wall." He pointed to the only other visible door across the room.

Gerald walked off, into the rows of weapons, picking up various swords and explosives to examine. The three of them weren't sure if they were supposed to follow suit, or if they were even allowed to touch anything. Ralph stood in front them, his grin wide.

"You guys, this entire room belongs to all of us. I just maintain it. You can go touch anything you want, and take anything you want—all you have to do is tell me for inventory purposes."

"Thanks, Ralph," Web said, and immediately dashed into the aisles. Brigham broke toward the walls, touching every gun within his reach as he skipped down the hall like a child in the toy aisle.

"How long have you been here?" Martin asked Ralph. He'd take any weapon that Gerald deemed necessary, but he didn't care about looking at all of the stock to make his own decision.

"I've been here for four years now," Ralph replied. "I love what I do and the people I get to meet from around the world and all throughout time."

"Do you never travel to other times, then?"

"I do on occasion, mainly on trips to get new weapons—they're much cheaper and more accessible in the past."

"Aren't there less laws now surrounding guns compared to the past?"

"If you're rich. If not, it's almost impossible to get your hands on a gun without going through the black market. Can't have poor people defending themselves against their murderous government." Ralph shook his head, his face scrunching as if he just bit into a sour grape.

"Is this your real time?" Martin asked.

"It is. I was born in 2034 and have lived all 30 years of my life here."

"You never thought about going back in time and not aging? Why live in a world like this?"

"I've thought about it. But, why live through any amount of time knowing it still ends like this? Even if I traveled back 500 years, it all leads back to this point in time. I'd rather just live my life and die when I'm supposed to. And it feels more refreshing doing my work in this era—it's more purposeful because I'm still fighting the good fight. I'm with the good guys, even if they bomb us in the middle of the night."

Martin scratched his head, unsure what to do with the life story Ralph threw his way, and decided to keep him talking—he had grown an immediate interest in the "history" of the future.

"So why do you have the Juice?"

"The Revolters damn near handed that stuff out after they took control. Once they wiped out the towns, they tried to sway any middle-class people the opportunity for a better life. They called it 'giving the gift of time.' Basically, they thought anyone who survived the attacks and still lived in the poor areas deserved a chance at a better life, as long as they weren't any type of minority."

"How generous of them. Did you lose any family?"

"Not through death," Ralph said, shaking his head. "See, I was part of the rich circle, a trust fund kid who never had to work a day in his life. But I wasn't your typical rich snob. I wanted to do good with the money. I spent my time researching various charitable organizations that I could donate both my time and money to, making sure it wasn't the sort of bullshit where seventy percent of your donation goes to some sleazy CEO. I had a good thing going with a dozen different organizations, but I didn't keep up with politics. If I had, I would've known that our fearless leader Poe had been slashing non-profit organizations for years already, squeezing them out of existence with different tax laws that made it impossible for them to stay in operation. By the time I knew what was going on, it was too late."

Ralph paused, head still shaking, as he retrieved a flask from his back pocket. Martin's eyes bulged at the sight.

"Relax," Ralph said. "This is a normal flask, with booze. A habit I took up recently; it really settles the nerves."

Martin knew that feeling, but put up a hand when Ralph offered some.

"I brought up the issue to my parents," Ralph continued. "Asking what they thought, if they agreed with me on how inhumane all of this was. What was the harm in letting non-profits run their businesses in peace? They weren't out taking potential money away from businesses run by the government. But my parents had become so brainwashed by this New

Age Revolution shit—something else I had apparently been too busy to notice. They and my sister supported every word that came out of the White House, and had become racist, anti-humanity pigs. So I did what any sensible person would've done and moved out in the middle of the night, after taking $100,000 out of my dad's safe, of course."

Ralph chuckled at himself, his eyes distant as he surely replayed that night in his head.

"And that's how you ended up here as a Road Runner?"

"Oh, there was resistance. They thought I was an undercover spy for the Revolters at first. I understood why, so I had to go through all sorts of tests to prove that I was more aligned with the Road Runners' values than the Revolters. They eventually let me in, and that's when I decided I wanted to keep helping where I could. These days, this is the only real way to help, short of risking my own life out in the public." Ralph tossed his hands in the air and pivoted around to admire the room of weapons. "I've had a lot of fun traveling back in time and gathering this collection. I've had enough face time with the past, that I don't think I could actually live there. I've grown conditioned to be paranoid and always looking over my shoulder, even though I know no one dangerous will come here. I suppose it's just part of growing up in this time. I wouldn't last in any other era being this way."

"That's an incredible story, Ralph. I don't know what to say. Thank you, I suppose."

"No, don't thank me. I want to thank *you*. You guys are the ones who come here ready to fight. I don't have half the courage as you do. Shit, I need to sleep with a rifle at my side to make sure I don't have any bad dreams. You guys are the real heroes, and I don't even know your backstories. You have a meeting to get to, though, so it'll have to wait for another time."

Ralph nodded across the room where Gerald and the others had gathered outside the conference room.

"Yes, thanks. I'd love to continue this conversation."

"I'll hold you to it." Ralph slapped Martin on the back before he rushed across the room.

Ralph had shown him that the world was as dangerous as advertised, but also, reassuringly, that there were still good people in these dark times. Even if they had to hide in the shadows, they were there, working to move forward and never giving up hope.

105

Chapter 13

Gerald paced around the conference room, shoving chairs aside with his hips, clearing the way for him to write on the dry-erase board that ran the length of the front wall. A long table faced the front where Martin, Brigham, and Web all sat and watched.

"I've been thinking about a plan," Gerald said, twisting the cap off of a marker and drawing a blue circle. "This is Denver. We're about thirty minutes away. I'm thinking we move to the edge of town and get a spot wherever we can find. There should be some hotels for cheap, and we can create a base there. Is that close enough to the city for you, Web?"

Web nodded, his hands folded and relaxed on the table. "I can try to hack the hospitals' security systems so we can look around their cameras," he said, pulling out a laptop from his bag and typing furiously as Gerald spoke. "I can break into anything."

Gerald smirked and nodded. "In that case, it'll be a waiting game until we get some more information on the insides of these buildings. Martin, we can use this downtime to have you explore downtown and get a sense for what's going on. Commander Strike believes Sonya has escaped to this era, so we might as well poke around and see what we can learn. I'm sure Web will have some insight on an escape route, but you might as well get familiar with the area—learn the hidden alleys and back doors, things like that."

Martin still felt out of place, essentially being thrown into the situation as a sort of spy. He had no experience doing such things aside from the James Bond movies he had seen. And there was no fancy car or beautiful woman to help him along the way.

"Alright, I can do that," he said, hoping he wouldn't be found out and shot dead like a rabid dog.

"And what can I do?" Brigham asked. "I know I'm just here for the medicine, but there's gotta be something I help with."

"I'd suggest you hang out with Web and pitch in where he might need help. If you're not comfortable with combat, then I'd advise you stay inside when we arrive downtown. You'll put yourself in danger if you don't have experience in fighting these people."

And I have experience? Martin wondered. *I didn't ask to be a part of this war, just to get my mom's medicine.*

It felt like he had left home months ago, even though they had been in 2064 for an entire hour. He imagined his mom at home, worrying about him, waiting to find out if he'd make it back.

I'll be back, and I'm pouring this damn Juice down the toilet so I never have to come back. I'll be long gone before the world goes to shit.

"I can help Web," Brigham said.

"Martin and I will go out and get a feel for the current situation. Like I mentioned, I'm from this era, but from Chicago. Things could be slightly different in Denver, but I wouldn't count on it. Either way, we'll find out for sure."

"Gerald," Martin said abruptly. "Do you think we might die?"

The room fell silent as everyone turned to Gerald, their fearless leader who seemed to have all the answers.

"It's definitely a better possibility than most missions," he replied, choosing words carefully. "But that's why we're going to put so much preparation into this. If we just went downtown and barged into the hospital without a plan, we'd be dead within minutes. Every decision we make will be carefully thought out, our plans regarding the medicine will be detailed to the exact second. We'll always know where each other is and how to get in contact."

Martin nodded, along with Brigham. Web continued typing away on his laptop, likely trying to hack the world's greatest computer servers for fun.

"Because of these plans, we need to get moving. It'll be best for us to arrive in the middle of the day and check in to a place. Everyone will be at work, and there's no need for us to get tangled with other Road Runners right now. The less people who know who we are, the better. We can't have people talking about the group of four men who showed up with their bags and guns. Word gets around fast, and once it's out, it'll eventually reach the Revolters."

"So we're going downtown already?" Web asked, not looking up from his screen.

"Yes, we'll plan to leave here in an hour, after you guys pick the weapons you want. I think the machine guns are pretty fun."

Web didn't acknowledge the response and remained entranced by his computer screen, glowing a blue haze across his face.

"Any questions?" Gerald asked, and when no one replied, "Let's get to it."

They exited the conference room and returned to the warehouse of weapons, none of them sure where to even begin their search.

* * *

Ralph had more than weapons. He provided them a busted old van to travel in, instead of the cramped sports car from 2019. "You'll blend right in," he said proudly. "Just wait till you see it. You'll be Gerald the soccer mom and his three kids." He cackled at himself, grabbing his belly as if he just told the funniest joke in history. They offered polite chuckles, except for Web—the researcher seemed to be in another universe at the moment, remaining distant and quiet.

"I understand you'll need a new wardrobe, so I've prepared a suitcase full of new attire." He rolled out a black suitcase and pushed it over to Martin, patting the top of it. "Everything you need. At the bottom is all of the fine attire: suits, shoes, ties, pocket squares, and a box of jewelry. Remember, the flashier your appearance, the more they think you'll belong. On top of that I packed your regular lounging clothes, which should only be worn when you're back at home base with these guys. Even the super-rich people in these times don't believe in relaxing in a pair of sweatpants. They'll stay in dress pants and a button-up right until bedtime."

"Do they sleep under gold sheets?" Martin asked, smirking.

"Some do, yes. Go somewhere like the governor's mansion, and you'll see everything in gold, all the way down to his very toothbrush."

"Obnoxious."

"Indeed, but that's the luxury of funneling all tax money to yourself. Politics has become even more of a cash grab than what I've heard about in your time. Politics is now a wealthy way of life for only the elite of society to participate. Everyone else just tries to mind their own business and pray they don't get killed for no apparent reason."

Every bit of information that both Gerald and Ralph mentioned felt like a new layer being peeled off an onion of fear. They were inching closer to the core, and the thought terrified Martin to his bones. Within the next hour he'd be arriving downtown with his small caravan of Road Runners, an easy target should they be discovered. He had seen downtown Denver grow from the 1980's all the way through 2019. He even had a taste of life in 1919, but none of that prepared him for whatever horror lived on this side of the century. Would the city look the same? Were all the familiar buildings and skyscrapers still standing strong? Did Revolters march around town with automatic firearms looking to shoot anyone who appeared as a threat? He tried to imagine such a world, but couldn't, refusing to accept that life could've taken such a dramatic twist during the course of history.

His flask throbbed like a hot cast iron in his back pocket, begging him to return to his normal life in 2019. It was a much different experience traveling forward compared to backward. Going back in time, he knew what would happen for the most part. There were no major surprises kept out of the history books, and life in general seemed more relaxed.

Jumping into the future sparked a constant tension that hung over every moment. An obvious sense of the unknowing tickled the back of his thoughts, creating fear and doubt. How was he supposed to return to 2019—even with the cure to Alzheimer's in hand—and pretend that everything was okay? How was he supposed to attempt to return to a normal life, knowing what lied ahead less than twenty years ahead when President Poe ran for office? It reminded Martin of a classic scene in many suspense movies where the protagonist found themselves strapped to a conveyor belt, inching closer to a pool of boiling water. The future was the water, time the conveyor belt, and Martin was strapped down, praying someone would come rescue him.

Will he make it before turning into a boiled lobster? Tune in tomorrow—same Bat-time, same Bat-channel!

"Briar!" Gerald shouted from across the warehouse. "It's time."

He locked eyes momentarily with Ralph and felt an odd sense of comfort. "I suppose I'll need to take your recommendation on a gun; I need to get going."

Ralph grinned and led Martin down the aisle.

106

Chapter 14

It hadn't even been twelve hours, so Chris jumped out of his seat when he saw a figure appear on the monitors. It was 9 p.m., hours after he had released half of the prisoners back into the wild. He resisted every temptation to jump forward a day in time to see what happened, but as he had learned in his decades of time travel, it was sometimes best to let time pass.

If good things come to those wait, then I'm about to receive the ultimate present.

And as long as the Road Runner wasn't bluffing, he would. He'd kept faith that his enemies were as true to their word as he was, and watching the figure approach from the distant woods caused a rapid heartbeat he hadn't felt in years.

His hands fumbled across his desk, batting papers and loose articles out of the way in search of the intercom control. "Duane, please come to my office. This is an emergency."

Chris couldn't think of a time where he had ever mentioned an emergency publicly over the intercom. For convenience, the intercom reached every inch of the mansion, including the basement. He imagined the remaining prisoners panicking like caged dogs on their way to the pound. Perhaps it was his heart's desire, but he swore he heard their shouts from two levels below.

Within a minute, Duane knocked and entered the office, unbothered as usual.

"What's going on?" Duane asked.

"Our friend is coming back."

"Already? Are you sure it's him?" Duane pulled his sleeve down to check his watch. "It's only been eleven hours."

"Perhaps they were giving us broad timelines as well. But I don't know who else would be walking from the woods in the middle of the night."

Duane hurried around the desk to look at the monitor, his face stretched into a studious gaze. "It's one person again, gotta be him."

"I *know* it's him, Duane, that's why I called you up here."

They watched in silence as the small figure on the screen once again grew larger with each approaching step. The distance between the mansion and the woods was much longer than Chris had remembered, as it took this man nearly three minutes to reach the front porch.

Duane had already opened the software that allowed two-way conversation with the outside world.

"Good evening," Chris said, unable to hide the grin on his face as he slid the headset on. One of two things were about to happen, both making him drool at the thought. The man was either back to disclose the plan for capturing Strike, or he was here to try and negotiate a new deal and back out of the old one, in which case he'd be killed within two minutes. No one backed out of a deal with Chris Speidel and lived to tell the tale.

"Hello, Chris," the familiar voice responded, and the man waved to the cameras he couldn't see.

"I see you're back so soon. Did you get your people back in the shape you wanted?"

"We did, yes."

The Road Runner said nothing further and stood in silence, staring at the steel barricade without any outward sign of emotion. He was again bundled up from head to toe, leaving them unable to make out a single detail aside from the man's height.

It's a fucking negotiation tactic, Chris realized. Refusing to speak first was one of the oldest tricks in the book, putting the pressure on whoever decided to utter the first words.

Chris muted his microphone and turned to Duane who had sat down across the desk. "I need you to round up everyone we have and make them wait at the front door. I think this guy is going to try and talk his way out of this, and we will not accept that."

Duane nodded and disappeared as effortlessly as he had arrived. Chris preferred having Duane at his side in this sort of situation, but he had to think ahead. This scum Road Runner was not going to walk away without giving Chris the promised information.

The man remained silent, each passing second growing more awkward, before Chris decided he had to say something. "Is there something I can help you with today?"

The question was vague enough to suggest the Road Runner had no negotiating power.

The man turned, the fuzz on his jacket blowing in the wind, and stared directly into the camera from behind his ski goggles.

"I'm ready to discuss the terms of our deal," he said in monotone. Chris had no way of knowing, but assumed this Road Runner was on the verge of shitting his pants. This could have all been some far-reaching goal for him, not expecting Chris to actually turn over the prisoners. But here they were, face to face, and he now had to turn in their one and only leader. "I'd like to come inside to talk—I don't want to say anything out here in the open."

Chris leaned back and thought. It was still possible this was all a big ploy to try and get into the mansion. There was no one visible in the distance, but that didn't mean they weren't nearby waiting for the barricade to drop.

"I've come here in peace," the Road Runner said, as if he could read Chris's thoughts. "No weapons, no backup. Just here on my own to work this out." He raised his hands in the air as if this proved all of his words as true.

"Give me a minute," Chris said, his arms crossed and head shaking. As much as he believed the Road Runner, it was still a Road Runner. One of the same lower species he'd been trying to exterminate for years like the filthy rats they were. "Wait right there, don't move."

Chris removed the headset and leaned over his intercom microphone. "Duane, please cancel what you're doing and return to the office immediately."

He planned to lower the barricade and let the Road Runner inside to discuss the next steps, but he didn't want to just drop their steel shield and leave everyone vulnerable without a warning.

Duane entered a minute later, calm and cool. "Why did you make me stop?"

"Our friend outside would like to come in to discuss the details. Says he doesn't want to say all of this outside where he can be heard. I'm going to let him in."

"Don't do it, Chris."

"I have no choice. He's not going to talk to us unless he comes inside. And we need Strike."

"You didn't even know you needed Strike until a couple days ago."

"Are you kidding me? Just because an active effort to capture her was never discussed doesn't mean we don't need her. This is a gift from God."

"No, it's a gift from the Road Runners, which is exactly why you should be suspicious of him acting so desperate to come inside."

Chris sighed and folded his hands on his desk. "Here's what's going to happen. I'm going to drop the barricade, and you're going to send two of our soldiers outside to greet our friend. Have them check him for any weapons and bring him inside to this office. No tours of the house, just straight here. Then I want three of our soldiers here in the room, guns cocked and aimed at Mr. Road Runner in case he tries to make any moves. Are we clear?"

"Yes, sir."

"Great. Head downstairs and gather the soldiers needed. I'm going to disarm the barricade in two minutes."

Duane left and Chris placed the headset back over his head and looked at the monitor where the Road Runner had indeed not moved. "Okay, sorry about that, just working out some logistics before we let you in."

"Understood."

"It'll be a couple minutes before we disarm the house, so hang tight. My team will meet you outside to pat you down before coming in."

"Fair enough."

The Road Runner said nothing further and stared blankly at the concealed mansion in front of him, small clouds of his breath slipping out through the ski mask stretched over his face.

Chris took off the headset and drummed his fingers on the desk, anticipating the upcoming encounter. He'd never had a Road Runner come to the upper floor of the mansion, and certainly had never sat down to have a civil discussion with one. They were never worthy of so much. He thought back to the dozens he had personally killed, and the millions murdered under his watch throughout time, causing a smirk he couldn't quite keep away.

What would happen if I flipped the script on this guy and shot him dead in my office? There's no better Road Runner than a dead Road Runner, right?

As delicious as it sounded, Chris would have to resist. If anything happened while the man was in his office, he'd end up dead anyway. Because if this wasn't some cheap setup, then the future became a lot brighter for his team and their goals.

He opened the software and punched in the code to drop the barricade. The familiar hum carried throughout the house as the steel shields lowered. The Road Runner didn't flinch.

When the humming stopped, Chris watched the monitor as the front door swung open and two of his soldiers stepped into the cold night, approaching the Road Runner with their guns drawn. The man returned his hands to the air and rotated to give his back to the Revolters.

One soldier kept his rifle fixed on the Road Runner while the other stepped up and began patting down his legs, working his way up to the neck. He nodded to the other soldier, and turned the Road Runner to lead him inside.

Chris could have changed the camera view to follow them through the entryway and up the stairs, but didn't bother. He'd be in his office within a minute anyway. A handful of soldiers stepped outside, rifles cocked and aimed into the distance, anticipating anything that might come from the woods. Duane must have given this order, clearly forgetting about the last time they had soldiers outside like sitting ducks.

The rumble of multiple footsteps coming up the stairs sent small vibrations into Chris's office, churning his stomach at the thought of an upcoming meeting with his enemy. He closed the software on his computer and pulled open a drawer to make sure his loaded revolver was still there, waiting to protect him from any attack.

The stomping grew louder and stopped outside the office door before a rapid knock banged on it.

"Come in," Chris shouted, hands trembling with excitement.

The door swung open with Duane leading the way, the masked Road Runner behind him, followed by three Revolters, each with a rifle pointed at the man's back.

"Hello, Chris," the Road Runner said, muffled through his mask.

"Please, have a seat." Chris gestured to the open seat where Duane normally sat during their sessions together. "Shall we begin?"

The man nodded. "Let's do it."

107

Chapter 15

The four men loaded into the van after wishing Ralph farewell. Ralph assured them he'd be in the same place should they need to come back for anything, although he hoped they wouldn't need to. They filled the trunk with six firearms, ten smoke bombs, one grenade, and a half dozen cases of ammunition, all at Gerald's instruction.

Gerald whistled once they reached the freeway toward downtown, leaving Martin to wonder how he could be so chipper. It was a few minutes past noon as they coasted down the empty road, and Martin couldn't recall the last time I-70 was free of any traffic.

"I want you guys to know you don't need to live in fear," Gerald said. "Stay alert, be aware of your surroundings, but no one will bother you unless you bother them. It's not *as* bad as you think."

"You said they gun down Road Runners for fun," Brigham snapped. "How am I supposed to *not* live in fear?"

Gerald chuckled a morbid sound. "We're covered. That's why I had us change to long sleeves and baggy pants. The only way anyone will see the glow from your skin is if they get right in your face. And the only reason they'll get in your face is if you bother them. Besides, where we're going there won't be many Revolters, if any. They don't exactly hang out in the slums looking for people to shoot. They stay in their area and protect their turf from outsiders."

"So it's like segregation is back?" Martin asked.

"One hundred years after it was abolished, yes, it's back. People have always been ignorant to the fact that history actually does repeat itself, and it's only become worse now that the Revolters have taken control of the education system and erased any details from the history lessons that paints what they're doing as a negative thing."

"What's the rest of the world like?" Martin asked. "Or is this just happening in America?"

"Well, I'm sure Brigham can tell you about Europe," Gerald replied. "They haven't been fully infiltrated yet, but they're on shaky ground."

"We're fighting," Brigham added nonchalantly.

"But as for Asia, Africa, and South America, they've all been taken over by the Revolters and are going through the same things we are here. Their plan is to rule the world in unison, which would be the end of civilization as we know it."

Martin shook his head. "What about Australia? You forgot them."

"Ah, the Aussies. Yeah, that's the one place they're having an incredibly difficult time taking control of. The Road Runners have a strong presence there, but I'd say ninety percent of the population has zero interest in picking a side between the two of us. They view us all as outsiders and want us to get the hell off their enormous island. They really are our last hope, and even though they reject the Road Runners, they're helping our cause by being as equally turned off by the Revolters. It's actually quite funny to watch the Revolters' leaders try to offer people the Juice down there. They usually return a blank stare and tell them to *fuck off, mate.*"

They all laughed at this, picturing someone like Chris being told to fuck off by a pissed off Australian.

"Won't they eventually just start executing people?" Martin asked. "Like if it comes down to them being the final country to take over, can't they just force their will at that point?"

"They could, but it wouldn't be wise. They'd be going up against two groups instead of one: the Road Runners *and* the Aussies. The people down there are already suspicious of any outsiders, and they have no issue unifying to protect their country. See, they actually read history books and take the lessons seriously. They would never allow something to happen to their people the way it did when the Europeans came to the Americas to rape and kill all the natives. The Revolters thrive on dividing and conquering populations of people, but the Aussies have proven resistant against such a threat."

The open fields gave way to city buildings, and Martin saw the skyscrapers of downtown in the distance, through a dark smog that hung over the city.

"We're about five minutes out," Gerald announced, shifting the mood immediately to the seriousness of the task at hand. Martin understood why Gerald was thought so highly of. He had a knack for calming the mood, making them forget where they were or why they were there.

They're all here because of me, Martin reminded himself, no longer sure if that was entirely true. Would they still have come on this mission without Martin? All across the spectrum of time, Revolters and Road Runners alike were working toward their lofty goals of ruling the world and protecting the world, respectively. Would the Road Runners really have granted a newcomer their own mission out of a simple gesture of appreciation for risking his life?

With the expanded knowledge he had gained about the Road Runners and their worldwide mission, it seemed less likely. He presumed this mission was already planned, and they took advantage of the situation to both please Martin and also add another foot soldier.

Regardless of whatever the truth might be, they trusted him enough to go into the future, something their very own leader refused to do. The group was there for both a common goal, but also their own individual reasons. If a choice came down to saving one of these men's lives or grabbing his mom's medicine, Martin wasn't entirely sure what he'd do. On the flip side, could he trust these men to save his life should a situation arise?

There were too many unknowns as they pulled into the city, but Martin pushed them aside and focused on one step at a time. And right now was all about exploring the city and knowing the best way to stay alive in it.

The van exited to I-25 southbound from I-70, the city now towering in front of them. The skyscrapers looked the same as Martin had known them from 2019, and there were even a handful more added to the skyline that overlapped the blue Rocky Mountains in the backdrop. A thick, gray haze clouded their vision.

"What's with the smog?" Martin asked. Being the only person in the vehicle who was a Denver native, he realized his responsibility to compare the city's 2064 version to the 2019 one he had left behind.

"Poe's biggest donors were from the coal industry. Once the Revolters had full control over Congress, they passed all sorts of tax breaks for companies who remained powered by coal. Such ridiculous incentives that clean energy has damn near disappeared."

"No one fought it?"

"Of course they tried. But any sort of environmental protection group run through the government had been terminated. And all the Earth-loving hippies were obviously seen as anti-Revolution and were executed. The government actually hires fake scientists to explain why coal is better for the world—and these morons believe every word of it."

They turned again off the interstate, this time taking the exit ramp for Park Avenue, and Martin's eyes bulged at the sight of a somewhat familiar building in front of them.

"Is that Coors Field?" Martin asked.

"Is that what it used to be called?" Gerald replied. "Today it's called Denver Energy Ballpark, named by the state's largest coal company, and owners of the team."

Gerald rolled his eyes as they pulled up to a stop light in front of the stadium. Martin looked out his window at the building that had undergone a transformation. Gone was its brick exterior and purple neon lighting, replaced with gold-tinted glass that shielded the view inside the stadium, a similar effect as Mandalay Bay in Las Vegas.

"Let me get this straight," Martin said. "While the rest of the country is going to shit, baseball stadiums got an upgrade?"

"All sports got an upgrade," Gerald said. "Two things happened: with the Revolters came a bunch of new billionaires, and President Poe openly admitted that sports were important to keep around so that the poor and middle class can remain distracted from what's actually going on in the government. Since the Revolters came from all eras of time to join the big takeover, these billionaires were essentially playing with fake money, as far as they were concerned. They bid against each other for ownership of all these sports franchises, and since they're playing with fake money, they simply paid athletes more while dropping the prices of the cheap seats for the general public to get in. As a group, they bought into the idea of controlling the poor and middle classes, and it worked."

"Of course it worked. All those people had a new opportunity to go catch a game; something they probably never thought possible."

"You got it. And inside you can register to vote, but only if you plan on voting for the Revolution. Poe praised himself for making it possible. He called it his gift to those less fortunate. It gets bad when Poe starts talking about himself in the third person. 'Thank President Poe. Enjoy all of the games, his treat!' he'd say. So fucked up, but people eat it up every season."

They drove away from the ballpark, and Martin thought it looked more like a palace than a baseball stadium. *I wonder what the inside looks like.*

As the luxurious, golden ballpark faded into the distance behind them, it became suddenly clear where they were. The skyscrapers stood tall and mighty a few blocks away, but the other buildings—the restaurants, stores, and small apartment complexes—were all decorated with graffiti and deteriorating from the inside out. Most of the buildings were constructed from brick, as they had always been, but now bricks had fallen out of place and were never repaired. Windows were shattered behind the iron bars that kept the thieves out. And the biggest surprise of all was the amount of homeless people crowding the sidewalks.

"Why do all of the homeless seem so organized?" Martin asked after they drove down a block where sleeping bags and tents filled the entire sidewalks on both sides of the street.

"They're restricted to camp out on certain blocks. Some of the businesses down here can pay the government extra tax money to ensure the homeless won't park themselves in front of their stores."

"How do they enforce that?"

"Quite simple. The business owner calls the police if they find a homeless person outside their store. The police department confirms that the business has paid its annual fee for this special privilege. Then they come out and shoot the homeless person, and take the body off to who knows where."

"Jesus Christ," Brigham uttered, having remained silent during the drive. Web gazed out the window, but they had grown expectant of his reticence.

"We can continue the history lesson another time," Gerald interrupted. "Because we're here, gentlemen."

He pulled the van to the side of the road and parked in front of a three-level building, a crooked, faded sign calling it *The Last Stop Hotel & Suites*. It appeared no different than the other buildings they had passed, only this one had a welcoming patch of two-foot tall grass, and black, dreary trees. Atop the building, a crow cawed into the quiet afternoon.

"Say hello to your home in 2064," Gerald said, killing the engine.

Martin pressed his face against the window to soak in his surroundings. The buildings were practically stacked on top of each other, separated only by narrow alleyways where groups of people huddle around each other, shooting dice on the ground with dollar bills in short piles.

Just remember why you're here, Martin reminded himself. *It's not that bad. When you get the medicine, all of this will be forgotten.*

He leaned back, knowing none of this would ever be forgotten. The images from his brief time in 2064 would already be burned into his memory forever, serving as a constant reminder of what waited for him later on in life.

108

Chapter 16

Commander Strike awoke in a dark hotel room. Sleeping in the Denver office had grown exhausting, as she never actually received a full night of sleep. The pull out beds had springs that dug into her back all night, and the temperature always seemed to be just off, either too hot or too cold, never perfect.

She had wished the team farewell before leaving, letting them know she was heading back to Alaska to plot the next steps of the war with Julian. While she could've slept on the plane ride home, all she really wanted was a moment alone. She had wandered down the street from the office and found a small hotel called the Jet Hotel. She could've stayed for free at the Oxford, but walking into any place filled with Road Runners always drew their attention and swarmed her in a mob of excited people.

At the Jet Hotel, she walked in the front door like any normal person looking for a room, minus the trailing security team who followed, blending in as if they didn't know her. When she checked in to her room, she immediately collapsed onto the fluffy bed, splaying her limbs in every direction and enjoying the room's perfect temperature. It had been at least ten days since she had a day off, and she'd plan on spending it in bed, watching trash TV, and ordering room service for all meals of the day.

Even on the brink of passing out from fatigue, she wondered how the crew was faring in 2064. Mainly she wondered about Martin. Something about him drove her a bit wild. He had a confidence that he didn't realize, yet a soothing presence equally oblivious to him.

She wondered what drove Martin Briar. After losing his daughter so many years ago and going back in time to helplessly witness it, *something* had to keep him moving forward. She'd seen similar scenarios play out where people had killed themselves or let their life spiral out of control with drugs, alcohol, and gambling. But not Martin Briar.

She didn't just think about him, but *worried* about him. She was in 2019, and he was in the dangerous year of 2064, 200 years after the Civil War had ended, yet seemed to be starting again. The Road Runners had statisticians who ran numbers throughout the spectrum of time. She pulled a report and found that anyone who traveled beyond the year 2050 had a six percent chance of being killed if they spent an entire day in any following year. Those numbers jumped up to ten percent and eighteen percent on days two and three, respectively.

She shared this data with Gerald, insisting they get in and out as quickly as possible. He projected a week's time to complete the mission, which carried a forty-five percent chance of death.

"They can run their numbers all they want," Gerald told her. "But they can't factor for me. Those odds don't mean shit to me. The crew will be safe as long as they listen and stay by my side."

Strike sighed in her silent room, thinking back to this brief conversation and only feeling temporarily relieved by Gerald. She wanted Martin back, not only to ensure his safety, but to ask him if he'd like to join her inner circle in leading the Road Runners. She had Julian and Bill to bring him up to speed, and believed he'd be the perfect fit with those two. Working alongside her would guarantee he'd never have to leave on a dangerous mission again, unless he really wanted to.

Thinking of them reminded her that she'd need to have a talk with both men. As a departing Commander next year, she was to endorse an individual to succeed her. Endorsed candidates had won the election ninety-five percent of the time throughout the Road Runners' history, and while Bill had plenty of seniority and wisdom, she believed Julian had the mettle and toughness to lead the organization into the next wave of the future.

Bill had always been laidback, so she hoped this scenario would be no different. He'd make a fantastic leader during a time of peace, but they simply weren't at that point yet. For her, she considered who would have the greatest odds of capturing Chris, and that was a no-brainer to choose Julian. He had the ambition, passion, and a wealth of fresh ideas. Deep down she knew she wouldn't be the one to get Chris, but had no issue imagining Julian pulling off the task.

Julian can end the war, and Bill can lead them into peace afterward, she thought, and would plan her pitch to them on exactly this.

A shallow knock came from the door, causing Strike to jump in the bed. The room was pitch-black except for the soft glow of the clock on the nightstand that read 6:42. She had breakfast scheduled for delivery at 7:30, and couldn't imagine they'd be this early with the food. Perhaps they thought she asked for her delivery at 6:30. Or it could have been one of her guards, but they never disrupted her, especially during sleep.

They'd either knock again, or leave, realizing their mistake. Strike rolled onto her back and stared into the darkness. The thick curtains had been drawn shut to keep any sunlight out. She turned to the door, where a sliver of light from the hallway seeped through the bottom gap. The light divided by the shadows of two feet as the person who knocked remained on the other side.

A second knock echoed throughout the room.

"Who is it?" she called.

"Room service. Breakfast delivery."

Dammit, she thought, dreading that she now had to get out of bed a whole 45 minutes earlier than planned. She had the room till noon and planned to eat herself into an early morning nap.

Strike rolled to the edge of the bed and swung her legs over where they landed into a pair of white slippers. A robe lay on the ground which she pulled over her naked body. "I'm coming!"

She shuffled across the room, tasting the sourness of her morning breath, and knowing her hair was a frazzled mess. The unpleasant sight of her opening the door was their fault for being so early. She flicked on the light switch in the entryway, splashing a soft glow across the room. A quick check through the door's peephole showed a young man dressed in a suit, a tray of breakfast held in his arms.

Strike pulled open the door to receive a warm smile from the man. "Good morning, Ms. Strike, we have your breakfast ready."

"Thank you, but I had asked for it at 7:30."

The man's face scrunched as he checked the receipt on the tray. "I show that as your regular request, but that you called in to request it earlier."

"I never called in. I've been asleep almost the entire time I've been here. It must have been a call for a different room."

The man peered at the paper, his arms trembling from the weight of the tray.

"Please, you can put the food down on the dresser. You don't need to hold it this whole time," Strike said. The young man entered the room and slid the tray on top of the nearest dresser.

"Of course, thank you. It just doesn't make sense. It was a handwritten note passed over to me about the change of time. I don't know who did it."

"I did," a voice called from the open door, and they both swiveled around to see Chris standing there with a wide grin.

"Who are you?" the man asked.

"Just an old friend of Ms. Strike," Chris replied calmly, his grin not fading.

The man looked from Chris to Strike. Strike had a stern expression smacked on her face.

"Ma'am, are you okay?" he asked. "Or should I stay?"

"You can stay," Chris cut in, lunging across the room and pulling a pocket knife from his coat.

The poor kid never saw it coming. Chris jammed the knife into his gut, getting a faint grunt sound as the hotel employee collapsed to his knees, eyes staring blankly at the crazy old man.

Strike balled her hands into fists, fighting off the urge to leap across the room and tackle Chris. He had a weapon, leaving her no option but to stand by and watch, her pistol tucked away in her suitcase.

Where the hell is my team? she wondered. It was completely unacceptable for Chris Speidel to even be in the same building as her, let alone standing at her room's door.

"So we're killing innocent civilians now?" she snapped.

Chris tipped the man on his back, his skull hitting the carpeted floor with a hollow *thock!*

"I'll kill whoever gets in my way," Chris said, turning his maniacal expression to her. "Especially with such a grand opportunity like this."

"What are you talking about?"

Beneath her confident tone, Strike shook with terror. This was her own mistake, insisting to stay in the hotel. *Where are they?!* Surely one of the guards had to have seen Chris slip into the building. Strike focused on her heart rate as it tried to leap out of her throat. She was alone in a private room with Chris Speidel where he could kill her and disappear without a trace. The weight of the entire war now hung on to her ability to talk her way out of this predicament.

"I'm talking about an end to this war," Chris said.

"I see, so you're here for a peace offering."

Chris giggled like a child. "Peace? I think too much blood has been shed for this to all end with peace. I always imagined the ending as more of an explosion. An ending of all endings. A big *boom*." He held his hands open and apart to mimic an explosion.

Chris returned the knife to his pocket after wiping the blood clean with his fingers, which he slurped off like barbecue sauce after attacking a rack of ribs. The sight sent instant chills down Strike's back.

"You see, Ms. Strike, I came here with two options. I can either kill you and watch your people flounder for leadership. Or, my preferred option, I take you with me, and we watch together as your people scramble. We can laugh at it like a good comedy movie."

"We have systems in place," Strike cut in. "This exact scenario has already been planned for. We have a chain of command that falls into place, and everyone moves up one position."

"How precious. That's a good sentiment, and I'm sure it'll resonate with the general population of your people, but what about your leadership? Your Lead Runners, as I believe they're called?"

"How do you know that term?" A tsunami started to form in her gut. Chris already knew too much.

"That's a fair question, but have you considered the other glaring one you've yet to ask? Aren't you curious as to *why* I'm here? *How* I got here?"

"Your people have been following me. It's no secret. And this is my own fault for insisting on a non-Road Runner hotel."

"I see. Thought you'd have a romantic getaway, eh? Well, I hate to be the bearer of bad news, but we have not been tailing you."

Chris paused, and his grin somehow widened even more, revealing his yellow-tinted teeth.

"I don't know what you're getting at."

"Strike, my dear, your own people turned you in. *Your* people told us where you'd be and how to get to you. *Your* people told us where your security team was, so I killed them all before coming to your room. We made a deal where I release the prisoners I've kept for so long, and they hand you over. I thought the offer was too good to be true, but here we are."

Strike studied Chris, unsure if she should believe him or not. He kept his childish grin, and that's what made her think it all true. He clearly enjoyed getting a reaction, and not a fake one. That was his purpose wasn't it, to feed off the raw emotion from those around him?

Her mind immediately jumped in circles, wondering who in the hell on her team would stoop this low. Her face softened with the sudden realization that she had no way out of this situation.

"I know, my dear – this must be sickening for you to hear. I never thought such a loyal group of people could carry out such huge betrayal."

"I don't believe you." Doubt clung to her every word.

"Let's cut the shit. You're coming with me and it's time to decide how. I can force you, or you can cooperate, and I just might spare you further down the road. So what will it be?"

Strike wanted nothing more than to grab her pistol in the closet and empty it into this old piece of shit's skull, but it wouldn't accomplish a thing. He'd just stand there, giggling through it like someone was tickling him with a feather.

She wondered what the nerds at the office would say of her chances of death right now. Her only chance of living now relied on Chris's mercy, and she had to do anything to increase those chances.

"Before I go with you, I want some sort of proof. I still don't believe someone on my team would do this."

"Certainly," Chris said as he rummaged in his pockets, pulling out a folded up piece of paper. He stepped toward her and held it out for her to grab.

She unfolded it and flattened it to read the scribbled handwriting.

"Holy shit," she gasped. The writing was the next 24 hours of her schedule neatly listed in bullet points, down to the minute. Her flight back to Alaska was the next thing shown, where they'd expect her in another five hours.

"The holiest of shits, I'd say," Chris added.

"This can't be."

"Let's go, my dear. We have work to get done."

Chris stepped to her and took the paper out of her trembling grip, sliding an arm around her shoulder.

This is actually happening, she thought, mind spinning. The deathly sensation of Chris's arm around made her want to vomit. He smelled like a funeral parlor, and his arm felt like a block of ice over her shoulders.

"Who did this?" she demanded, squirming to get out of his grip.

Only a handful of people had access to her complete schedule: Bill, Julian, and her security detail who trailed her every minute of the day. The security team consisted of a rotation of ten different members who typically traveled with her and stayed by her side when she left one of the offices. Except today when she demanded they stay in a hotel room down the hallway.

"I wish I could tell you," Chris said into her ear, the odor of death oozing from his pores. "It was a man, but he remained anonymous, insisting to never be known. And since he came to me with such a generous offer, I felt compelled to oblige to his request."

If it was a man, that only eliminated the two women on her security team, leaving eight others plus Bill and Julian. But why? Who would gain from having her kidnapped by the Revolters? Julian would step into her role as Commander, with Bill moving up one spot closer. But she couldn't imagine either of them orchestrating this, especially with her term up within a year.

It had to be someone on the security team. Just because Road Runners were sworn to loyalty, it didn't make them immune to the temptations of an offer. Who knows what Chris put on the table in exchange for her schedule, but it had better been worth it, because if she ever found her way out of this mess she wouldn't rest until the traitor was brought to justice.

Her fear and anxiety quietly slipped away and gave way to rage. Her fists had been balled, and she now felt her fingernails puncturing the inside of her palms.

"Let's get out of here, shall we?" Chris said with his smirk. "We've got so much work to do and so little time."

He pulled her in closer, daring her to make a move she would only regret.

"Let's get this over with," she said.

Chris nodded, and led them out of the room.

109

Chapter 17

The hotel suite reminded Martin of his old place in Larkwood. It had every feel of the bachelor pad that he had grown to love. The chipped walls had larger holes covered with tape and a half-hearted paint job. The blinds, crooked in the window sill, let the sunlight seep in through a slanted angle. The stench of cheap cleaning chemicals filled their noses when they entered the vacant space.

Web studied the space with his lips pursed and brow furrowed, and touched the furniture and countertops with such caution that he must have thought a diseased creature would jump up and kiss him.

"Don't fall in love with the place, gentlemen," Gerald said. "We're here to sleep and work—won't exactly be hanging out to watch football on Sundays. Web, you're going to have the master bedroom since you'll be doing the most work inside. Set up the room however you see fit. There are two other bedrooms, so who wants to sleep on the living room couch?"

Brigham and Martin locked eyes for a brief moment. "I'll do it," Brigham said. "My wife used to threaten me to sleep on the couch, but little did she know I liked it; my own private space where no one could steal the sheets."

Gerald snickered. "Suit yourself. Martin, I'll take the north facing bedroom since it has the best view of the front of the building."

"Sounds good."

The men split separate ways to examine their new living spaces. Bedroom doors creaked open as Brigham flopped down on the raggedy couch, kicking his shoes off and grinning the way only a free man could.

Martin entered his room to find a bed pushed into the corner next to a closet. A lone wooden desk sat below the window and faced the city. Forty years earlier the view would've been stunning, but with the gloom and smog, it was borderline depressing to see what had happened to Denver.

The walls were thin, as he heard Brigham whistling to himself and Gerald humming a tune. Martin pulled open the desk drawers to find nothing but some blank sheets of paper with pens and pencils. The closet also had no trace of life except for the empty hangers. He wondered if this building had been slaughtered like the one they had first visited to see Ralph, and decided he didn't really want to know, seeing as he had to sleep in this room.

"Gentlemen!" Gerald shouted loud enough to make Martin jump. "Living room right now."

Martin stepped out of the bedroom and met everyone around the couch where Brigham now sat up with his smile gone.

"We have a problem," Gerald continued once they all arrived. "I just got an email from headquarters. It appears Commander Strike has been kidnapped by Chris."

Web gasped, and Brigham shook his head in disgust.

"We don't know any of the details, other than she had checked into a hotel in Denver the night before her return flight to Alaska, and when she never showed up to the plane, the team started their search. She only had one bag of things she had packed, but it was still in the hotel room."

"How do we know it was Chris?" Martin asked.

"That bastard left a note. 'I have your girl,' was all it said, signed in his name.

"Jesus Christ," Brigham said, a sour look stuck on his face. "What does this mean for us?"

"At the moment, nothing. They're scrambling to figure out what to do next and deciding if they need to implement the chain of command that's written in our bylaws. They first want to see if there's even a chance of finding her before making that decision."

"You don't suppose she ran off?" Brigham asked. "Did they not check her tracker?"

"I'm sure they did, but they're not sharing all of the details."

"That means it's an inside job. They are transparent with everything. If they're hiding something, that means they don't want it to fall on the wrong ears."

"Let's settle down. This is how rumors start. They may have the details and just didn't tell me. It was more of a notice in case we happen to hear anything here in 2064."

"Right, because they would run off to this shithole," Brigham said, shaking his head. "No offense."

"None taken," Gerald snapped. "This does make our work a bit harder, more in the sense of our timeline. We'll need to hurry instead of taking our time. Just because we have a system in place doesn't mean this won't have an effect. There could be a ripple all the way to this year."

"What does that mean?" Martin asked.

"It means we need to get to work right now so we can help with whatever the Road Runners need. Let's get our thoughts in order and meet back here in fifteen minutes to start a plan."

"Fifteen minutes? I don't think you understand what I do," Web added, a tinge of anger in his voice. "I need at least an entire day to gather research on the area."

"I know that. I said to *start* a plan, not an entire strategy ready to go. I know this will all take time. I'd rather get started now instead of wasting a day doing nothing." Web stormed off to his bedroom and slammed the door like a moody teenager. Brigham giggled as Gerald sighed and crossed his arms. "Anyone else have any issues they'd like to discuss?"

Brigham stared to the ceiling and Martin shook his head.

"Great then. Martin, if you don't mind I'd like to meet in your room and go through that suitcase Ralph gave you. Knowing what's in there should help us plan what you'll be doing."

"Okay, let's go."

Martin pivoted and led the way to his bedroom. He had pushed the suitcase into the corner, and tossed it on the bed to examine its contents.

Gerald shuffled into the room and closed the door. "How are you doing?" He dropped his authoritative exterior, softening his voice and facial features as he watched Martin.

"I'm fine. Why do you ask?"

"I know this is your first mission with us, and it's one hell of a difficult one. I'm just making sure you're not having any regrets."

"No regrets. I just want this medicine. I *need* this medicine."

Gerald nodded. "I know. We're gonna try to get it as quickly as possible. What do you think of our team?"

"I don't know, everyone seems nice enough. I like Brigham, he keeps the mood light. Web stays to himself, so it's hard to get a good read on him."

Gerald chuckled. "Brigham is a character, that's for sure. He's scared shitless, that's why he's always saying things. He's keeping the mood light for himself, not us. And Web is a wizard, you'll see. He's honestly the key to everything. He'll get us into the hospital, or wherever we need."

And what do you think of me? Martin wondered. *That I'm in over my head? Are you wondering why you got stuck babysitting some newbie on a fool's mission?*

"So let's see inside this bag," Martin said, pushing his thoughts aside.

"Yes."

Martin stepped forward and unzipped the suitcase to reveal a stuffed bag of clothes.

Gerald reached in, pulling items out and examining them. It was mostly shirts and pants, but a few accessories like earrings, chains, and rings were found in a separate pouch. Martin studied the clothes that looked no different than polo shirts and jeans. Each article of clothing had a letter P sewn into it, small like a dime, but visible nonetheless.

"What's the P for on all of these?" Martin asked.

"Our fearless leader. Poe Enterprises is the name of his company, and they make a little bit of everything. It's easy when you're in charge of setting the regulations. Poe gives company stock to every single member of Congress—after he abolished all the rules against it, of course—that way he can ensure every decision made will have his company in mind."

"How did he manage that law?"

"Again, it's easy when your party is aligned in all three branches. Even the Supreme Court allowed it. He probably paid everyone off to get the votes. It's one of those things where no one says, and no one asks. If anyone dares to question Poe, they might as well sign their own death certificate."

"So these clothes are supposed to make me look like a supporter?"

"That's the idea. His brands are so heavily advertised—for free—that it's all anyone really buys. He damn near has a monopoly on every industry, and in the ones he doesn't, he only allows his friends to operate their businesses. He has no competition."

"So the law against monopolies has been erased, too?"

"The law? Try the entire SEC. There's only one group overlooking everything in the country, and it's the Revolters."

Martin stood in silence, looking to the clothes scattered across the bed. "You think they have Strike alive?"

"They do. I'm also in a hurry to join you guys back in 2019. I'll be volunteering for the mission to rescue her, and you should, too."

"I think I should see how this one goes first, don't you think?"

"Nonsense. I'll barge into any room for a chance to save Commander Strike, and I like my odds in most situations. But for you, it should be all about helping the Road Runners move forward. We can't truly move forward without our leader."

Martin remembered what he had heard about a major decision waiting after Strike's term had ended. How could Gerald not know? Or was he too brainwashed by the Road Runners to see clearly? Gerald would take a bullet for Strike, while Martin just wanted out of this situation. If only he could've left Izzy in the past, he'd never have met Sonya, his mother would've never come down with Alzheimer's, and he'd be happily blackout drunk in his apartment, dreading the day at the post office ahead.

It had been a while since he reminisced on his life before meeting Chris, and never thought he'd actually long for a return to the fuzzy days of his horrendous routine.

"This is all bigger than us. Remember that, Martin." Gerald spoke as he looked at the clothes piled on the bed. "You should head into town in the morning and get familiar with the area. You'll want a backstory, just in case. I think a good job to say you have is as an attorney. There are thousands of those now, and they all make ridiculous money. There are some suit jackets in the bag, throw one on. Do you know anything about lawyers?"

"Sure. I've gone through a divorce."

"Perfect, play off that. Say you're a divorce lawyer. That's even better because no one wants to go into those details, unlike a criminal attorney."

"What exactly am I looking for around town?"

"Since we know where the medicine is kept, I'd say to get familiar with the area around the hospitals. Learn any side doors, hidden streets, anything that can help in case we have to escape in a hurry."

"Question. Why aren't we planning on taking our Juice with us and drinking it as soon as we have the medicine in hand?"

"Brigham and Web will be here, and we can't leave without them."

"Can't we call them when we have it and take our drinks together? It just seems like an unnecessary risk to try and escape after stealing."

"Calling would be the risk. Privacy laws have been abolished, meaning the government listens to all phone calls that take place, read every e-mail and text message that are sent, and likely bug houses wherever they might have a suspicion. We have to pretend there is no way of communicating with each other once we leave this apartment."

Martin thought back to his brief trip to 1919 with Sonya where they also had no means of communication. Maybe if they had, he wouldn't have been sucked in as a Road Runner.

"In fact," Gerald continued. "If you brought your phone, I urge you to leave it here. There's no point in taking the risk of temptation. They might even be trying to track you. Unlikely they think you're in this year, but you never know."

Martin shook his head, the future becoming grimmer with every detail that was further revealed. At this point, he simply wanted to get the mission over with and return home, and that's what he told Gerald before changing into his new clothes and preparing to explore the city as an undercover Revolter.

110

Chapter 18

Julian pushed open Commander Strike's office door, letting it creak as it revealed the dark and abandoned space. Everything remained exactly as Strike had left it. Her desk was clear of any clutter, a lone framed picture of Strike's former family smiling as they posed at a local park. The filing cabinet on the back wall was covered with mementos from around the world and history. She had collected coins, which were spread across the surface, mixed in with handcrafted wooden and glass figurines.

Julian stepped in, flicking on the light switch, and planting himself on the couch that faced the desk where his boss always sat and vented to him. Being the second-in-command was as awful as it sounded. While he technically had the power to make sweeping decisions, he couldn't do so without the Commander's approval. Everything was run through the Commander, for better or worse.

He leaned back on the couch, falling into its soft embrace, and soaked in the office ambiance. A picture hung on the wall of the seven Commanders, standing strong together with stern expressions. Julian remembered this picture because he took it on a spur-of-the-moment trip where the leaders decided to meet to establish goals for the near and distant future, most of which surrounded the capturing of Chris.

It was the only picture of its kind, the past leaders of the Road Runners never having taken a photo together despite the dozens of times they met.

Strike insisted on the picture, and after seeing it printed, the organization decided it should hang in every Commander's office around the world, and updated whenever someone new was elected into the position.

It was getting late, 9 p.m. to be exact, but Julian wouldn't sleep, his mind flooded with excitement and angst. It wasn't the way he imagined it, but he was now in charge of the North American Road Runners thanks to the laws for an existing Commander unable to fill their role.

Julian was sworn in earlier in the day, taking the oath to protect and serve the Road Runners will all of his might, willpower, and mental fortitude. He thought these all meant the same thing, but said "I do" just the same.

From that moment on, he was free to assume his new role as Commander. The guilt, however, had kept him out of Strike's office at first. He could've spent the next week dwelling on the guilt, but that served or protected no one. As leader, decisions needed to be made quickly and with purpose. *The world must go on,* he thought, echoing a thought from his late grandfather.

Julian rose from the couch and crossed the office to the desk—*his* desk—now taking in the view from the other side. As he sat down, the cold leather chair welcomed him, screeching as he adjusted in the seat. He slung his arms on the armrests and enjoyed the private moment where he realized the weight of the world that had been gently placed on his shoulders.

Commander Strike had always told him about the pressures that came with the position. One decision could mean life or death, and while deploying Road Runners for dangerous missions was agreed upon as a necessity, it never made it easy to authorize, knowing the odds of survival in certain situations.

Even though she didn't make the greatest of leaders for their organization, she did serve as a great mentor for Julian—he couldn't deny that. Maybe she was the right leader at the wrong time, similar to Bill, who would make a fine Commander during a time of peace. She liked to beat around the bush when it came to the aforementioned sending of troops into danger.

Julian had to capitalize on the situation. A window would soon be opened, and he saw no reason to not take advantage of the chance to end this war once and for all.

"It's going to happen under my watch. Even if I have to do it myself." Julian spoke to the empty office in a calm voice, grinning as his legs bounced wildly beneath the desk. He closed his eyes and imagined the explosions, green and magnificent, glowing victorious in the silent Alaska air.

He pulled out his cell phone and sent a text message to Bill, asking him to bring Julian's laptop from his office and meet him immediately. Bill had become the new lieutenant commander after Strike's kidnapping, yet Julian hadn't heard from him beyond the day the news had broken.

Bill let him know he'd be there shortly, and Julian slouched back into the chair, enjoying the comforts of his new office space. Down the hallway, the security team was split into two, one half trying to find a way to get Strike back, and the other planning their security detail for Julian as the new Commander.

Bill knocked on the door and let himself in.

"Good evening, Julian."

"Good evening. How have you been? I feel like I haven't seen you in days."

"I've been fine. Working around the clock to try and get Strike back. It's not looking good."

No shit it's not looking good, Julian thought. *She's with Chris. It'll be impossible.*

"I'm sure we'll come up with something; we always do," Julian said.

"I don't think that applies to this situation. This is new to all of us. People are wondering why you're not making more of an effort to get her back."

"Christ, I've only been in charge for a day. I haven't even made a public speech yet to the organization. Besides, I've been toying around with another idea, and that's why I called you here."

"Alright, what's going on?"

Bill approached the desk and sat down across from Julian, sliding his laptop across the polished wood.

"Right now, Strike is in the air with Chris. We've been following Strike's tracking device. The connection has been lost, but that only means they're too high in elevation. He's either taking her back to his mansion, or his store in Nevada. The store has no protection compared to the mansion, so we believe they'll be landing here in Alaska in the next few hours."

Julian sat forward and smirked, his hands clasped on top of the desk. The light reflected off his slicked hair as he stared into Bill's soul.

"What are you getting at?" Bill finally asked.

"I know we have bombs. Lots of them."

"Those are strictly for use in a time of crisis, only to be deployed as a final resort."

"Is our leader being kidnapped *not* a time of crisis? Have we *not* tried shooting Chris multiple times in the head, only to see him live? I think we reached our final resort after he rose from the ground and laughed his way back into the mansion."

"Dropping bombs never ends well. There are too many innocent people who can die."

Julian sighed. Bill was very much cut from the same cloth as Strike. Neither of them had the balls to drop a bomb, all because of a false sense of morality.

"All I'm saying—and it should be considered— is that we take the chance since Chris is outside of his mansion. We can blow him up in the sky, or wait till he's on his way home."

"You want to bomb him with Strike by his side?"

"It's not that I *want* to, but we *need* to. Strike would die happy knowing she was sacrificed to kill Chris. Besides, if we don't have a way of getting her back, then she's only going to spend the rest of her life in his prison. Why make her suffer through that? What do you think?"

Bill stood up, his face curled into a snarl. "I think you've already gone

677

power-hungry on your second day. You need to think about what you're saying and come up with a better idea—one that doesn't involve killing *our* Commander." He turned to storm out of the room.

"Wait," Julian said with a hand raised. He stood to meet Bill's eye level. "I didn't ask for this. This isn't how I ever imagined I'd come into this position. I was going to run a fair campaign in the next election cycle. But none of that matters. She's not coming back, and the sooner we can accept that as an organization, the sooner we can get back to ending this war. That's why I'm up all night plotting away, and I thought you'd like to come along for the ride."

"You know if Strike lives this will never cease. Whether it's you or some future Commander, the people will expect an idea for getting her back."

"I know that, but I have my sights set on bigger things. We can end this war today if I can just get some support on these bombs."

Funny enough, the number two in charge had to give the final approval for deploying the bombs after authorization from the Commander. Julian technically had more influence on the decision as Strike's number two, compared to now as the Commander. *Goddamn checks and balances.*

But maybe he was closer now. Strike would never have authorized a bombing, even on the tragic day after Chris was shot and rose from the dead minutes later. Sure, the barricade went up and likely made the bombs useless, but why not give it a try? Or at least have a discussion? The worst case scenario was them stuck in the same exact position.

"A bomb will never be dropped under my leadership," she had told him when he first brought it up.

Now that the closed-mindedness was out of the way, Julian only had to convince Bill to approve the bombs. Bill was just as peaceful as Strike, but he had an open mind.

"Sit down, Bill. I want to discuss this."

Bill sighed, crossed his arms, and dragged himself back to the seat across Julian's desk. In the past, Bill could've stormed out of the room without a word, but Julian was now the Commander, leaving him no choice but to do as requested.

"Thank you," Julian said sharply. "Let's get the first matter out of the way. We don't need any tension. You and I are still friends and will continue to work together like we always have. I'm not here to boss you around, just to get shit done."

Bill clasped his hands on his lap, one leg bouncing as he stared at Julian with heavy, exhausted eyes. "I don't want this power to go to your head. I'll be here to support you every step of the way, but please don't overstep any boundaries."

"With all due respect, Bill, there are no more boundaries. I'm the Commander."

"Yes, we know that. But it doesn't give you the right to become a dictator. Don't lose your values."

Julian had met Bill when he was first recruited by the Road Runners. Bill saved Julian, more than he'd ever know, after the complete collapse of his life. Julian was a prodigy in his life before the Road Runners, leaving no wonder as to why he was sought out after he received the Juice from Chris.

Julian had risen as a shining star throughout high school, finishing as valedictorian and leading his football team to their second consecutive state championship as their quarterback. Scholarship offers flooded his mailbox, both athletic and academic. Deciding to enroll at Harvard ended up as the decision that shaped the rest of his life.

He didn't continue with football at the collegiate level, wanting to focus on economics in his schooling. But he remained in shape, and even got talked into running the Boston Marathon in 2013. Always up for a physical challenge, Julian trained every single night to get into top shape for the famous marathon.

Like everything else in his life up to that point, the training came naturally. He reached a point where he ran 15 miles every day after class. At nineteen years old, Julian had quickly found himself in the best shape of his life. He ate chicken and vegetables every single day for the four weeks leading up to the marathon, leaving nothing to chance. He passed on parties, drinking booze with his roommate, and made sure to get eight hours of sleep each night.

Everything led up to a successful day on April 15, 2013. He started with the 10:40 a.m. slate of runners, taking the morning to relax, stretch, and mentally prepare for the grueling task ahead. Always an analytical person, he projected four hours for him to complete the race, not bad for a first timer, but well off the mark of the winners who typically clocked in under two and a half hours.

He didn't join the race to win. There were plenty of runners who dedicated their lives to a chance at victory. Julian popped in his earphones and listened to the four hour playlist of songs he had created to carry him through the race. He maintained a steady pace that he had found to work, and focused on his breathing, letting the cool air fill his lungs as he timed his inhales every five seconds.

The race passed in a blur, and as he approached the finish line with a few minutes to spare before 3 p.m., everything changed forever.

The finish line waited over 100 yards away. Julian had taken out his earphones to hear the roaring crowd cheering on everyone who finished the race. People lined the sidewalks, jumping and waving at the hundreds of strangers who ran by on the street.

An explosion boomed from the left sidewalk, gray smoke immediately rising and filling the air, clouding the view of the upcoming finish line. The ground shook, causing Julian and many others to lose their footing and fall with their hands splayed out. His first thought was that an earthquake had just struck.

By the time he got back to his feet, a second explosion rang out, this one much closer as the thunderous force sent everyone flying through the air. Julian's ears reverberated as he threw his arms over his head to shield it from what felt like dozens of hailstones showering over him. He had fallen back to the ground.

He looked up to see blood speckled across his legs, as if he had just received 100 small paper cuts across his flesh. About thirty feet away was a sight that would never leave his memory. A man lay on his back, arms splayed to his sides as he cried and shouted to the skies. Both of his legs were gone, cut from the knee down where blood oozed like a river onto the asphalt.

"Somebody help me! It fucking burns!" the man had shouted, his shrieking voice lost in the commotion of hundreds of other people shouting and stampeding to safety.

Julian shook his head free of the shards of glass, crawling toward the man, but not moving. Each movement he made sent a jolt of pain down his back, all but paralyzing him. After five attempts to push off the ground, he gave up and rolled onto his back, looking to the smoke-filled sky and praying this wasn't how his life ended.

Life didn't end that day, but a new beginning waited on the horizon. Julian walked away with no serious injuries, merely a couple of broken ribs and bruising throughout his whole body. While this all seemed innocent on paper—and nothing compared to the man who lost his legs and the countless others who never made it home for supper—the recovery led Julian down a dark path of painkillers and an opioid addiction that would haunt the next three months of his life.

Until he met Chris Speidel.

111

Chapter 19

"Let me tell you why you should give the green light to the bombs," Julian said, sitting up stiffly. He had his cell phone on the desk, a software running in the background to record this conversation, needing at least one soundbite he could work with. "For starters, we've been sitting on these bombs for how many years? Are we ever going to use them?"

"They're intended to use in defense; not to proactively drop."

"I know that, and I understand why. Dropping a bomb can easily get regular people in the middle of this mess. But, Bill, we're in the middle of nowhere, the fucking North Pole. These aren't nuclear bombs, so it's not like we have to worry about any widespread harm to civilians. We can drop hundreds of these bombs and no one will even know."

"So you want to drop them on the mansion?"

"Precisely."

"You know it's barricaded with thick steel. Dropping a bomb would be a waste and do nothing but escalate this war."

"Or it can *end* this war. We're going to have a small window of opportunity when those barricades go down. The rest of our people are going to be released at some point in the next couple of days."

"How do you know this?" Bill asked, staring at his young counterpart with suspicious eyes.

"We have an insider, and that's all you need to know. I think we need to act quickly because no one knows how long this barricade will stay up once its closed again."

"He'll have Commander Strike in there. We need to get her out of there before any bomb is dropped. I won't approve it otherwise."

"I think we can make that work. So you will approve the dropping of a bomb on Chris's mansion?"

Bill sighed and crossed his arms. "Yes I will—"

Got it! Julian wanted to jump out of his chair for obtaining the recording he needed, but kept cool while Bill finished speaking.

"—but only under that one condition. If you can actually pull it off, then what can stop me from saying no?"

"Thanks, Bill. I knew we'd be able to come to an agreement. Shall we toast to our future as the leaders of the Road Runners?"

"Perhaps tomorrow. I don't remember the last time I've slept, and it's time for me to take a day off."

"I'll see you tomorrow, then. Go get some rest."

Bill nodded and bowed out of the office in a hurry, leaving Julian alone to stew in rage.

They both knew there was no chance of getting Strike out of that mansion. Julian had to bite his lip over the past few months as he watched Bill desperately try to win Strike's affection. Bill had the unconditional and blind loyalty of a puppy toward Strike, so it was no surprise for him to make such an outrageous offer.

Julian was also a step ahead, knowing Bill had cornered him with his proposal. If Strike actually escaped the mansion, she would immediately return to power and could override any decision implemented by Julian. And she would never approve of a missile strike on the mansion, even if it was confirmed empty of any Road Runners.

They deserve each other, Julian thought, trying to think of a way out of this virtual handcuffing of his plan.

He had the conversation recorded and could edit it to force the approval. To get to that stage, however, Bill needed to be completely out of the picture.

Julian leaned back and reflected on the difficult decision that now stood between him and his destiny as the Commander who killed Chris.

You can't stop this, Bill. There are too many moving parts, and this train has already left the station. Get off the tracks or else.

Julian tried to shake his head clear of evil thoughts, but they wouldn't leave. No, he didn't necessarily want to see Strike dead, but he also didn't want to see her alive. The Road Runners were in better hands now, under his guidance, and the population would see that soon enough.

"I just need to drop this bomb and end this war. Then they'll make statues of me and crown me as the best Commander ever." He looked at the office walls, dozens of portraits of past Commanders staring back at him with smug expressions, and years of failure hiding behind their eyes. "I can be the one. Someone has to be."

The pictures were in chronological order, leading up to Commander Strike, her portrait slightly larger than the rest to signify her current reign. In her picture, she had pursed lips, a cocked eyebrow, and long blond hair slung behind her shoulders. Her blue eyes pierced Julian, daring him to complete this side project he had been working on behind her back. She had to have known. Even though she was afraid to take chances, there was no denying her intelligence. She rose to power because of her mind and ability to communicate with people, traits that Julian needed to work on to add to his arsenal of talents as a strategist in the war against the Revolters.

Julian smiled and pulled open the desk drawer to retrieve a silver revolver. He spun the cylinder to ensure no bullets were loaded, cocked the hammer, and pointed it at Strike's portrait with a widening grin.

"We can't go on with you. I'm sorry. I know you didn't get us into this mess, but you'll never get us out of it. *I* have to do it."

He squeezed the trigger, a faint click leaving the revolver that trembled in his hand. Strike's portrait continued to stare at him, showing her disappointment with his sudden rise to corruption. Julian giggled, knowing tomorrow her portrait would be changed to a smaller version to make room for his own face. Tomorrow was the public ceremony where a big speech was expected, outlining his vision for the rest of the term. Julian had the unique opportunity to serve longer than the standard two-year term. Since he was succeeding Strike in her absence, he was technically finishing out her term, which had another year left. After that he could run for the following election and be solidified for another two years in power.

If he could get the bomb dropped within the next three months, his popularity would soar and easily carry him through the next election, leaving him to guide the Road Runners not only through the end of the war, but also the transition into peace that followed.

"I have to do it," he said again to Strike's portrait before loading the revolver and standing from the desk. "And there's not a damn thing you can do to stop me."

He cackled one final time before departing the office and turning down the hallway to Bill's office. The main floor had a handful of Road Runners scattered about at their desks, monitoring the screens, searching for a way to break Strike free. The majority were already sound asleep, snoring on the pull out beds underneath their desks.

The leadership team sometimes slept in their offices, but always tried to make it home at the end of the day. Bill's office waited three doors down, and if he was in there, Julian would try to talk him into going home. And if he wasn't there, Julian would head straight to his house for a nightcap.

He reached the door and rapped on it with a shaky fist. He'd never considered himself a nervous person, but with history looming on the other side of tomorrow, a pressure had bubbled up within himself that made it impossible to sit still.

No answer, so he knocked one more time for good measure. Julian checked behind to see if any of the other Road Runners were paying him any attention and was pleased to find they weren't.

He tried the door knob, and let himself into Bill's empty office. The computer screen splashed blue light across the office's back wall as the only source of light. The couch had not been turned into a bed and all the lights were turned off.

He went home.

Julian hadn't expected this to be so easy, knowing anything with Bill was always an uphill battle. The sight of the abandoned office created a fresh wave of nerves that fluttered from his toes to his throbbing temples. The revolver pulsed in his waistband like it had a life of its own.

Go to his house. The stars are aligned for all of your dreams to come true. Don't mess this up.

Julian nodded, stepping back into the hallway and gently closing the door to avoid any attention. Those who worked were too involved in their screens to see what was going on right in front of them. *Keep looking for Strike,* he thought. *You'll never get her out of that mansion.*

Julian retreated down the hall back to his new office. In case any wandering eyes had noticed him, he needed to put some time between his visit to Bill's office and his departure from the building to avoid any suspicion.

"Fifteen minutes," he said after closing his office door and pacing around the room. "Fifteen minutes and I'll go to Bill's house. Ask him if I can come in and talk a little more. He can't send me away; I'm the Commander."

No matter how many times he said it aloud, the ring of his new title never grew old, making him grin every time.

Stop stroking yourself and prepare for this meeting. You can't take that gun.

Julian stopped mid-step at this realization. If he planned to get away with murder, he had to think smarter than shooting Bill with a revolver that only a handful of people had access to, let alone knew about.

"Fuck," he barked. His plans were about to get messy, but his mind had already been made. He shuffled to the desk and frantically pulled open all of the drawers until he found a pair of gloves that belonged to Strike. He pulled them over his hands, stretching them to their limits as the stitching in the seams made cracking sounds.

"There," he said, examining his gloved hands under the lights. The technology in the future could identify a fingerprint within a matter of minutes, and if a highly ranked official of the Road Runners were to show up murdered, they would certainly send all evidence to the future to try and solve the case. "I think we're about set here, Commander Strike," he said to her portrait, patting it with the black gloves.

Julian closed all the desk drawers and arranged the papers on the desk in a neat pile, not wanting to leave a trace behind of his flustered presence. He tapped Strike's picture as he left the office, sure to turn off the lights and close the door silently before slipping out of the building into the night.

112

Chapter 20

Martin tugged at his crotch for the hundredth time as he sat in the passenger seat, Gerald driving him from the apartment to downtown Denver. Ralph had assured them the outfits in the suitcase were authentic for the times, but Martin wasn't sure if it was a prank or if men's testicles had shrunk in the last 40 years.

He wore faded jeans that leeched to his legs, waist, and groin, to go with a silky, shiny purple shirt that would surely glow under the city's bright lights at night. As if everything needed to be tighter, a belt fastened around his hips that matched his polished black shoes. Leather gloves covered his hands while a gray scarf wrapped around his neck to conceal his glowing skin.

I feel like an idiot, he thought.

Martin had rarely dressed up throughout his prior life, but understood the correct times and places to do so: weddings, funerals, rare nights out to fancy restaurants he couldn't afford. But for a casual stroll through the city, this seemed a bit over the top.

With the slums of their neighborhood far behind them, the van slowed as it approached the towering skyscrapers. Martin looked up at the handful of new buildings he didn't recognize, his stare working down to an electric fence standing twenty feet tall and wrapping around the perimeter of the city. The street narrowed to one lane that entered the city through a checkpoint of armed guards.

"What's this about?" Martin asked, no longer shocked by the things he saw.

"That is a 12,000 volt fence that will fry anyone who tries to go through on their own. You can no longer stroll into the big cities around the country. You have to go through the checkpoint and be cleared by the guards."

"What are they checking for?"

"Only that you look like you belong, or if you have official business in the city. I won't be able to get in because I'm black. Ralph is working on a city card for me but will need another day, so I'm planning on joining you tomorrow, at least in terms of getting in. We still can't be seen together or they'll take us both in for questioning."

"How does the city card get you in?"

"It's like a work visa. Says I have business in the city, likely as a cleaner, cook, or server at some fancy restaurant. Today, I'm gonna drop you off and you can go through the pedestrian entrance. You certainly look the part so you shouldn't run into any issues. Just walk through and start exploring. You'll see interactive maps throughout town, and you can also call a car to take you wherever you need."

"How long am I supposed to stay in there?"

Gerald swerved the van to the shoulder and turned on his emergency lights. "Meet right back here at nine. That gives you roughly five hours to get reacquainted with the city. Get a feel for what life is like and where things are. Tomorrow we'll focus more on a plan; hopefully Web will have something we can build off. Now get on out there, and enjoy. Remember, you're rich and belong – don't act any other way."

Martin nodded and patted Gerald on the shoulder before getting out of the van. The line of traffic went on for another quarter mile, but only a dozen or so people stood in line at the pedestrian entrance. He puffed out his chest, raised his shoulders, and walked to the line as if he had done it a hundred times before, jeans riding up his ass.

I belong here, he reminded himself as he approached the electric wall,

689

a faint burning smell radiating from its warmth. By the time Martin reached the line, everyone in front of him had already made their way inside the city, leaving him to pass through the security checkpoint alone. Security towers stood over the entrance and were spaced as far as he could see, roughly 300 yards apart. They looked no different than prison towers, with floodlights and pacing, armed guards.

It was apparently a major issue regarding who was allowed into the city. *Why have guards if there's already an electric fence?* Martin wondered.

The guard at the checkpoint, dressed in full camouflage and toting an M4 carbine assault rifle, watched Martin approach, his eyes concealed behind thick sunglasses.

"Good afternoon," Martin said, unsure if he was supposed to stop or walk through like he belonged. He chose the latter with a shaky confidence, and was relieved when the guard gave him a quick nod.

That's it? No ID? No questions? I could be anyone.

Gerald had dropped him off on the east side of downtown, where the state capitol stood in its usual location. Only something looked different as Martin passed through a small pedestrian tunnel and crossed to the other side of the fence. While it once had a golden dome, the capitol building was now made entirely of gold, blinding and difficult to look at as the setting sun glared off the exterior.

"Who the hell thought that was a good idea?" he muttered under his breath. The city entrance was nestled behind the rear of the capitol, and Martin strode down Colfax Avenue toward the front of the building and closer to the heart of downtown.

The sidewalks weren't crowded like he was used to for the middle of a workday, and there wasn't a single homeless person in sight. Civic Center Park, the space across from the capitol, was usually filled with the homeless, but only a few businessmen in suits sat on the park benches, talking on their cell phones.

Digital screens and billboards covered the exterior of many buildings, the capitol included, giving the city a feel similar to Times Square in New York with the constantly fluctuating advertisements for movies, sports, and clothing.

Martin continued along the sidewalk, reaching the front of the capitol from the lawn's furthest corner, and turned to look at the golden building. The American and state of Colorado flags both flapped in the breeze from a towering pole centered at the front entrance. A banner hung above the entrance's tall, golden pillars read: *KEEP COLORADO PURE.*

A group of students clearly on a field trip scattered across the lawn, some snapping pictures on their phones, others typing on handheld tablets as an instructor barked information about the building.

"In 2039, President Poe allocated a special budget to every state to decorate their capitol buildings with as much gold as possible, as part of his Purity Now initiative. As a state, our redecoration was completed in early 2041; at the same time, the Wall of Perfection was installed and activated to ensure that only those of pure American heritage are allowed into the city."

Martin shook his head after listening to the tour guide, feeling instantly out of place. Gerald had mentioned minorities weren't allowed without a special type of identification, and Martin now realized that the "purity" spoken of meant nothing more than white skin and a bank account full of money. Only luxury vehicles lined the metered parking along the roads, every car shiny and polished as if they had just pulled off the dealership lot.

Martin continued away from the capitol, crossing Colfax and approaching the old *Denver Post* building that had been overtaken by a new media outlet called *Revolutionary News Group.* The moving billboard on the structure flashed the words: *YOUR ONLY SOURCE FOR THE TRUTH!*

More people strolled down the sidewalks, mostly men in expensive suits, flashy watches, and polished briefcases dangling at their sides. Martin didn't see any women, but thought nothing of it at the time. Traffic hummed in the background, until a familiar tune blared out of speakers that seemed to be set up on every street corner. A trumpet blasted the opening notes of the Star-Spangled Banner as all of the video screens showed waving American flags.

Everyone who had been walking and minding their business stopped where they were and placed their right hand over their heart. Martin followed suit, not wanting to stick out as the only person not honoring the national anthem.

A woman's voice sang the words, high-pitched and perfect, as if it had been remastered in a music studio. She held the final note for a solid ten seconds as the trumpets faded and a male voiceover spoke to changing images on the screens.

"America," the baritone voice said. "We've come a long way from a once ugly history." The video flashed through images of Martin Luther King Jr., an American flag on fire in the street, and former athletes kneeling. "We've come a long way from the days of hatred when people thought it was okay to disrespect our country."

The screens changed to show a ghastly looking man, black hair slicked to the side, face powdered with too much makeup. He had a crooked smile in the image as he held a skinny thumb up.

"Thanks to the Revolution, we've been blessed with brilliant leaders like President Poe, who have kept America pure, and cleansed our blessed country of the hatred that almost took over God's land."

The still images gave way to video footage of this same man, who Martin presumed to be President Poe. In the video, he wore a black suit with a red tie, an American flag pin on one lapel, and a crucifix on the other. "You won't find a better Christian than me to lead our country back to pureness. Trust me." Poe spoke in a stern voice with a slight rasp underneath his words. "Trust in me is trust in a safe America. Never again will we have to fear our enemies, both domestic and international."

Martin watched the video that reminded him of a campaign commercial with the cheesy images and sound bites, and a wide-grinning President Poe giving a thumbs-up to the camera. The video cut to a live shot of President Poe standing at a podium in front of the White House. His lips pursed together as he winked to the camera before speaking.

"Good evening, citizens of America. Our daily briefing today will be short. As for yesterday's stats, nine people tried to sneak into our country illegally. All nine were shot dead."

The small crowds that had gathered on the sidewalks cheered and howled in excitement, pumping their fists into the air.

"Seventeen Road Runners were captured and sent immediately to the execution chamber for a most torturous end to their lives."

The mention of Road Runners sent an immediate chill down Martin's back, and he looked around suspiciously to ensure no one had an eye on him. The crowd again ruptured in applause at the mention of dead Road Runners.

"Lastly, the country of France is considering war with us. They think we can't take care of ourselves. Their president called me a power-hungry fool." The crowd booed. "Do you know what I did when he called me that? I hung up on that croissant-loving son-of-a-bitch, and increased our budget for more nuclear bombs. Nobody threatens war on God's country and gets away with it." President Poe stared directly into the camera, into the soul of America. "So if you still want to declare war on America, be ready for your country to turn into a hot pile of French fries!"

The crowd jumped and screamed. "Tell 'em, Poe," a man nearby shouted. "Nobody fucks with America!"

Poe hesitated, as if he knew the masses in the streets were cheering. "I want to thank you fine citizens, as I do every day, for giving me this chance to lead our country. Nobody loves America more than me. You can try, but I simply have more love to give. If I have to get in a cage and fight President French Fry, then that's exactly what I'll do, and you know I'll give him a good ol' American ass whooping."

More howling and fist pumping.

"Let this serve as a reminder that if anyone ever badmouths America, you have the right to take matters into your own hands. I can't be everywhere at once, so I have to rely on you, fine citizens, to keep our country pure. Now, I want you all to enjoy your evening, eat a nice dinner, and get a good night's sleep. Tomorrow is a new day with new opportunities to keep America pure. Our work is never done, but that's why we stay in business. I'll see you all tomorrow. God bless you, and

God bless the United States of America."

The crowds gave one more round of applause before promptly returning to their days.

Martin continued down the sidewalk—more leery and constantly looking over his shoulder—as he approached 16th Street Mall. He studied everyone he passed by, half expecting them to pull out a gun and shoot him simply because he was a Road Runner. But no one so much as looked in his direction.

The world as he knew it was gone, replaced by a totalitarian society where everyone likely lived in fear of one thing or another. Martin felt it walking down the street, the screams of the past radiating from the very concrete he walked on. An invisible hand was present above each and every person, providing both a sense of safety and a threatening tension to remain a loyal citizen. Or else.

For the first time he could ever recall, Martin felt terrified for his life.

I need to get this medicine and leave.

113

Chapter 21

Julian crouched behind a bush along the sidewalk, his heart drumming in his ears. eHe'd been to Bill's house a half dozen times before for dinner, typically with Commander Strike joining them. A black iron fence surrounded the property, enclosing a manicured front lawn split by an S-curve walkway to the front door. He stepped out from the bush, studying the house concealed by darkness. Inside Bill was lying peacefully in bed, dreaming about rescuing Strike and becoming an instant hero in the world of Road Runners. Julian still had no idea what to do once inside. *Do I try to break in and kill him in his sleep? Should I knock on the front door and have him let me in? I can always blackmail him with his recorded voice.* Julian shook his head, knowing Bill wouldn't fall for such a trap.

Even in the cold Alaska night, his palms turned slick with a nervous sweat underneath his gloves. He chose the latter option for entering the home, and checked over his shoulders for the hundredth time to ensure no wandering eyes were on him. It was almost midnight in the quiet, family neighborhood, leaving no one to mind him.

The front door seemed to scoot back with every step Julian took up the walkway, never seeming within reach until he actually pushed the doorbell with a shaky finger. The urge to vomit suddenly crept into his throat as he took a step back and waited for the door to open.

Nothing happened after a minute of waiting, prompting Julian to ring the doorbell a second time. *Wake up, old man.*

The waiting curbed his nerves to a dull, distant tremble, but they immediately returned when the sound of the door's lock rattled in front of him. The door swung open to more darkness, the tip of a long rifle extending out to Julian's face.

"God dammit, Bill!" he shouted. "Put that thing down, are you crazy?"

"Julian?" Bill's voice asked from inside. The rifle vanished and was replaced by a groggy-eyed Bill, gray hair splayed in every direction like someone had just run a rubber balloon over his head. "Are *you* crazy? Why are you ringing my doorbell in the middle of the night? You know how paranoid I am."

"I know, I'm sorry. I should've called first, but my head has been so flustered these last couple days. Can I come in?"

Bill sighed and turned on the inside light, revealing the living room behind him. "Come in," he mumbled, clearly wanting nothing more than returning to the deep sleep he had been so rudely awakened from.

"Thank you. I'm sorry for intruding on your night like this, but I know if we don't talk, I might never sleep again."

"Have a seat on the couch."

Julian stepped into the living room. Bill was a simple man with no wall decor or anything that showed signs of life. His living room consisted of the lone couch that faced the mounted flat screen TV on the wall. A loaded bookshelf collected dust in the back corner as the only other item in the living room. The house could've been staged for real estate showings as Bill kept it clean and spotless of any clutter.

"Can I get you a drink?" Bill asked, clearing his throat of his deep sleep.

"I'm okay, thank you."

"Well then, what can I do for you that couldn't wait until the morning?" Bill spoke with as much resentment as he could muster, but Julian was too nervous to notice.

"I feel like we're not seeing eye to eye right now, and I want to make sure we're on the same page. We have to be if we're expected to lead the Road Runners, and that's the part I feel you're not understanding."

"What part?"

"Leading. I may be the Commander now, but that means you're my lieutenant. I'm just as concerned about getting Strike back as you, but it's also now our responsibility to lead the Road Runners. We can't just leave our millions of members to run on autopilot, especially in a time like this."

"You haven't shown any effort to get Strike back. Someone needs to."

"Bill, we have entire teams dedicated to rescuing her. Eyes are on Chris's house around the clock, and meetings are constantly taking place to devise a plan to get her out of there. And she hasn't even arrived there yet. *You* need to trust what we have in place and help me lead the Road Runners through whatever comes next."

Bill nodded, his eyes gradually clearing of the fog from his snooze. "I see your point, but I feel like I owe it to Strike. After everything she's done for me, I'd feel guilty if I kicked back and waited for someone else to rescue her. I have to be involved."

"I know she saved you, and you certainly do owe her your life, but Bill, you can influence a lot from your new position of power. You can *lead* these groups working on her rescue and implement whatever strategy you want. You have my full blessing."

If I can get him to commit to the bomb right now, I won't need to get rid of him, Julian thought, a confident smirk spreading over his face.

"I know that, but it still seems wrong to not be the one out there physically doing something. I can't make myself sit still while all of this is going on."

"You can have it both ways. You can implement the strategy from the top, and join the troops out in the field. You'll be like a modern-day George Washington."

Bill chuckled a hoarse sound that could only come from a man in his seventies. "That's a generous offer, Julian, but I know what this is all about. You want me to approve that bomb and are offering me—*bribing* me—into doing it."

Julian's smile snapped into pursed lips, a flash of rage bursting through

697

his head. "Bill, I'm not bribing you. I'm making you an offer where we can both get what we want."

"Except what you want puts Commander Strike at an incredibly high risk. There are too many unknowns."

Julian fought the urge to shout, and kept his most professional face and composure. "Unknowns like what? This has been researched through and through."

"We can't drop a bomb on the mansion if Commander Strike is inside. That's essentially assassinating our own leader."

I'm your goddamn leader, Julian thought, hot anger tickling every nerve in his body. He thought Bill had smirked at him after the snide comment, but couldn't confirm if it was real or in his head. "She'll be in the basement," he replied in his calmest voice.

"We don't know that for sure. It's not like she's some regular Road Runner being held hostage; she's our leader, and Chris knows that. For all we know, she'll be held in a cage in his office. Besides, there has never been a study done at the mansion to know what effects a bomb would have. What if it blows up the basement with it?"

This was always a hot topic for the team who studied the mansion and spent many hours trying to find a way inside without putting lives at risk. The fact that they couldn't get close enough to the mansion without the risk of a bullet in the head spoke volumes to how effective their investigation had gone. The discussion of a bomb had come up before, after it was learned that fifty Road Runners were trapped within the house, and it wasn't until Martin had shared his knowledge of the basement's existence that the topic was revisited. The bombs the Road Runners had in storage would surely destroy the mansion, but their impact to the ground beneath it remained in doubt. Commander Strike refused to take the risk of dropping the bombs if it had a chance of killing the fifty hostages. Multiple simulations were run and bombs were dropped on replica structures to gauge an explosion's impact, but they simply lacked the knowledge of what the inside of the mansion was made of. Each material they tested returned various results, leaving them back at square one.

"The basement won't blow up. Besides, what's the alternative plan to get her out of that house? Are you going to knock on the steel barricade and ask nicely? He's never going to hand her over."

"We'll negotiate. And thank you for bringing up the barricade. Add that to the list of reasons we can't drop a bomb. What if the steel deflects it and it bounces back to us? Then what?"

"It's a *bomb*, Bill. It explodes on impact. I'm beginning to think there's nothing I can say to convince you."

"No shit. That's why I left the office tonight. Not only was I tired, I knew you'd be pressing this matter until four in the morning. And here we are. I'm not approving a bomb, Julian, so I suggest you move on to a different plan or meet the terms we discussed earlier."

"This is why you'll never be Commander." Julian spoke in a relaxed voice, no longer enraged by Bill's stubbornness, but rather clear-headed as he knew what had to be done next.

"Don't get all high and mighty. This new power has gone straight to your head. I used to think you were just young and arrogant, but now you're nothing but an asshole. It's a good thing we only have two-year terms, or you'd run us into the ground like Chris did with the Revolters."

"I'm sorry you feel that way, Bill. I *am* the Commander now, and I'm aware of my new role, that's all. I think leaders are misunderstood because they have to make the decisions that no one else will. We have to sleep at night with the weight of the world pressing down on us like an invisible slab of concrete on our chest. When's the last time you couldn't fall asleep because of a decision you had to make?"

"Every single night," Bill snapped. "Unlike you, I stay up every night worried about our leader and what our future looks like because of her kidnapping."

Julian stood from the couch. "I need to use your restroom."

The sudden change in subject caught Bill off guard as his jaw hung temporarily open. He clearly had more to say and was ready to explode, but Julian asking to leave the room made his mouth snap shut and left a dazed confusion splattered across his face.

"Be my guest," Bill said, defeated. He slouched into the nearby recliner and fidgeted with nervous fingers.

Julian stepped into the dark hallway, turning to Bill before disappearing. "Oh, and I do worry about Strike and our future, but I have a job to do now because of this mess. I wish you'd hurry up and realize that you do too, and help me make sure our future stays on track."

He left the living room without another word, grinning because he knew he just dropped a bomb of guilt on his old friend and mentor. It really was a shame how matters had to end for Bill, but the old man refused to give any support for the most obvious next phase of rescuing Strike *and* ending Chris.

Julian entered the bathroom and flicked on the light switch, closing and locking the door behind him. The mixture of nerves and anger caused a slight quiver in his hands, but he rummaged through the drawers and cabinets with intense concentration. There had to be something he could use to end Bill, and he didn't care how messy it ended up being. Razor blades were nowhere obvious, so Julian scoured through the mountain of toiletries piled on the sink counter.

Jesus Christ, he thought when he couldn't find anything sharper than a toothbrush. He paced around the bathroom, racking his brain for a new option. He could try to sneak into the kitchen, but that left him exposed as he didn't fully know his way around the house in the dark. Bill might also hear him heading the wrong way and come to investigate before he could find a knife.

He sat on the closed toilet and planted his face into his palms. Trying the kitchen might be his best chance, so he stood and ran through the mental map of the house, imagining how many steps it was to the kitchen through the dark hallway.

Does the floor creak? He couldn't recall, but these older hardwood floors likely had some noisy spots when stepped on.

He stepped to the door, and with his gloved hand on the knob, turned around one more time to make sure he didn't miss anything. His eyes scanned the room and settled back on the toilet.

"That's it," he whispered. "Easy."

Julian returned to the toilet, flushed it, pulled off the heavy porcelain lid from the tank, and reworked the chain that connected to the rubber flapper at the bottom so that it tightened to the point of not closing, forcing the water to run constantly. He had placed the tank lid on the sink countertop, and opened the door to shout down the hallway.

"Bill! We might have a small problem in here."

Julian returned to the toilet to give the appearance that he was studying inside the tank, even jiggling the handle for good measure.

"What's the matter?" Bill asked from behind.

Julian turned, fake worry as his expression. "I don't know. I took a leak and flushed, but the water won't stop running. I don't know too much about toilets."

"Let me take a look," Bill said confidently and approached as Julian stepped aside, toward the sink. He leaned over the tank, his gray hair exposed as a wide-open target.

The excitement bubbled up within Julian, who couldn't recall a time where he had ever felt so nervous and giddy in unison. Bill started whistling as he examined the toilet, and Julian knew he had a handful of seconds to take advantage of the old man with his back turned.

He tiptoed to his left, grabbing the tank lid as gently as possible, the inevitable sound of its clunky porcelain washed out by the toilet's running water. He held the lid vertically from the middle, hands fixed as if he were reading a thick, hardcover book, and raised it above his head, adrenaline drowning his veins, heart bulging into his throat.

"It looks like the chain got tangled and isn't letting it close," Bill said into the tank, oblivious to the world behind him.

"Is that so?" Julian replied, damn near laughing as he spoke.

You're doing this for the betterment of the Road Runners, not because you're a monster, he reminded himself, as if murder could be actually be justified.

His eyes throbbed as he tightened his grip and swung the lid down with all of his body's force behind it. The porcelain met Bill's skull with a

THUNK! sound, sending the old man's face briefly into the tank before his body collapsed to the floor in a heavy thud, knees hitting the ground before falling flat on his back to stare lifelessly at the ceiling.

Julian had struck him as square as a baseball bat connecting on a crisp home run swing, and he hoped the one hit was all it took. If the porcelain didn't break, then surely the skull had. Julian grinned at the sight of blood pooling behind Bill's head, and squatted for a closer look.

Bill's blue eyes remained open as his jaw hung, and Julian saw what he believed was a look of relief on his face. If you added up all the time Bill had spent traveling through time, he had likely been living for over 500 years. Perhaps Julian did him a favor by finally letting him get a deep sleep. Perhaps that was just the expression a dead person made after a surprise end to their life.

Julian closed Bill's eyes with his gloved hand and propped up his jaw to make him look somewhat peaceful. The blood continued to expand into an imperfect circle around Bill's head.

If he's not dead yet, he will be soon. That's too much blood to lose from your head, Julian thought, smirking.

"Sorry, old friend," he said to the body, standing back up. "This really was my last resort. You forced my hand, but I had to do what's right for the Road Runners. Now we can end this war, and I'll even dedicate it in your honor. Rest easy."

Julian turned and left the bathroom, the toilet's water still running, as it would until someone showed up to find the mess. He wanted to go back to the office and start preparing for the bombs, but had to wait. An investigation would soon be underway to solve Bill's death, and cameras at the office would show what time Julian had left and returned. He would already have questions to answer for leaving the office before the timeframe of Bill's death.

He left the house as quietly as he had arrived, whistling the same tune Bill had while examining the toilet, knowing a new fate waited ahead to change the course of this godawful war once and for all.

114

Chapter 22

Martin continued exploring the city, unable to shake what he had just witnessed from the live broadcast of President Poe. In his brief speech, Poe revealed his true colors and made it clear how the country had progressed to where it was today. If he had time, Martin would try to visit the library—if such thing still existed—and read up on this new president.

For now, though, he did as Gerald had instructed and explored downtown, avoiding eye contact with everyone he walked by, keeping his head down to blend in with the rest of society. Even the classy businessmen, dressed in their fine suits, had cheered and whistled at the nonsensical video that halted the middle of the day.

The buzz from the daily presidential address had died down and people continued their day as normal, businessmen on their cell phones, briefcases swinging in their grip as they skittered down the sidewalks. There wasn't a single homeless person on 16th Street Mall, an anomaly as far as Martin was concerned. The sidewalks were clean and even had a fresh smell oozing from the cracks, instead of the usual stench of piss and body odor he was accustomed to.

Martin spent the next hour walking up and down the mall, making mental notes of all the new stores and restaurants, none of which would provide any help on their mission. The hospital was another ten-minute walk south of downtown from his starting point at the capitol, and he planned to stroll by there after the sun went down. Knowing how all of the population felt about Road Runners, he decided it best to hide until the sun went down and move in the darkness.

He stepped into the next bar he approached, a two-level building with chatter pouring from the rooftop and music booming inside. The bar was called Viewpoint Pub, and inside looked no different from any bar Martin had ever been: neon lights in the windows, televisions showing sports, groups of coworkers taking rounds of shots together, and men hitting on women.

Women! He had passed a couple during his walk, but there were at least five within the bar, not counting the trio who pranced around in tight white shirts and shorts, balancing trays of drinks.

Martin worked his way through the bar, squeezing through rows of tables until he found a table for two in the back corner. He plopped down and immediately lifted the menu in front of his face, his eyes peering over the top to see if anyone was watching him.

A waitress skinny as a twig greeted Martin, her black ponytail swaying behind her head as she grinned pearly teeth. "Good evening, sir, my name is Cecilia. Is there something I can get started for you?"

Martin hesitated lowering his menu, but decided the room was dim enough and this young lady was not likely a headhunter for the Revolters. "I'll take a glass of scotch and a burger."

"Certainly, I'll bring those right out." Cecilia flashed one more smile before turning away, a nearby table of five men in suits watching her every step, howling like horny dogs after she disappeared into the back.

From the corner Martin could see the entire bar. He leaned back in his seat, trying to appear relaxed and blend in. So far no one had paid him any attention and he intended to keep it that way.

There were a couple others sitting alone, but they seemed content on their cell phones, something Martin wished he had to kill some time. Instead, he gazed at the nearest TV and watched football analysts discuss the week's upcoming games.

Over the next ten minutes, the bar filled with downtown workers escaping the office for the day. Cecilia brought him his drink and burger simultaneously, leaving him to eat as the noise level rose to the typical, blurred chaos common in bars and restaurants.

"Excuse me, sir," a man in a suit said, approaching Martin's table. "Can we borrow this chair?" The man placed a hand on the chair across from Martin.

"It's all yours." Martin's hand immediately fell to his waistband where his instincts thought a gun should have been, but remembered Gerald insisted he not carry one in the city.

"Thank you, have a good day," the man said with a quick smile before returning to a nearby table with the chair in hand.

Martin scarfed his burger while savoring every sip of the scotch, an incredibly smooth blend with a smoky flavor and subtle taste of the barrel. It was comforting to know that scotch improved even more in the future.

He ordered another round, having at least another 90 minutes before the sun would start setting. His life had turned into a never-ending cycle of chaos once he stepped into 1919 with Sonya, and he couldn't remember the last time he sat in a bar drinking scotch by himself, a pastime he enjoyed more than life. The alcohol left its tingling sensation from his throat all the way down to his stomach in a pit of delightful warmth. Martin's fingertips and lips turned numb halfway through the second drink, and that's when he knew he had the perfect buzz.

The man in the suit returned with the chair twenty minutes later as his group of friends all stood up to leave. "Are you having a good evening, sir?" he asked.

Martin had avoided eye contact during their first encounter, but looked at the man this time. He had wavy brown hair, green eyes, and a strong jaw bone. He was built much like Martin's new chiseled physique, but was at least 20 years younger.

"I am, thank you," Martin responded curtly, not wanting to leave the door open for a long conversation.

The man sat in the chair, planted his elbows on the table, and leaned within a foot of Martin's face as if he wanted to kiss him. "You're not from here, are you?" he whispered loud enough to be heard over the music that clashed with the chatter in symphony.

Martin immediately locked eyes with the man, his pulse jumping at least 30 extra beats.

"I was born and raised in Denver," he replied casually, focused on keeping his voice steady and confident.

"That's not what I mean, and you know it. Tell me what year you're from." The man returned his own confidence as he peered in Martin, demanding the truth.

"Are you feeling okay, young man?" Martin asked. "It's 2064, in case you've forgotten."

"What year were you born?"

Martin opened his lips to respond, but let his jaw hang. The young bastard caught him red-handed. Martin had never bothered to calculate what his year of birth should have been to go along with his lie.

"I knew it," the man said, unfazed. "Who sent you? Are you here on official Road Runner business?"

"What's a Road Runner?" Martin had no choice but to resort to the childish tactic of playing dumb. *Very* dumb, in this case.

"Cut the shit. We've heard rumors that there would be a few Road Runners around town this week." The young man inched even closer, the stench of booze seeping from his lips as he whispered in a practically inaudible voice. "I'm a Road Runner. You can trust me."

Martin wanted to believe the kid, but had no idea who to trust. Could the Revolters have been following him all along, inching him on like a donkey chasing a carrot? He looked down his arms, ensuring they had been properly covered up to hide his glowing skin.

"How did you know?" Martin asked, defeated and unable to look the man in the eyes.

"We can tell," the man replied. "A few of us have been undercover long enough to know when someone looks out of place."

"Can the Revolters tell?"

The man looked around the bar to be sure no one was looking at them suspiciously. "Not in a place like this. Maybe in a government building or somewhere with heavy security, but just around town, you'll blend in fine. I followed you from outside, asked my group of coworkers if they wanted to stop in here for a quick drink once I saw you come in. The moment I saw your reaction for the National Anthem, I knew you weren't from here. It's an honest mistake for anyone not from this time—Revolter or Road Runner— but the way you kept looking over your shoulder told me all I needed. So where are you from, and who are you here with?"

Martin had learned after mingling with plenty of Road Runners that when asked where you're from actually meant *when* you are from.

"I'm from 2019, sent here by Commander Strike with a group of three others. Who are you here with?"

The man nodded. "Straight from the Commander, huh? Impressive. I'm not here with anyone. I was born in 2040, right in the middle of this shit turning for the worse. My family stayed in hiding to survive, and raised me to be a Road Runner at heart, but a Revolter by all outer appearances. There's a lot of us like this, raised to survive. None of us have ever been to the fancy Road Runner headquarters. The only time we leave the city is to board a plane and fly to another wealthy city across the country."

"So you haven't seen your family since you left them?"

"That's right," the man nodded, staring distantly into the table. "It's impossible for us to know what's going on with the organization, all we have as resources are whatever the Revolters want to give us—which is never news about the Road Runners, unless one is getting murdered."

"Do the Road Runners even know about you guys?"

"They know we exist, but I don't think they realize how many of us there are. I wouldn't say we could overthrow the local government, but we would put up a fight. The Revolters are too consumed with themselves to ever know what's actually going on."

"What's your name?" Martin asked, the question itching since the man sat down and started accusing him of being a Road Runner.

"I'm so sorry, it's an instinct to not give my name. I'm Marcus."

"Pleasure to meet you, I'm Martin."

Martin didn't know what protocol was in 2064 and waited to see if Marcus stuck out a hand to shake, which he never did.

"I really should be going, though, Martin," Marcus said, standing from the table. "I've had a long day, but wanted to make sure I said hi. It's not every day we get to meet someone from the outside."

"It was a pleasure," Martin replied. "I hope to see you around again."

"Don't count on it. We have strict rules about mingling with anyone in public. I really shouldn't have come over here today, but to hell with rules, right? You take care of yourself, Martin, and stay strong."

Marcus turned and vanished through the bar with a rapid grace.

Martin watched as the young man weaved through the final tables, then his heart froze when his eyes caught something he thought they'd never see again.

Sitting alone at a table near the front door, facing Martin's direction, was Sonya.

115

Chapter 23

The room was illuminated by nothing more than a lone lamp tucked away in the far corner. The damp, murky smell of a basement filled Strike's nose as she woke up, all four limbs handcuffed to the chair in which she sat. She tugged with her legs to find they only had two inches of range. She flexed her arms and yanked, a piercing pain shooting up from her right forearm to her neck.

A white bandage was wrapped around her forearm, a small dot of blood appearing in the middle like the Japan flag. She stared at it, longing to touch it, but unable to soothe the pain that throbbed beneath. The pain came from where her tracking device had been, and she knew they had removed it.

"Good morning, Ms. Strike," Chris's voice called out, calm and steady. "We thought you were never going to wake up."

Strike felt the crazy old man behind her, and made a conscious effort to stay calm. Part of being elected to office was taking an intense training course on staying calm in the most strenuous of circumstances, including torture, which she suspected might be around the corner. She focused on maintaining her heart rate and breathing, taking long, calculated breaths and exhaling steadily.

"I will say this, Ms. Strike," Chris continued. "Your people love you. You should see the hell they're raising to find you. We dropped your tracking device in the middle of a field in Idaho, and a search crew arrived there within ten minutes. It was quite entertaining watching them flock like birds to a tiny piece of bread."

Strike kept her focus on her breathing while Chris spewed his nonsense.

"I've been dreaming about this day for a long time. The Commander of the Road Runners is in my house. I never knew which Commander it would be—you guys rotate out so quickly—but I knew sooner or later this time would come."

His footsteps whispered across the ground, approaching Strike until he stood in front of her, crouched down with his evil grin in front of her face. She'd never been this close to a Revolter.

"One of two things is going to happen today," Chris continued. "You're either going to surrender and allow the Revolution to claim its righteous victory, or we're going to force you to tell us all of your dirty secrets about the Road Runners. I suspect there's zero chance of you surrendering, so I'll let you know that option number two is not going to be very fun for you." Chris held his grin, stale breath seeping from his lips. "It's only a matter of time before your people come knocking on my front door demanding you back. Anyone who steps foot on my property will be shot dead, so I suggest you talk fast. And if you do decide to give us all of the information, you'll be free to go, but I can't say how well you'll be able to move."

Two men chuckled somewhere in the background.

"So what will it be, Commander?"

"I'll never surrender to you," she replied quickly and confidently, her faith waning. How the hell was she supposed to stay calm and talk her way out of *this*? She was strapped to a chair with no way out, and who knows what kind of torture on the way.

Focus away from the pain. Torturers never want to kill you; they need your information. Trust that you can buy the time necessary to be rescued.

She had never been one to rely on others, but had no choice. She prayed that Bill and Julian hadn't given up hope yet and would come busting through the door to save the day.

"Let's begin, shall we?" Chris said, nodding to someone in the corner. A bright light flashed like a strobe, reminding Strike of going through haunted houses as a teenager during Halloween season. Strobe lights were known to heighten fear, but since she knew this, she managed to block out the constant flashing.

"Tell me, Commander, where is your main headquarters?"

Strike had a tough decision to make. She could either feed him answers of things he should already know, to show cooperation, or she could play difficult and let the torture begin.

"You know where our headquarters are."

"I just want to know you'll work with me, Ms. Strike. Please tell me where your headquarters are." Chris spoke calmly.

"Down the street."

"Underneath that little shack? That's your *main* headquarters?" Chris threw his head back and laughed. "Why not your lavish New York office? Or Miami? Those places look like fun."

"Our headquarters is wherever makes sense, and right now it's keeping an eye on you here." Strike spoke with disgust dripping from every word.

"How nice of you people. Tell me, Ms. Strike, who's in charge or your little group while you're . . . occupied?"

Strike shrugged her shoulders immediately. "How would I know? I've been here with you."

"Please. Don't act like you don't have a system in place in case the Commander goes missing. You people have systems for everything."

"I'm sure there is, but I don't know the system for this; it's never been used before."

"Tell me right now who's in charge in your absence," Chris snapped like a scolding parent.

Stay strong, Strike reminded herself, and shrugged again.

Chris grinned and turned his face toward the corner, nodding to someone hiding in the darkness. Footsteps approached as Chris reached out to grab a pair of pliers. "Thank you," he said to the figure that was nothing but a dark blob from Strike's view.

"Pliers," Chris said, admiring the tool. "A universal tool of sorts. I can break toes, remove fingernails, even play dentist and take out some teeth." He stroked the pliers with a steady thumb as his grin grew wider. "So tell me, Ms. Strike, who's in charge of the Road Runners?"

It was a simple question, but telling him could put the entire organization in grave danger. Should Julian go missing, Bill would take control, but there was no one beyond Bill in the line of succession. Chris could play this game with the Road Runners until there was no one left to lead them.

"I told you I don't know."

"Very well, Commander," Chris said, reaching toward Strike's left hand with the pliers open. "Let's start at the pinky and work our way up."

The cool metal clasped around her pinky finger, right on her middle knuckle. Chris wiggled the pliers to make sure he had a good grip, and then twisted the finger backwards toward her wrist.

Strike clenched her jaw shut as the tendons stretched and popped, sparking an explosive pain that erupted all the way up to her shoulder. Tears welled in her eyes, but she managed to show no emotion aside from a subtle grunt through clenched teeth, choking down the urge to gag.

"Tell me who is in charge," Chris said calmly, moving the pliers to her ring finger.

She didn't respond, and Chris repeated the action. This time she couldn't help but shriek as her arm turned completely numb. She looked to her hand to see two fingers going the wrong direction while the others remained in place.

"Now, Ms. Strike, I already told you someone from your group handed you over. They came right up to my front door and told me what city you were in, what hotel you were staying at, and how to get around your guards."

"I don't believe you," Strike uttered, her head dizzy. She thought she could withstand more broken fingers if it came to it, as her entire hand was numb with adrenaline.

"I didn't believe it, either, but that's what happened. How else could I have gotten you here?"

"You're full of shit."

"It was a younger man. He kept a disguise so I can't tell you at all what he looked like. I don't suppose it's a young man who is now leading the Road Runners? Surely a Road Runner would never do such a thing just to get into a position of power." Chris howled with laughter.

"We wouldn't ever do that."

"Funny, that's what he said, too. But he also said you're too much of a stickler for the rules, that it holds you back from being a good leader. This young man questioned all of your decisions and came to the conclusion that he had to have you removed from office to further the Road Runner agenda. Now, I'm not as dumb as I look, but even I know the Road Runners' agenda is to kill me. That said, it's in your best interest to tell me who is in charge over there, because there are strict orders in place for your death should I get killed."

Strike paused, the pain in her fingers and arm constant, seemingly permanent. "I thought you can't die. You sound worried, Chris . . . is everything okay?" She managed a grin through the pain.

Chris responded with a stern face before nodding to his assistant in the darkness. The footsteps shuffled around as Chris reached out for a box with wires flowing from it. He quietly untangled the wires and pressed the adhesive ends of them onto Strike's flesh, scattering them across her arms, chest, and head.

"I'm done with the games, Ms. Strike," he said. "In my hands is a control panel that decides how many volts of electricity I want to send through your body. Let's give it a test run, shall we?"

She tried jerking her body out of it, but it was a waste of energy as her wiggle room remained within a couple inches.

Chris turned a dial, causing the machine to hum as he raised it in the air like a teasing child. His thumb settled over a red button the size of a half-dollar coin. He smiled like a lunatic, and then pushed the button.

Strike jolted, her every limb thrusting into the restraints for a quick second as the stinging shock hit her all at once. The sensation reminded her of the time she had stuck a finger in the outlet as a child, the emotional shock more dominant than the physical one sparked by electricity. It was a morbid feeling to get electrocuted, as a quick realization forms around the fragility of life.

"That was the lowest setting," Chris said grimly. "Shall I crank it up a notch?"

"You're a chickenshit," Strike replied, her mental stability wavering. She could handle most pain, like the broken fingers, but when electricity flowed, it left her body a seizing mess.

"Just tell me who is leading the Road Runners. Is this even worth your suffering? You know I'll find out who it is eventually. Why not just make this easy on both of us?"

"Go fuck yourself," she snapped, proud she could still muster the energy to push back against his demands.

"Okay, very well." Chris turned the dial again and held down the button.

The higher voltage created a burning sensation as Strike's body tensed from head to toe. It immediately felt like she was flexing every single muscle in unison as her head jerked backwards, thudding against the chair. Chris might have only held the button down for three seconds, but she would never know for sure, as it felt like an entire ten minutes.

Chris cackled when he released the button, even grabbing his stomach to hold in his guts from spilling out. "Oh, Commander, this is more fun than I thought." He walked circles in place, having virtually no slack from the wires connected to his console, and started conversing with himself. "Can I know who's leading the Road Runners? No? Okay!"

He pushed the button, waving the console in the air like a baton and dancing in front of Strike as he shrieked with laughter. Whoever hid in the shadows joined the chorus as electricity pulsed through Strike's body, leaving her stiff and motionless in the chair.

116

Chapter 24

The sunlight didn't seep through the windows as it normally did in the mornings. The sky remained gray, clouds pregnant with enough rain to downpour well into the afternoon. Julian still sprouted out of bed at eight o'clock, knowing a long and emotional day awaited.

He had arrived home shortly before one in the morning and popped a couple of sleeping pills, as he knew he wouldn't be able to drift away on his own. He felt guilty, but also accomplished and proud. The Road Runners were now free from their ultra-conservative ways and could proceed with a dramatic move to end the war.

"It's a great day to become an international hero," he said to his mirror as he prepared for the day. Everything would change after the realization of Bill's death. Currently, all of the security detail that followed the Commander was still focused on Strike, working around the clock to find a way to break her free from the mansion. They had offered their services to protect Julian right away, but he insisted that they resolve the Strike matter before making any changes. Once they discovered Bill had been murdered, Julian would no longer have a say in the matter, as the security team would have no choice but to follow and protect him.

It didn't matter to him at this point. He had Bill's recorded voice authorizing the bombs, and no Bill to deny it. It would take a few hours for the decision to be agreed upon by the Council, but he fully expected to see fireworks before dinner.

Julian lived in the city of Barrow, a quick five-minute drive to their secret entrance in the middle of nowhere. When he arrived, he jumped out of the car and rushed to the elevator. He entered the office and no one paid him any attention, an immediate good sign that the terrible news had yet to break about Bill, but concerning that his tracking device had not set off an alarm when he died.

He did die, right? Julian asked himself, remembering Bill had definitely stopped breathing. But what if he started breathing again after he left? That would be catastrophic if Bill somehow survived and remembered who had clocked him over the head with a slab of porcelain. Julian would immediately be put on trial and risk ex-communication from the organization.

He proceeded to his new office and entered to find a security team rummaging through the desk drawers. "What the hell's going on?"

A large man of at least six-and-a-half feet tall, with tattooed arms as big as his legs, crossed the office to meet Julian.

"Commander, I'm Garrett Anderson, the head of Protection in Europe," he said in a crisp British accent. "Your team called me in overnight. There's been a crisis, and they are still working on Commander Strike."

"Crisis? What kind of crisis?"

"I'm afraid Bill has been murdered."

Garrett paused. Julian had to make a conscious effort to react as a normal person would, so he moved a hand to his open mouth in shock.

"I was just talking with Bill last night, right in this office. Why wasn't I notified immediately?"

Garrett raised an open hand, fingers the size of bananas. "I'm afraid you're a suspect, since we believe you were the last person to see him alive. That's why we're in here, checking for any clues that might point to his death."

"Oh, I didn't realize I was the last person to see him—I thought he stayed here for a bit after he left my office."

"We have the video footage of him leaving your office, going to his office to grab his things, and then leaving. May I ask what you were speaking about with him?"

"We were discussing strategy, both on how to proceed with the war and in the rescue efforts for Strike."

"Did he seem worried at all?"

No," Julian said, rubbing his head as if in thought. "He seemed like himself—business as usual."

Garrett jotted notes down on his handheld pad.

"May I ask how he died?" Julian questioned, forcing what he believed to be concern in his voice.

"He was struck on the head with a toilet tank cover. The cover was off and the toilet water was running. We believe he had his head in the tank to try and fix it when someone struck him from behind."

Julian let his jaw drop again and moved a quick hand to cover it, acting speechless.

"Any thoughts on who might have done it?" Garrett asked, an eyebrow cocked at Julian.

Julian shook his head slowly and thoughtfully.

"I can't imagine it being anyone we know. Have you looked into the Revolters? They could very well be plotting revenge for the men we killed on Chris's property."

"We're looking into all possibilities. We're going to take his body into the future, study it in the labs there to see if we can find anything. In the meantime, Commander, I suggest you remain vague when explaining this situation to the public. It can create a widespread fear that is unwarranted. Our team is in complete control of the investigation, so there's nothing to worry about."

"Got it."

"And please keep your phone on you. We may have follow-up questions about your conversation with Bill."

"Of course."

Julian's heart thumped so hard he thought it might burst out of his ears. He shook Garrett's hand, worried the monstrous man would feel the adrenaline throbbing in his fingertips.

"Give us about ten more minutes to clear out of your office, then you'll be able to get back to work," Garrett said.

"Not a problem—take your time."

Minutes after the security team left the office, Julian returned to his desk and sat with his face buried in his hands. He closed and locked the door, not desiring any distractions as he prepared for the next phase in his rapidly advancing plan.

Garrett had raised a good point that he hadn't yet considered. A message would need to be delivered to the public. Those in the Alaska headquarters already saw the security team raid the office with no explanation. Did they even know Bill was dead? Surely rumors were already spreading across the world.

The office was equipped with a podium that pulled out of the closet in case the Commander needed to deliver an impromptu message to the nation, and this situation certainly called for it.

He crossed the room to the corner closet and pulled open the door that revealed the podium, among a couple of file cabinets and old campaign posters from Strike's last election that read *Don't Strike out, vote for me!* He wheeled the podium out and positioned it in front of the wall of the past Commanders. The Road Runners had no flag to call their own, believing a physical symbol could risk their cover in the general public, so the American and state of Alaska flags hung high on the walls above the portraits, creating a formal backdrop for the upcoming speech.

Julian pulled open the door to the rest of the office. "Danielle, can you come here when you have a moment, please?"

Danielle was the office manager and had the answers to anything in the building, including how to turn on the cameras to go live for a speech.

"Good morning, Commander," she said, strolling into the office on her short, pudgy legs. She was known for wearing excessive amounts of perfume and today was no exception as she entered with a fruity breeze that would linger for several minutes. Danielle offered a youthful smile as she brushed back her short brown hair. "Is there something I can help you with?"

"Yes. I need to broadcast live to the nation. I already set up the podium, but have no idea how to turn on the camera."

"Easy enough. Are you ready now?"

"How do I look?" Julian asked, having dressed casual in jeans and a button-up.

"Relaxed and confident," Danielle replied, reaching out to brush lint off his shoulders. "How long of a speech will you be giving? Should I get you a glass of water?"

"Shouldn't be more than five minutes; no need to worry about it. Thank you."

"Whenever you're ready, get behind the podium and I'll make sure the camera is centered before we broadcast."

Julian nodded and proceeded to the podium, grabbing the sides in a stern grip and looking straight ahead where a camera protruded from the wall behind his desk. Only a handful of people knew that a Commander's office also doubled as an underground bunker. Should there ever be an attack, Julian could seal up his office much like Chris did his house. Everything he needed to run the organization was available within the office, including a month supply of food for two people, should he decide to have someone stay with him.

Danielle pulled a tablet out of the top drawer beneath the camera and ran her fingers across the screen as she whistled. The camera made a robotic creaking sound as it moved up and down before centering on Julian. "That should do it," she said, and crossed the room with the tablet stretched out to Julian. "Push the green button to start the broadcast. It will show you the countdown until you actually come on the screen. After that, the same button will become red. Just push that when you're done."

"Perfect, I think I can handle that. Would you mind staying in here? I think it's weird to give a speech to an empty room."

"Whatever you need, Commander," Danielle said and took a seat behind the desk.

Julian fought off a slight tremor in his hands, knowing he needed to lie to everyone's face to move forward with the plan. He pushed the green button and watched as a fifteen-second countdown appeared.

Preceding a Commander's speech was a quick jingle and video that showed images of Road Runners hard at work around the world. The broadcast was sent out nationally to all offices, as well as direct to the other Commander offices on the different continents. The countdown struck zero and Julian stared into the camera's soul.

"Good morning, Road Runners. It's with a heavy heart that I must announce our very own Bill Jordan has passed away. He died in his home last night, and our team is working hard to investigate what exactly happened. We will not be slowed down by this tragedy. We will do what we always do, and keep moving forward.

"I was extremely close with Bill. He mentored me soon after I joined the Road Runners, and I know I wouldn't be here today if it weren't for him. Bill worked tirelessly for our organization – for our cause – and many times put us ahead of his own happiness. He had been working on finding a way to rescue Commander Strike, and I suspect he was getting close if the Revolters felt this was the best way to respond. I genuinely believe this attack was carried out by them."

Julian held his stare into the camera, but could see Danielle in his peripheral vision, her brown eyes bulging out of their sockets.

"We've come to a crossroads in our history and have arrived to a tough decision that needs to be made. Bill and I were just discussing the matter last night before he left the office, and we came to an agreement."

Julian paused and sighed to release the tension.

"We are going to deploy our bombs onto Chris's mansion and put an end to this war. It's been a decision many years in the making, and I feel this is the right time to move forward with it."

Julian thought he heard Danielle gasp, but it might have been the group of Road Runners huddled around the TV just outside his office walls. Either way, he knew the message was delivered with the authority he had hoped for. Once the shock wore off, he returned to the camera.

"Road Runners, right now is an extremely dangerous time for us.

No matter where you're located, it's imperative you keep an eye out for yourselves and your neighbors. Bill is just the start, so be vigilant, especially in the days following the bombing, as there will most certainly be retaliation from whoever is left of the Revolters. I wish you all the best. Good day."

Julian nodded and pushed the red button on the tablet to cut off the feed.

"How was that?" he asked Danielle, frozen in the desk chair.

"It was fine—I mean, it was great. But is it all true?"

"Is what true? Of course it's all true."

"Bill was killed by the Revolters in his own house?"

"We *believe* it was the Revolters," he lied. "The investigation is still taking place, but who else would do it? Bill was beloved by everyone within the Road Runners."

A tear trickled down Danielle's cheek, leaving a moist streak through her makeup.

"I can't believe it. I know we're in a war, but you never think something like this will actually happen, you know?"

"I know. They've done us enough harm by taking Commander Strike, and now Bill. We have no choice but to make a move."

Danielle nodded as she stood and moved to the door. "There was some worry among us about you taking over. But I think you'll have everyone's support with these bombs." She said this robotically, like a history teacher repeating random facts to a bored classroom.

"Thank you, Danielle."

She left without another word, and Julian returned to his desk, knowing that someone would shortly be in touch to try and talk him out of the dropping the bombs.

117

Chapter 25

Martin rose quietly from his seat, as if she could hear him approaching over the constant roar of the bar. His legs wobbled, a sensation of walking through wet cement. Sonya had her face down towards the menu while Martin approached her like a rare, exotic bird he didn't want to scare away.

He reached her table after what felt like ten minutes, even though it had only taken him ten seconds to move thirty feet. His arms shivered with anticipation as millions of thoughts ruptured his mind.

He was within arm's reach of the table and she still hadn't looked up. Her face appeared relaxed, free of the stress from their last encounter at her house. The thought of her bullets tearing apart his legs made him want to lunge across the table and strangle her. But he also remembered the time they had spent together in 1996, and no matter what anyone said, he knew their connection had been real.

Instead of lunging, Martin pulled out the seat across from Sonya and sat, remaining silent to not startle his bird into flapping away.

"Sonya," he said, watching her head jolt upright at the sound of his voice.

Her eyes grew another inch, head jerking side-to-side like a chicken as she scanned the bar behind him. "Martin," she whispered. "What the *hell* are you doing here?"

Her hands slapped the table as she jumped out of her chair. Martin raised his hands in self-defense, and waved her to sit back down.

"I could ask you the same thing," he said, his hands shaking underneath the table. Martin clenched his jaw shut, afraid his teeth might chatter and show his boiling rage. *Remember,* she *shot* you. She *left* you.

"I . . . I don't know what to say." She sat back down, but her hands remained planted on the tabletop.

"I think you and I need to have a long talk, and you can start by saying everything I don't already know."

"I don't know what you mean. I was just doing my job—you shouldn't be here. It's dangerous."

"Dammit, Sonya, we're way beyond that. I'm here. You're here. Now tell me what the hell happened!" These last words flew out of his lips with a snarl.

"Okay, okay. Relax. You need to tell me first why you're here and who sent you."

Her hands inched closer to her body, but remained on the table. Martin focused his stare to them, plotting his words wisely, as he no longer trusted the woman across the table.

"I'm here to get medicine for my mom. I was told it existed here and asked to come." Sonya nodded as if she knew this. "And no one sent me. Commander Strike gave me permission to come with a group of others, but I would've come either way. Now start talking."

Sonya looked around, her blond hair swinging behind in a ponytail. "We shouldn't talk here in the open. Can we go somewhere else?"

"Wow, so you're a Revolter now, huh? You're surely not one of these undercover Road Runners, since you betrayed me." She finally raised her hands, waving for Martin to shush. "Sorry, but I'm not going anywhere with you. You're crazy if you think I will, after that stunt you pulled at the Oxford."

Sonya gazed into him with her hazel eyes, and Martin thought he saw regret swimming beneath the surface.

"Okay," she said. "That's fine. But we can't talk here in a bar filled with Revolters. If one person hears the wrong part of our conversation, you'll be dead in seconds."

This much was true, and Martin had let his emotions get the best of him as soon as he saw Sonya. He needed to not lose track of where he was or who he was supposed to portray.

"Can we talk outside?" he asked. "Maybe go for a walk?"

Sonya nodded. "Yes, but if we walk by someone, anyone at all, you need to drop the conversation until we're clear. They're always listening in the city."

"Who's listening?"

"The government."

With this dramatic comment, Sonya stood again and pushed in her chair, prompting Martin to do the same.

When they stepped outside, nighttime had started to take its hold as the street lights illuminated the sidewalks, and the city's buildings glowed like candle flames. Golden spotlights danced across the sky, coming from the direction of the capitol.

"Where to?" Sonya asked.

"Is Civic Center Park safe at this time of day?"

"Everywhere is safe. There's no more crime in the city; it's all been pushed to the outside. Where are you staying?"

"None of your business," he snapped, pleasantly surprised by his own sternness.

They walked in awkward silence, a quick two blocks to downtown's biggest park across the street from the capitol steps.

They crossed Colfax to the park, prompting Martin to stop and admire the setting. The park was its usual self, only more attractive. New lighting ran along the pathways that cut across the grass. Additional benches had been added, along with a water fountain that provided a soothing background noise. Couples walked around, hands intertwined, while joggers ran by for their evening run through the park.

"There's not a homeless person in sight," Martin noted, remembering the park as a main hangout for those without a home.

"President Poe signed a law that forced all poor people out of the big cities," Sonya explained. "He claimed that cities were designed for the wealthy, not the suburbs, and as of now the, roles have reversed. Places like Highlands Ranch and Boulder belong to the poor now, and all of the rich reside in the city."

"Protected by guards and an electric fence. Don't tell me you agree with this."

"I don't have much of a choice. This is my home now. Forever."

"Why did you shoot me? Do you have any idea how long it took me to recover?" Martin tried to keep his tone soft, but his disgust leaked out just the same.

"I didn't want you coming after me. I knew if I didn't shoot you, you'd have followed me into the bedroom and grabbed me as soon as I drank my Juice. I couldn't have a single person know where I was going."

"Why here?"

"I'm protected here. I know the Road Runners want to kill me. Hell, I even understand *why* they need to, but I'm not going to just turn myself in. I don't want to die, even though I know it will save the world."

"Did you hear that Strike was kidnapped by Chris?"

"Of course."

"What do you plan on doing here for the rest of your life?"

"I don't know. Just living without fear. It would be a first, and it was peaceful until you showed up. I thought for sure you'd blast my head off."

"I could never kill you. The Road Runners sent me with that poison to your house, but I was never going to use it."

Sonya grinned. "I didn't think you would, but I had to play it safe."

"I need to know the truth, Sonya," Martin cut in, redirecting the conversation back to what he wanted. "I've heard all sorts of things about our relationship being a lie. Is it true?"

Sonya looked to the ground and kicked a rock out of the way. They hadn't moved since arriving to the park, standing on the sidewalk like nothing else in the world existed. "I don't know what you want me to say. I had a job to do. I may have fallen in love with you, but I couldn't give all the way into those feelings. Doing so would only put both of us at risk. I took this job because I'm emotionally scarred. My childhood was absolutely fucked up. Chris killed my mom when I was a kid. Nothing has been right ever since then. Then he injected his blood into me to keep himself immortal. I don't know how it all works, but it was supposed to give me purpose in life. Like he thinks I actually love him for being such a shitty father."

"Does he know you're here?"

"Of course. He set me up with the apartment."

"I don't understand your relationship. He's your father, but you hate him? But he also wants to keep you alive for his own reasons." Martin shook his head again, nothing making sense.

"We had to make a pact, him and I. When I ran away when I was 17, I joined the Road Runners—obviously this drove him crazy. I was trying to figure out life on my own and he'd just show up at the worst times, and he knew there was nothing I could do about it." Sonya shook her head while reminiscing. "Since his life depends on mine, I had to threaten suicide for him to leave me alone. And not just a verbal threat, I had to cut my wrists in front of him to show him I wasn't bluffing. Once he saw the blood he agreed to our pact."

"What's the pact?"

"To live and let live. He can no longer publicly acknowledge me as someone he knows. Even if I'm in the middle of important Road Runner business and he shows up, he has to pretend that everything is normal. Remember that date we went on to the steakhouse in 1996? He does shit like that all the time, showing up unannounced to mess with my head, never saying a word to me."

Martin nodded, remembering the encounter and his panic to ensure Sonya didn't find out that the two had known each other. Apparently, everyone already knew everything, Martin being the only oblivious party. He thought back to all the times Sonya had asked to not see the old man ever again, and the dots started connecting.

"When we returned to 2018 and went to the Wealth of Time store, you went inside with me. Why?"

"I wanted to surprise him the way he always did to me. It was a good idea in my head, but he wasn't fazed; probably knew I was coming." She shook her head in disgust.

"So now you both work for opposite teams, but have a mutual agreement to leave each other alone?"

"Well, we did. I don't know what I'm supposed to do now."

"Let me talk to them for you. I'll tell them you're alive and well and want to stay with the Road Runners."

"Are you shitting me? Want to stay? They sent you to kill me. At my own house! I don't want to stay."

"So you're joining the Revolters?"

"Hell no. I'm just living and waiting to see what happens. As long as my dad is alive, I have to stay in hiding. I'm at just as much risk as him to get killed by the Road Runners."

"So you hide out in the city where Road Runners aren't allowed. It actually makes sense. But did you know there are undercover Road Runners in the city? I got through just fine."

"Of course I know that. That's why I don't mingle with anyone unless I know for certain who they are."

"Is it just dumb luck that I happened to be sitting in the same bar as you?"

"I suppose it is. I go to new places for dinner every time I go out— I don't want to be seen as a regular anywhere. But Martin, you can't tell them about me. If the Road Runners know where I am they will hunt me until I'm dead. Who's in charge right now anyway, with Strike missing?"

"I have no idea. I was only told that Strike was missing, but they might already be onto you. Strike told us to keep an eye out for you before we came on this trip."

"It's logical to assume I would hide in this era within the walls. They know I can blend in with the Revolters if needed."

"So what am I supposed to do? Just go home and pretend like nothing happened?"

Sonya nodded. "Yes. But I know you won't actually do that, so I can sweeten the deal for you."

Martin's eyebrows raised in curiosity. "What do you mean?"

"I can get you that medicine."

"Are you shitting me? You've had access to the medicine this whole time?"

Sonya raised her hands for Martin to relax. "Look, I was just doing my job. I know it was a dirty thing to do, not telling you."

"You can say that again," Martin snapped, rage instantly flaring through his body. Not only had she laid the perfect trap for him in 1996, she had access to the most valuable medicine in the world, at least to Martin.

They paused as a couple of joggers passed them by on the park's trail.

"I'm sorry, Martin," she finally said. "Let me help you get the medicine. It's the least I can do."

"You can answer one question for me, actually," he responded dismissively. "Why did you drag me along for 6 months in 1996? Why did you come back with me to 2018, only to plan another trip into the past where you eventually led me into the trap? It seems like you had plenty of easy opportunities to turn me over."

"The Road Runners don't just recruit anyone," she said, her nervous stare returning to the ground while she spoke. "It's a long vetting process that often times can take an entire year."

"And what is it you're looking for during all that time?"

"Certain traits. I was actually on a special mission from Strike to find a worthy successor to her Commandership. She had trust issues with Julian, and wanted to see other options."

"Me as Commander? That's absurd." Martin shook his head, grinning at the thought of him leading the Road Runners in any capacity.

"It's not. You don't give yourself enough credit."

"I've never had any leadership qualities. Not in this sense."

"Really? Then why are you here? Where's the rest of the group you came with?"

Martin paused, thinking of a good response, but coming up short.

"Martin, you have the traits of a high-ranking Road Runner. You take initiative, are organized and extremely determined, and for the most part seem to be fearless. These are the things I had to judge as part of my job, getting to know you behind closed doors. When you came out of your coma ready to continue work, I knew you were the real deal. Anyone else would have called it quits at that point; you did not." Sonya let her words hang above Martin like a cloud of truth.

He thought back to their time together in 1996, mentally picking apart each moment and trying to categorize what had been real, and what had been a test. "Was the coma done on purpose?"

"Of course not. We would never cause a potential Road Runner any harm. But it was a unique opportunity for us to see how you'd respond in the most difficult of moments. Look, we can talk all night about this, but nothing will change. We're in 2064, and you're not even allowed to be in this city. Come back tomorrow morning. Let's meet in this same spot and I'll have your mom's medicine."

"What happens after that?" Martin asked, sensing a familiar desire to spend every waking moment by her side.

"You go home and save your mom, and we never see each other again. I'll be moving to another city. Even though I trust you, it's too risky having someone know where I am."

"Sonya, you don't have to do that. I'll leave you in peace."

"I think we both know that's a lie. I know in some other universe, where there's no such thing as Road Runners or Revolters, you and I probably have a life together. But that's not our reality, and it never will be. After tomorrow, we'll say goodbye forever." Sonya leaned in to Martin to kiss his cheek. "I'll see you in the morning. Please don't follow me home."

Martin watched her turn and walk across the street, back where they had come from. Somewhere in the city she lived her life, hiding out one day at a time. He checked his watch to find it was already nine o'clock, and Gerald was waiting for him outside the city walls.

118

Chapter 26

Julian locked himself in his office. Tension and pandemonium brewed outside as teams of Road Runners prepared for the upcoming attacks on Chris's mansion.

"Can he do this?" people murmured, excitement and angst heavy in their voices.

I certainly can, he thought. Only one group could attempt to stop him. The Council, a panel of seven Road Runners appointed by the commandership, served a role similar to the United States Supreme Court. With the Road Runners lacking a type of congress, the Council provided the only checks and balances on the commander, aside from the lieutenant commander.

Anyone within the organization could bring an issue to the Council for review. If interested, a member of the Council had to motion the topic for review, and it needed to be seconded by one other member. Once a motion was approved, The Council gathered in their private chambers to hash out a discussion before putting the matter up for a vote. Every Council member was required to vote, and not a single person could overturn their decision.

Julian had always found this unfair. Why should one group of Road Runners be able to wield all of the power? Not even the commander had any influence over them, so who was really in charge of the organization?

If there were only two Council members who felt strongly against dropping bombs on Chris, then the issue was already being discussed in New York City. All Julian needed was four Council members to side with him and everything would proceed without backlash. For whatever reason, the Road Runner community blindly accepted whatever decision the Council made.

It had only been thirty minutes since he delivered his speech, and his office phone began ringing constantly. The issue appeared more polarizing than killing Sonya, only this one had involvement from the public.

Julian left the phone off the hook, basking in silence as men and women worked in organized chaos to prepare the arsenal of bombs for deployment. He had decided to move forward as if nothing would stop him. Even if the Council ordered him to stop, he would still push forward, pretending to not receive the message. Disobeying the Council put him at risk of life in prison, but if the people could just see what a peaceful world looked like on the other side of the bombs, they'd have no choice but to forgive and forget.

"All leaders will be faced with one decision that defines them," Strike had told him once. "That decision forms how you're viewed by the public. It can turn you into a hero or the enemy of the people—there is no in-between."

He hadn't known why she shared this with him, but figured she was more talking to herself to arrive to a final decision on Sonya's fate, but he looked back at her words today with a wide grin.

"This is my grand decision," he said to the empty office. "Only my second day on the job, and the people will love me for ending this war."

Forty-five minutes had already passed since Julian authorized their preparation.

The Council was surely up in arms over the issue, hopefully equally split on the matter to burn more time while the rest of the world waited.

A knock rapped on the door, authoritative and rushed.

"Who is it?" Julian called out, not moving from his desk.

"Sir, Councilwoman Murray is on the phone for you. She needs to speak with you." The voice belonged to Danielle, and Julian sat in silence. "Sir?"

He wondered if he sat there long enough if she'd give up and tell Councilwoman Murray to call back later. But the call was too important; they would deliver the message to him one way or another. *No way they came to a decision that quickly.*

"Danielle, can you please give me two minutes?"

"Yes, sir, I will let her know."

Julian whipped out his cell phone and scrolled through his list of contacts until he found the one he needed, pressing on the call button with a shaky thumb.

"This is McGuire," a deep, hoarse voice answered.

"Mr. McGuire, this is Commander Caruso," Julian said.

"Hello, Commander, what can I do for you?"

"It's time to deploy the bombs to our target. I authorize you to do so immediately."

A brief silence filled the airwaves, and Julian sensed McGuire hesitating, debating to take the order or not.

"Mr. McGuire, right now, please."

"Yes, sir."

Julian hung up the cell phone and picked up the desk phone. "Danielle, you can patch through Councilwoman Murray."

"One moment," she replied before the phone cut to a brief silence.

"Commander Caruso," a woman's voice said, stern and disgusted.

"Good morning, Councilwoman, is everything okay?" Julian asked in the most laidback voice he could muster.

"No, Commander, it is not. We need you to cease all of your operations immediately. The Council has voted unanimously against dropping bombs on the Revolters' headquarters."

"Unanimous!" Julian jumped out of his chair, nearly choking on the word. He had expected this phone call after a long debate between the Council members, but a unanimous decision? "Why on Earth was it *unanimous?*"

"Commander, you're a suspect in Bill's murder. We can't have you making any major decisions until your name is cleared. There is support for the bombs in the Council, but this is the right thing for us to do. Once we clear your name, we can resume this discussion."

Julian checked the time to see two minutes had passed since he spoke with McGuire. In their prior conversations, McGuire had mentioned it would take four minutes for the bombs to be deployed upon receiving the order. Julian needed to stall two more minutes.

"Councilwoman, this isn't fair. I have a voice recording from Bill himself giving his approval. The Council has never reversed a decision agreed upon by a Commander *and* his lieutenant. Never."

"That is true, but this is an investigation. The recording will be part of it, and if our team determines the recording is real, we have no choice but to allow the bombs to move forward."

"How would I get a fake recording of Bill agreeing to this? Do you know how crazy you sound right now?"

"I know it's frustrating, and I know it's been an emotional morning for you," Murray responded calmly. "And I know this is probably the most difficult start to a Commandership we've ever had, but I need you to understand these are our laws, and this is how we have to enforce them."

"I understand," Julian said with a darkening grin. "By the way, Councilwoman, I already placed the call to authorize the bombs, the fireworks should begin in about thirty seconds."

Julian hung up the phone, leaned back in his chair, and clicked on the TV hanging on the wall. He flipped up one channel for the camera view showing Chris's mansion. It stood peacefully in the snow, moments away from its steel barriers being destroyed.

A helicopter flew above, rumbling their underground headquarters, signaling the start of the bombing. The crew in the helicopter studied the wind and relayed the information to the nearby arsenal where the bombs were loaded into futuristic cannons.

Julian dashed to the door to join the rest of the office huddled around the main screen. "It's time, everyone!" he cried. A few whispers spread through the office, but it remained otherwise deathly silent.

Julian leaned against a desk and crossed his arms, already proud at his decision and being the first to authorize the bombs that had been stored for years. He grinned, thinking about Councilwoman Murray on the opposite side of the country, running around in a panic trying to figure out a way to stop this already moving train of destruction. She could thank him later when they recovered Chris's body from the rubble.

Due to the silence, the rupture of four blasting cannons was heard clearly. Julian's heart raced as all eyes turned from the sound above their heads back to the big screen TV. It seemed ten minutes had passed with no action, but it had maybe only been ten seconds in reality.

The first bomb hit squarely on top of the mansion's barricade, exploding into a ball of flames and black smoke. The next three bombs followed within seconds, smoke filling up the entire screen in a blackout of doom. Julian giggled, but no one would ever hear it above the majestic explosions. More bombs struck the mansion in terrifying unison, rumbling the entire world.

One more round, Julian thought, smiling wide like a child walking into Disneyland for the first time.

Twenty seconds later the final bombs dropped, leaving them to wait for the smoke to clear and see the results. Surely the mansion was a pile of rubble. It took three treacherous minutes for the smoke to clear.

The mansion stood in its same place, undisturbed with the exception of black powder marks scattered across the steel barricade like a muddy child's handprints.

"Are you shitting me?" someone screamed out from the back. "Not even a dent?"

Julian watched in disbelief, nausea eating away his insides. With nothing to show for this bold stunt, the Council just might vote to remove him as Commander, or worse, send him to prison.

"No!" Julian screamed, barging back into his office and slamming the door shut behind him. "Goddammit!" he grabbed the phone from his desk and hurled it across the room, bits and pieces exploding in every direction. He debated running away, but had nowhere to go with the tracking device lodged in his arm, a virtual handcuff that kept him in place.

After all of the risks of going to the mansion to negotiate with Chris, turning Strike over to their greatest enemy, murdering Bill, and ignoring orders directly from the Council, the reality sunk in that Julian was fucked. All of these truths would be uncovered during an investigation that would surely be underway by the evening, and he had violated nearly every major rule in the book.

The screens cut out, flickering as if searching for a signal. After a few seconds, the signal strengthened, but showed Chris sitting in an office, the same office Julian had met him.

"Hello, Road Runners," Chris said, grinning into the camera. "I hope you're all having as pleasant of a day as I am. I have Commander Strike here, and she is fine and well. For now."

He paused and took a drink of water he didn't need, only doing so to add dramatics.

"I need whoever ordered these silly bombs to come over here right now. If you do, we can all carry on business as usual. If you don't, I'm afraid I have no choice but to respond to your malicious attacks. And trust me when I tell you this, there will be no more Road Runners by sunrise tomorrow. So, I suggest you turn yourself in and save thousands of lives. You have six hours to arrive before I unleash every weapon you can imagine on your little hideouts. *Ta-ta* for now." Chris winked and blew a kiss to the camera before the screen cut back to the still image of his charred mansion.

Julian sunk into his chair, an invisible fist pressing into his gut as a million thoughts flooded his mind. *The next six hours won't end well for me.*

The Road Runners had no time to grow an allegiance to him, and they would absolutely turn him in to spare their own lives. Stepping foot outside of his office all but guaranteed his death by Chris's hands, probably in a public humiliation for all of the world of Revolters and Road

Runners to see. If he stayed in the office, a crew sent from the Council was surely on its way to arrest him. If found guilty of Bill's murder, the penalty for killing a fellow Road Runner was death by firing squad.

He briefly debated making a run for it, but how far would he honestly make it with both Road Runners and Revolters chasing after him? There wasn't a place in the world to hide and feel safe.

Julian looked around the office, the wall of past Commanders gazing into his soul. They would never hang his portrait, even though he was soon to be the shortest-tenured Commander in history. The walls closed in around him, barricading him within his own mental prison. He heard the initial banging on the door from those in the office, surely trying to break in and take him to Chris's house. They punched and kicked the door, shouting mumbled phrases that he'd never hear.

No one was going to dictate how Julian Caruso left this world, so he pulled the pistol out from its drawer and pointed it at the door that would soon burst open, his hand steady on the desk.

The tumultuous knocking and banging ceased and was replaced by the sound of a bigger, quaking thud that rattled the door in its hinges, dust and debris puffing from the edges of the door frame in little clouds.

Here we go, Julian thought as he cocked the pistol.

With the next bang, the door burst open, revealing a desk they had used as a battering ram. At least twenty Road Runners stood behind it, all peering into Julian's office, shouting in such disarray that it was impossible to know what anyone said.

Six rounds of ammunition had no chance at holding off two dozen pissed-off Road Runners. As the first of them lunged into the room, Julian slipped the pistol into his mouth and squeezed the trigger.

119

Chapter 27

Martin didn't speak much on the ride home with Gerald, his encounter with Sonya gnawing at his conscience like a rabid goat. Gerald filled in Martin with everything he had learned about Commander Strike's disappearance and the ensuing catastrophe with Julian.

"It's complete turmoil for us right now," Gerald said. "We have no leader. The next in the chain of command is the head of security, I think, until we have a special election."

"I can't believe all of this has happened since we left. We haven't even been here a full 24 hours."

"This is poor judgment on Strike's behalf. Julian should have never been her lieutenant commander. He was too young to be in such a position, and already lacked respect from others. Bill would've been the better choice, even if most saw him as too soft; we wouldn't be in this mess right now, that's for sure."

They pulled into their hotel parking lot, a tall lamp post flickering to provide the dimmest of light.

"I need to tell you something," Martin said when Gerald turned the van off. "Something happened downtown today."

"Something is always happening downtown." Gerald chuckled.

"No, not like that. I met some people. Some Road Runners."

The grin on Gerald's face vanished immediately. "How do you know they were Road Runners?"

"They told me."

"Martin, you're lucky to be sitting here. That's a common line for Revolters to use to sniff out the real Road Runners." Gerald bolted upright, raising his voice like a disappointed parent. "If that had been a Revolter, you'd be dead—I warned you about this."

"Well, then it must have really been a Road Runner. It was one man who came over to me in a restaurant and we spoke privately at my table. I didn't think anything of it. He told me he was one of the undercover Road Runners living in this year, and wanted to wish me the best."

"How did he know?"

"No idea. All he said was that he could tell I wasn't from here."

Gerald shook his head. "Doesn't make sense. There were others?"

"Yes, I met one other. Someone who said they can help me get the medicine. In fact, said we can get it tomorrow morning."

"Why does someone inside the city know about the medicine?" Martin sensed that Gerald would stand up if physically possible, but they remained trapped in the vehicle. "They said you were smart, but it sounds like you made nothing but horrible decisions today. Are you trying to end up next to Strike? Or worse?"

Martin recalled being somewhat of a prisoner in Chris's mansion, and imagined there weren't many things worse. Even death was more attractive than becoming a robotic soldier for Chris.

"It was an old friend, quite a coincidence that I ran into her."

"*Her*? Don't tell me—"

"Yes, it's her. She's hiding inside the city, and just happened to be in the same bar as me tonight."

Gerald sat quietly, his thick fingers rubbing his lips in discomfort. "You know we have to kill her. That's our order."

"Order from who? We don't have to kill her. She made a promise to help me, and she will. I'm not going to be involved in killing her. I'm going to get this medicine that I came for, and go back home. She already knows she's being hunted."

Gerald shook his head. "I don't like the sound of this. She betrayed the Road Runners and now lives in the city. She's clearly in contact with Chris and can't be trusted."

"I can trust her."

"Oh, so you're an expert now? You can tell when she's telling the truth or leading you on for six months of your life?"

"That's low."

"That's the truth."

"She feels guilty. She knows my mom, and doesn't like what Chris did; that's why she offered to help."

"As the leader of this mission, I'm telling you this is a bad idea. It smells like a setup, especially with how valuable you are. I strongly advise you do not move forward this. However, as a human being, I understand you trying to save your mother, and I know you need to take some risks to do so. If you feel you need to do this, then I won't get in your way, but just know you'll be meeting her alone."

"Thank you, Gerald."

Gerald nodded, staring out the windshield into the darkness. "You can still reject her offer and I'll go in with you as planned. We can get this medicine without her."

"I don't doubt that, but she told me she can get it without any trouble. Why put all of us at risk if we don't need to?"

"If you trust her—which you shouldn't—then I can't stop you. I'll look the other way, and if anything bad happens, I'll tell them you went off on your own."

"There is no *them* right now."

Gerald nodded calmly. "Ain't that the truth? Well, best of luck to you. I'll give you a ride in the morning and we'll see what happens."

"Thanks again, I don't know how to ever repay you."

"Just don't get killed, and we'll call it even."

Gerald pushed open the van's door and stepped out into the cool night. A man sat in a lawn chair in the patch of dirt in front of the complex, puffing a cigarette and blowing smoke to the sky. Martin joined Gerald and walked by his side into the hotel.

They strolled down the main hallway, its peeling carpet and chipped walls welcoming them home. The odor of cigarette smoke filled the halls as if it were once a smoking lounge.

Gerald jolted to a stop when they reached their door, his hand swinging up to tell Martin to stay put.

Martin followed Gerald's gaze to the ground, where three droplets of blood splashed on the floor.

"Were those there this whole time?" Gerald whispered, his other hand whipping a pistol out of his waistband.

Martin froze in his tracks and shrugged.

Gerald studied the door, but found nothing out of the ordinary. He lowered his hand and slid it quietly onto the doorknob. "Stay out here."

Martin reached into his waistband, forgetting that he had left his gun inside the room, advised by Gerald to do so. The insecurity of having no protection besides his fists sent instant panic through his core.

Gerald turned the knob as gently as possible, the sounds of old springs creaking before he thrust open the door and immediately raised his gun in the air. "Jesus Christ!" he shouted as the door banged against the inside wall. "Stay here!"

Martin watched Gerald disappear inside, leaving him paranoid and clueless in the hallway. Not sensing any immediate danger, Martin took a soft step toward the door frame and craned his neck for a view inside.

Web sat on the couch, facing the door, a hole in the middle of his forehead, blood splattered behind him like a bucket of red paint had been thrown on the wall. Web's eyes remained open, glossy as they stared at Martin. His arms splayed by his side as his head hung slightly to the left, held upright by the couch.

"Should I call someone?" Martin asked.

Gerald whipped around, snarling. "I said to stay outside. I need to make sure the suite is clear."

Martin backed away, subconsciously raising his hands in the air. He waited in the hallway, feeling like a sitting duck for any attacker willing to swoop by and take him out. The rest of the hotel was eerily quiet, too quiet considering it was barely nine o'clock. He wondered if their neighbors had also been attacked. But wouldn't the man smoking in front of the building have mentioned something about people barging in with guns?

"Come in, Martin!" Gerald called out.

Martin shuffled back to the door, fighting to keep his eyes off the dead body on their couch, but failing miserably.

Gerald stood in the kitchen, joined by a shivering Brigham.

"I found Brigham hiding in his closet," Gerald said, putting an arm over the traumatized scientist's shoulder. "Are you ready to talk about what happened?"

Martin watched Brigham's hands tremble like he had uncontrollable Parkinson's disorder.

"I'm not ready, but I need to talk about it," Brigham said, his voice matching his hands.

"Take your time, start from the beginning and go slow. We're safe right now."

Martin noticed the choice of the words *right now*, leading him to believe that they weren't necessarily safe moving forward.

"I was in my room," Brigham said. "Wrapping up a couple of things for research and about to lie down. Web was in the living room, working on his laptop. I heard a loud bang and two men yelling at Web. He yelled back, and that's when the gun went off. I panicked and went into my closet, praying they wouldn't open it. I heard their footsteps moving through every room, even mine, but they didn't touch anything from what I could tell."

Brigham's voice teetered off as he broke into heavy sobs, burying his face in open palms. Gerald rubbed his back to try and console him, shaking his head as he studied the ground.

"We need to get Web's body out of here," Gerald said. "If you can help me load him into the van, I'll drive and take him back to 2019." He spoke to Martin, who nodded.

"Are we safe here?" Martin asked.

"Yes. Assuming these were Revolters, they don't ever come back to a place for a second time unless a few months have passed."

"Shouldn't we call the police? Or check on the others in the building?"

"There are no police outside of the city. It's everyone for themselves. If they came in and did this to Web, then it's probably too late to help anyone else. All we can do is clean up, and make sure we complete our mission this week, so we can get out of here."

"How do you want to do this?"

Gerald released Brigham, who had started to slow down with the water works. "Let's wrap his body and lay him in the back seat. I'll drive to Ralph's place and will take Web back to 2019 where they can proceed with getting him back to Europe." He shook his head, unable to hide the disgust plaguing him.

"Don't beat yourself up over this," Martin said. "It's not your fault."

"It's always my fault when someone on my crew dies. Especially when it's someone who has never gone through field training. My only job is to keep them safe, and I failed. You'll understand one day when you have to lead a crew of your own."

Martin felt guilt creep into his thoughts. These men were all here because he wanted medicine for his mother. If not for him, Web would be alive and Brigham wouldn't be traumatized. All of this had happened and he hadn't even seen the medicine yet. Would the Road Runners have sent this group on a mission together if Martin had never asked about medicine? He didn't know for sure, but assumed not. Brigham and Web had volunteered to come along, and now one of them was dead. While Martin didn't believe he'd ever lead a crew on a future mission, he assumed responsibility on this trip.

"Let's do it," Martin said. "I'll help you, and I'll stay here with Brigham to make sure nothing else happens. And tomorrow I'm getting that medicine so we can leave." He spoke in his most authoritative voice. He had been warned of how dangerous the future was, and now seeing it firsthand, the reality sparked a new urgency. There was no time to waste.

"Grab a couple of sheets from your bedroom closet," Gerald said. "We'll wrap him in that."

Martin retrieved the sheets and returned within a minute. Gerald had made his way to the couch to lay Web on his side, tipping him over like a lifeless stuffed animal. He took a sheet from Martin and draped it over Web's face, stretching it down to cover the entirety of his body.

Gerald worked with the ease of a hotel maid, and Martin wondered if this was something he had done in the past. He lifted the dead body, tucking the loose sheet underneath, starting from the head and working down to the feet, until Web was wrapped in what looked like a cocoon. He repeated the same process with the second sheet, covering the red splotch that had seeped through the first layer.

Gerald stepped back to ensure his work was complete. Just like that, Web had become a mummy on the couch, lifeless under wraps, another casualty of the never-ending war between good and evil.

"May I?" Brigham asked, stepping toward his old colleague. He placed a hand softly on top of the white lump, shaking his head. "We weren't the best of friends, but we worked together on many projects. You were always easy to work with and kept the mood light. You'll be missed. Rest easy."

His words were brief, but meaningful, and he sniffled away more tears as he turned to join Gerald and Martin.

"You ready?" Gerald asked.

"Yes," Martin said, taking the first step toward Web.

"You take him by the legs, I'll take him by his shoulders."

They positioned themselves and hoisted Web upward, the sheets' tight wrapping undisturbed. Martin had never understood the term "dead weight" until this moment. Sure, he had carried Izzy from room to room when she fell asleep on the couch, but that paled in comparison to lifting an actual dead body. If he had never been whipped into shape, poor Web would be splayed across the floor, but Martin's new muscles bulged as they started out the door and down the hallway.

"Brigham, you'll need to come open the van door for us," Gerald said through gritted teeth.

They made their way toward the building's exit, Martin and Gerald thudding down the hall like they were moving a heavy couch. Martin broke a sweat during that short time, the outside air cooling him immediately. The smoker from earlier was gone, leaving just the three of them as they crossed the walkway to the van.

Brigham ran ahead and opened the door to the back seat, looking away from the sight as they lowered Web inside.

Gerald lowered the head in first, pushing it as far in as he could reach. He pulled himself out, leaving Martin to hold the legs like a wheelbarrow, as he rounded the van to open the door on the other side and continue pulling Web in all the way. Martin bent Web's knees to allow both doors to shut without slamming into the corpse.

"You guys head back inside," Gerald instructed. "Order some dinner, try to take your mind off things. I'll be back in about 90 minutes."

Gerald hopped in and sped off like a man on a mission.

"I'm glad you're okay," Martin said to Brigham as they started back inside.

"Me too. I still can't believe any of this happened."

"I've got some things in place where we can hopefully leave tomorrow morning."

They walked in silence back into the hotel, the tension of their mission feeling like the least important thing as they cleaned the blood splatters off the walls and floor.

120

Chapter 28

Strike woke to the sensation of a stake rammed through her head. She lay on a couch in Chris's office, her eyes shifting in and out of focus as they peered around the empty room.

Would Chris actually leave me unattended? she wondered, knowing damn well he'd never let her escape. Perhaps he was laying a trap.

None of it mattered, as her arms and legs throbbed in excruciating pain. Her muscles had tensed unlike anything before, and she was happy to simply wiggle her toes and know she hadn't been paralyzed. She lay as limp as a sloth on a Sunday afternoon, attempting to lift her head, but unable to, new waves of pain shooting down her spine. She tried moving her legs, but couldn't. He may have not paralyzed her, but Chris made sure she wouldn't move from the couch.

The office looked as if it had been suddenly abandoned. Chris's chair faced the open door, computer monitors glowed, and a fireplace crackled in the distance. Surely they wouldn't have left her alone without the intent of coming right back. Strike was, after all, the most prized possession according to Chris.

Muffled voices and heavy thuds came from the other side of the wall, in the hallway. It sounded like a group of men chattering, moving something heavy down the hall by the sounds of their slow approaching footsteps.

"Right in here," Chris called out before appearing in the doorway. "Ah,

Commander Strike, good morning."

She hated when he called her commander, but there wasn't much she could do about it while being a useless pile of flesh on the couch. She tried pulling herself up through her abdomen, again failing. Even though she wasn't constrained, she was still a prisoner.

Chris entered with a giddy smile and extra hop in his step. Four men followed behind him, grunting as they held a body between them, one holding each limb.

"This way, gentlemen – go ahead and drop him in front of the Commander." Chris clapped his hands and skipped toward Strike.

She watched the men haul the body over. It was dressed in jeans and a flannel shirt, snow frosting the top of black hair. The men lowered the body to the ground directly in front of Strike, and her eyes bulged at the sight of the cold, dead face.

"Ahh, so you do know this person," Chris said. "Your people dropped him in front of the house like a sacrifice. They left a note." Chris reached into his pocket and pulled out a piece of paper, unfolded it, and began reading. "Mr. Speidel, please accept our sincerest apologies. This is the body of the traitor who decided to drop bombs on your mansion. He did this without any approval. We don't want any trouble, just to have Commander Strike returned safely. Thank you."

Chris giggled madly while he folded the note and returned it to his pocket. "So, tell me, Commander. What was his name?"

A tear ran down Strike's cheek, seemingly the only thing moving on her body. "Julian Caruso. He would've taken over when I went missing."

Chris nodded to the men who had stood awkwardly in the corner, and they left the room.

"So I have the pleasure of two Commanders in my house at the same time," Chris said to himself. "What a blessed day. You slept through the bombing. I counted over 15 that he dropped on us. It was hard to tell; at one point the house was just constantly shaking and the sounds of explosions were nonstop. I didn't know you peaceful people had access to such bombs."

"We have them, but never planned to use them," Strike said, wanting so desperately to simply sit up.

"Well, it appears Commander Caruso here had different plans. And look at him now." Chris laughed. "So who is in charge now when both Mommy and Daddy aren't home?"

"We hold a special election." Strike lied. Bill would be in charge right now, but she wasn't going to give this lunatic anyone's name. "There should be a new Commander selected within the next two days."

"An election, huh? Think I have a shot?" Chris howled, his laughter echoing around the walls and sending chills through Strike's motionless body. When he settled down, he returned his attention to Strike. "This is unfortunate, though. I was hoping to give whoever dropped the bombs the same welcoming hospitality you received. It's only fair. But he's dead, so that won't be very fun."

Chris paced around Julian's body, studying the corpse like a scientist. "You don't suppose this is our guy, do you, Commander?"

"What do you mean? He's one of my people."

"Yes, we know that. I mean the man who came over and sold you out. The man was about this size, and his voice sounded younger, much like our friend here."

Strike still didn't believe anyone in the Road Runners would do such a thing. Surely Chris was bluffing, but she studied Julian with suspicious eyes just the same. How else would Chris have been able to get her so easily?

"I guess since he's already dead," Chris continued. "I'll have to move forward with retaliation. His body is a lovely gift—I'll be sure to thank your people—but it's not what I was hoping for. Did you know we have enough bombs to end civilization? And they are all over the world. Talk about a fireworks show you don't wanna miss."

Chris giggled while he shook his head.

"Why would you blow up the world?" Strike asked. "You live here."

"Oh, Commander, I have no plans on blowing up the world. I just like having the option in my back pocket. It's a strong wagering chip, as you might imagine, and most people are smart enough to know I never lie."

"Are you going to tell me what you want? Or just keep talking nonsense?"

"I love your eagerness, Commander, but you really should relax. It's going to be at least two more days before you can lift yourself off that couch. I must say you do look quite comfortable, like a cat taking a day off from its hectic life."

"And what is your retaliation?" She tried to sound unimpressed, but was terrified at learning how many explosives Chris had access to.

"Eye for an eye, Commander. I don't try to one up my enemies, just return the favor. They tried to blow up my house, so I have no choice but to blow up one of yours. Where is your election going to be held?"

"It's not held anywhere. Everyone votes from whatever office they're in."

"I see. Election day might be a fun time to rattle your little underground forts. It would be a shame for the rest of the world to find out about this secret society you've kept hidden for so long."

"What do you want from me?" Her body may have not been able to move, but her voice came out sharp and demanding. "Tell me, dammit!"

"It's not so much what I want from *you*, Commander. See, you and I want the same thing: to end this war. Now that I have you in my possession, that is becoming a reality as we speak. Your pathetic group of warriors are now flailing around like headless chickens. Their leader is gone and their backup leader is dead on my floor. Forgive me for saying this, but you silly Road Runners have never had a day as bad as this, and it makes me beyond tickled."

"You know most wars end with a sort of peace treaty, not destruction."

"Commander, I've *been* to most of the wars throughout history, and destruction is what *leads* to the peace treaty. Trust me. No one is asking for peace until their backs are against the wall. Much like yourself right now." Chris grinned and sat down in a love seat opposite the couch, Julian's corpse between them. "We can work out a deal, but I want to have my fun first. I can't let you walk out of here looking like a hero who negotiated a deal. I have to blow some things up, kill some of your people, and paint the picture that I drove you to surrender."

"You're a twisted piece of shit," she snarled. "All we've ever done is try to keep the world safe from your lunatic ideologies."

Chris threw his head back and chuckled. "Commander, people *love* my ideology. You've seen the future, the whole world loves it. Humans only worry about themselves and not others. I've found a way to stroke those selfish desires and turn the world on its axis. Chaos is the world naturally cleansing itself, resetting us back to our barbaric roots."

"You're wrong. People will always strive to be better and improve. Nobody wants to go backwards."

"I'd say Mr. Caruso here took a step backwards, wouldn't you? I didn't even have the pleasure of killing him myself. I was gonna televise it for all of your people to see what happens when you try to disrupt my life. Perhaps you can fill that role, or maybe we can work out a deal. Maybe both?"

Chris leaned back and stroked his chin, the dials turning in his sick mind. Strike would happily offer both of her legs if it meant getting out of this mansion, but knew even Chris wouldn't accept those terms. He enjoyed mind games more than dead bodies.

"I'll have to get back to you, Commander." Chris pulled up his sleeve and checked his watch. "I'm gonna head to bed, it's about that time. I'll leave you here to catch up with your friend, maybe he'll answer to you why he decided to drop bombs on my beautiful mansion. Have a great night."

Chris stood, winked, and left the office, closing the door behind him.

Strike remained on her side and cried as an earthy odor rose from Julian's dead body, his perished eyes open and gawking at the ceiling. A long night awaited as she would need to decide how to best surrender the war.

121

Chapter 29

Martin woke up the next morning and vomited in the toilet. Gerald had planted the idea of Sonya playing mind games, and he couldn't shake the thought, having woken up in a nervous sweat multiple times throughout the night. His morning meeting with Sonya loomed, and as the hours ticked away each time he woke up, a sense of doom crept into his conscience like a slow moving funnel cloud waiting to demolish a small town.

Sonya had left the Road Runners behind, having no choice, but would she go as far as reuniting and with her estranged, demented father? And actually do him a favor by trying to capture Martin?

He doubted it, but crazier shit had already happened on this brief adventure to the future. Martin owed it to himself to meet with Sonya. At this point, what did he have to lose? He had already braced his mother for the possibility that he might not return. It was a classic high-risk, high-reward scenario, with the reward being a return to 2019 with the cure for Alzheimer's.

Web was dead, so he at least owed it to him to not have his death pass in vain.

After rinsing off under the sink, Martin returned to his room to dress in his Revolter attire of dark jeans and a long sleeve, plaid button-up. His suitcase was filled with plenty of similar outfits to blend in around the city for at least another week.

Today's the day, Martin thought as a knock came from his door. He expected Gerald, and pulled open the door to confirm.

"How did you sleep?" Gerald asked.

"I hardly slept. I just wanna get this medicine and go home."

"If all goes well, hopefully we'll be on our way in the next couple of hours."

"I know." Martin slipped into his shoes and looked in the mirror, wondering if this was the final time he would see himself alive.

"What's bothering you?" Gerald asked, monotone like always.

Martin sighed. "Am I making a mistake, Gerald? Part of me is starting to think that I might not make it back."

"That's always a risk living in this era. Being a Road Runner after the year 2030 is basically a death sentence. But that's beside the point. I take it you thought about what I said about Sonya."

Martin nodded. "I did. I still don't buy it—I don't think she would do that to me after all we've been through. But I still can't make myself rule it out as a possibility. I might show up expecting the medicine and end up back in Alaska with Chris, to never see the light of day again."

"I wish there was more I could do to help, but we can't risk it. If only you could've had her agree to meet you outside of the city, but I doubt she would fall for that."

"It's too late now, so let's head out."

Gerald stepped aside and let Martin pass into the living room. The blood splatters had been wiped off the wall, but the stains in the couch would never come out, appearing like a deep, black hole in the center cushion, ready to suck another life into it.

"Is Brigham still sleeping?" Martin asked.

"Trying to. I checked on him just now, said he's been staring at the walls all night, going to try and fall asleep now."

"Poor guy must be horrified."

"Yeah, he'll be okay as soon as we get back home."

Thanks for the extra pressure.

Gerald pulled the van keys out of his pocket, and they left the hotel and Brigham behind, oblivious to what the next few hours had in store.

The abandoned roads at seven in the morning surprised Martin as they headed toward downtown. It made sense, though, since everyone who worked downtown already lived there. Those on the outside had no business in town, unless authorized.

Gerald pulled over to the same spot as yesterday to let Martin out. "I'll wait here," he said after not speaking a word during the tense ride over. "One hour, then I'm going back. If it takes you longer than that, I'll be back at noon. That sound good?"

"Yes."

"Good luck." Gerald shook Martin's hand before he headed off to his date with Sonya.

Martin stepped out of the van and never looked back, starting down the long sidewalk toward the checkpoint where a handful of people formed a short line to get through security. He only waited two minutes before stepping through the metal detector and getting the green light to enter the city. He wondered if he had never met Chris, what side of the electric fence he would have ended up living on. Would he have even survived the initial wave of genocide that occurred after the Revolters snaked their way into government?

He shook off the thought as he passed through security and stepped into the bustling city. Even though no one had to commute into the city, there were still thousands who needed to get across town, leaving the roads clogged and jammed like rush hour in Manhattan.

Martin entered through the same location as yesterday, a couple blocks behind the capitol. On the other side of the golden structure would be Sonya, hopefully alone and holding a bottle of medicine. He walked down Colfax, the cars on the street a sitting parking lot that shimmered under the morning sun. Birds soared above, chirping, while Martin fought to keep the weight of his upcoming encounter off his mind.

Within a couple minutes, Civic Center Park appeared, dozens of businessmen crossing it on their way to work, coffee in hand and briefcases at their sides. Martin started straight for the same location where he had left Sonya last night, and believed he saw her sitting on a park bench.

If it was her, then she was alone, easing his mind. Martin had half-expected her to show up with someone else, either to escort the medicine that was apparently a hidden treasure, or to help take him away so Chris could feast on his soul forever.

The walk toward her felt like an eternity, but when he finally reached her, all sense of doom vanished. She sat on the bench, peaceful as she watched a group of butterflies flutter across the park. She was the same girl he had fallen in love with; nothing would ever change that.

"Good morning," he said when he reached the bench, sitting down next to her.

"Hi, Martin," she said, her face lighting up with a wide smile.

She's either excited to see me, or happy knowing this is the last time.

Martin pushed the thoughts aside, knowing how the mind played tricks on itself when paranoia ran wild. "How was your night?"

"It was fine. Yours?"

"It was okay." Martin debated telling her about coming home to a murder, but decided against it. He couldn't afford to let anything derail them from the task at hand.

They sat in awkward silence for a few seconds, neither wanting to speak next while they absentmindedly watched people pass through the park.

"I have the medicine," she finally said.

Martin exhaled, not realizing he had been holding his breath. "Thank you. I don't know how to ever repay you."

"You don't owe me a thing. Just remember our deal."

Martin slouched on the bench, all tension leaving his body. "Can I ask how you got the medicine so easily? They made it sound like an impossible mission for us to get it."

"Let's just say I have connections being Chris's daughter—as much as I hate saying it. I've never used it to my advantage until last night when I went to pick up the medicine. It felt gross dropping his name, but I had no choice. Your mother didn't deserve this."

"Thank you. I'll tell her it was you."

"Please, just forget about me."

"Sonya, you don't have to live the rest of your life in this world. This doesn't need to be your new normal."

"Easy for you to say. I don't have many options if I'm supposed to dodge Road Runners trying to kill me."

"I still don't understand why this became a thing all of a sudden. Haven't you been a Road Runner for years?"

She nodded. "They didn't always know about my life being linked to Chris's mortality. When it became clear that he can't be killed through any conventional means, they branched out their research to find other ways. And that's how they discovered this."

"How did you find out?"

"They told me. That's the Road Runner way, you know, being transparent with everything. They never made plans to kill me; in fact, they wanted to study me and see what they could learn. Maybe there was a way to kill Chris by removing a part of my body or something, but nothing ever came out of it. Just recently is when these conversations started, but I had friends in high places who warned me."

"Was it Bill?"

She nodded slowly, her hair swaying in a silent breeze. "Bill had become like a father to me during my time with the Road Runners. He was never going to let anything bad happen to me. He tipped me off seconds after the vote was cast to decide my fate, and had an escape plan in place. It was his idea for me to hide out here. He said it was the only logical place where a Road Runner wouldn't be able to get their hands on me. He deserves to be the next Commander if things don't work out with Strike. He may be a bit reserved, but he has such a bright vision for the future."

"I'll be sure to vote for him." Martin couldn't bring himself to tell Sonya that Bill had been murdered; she had been through enough already.

"Whatever ends up happening, just be ready to make a huge decision when you get back."

"What do you mean?"

"This mission you're on is a test. The other Commanders around the world are watching to see if you succeed or not, and how you are when you get back to 2019. I told you, there is consideration for you to run for the Commandership."

"It doesn't make any sense, I just joined not even a week ago."

"And that's exactly what they want: a fresh perspective. There are lots of lifetime Road Runners who will throw their name into the mix, but they want someone with more of an outsider's perspective, and who also has the merit to take on the role. When you return with this medicine, you'll basically be sealing your fate as a future Commander. Once you have the support of other Commanders, it's nearly impossible to lose an election."

"But I don't want to be a Commander. I just want to go back to my normal life."

Sonya sighed, staring straight ahead, but speaking out of the side of her mouth. "Your normal life is gone. You're a Road Runner now, an important one with a special gift. You either stay with the organization, or get hunted by Chris. And he will catch you if you leave the protection the Road Runners provide."

Martin stood up, needing to move around, and rocked on his wobbly legs. *Is she going to give me the medicine? Or keep trying to tell me the future?*

She joined him, reaching into the purse that had been hidden by her side. "I guess this is where we say goodbye."

"It doesn't have to be," Martin pleaded.

"But it is. You're going home and your life is going to change forever. And I'll be staying, living here until I'm an old lady. That's the way it is, and there's nothing you can change about it."

Martin's face flushed, his eyes growing heavy with tears as a lump bubbled his throat.

"Don't cry. I'll never forget you, Martin Briar. You're going to do big things."

"This isn't goodbye," Martin said, his voice shaky while a lone teardrop streamed down his cheek. "If I have any sort of influence with the Road

Runners, I'll make sure they drop their mission to kill you, and you can return home safely."

"I'm sure you will, but I'll be staying here. I hope one day, in another life, our paths cross again."

Sonya stepped into his embrace and planted her lips on his. Their kiss lasted a couple seconds, but her flavor would forever remain in Martin's memory. As she pulled away, she slipped a brown paper bag into Martin's hand, closing his fingers around it with her own.

"Go take care of your mother. She needs you. Goodbye."

Sonya stared into Martin's soul with her hazel eyes, and he held on to the moment, storing it for the rest of his life.

"Bye, Sonya."

She walked away, crossing Colfax toward the downtown skyscrapers. Martin's heart insisted she wasn't really leaving forever, but his mind said otherwise. It only took a minute for her to walk out of his life, just as quickly as she had come into it.

122

Chapter 30

Martin dragged himself out of the city, a throbbing sensation radiating from his gut. Every particle of his heart told him to turn around and spend the rest of his life with Sonya. Even his mother would give her blessing if that was what he desired. Passing by all the robotic businessmen convinced him to keep walking. *This is no world to live in.*

Gerald was waiting in the same spot like he said, and perked up behind the wheel upon seeing Martin return so soon. The van idled, and as he approached, Martin heard music for the first time in this futuristic hellhole. The beat was a clash of electronic dance music and hip-hop, notably with no lyrics.

Gerald punched off the radio when Martin opened the door and sat down, the brown bag clutched depressingly in his grip.

"That's it?" Gerald asked, staring at the bag.

Martin nodded and opened the bag for the first time, pulling out a white pill bottle that looked no different from something you'd pick up at the local pharmacy. There was no label, just a scribble on the bottle that read *Take one pill every day for 30 days.*

"What's wrong?" Gerald asked as Martin sulked silently in his seat.

"It was hard, okay. You may all be trained to murder Sonya, but I love her. Saying goodbye wasn't easy."

"I'm sorry, Martin. It's not that I'm not sympathetic—please understand that. I feel for you, and under normal circumstances I'd say let's take a few days off and go drink at a bar. But we gotta get you and Brigham the hell out of here. It's not safe. They stole Web's laptop when they killed him. So it's only a matter of time before they break through his security and find out what we are doing here. They'll be back within the next few days, and it's best that none of us are around."

"I understand. We're all just doing our jobs."

Martin studied the pill bottle, his chest empty of emotion. Could this be the pain Chris was referring to? Was setting up his mother with Alzheimer's just a step to get him to this lovesick point of near depression? Chris was certainly crafty enough to orchestrate such a drawn-out plan.

He shook his head free of the thoughts, knowing they'd creep back in plenty of times over the next few days.

"When we get back to the hotel, we'll take about ten minutes to make sure all of our stuff is gathered, then we're leaving." Gerald spoke as he started driving, leaving Sonya and futuristic Denver in the rear view.

Martin leaned on the van door and wished nothing more than to go back to that day in 2018 when his mother asked him to take her to the new antique store in town. He rarely told her no, but it would have been worth every ounce of joy today. Would she have still developed Alzheimer's? Would he have eventually shot himself? Would Izzy's body ever have been found, sending Lela to prison?

It was impossible to answer these questions, so he had to trust that things worked out the way they were supposed to, regardless of what he actually wanted.

"Gerald, can I ask you something?" Martin spoke like a nervous child.

"Of course."

"Sonya said some things about me being considered for commander. Do you know anything about that?"

Gerald nodded. "It's true," he said, nonchalant.

"Were you going to tell me?"

"It's not for me to tell. I'm a soldier, Martin. I take orders. I was given strict orders to protect you at all costs, even sacrificing my life if need be. That type of protection is only given to the highest ranking Road Runners, mainly the commanders. They never told me directly that you're in consideration for the job, but the protection order speaks for itself."

"What am I supposed to do?"

"What do you mean? You run for Commander, win that election, and lead this organization. There's nothing else to do."

Gerald spoke of the situation as if it were a no-brainer type of decision. Was Martin the only person who didn't see himself as a commander? Sometimes people perceive you in a way that you never thought possible. But that doesn't make them right.

"Look, Martin, I can't tell you what to do. But if there are people higher up who believe you're fit for the job, then you're fit for the job. It's that simple. We've never even had a questionable candidate run for the position. There have been some with agendas we don't agree with, but never someone who we would ever question their ability to lead us toward an end to this war. You're not giving yourself enough credit."

Everyone keeps saying that.

Martin didn't respond, opting to gaze out the window as his unfamiliar hometown passed by in a blur. It seemed he didn't even have a say in the matter. When he arrived back to 2019, someone within the Road Runners' organization would be waiting with plans for him to run for commander, and he still didn't know why.

Gerald whistled a tune while they drove, clearly wanting Martin to have the moment to allow the reality of both the past and future to settle. When they pulled up to the hotel ten minutes later, Gerald spoke.

"Martin, one thing I want to be clear is that you're never alone when you're a Road Runner. Even if you're somebody like myself or Ralph. We may physically live by ourselves, but we're not alone. Thousands of Road Runners are ready to support and help with anything. Even more so when you enter a leadership position."

"Then why is Strike gone?" Martin asked coldly.

"Strike is gone because of her own recklessness. She should have gone home. But it shouldn't have been that easy for Chris to get to her, either. Something isn't adding up."

"And that's the position you expect me to welcome with open arms?"

"Nothing is guaranteed. You can't be forced into the position—it's an election, and you're not even well known around the community. At this point, I'd say you're a dark horse. Now, let's go inside and prepare to leave this place before we all end up dead."

Gerald killed the engine and stepped out of the van without another word. Martin followed him into the building and to their suite, where Brigham stood against the wall, sweat glistening on his skin, and four suitcases lined in front of him.

"I hope you guys don't mind," he said. "I packed all of your bags after I finished mine. I've had so much nervous energy all morning, I had to put it to use. I still feel like I could go on a 20 mile run and not bat an eye." Brigham spoke rapidly, like a teenage girl filling in her friends on the recent gossip from the high school hallways. "Let's just say I'm ready to go home. I almost drank my Juice and left a note for you, but I know that's not the way we do things."

He giggled at this last statement, like it had been an inside joke with himself.

"Well, thank you," Gerald said, stepping up to grab his bag. "I'm just gonna do a quick sweep of my room to make sure nothing got missed. Martin you should do the same."

"I've checked five times already," Brigham said. "But be my guest." He held out his arm toward Gerald's room, grinning madly at Martin, who returned a quick smile before turning to his room.

His bedroom was immaculate as he checked in the closet and under the bed for any straggling items. They had only been here a whole two days, so it was by no means an impossible task to have a clean sweep done within a few seconds.

Martin checked Web's room, also clear of any belongings, and wondered if packing up Web's things sent Brigham into the mental breakdown he seemed to be currently fighting. All three of them were still on edge about the situation, but Brigham had survived it, and had to listen to his friend get murdered in the living room. Brigham might never be the same, and Martin hoped the Road Runners had an extensive mental health team to help him recover from this tragedy.

Martin returned to the living room where Brigham had pulled the suitcases to the front door.

"I guess we're ready to go. Thank you for packing everything," Gerald said.

"Glad to help. It's the least I can do while you two are out saving the world. Did we get the medicine? I almost forgot that's what we came for."

"We have the medicine," Martin said, never releasing his death grip from the paper bag. "Our mission here is complete. Let's go home."

Brigham smiled like a surprised child and pulled open the front door. Martin expected something to go wrong. Sonya had handed over the medicine with no hesitation, and Gerald's voice kept shouting in his head that it was all a set up. Surely she had set him up to send an army of Revolters to their doorstep before they tried to leave.

But no one waited in the hallway as they made their way to the van and loaded the suitcases in the trunk. No guns fired as they pulled out of the parking lot. No bombs exploded as they turned onto the highway and headed east to the plains where they had arrived only two days earlier.

Martin leaned back in his seat, staring at the blue sky passing above as the rest of the world seemed to vanish into the background of his thoughts. His mind raced as quickly as the van blazing down I-70.

The truth he had longed for—and didn't know he'd learn on this trip—became clear. Sonya gave him the medicine with no strings attached, no hidden agenda. Even if she didn't say it, Martin knew that she loved him. And as they returned home to 2019, where a new chapter waited in his chaotic life as a Road Runner, the thought warmed his soul and provided him a fresh boost in confidence for whatever came next.

123

Chapter 31

Strike had a bit more strength the next morning. She managed to roll from side to side, but trying to pull herself up sent biting waves of pain from her abdomen to her neck.

Falling asleep the night before hadn't been too difficult, as she started snoring twenty minutes after Chris left her alone with Julian's corpse. Her mind and body were drained, having zero energy to even consider staying awake. They must have carried Julian out in the middle of the night, for he was gone by the morning when she woke up refreshed and mentally energetic.

The mansion had a relaxing mood about it, something she'd never admit. The couch, wide and soft, swallowed her in its comfort. The room temperature held at a consistent 72 degrees, perfect to sleep without a blanket. And lastly, all worries seemed to vanish overnight. She knew she was trapped in Chris's lair, a prisoner who would likely die in this same mansion, but none of that concerned her. Could Chris be pumping a sort of relaxant through the vents? It was possible, especially considering he was immune to just about everything as an immortal being. That could be why his soldiers obeyed him like desperate puppies.

Don't fall for any of his bullshit, she reminded herself. Years of studying Chris had led her to know that whenever the old bastard did any act of kindness, it was always motivated by slimy intent. She thought this as soon as the aroma of bacon, eggs, and waffles carried into the room. Footsteps followed shortly behind, before Chris swung the door open with a tray held in one skinny arm.

"Rise and shine, Commander," he greeted, both chipper and psychotic. "I've learned some exciting news this morning, and I couldn't wait to share it with you."

She tried willing herself to sit up, but only managed to roll onto her back with a drawn-out groan.

"What is it, Chris?" she asked, trying to sound uninterested despite the curiosity bubbling beneath her surface.

He placed the tray of food on his desk, clapped his hands, and skipped across the room, planting himself in the seat opposite the couch. "It appears my dearest Sonya has sided with Martin Briar. I've had my people following her since she moved to her newest location and she just happened to cross paths with Mr. Briar—total coincidence, from what we can tell—and has aided him."

Without him saying it, Strike knew what this all meant. She had authorized Martin's mission to go to 2064 for the Alzheimer's cure. What else would Sonya have aided him in doing?

"Why is this news? I'm here and can't do anything about it."

"I just thought you'd like to know since these are people you've been heavily invested in. They're still out there carrying on their lives. I don't suppose either of them even know about your disappearance, since they've been frolicking about in the future. How does that make you feel?"

He was clearly trying to bait her into a reaction, perhaps trying to set the tone for a rough day. But fuck him.

"It makes me proud to know that my Road Runners still care for each other and are willing to help each other. Even in the ugliest of places."

"Interesting take. It makes me quite disgusted, frankly. My own daughter betrayed my trust—"

"She hates you, you know. Wishes you would die without her having to die. She worked around the clock for two years trying to find a way to release this curse you've placed on her. *You* drove your own daughter to the brink of suicide, and *you're* the one disgusted?"

"Don't flatter me with these pity stories, Commander." Chris grinned as he slid a balled fist under his chin. "I made my daughter an offer to live under my protection, in a situation where she still didn't have to encounter me, and this is how she thanks me. It's a stab in the back."

"Like when you stabbed her mother in the back." Strike may have been relaxed, but her mind was quick and locked in, ready to dance with the devil.

"Ahhh, more nonsense to try and rattle me. It will never work."

"It'll work one day. We may not be able to get to you with words, but you've made enough people in this world furious. One day someone is going to wipe that stupid grin off your face and remove you from this world like the scum you are."

"Commander." Chris grinned even wider. "Please stop it, you're arousing me."

"You're sick. What is it you want from me?"

"Since we're growing our relationship and being so honest with each other, I suppose I can tell you. Martin has gotten away with too much. Yes, it's my mistake for not throwing him in the basement like I wanted—sometimes you gotta trust your instincts, right? I trusted him by giving him freedom within the mansion and on the property. You have to understand, from my point of view, he appeared ready to commit his life to the Revolution. He was either really smart and outplayed me, or too naive to know better. I say the latter, but it doesn't matter at this point."

"Get to the point, then."

"The point is he betrayed my trust. Used it against me for his own gain. Now, I'm equally as pissed at Sonya, but I can't do anything to her for obvious reasons. With Mr. Briar, though, I can make the next move in the war, and it won't be pretty. A violation of one of our unwritten rules, you could say."

"Don't you fucking dare," Strike snapped, and this time she was able to sit up a couple of inches before falling back into the couch.

"I absolutely dare, and I will. It's time to send a message, and I thought you should be the first to know, since there's nothing you can do about it from that couch. Do you care to watch, or shall I just fill you in on the juicy details when it's done?"

"You're sick. If you do this, we'll have no choice but to bomb the living hell out of every one of your hideouts."

"The only person with the balls to send the bombs was lying in this room with you last night. Where is he today?"

"You're a coward."

"Not the first time I've been called that, and not the last I'm sure." Chris giggled as he stood up. "I've brought you breakfast. Our cooks are some of the best. I'll send someone up to feed you."

"I'd rather starve to death than live another day in your shithole world."

"Well, I don't want you to die, Commander. If you refuse to eat, we'll just give you a new treatment in the electric chair and then force a tube into your stomach. Please don't make me do that, and just eat your breakfast like a good girl."

Condescending piece of shit, Strike thought, mentally lunging from the couch and squeezing the life out of the old man's throat.

Chris crossed the room to the door and turned around. "Don't worry, Commander. You and I will enjoy a front row seat to the madness. I gotta run, though – need to make sure everything has been settled for Martin's homecoming. Would hate to see his optimism run any higher than it already is."

He turned back and left the room, sure to slam the door shut behind him.

Strike thought she heard howling laughter coming from the hallway, but it might have been her imagination. Either way, she knew what Chris planned to do without him even saying it, and the thought disturbed her to the core as she lay on her back, staring at the ceiling.

Please don't let him do this.

124

Chapter 32

Martin woke up in 2019, his mind foggy and begging for actual sleep. They were still in the van, back in Watkins, in the middle of an open field beside a frontage road. Gerald mumbled, still coming to, and Brigham sat stiffly in the back seat, eyes bulging, grateful to be alive and far away from the year 2064.

While Gerald shook himself awake, Martin scanned the area, still half-expecting a group of Revolters waiting to execute them. "Coast is clear," he said, the spike of tension fading away.

"I just want to go home," Brigham said.

"We're on our way," Martin replied, nudging Gerald in the shoulder.

Gerald's eyes shot open and looked around the vehicle to gather his surroundings. "We all okay?"

"Yes. Let's get back to headquarters."

Gerald turned the van on without hesitation and reversed out of the field toward the frontage road. "Let me do all the talking when we get back. When I dropped off Web, I sort of left in a hurry; they're going to have hundreds of questions."

"Good with me, I'm gonna take a shot and go to sleep," Brigham said, no sign of joking in his voice.

That's all Martin wanted too. He hadn't had a solid night's sleep in a few days and it was starting to take a toll on his ability to think straight.

One more skipped snooze session and he might grow crazy enough to run for Commander. He laughed, a bit slaphappy.

"What's so funny?" Gerald asked.

"Oh, nothing. Just can't believe how easily we got the medicine. It was supposed to be this big secret operation, and then someone just hands it over."

"I'm glad you think this is funny," Gerald snapped, clearly tired and cranky as well. They drove silently, thankful for the break in stress, enjoying a quiet morning into the city.

Within thirty minutes they pulled into downtown, working their way through the bustling traffic that was always present in 2019, regardless of the time of day. They pulled up to the marketing office, and Gerald let out a long sigh as he turned the engine off.

"We might have some visitors," he said, scanning the area.

"What do you mean?" Martin asked, reaching for a gun that wasn't on his waist, but packed somewhere in his suitcase.

"I think there are some high-ranking Road Runners in town, likely to see you, Martin."

Do these people not believe in resting? Martin wondered. *I just survived the future and want to go to bed. But all they want to talk about is what to do next.*

The fatigue created a short fuse for his irritability, but he understood the widespread panic across the organization with Strike being held hostage. He'd try to answer their questions, but if they wanted him to ever run for Commander they needed to respect his basic wishes of a private bed to sleep in.

Gerald kicked his door open and stepped outside, his back cracking as he stretched his beefy arms above his head. Martin joined him while Brigham pulled himself out of the back seat.

"It does feel good to be back in my city without worrying about stepping on a Revolter on the sidewalk," Martin said as he rounded the van to meet Gerald in front of the building.

"I've nearly forgotten the sensation," Gerald replied with a forced chuckle. "Shall we?"

Martin nodded and the three of them trudged up the steps and entered. The marketing office hummed with energy he hadn't seen before, and he wondered if everyone was actually working on their marketing projects, or looking for Strike. Eyes followed them as they passed through the hallway toward the back office.

No one said a word as they entered the manager's office where the secret staircase waited. A brief, sick thought popped into Martin's mind where he questioned the use of a basement as their hideout. Chris also used a basement for a hideout of Road Runners, and the connection made his mind spin.

As they descended the stairs, the sound of voices grew even louder than they had been in the marketing office. The Road Runners seemed to have doubled in population as dozens of people ran frantically through the office, papers in hand, phones to their ears, and not a soul paying attention to the three men who just returned from the future.

"Let's see if Tarik's in his office," Gerald said, and led the way toward his office where the door stood open. Tarik sat behind his desk, two other men standing along the walls in the middle of an intense conversation.

"Gentlemen!" Tarik said, standing up to meet them at the door. "So glad you made it out of there alive. They bombed your hotel this morning, and we temporarily lost the signal on your tracking devices. Let's just say there was a good five minutes of complete panic until the signal came back and we saw you were safe."

Martin looked behind to see Brigham turn white as paper. Gerald stepped into the room, with Martin following. Brigham remained in the hallway, frozen as if he had just seen a ghost.

"I figured as much after they killed Web," Gerald said, unfazed by the news. "Have we learned anything more about his death?"

"I'm afraid not," Tarik said. "They didn't leave a trace beyond the bullet wound. It appears they never even touched him. We did learn his laptop was designed to self-destruct if any false attempts were made to access it, so they wouldn't have gained any information from that."

An older Asian man cleared his throat from the corner of the room.

"Gentlemen, this is Commander Quang, the leader of our Asia chapter," Tarik said. "And this is Commander Blair from Europe."

Commander Blair stepped forward and stuck out a hand to both Gerald and Martin. He appeared to be in his early 40's, with a head of light brown hair, and glowing white skin to complement a charming smile. "Always nice to meet a fellow Warm Soul," he said to Martin in a British accent.

Commander Quang followed suit, his bony hands fragile with age, but stern. He was bald and clean shaven, making him appear younger than he really was. "It's nice to meet you both," he said in a low raspy voice. "We have a lot to discuss, so if you wouldn't mind us beginning."

He directed this last statement to Tarik, who hurriedly escorted Gerald into the hallway and closed the office door. Tarik returned to his seat behind the desk and gestured for Martin to sit down.

This must be it, Martin thought, knowing what these Commanders wanted to discuss.

"Commander Iglesia was going to join us, but something came up in Argentina that he needed to tend to," Tarik explained.

Just cut to the chase already, Martin thought. *I need to get this medicine to my mom.* He had finally released his death grip on the pill bottle when they entered the office, trusting his back pocket to keep it safe while these men tried to convince him to run for the Commandership.

"Mr. Briar," Quang said. "Commander Strike thought very highly of you. Her reports call you a perfect fit for a future commander position within our organization. We're close to calling her rescue mission a failure, and need to have certain plans in place before that decision is announced."

Martin decided to play dumb.

"I'm sorry, did you say you want *me* to be a commander?" he asked, placing an open hand across his chest.

"Yes, sir," Commander Blair added. "You've progressed quickly through our training program, and now have a futuristic mission under your belt. We assume you have the medicine you sought to get, yes?"

"I have it, sure, but that doesn't mean I'm a commander."

"Not yet," Quang continued. "It's an election, and sure to be a crowded one. But an endorsement from each of us can basically guarantee your election. Is this something you're interested in?"

"Honestly, no," Martin said sternly. "I don't want to be responsible for people's lives. I don't even want to deal with time travel anymore."

"With all due respect, Mr. Briar," Blair said. "We are beyond that point. You're in this life until you die, especially now that Chris has a target on your back, but I'm sure you already know that by now."

Martin's face flushed, the inevitable gnawing at his soul no matter how badly he wanted to refuse. He now realized that stepping out of Chris's mansion both simultaneously liberated and trapped him.

"I haven't even been a Road Runner for a year – why would anyone take me seriously?"

Blair nodded. "Same scenario as me. I was a Road Runner for six weeks when the election came up. They asked me, endorsed me, and I won. Now I've been the Commander for a little under a year. It's very much a job you learn on the fly, not much any one can do to prepare you for it."

"I just don't understand why *I'm* the one you want out of all the people who are surely more qualified."

Tarik pulled open a drawer and dropped a file on the desk. "This is Commander Strike's report on you. We've had eyes on you since the very first time you took the pill from Chris and traveled two hours back in time at his store."

Martin peered at the file, bloated with an inch thick of papers.

Commander Quang stepped forward. "Chris doesn't know that we follow everyone he brings into this world of time travel—at least in recent years since we've started doing so. You were followed during your attempt at Columbine, saving your daughter, and all the way up to your trip to 1919. We look for people who have a natural feel for adapting to different eras, finding ways to survive, and you passed every test. You're a natural time traveler."

"But I'm not a leader."

"Wrong. You don't have leadership experience. There is a big difference. Your raw ability to adapt and strategize will translate into strong leadership qualities. You'll never grow into a leader without trying."

"And putting me in charge of the entire organization is the best option to do that?"

Quang smiled, the wisdom of thousands of years swimming behind his eyes. "We like to move quickly and boldly."

The room fell silent, waiting for Martin to make the next move, but all he did was look from Tarik to Quang to Blair, then back to his twiddling thumbs. After two minutes, he realized they had dug their feet in and wouldn't say a word until he did, the medicine burning a hole in his back pocket.

"I don't have much of a say in this, do I?" he finally asked.

"Anyone in the organization can nominate anyone for the position," Blair said. "I guess you could say we're seeking your blessing before doing so. But we have every intent of nominating you unless you give us a compelling reason as to why we shouldn't."

Blair crossed his arms and leaned against the wall. Martin felt Quang's eyes burning into his soul. His Warm Soul. The damned reason he was in this mess to begin with.

"I suppose the fact that I don't want to do it isn't compelling enough?"

Blair shook his head, grinning as if he knew he had won this debate. Which he had. They had him backed into a corner with no way out. Martin Briar was going to be a nominee to lead the North American Road Runners, and had endorsements in place from the commanders around the globe.

He wanted to start laughing at the thought, growing more punchy by the second, but the tension in the room was ready to burst at the seams. He was pretty sure Quang was trying to hypnotize him, as the old Asian man had still refused to break his glare toward him.

Martin's mind raced for something—anything—to say that would make them leave him alone, but there was nothing.

"Okay. So what happens next?"

125

Chapter 33

Martin wasted no time bolting out of the office. He promised the Commanders to return as soon as he delivered the medicine to his mother. And yes, he would bring a pill back for them to reverse engineer.

His car waited outside, and he jumped in, speeding off like he had just robbed a bank. His mind kept trying to tug him to sleep, but it had no chance against the anticipation of saving his mother's ailing brain. Martin drove like a maniac, weaving through traffic, honking at anyone who dared touch their brakes. By habit, he reached into his pocket for his cell phone, but it wasn't there. He didn't remember where he left the damn thing, or if it was even in the correct year. He wanted to call his mom and let her know that he was on the way with the medicine in hand.

"I'm coming!" he barked into the empty car.

He briefly wondered how painful it was for Sonya to cut the tracking device out of her arm. Any amount of pain would be worth the freedom of getting his mother and disappearing to an island in the Caribbean with his millions, never to be seen again. Sooner or later, the Revolters and Road Runners would give up searching and move on to the next schmuck they learned had a special ability.

He rolled down the windows on the freeway, the day's warmth magnified in the enclosed car. The wind ripped through the car, splaying his hair in a wild mess, and drowning out the silence with the whipping white noise that accompanied driving 75 miles per hour with the windows down.

As much as he hated traffic, Martin was relieved to see other cars on the road, driving slowly without a care in the world. The way it should be. Even the bustle of life could be taken for granted when you saw the darkness of the future where zero traffic existed because everyone was dead.

Martin brought his mind back from that dismal setting, taking his exit that faced the stunning Rockies in the near distance. As he weaved down the side streets and toward his neighborhood, butterflies started to flutter in his stomach. He had subconsciously accepted his death on the journey to the future, and never expected to be driving home right now with the medicine.

He turned into his driveway, heart thumping as he parked and jumped out, hands flailing for the medicine bottle in his pocket as he rushed to the front door and burst inside.

"Mom!" he shouted. "I did it. I have your medicine!" The house was silent. Too silent, he thought. "Mom?"

She could just be napping.

He dashed down the hallway to her bedroom and flung open the door. Martin gasped and sprung back, tumbling across the hall and banging into the wall as all feeling drained out of his legs, causing him to collapse to the ground. The door banged against the inside of her bedroom and swung back toward its closed position, stopping ajar with a three-inch gap of visibility. Martin saw his mother lying in bed, her throat slashed in the shape of a red smiley face, her intestines oozing out of her stomach like a gutted deer.

The room spun around Martin as his mind worked in overdrive to make sense of what his eyes were seeing. His entire body trembled as his throat swelled like it had an inflated balloon inside.

You're dreaming, he told himself. *You've done too much time traveling and your brain doesn't know what's what any more. You're asleep and will wake up soon, back in bed with Sonya, because none of this has actually happened.*

The lie to himself gave him enough strength to rise to his feet and step toward his mom's room. No, he didn't actually believe he was dreaming, but wasn't that how dreams normally worked? His body shuddered when he entered the room, the stillness of death thick in the air. He glanced around, looking for anything to keep his eyes from returning to his torn open mother. She kept a table by the window, stacks of her puzzle books and novels standing neatly on the edge. A single sheet of paper in the center caught his attention.

Martin forced his legs to cross the room, Marilyn to his left where the darkness of blood soaking into the sheets was impossible to ignore. He cleared his throat and gulped as he leaned over the table to read the paper:

Hello old friend,

I thought we had an agreement after I saved you from the Road Runners. I brought you into my home, my private domain, and you betrayed my trust by running away a few hours later. I'll admit, it's my own fault for not being more cautious, and thanks to you, future residents will have zero privileges as far as roaming the house and the grounds.

We could've made a great team. I had a grand vision for how to use your special ability to make the world a better place, but it appears you've fallen into the familiar trap laid out by the Road Runners. It's a shame, because now our relationship can only end with your death.

I was ready to let it all go since I had only myself to blame. But then I heard you used Sonya to get the medicine to cure your mother. How dare you try to find a workaround to our deal. I exchanged a lifetime supply of the Juice (which you still have) for your pain. By avoiding the pain of watching your mother fade into a shell of her former self, you violated our agreement.

I'm sure you understand why I had to carry out this drastic action. If it puts your mind at ease, she was sleeping when we did this, so she shouldn't have felt a thing.

I'm not a monster, just a man of my word. Until next time.

Your friend,

Chris

Martin's lips quivered as he read the note, clenching the paper tighter

774

in his grip with each passing line. Tears spilled down his face onto the paper, blotting parts of the hand-written ink. Reality sunk in that this was no dream.

I can go back in time and stop this from happening.

The thought jumped into Martin's head with such fierceness that he sprinted out of the bedroom in search of his bottle of Juice. He couldn't remember if he had left it hidden in the basement bar or somewhere in his bedroom, sprinting to the basement first since it was the closest door.

But like most ideas that come to fruition in the middle of panic, the possibility quickly faded, taking along every ounce of hope with it. There was nothing he could do about his mother's death—Chris would never allow it. If he had gone through this much trouble to prove a point, anything further would only result in Martin's own demise.

That doesn't sound so awful right now, Martin thought, memories of his mother flooding his mind. It had been a while since he contemplated taking his own life, and much had happened since that last time at his old apartment in Larkwood. But the temptation always stood silently in the corner of his thoughts, in case he needed an easy way out.

He had left his suitcase in the car, containing his flask and pistol. He debated running to the car and flipping open the suitcase in dramatic fashion, to face the ultimate crossroads of his life within the same bag. Drink the Juice to go back and save his mother, or slide the pistol between his teeth and squeeze the trigger, once and for all.

The days of flirting with suicide were behind him, though. If there was anything Chris had done, it was reform Martin into a person who longer toyed with the idea of ending his own life. He now tried to contribute to the world after coming out of Izzy's death a changed man. Even if Sonya and the Road Runners were the ones who *actually* reformed him, it was Chris who had given him the opportunity to ever meet them.

Chris had indirectly saved his life—something he would never admit out loud. Before he met Chris, his life had dragged through the shambled mess it had always been since Izzy's death. Even after learning the gruesome truth of what had happened to his daughter, Martin found peace in the closure he had received.

Defeated, Martin returned upstairs with his head hung low, reality's cold and unforgiving grasp squeezing his heart. For the moment, his past with Chris was forgotten, his future with the Road Runners buried in his thoughts. All he cared about was the present.

When he reached the landing at the top of the stairs, he looked into the living room, spinning around to admire the mansion he was able to buy with hopes of starting a new life with his mother and Sonya. A steady breeze howled outside, providing the only sound in the silent house.

He shuffled across the living room, looking to what could have been. It seemed like yesterday when his mother was boiling water in the kitchen, wanting to make noodles they didn't have. Martin sunk into the couch and gazed to the dining room where he had sat with his mom and told her the truth about his unique opportunity to travel through time. It was the same table where he and Sonya had scarfed down lunch before beginning their journey to 1919, the same trip that had led him to becoming a Road Runner and to this very moment.

"You win, Sonya," he said, his voice echoing off the vaulted ceiling above. "Your mission is complete."

Sonya was gone. His mother was dead. The future waited, whether he liked it or not.

Martin Briar had been delivered to the Road Runners exactly as planned. They expected him to lead, to change the future for an entire organization working around the clock to defeat their nemesis who had, in some way, hurt each individual person, whether physically or emotionally.

He hadn't yet processed everything that had happened since Sonya led him into a trap. And he'd be damned if he'd miss the opportunity to grieve his mother's death. Grateful to be alone, disconnected from the world and any technology in it, Martin buried his face into his open hands and cried.

126

Chapter 34

Martin later found his cellphone in his bedroom, waiting peacefully on his nightstand as if he had never taken a dangerous trip into the future. He called Tarik and explained the scene at the house, the words causing fresh outbursts of tears.

It felt good to cry, relieving. Ever since he had gone back to 1996 and followed Lela to the lake where she threw Izzy's body, Martin hadn't had a chance to sit in solitude and grieve. This particular afternoon served as the perfect time to catch up while he shed tears for Izzy, the hundreds of lives lost in the Columbine High School fire, Sonya, and now Marilyn.

It wasn't the fact that his mother had died that bothered him—he had mentally prepared for that inevitability at the end of a painful Alzheimer's tunnel. It was the gruesome nature in which she had been murdered that sent shockwaves of pain throughout his body. Even though he had only caught a glimpse, it was enough to burn the image of her bloodied and mutilated body into his memory forever. Perhaps that was a good thing. Being motivated by such a disturbing memory would surely end Chris one day, but now wasn't the time to plot revenge. There was plenty of time for that.

Tarik sent a squad of Road Runners to clean up the mess in Martin's house, and offered to handle the burial arrangement and services. There were a few relatives Martin had to inform of Marilyn's death, but he needed to brainstorm a cover-up story first.

The crew Tarik had sent worked quietly and respectfully, as if this was something they had done hundreds of times. A morbid thought popped into Martin's mind as he wondered if these were the same men who would have come to clean him up if something went terribly wrong.

Tarik joined the crew and stood outside Martin's house, pacing while he spoke on his cell phone. Martin pulled himself off the couch and joined him after he hung up.

"How are you doing?" Tarik asked, slinging an arm around Martin's shoulders.

"Aside from regretting every decision I've ever made, I feel okay." Mucus clogged his nose and throat, prompting him to clear it out after every sentence he spoke.

"Look, Martin, we want you to do whatever you need, take your time recovering from this. The Road Runners will be here for you every step of the way."

"I appreciate that. What about the election?"

"We're delaying the special election, until you're ready. Technically we can because Commander Strike is still alive; we know that much."

Martin nodded, knowing there was no way out of it now. They wanted him in that position, and went as far as postponing the election to let him grieve.

"What am I supposed to do until then?" Martin asked.

"Whatever you want. Take a trip, get out of town. Go do whatever makes you happy and helps you find yourself."

"Will I be followed?"

"Of course. Chris is too busy with Commander Strike at the moment, but he still wants you. You'll have eyes on you at all times, and a couple of our soldiers within close proximity no matter where you go. Carry on as if we're not there. We'll only intervene should something arise."

The thought of not having any true privacy would have normally bothered Martin, but he had no more emotional energy to give a shit. The Road Runners were going to do as they saw fit.

"I just want my mom situated, and then I'll worry about what to do with my time."

"Of course. Commanders Quang and Blair send their condolences; they had to return home, but look forward to meeting with you again in the future."

"Are we still trying to save Commander Strike?"

"We're exploring all options, but it's not looking good. The attack that Julian authorized on Chris's mansion didn't even leave a dent. He's clearly using some sort of steel from the future—it's indestructible. There's not much we can do if we can't even penetrate his fort. We're looking into tunnels, but are hesitant because we don't know what we'll run into as we start digging toward the mansion."

Deep down, Martin wished they would rescue Strike and let him off the hook for this damned election, at least for the immediate future.

"I don't want you to worry about these things right now," Tarik said. "Worry about yourself, we'll be just fine when you're ready to come back. Give me a call if you need anything at all."

Tarik offered his hand, and Martin shook it. "Thank you. I'll be in touch."

Tarik nodded before turning back down the driveway where his car waited, leaving Martin as the crew worked as silently as mice in his mother's bedroom. They would have everything cleaned up within two hours.

Martin needed to get out of the house, wanting to get far away from his life as a Road Runner. He wanted to remember what a normal life felt like. A life where there was no secretive global war. No Chris hunting him down like a prized animal. No Road Runners forcing him into a leadership position he didn't want.

Let them follow me. I'm getting the hell out of town.

Without a word to the crew down the hallway, Martin swiped his keys off the kitchen counter and bolted out of the house.

He slid behind his steering wheel, reaching over the suitcase in the passenger seat, and opened it, rummaging through the layers of clothes until his fingers grasped his flask of Juice.

With the Juice in his possession, Martin wasted no time turning on the car and pulling out of the driveway. He stopped before driving away, taking one last look at the house he had purchased thanks to his time travel capabilities. The ghosts of his lost future cried for him to stay, but he couldn't. Not right now.

He nodded to the house, genuinely unsure if he would ever return to see it. He had no plans for where he'd go, but would travel as far as he could until he found somewhere that called to him. The tank was full, so he had plenty of hours ahead.

The spontaneity made his heart race in a way he didn't remember. Time traveling gave him a rush, sure, but nothing compared to diving into an unknown adventure.

Martin drove away, leaving his life in the rear view mirror. It would always be there, and he could always return to it. For now, all he cared about was the future and honoring his mother's life. He requested they cremate her remains, and have them deliver those remains to wherever he ended up.

Maybe I'll finally go to a beach and drink fruity drinks all day.

Martin grinned as he pulled out of his neighborhood and made his way toward the freeway. He drove quickly, the freedom of the open road ahead. Headlights appeared behind him in the distance. They may have been random, or possibly the Road Runners keeping their invisible hand over him.

He didn't care. Let them follow. He had plenty to contemplate and would take his time doing so. The future, much like the past, wasn't going anywhere. And much like he'd done since meeting Chris, Martin kept moving forward, waiting for what would come next.

Keeper of Time

Keeper of Time is the fourth installation of the Wealth of Time series. This book continues the story from where Bad Faith ended, as well as takes a deep dive into Chris Speidel's past in a first-ever look at his rise as the Keeper of Time.

Get Keeper of Time on Amazon today!

You can also pre-order the second boxed set collection of the Wealth of Time Series. This bundle includes books 4-6, the final three of the series! This will not be available until the final book, Time of Fate is release in the spring. Please disregard the date listed on Amazon, as the book will release in April.

Pre-order the second bundle at a limited time discounted price!

GET EXCLUSIVE BONUS CONTENT

Connecting with readers is the best part of this job. Releasing a book into the world is a truly frightening moment every time it happens! Hearing your feedback, whether good or bad, goes a long in shaping future projects and helping me grow as a writer. I also like to take readers behind the scenes on occasion and share what is happening in my wild world of writing. If you're interested, please consider joining my mailing list. If you do so, I'll send you the following as a thank you:

1. A free copy of *Revolution,* a prequel story that goes back in time before Chris Speidel ever knew about the mysterious world of time travel.
2. A free copy of *Road Runners*, a prequel story that looks at the rise of the Road Runners.

You can get your content **for free,** by signing up HERE.
https://dl.bookfunnel.com/zbo3c72679

Now enjoy a sneak peek of the prequel story, Road Runners:

Maxwell Hart leaned against the wall, heart drumming against his rib cage, nervous sweat streaming down his face.

Pull the pin, throw it, and run.

He'd repeated this line to himself at least four hundred times in the last two minutes. The grenade felt no different than a baseball in his grip. But tossing a baseball into a sleeping man's bedroom never killed anyone.

Yeah, but that backstabbing piece of shit deserves the most painful death.

Max had worked diligently behind the scenes to arrive at this precise moment in December of 1974. One quick toss of the grenade would avenge the death of his wife and two children. Sure, he'd still live the rest of his life in a state of emotional anguish, but as long as the bastard responsible for it was dead, that was all that mattered.

Pull, throw, run.

He'd have to run like hell. As soon as the explosion sounded, there would be a dozen Revolters sweeping the grounds for the perpetrator. His planned escape route minimized the distance from the grenade to the nearest outdoor exit. From there it was a straight sprint three blocks to where his car waited, parked out of sight.

His hand trembled to the point of almost dropping the grenade a couple of times. That would have been ironic, coming this far in such an elaborate plan, only to wake up his target with the sound of metal hitting the tile floor and rolling around like a bowling ball.

The bedroom door stood ajar, but he hadn't looked inside. The steady cadence of heavy snoring echoed from within the darkness. He knew the layout of the bedroom and where exactly to lob the grenade, even in the blackness.

He wore all-black clothing to hide every inch of his light skin, blending into the night as he shuffled through the halls where his old friend awaited his unforeseen death. A black balaclava covered his head and face, an inch-wide slit open for his eyes and nothing more. The orange glow from the street lights outside splashed across the hallway, but didn't provide nearly enough light for visibility.

The breeze outside ceased, leaving the building silent. It felt as if the world came to a halt, the opportunity to toss the grenade and save innumerable future lives from the scam artist known as Chris Speidel lying in wait, tantalizing and tangible.

He pulled the pin, and the grenade throbbed in his hand now that it had become a deadly weapon. He only had to throw it into the bedroom and it would explode in a confetti of metal shards, piercing every organ in that murdering bastard's body.

There had been prior attempts to kill Chris from long distance with snipers, but all had failed. Some had wondered if the self-proclaimed keeper of time was indeed invincible. While the ability to time travel prolonged lives by hundreds of years, no one had ever proven immortal. Max rode this belief into devising his plan to get up close and personal in his assassination attempt.

He needed to toss the grenade before his hand accidentally fell off the lever and splattered his own guts across the hallway. He raised it to his lips and kissed it, the metal cool to the touch.

Max slid his feet into the doorway, looking into the black hole of the bedroom and tossing the grenade with the touch of a basketball player dropping in a soft layup. If the grenade hit the ground, it might not work, as it would have to explode *through* the bed. But it made no such sound as it landed with a soft thud on the mattress.

Four seconds, he thought as he pivoted and sprinted down the hallway. He had practiced this exact routine a dozen times in the last week at the basketball gym, from the blind toss eight feet into the dark bedroom, to the exact footwork he'd use to escape. It all needed to come naturally, and it had paid off. The grenade would explode four seconds after making contact with the bed, and he mentally counted as he ran down the hall.

The hallway stretched exactly eighty-five feet to the corner that turned into another hallway that ran fifty feet to the exit door. In his drills, he wanted to be turning the corner as the explosion sounded, leaving him an estimated ten-second delay for those sleeping in the other rooms to hear the sound and jump out of bed. Fourteen seconds after throwing the bomb should have him at least 150 feet away from the building and out of sight.

Even though his legs quivered with nerves, the adrenaline kept them strong and propelling forward. The timing all went according to plan as he turned the corner simultaneously with the booming explosion that shook the entire hallway. Grenades weren't as loud as he originally thought, but the sound may as well have been a cannon in the midst of a silent building.

Max sprinted for the exit door, lunging into it like an Olympic hurdler and bursting it open as he briefly tumbled outside, never completely losing his balance. He put his head down and ran, trusting his internal compass and never looking back.

Chris is dead! Chris is dead! he thought as his legs pumped for three more blocks. There was no way he survived a grenade rolled up next to him in bed like a cat. It would have sent its deadly fragments from his toes to his head, leaving him with no chance of survival.

Three minutes after escaping, Max's silver BMW sedan became visible, parked on the street where he had left it, strategically facing the direction he needed to drive. The sight of it moved his legs a little faster.

When he fell into the driver's seat, he finally looked back and saw three figures running in the dark, at least a block away. *Did they see me or are they just looking around?* Max didn't waste another second to find out, and fired up the engine, speeding away with smoke blowing from his screeching tires. They'd never catch him on foot and had no chance of getting so much as a glimpse of the car.

Sweat dripped down his back, his shirt clinging to his flesh, as he sped away, panting for breath in heavy gasps. The roads were deserted, as they should be at two in the morning.

"I did it!" he shouted once the tension had faded, and the realization settled that he had actually gotten away with it. "I fucking did it!"

The loss of his family seemed like a distant memory as he turned onto the freeway, heading back to New York City. The pain would resurface once the excitement faded, but for now all he could do was celebrate the death of Chris.

Surely a massive party awaited the next day. They had been working for months on this mission. Max had gone plenty of days without sleep and now intended to stay in bed as long as his body desired.

Sleep, drink, and party. In their honor.

Max patted his pocket where he kept his most recent family picture. Their life together seemed sixty years in the past, not a mere sixteen months. He often wondered what they would all being doing at any given moment. Right now they'd all be asleep in their private Tudor home in upstate New York. But during the day, a cold one with temperatures in the upper 30's, they might have gone to a local ice skating rink, or perhaps light a fire in the living room as they watched movies. Abby loved anything Disney, and James always giggled watching along with her.

These fabricated memories flashed and disappeared in his mind like a bolt of lightning. Months earlier this same scenario would play out with him pulling the car to the side of the road and crying for the next hour, cursing God—and Chris—for letting such a tragedy happen. Every one of these crying sessions ended with him returning home to his office in a fit of rage, determined to plot the master plan to kill Chris.

But now it was done, and the burden that weighed on his shoulders like boulders had lifted. Was it relief he felt? Closure? Max didn't know, but the constant urge to cry and destroy random household items had vanished.

"Chris is dead and he can no longer hurt me," Max cried gleefully as he cruised along the freeway. "He's dead, he's gone, and he will never hurt *anyone* ever again."

He laughed like a madman, oblivious that Chris was indeed far from dead.

Acknowledgements

I can't believe this is already my eighth book since starting this journey back in October 2016. Back then I had clue what to expect. If you told me I'd be eight books in before the turn of the decade, I probably wouldn't have believed you. But here we are. This whole career is sort of like jumping off a cliff and hoping for the best, much like Mike in *Stranger Things*, taking that leap of faith and trusting that Eleven would save him.

My Eleven is very much you, the readers. With every new release I get to connect with old fans and new fans alike, slowly accumulating a following as we move along, and seeing this career really being to flourish. I still connect—quite often—with those loyal readers who have been with me since that October of 2016, and seeing them excited for each new book keeps the fire roaring within. If you've ever left a review or messaged me about your enjoyment of a book, please know it goes noticed and helps this author maintain that trust each time I jump off a new cliff.

Bad Faith wraps up the most recent installment of this *Wealth of Time* series, and I'm blown away at the positive reception this series has received. Please know that I have many plans (in a steel-trap box in my head) for this series. It has endless possibilities with both Martin's main story line and so many potential spinoffs.

I'd like to first thank my editor, Stephanie Cohen. She is just as vested in this series as me, and her hard-work and timely delivery helps keep me on an aggressive release schedule. I hope she doesn't mind me bragging for her, but she just landed a big editing job for a major publisher in NYC. Congrats, and I can't wait to keep working with you!

Thank you to Dane Low at EbookLaunch. As always, you have the perfect vision for these covers. Keep them coming!

Thank you to the Dizzy Dragons. It's so much fun "working" with others with the same drive and vision.

Arielle, Felix, and Selena for providing that constant motivation to keep going and never settle.

And as always, thank you to my wife, Natasha. I know you sacrifice a bit for this dream, I'm just glad to have you in my corner. I love you.

Andre Gonzalez
    Denver, CO
    December 2, 2019

Enjoy this book?

You can make a difference!

Reviews are the most helpful tools in getting new readers for any books. I don't have the financial backing of a New York publishing house and can't afford to blast my book on billboards or bus stops.

(Not yet!)

That said, your honest review can go a long way in helping me reach new readers. If you've enjoyed this book, I'd be forever grateful if you could spend a couple minutes leaving it a review (it can be as short as you like) on the Amazon page. You can jump right to the page by clicking below:

US

UK

Thank you so much!

Also by Andre Gonzalez

Wealth of Time Series:

Keeper of Time (Wealth of Time Series, Book #4)

Bad Faith (Wealth of Time Series, Book #3)

Warm Souls (Wealth of Time Series, Book #2)

Wealth of Time (Wealth of Time Series, Book #1)

Wealth of Time Series: Books 1-3 (Box Set)

Road Runners (Wealth of Time Series, Short Story)

Revolution (Wealth of Time Series, Short Story)

Insanity Series:

The Insanity Series (Books 1-3)

Replicate (Insanity Series, Book #3)

The Burden (Insanity Series, Book #2)

Insanity (Insanity Series, Book #1)

Erased (Insanity Series, Prequel) (Short Story)

The Exalls Attacks:

Followed Home

A Poisoned Mind (Short Story)

Standalone books:

Snowball: A Christmas Horror Story

About the Author

Born in Denver, CO, Andre Gonzalez has always had a fascination with horror and the supernatural starting at a young age. He spent many nights wide-eyed and awake, his mind racing with the many images of terror he witnessed in books and movies. Ideas of his own morphed out of movies like *Halloween* and books such as *Pet Sematary* by Stephen King. These thoughts eventually made their way to paper, as he always wrote dark stories for school assignments or just for fun. Followed Home is his debut novel based off of a terrifying dream he had many years ago at the age of 12. His reading and writing of horror stories evolved into a pursuit of a career as an author, where Andre hopes to keep others awake at night with his frightening tales. The world we live in today is filled with horror stories, and he looks forward to capturing the raw emotion of these events, twisting them into new tales, and preserving a legacy in between the crisp bindings of novels.

Andre graduated from Metropolitan State University of Denver with a degree in business in 2011. During his free time, he enjoys baseball, poker, golf, and traveling the world with his family. He believes that seeing the world is the only true way to stretch the imagination by experiencing new cultures and meeting new people.

Andre still lives in Denver with his wife, Natasha, and their three kids.

You can connect with me on:

- https://andregonzalez.net
- http://twitter.com/monito0408
- http://facebook.com/AndreGonzalezAuthor
- http://instagram.com/monito0408

Subscribe to my newsletter:

- https://andregonzalez.net

Made in United States
Orlando, FL
12 November 2021